ABOUT THE AUTHOR

Markus Heitz was born in 1971; he studied history and German language and literature. His debut novel, *Schatten über Ulldart* (the first in a series of epic fantasy novels), won the Deutscher Phantastik Preis (German Fantasy Award) in 2003. His bestselling *Dwarves* trilogy has earned him a place among Germany's most successful fantasy authors. He currently lives in Zweibrücken, Germany.

Also by Markus Heitz

The Legends of the Älfar
Righteous Fury
Devastating Hate

Oneiros

THE LEGENDS OF THE ÄLFAR
BOOK III
DARK
PATHS

MARKUS HEITZ

Translated by Sheelagh Alabaster

Jo Fletcher
BOOKS

First published in Germany in 2012 by Piper Verlag GmbH
First published in English in Great Britain in 2016 by

Jo Fletcher Books
an imprint of
Quercus Publishing Ltd
Carmelite House
50 Victoria Embankment
London EC4Y 0DZ

An Hachette UK company

A CIP catalogue record for this book is available from the British Library

PB ISBN 978 1 78206 594 4
EBOOK ISBN 978 1 78429 970 5

10 9 8 7 6 5 4 3 2 1

Typeset by Jouve (UK), Milton Keynes
Printed and bound in Great Britain by
Clays Ltd, St Ives plc

To all who love life.
Smile when you are envied –
it will heighten your pleasure.
The jealous will never admit
that your luck is deserved.

Dramatis Personae

The Älfar

Firûsha	
Sisaroth	triplets
Tirîgon	
Aïsolon	their father, governor of Dsôn Sòmran
Ranôria	their mother, a celebrated singer
Gàlaidon	Aïsolon's deputy
Tênnegor	älf in Dsôn Sòmran
Sémaina	älf in Dsôn Sòmran, Tênnegor's partner
Liphelis	älf in Dsôn Sòmran, Tênnegor's daughter
Wènelon	älf in Dsôn Sòmran
Nomirôs	älf in Dsôn Sòmran
Phodrôis	älf in Dsôn Sòmran
Helîstra	glass-craftswoman in Dsôn Sòmran
Acòrhia	tale-weaver in Dsôn Sòmran
Cèlantra	female älf in Dsôn Sòmran
Iòsunta	female älf in Dsôn Sòmran
Naïgonor	älf in Dsôn Sòmran
Marandëi	female älf in Phondrasôn
Crotàgon	älf in Phondrasôn
Hamîna	female älf in Phondrasôn

Esmonäe	female älf in Phondrasôn
Bephaigòn	älf in Phondrasôn
Draïlor, Horogòn	wound-healers in Phondrasôn
Sintholor	young älf in Phondrasôn
Tossàlor	älf in Phondrasôn
Carmondai	master of word and image

Miscellaneous

Tungdil Goldhand	groundling in Phondrasôn, master armourer
Jamenusîl	elf in Phondrasôn
Hopiash	karderier shapeshifter in Phondrasôn
Veyn	creature in Phondrasôn
Shucto	barbarian from the tribe of the Shuctanides
Korhnoj	Zhadar army commander
Ehiow	Zhadar envoy
Kiumê	rebel
The Zhadar	prince of Phondrasôn

Concepts

Sytràp	älfar rank of officer in Dsôn Sòmran
First Sytràp	highest rank below deputy in Dsôn Sòmran
cîanai/cîanoi	älfar magician (sorcerer/sorceress, extremely rare)

Places

Efrigûr	province cave in Phondrasôn
Cjash	region in Phondrasôn
Whifis	triple cave system
Sojól	cave in Phondrasôn

Creatures

ukormoriers	magic humanoids in Phondrasôn
karderiers or rîconiers	magic shapeshifters
wyde hornets	insects with lethal sting
hangbear	predator in the Dsôn Sòmran mountains
shadow-wolf	predator in the Dsôn Sòmran mountains
amdiu	worm lizard in Phondrasôn, occurring in several different colours
gålran zhadar	race of magicians of squat stature, often mistaken for dwarves
Shëidogîs	one of the gods of infamy

They are said as a people to show more cruelty than any other.

They are said to hate elves, humans, dwarves and every other creature so much that the blood runs black in their veins and darkens their eyes in the light of the sun.

They are said to dedicate their lives exclusively to death and to art.

They are said to use black magic.

They are said to be immortal . . .

Much has been said about the Älfar.

Read now these tales that follow and decide for yourselves what is true and what is not. These are stories of unspeakable horror, unimaginable battles, gross treachery, glorious triumphs and crushing defeats.

But they are also tales of courage, integrity and valour.

Of friendship.

And of love.

These are the Legends of the Älfar.

Preface from the forbidden books which transfigure the truth,
The Legends of the Älfar,
unknown author,
undated.

Prologue

Ishím Voróo (Outer Lands), Dsôn Sòmran, Dsôn, in the northern foothills of the Grey Mountains, 5427th division of unendingness (6241st solar cycle), spring.

The soft music of bone flutes, drums, fiddles and many other instruments came drifting up to Firûsha's open window.

She revelled in the nocturnal serenade, the strands of sound weaving harmoniously. As she listened with eyes closed, it seemed the musicians were vying with each other to achieve perfection, embodying heart, soul and a deep longing to reunite with distant älfar.

The musicians are excelling themselves tonight. It is as if they know. Firûsha's excitement grew. Soon the three siblings would be together again; as triplets they had always enjoyed a special status in the city.

Firûsha had taken care in choosing her attire. She was dressed in a white robe with black embroidery that emphasised her slim figure. The long sleeves and train rustled slightly when she moved.

She was keen to enjoy every instant of her siblings' company, aware they would not be staying long. After this short break for physical and intellectual rest they were all due to return to the next stage of their demanding apprenticeships with the masters of their chosen paths. She was training to be a singer; her brother Sisaroth was to become a priest for the gods of infamy, while Tirîgon was proving a promising warrior.

It can't be long now. Firûsha did not have to open her eyes to see Dsôn. She knew the city view as well as she knew her childhood home, which she would soon be leaving to further her education in the art of song, with which to delight Dsôn Sòmran's citizens.

The building where Firûsha had spent her early life was composed of eleven modest rooms for her family. Of course, there were also the slave quarters, guest lodgings, reception galleries and the halls for martial arts practice.

Their house was situated at the highest point of Dsôn's stone basin, towering over most of the other buildings and emphasising the family's status. There were no more than a score of other älfar families with names more important than theirs.

Mother never liked to boast about her rank and fame. Firûsha's thoughts turned to those envious souls who had tried and failed to find grounds to topple Ranôria and to turn the city's governor Aïsolon against her. Live births were so rare that producing the triplets had enhanced Ranôria's reputation; she was now almost akin to a deity, held in nearly as high esteem as the Inextinguishables.

No one will be able to denigrate her in Aïsolon's eyes – he still holds her in great affection. She is the mother of his children, after all. This made Firûsha laugh. *My father will love her forever. I'm sure he'll be thinking of her when he hears the songs of the bards.*

Firûsha heard the door handle being quietly turned, as if

someone were hoping to surprise her, but her hearing was far too acute for that. She turned her head towards the entrance, where fine tapestries hung from the wall. The carpets were hand-knotted by guild masters of the craft, presented to her mother in honour of her wonderful singing voice.

The door swung open to reveal a tall älf of serious mien, trying to hide the joy sparkling in his steel-blue eyes. He had chosen a shimmering dark red robe for his meeting with his siblings, and an elaborately worked ceremonial dagger hung at his side.

'By all the gods of infamy! Sisaroth, you look so . . . *different*!' Firûsha hurried from the window and ran into her brother's embrace. Her bare feet made no sound on the grey patterned mosaic floor. 'But you're finally here!'

He laughed, kissing her brow under the diamond tiara perched on her long black hair. 'I know what you mean. My physique has improved with all the training – my muscles are like taut ropes! They work us hard, but I have no complaints.' He hugged her. 'My darling sister!'

Firûsha gave a sigh of relief, stroking his face, so like her own, but manly and distinguished. 'It feels like so long since I've seen you, but I suppose it is really only a hundred moments of unendingness.'

Sisaroth released her from his embrace, took her hands and looked her up and down approvingly. 'A proper grown-up älf-woman now. How many hearts lie shattered at your feet? I bet you're fighting off every älf in Dsôn Sòmran capable of passion for a female.'

She grinned in delight. 'No, not quite all of them. But come and see what Dsôn has in store for us tonight.' Hand in hand they strolled across the long gallery to the open window, breathing in the blossom-perfumed air the south wind had sent.

Sisaroth wondered what to expect. *It can't be anything more delightful than Firûsha herself.* As he walked, his new dagger bumped against his thigh. He had received the award only two moments of unendingness previously, for bravery and fighting prowess. He was immensely proud to know that, in spite of his youth, he was as good as many more experienced warriors. *It can't hurt, can it, to be known for my swordsmanship, even if I am going to be a priest?*

He was delighted to see how well his sister was looking. She had remained in Dsôn, to be tutored in singing by their mother. Her voice was already magical. *What will she sound like once her training is complete?*

'Would you sing for me tonight?' he asked. 'Show me what Mother has taught you.'

She hesitated. 'Let's wait for Tirîgon. I'll have to owe you a song for now.' She led him over to the cushioned window seat and together they looked out onto the majestic city, enclosed on all sides by the high grey rock walls of the vast natural basin. Dsôn – the centre of the älfar empire, Dsôn Sòmran, spread out before them in all its sparkling glory.

Light from windows, candles, torches and lanterns shone through the darkness and reflected on the clouds of smoke released from the flammable powder and burning fuses that had been catapulted into the sky for effect.

The festival was in honour of the west wind: the more lavish their offerings of fire and light, the more favour they hoped to receive from the god of wind, Samusin. Extravagant handfuls of petals and coloured feathers were also tossed in the air, to be burned by the fireworks or to drift upwards to land on rooftops and cliffs. It was a fascinating spectacle, full of grace and poetry.

How wonderful it all looks. Firûsha clasped her brother's hand for a moment. 'Would you ever have thought we could enjoy such harmony and freedom after the destruction of Dsôn Faïmon?' she asked, leaning out into the night, her blue eyes lit with enthusiasm as the wind played with strands of her long black hair.

'We might be too young to have known the old älfar empire,' Sisaroth replied, moved by the beauty of the scene, 'but it can't have been more beautiful than our own Dsôn.' He looked out towards Tark Draan in the north, where another älfar realm lay and the Inextinguishables remained.

Every time he thought about the distant Sibling Rulers on the other side of the Grey Mountains, he was filled with resentment. They had fled the plague of sickness affecting their people and had never shown any interest in the survivors. Sisaroth imagined their fame and glory in their extensive empire while he and his siblings were stuck in the claustrophobic confines of Dsôn Sòmran. *It's like living in a glorified dungeon – it might have magnificently decorated walls, but it's still a prison.*

His father Aïsolon had occasionally spoken to him about the heroes, Sinthoras and Caphalor, who had once been highly placed nostàroi commanding the älfar army in the victorious campaign against Tark Draan. His father and Caphalor had been close friends, until, all of a sudden, all communication with the other side of the mountains had ceased. There had been no news for dozens of divisions of unendingness.

Troops that had been sent to Tark Draan through the Stone Gateway either never returned or had been forced back by vicious attacks from monsters – and Dsôn needed every single soldier to protect its citizens from the hordes of óarcos determined to wipe out the city.

Sisaroth battled dejectedly with his thoughts.

He knew he shouldn't hate the Inextinguishables and those älfar safely ensconced in Tark Draan – but why had they not come to Dsôn Sòmran's aid? What was stopping the rulers from returning to their subjects – or at least sending messages of hope and support?

I bet I know what happened: they just forgot all about us. They're all fine, revelling in luxury there – but it's not right. We were supposed to be one people. We are älfar too, and we deserve a better existence than this.

The optimists among them called Dsôn Sòmran the 'Empire', while cynics had termed it the 'Offshoot', though the settlement had been founded and commanded by Aïsolon and defended by courageous warriors.

The city had been constructed here, deep in the mountains, in this funnel-shaped hollow only half a division of unendingness after the catastrophe that destroyed the Star State. It was isolated and impregnable – and totally insignificant. It was just a colony, a mere enclave – that was how many of its citizens saw it.

We are wasting away here. Sisaroth laid his hand absentmindedly on Firûsha's shoulder. *The plague survivors buried themselves here, where they live like groundlings. We're just clinging to our houses chiselled into the cliff, waiting for the Inextinguishables to come and save us and lead us to Tark Draan – if the new älfar realms even exist. They'd be magnificent great empires – nothing like this pathetic little settlement in Ishím Voróo.* Dsôn Sòmran was surrounded by dangerously unpredictable mountains that hung over them like dark storm clouds, and almost constant rain that felt like it wanted to wash the älfar off the mountainsides. Whole families had been already wiped out, homes swept away in mudslides that ripped out foundations and dragged the victims to their deaths.

Sisaroth clenched his hand into a fist. *We are not groundlings and we shouldn't have to live like them. What do the Inextinguishables think they are doing?*

As if the dark grey clouds above their heads had intercepted his thoughts, fat drops of rain began to clatter against the panes of the open window.

Sisaroth stared down at the festive flames, his face a dark, immobile mask. 'It's time they returned,' he muttered. 'They owe it to us.'

'Who?' Firûsha turned to face him.

Don't spoil things for her. She's been looking forward to this. 'I'm sorry. My thoughts were wandering,' he said, forcing a smile. 'I was just thinking that it's time Tirîgon turned up. Our brother should be here by now.'

'He'll have his reasons.' She caught raindrops in her outstretched hand. 'The west wind doesn't like our festival, does it? What a shame. I hope this isn't a bad omen—'

The door crashed open and the two of them whirled around in surprise, Sisaroth's hand flying to the hilt of his ceremonial dagger.

Instead of being joined by the brother they had been expecting, they found themselves confronted by the drawn swords of a troop of armed soldiers fierce enough to repel an army of wild óarcos.

Their leader, a blond älf with bright green eyes, was the only one not carrying a weapon. His elaborately decorated coat of black tionium armour and the silver chain he wore around his neck signified that he was the deputy governor of Dsôn Sòmran and that his orders carried practically the same weight as Aïsolon's.

'Gàlaidon?' Firûsha mouthed his name. *But he is the First Sytràp. What can he want from us?* The warriors surrounded Sisaroth and Firûsha, their swords raised threateningly, looking as if they meant business.

What can have happened? 'You must have a very good reason for this,' said Sisaroth sharply, stepping in front of his sister to protect her, his hand firmly on the hilt of his dagger.

Gàlaidon held up his hand for silence. 'I am here at the behest of Aïsolon, Governor of Dsôn Sòmran. I have come to arrest you in the name of the law,' he declared.

Sisaroth frowned. 'There must be some mistake – we have not been accused of anything.' He looked over to the doorway to see his mother emerge, evidently attracted by the noise.

Ranôria, an older version of her daughter, looked over at her children with obvious concern. She was wearing a black dress with white embroidery and had fine bone jewellery at neck and wrists; eleven white strands in her black hair indicated the number of children she had given birth to. She was accompanied by two veiled slave-girls. 'What is happening here?'

The soldiers stepped forward to block their way, knocking one of the slaves to the ground.

'Ranôria, I insist you keep out of this,' said Gàlaidon sternly, speaking over his shoulder. 'It was Aïsolon himself who sent me. Only he can rescind his own orders.'

I must put a stop to this. Sisaroth stepped forward. 'Show some respect towards my mother. Who do you think you are? Behave yourselves, or—'

'Hold your tongue, Sisaroth. Accept your punishment!' thundered Gàlaidon, hurling two white stones to the ground. The stones shattered on the mosaic floor, leaving pale dust on the leather of Sisaroth's fine shoes and the immaculate skin of his sister's feet.

'No,' whispered Firûsha in horror, covering her mouth with her hand to stop herself from screaming. 'Not . . . that! NO!' *I don't understand what's happening* – banishment? She cast a terrified glance in her brother's direction.

Sisaroth held a hand up to their mother, indicating she should not worry. 'Sytràp, I demand to know what this is about. You need to tell us what this performance is in aid of.' He searched feverishly for some reason for the verdict. *It makes absolutely no sense. Why are we being sent to Phondrasôn?*

Gàlaidon met his gaze. 'Three murders have been committed this evening: the venerable Tênnegor, his life-partner Sémaina, and their daughter Liphelis. There are witnesses,' he said, his voice level and cold, 'who saw you kill them.'

'What? I contest this.' Sisaroth drew his dagger out of its sheath and pointed it at the First Sytràp. In a flash, the soldiers stepped forward to aim their blades at the young älf's throat.

'The witnesses have given sworn evidence to Aïsolon and proof of your involvement was found at the scene.'

'Someone is lying!' *It must be some conspiracy to harm our mother – if we are both sent into exile it will be she who suffers most.*

Gàlaidon remained unmoved, his eyes devoid of sympathy.

'The decision is Aïsolon's, not mine,' he retorted. 'We could all see it was not made lightly. But he interrogated the witnesses at some length and apparently their testimony left no room for any doubt in the matter.'

'I don't believe it!' Ranôria spoke up. 'I'm going to see Aïsolon straight away. He must be made to see that this is all a mistake. They're all wrong – him and the witnesses! Sytràp, I implore you, do nothing until you hear from me!' She turned and rushed away with her slaves.

Gàlaidon looked round. 'Do you know where your brother is?'

'Is he accused with us?' Sisaroth almost laughed. *This is utter madness!* He found himself unable to think clearly. He certainly hadn't killed anyone, and he couldn't imagine that his brother or sister had either. They were surely not capable of such an outrage. His brother was the most rational being he knew and he never rose to provocation. 'This is—'

'I don't know why you are denying it.' Gàlaidon lowered his voice. 'As I see it, the two of you were protecting your mother's name, trying to stop the scandalous tongues once and for all. But however much I might approve of your actions privately, there is no way you'll escape banishment for it.' Ranôria's pleas had obviously left him cold. 'I am tasked with taking you both straight to the tunnels,' he went on. 'Your exile in Phondrasôn begins this very night. And you will go there separately.'

No – I will never survive on my own! 'But our mother begged you to wait,' Firûsha objected.

'And I told you only Aïsolon can change my orders. No one else.' Gàlaidon gave a signal to the troops and the soldiers strode forward and surrounded the condemned pair.

How could Aïsolon condemn his own flesh and blood? And what is all this 'evidence' he mentioned? 'We are innocent!' Dark lines like cracks in old porcelain crossed Sisaroth's furious face, and his steel-blue eyes turned black. His feelings overwhelmed him and he sprang forward to attack the nearest soldier.

The warrior warded off the dagger thrust with his own blade and his comrade in arms brought Sisaroth down with a blow to the back of the knees. A third soldier stepped in, his sword raised.

'Stop!' shrieked Firûsha, tears streaming down her face. *They must not kill him!* But the soldier, ignoring her, gave Sisaroth a deep cut to his right leg and blood seeped out through his boot to drip onto the mosaic floor, covering the grey and black pattern in bright red spots.

'My orders are *not* to kill you,' was Gàlaidon's unsympathetic comment as he struck Sisaroth in the face with his gauntleted fist, cutting the flesh over his cheekbone, 'but I am at liberty to inflict as many injuries as necessary, if that is the way you want it. *That* was for hitting my man. Stop struggling or you'll be sorry. You'll need your strength to survive in Phondrasôn. There are creatures down there that can smell blood a hundred miles away.'

If I give up they will have me and Firûsha dragged off before our mother has had a chance to talk Father round. We need time. 'I will not give in!' yelled Sisaroth, struggling to his feet, about to launch himself on the soldiers again, but his sister moved to stand between them. They were armed with swords – there was no chance of Sisaroth defeating them with his paltry dagger. *He must not, cannot, die in a fit of anger.*

'How long are we to be exiled?' Firûsha croaked, unable to

comprehend the harsh sentence. 'How many divisions of unendingness are we to be banished from Dsôn Sòmran for something
we haven't done?'

Gàlaidon replied, 'You can return to Dsôn after twenty divisions of unendingness. That is your sentence.'

Twenty? She groaned. 'By all the gods of infamy! We'll never
survive that long down there, especially if we are not even
together.' She had heard enough ghastly stories about the netherworld of Phondrasôn to be petrified at the idea; the prospect
of being killed by beasts might be the least of her worries.

I'm not much good at fighting, and ...

Firûsha turned to Sisaroth, who was glaring at the soldiers.
His leg appeared to have stopped bleeding. 'You have to find me
below, brother. You have to!' She hated sounding so pathetic
but couldn't stop herself. 'Please! I'll never survive on my own.
All I have is my voice and my songs – what good will they be
against monsters and their weapons?'

She speaks the truth, I— His face still crisscrossed by anger
lines, Sisaroth was about to answer her when a gust of wind
swept through the room, lifting the curtains.

'Is our mother giving a party tonight? What are all these people
doing here?' Tirîgon's voice from the corridor cut through the
evening air. 'What is this? Some sort of joust for the festival of the
west wind?'

Firûsha whirled to see Tirîgon stride into the room in tionium-
reinforced leather armour, helmet under his arm and his left
hand on the pommel of his sword. She screamed a warning at
him: 'Run, brother, run! They're sending us to Phondrasôn!'

'What is this nonesense?' Tirîgon stared at Gàlaidon in challenge. 'I'm curious as to what we are supposed to be guilty of?'

Perhaps we didn't kill enough óarcos last time we were on defence duty at the wall?'

The Sytràp nodded a curt acknowledgement of his presence. He gave a brief summary of the charges. 'But you are not charged, Tirîgon,' he stressed. 'Only your brother and sister are accused. Perhaps you should go and help your mother? She's on her way to see the Governor.'

Any question about this being a silly prank disappeared when he saw his sister's terrified expression. Tirîgon scowled as he took in the sheer number of armed älfar surrounding his siblings; for a brief, automatic moment he considered who he'd attack first in order to liberate them.

'I advise you not to try anything, young älf,' Gàlaidon warned. 'My men here are veteran soldiers. Children stand no chance against them. Your brother has already learned that the hard way. Don't do anything stupid.'

May the infamous ones be praised! At least Tirîgon will be spared. 'He is right,' said Sisaroth. 'Go and find out who is behind this plot – it must be aimed at our mother. She is the true target, I'm sure. We all know how she will suffer if she loses us.'

It's already decided, then? Tirîgon slowly put on his helmet. Four of the warrior escort turned towards him. Leather armour creaked and there was the sound of metal scraping on metal as they took up fighting stances.

A deathly hush fell inside the room. The only sound to be heard was the rain splashing onto the windowsill outside. The festival musicians had long ceased playing so they could take refuge from the torrential downpour.

He is getting ready to fight – but he cannot win. 'No, brother!'

Firûsha's frightened cry broke the silence. She could not bear the tension. 'You'll never—'

Tirîgon strode past the warriors, shoving three of them out of his path, pushing their drawn swords aside with his gauntleted right hand. He moved to stand by his siblings. 'I have no intention of fighting against Gàlaidon and his troops,' he declared, his voice muffled by his helmet, 'but there's no way I'm letting the two of you face the horrors of Phondrasôn on your own. I shall follow you there.'

But— Sisaroth was lost for words.

Firûsha sobbed. *If only this were all just a terrible dream. O great Samusin, I beseech you: let me wake up now in my own bed.*

'The three of us have always stood side by side and nothing will change that. Mother will get to the bottom of all this and will clear your names.' He drew a circle round them in the air with his hand. 'Our task is to survive this ordeal and return to take our revenge on those evil älfar who have treated us so shamefully.' He held his hand out flat. 'Let us swear to find each other in Phondrasôn.'

Sisaroth laid his own hand on Tirîgon's. Firûsha followed suit.

'Let us swear that we will spare nobody when we return to take our revenge, no matter who the guilty party may prove to be.'

'We swear it,' they intoned solemnly.

I am so relieved, though my heart is hammering away in my breast. Tirîgon was only at the beginning of his military training, but the prospect of having to fight his way through the labyrinths of Phondrasôn did not dismay him, for he knew he could always rely on his native ingenuity when faced with a difficult situation. He had a fertile imagination, steadfast reason and an adamantine will. *I shall not leave them*, he swore to himself. *Firûsha is even less of a warrior than me, and Sisaroth will need my help. We'll be spending a very long time in that maze of passages and tunnels.*

He turned to Gàlaidon. 'You have heard that I go with them of my own free will. I am thus free to return at any point to learn how investigations into these false accusations are proceeding.'

'Of course,' the Sytràp agreed, showing respect for Tirîgon's selfless decision. He ordered his troops to stand in formation, enclosing the triplet siblings in a prison cell of living black steel. 'Move on.'

'Can't we take—?' Firûsha started, unable to believe that they wouldn't be allowed to take *anything*, not even food to eat on the journey, but Gàlaidon was already striding off.

He turned back and said, 'I regret that my orders are to take you directly to the entrance.'

The small procession left the house and marched up the steep cliff path to the north, turning away from Dsôn and towards the massive defensive wall that kept the compact city safe from attack.

The walls were five hundred paces high: a combination of chiselled stone blocks and natural rock. There were periodic watchtowers and lifts to the walkways on top. Älfar runes invoking protection from Tion, a god of infamy, and the Inextinguishables were carved into the stone.

The monsters on the far side did not possess catapults powerful enough to send missiles over this great defensive structure. There was no gate that could ever be stormed. Älfar troops going out on scouting missions had to be conveyed to Ishím Voróo in freight containers lifted and let down by huge cranes.

This was how the three young älfar would begin their exile.

Sisaroth, Firûsha and Tirîgon were soaked to the skin by the time they reached the wall. Their hands were clasped firmly, as Firûsha trembled with cold and fear.

Sisaroth clenched his jaw as he vowed to himself, *I shall kill the evildoers who have borne false witness.* He was determined to show no weakness from his injury even though red-hot pain shot up his leg with each step. The chilling rain had cooled his fury but not his resolve.

Gàlaidon turned his party of condemned älfar and their escorts to the west, where a huge crane could be seen. It was constructed from heavy wooden beams reinforced with iron cross-bars and metal plates. It was obviously strong enough to lift the heaviest weights into the air, using a series of interlocking gear wheels.

They approached the base of the crane and after a shouted exchange of orders, the sound of chains moving over cogwheels greeted them. The crane tower swung slowly round through the cold night air. They were obviously expected: instead of the usual freight container, three älf-size cages hung from the crane cables. They were lowered onto the walkway and the soldiers rushed to open their heavy, metal doors. Gàlaidon locked the siblings into their separate cages and gave a signal.

As the cages were hoisted up, icy gusts of wind tugged at the triplets' drenched clothing.

Cupping his hands to make his voice carry against the wind, Gàlaidon called up to them, 'May the gods of infamy support you on the other side. They will decide whether or not you can survive in Phondrasôn. And may you soon find each other.'

Let me wake up safe now! Please, Samusin and all the gods of infamy, help me! Firûsha dropped sobbing to the floor of her cage.

Sisaroth grabbed the iron bars and gave a cry of helpless rage while Tirîgon stood resolute and calm, his natural balance countering the sway of the cage floor.

The crane arm swung out over the wall until the cages, rocking and colliding with each other, had travelled forty paces and were suspended over a yawning black chasm. Nothing could be distinguished in the utter darkness – even the stars were hidden by clouds.

This will not be the end of things. 'You still owe Tirîgon and I a song, sister!' said Sisaroth, though he was well aware of what lay in wait for them: a narrow cleft in the mountain base, a smooth fissure that could have been formed by a god's piercing spear. At the bottom of that chimney in the rock there was a second ravine leading directly down to Phondrasôn itself.

'You shall have your song,' she vowed quietly. 'And it will be—'

The cages shot vertically down into the abyss.

Firûsha screamed, and her brothers' voices echoed her.

The fall ended abruptly as the cages broke from the retaining hooks and tumbled down the slope, somersaulting over and over into the dark.

'We will find each other,' Tirîgon shouted. 'We *will*! Can you hear me? We *will* find each other. We have to!'

But Firûsha's reply came from far away and he could not hear his brother's voice at all.

His own cage crashed into a rock face, rolled over and slid through a loose scree before slowing and finally coming to a halt.

Everything is going round . . . and . . . have I broken any bones? Tirîgon peered out into the blackness.

And then his cage tipped over the edge . . .

FIRST BOOK

The Lost Ones

FIRST BOOK

The Lost Ones

Much happened to me.

I founded glorious cities – and saw them fall.

I loved the most beautiful älfar women – and saw them killed.

I followed the Inextinguishable rulers – and saw them pass.

Yet in those splinters of unending time, in the depths of Phondrasôn, where terror and thousandfold death lurk, I walked dark paths, seeing monsters and the strangest things – and suddenly came across Young Gods in a place where I had not expected to find anything at all.

I realised that the Young Gods had much to learn – before becoming True Gods.

Excerpt from the epic poem *Young Gods*
composed by Carmondai, master of word and image

Chapter I

Born from urgent necessity
a refuge for the healthy
a place of hope, in the midst of surging madness
among the mountains of Ishím Voróo
hoping they might hear news of their own kind,
the älfar in command in Tark Draan.

Know this: waiting is worse
than death if you live forever.

Excerpt from the epic poem *Young Gods*
composed by Carmondai, master of word and image

Phondrasôn, 5427th division of unendingness (6241st solar cycle), spring.

Firûsha blinked in the warm, honey-coloured light. At first she thought she was looking at a lantern, then the sun. *How ever did I get back to the surface?*

Her senses returned slowly and she shaded her eyes from the glare. There was none of the usual tightening in her face and her eyes did not turn black, as they did in daylight. It could not be the daystar after all.

What can it be? Peering through her fingers, Firûsha could see the bars of her cage and long, reddish-green stalks of grass swaying in the breeze round her prison. She could smell the earth, sweet blossoms and ripe fruit.

Then the pain surged in. Her whole body must be covered in bruises and she could feel the sting of a cut on her forehead. Luckily, the wound seemed to have stopped bleeding of its own accord and she did not think she had any broken bones.

'Sisaroth? Tirîgon?' Her cage had landed on its side so she couldn't stand up. She propped herself up on her elbows and looked around.

She was surrounded by giant vegetation and in the distance she caught sight of blue sky peering over a crumbling grey wall. A broad track of flattened grass showed where the cage had travelled. *It looks like that's where I've come from.*

Firûsha tried the padlock on the bolt of her cage. It was not locked, as the condemned exiles were expected to leave their cages on arrival in Phondrasôn, but it was stuck. She could only guess just how rough her trip had been, as she had obviously passed out, but the bumpy passage must have damaged the catch.

No! Firûsha shook the cage bars frantically. There was no way she could force the door open. She cursed under her breath.

'Sisaroth? Tirîgon?' she called, hoping her brothers were close. *What do I do if they're too far away to hear me? I'll starve and die here, despite the fruit that smells so close!*

Her cries for help echoed back down to her and Firûsha realised she must be in a cave. That wasn't the sky she could see overhead after all, but a strange blue roof – perhaps it was the natural colour of the stone. *Or has it been painted? Who would do such a thing?*

None of this would matter if she could not free herself from her metal prison. Without her brothers, who was going to get her out? Were there any living beings here at all? And if so, how would they react to visitors?

According to the stories told about Phondrasôn, it was highly unlikely anyone would come to her aid, but if she just sat there quietly she'd probably starve to death. 'By all the gods of infamy!' She attacked the cage bars with renewed vigour, shaking the door and kicking it. The only results were exhaustion and further grazes on her hands and legs.

It is too strong. I'm having absolutely no effect on it whatsoever. She lay down to get a little rest, closing her eyes and deliberately slowing her breathing, trying to decide whether to risk calling for help or to carry on waiting.

The cavern's light had begun to grow dim and the pleasant warmth was disappearing – she had goose pimples on her arms and legs. Her dress was badly torn and her costly tiara must have rolled only the gods knew where. Maybe one of Phondrasôn's more discerning beasts would be seen wearing it. When she opened her eyes again, she noticed her breath steaming in the cold air.

This sudden drop in temperature surprised her. *There must be a strong draught from the upper world.* Despite the springtime there had still been plenty of snow on the ground in the älfar empire. The icy mountain wind must blow in through cracks in the tunnel. Frost started to form on the grass stalks as she watched.

Firûsha shivered. *If it gets any colder I'll freeze to death.* With her body starting to shake uncontrollably and her teeth chattering, she realised she had no choice; she shouted for help. Grateful for her training in languages, she yelled in the älfar tongue at first and then in the lingua franca the barbarians used. Her voice eventually gave out. Nobody came.

Sometimes she thought she heard footsteps, but no one ever materialised. The grass rustled and cracked as the layer of frost grew, ice forming on her belt and hair.

She was near tears in her desperation, but did not give in. Defiance took over.

I will not die. Tirîgon, Sisaroth and I vowed we would find each other. I'm sure they will come and find me. She rubbed her slim hands together to keep the circulation going; her rings were bitterly cold on her fingers. *They will find me.*

Rustling steps approached and she saw a creature drawing near. Though it walked on two hind legs, its eyes were similar to those of a hungry hunting cat – except that there were three of them. The creature's throat emitted a clicking purr.

Firûsha couldn't stop herself shrieking as she struggled against the bars of her cage, but after a few seconds she realised how futile it was. She slumped against the metal bars on the far side of the cage and asked quietly, 'Can you understand me?' in the barbarian language.

The creature had a simple fur mantle tied around its middle and it bared its teeth as it pushed at her with its filthy calloused paws through the bars of her cage. 'Soft,' it muttered. 'Good!'

What does that mean? Firûsha pointed to the damaged door latch. 'Can you open it? I am stuck!'

The creature hopped on top of the cage and jumped around

for all it was worth, kicking at the door with its shabby boots. There was no end of noise and a lot of dirt but the door release mechanism remained unimpressed.

The disappointed creature hissed and screamed with anger and frustration. As it slid back down to the ground and pummelled the bars with hairy fists, Firûsha was almost overcome by the pungent smell from its body.

The beast can't be very bright. Its boots don't match and that cloak is probably stolen. Firûsha tried to calm the creature down. 'No, wait. Slow down. Shhh. It's okay – why don't you find a stick?' She attempted to make her meaning clear by the use of gestures and pointing. 'Stick. To break door. I show you how.'

The creature paid no attention to her but instead pulled out a little trumpet and blew on it, producing a quavering note that reverberated through the cavern.

The response was an answering tone from many similar bugles. Monsters came running up on all sides, trampling the grasses flat. Frost sprayed into Firûsha's face and she found herself being sniffed and stared at by several specimens of the same type of creature. They reached through the bars to poke her arms and legs and pull at her dress, tearing it even further.

'Stop it! Stop! Go away!' *It was stupid of me to shout for help like that.* The new creatures were dressed just as strangely as the first, wearing a mixture of random, ill-fitting cast-offs. They continued to rattle the bars of her cage angrily as they tried to reach her, tugging at her hair. 'Get out of here and leave me be or my brothers will— '

Suddenly, the monster who first discovered her sprang on top of the cage and shoved all the others away. He shrieked something unintelligible, pointing at Firûsha as he did so.

Whatever he was shouting seemed to find favour with the others and they took hold of Firûsha's prison and lifted it into the air with their leader still on top.

'What are you doing?' she cried, her long hair finally free from their clasping fingers as they carried her away. The cold was intolerable – it was vital that she get out of the cage and find something warm to put on. The overpowering stink of the creatures was making her feel sick. *I hope Sisaroth and Tirígon aren't far away. They should be able to follow these tracks.*

The beasts lugged her to a clearing where a number of odd-looking shelters had been erected from animal skins. In the centre of the camp, a crowd of monsters were roasting meat on long spits over a blazing open fire. When the group arrived, they were greeted with enthusiastic cheers and ridiculous trumpet blasts that sounded like the toys barbarians gave their children to play with. Their strident tones were far too harsh for älfar ears.

With Firûsha still inside, they put the cage down and rolled it toward the fire. It was like being spun round in a bee-keeper's centrifuge. She was momentarily relieved that they were pushing her closer to a heat source until she realised they weren't slowing down.

The cage continued to roll, starting to get very close to the flames. It wasn't slowing down at all . . .

Do they want to cook me? 'No! I'm not an animal. You can't eat me!' she shouted in desperation. Her plea fell on deaf ears. She tried to use one of her älfar magic gifts – the ability to douse flames and extinguish lights – but she was being rattled around too much to concentrate. The fire remained unaffected.

She attempted another of her gifts – the ability to instil

fear – in order to drive the beasts away. This was equally unsuccessful. She had spent too much time recently on her singing and had neglected her magic arts practice.

The monsters danced around, as excited as ever, anticipating a good feast. The cage was now perilously close to the fire.

There's only one thing for it. Aware of the extreme danger she was in, Firûsha raised her voice in song. She did not sing any song in particular – merely a simple series of notes that occurred to her on the spur of the moment. The sound cut through the noisy atmosphere like a diamond slicing through glass.

The monsters fell silent.

They stopped rolling the cage half an arm's length from the fire and stood it upright. A hundred triple eyes stared at the älf-girl as she sang. Enraptured, the creatures pushed closer to their captive and shushed each other.

It's working! Firûsha forced herself to carry on in spite of her sore throat and the flames scorching her back. In a stroke of genius she decided to base her tune on the crude melody she had heard their trumpets make as she entered the camp, elaborating and refining the simple theme. She put her heart and soul into the performance – her life depended on it.

While Firûsha appreciated being out of the cold, her proximity to the fire was becoming rather disturbing – her exposed skin felt as if it were being burned and she was afraid her hair would catch fire. The metal cage bars were extremely hot and scorching the soles of her feet.

Her vocal cords were also suffering and in danger of failing her.

I can't go on singing indefinitely. O gods of infamy, help me! Send my brothers to find me! She ceased her song with one final long drawn-out note and begged her audience to drag her further from the fire and to give her some water. The request was met with angry hissing; half-chewed bones were flung her way, as were handfuls of dirt. It was obvious that they wanted her to start singing again.

But Firûsha refused – her throat would not let her. 'Please get me away from the fire,' she croaked.

The creature that had found her originally pushed and poked at her to get her to sing. When Firûsha shook her head he screamed in fury and grabbed hold of the bars of the cage. His comrades joined him and they began to tip the cage into the fire.

They'll eat me! 'Wait! Wait, I'll— ' She tried a new tune but her voice had been overworked – she could barely produce a sound.

Firûsha bent to avoid the sparks that were darting in through the top half of the cage, making herself as small as possible and hiding her face and hair in her arms.

Just then, Firûsha heard a dark, roaring sound above the beasts' shouts and cries. It was like the wind howling in a deep chasm and was quickly followed by the death screams from the first of the creatures.

Those closest to her let go of the cage, sending it teetering back and forth. *My brothers!* Firûsha got to her feet and tried to stabilise her tiny prison. *My thanks to you, o gods of infamy! So even in such a place as Phondrasôn you do watch over your children.*

All around her the beasts were frantically running about, picking up stones to defend themselves, while others howled a war cry.

'You'll be easy prey for Sisaroth and Tirîgon!' she called out, laughing. 'Not a single one of you will survive the night. You'll be made to pay for what you've done to me, you scum!' She made use of the utter chaos to try her fire-dousing skills again. This time the flames sputtered and shrank, though they still didn't extinguish entirely.

The creatures' screams were changing. Their shouts of excitement and battle-fever had reduced to the sound of pure terror. Some of the tents had caught fire and the smoke made it impossible for Firûsha to see what was happening. She could hear bodies falling, liquids spraying; she heard yells of pain and groans of agony and the sounds of death.

Her tormentors' cries gave way to thundering footsteps as they fled in all directions to get away from the two älfar who had arrived to save their sister. 'Over here!' she called through the haze of smoke. 'Sisaroth! Tirîgon! I'm here! By the fire! Please, get me out before I burn!'

A wounded monster came stumbling out of a cloud of whirling, grey smoke, its three eyes open wide in horror. It was whimpering pitifully and its forepaws were clenched tight over a jagged cut in its side, unsuccessfully trying to prevent its guts spilling out. It staggered drunkenly and crashed into the cage.

'No!' shouted Firûsha, throwing herself against the front of the cage to counter the impact. The beast sank down, howling, and vomited dark red blood onto the sandy ground.

The älf-girl was able to reach a fragment of bone that lay discarded near the fire. She grabbed it and dragged it across the creature's throat. *There's no way I'm letting you topple me into the fire.*

Then she caught sight of a silhouette approaching through the smoke. It was too tall and broad to be either of her brothers.

As the monster below her gasped and gurgled, desperately

clinging to the sides of the cage, a mighty spear came winging through the air. The weapon narrowly missed Firûsha and hit the creature, which juddered and kicked out with its feet in its final throes – spraying her with blood and pushing the cage towards the fire.

'No! Please no!' Firûsha was powerless to prevent the cage toppling.

But before it fell on the glowing coals, it was arrested, jerked upright and pulled to one side.

Icy winds dispersed the smoke and Firûsha saw the stranger who had rescued her. A tall creature, dressed head to toe in beast-skins. An uncanny mask on its face was elaborately crafted from pieces of skull with only a narrow slit to leave its grey eyes uncovered.

So one monster saves me from all the others. O gods, what are you thinking? Keeping tight hold of the fragment of bone in her hand, she felt her survival instincts coming to the fore despite her precarious situation. 'You probably won't understand what I'm saying, but I swear I'll slit you in half if you try to touch me!' she exclaimed.

The unknown figure, at least a head and shoulders taller than she was, tugged his spear out of the victim's body and wiped it clean on the corpse's fur. 'Why should I want to touch you?' came the amused retort from behind the mask. It was a man's voice.

Firûsha stared at the figure in disbelief. *He spoke älfar! My language!* 'Who are you? Why are you keeping your face hidden? What is your name?'

'I choose who I show my face to – and when I wear a mask the beasts are afraid of me,' he replied, studying the door of the cage. 'The catch has broken off.'

'Yes, I know that,' snapped Firûsha. 'Can you get me out of here?'

'Of course.' He slid the shaft of a giant spear through the bars at the top of the cage and looping his arms around the pole, hoisted the cage on to his back. He set off, moving through the smoke and treading on bodies as he went, heading deeper into the cave. It was growing darker by the minute.

'So why don't you?' The älf-girl almost sobbed with frustration. *I'm such a fool. This is Phondrasôn – where my people's worst criminals are sent. He'll be expecting something in return for his help.* She had a good idea what that might be. She stared at her kidnapper's broad back with trepidation. *I will not let him have his way with me, but I can't stab the bone fragment into his neck from here.* 'What do you intend to do with me?' She was struck once more by how cold it was. She started to shiver.

'I'm going to take you to where I live before you freeze to death,' was his response.

Not a bad idea. She turned the weapon in her hand. *And there's bound to be an opportunity for escape sooner or later.* 'And then?'

'What's your name?'

'Firûsha.'

'Nice name. Suits an artist like yourself. I shall give you something to eat. Warm soup will help your poor throat recover.'

'And then will you release me?'

The masked figure stopped and turned his head; she heard a quiet, muffled laugh. 'Oh, I don't think so. You shall be *my* little singing bird now. I have been quite homesick for the songs of our people.'

'Songs?'

'Your voice was why I saved you, and I want to keep it.' He set off once more. 'Don't worry. I'll make sure you're well looked after. You will be my personal entertainment – I hope you know many, many tunes. It would be such a shame if I got bored with you too quickly.'

I've ended up being rescued by a mad älf. Firûsha groaned with despair and sank down onto the floor of her wildly swinging cage. *Wherever you've got to, brothers mine, it's high time you turned up. I need you.*

Phondrasôn, 5427th division of unendingness (6241st solar cycle), spring.

The soothing noise and the pleasant sensation of warmth meant that Tirîgon was in no hurry to open his eyes.

The noise grew louder, swelled and then fell, rose and then fell again . . .

In the spaces between, the sound of birdsong trickled through and reminded him of the one of the few happy times he'd had in Dsôn. It had been summertime, and he'd been playing with his siblings down by the stream that ran through the bottom of Dsôn's natural basin. They'd shared their dreams for the future.

Am I beside a river now? He opened his eyes and watched waves roll towards a beach, seeping into the white sand to make way for the next. Light glinted off the water. A small crab scuttled across the sand, its pincers aloft and snapping wildly, as if it were battling with a whole army of invisible foes.

Am I dreaming? Tirîgon was wide awake now. He sat up.

He found himself on a bright sandy beach, less than three paces from the waterline and in the shadow of a tree with large foliage. A little further away he could see the remains of the cage he had travelled in, broken and squashed out of shape, as if it had withstood tremendous forces. The door hung open.

I must have been thrown clear. He sat up gingerly, groping for something to hold on to. He leaned against the smooth bark of the tree. *I wonder where I am?*

The light originated from countless little spots above his head glowing through low clouds and it was indeed as warm as a summer's day. His armour, his long black hair and his clothes all seemed to be dry; his helmet was lost, he noted. *No idea where Sisaroth and Firûsha have ended up.*

He decided to climb the tree to get a better idea of where he was. The view was amazing – but deeply worrying. He was on an island, no more than four hundred paces by four hundred in size.

Nothing but water all around.

It shimmered turquoise, green and dark blue in the light, intensely beautiful but completely empty.

I must be dreaming. He strained to see if he could make out anything in the distance. *I'm supposed to be in Phondrasôn, not on an island – how did I get here?*

Feeling rather more sober, Tirîgon climbed down and explored the tiny plot of land, looking for any other living creatures. But apart from the trees, a few malodorous flowers and an inexplicable skeleton, he found nothing. *Nothing to eat. Nothing to drink.* He didn't care how he had got there, but it was clear he must get away before his strength failed him. He'd have to build himself a raft out of tree trunks. If necessary, he could take his armour apart and use that. With plant fibres to bind the tree trunks together, it could work. There were already two fallen trees at the edge of the water, he'd start with those.

He took off his armour and all his clothing, apart from his undergarments, and started work. He managed to fell another tree and cut the three trunks into pieces the length of a man, slicing off the enormous leaves. He took a short rest every so often to conserve energy.

A sword isn't the best tool for logging. If I were a blade I'd be furious at being used so disrespectfully. Hot from his work, he eyed the cool waves. It was as warm and bright as ever – the lighting shone down on him, but strangely, did not turn the whites of his eyes to black.

He walked down to the water's edge, removed his boots and dived in.

The water refreshed his body as he rinsed off the sweat, but he quickly spat out the mouthful he had taken. *Salt. It won't be any use to me at all. It will pickle me from the inside if I drink that.*

He came up to the surface and swam until he was out of his depth. Looking back at the island he laughed to himself as he realised it represented an exile within an exile. Brilliant low-hanging white clouds swept slowly across overhead. *I wonder if it gets dark here?* He was pretty sure he was underground, despite all the signs to the contrary.

Their mother used to tell them stories about the miraculous and horrendous landscapes of Phondrasôn and he had always loved to listen to her tales. He wasn't frightened by being in one of the idiosyncrasies of the place, but he was forced to admit he had no idea how to find his siblings – or how to get out.

It doesn't make a blind bit of difference that I told Gàlaidon I was coming here of my own free will; if I can't find the way out, I might as well be an exiled criminal.

Feeling refreshed, Tirîgon began the swim back to the island to get on with his raft building. Within a couple of strokes, he caught sight of a long shadow, and then a second. Three parallel rows of dorsal fins cut swiftly through the water's surface as the creatures increased their speed and he realised he was being hunted. More fins appeared: the predators scented their prey.

With a curse Tirîgon accelerated to a fast crawl, not stopping till he was safely sprawled on the beach. But a hasty glance over his shoulder ascertained that his pursuers had fanned out in a wide arc, driving a foaming, two-pace-high wave ahead of them. He could vaguely see their fish-like forms and the dorsal fins through the water, their long, gaping muzzles rearing up, ready to bite.

Tirîgon realised their intention. *That wave they're making will carry them right up onto the shore!*

He struggled to his feet, panting heavily, and raced up the sandy slope towards the trees, but the rushing water overtook him and he was swept off his feet.

He managed to avoid the first two sets of snapping jaws and sharp teeth before the world transformed itself into spray and the wave sucked him under.

He could see almost nothing, but he pushed against his pursuers as they buffeted him, scraping his sides painfully.

He went down, head over heels, but then felt solid ground under his feet. Propelling himself out of the water with a spurt, he turned and narrowly avoided the next wave and a huge set of jaws snapping in vain at his legs – his whole body could have fitted inside that giant maw. But before he could make his escape for good, he was dealt a powerful tail-fin blow that sent him hurtling through the air into the safety of the trees.

He lay there groaning for some time trying to catch his breath.

Why did I think swimming was a good idea? Examining the grazes on his body, he saw he was bruised and bleeding. Stumbling to his feet, he studied the sea and horizon.

His attackers seemed to have disappeared. Waves were lapping innocently on the sand, but there were plenty of tracks and marks on the shore that proved how close the monsters had been to devouring him. If he hadn't reacted so quickly, his hero's adventure in Phondrasôn would have been very short indeed.

This makes the crossing more difficult. He swept his hair back out of his eyes. *I wonder how far I'll get before they attack me again?* Tirîgon returned to the place where he had left his armour and sword after felling the tree. *I hope the sword isn't too blunt.* He was hungry and thirsty now. *That's it. I have no choice.*

He was heading towards the flowers he found earlier, to see if their stems would be strong enough to make ropes, when he heard the low thunder of a mighty waterfall. *What can that be?* He raised his head and looked around.

A short distance away from his sanctuary, water was cascading down from the clouds into the sea, causing it to boil and froth. The previously gentle waves grew wilder and began to creep up the shore.

By the gods of infamy! What . . . ? There was a new noise and Tirîgon spun to see a second waterfall, this one even closer to the island. Wiping spray from his face, he noticed that this water was not salty. *Fresh water!*

He quickly grabbed one of the enormous leaves and folded it to collect enough water to slake his thirst, but his immediate sense of relief turned to dismay when he saw how quickly the water level was rising.

Whilst he had been distracted, other huge waterfalls had

appeared, pouring down through the cloudscape, adding to the problem.

Tirîgon cried out in horror as he realised the shoal that had attacked him was circling the island, waiting for a second chance at their prey. The water was now lapping around the base of the tree trunks.

The young älf hurriedly donned his clothing, boots, armour and weapons belt, realising he wouldn't have time to finish making even the most rudimentary of crafts. The fish-like beasts were no doubt capable of easily overturning a raft. Climbing the tallest of the trees, he drew his sword in readiness. He had no time to make a plan, he knew he was dead. *I'll kill at least one of them before the others pull me down and devour me.*

From his vantage point he had an impressive view of the waterfalls. As he gazed out, a gap in the low clouds opened up, allowing Tirîgon a glimpse of the cavern's ceiling. *It must be miles high!*

A layer of shining mist coated the ceiling, hanging like a translucent veil and producing the light and warmth that kept the cavern feeling like a summer's day. The cascades of water came from clefts in the exterior dome. Clouds of spray shimmered brightly where they impacted the sea.

Is there no limit to this cave system?

The water level continued to rise until only the topmost branches of his tree were above the water.

Below him, Tirîgon could see the predator shoal crashing against the trunk, frustrated that he was still out of their reach. They snapped at branches lying on the surface and dragged them into the depths.

Clinging to the treetop, he was under no illusion that it would save him. This was it. *But I had such plans for the future.*

Out of the corner of his eye he saw movement. Turning, he saw a shape gliding towards him. A ship!

It appeared to be a metal-hulled ferry boat, fifty or sixty paces long. The craft wove skilfully through the enormous gouts of falling water, using the ensuing down-draughts to fill its sails. Its course, however, was not going to bring it within the älf's reach.

'Hey!' he shouted. Tirîgon waved wildly. 'Hey! Over here!'

The water crept closer to the top of his tree.

If the crew don't spot me, I'm done for! He took the risk of balancing on two narrow branches. 'Over here! Can you see me?' he yelled for all he was worth. 'I'll give you ... riches ... gold! I've gold for you!' he lied, to entice the helmsman to come to his rescue.

Finally, the vessel changed course, skirting around the closest waterfall; the sharp ramming spar on the prow now pointed straight at him, only two hundred paces away.

The surface below him foamed violently as one of the fish monsters surged up out of the water, showing its armoured back and three dorsal fins. It sank back under the water and Tirîgon knew it was about to leap for him.

If I don't get out of the way, it will— Tirîgon was about to duck to avoid the creature's snapping jaws when he noticed another of the beasts shooting up directly underneath his precarious perch.

Launching himself up into the air, he pulled his feet close to his body. The fish scraped the soles of his boots with its dorsal fin.

This knocked him off balance and he fell awkwardly – narrowly avoiding the snapping jaws of the second beast. He crashed down into the turbulent waves. Lashing out, sword still in hand, he forced his way up to the surface, where he could see the ship's broad keel was finally within reach.

He grabbing the bowsprit and let himself be dragged along, yelling for a rope to be thrown before the ravenous creatures reached him. He was at a hopeless disadvantage.

No rope came, so Tirîgon scanned the runed sides of the hull for crevices and scaled the ship's side with the aid of his dagger and his sword. It cost him enormous effort, but he reached the railing. He tumbled onto the deck, the muscles in his arms burning and his legs shaking with the exertion. He lay there for a moment, catching his breath and looking around.

There were no armed soldiers, no crew, and no captain. The sail overhead was richly decorated with symbols and suspended from brightly coloured ropes in the absence of complex rigging. *Whose abandoned ship have I landed on?*

Tirîgon felt the ship judder under him and he struggled to his feet to look down over the gunwale.

One of the monsters must have attempted to ram it. Two of the runes on the iron cladding flared and the fish-creature's ugly head exploded. Bloody bits of brain drifted on the water and the corpse floated away, with the rest of the shoal following in a feeding frenzy.

A spell! That must be how the boat protects itself. As an älf he could perceive the presence of magic energy. His hands had tingled as he'd climbed up the sides of the ship, but at the time he had put it down to adrenaline.

'Welcome on board,' said a voice behind him, speaking in the language of the barbarians. 'I hope you don't mind if I take you to my home? You can rest, my friend.'

Tirîgon turned, and froze: the stranger's white clothing, false smile and the way his long blond hair was dressed made it all too clear that Tirîgon was facing his kind's arch enemy: an elf.

'Come with me, I'll show you—'

Sitalia's brood are here? His sword flashed.

The blade whirred through the air and severed the elf's head from his shoulders before he could even finish his sentence. The arm that had been held out in welcome dropped to the elf's side as his head rolled off, then the torso itself crashed to the deck.

Blood soaked into the weathered planking.

Chapter II

Aïsolon, brave comrade of the hero Caphalor,
was a robust and loyal governor,
known for uniting his people and
representing order and the law.
He led his kind and chose a place where survivors would
be safe.
Thus he created Dsôn Sòmran,
no more than a dip, a funnel in the rock,
but the site rendered it invulnerable.
The surrounding wall he built
protected the city
but caused its isolation.
No one entered it and no one left.
Splinters of time turned into moments,
moments became divisions,
and the waiting went on, and on.
Whatever projects älfar undertook
seemed doomed to fail.
No road led towards Tark Draan

to others of their kind.
Yet one expedition dared to break out.

Excerpt from the epic poem *Young Gods*
composed by Carmondai, master of word and image

Phondrasôn, 5427th division of unendingness (6241st solar cycle), spring.

Sisaroth opened the door of his cage and crawled out.

It was darker than a sealed well-shaft. The damp warmth meant he was not cold, but it offered no protection against hunger and thirst.

Curses. Where am I? His leg wound hurt more than ever and he seemed to have injured his right shoulder in the fall. The slightest movement caused him to grunt with pain and the wound throbbed terribly. There was absolutely no way he could fight in this condition. *And in Phondrasôn, there will be enemies round every corner. . .*

He got to his feet and felt his way forward gingerly until he reached a wall. Feeling his way along it, he tried to make as little noise as possible. Älfar could move silently when they needed to, but here, a single stone displaced by a foot could betray his presence.

Occasionally he caught the smell of fresh blood; not a good sign. Nobody liked to bleed, not even monsters. Then his foot struck something on the ground and made a clattering noise. He froze, but it didn't seem like anyone heard him.

I've got to find some light. He didn't dare call out to his brother and sister for fear of what else he might attract and his concern for his siblings' welfare grew with each beat of his heart. *What do I do if I'm attacked? I've only got one serviceable arm, a leg that doesn't work, and a dagger.*

He had no idea how long he had been moving along like this. In the blackness he had no sense of time or space. The surrounding odours didn't change and there were no other clues to be garnered. He limped on.

At the sound of a low rumble, like the thump of a millwheel or the workings of a pulley, he stood stock still. *What is that?*

Multiple rays of light without warning shone down on him and his surroundings were revealed. He heard guttural voices coming from behind him, arguing, and he wheeled towards the sound.

He saw that he was at the bottom of an extensive cave with hundreds of stalagmites, their ends sharpened artificially to look like spears. *It's a wonder I wasn't impaled when the cage fell!*

Dozens of rope bridges were suspended overhead, crisscrossing the expanse of the upper cave in all directions. Sisaroth couldn't see any exits at floor level so he guessed the only way out would be those rope walkways. But some of them didn't look very safe. Whilst many were brand-new or appeared to have recently undergone repairs, others were distinctly moth-eaten.

What is this place? Is this the central hub of Phondrasôn? He ducked into a niche and was about to use his älfar powers to hide in a cloak of darkness when something approached his position. He froze. His physical state would not allow him to join battle with any assailant.

The torchbearers came nearer, travelling upwards in some sort of lift, yelling orders at each other every few moments. *What an ugly language.*

With the torches lighting the scene, Sisaroth saw why they had come into the cave: piles of bones lay between the stalagmites. That was what he'd kicked earlier. The blood he'd smelt had come from an óarco stuck on two stalagmites under one of the rope walkways.

The unknown figures approaching seemed to be human. The barbarians were wearing crude chainmail over their leather clothing and they had apparently come to scavenge what they could from the injured beast.

The óarco's few possessions disappeared into the barbarians' pockets and bags. When the badly injured creature groaned and tried to move, they slit its throat and took its armour apart while it uttered its death-rattle. Finally, the great óarco mouth-tusks were broken off and distributed.

So it's a carefully arranged trap. Sisaroth looked up at the walkways. *They've arranged it so wayfarers will fall to their death, then they can steal their belongings at leisure.*

Once the óarco's loot was exhausted, the humans began to look around for further trophies. Sisaroth suddenly realised they would come across the cage and know—

'Men!' one of the barbarians shouted from a far corner. 'Come over here. I've found a cage.' His speech was crude and ugly but easy enough to understand.

'Great! It'll be another of those pointy-ears. Is it still inside?' barked one of the others.

'They always have good stuff with them,' chuckled a woman. 'I want the shiny things – got it, you lot? I want it all.'

Sisaroth fumed. No imagination was needed to see how these unscrupulous robbers would deal with a helpless or badly wounded älf. *I ought to slay the lot of you!* He pulled out his dagger, but the sudden movement caused pain to shoot through his shoulder joint. He couldn't fight like this.

'Do you think it'll still be here?' whispered one of the others. 'You know they love to hide in the shadows.'

The barbarians erupted into coarse laughter.

'We'd have noticed,' responded the woman crossly. 'The pointy-ears is long gone.'

'That's enough talk,' roared a dark voice, his words echoing round the hall. 'There's not enough here to share. Get rid of the cage and drag that stinking óarco out of here. Two of you get bridge eleven sorted. Remember, the planks have to give way the instant they're stepped on, even if it's only a fly. You three, go and loosen the ropes on bridge two. It seems a whole band of kobolds managed to get across unharmed. We can't have that happening again – the little squirts usually have gold! I want kobold corpses stuck on my stalagmites next time!'

'Understood!' The barbarians split up and soon hammering and sawing noises indicated they were preparing the next trap.

As soon as I can, I'll follow them. They must have provisions with them. Sisaroth's mouth was dry and he was suffering from acute hunger pangs.

While the workforce prepared to move on, he crept out of his niche, now concealed in his cloak of darkness. He hobbled over to the lift column and sat on one of the rungs under the platform. On the other side of the thin planking the barbarians were talking and laughing.

The lift came to a halt several paces above his head and the scavengers stepped out, leaving Sisaroth free to climb onto the vacated platform, biting his lip to suppress a groan of pain. Following behind, he concentrated on not losing the light of their torches.

They're not taking any special precautions – they feel perfectly at ease here. But really, there's only a few of them. An óarco horde would soon dispense with them.

He shadowed them through several caves, crossing the same bridges and taking the turns they chose at crossroads.

A few minutes into the journey, he began to notice markings on the walls – *these must enable the barbarians to find their way around in the maze.* He took it upon himself to destroy any signs he passed. *That's for the älfar you've slaughtered. May you hopelessly wander these tunnels and fall into your own traps.*

His protracted and painful trailing ended when the barbarians reached an iron-reinforced gate and closed it behind themselves. Arrow slits in the walls made it plain that the humans were well placed to defend their settlement against attack.

Only a little light escaped through the edge of the gate, but Sisaroth knew that his only chance for food, shelter and revenge was on the other side. Uninjured, he would have marched straight to the barbarians and slit their throats. As it was, he would need a plan.

He was still considering his strategy when he heard footsteps echoing from the tunnel behind him. *More of them? Perhaps I can use this to my advantage.* Sisaroth pressed himself deep into the shadow of the wall. *I know exactly what to do.* He would jump this latecomer, take his clothing and fool the sentries on the gate. *That will compensate for my injuries.*

But instead of another barbarian, he saw that the figure approaching was a short-bearded dwarf carrying a lantern.

A mountain maggot! That ruined his plan. *I refuse to crawl around on my knees impersonating a dwarf.* He played with the notion of a quick killing but then let him pass unhindered. *He can show me the best way to get through.*

It was obvious that the brown-haired groundling had been involved in some heavy hand-to-hand combat recently. Over his left eye he wore a filthy, bloodied patch that must once have been white and there were gaping holes in his chainmail shirt, hacked out by a battleaxe. Red bloodstains soaked through – stark signs of the dwarf's many injuries. His gait was puzzling. It was different from the clumsy lolloping stride of most dwarves; he moved more like a human.

Sisaroth noted the sword-like weapon the groundling carried. *What's that at your side, I wonder? I've never seen anything like it.*

The heavy black blade reminded him of älfar weaponry. It was as long as Sisaroth's arm and, whilst one edge was straight and conventional, sharp spines like fish bones protruded from the other.

The point of balance would be just past the hilt, meaning it would need to be used with two hands. *Wielded like that, the blade would cut through almost any metal.*

The dwarf passed close by Sisaroth and his lantern's angle illuminated the weapon's details clearly.

Sisaroth recognised the fine grooving on the metal and there was no doubt in his mind: it was the same metal the älfar used to forge their swords. *What an interesting little fellow you are. That weapon would be far better suited to me. I wonder who you stole it from?*

The dwarf stopped abruptly, turning to shine the lamp directly in Sisaroth's face and raising his sword to point at the älf's neck. 'I've sent too many of your kind to greet Tion to be fooled by a shadow cloak,' he growled, surging forward and attacking.

Sisaroth dodged the blade and it struck the rock close to his neck. The groundling followed with thrust after thrust, and Sisaroth felt his injuries taking a toll on his speed and precision. On the dwarf's third thrust, Sisaroth's dagger shattered. His opponent did not let up.

How is this happening? I'm going to lose! How is he doing this . . . ? Sisaroth attempted a kick, but was again forced to dodge a deadly thrust from the sword, and his follow-up blow met only air. He back-tracked desperately into a narrow downward-sloping opening, trying to get some breathing room, but he stumbled, yelling with pain when his damaged shoulder hit the ground.

Checking his surroundings, he realised he had ended up in a dimly lit side shaft. Piles of old bones from all kinds of creatures littered the floor and what little light there was came from amber, glowing seed capsules along the walls. *It's a rubbish tip.*

'Where are you going, black-eyes?' the dwarf sneered. 'Let Bloodthirster split you in half!' He raced towards Sisaroth, sword raised. 'Did I go through the Black Abyss only to find an älf here?' he complained. 'I made sure there were none of your kind left in Girdlegard. I'll have to wipe you out down here as well.' He drew closer, a malicious smile on his face. 'Where are you from, black-eyes? How did you get down here? Were you hiding from the Testing Star and got lost?'

Sisaroth didn't understand anything the dwarf was saying. *What is he talking about? Wait, Girdlegard . . . He must be from Tark Draan!*

Despite the pain and danger he was in, Sisaroth felt excitement take over: so there *was* a path between Phondrasôn and Tark Draan!

We won't have to follow the old route. If I can take him captive, this groundling could show me the way. His kind know more about tunnels, mine shafts and caves, after all. Sisaroth's brain whirred, feverishly trying to work out a way to disarm his opponent and gain the advantage. He glanced round.

'So, are you looking for the exit or trying to trick me?' The dwarf halted, five paces away, sword pointed at Sisaroth. 'You will die, älf. Here and now, slain with the weapon that once belonged to your rulers. The Inextinguishables had no further use for it once I was done with them.' He continued forward with a rasping laugh.

'You must be mad!' cried the älf, limping as he crunched his way backwards through the pile of bones. 'The Inextinguishables could not perish!'

The one-eyed dwarf grinned. 'Where have you been, black-eyes? The Testing Star eradicated most of the monsters and the majority of the älfar. Your Sibling Rulers hid under the earth like the cowards they were. We found them and killed them.' He whirled his sword. 'Look what I've made from your sovereign's weapon: I took Nagsor Inàste's sword and forged it anew. See the älfar metal – black and evil, but it has served me well. It cuts through anything: armour, flesh, bone. Wait and you'll see for yourself!'

Sisaroth refused to believe what he was hearing. *It can't be true! He must have been banished for being a complete lunatic!*

The dwarf's next attack put a stop to such thoughts. He stumbled through the bones at his feet, picking up jagged fragments to fling at the groundling, and scavenging for something to serve as a weapon.

'Are you ready for your end, black-eyes?' The one-eyed figure towered over him, both hands gripping the hilt of the sword, arm muscles rippling.

As the blade descended, Sisaroth noticed a strange phenomenon in the air. His whole body tingled. *Magic? Is it the swo—?*

Opalescent light suddenly flooded the shaft and the groundling froze mid-strike.

As the light touched them, the älf's eyes turned black and lines of fury criss-crossed his face as Sisaroth realised he was unable to move. It felt as if a thousand tiny needles were pricking his skin, seeming to gouge at it in a pattern. He cried out in pain and tried in vain to flee but there was no escape. Dwarf and älf alike were paralysed and tortured by the magic field that surrounded them.

A trap? Sisaroth's eyes were streaming and he panted, struggling to catch his breath. *Is this the work of those barbarians I saw?*

Before he could find out, the floor under his feet gave way, swallowing him whole and leaving the groundling behind, showered with bone fragments. The älf slid over skulls, bits of rib and other remains, falling down, down, down. *What if the tunnel has no solid floor at all?*

He groped the walls as he fell, trying to slow his descent, and his fingers grasped a cleft in the rock face. Scrabbling at the surface, his feet found a small ledge and he spotted a small gap in the wall at knee level. The opening gave way to a narrow horizontal shaft. Carefully lowering himself, he crawled through it.

The appearance of the magic force field, or whatever it had been, may have saved him from almost certain death at the hand of the groundling, but it had also made his entire body feel like it was going to burst. *I need to get out of here.*

He wriggled through the dark for some time, until the corridor widened enough for him to stand upright. For a moment he stayed on the floor, slumped against the wall, his eyes closed. He tried to regulate his breathing. *Gods of infamy! What were you thinking when you created Phondrasôn?* Gradually the fury lines softened and faded away, and he felt the black leave his eyeballs. His whole body throbbed with pain.

He opened his eyes and examined his injuries in the dim light emitted by shimmering plant life on the walls.

He was covered in cuts and grazes from the broken bones he slid through, his injured leg was bleeding again and his shoulder was hot and swollen. He was feeling worse than ever; in pain, plagued by hunger, and severely dehydrated.

This is truly a place fit for vicious, hardened criminals, not the innocent wrongfully sent into exile! Sisaroth pulled himself up and began to make his way along the corridor. It didn't matter where he was headed or who he might meet on the way – he just desperately needed some water.

To distract himself from his thirst, Sisaroth concentrated on thoughts of sweet revenge. *I shall slay the evil-tongued älfar who bore false witness against my sister and me. They'll be granted no time to beg for mercy.*

Shaking with every step, he limped courageously on.

I will not die here! he told himself again and again, clenching his teeth when his injuries sent waves of agony through him.

Gradually, he became aware of a sweet sound wafting through the tunnels: a female singing voice. No barbarian could sing like that. The vocal artistry must be that of an älf.

Firûsha! Still limping, Sisaroth sped up. *It's coming from dead ahead!* 'Sister!' he called, ecstatically. Joy gave him wings and numbed the pain that had been torturing him.

The tunnel opened into a hall with seven galleries leading from it.

Firûsha's voice echoed all around him and, no matter how hard he concentrated, it was impossible to tell which tunnel the singing was coming from.

He circled the hall, calling his sister's name into each opening as he reached it. 'Firûsha! Where are you?'

The melody stopped.

'Brother, is that you? Here I am! I'm here! Here!' Her voice continued to echo.

It all sounds the same. Which one should I take? Sisaroth hesitated, chose one of the tunnels at random and set off. 'Hang on! I'll be with you very soon!'

Ishím Voróo (Outer Lands), Dsôn Sòmran, in the northern foothills of the Grey Mountains, 5427th division of unendingness (6241st solar cycle), spring.

Ranôria was standing at the bottom of the deep valley in which Dsôn Sòmran had been constructed. *Being down here always makes me feel so small.* The steep cliff walls rose up all around her, älfar houses clinging precariously to their sides.

Some audacious citizen had put up bridges to connect various parts of the town, but, even supported by columns, the slightest earth tremor or minor landslide wreaked havoc. If you were unlucky enough to be on one of the bridges when that occurred you could end up under a heap of rubble, hundreds of paces below the foot of the defence wall.

Ironically enough, the reservoir of broken stone that collected here served as a quarry source for new builds. All thanks
to the constant losses.

*It's a cycle we can't break, not until the Inextinguishables sum-
mon us to join them and we leave this place.* Ranôria had used a
series of transport container lifts and platforms to travel down
to this level. There were steps at the quarry's edge, where thick
stone walls had been put up to protect against falling rocks, but
if she took that path there was a possibility she could run into
Aïsolon, and she had no wish to confront him again, especially
when looking less than her best. She needed to impress him, not
arouse his pity or cause him to turn away in distaste.

After her rushed and frantic audience with him on the fateful
night when he'd had their children arrested and banished, she'd
realised that her conduct had perhaps been unwise. He had walked
away and suggested she come back when she was feeling calmer.

One moment of unendingness later, Ranôria felt decidedly
more tranquil, and more determined than ever to not be fobbed
off with unsatisfactory answers. She would *demand* precise
information from the city governor. He had been her life partner
for a long time and together they had produced three children.
What could have possessed him to issue an order like that?

Ranôria stepped away from the roadway and through a gate
into the small courtyard situated at the base of the high defence
wall. Drizzle was still falling and the paving stones were wet.

Guards saluted as she approached the entrance to the main
building and one opened the door for her. She was greeted by a
sytràp who relieved her of her damp cloak and handed it to a
waiting slave.

'Follow me. Aïsolon is expecting you.' The sytràp strode

ahead, leading her through the corridors and past doors decorated with metal plates. The teams responsible for state security had their quarters here, while soldiers doing border patrol duty had a dormitory inside the wall surrounding Dsôn Sòmran. The corridor led to a set of double doors that smelled like the oil used by the warriors to grease their weapons. It was softly illuminated by ceiling lamps.

Her escort knocked at the door and opened it after a quiet command from inside. Ranôria walked into the hall, sedate and confident.

Aïsolon was seated at a desk patterned with tiny bone platelets and inlaid with shapes worked in gold and set with semi-precious gems. The walls of the large chamber were hung with captured enemy weaponry. Ranôria knew that each item was unique.

Aïsolon indicated she should sit. 'Please approach. May I offer you some refreshment?' He was holding a writing implement made from flexible metal and was in the act of signing a document. 'I'll be with you very shortly.' He looked resplendent in his midnight-blue robes and the grey sleeveless garment he wore over it.

'No, thank you. Please don't trouble yourself.' Looking over at the trophy wall, she commented on the lack of recent acquisitions.

'That's fine by me. It means the óarcos have decided they don't want to lose any more of their troops for now.' Aïsolon placed his pen in a holder and sighed. 'Word has spread that our defences are impregnable, and so things are peaceful. So peaceful,' he went on, 'that some of our empire's citizens are apparently so bored they have taken to killing each other.'

'Oh, so you still refer to the city as part of the *empire*?' Ranôria gave a sympathetic smile. 'In my eyes the place has become nothing more than a prison. A second Phondrasôn, just with fewer beasts in it. We're no longer waiting for rescue. In reality, we're exiles here.'

Aïsolon raised his eyebrows. 'Aren't you overreacting slightly?'

'It's no more of an overreaction than your decision to banish our children and have them hurled into the abyss!' she said cuttingly, emphasising each word.

'Did I not suggest we should postpone our talk until you had calmed down?'

'Tell me, do I seem out of control?' she countered coolly. 'Now, what do you have to say about this absolutely ludicrous murder accusation?'

'Firûsha and Sisaroth were accused of not just one, but multiple murders,' he corrected her, reaching into a drawer to extract a leather folder. He untied the string carefully, opened it and placed a hand on the pages it contained. 'I shouldn't really let you read this, but I need you to understand that I had no other choice in the matter—'

'But you are their father!' she stressed, without raising her voice – but only just. *I feel like shouting at him.*

'And that is precisely why I cannot be seen to be lenient. Or weak,' he responded. A muscle twitched at the side of his mouth and Ranôria realised he was fighting his emotions. 'It tore my soul to give Gàlaidon the order to arrest my own flesh and blood and send them to Phondrasôn. And when I heard that Tirîgon had offered to go with them . . .' He faltered and turned his face away. He passed the folder over to her without a further word, got to his feet and began to pace, looking at his weapons collection.

Ranôria had known he wouldn't have spoken the verdict easily, but she hadn't been prepared to feel sorry for him. She looked down at the folder and her eyes raced over the testimony notes.

The evidence against Firûsha and Sisaroth was overwhelming.

Aïsolon had recorded every word of the sworn statements meticulously and the witnesses themselves, seven of them, were all of high status and impeccable reputation.

According to the report, on the evening in question Sémaina had held a celebratory supper at the house she shared with Tênnegor. The seven witnesses had been among the attendees. Everyone had been enjoying themselves immensely and things had been going well – the guests had been laughing about the beasts, the terrible weather, the god Samusin and . . .

Me? They were laughing about me? She was indignant.

She knew she was envied for having birthed triplets – truly a miracle in Dsôn – and for her singing talent, but it didn't make it any easier to bear. Sémaina had never tried to hide her feelings and was convinced her own voice was superior, often spreading the rumour that Ranôria's talent had faded after the birth of her last three children.

The notes said that when the laughter was at its highest, the doors flew open and Sisaroth had come storming in, dagger in hand. He had looked furious and demanded a public apology from Sémaina for the insult to his mother.

Sémaina had refused to back down and had assumed Sisaroth's threatening behaviour was either a prank or youthful overreaction, but the young älf had seized her, pushed her down against the table, pulled out her tongue and sliced it off, shouting, 'You will not insult my mother again!'

Could it be true? He certainly has a temper on him, but surely he would never do anything like this! Her hands shook as she turned the page.

It went on. All the witnesses agreed that Firûsha had then joined in, holding the supper guests back with a fragile petroleum lamp, threatening to throw it and set the place on fire if anyone intervened. When one of the guests had doused the candle flame Sisaroth had slit Sémaina's throat.

The siblings had escaped under cover of darkness. Later, the bodies of the other members of Sémaina's family were found in an upstairs room.

Seven witnesses. Ranôria felt giddy and faint. *They can't all have been mistaken. And they can't all have been lying.*

She knew three of the witnesses personally and the others were all well known and well respected members of the community. She might have suspected some kind of rivalry with her children in the case of a couple of the younger ones but the sheer number of statements made her dismiss this idea.

She raised her head and looked at Aïsolon. 'Now I understand why you acted as you did,' she said, hoping he heard the unspoken apology for her conduct in her voice. 'I should have asked to read the records before accusing you of heartlessness.'

He nodded and sat down, pouring flavoured water into a cut-glass beaker and drinking it. 'Can you imagine how I felt when I condemned our own children to exile in the dark realm of Phondrasôn?'

'I only wish I could have said my farewells.'

'I had to move swiftly, to stop an outraged mob stringing Firûsha and Sisaroth up before my guards could get there,' Aïsolon answered. 'I had to protect them.' He leaned back and stared at the weapons on the walls. 'It sounds strange, but it is the truth.'

What could have led them to commit such a violent crime? Others have spoken harshly of me before.

Sisaroth was well known for his temper and she could almost believe him capable of the offence. During training exercises he had once become so angry he had killed two of the household slaves. Aïsolon had been forced to wrestle his weapons away before their son could rampage through the servants' quarters.

Firûsha also occasionally acted unwisely, but only where her singing was concerned. She would disappear for long periods while practising and often might forget to eat and sleep, until she collapsed with exhaustion. But Ranôria couldn't imagine her gentle daughter threatening anyone, let alone holding off seven grown älfar intent on restraining her brother. *And no one would leave their weapons behind just because they were at a formal dinner in the house of someone like Těnnegor.* Weapons were one's status symbols – she carried a decorative dagger at all times. *Everyone knows Firûsha is no warrior. They should have overpowered her easily.*

The more she tried to picture the events of that night the less convincing it all sounded. *Something is wrong.* She read through the list of witness names. 'Did you conduct the interrogations yourself or was it a sytràp?'

Aïsolon was intently studying a triple-hooked knife with a broken grip. He stroked the broad side of the blade absentmindedly. 'I took their statements. They gave exactly the same account and I could tell from their expressions that the incident had shocked them severely. It was a ghastly crime, the like of which has never occurred before in our empire.'

'Their stories were the same, word for word? Exactly? *All of them?* No slight deviations? That's very odd.'

'What are you implying?' He turned to face her. 'We found a piece of Sisaroth's shirt at the scene and a talisman ...'

'Do you think they could have colluded? Could it be a conspiracy?'

'No, I don't. They were just in shock from witnessing the attack.' Aïsolon shook his head slowly. 'I thought the same as you at first and refused to believe them. But I went there, saw the evidence, saw the tongue that had been cut off, saw the bodies. It was all exactly as described. However unlikely the whole incident sounds, it can't be disputed. There's no question: Sisaroth and Firûsha carried out these murders.' He picked up his drink and turned the glass in his fingers.

He is horrified by this. Ranôria learned the witness names off by heart, replaced the sheets of paper into the folder and tied the bundle neatly. 'Thank you for your time.'

Aïsolon turned to her. 'Thank you for your understanding. And for forgiving me.'

'Did I say I had forgiven you?' Ranôria stood up. 'I do understand, Aïsolon. You can stop worrying. I wouldn't wish to carry your burdens on my shoulders.' She sketched a bow. 'Just keep your guards close at hand.'

'What do you mean?' he asked, surprised.

'In case I return with new information that makes it necessary to arrest someone.' As she started across the room, she said, 'I think our children have been framed and that we have been deceived. I shall find out the truth.'

'What are you going to do?' he called after her. 'Don't let your feelings run away with you and do something rash.'

She turned to face him. 'I will find out what happened. What *really* happened. Even if it means I have to admit my children are guilty of murder and deserve their punishment.' *But that won't be the case. I'm sure of it.* Ranôria closed the door behind her and put on her cloak when the sytràp handed it to her. *Gods of infamy, bear witness: I shall kill whoever plotted against my children. I shall fling their pernicious hearts into the abyss for the monsters to devour.*

She crossed the courtyard. Gàlaidon walked out of an adjacent building and lifted his hand in greeting, but she ignored him. It was ridiculous to snub the First Sytràp – he had only being carrying out the governor's orders – but she couldn't bring herself to trust him.

She strode out through the main gate and made her way to one of the funicular lifts the älfar used to reach different levels.

The weather had worsened and heavy rain poured down from the dark clouds that often hung at the top of Dsôn's cliffs. The rain spattered on the paving stones and ran from her waxed cloak in rivulets.

The names of those who had borne witness against her children had burned their way deep into her memory. *Who shall I start with?*

She stepped onto the gondola-like lift platform, deciding to visit Wènelon first. He was not an älf she would have described as an enemy. He normally kept well clear of unpleasant arguments and intrigues and she thought he might listen to her with an open mind.

'Fourth circle up, please,' she instructed the attendant. He nodded and moved the levers to put the lift in motion.

Ranôria pushed back her hood. *I wonder what Wènelon was doing at a dinner like that? He doesn't normally socialise much*

and he never takes sides in a dispute. And what was Sémaina cel-
ebrating? There had been no indication in Aïsolon's records. *I'm*
sure Wènelon will fill me in.

The lift slowly worked its way upward, stopping occasionally
to take on or let off more passengers. The älfar city was divided
into eleven rings, each one designating the approximate status
of any particular family. The higher your circle, the grander
you were.

Ranôria thought back to Dsôn Faïmon with nostalgia.
She was homesick for the old capital of the empire, with its radial
arms, each dedicated to a different aspect of their civilisation –
warriors, artists, scholars, and more.

The same divisions did not apply to this interim state – the
different professions were all mixed up together. She didn't
approve. *We have no clear ethos, no distinct leadership and no*
real home.

She respected what Aïsolon had managed to achieve here. He
had imposed a certain amount of order in the chaos of the initial
settlement, but Ranôria had always been aware that something
was missing. She saw it each and every day.

Waiting made them disheartened. The älfar had lost confidence and were abandoning traditional ideals and attitudes.
Society had changed and so had the älfar way of thinking.

Her race was in danger. Particularly the young älfar being
born in Dsôn Sòmran and only knowing this life and these
oppressive and demoralising surroundings.

She had tried to bring up her youngest children – the triplets – in
the old ways, but now it was all for nothing. Her joy, her pride, had
been banished to Phondrasôn.

I shall bring you back!

The platform stopped; they had arrived at the fourth circle.

She stepped off, pulling her hood back over her dark hair, covering her eleven white strands. She wondered how Wènelon would react when she questioned him about the fateful evening.

And what she would do if the witnesses were telling the truth.

Chapter III

The expedition made its way through the Stone Gateway
  where the beasts were now no more.
  The dust lay knee deep
  and the discarded óarco armour and weaponry
  made it difficult to proceed
  along the tunnels and through the shafts.
  The monsters must have been destroyed by some magic power!
They marched through the groundlings' deserted realm
  and just as they reached the gate
  in order to enter Tark Dràan and find the Inextinguishables
  a new dwarf army confronted them.
Although they defended themselves courageously
  the älfar were forced to withdraw,
  with heavy hearts and the knowledge
  they had been routed so close to their goal.
The doors of the Stone Gateway
  closed again behind them.

Excerpt from the epic poem *Young Gods*
composed by Carmondai, master of word and image

Phondrasôn, 5427ᵗʰ division of unendingness (6241ˢᵗ solar cycle), spring.

Tirîgon wasted no time contemplating the decapitated elf. He looked round quickly, expecting to be attacked by the captain's crew.

But nobody came to exact revenge.

Where did the elf come from? Looking around, Tirîgon noticed a small door in the forecastle. There was no sign of a ship's wheel either. *How is this thing steered? Levers, perhaps, like the lifts at home?*

He hurried up the steps to find out.

What little he knew about ships and sailing had been picked up from books or pictures. Boats had no place in land-locked Dsôn Sòmran. They only had one stream, crossed by seven short bridges. They didn't even have a ferry. So he didn't have the slightest idea about shipboard procedure. But even *he* knew it was odd not to have any rigging.

The ship carried on, moving past the few branches that were now the only visible sign of Tirîgon's little island. The vessel seemed to know its course and destination – with or without its master to direct it.

Tirîgon reached the upper deck and still saw nothing that looked like it might be used for steering the ship. In fact, the entire deck seemed to be bare. *It's as if they forgot to equip the ship.*

He listened out for any sounds from below decks.

Nothing. Could that elf have been by himself? He must have thought I was an elf too, otherwise he wouldn't have been so welcoming.

He stood there, confused, watching the mighty waterfalls discharge themselves into the turbulent sea. Spray continued to be tossed into the air while the waves grew more powerful. *What a bizarre world! Phondrasôn is too strange for words.*

He needed a plan of action. He must find his siblings. They obviously hadn't landed on the same island as him, but he had no way of knowing if they could be floating somewhere in these dangerous waters, nearby but unseen.

The ship creaked and swung suddenly to the right, the sail sweeping over the deck. As it did so, a selection of unfamiliar runes flickered. *That must be what controls the ship. Where are we heading?*

The bow cut through the water as the craft gathered speed. Tirîgon jumped down to the main deck, searched the dead body of the elf – finding three rings and a neck-chain with a key-shaped pendant – and then threw the corpse over the side. He would scrub the blood away using a bucket of sea water – he didn't want to leave proof of his own guilt on board.

A loud splash had him whirling round – behind the ship he saw a huge marine monster rearing up out of the waves. It looked like a giant pike but with a flatter head. It was twice the length of the ship and currently devouring the body of the elf. After swallowing, it uttered a roar and dived back down towards the seabed.

Have I attracted the monster by feeding it the elf's body? He followed the shape under the water as it approached the ship once more. *It's fast, I must make sure I'm faster! Perhaps I could charge it and spear it on the bowsprit?* He studied the mast. *But how do I control the ship?* A mighty thump echoed through the vessel and the deck started to tilt, the planks creaking and protesting but holding up. The hull's metal plates were standing it in good stead.

Another blow reverberated through the ship and Tirîgon was knocked off his feet, colliding with the bulwark. The craft righted herself and raced across the water, but the runes didn't seem to have much of an effect on the creature.

The älf got to his feet and made his way to the quarterdeck, but was horrified to see a huge chasm opening up ahead of the vessel. The ship was heading straight for the top of a waterfall.

Theoretically it should be possible to steer the ship round this danger. *Infamous ones! How am I expected to manage that?* Tirîgon had no idea what to do. If he jumped overboard he'd either be eaten by the monster or sucked into the abyss, but if he stayed on board he would be lost with the ship.

I need a barrel! Maybe there's one in the hold. I might survive the fall inside it and with luck get back to the surface – wherever that might be.

He ran for the companionway but there was a bellowing roar and the ship was rammed again. He fell over the railing onto the main deck, and lay for a moment, stunned and winded. It was too late. The ship tilted and began to plunge over the edge.

And then a miracle occurred. The vessel sank a mere handful of paces before the magic runes on the mast flashed, and the ship rose above the water.

We're sailing . . . through the air! Tirîgon gave up trying to make plans and decided to wait and see where the voyage would take him: a voyage with no helmsman and no crew.

He glanced over the railings, down into the foaming chasm. The amount of water plunging over the edge seemed to make no difference to the upper sea level because of the waterfalls still gushing behind him.

The ship carried him up, past the falls and through shimmering clouds of spray.

'Hey! Pointy-Ears!'

He spun round.

'What's happening? Are you trying to sink the ship? Will it take much longer?' The discourteous voice peppered him with questions. It sounded like a female barbarian and seemed to be coming from the lower deck. Her accent was atrocious, but she was using the älfar tongue. 'I don't want to hang around forever. Hurry up and take me to your people to be killed!'

So the elf wasn't alone. Tirîgon drew his sword and moved down the ladder, noting the smell of damp wood and metal. *Who was he holding prisoner down here?* The interior of the ship appeared to consist of a single corridor with rows of doors on each side.

'So, what's the story, Pointy-Ears?' she went on, this time in her own language. 'Cat got your tongue?' Tirîgon's acute hearing located the female at the end of the corridor, behind a slightly ajar door. A dim light shone from inside the cabin. He headed over. He would check the other rooms later.

Thin wisps of grey smoke stole from the bunk and there was a definite smell of incense and dried herbs, together with a further, unidentifiable sweet tang. *Did the captain not store his meat provisions correctly?*

He kicked the door open and levelled his sword at the figure inside. She stood in a cage and emitted a strong stench of decay, not quite covered by the burning incense in the corner.

Tall and slim, the barbarian female took a step back in surprise. 'You're an älf?'

Her clothing was made from scraps of skin, roughly sewn together to make a tight-fitting body suit. Her hollowed-out face was crossed with scars and the cheekbones were set too high; it was clear that she had experimented in altering her appearance. The sharp ends on her ears were false and had been stitched to her own flesh with ugly black thread, and her eyes had been coloured with dark dye.

An obboona! Tirîgon felt close to vomiting with disgust.

His mother had told him about these creatures. They worshipped the älfar as quasi-divine beings and wanted, in their sick fantasies, to resemble them bodily. But they also hunted the objects of their desire, flaying them in order to steal their skin, their organs, their hair.

Is she dressed in my brother and sister's skins? No, the garment is too old and decayed. He raised his sword with both hands to strike the obboona from above. 'I should be grateful to the elf who took you captive. Now I have the pleasure of dispatching you.'

She raised her hands in protest. 'No! Please! Revered godhead, spare me! I am not wearing the skins of your kind! I would never presume! I would gladly give my life to save yours.' She stroked her ears. 'I hunt elves and give them to the god I worship! That's why the Pointy-Ears took me prisoner!'

She'd lie through her teeth to save herself. He refrained from answering. *But perhaps she can be useful and tell me how the ship is steered.* 'How many did you kill?'

'I stopped counting when I got to ten times ten hands,' she told him excitedly, pressing her body up against the bars of the cage. Madness shone in her eyes. 'Oh, what a blessing I am granted,' she enthused, looking him up and down. 'You have not been in the netherworld long, I see. Why did they banish you, young god?'

Tirîgon ignored her question. 'Can you tell me how to steer the ship?'

She shook her head, and the dead skin she wore rustled as she did so. Her ugly face took on a sly expression. 'I can't explain, young god. But I can show you. I've stolen some of their ships and used them on foraging trips. It's the signs on the mast that control everything. They have to be selected in a certain order.' She laughed. 'We're flying right now, aren't we?'

I know she just wants me to release her from the cage. He looked at her intently. *But do I really have a choice?* Her wording implied she served another älf in Phondrasôn and had been killing elves for him. 'Who is your master?'

'You mean my *god*? His name is Tossàlor!' she said, enthusiastically. 'I'll take you to him. He knows everything.'

'Apart from the way out of here, obviously.'

'No, he knows that too. He told me so. But he doesn't want to leave.'

'What? Why not? Who in their right mind would choose to remain in Phondrasôn?' Tirîgon didn't believe anything she was telling him. *But that name is familiar. Tossàlor. Where have I heard it before?*

'You can ask him yourself.' She indicated the cage, craftily. 'But you'll have to let me out first. My god is sure to like you and treat you well.'

Tirîgon suddenly realised where he knew the name from. Tossàlor was an älf who had been banished long ago, after a spectacular court case that had kept Dsôn in an uproar for many moments of unendingness. And not because the charge was unfounded, but because his arguments in his own defence had been so brilliant that many älfar thought he should be pardoned.

His father had once related these events, holding a small box in his hands while he shared the story with his children. The inlay pattern on the lid was composed of sliding panels that could be moved and rearranged. The shape of the box was also flexible, changing from a square to an egg-shape that stood upright due to its centre of gravity.

Aïsolon had told them the box was brilliantly designed, extremely valuable and made by Tossàlor's own hand. But despite the fact that it had been given to him as a gift, he was going to burn it as a sacrifice because it had been made from the corpses of his own people. Using slaves or beasts as his raw material was one thing, but using his own people was a step too far. Art shouldn't overstep the mark.

Originally, he had stolen corpses to use their bones, Tirîgon remembered. But when he ran out of legitimate sources he had killed half a dozen älfar, including several wall guards, and attributed their deaths to monsters. He had been caught red-handed and arrested.

Until the moment of unendingness when the true origins of his materials were discovered, his art had sold for extremely high prices. *I wonder how many älfar in Dsôn still have work that he produced?*

It had to be the same Tossàlor. Could he truly know the way home?

However unlikely, I have to investigate. At the very least I should be able to convince him to point me in the right direction. But what he really wanted from Tossàlor was his knowledge of Phondrasôn. The artist had survived here a very long time and he'd know much about the tunnels and shafts . . . and where his brother and sister might be.

His only concern was that Tossàlor might want to make art out of him and his siblings, but he would worry about that when he actually came face to face with the artist-älf. It might not be an issue; it seemed he was specialising in elves nowadays. *I wonder if it was a change of heart or if he just ran out of älfar down here?*

'Swear by your god you will not try to trick me,' demanded Tirîgon, using his älfar powers to instil fear in the obboona.

'Of course, young god! I swear in the name of Tossàlor. I would never even entertain the idea of deceiving you!' She swore, bowing.

Using the key-shaped pendant he had taken from the elf's corpse, he opened her cage door. 'Now take me to Tossàlor.'

'Of course. There's nothing I would rather do.' The obboona ran past him into the corridor, dashed into one of the cabins and came out with a sword. 'In case we need to defend ourselves,' she said in answer to Tirîgon's suspicious glare.

He kept a careful eye on her as they continued to the main deck. *I would be a fool to trust her word.*

The obboona moved to the base of the mast and knelt, caressing it gently and mumbling some unintelligible syllables that vaguely resembled the älfar language.

Over the rails, Phondrasôn continued to produce a range of miracles as they sailed through the sky. Massive islands drifted past the ship as if a giant had torn them from the ground, hurled them into the air, and for some unfathomable reason they stayed there, floating like clouds. Dark soil and roots trailed from their undersides.

Tirîgon made his way to the edge of the ship and looked down.

For a good hundred paces below them there was nothing but the flying islands and the sea, huge waterfalls still gushing into it. *How high is the ceiling in this confounded cavern, anyway?*

Whatever the obboona was doing seemed to work, as the runes changed colour and the ship's bow swung to one side. The ship changed course and began to move towards an island that had several buildings with smoke coming out of the chimneys. 'Is that it?'

The obboona nodded. 'Yes, young god,' she said happily. 'We'll arrive any minute.' She stood up and marched forward to the bow of the ship, showing no fear of the dizzying drop and held her sword up like a conquering heroine. 'Make ready!'

She was too confrontational for Tirîgon's liking; she didn't sound much like a servant returning to her master. The ship turned again and headed directly for what appeared to be a landing stage on the edge of the island. He could see five other vessels moored at the jetty, floating just like theirs. 'So, where is your god?'

The obboona gave no answer.

It was a trick. 'Your word is short-lived indeed.' She walked to the rails and he followed swiftly on her heels. 'Pernicious scum! What is this place? Have you brought me to an obboona settlement so you and your friends ... ?'

'This is where Jamenusîl lived,' she interrupted him gleefully.

'Jamenusîl?' Tirîgon lowered his sword.

'The elf you killed,' she explained without turning round to face him. He didn't know what to make of her – her crazy state of mind coupled with her frenzied excitement made her reckless and unpredictable. 'Tossàlor instructed me to find the village where the pointy-eared filth live, kill them all and bring him the bones. But Jamenusîl took me by surprise when I was off guard and captured me. Now they all know who I am.'

She fought all of them? She must be more of a warrior than I first thought. 'How many live there?'

She shrugged, and the top layer of stolen decaying skin crackled. 'A lot, I hope! They'll be waiting for us on the quay, young god. Well . . . They're expecting Jamenusîl, but we'll make a nice suprise. We'll be swifter and stronger than all of them and after I'll take you to Tossàlor.' She raised her weapon. 'It was Tossàlor who trained me in combat. Just wait and see how good I am.'

The ship slowed and came to rest against the jetty, where Tirîgon saw four long-haired elves in white robes, waiting. He had no idea what elves were doing in Phondrasôn in the first place.

She's completely mad! Against his better judgment he followed her. She alighted, laughing, and ran to the elves, stabbing each one through the heart before they had time to react. *I'll have to stay with her and keep myself alive or I'll never get off this island.*

Her surprise tactics had worked and she met no resistance. The stricken elves sank to the wooden planks of the jetty, blood soaking through their robes.

As Tirîgon joined her on the quayside, a bugle sounded and elves began to pour out of their houses to stand in formation on the village square, armed with spears and bows.

Ten, twenty, thirty . . . far too many. Tirîgon stopped counting. 'Are you good enough to take on this kind of number?'

'I was taught by a god! How could you doubt me?' The obboona gave a loud laugh and ran towards the heavily-armoured elves, her bloodied sword in her right hand. *Tossàlor is an artist, not a warrior.* He took a deep breath and raced after her. He had no other choice.

He would never have admitted it to his siblings or his mother but he was frightened. His hands felt icy cold and his forehead was bathed in sweat. More than fifty elves had gathered in the square, all appearing to be experienced warriors.

But Tirîgon had to stay alive. He had to find Sisaroth and Firûsha. *I will overcome any hurdle and vanquish any foe in Phondrasôn for the chance to see them again, o gods of infamy!*

He ran faster.

Badly aimed arrows hissed past his head, but two grazed his leather body armour. One nicked his throat and a second lodged in his breastplate without hurting him.

He stepped aside to avoid a spear and then threw himself into the fray with a resounding battle cry.

Phondrasôn, 5427th division of unendingness (6241st solar cycle), spring.

Firûsha crouched at the bottom of the cage and let the flames warm her. *At least I won't freeze to death.*

There was a crudely fashioned platter next to her covered in crumbs that were the only remains of her meal. Bread and salted butter had never tasted so good. Her captor had also made her a hot drink, sweetened with honey to help her voice and relieve her sore throat.

Her masked rescuer had brought her here after a long march through icy caves. The stone house was solidly built and its walls were thick enough to withstand a battering ram. He had carried her, prison cell and all, into the kitchen and lit a fire. She had seen no sign of him since.

She considered the demands he had made of her. *I'm to be his little singing bird, am I?* Firûsha smoothed down what was left of her dress to ensure she was not unwittingly revealing too much. She didn't mind singing but didn't want him to get the idea he was entitled to more than a few songs from the homeland. Unfortunately, her tugs didn't do much – the dress was in rags and barely covered her. *I'll have to sing particularly well to distract him.*

Firûsha sighed and turned her back to the fire to dry her long hair, still partly frozen from the journey. She drank more of her tea and tried to think.

She had, of course, tried to get the door of the cage open again, using the knife from her supper, but her efforts were in vain. If her brothers didn't find her soon she'd be facing life as an entertainer.

And what happens if he dies? she wondered. A festering wound, a fall, an arrow – anything could put an end to his life. And that would mean an end to her own. She'd starve to death without him.

She pulled herself together. *I am the daughter of Ranôria and Aïsolon, and I am not giving up. My brothers and I will be reunited and return to Dsôn. I am innocent of the crime I was banished for and we will see that whoever accused us is punished. We'll do it together! United and unbeatable.*

Firûsha replaced her mug and dragged her fingers through her hair. As she did so the bodice of her dress slipped down. Glad of the warmth of the flames on her naked skin, she didn't pull it back up. *I'll notice if he—*

'Would you like a comb?' Her captor's voice came from the shadows.

Startled, she quickly spread her hair over her exposed breasts and rearranged her clothing to cover herself as well as she could. *He's seen too much!* She had that little knife in her cage but she was not confident she'd be able to repel any unwelcome advances.

'Surely it would help with those wonderful tresses.' His laugh was friendly and reassuring. He was standing in the dark by the door. 'Did I frighten you? You are an älf, surely you're not frightened of anything?'

'I was startled by your lack of manners, watching me when I thought myself alone,' she responded, unsure whether she would get away with this recrimination.

'Well said.' He stepped out of the gloom. He had discarded the mask and Firûsha was surprised to see that his features conformed to the highest älfar standards of attractiveness. Only a sculptor could have produced more symmetry. 'I know you are afraid of me.' He was considerably older than Firûsha – around the same age as Aïsolon. His body was hidden in the darkness, but she assumed he was no longer wearing that unspeakably awful fur costume. 'You don't need to be . . . as long as you do what I ask.' He smiled. 'And by that I mean that I want you to sing for me, nothing more.'

I'd be a fool to trust him. She sniffed and reached for her drink. 'I'm sure my voice will recover.'

'I am looking forward to hearing songs from my homeland, but I can wait.' He ran his light brown gaze over her approvingly. 'You are obviously from a good family where polite behaviour is important. Riphâlgis, I'm guessing.'

Riphâlgis? He must have been exiled in the time of the previous empire, when the Inextinguishables still reigned over Dsôn Faïmon. 'No, not Riphâlgis. It was destroyed. The radial arms . . . they're all gone,' she ventured. 'Well, they did not disappear exactly, but the whole city was flooded with a toxic brew—'

'What are you talking about?' He strode into the firelight and she saw that apart from a black loin cloth, he was naked, his skin recently oiled with a fragranced herbal salve. He had bound his long grey hair into a braid fastened around his head. 'When did this happen?'

Firûsha was impressed with his appearance; he was taller and more powerfully built than any älf she knew. *It's as if the strange light in Phondrasôn has made him grow.* She reckoned he was at least half a head taller than her father, and when he moved, the muscles on his arms and upper body rippled.

'So you don't know?' she said, deeply affected. 'It happened many divisions of unendingness ago. We all had to flee Dsôn Faïmon. The Dorón Ashont attacked, and then there was a plague . . . and then a river of acid destroyed the entire city.' She related what her parents had told her about their former homeland. 'Ever since, the survivors have been waiting in Dsôn Sòmran, waiting for the Inextinguishables to come for us.' *I don't know his name.* 'So you see we share a certain fate, you and I; we are both imprisoned in places we are not supposed to be.' Her tone was sweetly appealing. *I will pretend to be docile until I can convince him to open the bars of my cage. There'll be an opportunity to escape at some point, I'm sure.*

He sat down heavily on a vacant chair near the table and put his head in his hands. He gazed at the fire with empty eyes. 'I . . . all my friends, family were in Dsôn Faïmon . . . I can't believe they've all been swept away, expunged from the earth. Dissolved in acid,' he repeated.

'There is no one left to send you back here if you came to

Dsôn Sòmran,' she wheedled. 'Your judges are dead. And even if they weren't, they'd be glad to welcome the return of such a strong warrior.'

'Dsôn,' murmured the älf. 'I only know of one Dsôn and it is not the one you name.' He closed his eyes and the muscles on his back twitched. 'Why would I want to go there? My home has gone. I might as well stay where I am. It is not a bad life, all things considered, if you know the rules.'

'But the survivors need älfar like you,' Firûsha slipped closer, holding the bars tightly. 'The monsters of Ishím Voróo threaten our city every day. If we had a warrior such as yourself . . . we all long for strong leadership!' She gave him an encouraging smile. 'My father can get you pardoned – he is a powerful älf, the governor.'

He shot her a tired, sad look. 'You have no idea what I was banished for and yet you assure me I shall be pardoned?' He gave a bitter laugh. 'I can see you are terribly young, but you are quite clever.' There was a pause while he stretched out to take a cup from the table and fill it with tea from a pot by the fire. He drank. 'Tell me. What were *you* guilty of? I'm wondering what sort of horror you hide behind that pretty face.'

'I am innocent.'

He gave a patronising laugh.

'It's the truth! My brother and I were framed for murder and our other brother came down with us for protection,' she protested. 'Someone schemed against us to break our mother's heart by getting us exiled. There are many in Dsôn who envy her.' She emptied her own beaker of tea. 'She must not be allowed to suffer. I beg you: let me go, and help me find my brothers and return home so I can find those who plotted this.

They must be punished. If you help me I'll make sure you are given everything you could possibly want when we are back.'

'And yet you still choose not to ask me why I was banished.' He got to his feet, put down his cup and came up close to the bars of her cage. 'What do you think?' His eyes narrowed. His features took on a threatening aspect. Intimidating.

Firûsha started to doubt she wanted his help. She leaned back and gulped; it was difficult to swallow. 'Murder?' she stuttered.

'Do you think I'm capable of it?' he asked her.

She had the impression that her answer would be completely immaterial. 'Does it matter? If I'm falsely accused of the crime, I'm sure the same might be said of you.'

He broke into a grin. 'You are beautiful, wise and quick-witted, even though you find yourself in a difficult situation where you might be well advised to act in a more subservient manner. I believe you; I don't think you killed anyone. But being innocent doesn't help you. You're still stuck in a cage and I decide what happens to you now.' The älf turned and placed more wood on the fire. 'Sing for me.'

'Are you not going to help me?' she said, discouraged by his behaviour.

'Did I say I would?'

'No, but I thought . . .' She sighed. The faint hope that she might be released and return home went up in smoke. Firûsha watched the sparks fly up the chimney. She raised her voice and sang a song her mother had taught her.

The flower needs blood,
battlefields, butchery,

suffering and slaughter:
death will nourish it better than water.

Bloodflower black
bloodflower red
the strongest of plants
thrives near the dead

It flourishes on disasters
entwines a rotting corpse
grows up straight and tall
the fairest flower of all

Bloodflower black
bloodflower red
the strongest of plants
thrives near the dead

Bursts into blossom, heavily scented,
it swamps every battlefield with poison and beauty
a deadly sight to all within range
if you smell this perfume
know, your time will come soon.

Firûsha sustained the final note for as long as she could, then hummed a refrain before allowing the melody to die away.

It took her a few heartbeats to return to reality. Whenever she sang, she immersed herself in the world of the song, visualising everything described in the lyrics. In her mind she experienced the emotions of the music – suffering, delight, ecstasy – and she would follow the story in her heart. Her mother had always stressed that the best singer would be able to take her audience with her on the journey.

The burning wood in the fireplace crackled its enthusiastic applause.

The silent älf had not moved.

It looks like I have not been able to charm him with my song. Firûsha quickly poured herself something to drink before apologising. 'Forgive me. My throat is sore.'

'Wonderful,' he breathed, still facing away from her. 'Just wonderful. I know the song. It was often performed in Dsôn. In *my* Dsôn, I mean. I never heard it sung like that, as a ballad. It was always a battle-song we used to sing on campaign.' When he turned round she saw there were tears in his eyes. His heart had been touched. 'My name is Crotàgon,' he told her softly. 'I used to belong to the ranks of the Goldsteel warriors. You know about our unit?'

At last he has told me his name. Firûsha nodded. The Inextinguishables had created that elite fighting company. The Goldsteel warriors had a reputation for being the finest in the whole älfar army; same-sex couples who had proved themselves against the fiercest marauding monsters. Male and male, female with female, these warrior pairings were inseperable in combat, standing up for each other, keen to speed to a decisive victory and eager to end the fighting with honour.

'The regiment no longer exists,' Firûsha told him. 'The few who survived the plague and came to us now serve with the wall sentries along with all the other soldiers.' She was mightily relieved to learn that Crotàgon had belonged to that exclusive group. *I won't have to worry about his having physical designs on me.*

'I was banished from Dsôn because I fell out of favour with the Inextinguishables. I once commanded a company of forty same-sex fighting couples. We were the best. It was at the start of the Tark Draan campaign. I was given an audience because of my military success and I confronted our rulers, making no bones about my conviction that the proposed attack deep into Tark Draan was a dangerous mistake. I told them the army had not had sufficient training. We would have been in unknown territory and commanded by Sinthoras, who always put his own good over that of his soldiers. I considered him incapable of proper military strategic thought. Instead of the planned attack I recommended a gradual expansion of Dsôn Faïmon territory on the other side of the defence moat.'

'That would have been a good idea,' was Firûsha's comment. *If they had taken that advice then the Dorón Ashont would never have invaded the heart of our empire.* 'And that was why they sent you to Phondrasôn? Because you spoke out? Did they exile you? Or did you come here to escape their anger?'

Crotàgon hesitated. 'It wasn't that,' he said. 'I had been trying to persuade the rest of the Goldsteel warriors to use their influence with the Inextinguishables. I wanted us to all go together to the Bone Tower to petition our point. At the very least I wanted to demand that a different nostàroi be appointed. There was no objection to Caphalor, but Sinthoras had to go.'

Firûsha weighed up what he had told her. *But he was practically criticising the Inextinguishables publicly. Criticising the rulers' decisions. That's treason.*

He looked down. 'But I . . .' He faltered and a shudder ran through his powerful body. 'My plans were betrayed. Betrayed by a person very dear to me and whose life I had often saved in combat.' He closed his eyes. 'I was dragged out of camp by night and hurled off into exile.' Crotàgon's hazel eyes showed his pain.

Being betrayed by his partner hit him harder than being sent to Phondrasôn. Firûsha felt a surge of sympathy. *He is still mourning that loss.*

'I can never go back to Dsôn as long as the Inextinguishables are alive. They will remember exactly what happened.' He turned his face to one side, revealing a handsome profile. 'But you are right: you should go back. Get up to the surface again and go back to your Dsôn.'

'Oh, that would be amazing, Crotàgon!' she exclaimed, but her face fell when he strode past without releasing her from the cage. 'Wait – where are you going?'

'I've got to think. I'll sleep on it. I can't decide right now. I can't let you travel through Phondrasôn on your own. You'd be killed quicker than a newborn barbarian in a pit full of óarcos. You're no warrior. And your singing is too good for you to be able to kill anything with your voice.' He laughed at his own joke.

Firûsha was not inclined to join in the merriment. She glared at him balefully. 'You're going to make me spend the night in this thing?'

'If I accompanied you I'd be giving up a lot. I have to consider it carefully. As long as you are in the cage you won't be running off, trying to find your way home or your brothers on your own. I'm honestly only protecting you, saving your life a second time. Really, you should be thanking me.'

'What is there to consider?' she retorted, unable to believe her ears. 'Look around you! You live in a shed my father would be ashamed to house the worst of his slaves in.'

'How do you know what the rest of my house looks like?'

'You're unlikely to have bathrooms and princely bedchambers hidden behind that door!'

He grinned and stroked his naked torso. 'You will have noticed that I bathed after the fighting? Behind that wall I have rooms more magnificent than you can imagine. I'm sure you would be glad to have a nice warm bath with herbs and perfumed oils. You shall be accorded that pleasure after one more night in the cage. And I'll give you a guided tour of the house. Then you will understand why I am taking my time about the decision.' He pushed a pot into the cage. 'For when you need it.' The stately älf left the room, closing the door quietly behind him.

Firûsha was so angry that she hurled her cup at the closing door. It shattered satisfyingly. She bit her lip instead of hurling imprecations and insults after him.

She slumped down against the bars and sat staring into the flames. *You shall take me back home, you steelygold monster of an älf! I will sing you into submission, just see if I don't. You'll be under my thumb before this is over.*

She did not know what she would say to her brothers if she met up with them now. *Should I have them kill Crotàgon or should I spare him in case he proves useful? If he knows the way out . . .*

She tried to get comfortable and rolled herself into a sleeping position. *You'll pay for this, one way or another. You've treated me like some filthy slave.* She closed her eyes.

Chapter IV

Dsôn Sòmran,
merely a city.
Not the pride of an empire
not the black heart of an empire
vibrant with affluence and powerful in battle,
but a grey refuge.
In grey mountains, under grey clouds and wet with grey
rain
the place gives rise to grey thoughts.
Immanent despair, the wearing-down of souls.
They told me that unspeakable things happened in Dsôn Sòmran.
The greatest blasphemy was committed by many:
Acting selfishly, they squandered the gift of immortality
and themselves. Eighty-eight of them.
They jumped off the wall,
impaled themselves on swords or hung themselves.
Their names were expunged from the records
and were not even carved on the Roll of Shame.

Excerpt from the epic poem *Young Gods*
composed by Carmondai, master of word and image

Phondrasôn, 5427th division of unendingness (6241st solar cycle), spring.

But I heard her! Sisaroth limped along the constricted tunnel, its hot air difficult to breathe. A faltering dim light came from the walls themselves. Was there a lava stream on the other side of the rock? It would explain the heat.

I'm stumbling around in the half-dark trying to find my way out of some damn oven! 'Firûsha!' he called, running his hand over his face and then licking the sweat. There had been nothing to drink and he must not waste a drop of moisture.

But the voice of his beloved sister was no longer to be heard.

It seemed to make no difference whether he continued down this passage or went back to the main hall. The other tunnels could not be much better. He continued in the same direction, hoping it would lead somewhere eventually.

He was still in a great deal of pain from his leg and shoulder injuries. He needed to find a place where he could be treated, or at least get water to clean the wound on his leg. If the cut remained dirty it could develop into the dreaded gangrene that eats its way through flesh and bone. He quickened his pace.

Sisaroth was afraid that it was fever and not just the heat in the tunnel making him sweat. *I must find water.*

At his next step he looked down and noticed painted, carved runes on the stone floor, partially obscured with dirt.

Bending down, he felt the deep grooves. At the edges the colour had been rubbed away by the passing of many feet. He wiped the dirt aside.

Älfar signs. Sisaroth recognised the characteristic script used by his own folk but these runes were unusual, probably from the distant past. He was only able to decipher a few words of warning about *danger of a spirit.*

With each step he uncovered more of the writing: *magic, infamy, eternal life, resistance, fire from the sky,* he read, tense with apprehension. *Is this a place of sanctuary?*

He decided to follow this tunnel to its end. Whoever had created the runes had been one of the älfar. So whatever awaited him would be positive.

In the meantime he was sweating as much as he would have done under the hottest midday summer sun. His mouth was gritty, his tongue swollen, his throat dry and painful. His progress was slow and laboured as he fought for breath.

The tunnel in front of him seemed to sway and fade and his legs trembled.

At that moment his right foot touched a symbol that flared up, bathing the whole tunnel in a violet glow.

Then all the runes lit up, one after the other, showing him the way. A wind rose and blew the dirt from the half-hidden symbols, sending sand into his eyes. He shielded his face with his arm.

'Come to me, Child of Inàste,' a female voice welcomed him. 'I am expecting you.'

'Who are you?' he called back.

'Come, come to me, Child of Inàste. I am waiting for you.'

With the last of his remaining strength, Sisaroth stepped over the signs, surrendering to his fate, whether it be protection or a trap.

The guide-lights led him to a cave in the middle of which was a circular arrangement of columns with an elegant tower at its centre. Support beams were anchored in the cave wall to ensure the edifice was secure.

The row of lights led directly to the tower and around it. The tower itself glowed and illuminated the entire cave, revealing a colossal mural depicting a hunting scene with an älfar city in the background.

Sisaroth was too weary to be impressed by the skill of the painting, the vivid colours, the accuracy in the detail. He no longer cared if there was anyone here or who it might be. He was in urgent need of water – and then he heard the gurgling sound coming from between the columns and saw the rippling brightness.

At last! Sisaroth limped over as quickly as he could, going past the columns to find himself in front of a wide basin, the tower at its centre.

He knelt down, moaning with pain, and sniffed the flowing water. Fresh, and clearly not stagnant. Nothing to indicate that it was not safe.

He scooped up a handful and tasted the liquid. *Incredible, fresh water! My thanks to the gods of infamy!* He held on to the side of the pool and dipped his face into the water to drink in long draughts. The water seemed to turn to steam in his mouth, he was so hot.

Sisaroth raised his head, gasping. *That's better.* He soaked his hair and tossed it back over his shoulder. Feeling refreshed, he leaned back against one of the columns and studied the incandescent tower. *And now for this next Phondrasôn miracle. I wonder if there is anything to eat in there. How do I get inside?*

The building must have been at least sixty paces high and fifteen in diameter; it was made from crude layers of rough-hewn stone blocks with intricately chiselled runes on the side. Sisaroth deduced that constructor and engraver had not been the same.

On close study it was obvious that the tower inclined slightly to one side. This would be the reason for the support struts. The immense weight of the edifice must be causing the foundation to sag. The cave vault, forty paces above the top of the tower, showed signs of having been altered to give extra height.

Were they trying to break through the cave ceiling or was the aim to increase the height of the tower? Sisaroth got to his feet and circled it. There was no access except over the water. No door that he could see. He speculated ruefully whether this might be the memorial tomb of some bewildered oligarch with delusions of grandeur. The dead would not be able to help him with food or medical attention.

Did some spirit lure me here to make a fool of me? 'Hey!' he shouted. 'Hallo! I am a child of Inàste and I followed your invitation. The runes led me hither. Here I am!'

Nothing.

He had not seriously expected to hear a response. *But it had been worth a try.*

He was uneasy now: very keen to solve the riddle and get into the building. There might be useful stores inside: provisions, weaponry or clothing. In Phondrasôn the principle of survival favoured the fittest – the strongest, the swiftest, the best. His chances would surely improve if he could pick up some decent armour.

His stomach rumbled.

For infamy's sake! What's the trick here? Sisaroth stood still and studied the columns with their glowing symbols. He could tell from the tingling on his face that the runes were imbued with magic. Two of the signs were badly damaged. Deliberately attacked with a hammer or an axe?

I'll give it one more try before giving up. He turned back to the windowless tower and shouted in a mixture of disappointment and fury. 'Hallo! Anyone in there? I am injured! I need help!' He bent down to pick up a pebble and hurled it against the side of the building. 'Do you hear me? By Inàste and all the gods of infamy, I need ...'

As soon as the pebble struck home, the tower's magic runes flashed a dangerous red. White lightning played along the length of the supporting girders. There was a loud humming seeming to originate from inside the tower, just as the energy was released.

A broad shaft of ruby-coloured light shot out from one of the stone blocks at the base of the turret, targeting the älf. His surroundings seemed to fizzle and disappear.

What's happening? Dazzled, he tried to shield himself from the light. Then it all went dark.

When he was able to open his eyes, he found himself hovering in a barred cell for two or three heartbeats before he was plonked down on a heap of old bones which crumbled under his weight. The injuries on his leg and on his shoulder sent waves of unbearable pain coursing through his body. He screamed and was forced to inhale polluted air which induced paroxysms of coughing.

'What a turbulent approach,' said a disapproving female voice, employing an ancient älfar idiom. 'You could hardly wait to get here, could you? What is your name?'

Where am I? Sisaroth tried to grab the bars in order to pull himself upright. Water, he realised, would quench thirst but it would not restore energy and he was eager not to appear weak. 'My name is Sisaroth,' he said, peering through the dust to see who he was talking to.

The älf-woman was standing at the foot of a staircase, draped in a light brown mantle over an embroidered robe; her long blonde hair gleamed in the light of her lantern. 'Where have you come from?'

'From Dsôn Sòmran. I am looking for my siblings.'

'You are the first, for . . .' She thought hard. 'It's impossible to keep track of time in this confounded place. At any rate it is absolutely ages since I had a visitor. A visitor who wouldn't try to eat me, I mean.' She gestured towards the heap of bones. 'Please excuse the initial greeting. I shall release you at once. The cage was for my own protection. The tower has tested me more than once with ghastly beasts living in the cellar slavering for my blood.' She came closer, a charming smile on her face. 'My name is Marandëi. Welcome to my unchosen realm.'

As if by a ghostly hand the lock on the door of his cell opened. *She must be a . . . cîanai!* He stumbled out, limping badly, and bowed. 'Thank you for bringing me here.' The wrinkles on her face, throat and hands showed she must be considerably older than his mother.

The only cîanai Sisaroth knew about were from the old legends. The same legends that told the history of Dsôn Faïmon and spoke of the research schools in the radial arm Welèron, where it was said that magic arts had been practised. It was incredibly rare to develop the gift of magic beyond the normal älfar ability to spread fear and darkness.

'Don't thank me. Thank the tower,' Marandëi said. 'Phondrasôn has been treating you badly, it seems. Come upstairs with me. You need food and drink first of all and then I'll examine your injuries.' She led the way. 'There are quite a few steps. Will you be able to manage?'

'Of course, Cîanai.' Sisaroth was relieved. *The pain and the hunger will soon be over. Thanks be to the infamous ones.*

'Cîanai.' Marandëi chuckled. 'That's a high honour for an älf when all she did was open the door of your cage.'

'What did you mean when you said it was the tower that summoned me?'

'Exactly that.' As the metal-reinforced tip of her tall stick tapped on the stairs, the lantern suspended from it swung to and fro. 'The tower could just as easily have turned you to ashes. The tower always decides what it wants to do with those that come here.'

Sisaroth did not understand. 'I thought *you* . . .'

Marandëi felt her way along the wall as she climbed the stairs. 'This is my home. My prison. My everything. You shall share it with me. I am sure we will get along famously. We have all the time in the world, after all.'

Sisaroth stood rooted to the spot. 'You don't mean . . .'

She turned round, her white eyes full of surprise. 'You don't think you're leaving, do you? There is no escape. The walls resist everything. I've tried it all. Nothing works. I am forced to wait here and occasionally there will be a visitor and I can watch him die.' She came down one step, leaning forward to put her face close to his. 'I don't live in this tower because I want to, Sisaroth. I am stuck here.'

It can't be true. He snorted with laughter. 'You're a cîanai and you can't get out of a prison? I don't believe it.'

'There you are, that's the impetuosity of youth talking. You have absolutely no idea, have you?' She whacked the stone with her stick in anger. 'I have attempted everything. But here's a suggestion, my young hothead. If you find the way to free us both from this misery, I'll follow you, and for five divisions of unendingness I promise to fulfil your every wish, as long as what you command is within my power.' The harsh expression on Marandëi's face softened. 'But first let us see to your wounds. You will need all your strength. And before I forget: the tower is resentful and never forgets if someone attempts to harm it. It has punished me every time I tried to get away.' She turned and continued up the stairs.

Sisaroth's thoughts were swirling round his head. 'Do you know who built it?'

'Some älf or other, I expect. The runes show it was built a very long time ago. The language used is a type of script no longer practised in Dsôn Faïmon. And whoever it was must have been off his head to think up all these traps.' Marandëi reached a door that opened as she approached. She reassured herself that Sisaroth was directly behind her. 'We are surrounded by a magic force field that feeds the tower. You saw those supports that are anchored in the mountain?' He nodded. 'They function as energy channels. The building has a permanent source of energy. It will never run out.'

'Unless the force field dries up.'

Marandëi laughed. 'How many divisions of unendingness do you think I've been waiting for that to happen? Don't hold your breath.'

Sisaroth remembered the damaged runes on one of the columns and told her what he had seen. 'Maybe that is why the tower does not want to release us? Or maybe it can't let us go?'

She looked interested. 'Maybe you are right. Let's discuss it. But first let's get you sorted.' She stood back to let him pass. 'Welcome to your new home, Sisaroth.'

**Ishím Voróo (Outer Lands), Dsôn Sòmran, Dsôn, in the
northern foothills of the Grey Mountains, 5427ᵗʰ division
of unendingness (6241ˢᵗ solar cycle), spring.**

'But I do not wish to speak to you!' Wènelon tried to close
the door.

Ranôria was not foolish enough to put her foot in the opening. Instead she leaned her shoulder against the door's carved
wooden surface. 'Only a little of your time. Then I will leave you
in peace,' she said firmly, not wanting to sound as if she were
begging a favour. She was standing in the small street outside
Wènelon's house. He was one of the älfar who had been present
on the murder evening and one of the seven witnesses whose
evidence had condemned her children. She would be speaking
with him.

A fresh wind had brought more rain, mixed now with snow,
despite the approach of spring. Ranôria's face was cold, but she
welcomed it.

'Aïsolon interrogated me for ages. I don't owe you any
explanations.'

*Is that the truth or can I hear an anxious tone in his voice? Is he
afraid?* 'Of course you don't.' She spoke more gently this time.
His vehement refusal to speak to her made her suspicious. 'I'm
just trying to understand how my two children could have
turned into bestial murderers. That is all.'

There was increased pressure from the other side and the
door was pushed shut.

You coward! Ranôria took two steps back and looked up at
the house façade. The buildings here were closely packed
together. Dsôn had so little space at its disposal. She could see

silhouettes moving behind the windows. She was being observed from behind the curtains.

I got absolutely nowhere with him. There were still six more names to try. She waved goodbye and called out her thanks. She wanted people to think they had had a successful conversation.

The fact he was afraid of her strengthened her conviction that the witnesses had something to hide. They had passed the governor's interrogation and did not want to risk giving anything away.

I swear I'll find out what happened and who is behind it. Ranôria strolled off, head down against the driving sleet. She was still dressed up from her earlier meeting with Aïsolon, and after getting off the lift had hastily applied grey cosmetics as a sign of mourning. It had the added benefit of making her look more threatening.

She had to step quickly out of the path of a heavily loaded cart.

She paid it no attention but when it stopped, she looked round. The wagon had come to a halt in front of Wènelon's house and the goods were being delivered via the door that had stayed resolutely shut to her.

Ranôria walked back to the house to discover what was in the crates.

The carter, more than happy to chat, told her the delivery was of exclusive wines and cut-glass carafes from the luxury craft workshop in Helîstra. And that this was the second consignment. A third was due later on.

Wènelon can't afford things like that, surely. The information she was given backed up her conspiracy theory. Wènelon's house was situated in the fourth ring. The people here were of the simple sort. His partner worked hard at her craft and she certainly did not earn enough to pay for a single cask of this wine.

Ranôria hurried off to the fifth ring. This time she would not take no for an answer.

The next name on the list was Acòrhia, an älf celebrated for her skill in story-telling. When she talked to young people she brought the beauty of old Dsôn to life; her descriptions of the battles against the Dorón Ashont were masterly and her tales emphasised the brave and generous conduct of the survivors who came to Dsôn Sòmran. Acòrhia had the gift of inspiring her audience with her vivid stories, and she could dispel the greyness in their hearts and minds. For a story-weaver she was extraordinarily young; she could hardly have seen the vanished Dsôn Faïmon empire with her own eyes.

Of course, she is expert at spinning a yarn. With her talents it will have been easy for her to persuade Aïsolon of her version of events. Ranôria was going to be more difficult to convince.

After a short walk and a long climb, she reached the fifth ring, where the houses were smarter and not so huddled together.

In this part of the city, residents could afford the luxury of a tiny garden. Climbing plants and creepers adorned buildings and roofs with black, white and red leaves.

Acòrhia's house seemed to be in competition with the whole neighbourhood judging by her luxuriant foliage display. The colours were vibrant and varied: a deep blood-red, an intense golden yellow and a subtle shade of grey.

She had placed delicate bone carvings and statues artfully throughout the plot; leaves draped themselves over a little nightmare to form its mane; a creeper encircled the body of a miniature óarco like a throttling snake.

Ranôria approved of the decorative aspect homes had been given in this neighbourhood. *I should come down here more often.* She used a doorknocker in the shape of two hands holding a silver skull.

The door was soon opened.

For two heartbeats Ranôria thought she recognised her own daughter's face – so similar except for that bright red hair. *I wonder if Aïsolon could be the story-teller's father, too?* she mused, without any feelings of jealousy. It was perfectly natural for älfar to change partners several times over the course of their lives.

Ranôria greeted her politely and started to introduce herself but Acòrhia broke in. 'I know who you are. Do come in.' She was dressed in a red gown with a short black tunic on top embroidered with pearls. 'It is an honour to welcome you to my home.' She stood aside for Ranôria to walk past into a hallway that smelt of ink and parchment. Ranôria gave a friendly smile of acknowledgment. *I shan't let you charm me with your courtesy.* 'How kind of you.'

After closing the front door Acòrhia took Ranôria into her library, where a large, dead tree dominated the centre of the room. Planks set on the upper branches gave access to the weighty tomes on the higher shelves. Other books stood in niches in the tree trunk and a swing-seat was suspended from one of the horizontal branches. On one side of the room there was a big desk with quill pens, glass writing sticks and little pots of coloured inks.

Ranôria admired how, instead of leaves, the tree was hung with pieces of paper covered in writing. They had been fastened to the twigs by wires and twisted into the shape of leaves, buds or open flowers. A pleasant almond and honey perfume from

the ink Acòrhia used pervaded the room. A slight waft of air
from the window set the paper foliage in delicate, rustling
motion. One of the pages came loose and fluttered to the floor.

'It's fantastic!' Ranôria exclaimed.

'Why, thank you! I use old versions of stories, first drafts that
I don't need any more. I give them their final place of honour
here on my tree,' Acòrhia explained. 'I prefer not to fix them
tightly. That way chance decides which ones are swept up and
burned.' She pulled out a chair for her visitor at the fireside.

Ranôria moved to the chair and hung up her cloak. 'What a
lovely idea,' she said enthusiastically. She took in the rest of the
surroundings: the library extended up through all four floors of
the house.

'I think of this collection as my own personal word-quarry, if
you like.' Acòrhia sat down opposite with a smile. 'In the books
and scrolls here there are many old Dsôn treasures which were
donated by survivors; and then I have all my records and writings here as well, of course.'

'Made-up stories?'

'Some of them. I ask people to tell me legends and folk tales
and true stories and I write them down. Some of it I adapt into
new forms. It's a rich source of material for me.' She leaned back
in her chair, her red hair tossed over her shoulders. 'But that's
not why you've come. You want to hear about the murder.'

'People are talking?' *I've only just been at Wènelon's house; it
looks like word is getting round surprisingly fast. I assume they are
afraid of what I might find out.*

Acòrhia nodded. 'I've never had children myself but I can certainly understand why you'd want to know more. If this happened
to a member of my own family I'm sure I would do everything in

my power to get them back from Phondrasôn – that is, if the accusations were false.' She looked unhappy. 'May I make you some tea before I begin?'

'Don't you have any slaves?'

'Slaves are expensive and require discipline, plus they get to know all your secrets,' Acòrhia replied. 'I live on my own and it's far too much bother to supervise them. I'd rather do the work myself.' She smiled. 'This is only the fifth ring, Ranôria. I'm not so high up as you are.'

'I understand. No tea, though, thank you.' She sat upright in her chair. 'Since you already know why I'm here, please tell me exactly what happened that night. I want all the details!' *I'm good at spotting a lie. Even from a gifted story-spinner.*

'You won't like what you hear.' Acòrhia began the tale. She did not recount the events as if she were giving a witness statement, but rather as if she were telling an exciting story. She was word perfect and had everything covered, leaving nothing open to question.

She even described in detail what the dagger looked like, how quickly Firûsha and her brother had been breathing, how fast they had spoken, and what gestures they had made. Her version of events was so rich in detail that Ranôria was able to picture it all. Nothing was missing. It all made horrible sense. 'And then we called the guards,' she finished. 'You know the rest.'

'Yes,' said Ranôria absently, trying to suppress the violent images in her mind. She did not trust them. Her heart refused to believe it but her reason whispered that this was exactly how it must all have happened. 'You were quite right. I don't like what I heard.' She studied the young story-teller's face.

'That's the drawback of the truth.' Acòrhia was sympathetic.

'It has the power to hurt us. Your children were given a harsh punishment, but it was one they both deserved. I still regret that it had to be like that. If Sémaina had not poured scorn on you and mocked you without any provocation, she would be alive today and your young ones would be with you.' She laid a hand on her breast. 'I was at your last concert. You have the gift of sending music directly into the soul of those who hear your songs. My words can never really compare with that.'

'Each of us nurtures the talent he or she is given,' Ranôria replied automatically. She had not found any indication of a lie, and could not detect any sign of fear in the younger woman's expression. *Can it really be the truth? Is that really what happened that night at Tênnegor's house?*

The thought was like a stab to her heart, as if her body wanted to punish her for doubting her own offspring.

I mustn't believe it! Firûsha could never have done that. Never! She wanted to stay longer and cross-examine her hostess. 'You know what, I think I will have that cup of tea after all.' Shivering, she reached her hands out to the warmth of the fire. 'It's far too cold for the time of year, isn't it?'

'I'll be glad to make you some. A friend gave me some revitalising herbs. She goes collecting over in the quarry and she swears those are the purest specimens.' Acôrhia stood up. 'Do feel free to look around,' she threw over her shoulder as she left the library.

I certainly shall. Ranôria got up and wandered about on the ground floor looking at the book titles, then she climbed the stairs that spiralled round the tree trunk and reached the uppermost branches that were level with the fourth floor.

Now she was a good fifteen paces up and there was so much

paper foliage that she could not see down to the desk. A wintry light seeped in through the glass dome, but rain and snow were still falling on it.

Ranôria had been counting on the story-teller making a mistake in her recitation, but she had been optimally prepared, it seemed.

The only criticism one could make was the fact her story was almost word for word identical to the notes that Aïsolon had made in his report.

Acòrhia could have thought the whole thing up and then made sure the others all knew exactly what to say. Of course there was no proof at all. She reversed her approach to the problem – and came up with a theory. *I'm going to test it out straight away.*

'Ranôria?' Acòrhia had returned with the tea.

'Coming,' she called, hurrying down the steps and over to the fireplace where the story-weaver was waiting for her.

The hot, fragrant infusion was served steaming in a glass bowl. Crystal beakers stood next to it on the side table. The smell reminded Ranôria a little of damp earth, roots and fungi. 'I hope it tastes better than it smells?'

'Yes. People often forget to place a fragment of slate in the pot.'

'Slate? You mean that stone that easily splits into layers?'

'Watch!' Acòrhia took a tiny bag out of the pocket of her robe and put a small spoonful of its contents into each beaker. While the tea was being poured, the brown liquid changed colour to an attractive golden beige. All the floating residue had dissolved. 'It's useful to know that the stone has this effect. Otherwise the first sip of tea would be difficult to swallow and it might make you gag.'

Ranôria tried the brew and was surprised to find it similar to red berries in taste. 'Fruity and sweet, almost like juice! I would never have expected that.'

Acòrhia lifted her own cup. 'Will you be visiting the other witnesses or do you believe me?' she asked as she stirred her drink.

'I've been asking myself from dawn to dusk what can have possessed Sisaroth to lose his temper like that,' Ranôria answered, pretending to be at a complete loss. 'Everyone assumes he did it to avenge an insult, some slur Sémaina made against me.'

Acòrhia frowned and played with a tendril of her long red hair. 'What other motivation could he have had? He was defending his mother's honour, although the lengths he went to were out of all proportion . . .'

'What if someone had been egging him on?'

'I see. You think someone might have wanted him to overstep the mark and get into serious trouble? Someone who wanted to get Firûsha and Sisaroth out of the way?' She tapped the slatestone spoon against her lips as she considered this possibility. 'A plot against your son is an interesting thought. Also terrible, of course. It could be useful to find out who had crossed swords with Sisaroth lately.'

'Not just Sisaroth. His siblings as well.'

'But Tirîgon didn't have anything to do with the killing.'

'But he still went to Phondrasôn to protect them and enable them to stay in contact with Dsôn. That could have been predicted.' Ranôria continued her musings, hoping to see Acòrhia's features betray her if she stumbled on a true version of events. *Give me a hint. Just a flinch and I'll know more.* 'Or how about this: maybe Sémaina had enemies who encouraged Sisaroth to kill her because they knew how hot-tempered he can be?'

'So you think Sémaina might have died for a completely different reason? Nothing at all to do with defending your reputation?' The story-weaver nodded slowly. 'Possible. We'd need to know what rumours are going around concerning Tênnegor and his family. Perhaps there are old scores that wanted settling?' She sipped her tea. 'I can see a whole lot of work for poor Aïsolon here. And for you, of course.' Acòrhia raised her beaker in a toast to her guest. 'I wish from the depths of my very heart that Sisaroth and Firûsha prove to have been innocent pawns. Without Sisaroth's testimony, though, it will be difficult to work out who was pulling the strings. Only your son would know who the älf was that drove him to murder on that fateful evening he burst in on Sémaina's gathering. May he be caught for Sisaroth's sake.'

Ranôria gave her a grateful smile. 'The gods of infamy will stand by me.' She placed her empty beaker on the little table and got to her feet, wrapping her shawl around her. The damp fabric had dried nicely in the heat of the fire. 'It is late and I must get on with my enquiries.'

'The governor will be sure to give you a listening ear.' Acòrhia stood up to accompany her guest to the door. 'My best thoughts go with you.'

Ranôria gestured to her hostess to remain. She would find her own way out. 'We will meet again soon. I shan't want to miss your next performance.' She said goodbye and made her way through the hall to the front door. Many things had become clear to her in the course of this visit.

Acòrhia has been lying to me. It was she who worked out the story about the murder and she told the others what to say.

Ranôria based this assumption on an observation: the

story-teller had not seemed surprised about any of the new theories being voiced, nor had she offered to help solve the puzzle. Surely in her professional life it must be more or less essential to keep herself informed; if she were truly an objective witness, she would have been willing to spin a tale about these peculiar events. Instead she had remained extremely calm and had offered no assistance. She also encouraged the theory of a third party being behind the incident – notably a male.

She stayed calm because she saw I was following a line of enquiry which did not involve her. Ranôria hurried through the streets of the fifth ring and made her way quickly to the lift to get home. *Acòrhia knows more than she is letting on.*

She had learnt a good deal, she felt, and there was a lot of new material to process if she was to find the real killer and send him to exile in Phondrasôn in place of her children.

Ranôria planned to visit all her friends and ask for their help. There was a lot to do: people to shadow, investigations and enquiries to be made, rumours to gather and evaluate. She would be close on Acòrhia's heels at all times, as soon as she had finished interviewing the remaining witnesses.

I will watch every step she takes! Sooner or later the young story-spinner would make contact with the cunning and malicious man who was behind the conspiracy. *If I can work out who is to blame we will have cleared up the mystery surrounding Sémaina's death.*

Ranôria reached the lift and moved the lever to summon the platform.

The rain had eased off. Fog rose up from the lower rings of the city and mingled with the smoke from the chimneys. The upper rings, the wall and the mountain peaks lay hidden in the mist.

Ranôria went on hatching her plans.

The next witness she would visit was Nomirôs, one of her neighbours, albeit not a close one. She was in possession of a piece of information that might make him more ready to talk. *I'll do it right now.* She stepped into the gondola that stopped in front of her. *I will have done a great deal today, if I make this next visit.*

Someone barged into her and shoved her against the wall of the cabin.

A male älf in a long woollen mantle covering his attire pushed inside. 'Excuse me,' he murmured, turning his face away as if wishing to conceal his identity from her. He was followed at close quarters by a guard whose face behind his helmet visor seemed strangely stiff. He was gripping his sword so tightly that his knuckles were white.

That's strange. Ranôria shuffled back into the corner in such a way that she would not have her back to either of the passengers. She did not like the look of them. *Perhaps it's wiser if I get out . . .* But it was too late for that. The platform had already moved off.

Into the heart of the fog.

Chapter V

And so it was
  the Young Gods sought their own paths
  through the darkness.
  They had been wrenched apart
  but hearts and souls
  clung close.
Fate willed
  they should find other älfar
  in this place.
Can you guess what came of it?
Friendship or betrayal?
Desire or love?
Future or death?

Excerpt from the epic poem *Young Gods*
composed by Carmondai, master of word and image

Phondrasôn, 5427ᵗʰ division of unendingness (6241ˢᵗ solar cycle), spring.

Tirîgon ducked to avoid the axe-blow aimed at his head and stabbed the elf with an upward thrust to the chin, through the mouth cavity and directly into the brain; at the same time he pulled the elf's dagger out of its sheath and cut the next opponent viciously across his bare thighs, slicing through a main artery.

'You are far too slow!' he mocked. As he straightened, he grabbed his sword from his first victim's head and struck another elf through the collarbone. 'Your deaths bear the name of Tirîgon!'

He was covered from head to toe in his enemies' blood. The sickly metallic smell encouraged his killing spree and gave him the strength and swiftness to gain the upper hand, even though he was heavily outnumbered.

Tirîgon moved through the advancing ranks of his adversaries like a dancer following a secret tune. His sword found the gaps in his foes' defences, while his armour protected him from their hail of arrows. He could not avoid injury completely but he sustained only surface wounds.

He had lost sight of the obboona but he could hear the clash of weapons and her triumphant laughter, so he assumed she was still dealing out death.

She's utterly mad! She took us right into the heart of their settlement. Tirîgon swerved to dodge an attack, kicked his opponent in the face and slit the elf's throat with his dagger.

The spurt of blood blinded the next elf and Tirîgon was able to open his belly with an easy stroke. The foe fell screaming to the ground, slipping on his own spilled guts; two further warriors came stumbling over their dying comrade and fell straight into the sweep of Tirîgon's mighty sword, which knocked their own weapons out of their hands and cut open their chests.

The final four elves withdrew hurriedly.

Distance won't save you. Tirîgon jammed his blade into a handy corpse, snatched up an owner-less bow and notched an arrow which went whistling through the air to pierce a fleeing elf through the back of the neck.

'Cowards!' he shouted at them as they ran. 'Cowards get struck from behind!' He felled another, his arrow finding the mark in spite of a raised shield. The elf screamed and did not get back to his feet.

He was surprised that the elves did not present a worthier challenge. *Phondrasôn's terrors have weakened them or else they were overconfident of the security factor of the floating island.* Tirîgon pulled his sword out of the corpse and used the dripping blade to brush the arrows from his armour. *You must always be vigilant. Attack can come from any quarter. As we had to learn to our cost.* Then he bounded after the last two elves, who were heading for the buildings.

The obboona did the same. He saw there were many slashes in the skin garment she wore; he could not tell whether the blood on her was her own. 'What a splendid harvest,' she chortled. 'My god will be pleased with us. Let's get these two alive. I know that he likes living specimens.'

'We'll see how we go.' He saw one of the elves disappear inside the largest house, which was fortified. The door slammed shut. *Where are their women and children hiding? Is that where they all are?*

He did not bother to try to force the door. He vaulted up from one of the window frames, grabbed the edge of the wooden guttering and pulled himself up onto the roof.

He could see straight away that breaking his way through would be difficult. The roof was solidly constructed, with stone tiles offering the elves protection from aerial attack.

He soon gave a satisfied smile. *People never think, do they?*

He went over to the smoking chimney. This was the vulnerable point. He could see that it was narrow inside and there was a wire grating with a hinged cover to prevent debris falling in. *But they need the ventilation so they can breathe.*

'Hand me up a bow, a quiver full of arrows, and a shield,' he hissed to the obboona, who was noisily belabouring the front door. 'And give me your skin.'

'What for?'

'You'll see. If you want to see your god happy, do what you are told.'

She slipped out of the bloodied garment, now in tatters. Her own pale skin was revealed, crisscrossed with slashes and obviously deep stab wounds. She did not have long to live, Tirîgon thought. *If she doesn't bleed to death she'll die when the infections set in.*

Thus far, however, the obboona seemed oblivious of her injuries. She handed up the various items and then continued her vain onslaught at the door.

That was fine by Tirîgon. All that commotion would occupy the elves' attention.

He tore the garment into tiny pieces to scatter through the chimney aperture. Then he placed the shield over the opening. *You won't stick around for long in there.*

He sat waiting, an arrow ready on his bowstring.

He soon noticed the stink of burning skin. Acrid smoke began seeping out from round the window shutters. Inside, elf women and children were starting to cough and sob uncontrollably.

The obboona greeted the sound with laughter and she swung the two elf swords she had garnered in combat. 'Hey, you there! I can smell bacon-elves! Come on out! I'll . . .'

A whirring sound and a thwack. An arrow quivered in her breast. She hit at it vaguely with the weapon in her right hand, but then toppled backwards and lay convulsing on the ground.

Shame, really. She could still have been useful for a bit.

The front door flew open with a crash and the elves surged out, desperate for air. Tirîgon had a good view. The two armed elves were protecting the group of women and children who were hastening down towards the ship. They were not making any attempt to defend their island stronghold. Their only thought was to get away.

That's another surprise. He felled the two warrior elves with quick shots before they had a chance to look up and see him on the roof.

He still had eleven arrows but there were at least seventy elves to deal with.

The first of the group had already reached the vessel and the mast runes were glowing.

They're just leaving me here! I'll never get away if they take the ship! 'Wait!' he shouted. 'I swear I'll kill all of you if you . . .' He was about to leap down from the rooftop when there was a rumble and a crash from inside the building and the chimney collapsed in on itself, belching up acrid smoke that made it impossible to see.

His eyes were stinging badly but he could hear a noise like a landslide on a mountain. Any resident of Dsôn Sòmran was horribly well acquainted with that sound.

The stone-decked roof tilted under his feet before he could save himself.

The älf landed in the hall, leaping to avoid falling debris. As the smoke cleared he was able to see – to his utter horror – that a huge gap had opened up where the fireplace had been. Underneath, there was – absolutely nothing!

The island is crumbling away! Tirîgon suddenly understood why the elves had been so keen to abandon it. *Was it sabotage?*

The hole was increasing in size, with the earth breaking away under the building. He saw soil, tiles, stone slabs plunging down into the void. Any moment now and the whole island would completely disappear.

Top priority: get myself a boat, now! He ran, noticing as he did so a map with elven markings attached to one of the last remaining walls. He pulled it off and shoved it into his pocket. Part of it tore but he didn't care.

Tirîgon stormed out of the ruined building. The obboona was writhing in pain and implored him to help her, but he ignored her cries. All the big ships and the medium-sized boats had moved away from the jetty. They sailed off majestically as if carried by invisible waters.

'Don't leave me here like this,' the obboona called weakly. 'I beg of you, take me to my own god. And don't forget the elf cadavers. I'm sure he will repay you for your trouble.'

I wonder if she might still be useful to me in some way? He turned back and knelt at her side, thrusting the map in front of her face. 'Show me where I can find him.'

'If I show you on the map you will go away and abandon me, I know.'

'Tell me! What if you pass out on the way? How would I reach him?' *Come on, hurry up. You know it makes sense.* Tirîgon suppressed a smile of triumph when she poked at the map with a blood-smeared finger. 'Wait here. I'll go and find us a boat.' He jumped up and raced off. Not for a single splinter of unendingness had he really considered taking the obboona with him.

He saw two elves casting off.

He had never run so fast in all his life. Behind him the last of the village houses were crashing down. The landslide rumblings grew ever louder.

'Stay where you are!' he gasped. His scrapes and cuts were causing him intense discomfort. He felt ridiculous. Here was the butcher calling out to the lambs to hold steady while he fetched his chopper. Why would they stop and let him on board? *Oh well, it was worth a try: lambs are pretty stupid animals, after all.*

The elves, however, were not stupid. They threw the ropes off and moved away from the quayside. The navigation runes glowed efficiently.

Tirîgon had his boot on the jetty. It seemed too great a distance for him to attempt to leap it. It could just work . . . *But if it doesn't, it's a heck of a long way down. On the other hand, that's exactly the risk I face if I don't try.*

He looked back.

Most of the island had disintegrated. A whole house collapsed while its chimney was still puffing out smoke; it was as if the elves inside were cooking away as normal, supremely indifferent to the catastrophe striking their settlement. A thin layer of soil and grass transformed itself into a flying carpet. Now the jetty was affected – it was too late. There was no landing stage left to launch himself from.

Overweening ambition comes before a fall. Tirîgon's heart seemed to stop but the jetty was marooned in mid-air.

What . . . ? He looked down and saw the planking shimmer slightly. He bent down and wiped away the dirt. The wood here also had inset runes – presumably to ensure the pier did not share the fate of the rest of the island. He raised his head and studied the quay. *Eight paces long and three paces wide. It will be my new home. Whatever else, I must admit this is a fantastic view.*

The ships full of female elves and children were heading for a distant island.

They won't want to land on the island without their husbands. I expect they'll find someone who can avenge them by killing me. Tirîgon's situation had not improved a jot. He would be swapping one island for another. The fighting had taken its toll. He had no rations. He had no water.

He spread out the map he had taken from the house.

It did not matter about the script being in elvish; he could work out most of what he needed from the illustrations.

He quickly found his own location. The elves had marked it with a red spot, as he was able to verify by looking at the lie of neighbouring islands. The huge cave they were all enclosed in had been indicated by a large oval shape and wavy line symbols depicted the lake.

He was relieved to discover that routes or channels had been drawn in and that one of them was not far from where he was. If he were interpreting the map correctly, it meant the path branched off just before a secondary cave with six outlets. The scale at the edge of map showed that he had about eighty miles to cover on foot once he got off this raft and onto land.

A bloodied fingerprint on that little cave marked where the obboona had said Tossàlor was.

That's an excellent turn of events. But eighty miles is a long way and I shan't even get started if I can't get this platform underway. Tirîgon placed his hand on a wooden symbol and called out an order. 'Forwards!'

Nothing budged.

He tried all ten fingers. He tried every command he could come up with. He tried a harsh voice, a wheedling tone, a friendly request.

Nothing.

Tirîgon scratched his head. *I wonder if the number of runes says something about the load-bearing capacity? If so, I have an idea . . .* He grabbed his sword and started hacking at the planks which constituted the jetty, and discarding them over the edge. *Are we going down at all?*

His actions had no effect, so he jettisoned more pieces of wood. Gradually the deck started to sink.

I was right! He looked down.

The cascades had ceased flowing and the lake was calm with a gently ruffled surface.

According to the map it was about three miles to the other bank. But it was still out of sight. The cave seemed to be of endless dimensions.

The platform is wooden, so it will float. He would be able to move it in the water. He continued to cast planks from the back of the platform with his sword, increasing the speed of their descent. His only hope was to use the quay-fragment as a raft.

He had no intention of dying here in Phondrasôn. What he wanted was to find his brother and sister. And then he would seek his fortune: fame, wealth and glory.

Phondrasôn, 5427th division of unendingness (6241st solar cycle), spring.

Firûsha had to admit that Crotàgon had not exaggerated: she lay in a smoothly polished stone basin full of warm water made fragrant with summer blossoms. *If I didn't already have a perfectly good home – oh, and if my brothers were here too – I'd be quite happy to stay here.*

This room, where the Goldsteel warrior Crotàgon had brought her first thing, must have been designed for a king; it bore absolutely no resemblance to the shabby hovel she had spent the night in. The floors were of polished marble and there were shiny water inlets directly over the tub. A fire, strewn with herbs and resinous wood, gave constant sweet-scented warmth. She wallowed in the bath, letting her recent ordeals and hardships float away.

Firûsha got out of the basin and dried herself with the soft towels Crotàgon had provided. There was a deep-gold dress to put on, and a pair of soft shoes.

She then went to join her captor – not in the kitchen this time, but through a side door he had previously pointed out to her. She had no idea what to expect.

She knocked and opened the door.

He greeted her, approval at her appearance in his voice. He was dressed in a flowing black robe with grey and yellow embroidery. 'I can see you are feeling better now.'

'Indeed.' Firûsha felt immediately at home in this room, decorated as it was with familiar älfar runes. The lighting came from bone candelabra. She was surprised to find he even had three fine abstract paintings hanging on the walls. Apart from a long table and four chairs there were two elegant couches. *I would not have expected him to be so aesthetically minded!* 'I am starting to understand what you meant when you spoke of what you would be leaving behind if you returned to Dsôn.'

Suddenly she was homesick. She wondered about her siblings and what might have befallen them both.

When Crotàgon nodded in response, his long, dark-grey hair fell forward and he brushed it away from his face. 'I have come to a decision. But sing for me first, little älf-girl.'

I might make you regret that. That nice bath and the lovely dress aren't going to make up for the way you order me about. I am not your slave. She comforted herself with the thought that her singing would bind Crotàgon more completely to her. *Of course I shall sing for you. You will come to wish you had never even heard my voice.*

Firûsha stood with her eyes closed and her arms relaxed at her sides; she concentrated on her song.

First she gave him *The Bloodflower* again. And then a children's song, a lullaby her own mother used to sing to her. She looked at him boldly when she was finished. 'I shall sing some more once we have eaten and you have let me know your decision.'

He stared at her absently. His soul was still captive in the world of sound she had created. He cleared his throat. 'Yes, of course. I'll go and get our food.'

Crotàgon served her dishes that were delicious and filling, though they were not as good as what her own cook would produce back home. The meat was tender, the vegetables garnished with herbs and there was a cereal with fresh mint. 'Do you like it?' he enquired.

She did not want to upset him so she smiled. *I really don't want to ask what sort of meat I'm eating.*

He laughed. 'A diplomatic response. But I can see through you.' He threw down his fork. 'Try as I may to make the place like home, the food available here in Phondrasôn is awful, isn't it? We simply don't have the spices. And there's no wine in these parts. Not to mention the quality of the meat.'

'Yes, I was trying not to dwell on that. Oh well. It seems to be dead and it's cooked all the way through, so I'm sure it won't kill me.'

'Would I want to poison my little songbird?' He raised his goblet of flavoured water to drink her health. 'Here's to you, and your wonderfully pure voice. I cannot think of any better entertainment.'

Firûsha raised her own beaker and took a tiny sip. She was eager to know his decision. 'Now for my dessert – what have you concluded?'

He was serious now. 'I have thought deeply about it. If what you tell me is true, then Dsôn Sòmran would be better for me than staying here, however opulent my surroundings. I can be useful to my own people if I go back. I will take you with me.'

'That's marvellous news!' Every fibre of her being quivered

with joy. *I shall be able to see Mother again. And my brothers.* 'When do we leave?'

'As soon as possible. I will make arrangements. We need provisions and a sledge to carry everything. The journey will be a hard one.' He spread his hands. 'What you see here was not all my own work, of course.'

'So you found it?'

'A friend did it all for me. He wanted me to have a lovely home. He designed everything and I followed the plans. He made all the furniture and the lamps and created the artwork. He did all that in return for the promise I made him.'

'And that promise . . . ?'

'To take him with me if I ever left Phondrasôn.'

'So he is your partner?'

At this Crotàgon burst out laughing. 'No! Certainly not! If *he* had been my partner I would have killed him long ago. He is too much like hard work. Very moody, always changing his mind. He knows he's difficult to live with and he enjoys his own company. And I'm the same, really. I visit him often and I take him fresh meat.'

So far Firûsha could not see any problem. 'But that's fine; all three of us will travel together. There'll be two swords instead of one. It'll be safer.'

He laughed. 'He's no warrior. He's an artist. If you gave him a weapon he'd turn it into some kind of statue on a pedestal, I suppose. He would want you.' He leaned forward and touched her on the arm, on the shoulder and on the neck. 'Not interested in you in the way you might think, but for a sculpture, perhaps. That sort of desire is more dangerous.'

My BONES! Firûsha's eyes were wide with horror. 'But I'm the same race! How could he?'

'Because he thinks that älfar bones are the height of perfection. That's why they banished him in the first place.'

She vaguely remembered her father telling a story.

'Tossàlor.'

'That's him.'

Her optimism disappeared. 'Do we have to take him?'

'He is my ... friend.'

'He's a serial killer!'

'I like him, though.'

He likes him? What sort of a stupid argument is that? 'But ... he never told you what had become of Dsôn Faïmon. Why in the name of everything infamous do you think that was? He must have had his own agenda to pursue.' Firûsha was not mastering her dislike of the murderous artist she had not, as yet, met. 'I don't want Tossàlor to come. And anyway, he won't be let into Dsôn. What he did was absolutely unforgivable. My father will never pardon him.'

Crotàgon grinned. 'That's a thought. Luckily we'll have the governor's daughter with us when we get there. Your father will be so delighted to have you back that I'm sure he'd stretch his generous feelings to a pardon for Tossàlor.'

Firûsha sighed. 'I very much doubt it.' *I never should have made those boasts. I must ensure he doesn't think I can do it all.* 'When all's said and done you must appreciate that it was him who banished me in the first place. He always takes his position extremely seriously. He would never put personal matters above the law he represents.'

It was clear from Crotàgon's expression that he would be standing by his decision. 'We shall see,' he replied, unimpressed by what she had said. 'Regardless, I promised Tossàlor I would take him with me if I went home. Let's go and find him and see what he wants to do. If the gods are on your side, who knows, maybe he'll opt to stay behind.' He indicated her plate. 'Have you finished?' His mood had changed for the worse. He was displeased by her vehement stance against the artist.

'Yes.' Firûsha put on her most winning smile. 'Thank you. And thank you for the dress, too.' She smoothed the material down. 'Where is it from?' She could have bitten her tongue. *I think I can guess.*

'Tossàlor gave me a chest full of clothes to store. He said he didn't want it any more. I was going to use some of the textiles for towels and linens.'

Firûsha had little difficulty imaging how Tossàlor had obtained the clothes. *I'm wearing the apparel of a murder victim.* She scanned the room, taking in the sight of the bones used in the fashioning of the lamps and chandeliers. *The remains of dead älfar?* She gave herself a shake; Crotàgon was clearing the table. She asked him where she was to spend the evening.

'Where you slept last night,' he answered coldly.

'In the cage?' She stared at him incredulously. 'You can't be serious! It's not as if I were planning to run off!'

'Think of it as a measure to protect you from the clutches of Tossàlor. This way he can't get at your lovely bones while you are asleep,' he teased her, pointing firmly at the door. 'Off you go.'

He's treating me like his slave. 'But I shan't sleep a wink! I'll be huddled on that hard floor . . .' She was desperate to get back to Dsôn. *I'll have him humiliated just like he humiliated me!* The fact that he had saved her life was beside the point. She was not feeling grateful and she was not prepared to overlook or excuse his attitude.

'You are young. You'll be fine.' He moved towards her and made plain that he would brook no arguing on the subject. 'I can't be getting things ready for the trip and looking after your safety at the same time. I prefer to know you are protected.'

Firûsha cursed and left the room, going back through the corridor to the wretched kitchen. She clambered back into the cage and sat down on the floor, her arms crossed defiantly. 'You are some kind of a monster,' she hissed at Crotàgon. He grinned and laid more wood on to burn before slamming and bolting the cage door. He had fixed a new locking mechanism to the iron bars, she saw. Then he turned around, humming. 'Why don't you give me a song? The one about . . .'

'You can sing to yourself till you're blue in the face,' she snapped. She watched him assemble equipment on the table.

'My dear young älf-girl. I am leaving this house for the sake of my people. I want to stand by them and support them, since I was not there in their hour of need when Dsôn Faïmon was destroyed.' He did not stop what he was doing. 'You should have grasped by now that I do not need you at all. I am only taking you with me because I want to and because your status as governor's daughter might be of use. When you sing, it reminds me not to forget to take you along when I leave. Do you understand?'

She snorted with anger but she took up her song once more. She was actually delighted that they would be leaving so soon. Her sweet revenge would come.

She was aware of the sharp piece of bone she had previously set aside to use as a dagger and the thought calmed her. *If Tossàlor comes within a pace of me, I'll plunge this into his neck.*

*

Two more nights' sleep and another nice bath brought her nearer their departure.

Crotàgon of the Goldsteel Unit wore a heavy suit of armour he had constructed himself: a combination of armour plating and steel rings fixed onto a leather base. He did not put on the mask or the stinking fur garment. He was now to travel as a self-acknowledged älf, not longer disguising his identity. His broad-tipped spear would serve as a walking staff. 'Are you ready?'

The transport sledge was loaded with tightly closed sacks. A space had been left for her cage.

'Get going,' she said crossly. 'I'll enjoy watching you struggle like a packhorse.' He had allowed another blanket for her against the cold. She gathered it around her shoulders.

Taking the straps over his shoulders he strode off, pulling the sledge behind him.

They left the steppe with its red and green grasses, leaving an all-too-obvious track, and headed into the forest. As they travelled over the undergrowth, aromatic smells of mint and warm amber rose up.

Firûsha turned round and saw the house behind them. *He has really made the break and given all that up.*

She sang a jolly marching song to spur him on and to pass the time. She wanted him addicted to her voice so she could exercise power over him. *I shall train him like you train a dog.*

She knew it could be done. Her mother had talked about it and instructed her, but it was difficult. Very difficult.

Simple souls such as barbarians or óarcos would quickly fall under the spell of an älfar voice. It only took a few notes and you could make them do nearly anything you wanted, her mother had told her. Female singers with perfect pitch could plunge these simple minds into total confusion and make them permanently mad.

But to charm an älf in this way, so that he would fulfil your every wish and happily sacrifice his own life for you – that was significantly harder.

I'll have plenty of time to practise while we're travelling. Firûsha was aware that Crotàgon was the only protection she had. He alone would keep her from being devoured by Phondrasôn's monsters and would ensure her safety with Tossàlor.

There was no sun and no stars here in the cave they were crossing, so it was impossible to gauge how the time might be passing. 'What makes the temperature change? And where does the light come from?' she asked.

'I have no idea,' Crotàgon replied without turning round. He found it difficult to talk; pulling the loaded sledge required enormous effort. 'Magic, I expect. But don't worry your pretty little head about the kind of things we'll come across. A lot cannot be explained away. All the gods – the ones we know and the ones we've never heard of – have gone to absolute excess down here. Perhaps they were showing off. Perhaps it was some kind of contest, to see who could come up with the most extraordinary phenomenon.'

'Oh yes? For example?'

He stopped, dropped the reins and drank from his leather flask. The grey hair adhered to the sweat on his brow. 'I've found caverns where the water flowed upside down. I've been places you could walk up walls without falling off and do a somersault on the roof. Once I stumbled upon a hall of mirrors it was almost impossible to find my way out of.'

'That sounds . . . fascinating.'

'It's not fascinating at all if you're desperate to get out and there are skeletons round each corner. People who failed to find the exits. Death comes in many different guises. As a monster, in the form of poison gas, a sudden abyss, a tiny insect with a lethal sting, a spirit. The list is endless. That's why I chose to defend my own small region. I restricted my outings to the immediate vicinity of my house and the tunnels near it. Tossàlor's attitude to risk is quite different.' He took up the leather straps once more. They set off.

'Isn't he safer staying in the confines of his house if he's no fighter?'

'Yes. He's so obsessed with his art that he doesn't see the dangers a warrior does,' he answered. 'But that doesn't stop him from exploring. He's drawn up a map of all his journeys. If there's anyone who knows how to get out of here, it'll be him. That's another good reason for taking him along.'

'I'd have thought it would be enough to get the map. Why would we need him?' Firûsha mused, looking at the landscape.

The grass was getting sparser and little, skeletal bushes with branches like claws snagged at their sledge. They hung heavy with fat blue berries.

Firûsha was just wondering if they tasted good when one burst open, releasing a long flying insect with spikes on its body. It buzzed around, scattering dark yellow droplets in its wake.

Crotàgon smashed it with a gloved hand and quickened his pace. 'I'd forgotten these horrors hatch around now,' he said, puffing with effort. 'Take care! If you see any more of them, let me know at once.'

'Of course. What's with these flies?'

'They kill you. The poison they carry thins your blood and it seeps out through the pores in your skin. You bleed to death.' He started a steady jog. 'I'll try to get away from here as fast as possible. Once we get to where Tossàlor lives, we'll be safe from these insects.'

So we go and seek protection with an älf that likes to kill älfar and harvest their bones? Firûsha gulped, huddling down deeper into her blankets.

More of the blue buds started to pop open on the strange shrubs.

The concert of buzzing grew louder on all sides.

Chapter VI

Red wetness on grey stone I spill
spurting from arteries I sever.
Hatred glows in the eyes I kill.
My blades are sharp, as sharp as ever.
My name is End
and Death beside.
I murder at will.
With Fate I ride.
At night, by day,
unlooked-for guest.
A silent gust
blows my victims away.
It cannot last. I shall be killed.
I have broken every law.
My punishment comes, my blood will be spilled.
Eternal darkness opens its door.
But until that befall
my name shall be Death.
My Name shall be the End of All.

Excerpt from the epic poem *Young Gods*
composed by Carmondai, master of word and image

Phondrasôn, 5427ᵗʰ Division of unendingness (6241ˢᵗ solar cycle), spring.

Marandëi unwound the bandage from Sisaroth's leg. 'That's looking better. The wound is healing, and with this salve there should not even be a scar.' She smiled encouragingly at him. 'You won't need to put on another dressing.'

'Good.' He nodded, thin-lipped. *But where does this get me?*

His nerves were in shreds from the enforced stay. He had slept. He had eaten. He had many long talks with the cîanai; he told her how he and his siblings came to Phondrasôn. He had explored the tower but still had absolutely no clue how to escape. He was seething with impatience.

Within these walls time passed with no indication of day and night. There were no windows and their only light came from candles and petroleum lamps, as well as the magical shimmer from the runes on the stone walls. Fresh air circulated from an unseen source.

How does Marandëi stand it? How Sisaroth hated their prison! One could not fault the accommodation for comfort and convenience. The tower seemed able to provide any sustenance they needed; the larder cupboards were never empty. All the ingredients for flavoursome meals were at hand.

But nothing made up for the loss of liberty.

Marandëi gave him another smile. 'You'll get used to it.'

'No, I refuse. I have to find my brother and sister and I have to get back to Dsôn.' *I'll construct some sort of siege equipment strong enough to break down the walls. I'll do it without recourse to magic. But I need tools to hollow out the stones.* 'I'm not giving up.'

There were sitting in what Marandëi called the library, although there were only four volumes on the shelves.

These she had written herself: a discourse on magic that Sisaroth could not understand, a collection of recipes, episodes from the lives of the cîanai, and some poems he did not think much of. The älf-woman had also done some drawing and painting, but he considered her output childish rather than gifted. Barbarians might go for that kind of thing but it did not impress him.

Marandëi had told him about her attempts to get away from the tower. She had tried magic, she had tried brute force, she had tried begging and pleading – all to no avail. He could see she was resigned to her captivity and that she was delighted to have someone to talk to after countless divisions of unendingness with beasts as her only visitors. Now she had an älf at her side with whom she could pass the time, and in whose company she could grow old. *For eternity*.

The prospect appalled him.

His father might have been attracted to Marandëi, he thought. He might even have selected her as a life-partner. But Sisaroth was not interested in a relationship; that would only complicate things further. He had to find his siblings and return to Dsôn.

He had to find a way to escape this tower.

He got to his feet. 'I'm going to carry on looking for a way out,' he announced, heading for the door.

She followed him with her gaze. 'And for that I admire you. You keep hoping you'll discover something I've missed.'

'No. I'm hoping to discover something that might have changed,' he corrected tactfully. 'Tell me, was the tower leaning like this when you arrived, when it first pulled you in?'

She looked taken aback at his words. 'No. No, I don't think it was,' she replied. She poured out onto the floor a little water from the basin she had used to attend to his injury.

The drops shimmered in place for a moment before they started to roll gently towards one side of the room, sinking into the bare wood of the floor.

'You are right,' she said, sounding surprised. 'I never noticed that.'

'You didn't notice because the change has been infinitesimal and gradual.' A vague idea began to form in Sisaroth's mind. 'Let's see what I come up with when I've climbed the stairs. Hand me a glass of water, please.'

He took the steps until he reached the highest room in the tower and then he came down again, going all the way to the dungeons. On each level he observed how the water behaved when the glassy beads were spilt. *It will work!*

He came back to where the cîanai was preparing their next meal.

She could tell from the satisfied smile on his face that his inspired guess had developed into a plan. 'He's only just arrived in the tower and already he has worked out how we can escape. How superb,' she said, with heavy sarcasm. 'Admit it: you are trying to impress me.' She winked at him.

Sisaroth sat down at the table and waited while Marandëi passed him a plate of lightly grilled meat and spiced cereal mash. 'I don't want to get your hopes up,' he said modestly. 'But I do think we can get out of here. Not without considerable risk to ourselves, of course. We could be badly hurt in the attempt.'

Marandëi brought her own plate over to the table and sat opposite him. 'You don't want to let me in on the secret?'

'On the contrary. I'll need your help. But be prepared for the possibility of failure.' He was impatient to get started. 'Are there any tools I could use?'

'I did find a hammer. And there's some equipment the beasts left behind in the dungeon. We could adapt it.' Her curiosity was aroused and her pale eyes sparkled. 'Tell me what you have in mind.'

'We are going to make the tower's weakness work in our favour.'

'But the tower is invulnerable.'

'No, it's not,' Sisaroth contradicted, with a grin. 'You'll see what I mean when we've finished eating.' He tucked into the meal, keen to build up his strength for the coming exertions.

He and Marandëi spent the next few hours moving all the furniture into the top room and piling it up against the far wall.

The cîanai's magic powers were no help to her with the manual labour. As she dragged the heavy wooden items she sweated and swore like a barbarian trooper, as Sisaroth noted to his delight.

They left an opening in the pile of furniture where they could slide the heavy wooden chest from the kitchen.

Sisaroth fastened eight small wheels to the chest so it would be easier to move. He and Marandëi managed to haul it upstairs, where they then filled it with stones and rubble from the dungeon at the base of the tower. Now they had the makings of a battering ram. They strengthened the construction by covering it with pieces of armour left by marauding monsters who had died there in the past. This would prevent the wood from breaking on impact. The two of them took occasional breaks for food and rest.

At regular intervals Sisaroth repeated the water droplet experiment. The tower's inclination had increased. Their efforts had been worthwhile. 'It's sloping a bit more now!' he shouted over to Marandëi.

'Then let's get to work,' she said with a groan, rubbing her neck. 'My back and legs are killing me.'

'I need you to fetch the blankets from your bedchamber.' Marandëi nodded and set off, while Sisaroth gathered a number of sacks from the ground floor.

With these items, they padded the wall they intended to assail.

The intention was to change the weight distribution in the tower, rather than attempt to destroy the stonework. If there was damage to the stones, the tower knew how to protect itself with magic. *But it won't be expecting to ward against toppling over.* 'We can begin.' Sisaroth started to roll the trunk across the room. 'Help me push. Or do you have a spell?'

The cîanai gave an embarrassed laugh. 'No. My magic's not much use, is it? I can make monsters explode, I can command water and fire at will, and I can bring down the night . . . but I can't push a cabinet on wheels. Look at me now.' Marandëi indicated her filthy sweat-soaked clothes. 'I've never had to work so hard. Like normal people.'

Sisaroth grinned. Taking a glass he placed it on the floor and marked the water level with a piece of charcoal. *That way we can measure the effect of our efforts.* 'You're doing fine.' He patted the lid of the kitchen storage chest. 'It won't be long now. Soon we'll be celebrating our release.'

'If we survive the fall!' She spoke these words with no trace of fear or doubt in her voice. She came over to his side and placed her hands next to his on the fortified wooden trunk. 'Ready?'

'Ready!'

Together they charged, trundling the heavy chest before them as they ran the width of the room, letting it crash into the padding on the opposing wall.

There was a loud noise and the wood protested but the metal armour held firm.

The wall quivered. The tower was reacting to the attack, doing its best to protect the masonry. Tiny cracks in the mortar closed up.

No matter. We're not trying to make a hole. We want the whole thing to collapse. Sisaroth glanced at the water in the glass. *No change there as yet.* He had not expected immediate success.

'Let's try again.' He grabbed hold of the handle and he and Marandëi lugged the chest back to the far side of the room for their next attempt. 'I think we may be doing this for some time.'

'That's all right by me,' she said. 'I don't have any other plans for today.' She put her hand on his shoulder. 'And thanks.'

'What for?' he asked, astonished.

'For giving me hope. Even if we never manage to escape you have taught me it's wrong to give up and simply accept one's fate.' She breathed a kiss onto his cheek and then leaned back to pull at the leather straps, helping drag the trunk over for the next onslaught on the tower's equilibrium. 'Let's show these stones what we're made of. We're cleverer than they are.'

Sisaroth smiled – and felt some degree of confusion. The warmth of her lips seemed to have permeated his skin and a strange tingling sensation had suffused his body. *That'll be her magic, I suppose.* He glanced over at her while she wasn't looking. *I'm not sure. Did she look that alluring before?* He shook himself to get rid of the vexing thought.

The two of them charged the wall again and again with the heavy improvised battering ram; they panted and cursed and hardly allowed themselves any respite. They were both obsessed with forcing the water in the glass to show their efforts were having an effect.

So far there had been no change.

'Wait,' said Marandëi. She leaned against the trunk, exhausted. 'I can't go on.'

Sisaroth used the pause to adjust the leather straps and inspect the wood and armour. The chest had held up well but cracks were showing in the metal fastenings. 'Let's try one more time.' He was extremely reluctant to give up despite his protesting muscles.

'It's no use,' she whispered. 'Nothing has happened.' She pointed to the glass. 'See for yourself.'

'I never said it would work on the first day.' *I'm not stopping.* 'Go ahead and lie down for a bit.'

'What about you?'

He pointed at the trunk.

'You won't let yourself entertain the slightest doubt, will you?' Marandëi tutted. 'You'll utterly exhaust yourself and you won't be able to move tomorrow, however young you are.' She touched him on the shoulder again. It did not feel like a motherly gesture. 'Come on. Let's both get some rest. We have plenty of time.'

'We may have plenty of time, but my poor siblings may not. My sister is no fighter. We're all stuck here in Phondrasôn and not safely behind the protective wall in Dsôn Sòmran where we belong.' Sisaroth took a deep breath and tightened his grip on the trunk handle. 'One more go. Please.'

But Marandëi plonked herself down on the lid in protest. 'You know what I think is odd?' She didn't wait for a response. 'You never asked me why I was sent here.'

'Why should I?' He was tempted to push her off. 'What good would that do? You could lie or use a spell.' He could not help thinking about her kiss. 'I'd have to believe anything you told me. I don't care why they exiled you.' Sisaroth pointed to the wall. 'I'm going to get us out of here and then you've undertaken to serve me for five divisions of unendingness. Plenty of time to ask you questions later, Marandëi.'

She laughed quietly. 'You are clever, aren't you? I think you are a young älf with a bright future.' She slid down from the top of the chest and grabbed hold of the handle. 'This is the very last try, or my back will . . .'

They heard a metallic clanging noise followed by a deep roar. The floor under their feet started to shake and then stopped. This sequence of events was repeated several times.

'What was that?' Sisaroth stared at the cîanai.

'The tower has brought us visitors,' she answered, horrified. 'Each time that noise happens something has arrived.'

The noises recurred and never seemed to stop.

Sisaroth counted forty-two instances of these new arrivals before silence returned. *What is the tower bringing us?* He did not assume the newcomers to the stronghold would be peace-loving.

'Did you lock the door after we collected the stones?' Marandëi asked him urgently.

No, I didn't. 'I'll go and take a look,' he answered swiftly, running out, the sword he had found below in his hand.

'Sisaroth!'

Something in the tone of her voice made him swivel round to face her.

'Look! The glass!'

He saw that the tower had started to lean further. The inclination had increased by a considerable number of degrees. The magic activity must have had an effect on the foundations; it was working in their favour. But her delight was premature – the price could well be too high.

'I must go downstairs. Wait here.' Sisaroth flew down and tried to reach the dungeon before the new arrivals could get over their surprise at landing in the tower.

He got as far as the kitchen.

Horrific creatures with the bodies of óarcos and the heads of animals charged him, screaming ferociously. They wore body armour and they were thirsting for a kill.

More came surging out of the corridor waving axes and other formidable-looking weapons.

I can't hold them back! Sisaroth retreated, fighting as hard as he could. He sliced off the top of one monster's head, stabbed another in the muzzle, and cut off a third's arm – then his sword became wedged in a bone and broke off.

The aggressive horde swept on, their approach heralded by an appalling stench and a tremendous racket.

The tower started to vibrate. More beasts were being brought in as reinforcements.

The tower is taking its revenge! Sisaroth leaped out of the kitchen and hurled the heavy oak door closed, bolting it fast. He took two steps back to catch his breath. *The tower wants us finished off by these ghastly fiends before we can tip it over.*

The door shook from the mass onslaught on the other side.

The hinges started to buckle and splinters of stone burst away from the frame. The noise from the beasts was ear-splitting.

He glanced around. *What can I do without a weapon?*

If only there were something to drag over and block the entrance! But he and Marandëi had taken everything to the top of the tower.

An axe blade was thrust through the door and torn back out for a second blow. A malicious eye glowed red through the hole in the splintered wood. 'Is alv!' came a guttural cry. 'Look, alv!'

Sisaroth turned and fled up the stairway.

Ishím Voróo (Outer Lands), Dsôn Sòmran, Dsôn, in the northern foothills of the Grey Mountains, 5427th division of unendingness (6241st solar cycle), spring.

The enclosed platform plunged into the mist. It was as if all that existed in the world were this cabin with its three passengers and the älf at the controls.

Droplets formed on the window panes, quickly giving way to a steady rainfall that drummed on the cabin roof.

Ranôria pressed herself into the corner by the door. From there she could keep an eye on the älf who had pushed past her on the way in. He was standing with his back to her.

I'm sure he was following me. Did Acòrhia send him? She wants to know what I'm up to. She was half-convinced that she was right to be so nervous. She was on the verge of uncovering a plot and the story-teller was at the heart of the conspiracy. But was someone else behind it all?

The other half of her brain kept telling her she was being stupid and she should not give in to paranoia.

What could really happen? She told herself to calm down. *So he's wearing a cloak. Of course he is. It's only because of the rain ... Lots of people cover their faces when the weather's bad like this.*

'Hey!' A loud voice called out from the greyness. They had nearly passed someone on the sixth ring who wanted to get in. 'Stop! Let me on!'

'Keep going!' the soldier commanded gruffly when he saw the operator was about to pull the lever.

'But I...'

Ranôria pricked up her ears. *This is my chance. As soon as we come to a stop I'll jump out and find another way to the top.*

The warrior raised his hand and shook his finger in a warning. 'No, you don't! I've got to get up to the wall for duty. How can I explain to the sytràp why I'm late? Shall I give him your name, so that the punishment comes down on you rather than me?'

Ranôria was struck by the appearance of a ring on the soldier's hand. It was made of tionium and silver, with an inlaid bone pattern and an amethyst-coloured stone. She did not recognise the symbol on it. The strange piece was not one of the normal military adornments and there was no indication of what family the soldier belonged to.

'Hey! Stop!' the person outside called again. 'It's raining hard and I can't walk very far!'

The soldier stared out through his visor, and lowered his arm.

'No, sorry. Can't stop here!' the intimidated operator called, as he moved the platform on its way. 'Sorry! You'll have to wait for the next one.'

Pity. Ranôria was annoyed she didn't have the chance to get out. She suppressed the uncomfortable feeling that something was amiss and turned her attention to the other älfar. *But at least this means I won't get wet.*

Nobody spoke.

The fog encroached on all sides, lifting occasionally, only to thicken and grow dark again, obliterating the view of rooftops.

Nearly there. Ranôria concentrated on the questions she wanted to ask Nomirôs. *I'll threaten him. I'll make him talk. I can swear that Aïsolon will protect him.* She remained convinced that the story-teller was playing a central role. *I've got to get Nomirôs to bear witness against her. I don't care if it's a lie or not, as long as she is implicated.*

The älf at the window suddenly turned round. He crossed his arms and stared at the tips of his boots. They were filthy. 'Will you look at that? I've only just cleaned them and they're already dirty again from the muddy streets.' He smiled at Ranôria. 'The slaves need to sweep better.' He bent down and polished his boots with the hem of his cloak. 'It would have to be today! I wanted to make a really good impression on her.'

So he's harmless enough. She returned the smile. 'You wanted to impress your partner?'

'She's not my partner yet,' he replied, still bent forward. 'And with my boots in this condition I stand no chance at all with her.'

The älf at the controls joined in their laughter. The guard cursed under his helmet and looked out at the rain. 'I thought it was supposed to be springtime,' he muttered crossly. 'The sun should be out and it should have started to warm up by now. When I'm on wall patrol I'll be soaked to the skin in no time.'

The ice was broken.

A dull thud, an impact against the pod and a shadow flitting past the window.

'What was that?' The hairs on the back of Ranôria's neck stood on end.

'That was a stone falling,' said the operative, moving two levers to speed up their progress.

'Start of a landslide, then?' The guard exchanged startled looks with the other passengers.

'Could be. Let's get ourselves up to the next level. We'll get out and I'll check the situation.' He stared out nervously. 'This stretch was thoroughly examined only a very short time ago. They said it was fine. That's why that loose stone makes me uneasy. They've recently renewed all the netting so it shouldn't be possible.'

'There were problems the other day on the north side. There's been far too much rain,' said the älf with the muddy boots. 'Slate can't take all that water.'

As if in confirmation of what he was saying there was a loud noise and a small boulder crashed down onto their roof; another burst through the windscreen in a shower of glass fragments and rolled over to where they were standing.

Ranôria shrieked and tried to get to safety; the operative at the controls was lying on the floor, his neck badly cut and his face covered in blood from the broken glass.

The platform had halted; the stone must have damaged one of the levers. The mist seeped into the cabin, clouding their view and letting in the damp and the cold.

The soldier moved over and examined the älf's injuries. 'We've got to get this going again. He may bleed to death.'

I don't think that was a normal landslide. Ranôria studied the stone that had come through the window. *Just the right size for throwing.* She did not look up. *Maybe someone was keen the cabin should stop just here?* She looked at the älf with the dirty boots; he was trying to work out how to master the controls. *I wonder if he has something to do with it after all?*

'Any idea how to drive this thing?' he asked Ranôria. 'This is ridiculous. I've been living here for eleven divisions of unendingness and I use the lifts all the time but I haven't got the foggiest idea how they work.'

The soldier let go of the wounded man, sprang to his feet and drew his sword. In one swift movement, he drove it through the other älf's body, clamping his hand over his mouth to stop him calling out. The mortally injured victim fell to the floor next to the wounded operative. The soldier finished off the lift-controller with a sword thrust through the neck.

This must be Acòrhia's doing! Ranôria looked out of the window to see where she would land if she jumped out to escape the murderous soldier. The fog gave no clear answers. It could have been half a pace down or thirty paces.

The älf towered over her in his armour, his sword pointed at her belly. His face was still hidden behind his visor. 'I've a message for you. You should never have doubted the guilt of your offspring.' His voice was threatening.

She could not think of a way out of this trap apart from an attack – and any attempt would surely cost her her life.

I should have smelled a rat when he said he had to get to the wall. The guards on duty there always stay in special quarters underneath the fortifications.

'And having passed on the message,' he said, loosening the muscles in his shoulders, 'I come to the second part of my assignment.' And he thrust at her with his sword.

Ranôria leaped aside and the sword narrowly missed her,

burying itself in the wood of the cabin wall. With all the strength she could muster she kicked the assassin in the side to knock him off balance. She sprang past him, out through the door opening.

She fell several paces down through rain and fog before meeting a solid surface. From the sound her feet made she guessed she had landed on the slates of a roof; she could get no purchase on the slippery tiles.

She slid down the incline on her seat, her fingers grabbing in vain at the damp roof. Her fall was broken when she crashed against a chimney pot. There was a crack and a searing pain went up her leg.

My ankle! Clutching at the chimney for all she was worth, she shifted her weight. 'Hallo? Can anyone hear me?' She was desperate. The fog prevented her seeing where she was – she had no idea where the house was in relation to others, nor which level she was in.

Her voice did not seem to carry at all in the mist.

Ranôria took a look down the chimney. *Surely whoever lives here ought to be able to hear me?* She shouted down through the warm smoke that made her cough. 'Hey, you down there! I need your help! I fell out from the lift pod and I landed on your roof and I've . . .'

There was a clink and a dark shadow landed on the tiles next to her.

The murderer! He's not given up. She fell silent and clung to the brickwork, trying to hide.

Everything was quiet. Each of them was listening for the sound of the other's movements.

The wind made little noise, but whirled the mist around, taking pleasure in forming lifelike figures with it.

The rain continued to sheet down on the city and Ranôria's clothes and hair were soaked. Her ankle was causing her a great deal of distress and she gritted her teeth to avoid groaning with pain and betraying her position.

'I shall find you,' whispered the killer. 'The fog can't protect you from me.'

Bolts were shot back and a trapdoor opened. Warm yellow light from a lantern spilled across the tiles. It signified relief, and safety.

'Is anyone there?' called a female älfar voice. The lamp moved from side to side.

Only four paces and I'd be inside, Ranôria guessed. At the same time she was horribly aware that the murderer would immediately know her whereabouts as soon as she moved. The broken ankle would make it impossible to move nimbly.

The lantern moved. A hand and an arm were just visible through the misty air. 'Is this some kind of a joke? Who's there?'

Ranôria decided to risk it.

Without answering, she left the comparative safety behind the chimney pot and slid towards the opening, moaning with pain when she put her injured foot down to help keep her balance.

The light swung round. 'Who is it?' demanded the voice.

The assassin rushed down the steep roof, clattering over the slate. He dived towards her like a bird of prey.

There he is! Ranôria could see his shadow; she rolled to the side.

The blade missed her heart but pierced her right arm. She screamed. The impact made her spin round and she slid down headfirst into the greyness, rapidly approaching the edge of the roof – until someone grabbed her foot. Her fall was halted.

'I've got you,' said the female älfar voice.

'Thank you,' Ranôria sobbed, feeling the hot blood stream out from the wound in her arm. *But where is the killer?* Terrified, she raised her head and stared into the fog, her heart beating fit to burst.

'Can you move?'

'No, I can't. Please don't let go.'

Other voices joined in. 'We're going to pull you in. Don't be afraid.'

'Whatever, in the name of all infamy, are you doing up there on my roof?' This time it was a male voice. 'I hope this is not some trick to break into my house.'

'Father, just help us,' said the girl firmly, 'before you start accusing anybody . . .' Her sentence ended in a scream, quickly followed by a groan from her father.

'What?' Ranôria was being pulled up. 'Has something happened?'

The lantern rolled down the roof past her and went over the edge.

'It certainly has.' The killer was speaking now. 'But it's nothing to worry your little head about.'

'Let me go!' Ranôria shouted, as she slowly approached the skylight.

Her struggle was all in vain. The slate she had been grasping came away in her hand.

Her legs were being pulled through the skylight and a hand grabbed her cloak, pulling at her upper body. It was the soldier. He was in the attic. 'Let me finish what I started . . .'

'Not as long as I have breath in my body to fight back.' Ranôria jabbed at him with the broken slate in her grip. It shattered against his helmet, but some splinters found their way through the visor.

He jerked his head to one side with a grunt and fell back through the roof window. He did not release his grasp of her leg, and Ranôria was pulled into the attic with him.

You haven't won yet. She landed on him as she fell. A second lamp hanging on one of the beams illuminated the scene.

I've got to kill him first, before he can – She managed to get her uninjured hand on his dagger and pull it out. She moved to plunge the blade into his neck.

The älfar reached up and held her hand fast, so that the blade merely scratched the skin of his throat. 'Not bad.' He punched her in the face and pushed her off.

She landed on the dead body of the owner of the house. His throat had been cut. His daughter lay crumpled at his side. She was too giddy with pain to think clearly and she moved clumsily. She had lost too much blood.

I have to save my children. Ranôria made a futile attempt to drag herself to the stairs but she was kicked in the head and nearly passed out. It was as if she were wearing a red veil; she realised it was her own blood flowing into her eyes.

'In recognition of your near escape from me, I'm inclined to let you live,' her attacker said. 'But the woman who commissioned my services was adamant, so I regret I must carry out the task in full.'

Ranôria was thrown onto her back, but she could only see her killer vaguely. 'Please,' she whispered, 'I beg you. Let me live so I can save my innocent children.'

'You are a good mother. What a pity.'

'Then at least let me die knowing the truth. Were you the one who killed Sémaina's family?'

There was a short pause. 'No. I had nothing to do with that.'

'Who ordered my death?' Ranôria was cold. She could no longer feel her back at all. She was so tired that all the pain ebbed away. Neither her ankle nor her arm hurt her now. *Death has come and he will take me to endingness.*

'Can't you work out who it was?'

'Acòrhia?'

His response was a movement of his head but with her sight failing she was unable to read the sign. *Was that a yes or a no?* 'Speak the name . . .'

Before she could repeat the request, he had driven his sword into her floundering heart. He destroyed the organ with a twist of the blade. The muscle of life ceased to beat.

Rain from the open skylight dampened her face. The murderer smashed the lantern on the floor and set the attic alight. Fire would consume her body and eliminate any traces of his crime.

Her eyes lost their warmth. The unique singing voice, which had captivated thousands of älfar in her time, making them laugh and cry, had faded forever.

Chapter VII

Isolated and remote,
*   uncanny and bleak-hearted.*
*   This place alone can sunder*
*   what can never else be parted.*
Vale of shadows
*   . . . come to me, dark sister*
Vale of shadows
*   . . . come to me, dark brother*
Vale of shadows
*   . . . come, join hands for the dance*
*   in the vale of shadows*
Released, unchained, unfettered:
*   shadows are beyond recapture.*
*   They dance with any that they find*
*   and seek new ties of rapture.*
Vale of shadows
*   . . . come to me, dark sister*
Vale of shadows
*   . . . come to me, dark brother*
Vale of shadows

. . . come, join hands for the dance
in the vale of shadows.

Watch out, hold fast!
You tether him in vain –
he will break free.
Until the last
you must remain.
in the vale of shadows,
vale of pain . . .

'Vale of Shadows' from the epic poem *Young Gods*
composed by Carmondai, master of word and image

Phondrasôn, some time after the 5427th division of unendingness.

I hope it tastes better this time. Everything else has been mouldy.
Tirîgon gutted the fish and roasted his catch over the fire,
skewered on a piece of bone. It would be his first proper food for
ages; even if it had more bones than flesh, it was decidedly better
than nothing.

He turned the fish patiently on the makeshift spit while
studying the map he held carefully in his other hand. It had
served him well up to now.

The elves of the floating island had gone to great lengths
to make an exact cartographic record of their immediate environment, but Tirîgon was starting to suspect that Phondrasôn
was not a single place but a multiplicity. *Like a box within a*

box within a box. One cave opened up into another, or into a tunnel. Steps branched off corridors, giving access to different levels.

He had passed chasms spanned by mile-long bridges suspended from chains originating up in the impenetrable blackness. Tirîgon could not imagine what the chains were fastened to and had no idea whether the bridges would bear his weight. *Take the risk* seemed to be the motto for travel in Phondrasôn.

Because he was keeping strictly to the map, avoiding any deviations or confrontations of any kind, he had made reasonable progress. Hunger and thirst were his chief adversaries.

The fish gave off an appetising smell. It was done.

At last! Something to eat! Tirîgon settled back into the niche at the side of the path and tucked in, being careful to remove the bones. He tried to work out how much longer his journey to Tossàlor would take.

He reckoned he had already covered about seventy-one miles. *So there are still nine to go.*

He did not know how much time had passed. A glow from shimmering moss was the only light source in the tunnels, and even that was occasional. Once he came across a discarded torch he could light. He created sparks by rubbing together fragments of dried bone. With no discernible night and day, he became accustomed to sleeping when he was tired and moving when he woke.

I must stink by now. Cleanliness was of vital importance to the älfar race; he was uncomfortable with his filth. Phondrasôn was extremely unhelpful in this regard.

Tirîgon chucked the remains of the fish into the fire and then picked up a fragment of wood, one of the last salvageable pieces he still had from his raft. He began to carve it out. He liked to fashion little figurines with his knife to distract himself from his worries. This had always been his favourite leisure pursuit back in Dsôn.

What do I do once I've found Tossàlor? Say hallo politely and hope he doesn't want my skeleton for artwork? He had whittled the rough likeness of an älf with a little sword and spear to complete it. He could not provide more intricate detail with the tools at hand. *Maybe I should overpower him and tie him up before I try to talk to him.*

He placed the little figure on the ground next to him and tossed a couple of old animal bones into the flames, together with two of the yellow stones he had come across. They gave off an intense heat and must, he thought, be somehow related to the coal used in Dsôn as fuel. It had been a lucky find; a lucky charm. So far nothing had tried to attack him as he slept.

He laid his head on his arm and watched the flames, listening to the crackle of the fire. He wondered about his siblings and how they might be faring.

He hoped that Tion and the gods of infamy were supporting them in the way he himself had been helped. He had landed safely on the lake with his landing stage remnant and had eventually floated to land, where he had traveled through tunnels, shafts and galleries without encountering resistance or danger. He had lost a lot of weight – his clothes and armour now hung on him – but he was alive.

They have to survive. They have to! We will find each other. He clenched his fist. *Even if Phondrasôn were a thousand times bigger we would find each other. We are bonded.*

A pebble clattered down the rock and rolled to a stop near his head.

It could be nothing – or it might announce the arrival of someone attracted by the fire.

Tirîgon scrambled to his feet and climbed up the rock wall onto a narrow ledge. From here he could watch the niche he had been sitting in.

A dark-clad figure the size of a human was silently approaching, drawn dagger in hand.

From his vantage point Tirîgon could not tell if it was a barbarian, man or woman. But it was clear the intentions were not friendly.

The figure came close to the fire and, obviously hungry, grabbed the fish skin that Tirîgon had rejected. It knelt down cautiously and stopped chewing every so often to listen, head swivelling.

When all the tough skin had finally been eaten, the figure's gaze fell on the little carving Tirîgon had made. It lifted it up and held it to the flames for closer examination; the light fell on the dirty features of a female.

Is she wearing a mask? Tirîgon tried to get a closer look. What he had thought to be gloves turned out to be a gauntlet of skin. *Is this another obboona? If so, she needs killing at once!*

She blew the dust gently off the little figurine, put away her dagger and pulled out a needle-thin stiletto blade from the folds of her garment. She continued the work Tirîgon had started.

She'll ruin it! He rolled off the ledge and landed behind her, his sword drawn. 'Leave it,' he ordered in barbarian. 'I don't want you to touch my artwork with your stinking hands.'

She froze, then slowly rose to her feet. She seemed to grow in stature. 'Do I hear right? Is that perhaps the commanding voice of an älf?' she responded with perfect älfar diction. She raised her hand. 'So this is something you made?'

Tirîgon came round to stand in front of her, blade still poised threateningly. 'Yes.'

'It's very good. Under these conditions. You'd need better tools, of course, but I can see you would make an excellent master sculptor.' The female watched him closely from behind the wrinkled old skin she had covered her face with. 'Oh, how young you are! Very young indeed!'

'I may be young but I know how to kill.' The expression in her reddish-brown eyes was cold and cruel in a way Tirîgon was not familiar with, even among his own personal enemies. *She is clever. That's obvious.* 'Put it down!'

'And then you will kill me, I suppose,' she said, keeping hold of the carving. 'So I'd be ill-advised to do what you say.' Her tone was mocking. 'Is the little älf scared his tiny dolly might get hurt? Perhaps you need it so's you can get to sleep. It's such a horrid place, Phondrasôn, isn't it?'

This is not how an obboona would behave. 'No, I need it to plunge into your heart.' He brought the sharp sword-blade right up to her throat. The filthy covering of wrinkled skin fell apart with a dry rustle, revealing cleaner, lighter flesh underneath.

'Well said!' She waved the little bodkin. 'But do you think I'll let you do that? Or might I open your carotid artery first?' To his surprise, her eyes turned black.

The campfire extinguished with a rush of sound and a cloud of sparks flew at Tirîgon.

She's an älf! He sprang backwards to avoid the glowing shower of embers and struck out, his sword making a powerful horizontal arc. *She must have lost her mind if she's dressing as an obboona!*

A hand grabbed his long black hair and hurled him around into the cliff face, briefly stunning him. He thrust his weapon out behind him.

A cool laugh sounded in his left ear. 'That's not going to get you anywhere, young älf!' Her slim blade caressed the skin on his throat. 'Here's a little souvenir for you.'

He threw himself backward, breathing hard, trying to knock her over with his weight, but there was nothing behind him. Before he could recover his balance, the stranger pulled his feet from under him and he landed on his back in the dying embers. The heat went straight through his armour.

Is she some kind of warrior woman? Tirîgon rolled over and sprang to his feet, plunging his sword into the darkness without meeting its target.

This time her laughter seemed maliciously joyful. The flames jumped up again. Light returned to the little niche and illuminated the two älfar standing face to face.

Tirîgon put his fingers to the wound on his neck. *A scratch. Carefully delivered.* He stared at her. 'Who are you?'

'Names are nothing here in Phondrasôn,' she replied. 'It is deeds that count. Deeds we do or deeds we leave undone.' She was still holding the little carving but had stowed the stiletto knife. 'I have decided not to take your life, young älf. You have noticed I would have no difficulties on that score.'

'You must have been exiled for being completely mad,' said Tirîgon. He lowered his sword, aware the weapon was of no use. She had showed her superiority clearly enough. *What will result from this meeting?*

'For pretending I am an obboona? No. I only started to do

that when I got to Phondrasôn. Nobody likes them so I get left alone. It saves a lot of trouble, this get-up.'

She is very beautiful, even though she's covered in dirt. Tirîgon sheathed his sword. *If I'd met her back in Dsôn and she'd been nicely dressed – and clean – I could imagine wanting her for my partner!* 'If you won't tell me your name, how about telling me why you got banished?'

'I am the older of us two and I've clearly been in this ghastly place a whole lot longer than you have. I insist on hearing your story first. It will be quicker in the telling than my own.' The älf-woman looked round. 'I don't suppose you've got another of those fish anywhere?'

'No, but I can show you where I caught it. There's a pond near here and the water's shallow. It was quite easy.' Tirîgon sat down and she did the same. 'I came here of my own free will.'

'Aha. So you are a brave little soldier wanting to gain his combat colours,' she laughed. 'Why don't you people ever do anything sensible as a rite of passage? If I were a monster or some mad woman I'd have finished you off with no trouble at all. Your family would be waiting a very long time for you to come back.' She touched her own throat to remind him of the wound she had inflicted.

'No. It's not some coming-of-age ritual. I'm here to look after my brother and my sister, who've been exiled. They're innocent of the crime they've been accused of.'

'And your siblings must be powerful sorcerers.'

'Why do you say that?'

'Because I don't see them here.' The älf-woman smiled. For the first time her expression looked genuine.

Tirîgon sighed.

'We were separated. I am looking for them.' *And all I've got to guide me are my own good intentions and two-thirds of a map that probably only shows a fraction of these maze-like paths.* 'I don't feel like joking about it.'

'You have my sympathies.' She tossed the little figurine over to him and he caught it. 'I really meant it when I said you would make a good carver. Not many have the ability to work in such detail using only a common dagger. If you created this from wood, I can only imagine your skill with bone. Do you know Tossàlor?'

'The murderer?' The words slipped out.

She grinned. 'He prefers to be known as *Master* and he insists that he is a misunderstood artist. He lives down here and I'm positive he wants an apprentice to train. And if you're not suitable as a pupil he can make you famous by using your bones in a sculpture.' The älf-woman peeled off the rest of the false skin veil, revealing long brown hair encrusted with brilliants.

It's as if she has all the stars of the firmament in her hair. Tirîgon stared in fascination. 'I . . . what . . . ?'

'That's why I keep my head covered,' she stammered, embarrassed.

'Were you born like that?'

'No. It was a silly mistake. Soon after I arrived in Phondrasôn I got stuck in one of the magic fields. There are lots of them here. You never know in advance what their effect will be. Sometimes they'll cause a creature to explode in mid-air, sometimes they'll make a beast grow three times its natural size, and sometimes they'll cripple you by stealing your limbs. They give you the strangest characteristics. There are infinite possibilities. You must be careful. Watch out for magic and keep well away.' She pushed her shining hair back; it reflected the firelight. 'And this is what the magic fields did to me. Amongst other things, of course.' She threw a couple of bones into the flames. 'If you like, I can take you to Tossàlor.'

'I would like to see him, but I have no intention of living near someone who has murdered people of our own race. And I certainly don't want to learn his craft. But thank you. So now you know my story ...'

'You'd like to hear mine?'

Tirîgon nodded.

'It was a trivial matter. I defended myself against an importunate suitor, that's all. But he died in the fight. And since the weapon he had used against me couldn't be located – ' She looked at him. 'They accused me of having committed murder rather than acting in self-defence. All the evidence went against me and there hadn't been any witnesses, so I ended up here, in exile.'

Tirîgon tried to read her expression, but her features were coated in dirt. He wanted to know if she were telling the truth.

'What was your trade, back in Dsôn?'

'Why do you want to know?'

'Because you move like a highly trained warrior. My father ...' He stopped himself from mentioning Aïsolon was the governor. 'My father was one of the wall sentries for a long time. He taught me everything I know.'

'He gave up too soon, if you ask me,' she objected. 'No, I served a high-born älf-woman. I was her personal bodyguard.'

'Aha? And who was she?'

'It is not important. She did not stand up for me when I needed her support. I was bitterly disappointed.'

Tirîgon was not convinced by the story she was telling him.

She's refusing to name names. I think she's lying. Nobody in Dsôn kept a personal bodyguard as protection against other älfar. Any feuds were fought in secret, and it was words that were used, not violent deeds: rumours, of course, and lawsuits. Nobody would order an assassin to get rid of a rival.

Properly trained hit men were very rare nowadays. They had all gone to Tark Draan, Aïsolon had told him. Virssagòn had been the best of them. He had specialised in inventing new weaponry and developing techniques for their use.

A thought made him sit upright.

By all the gods of infamy! Tirîgon tried to control his reaction but he couldn't help staring at her intently. This time he was not concentrating on her brilliant shimmering hair. *I wonder if she was one of Virssagòn's former pupils?*

She could tell that he was trying to work out who she was. 'Well, there we have it. We're both stuck here in Phondrasôn,' she said quietly, laying a hand on her stomach. 'I'd like to get back to the offer you made me.'

'What offer?'

'For the fish. You were going to show me the pond where you can catch them easily. We've already got a nice fire going.' She got to her feet. 'After that I'll let you sleep. I'll keep watch.'

All right by me. He did not think she was trying to trick him. *If she'd wanted to kill me she could have done it several times over by now.* Tirîgon agreed and led her to the spot where he had caught the fish for his dinner.

The girl walked a little apart from him, and wondered aloud how he found his way so surely. 'You seem to know exactly where to go. Which tunnel goes where and how the paths interconnect.'

He tapped the map in his pocket. 'I've got – ' *no, best not tell her that* ' – an excellent sense of direction.'

'I see.' She seemed happy with that answer. 'Then maybe I should stick close to you.'

'All the way to Dsôn Sòmran? Are you going to be allowed back? It's different for me since I came down to the caves voluntarily.'

'Of course,' she nodded. 'I've finished serving my time. It's just I've never been able to find the way back.'

Tirîgon was not thrilled with the idea of having an älf-woman disguised as an obboona as a travelling companion. He still had nagging doubts about her state of mind. *But I must admit she has powerful combat skills. That could be useful.*

When they reached the pond he showed her the fish swimming under the shelter of a narrow overhang. 'I look forward to seeing how long it'll take you to catch one,' he challenged her.

She bounded past him, diving into the water and reappearing at the surface a few seconds later with a fish wriggling in her hand. The water had removed most of the filth from her appearance and allowed her natural gracefulness to shine through. 'I think I've just won,' she crowed, tossing the fish onto the bank. 'Lightly grilled fish! Delicious! My mouth's watering already.'

Tirîgon watched while she stripped off her wet clothes and the false skin. She sank back into the water to bathe properly, her brown hair sparkling like the stars. The swim turned her into a completely different, fascinating being.

She's irresistible!

When she invited him to join her with a playful gesture, he did not hesitate. He was consumed with desire.

In recent days caution had been his constant watchword, but

now he ripped off his armour and his garments and stepped into the pond.

Phondrasôn, some time after the 5427th division of unendingness.

Sisaroth ran up the stairs and locked all the doors behind him. There were no items of furniture left which could be used as barricades. *The tower must have known this was the right time to strike with the beasts.*

He dashed through to the top room where Marandëi was struggling to get the chest into position by herself. 'It's a horde of monsters! Nearly fifty, I'd say!'

'I'd burn them to ashes if we weren't in this tower. It always knows when I try to use magic.'

There was another rumbling sound and the floor shook.

Yet more of them. But the vibrations they cause should work for us. He went over to the cîanai's side and put his shoulder to the heavy trunk. 'We've no choice but to succeed in toppling the tower.'

Their battering ram crashed into the wall.

This latest impact brought more dramatic results. The whole building juddered and tilted to one side like a falling tree.

The glass of water slid across the floor and shattered against the wall. Sisaroth and Marandëi were forced to lean to keep their balance, as if climbing a steep incline. It was almost impossible to drag the heavy chest away from the side.

But in spite of the pronounced slope, the tower refused to fall.

'The support beams must still be holding it,' said Sisaroth. 'A last bit of resistance before it collapses.'

'But what are we going to do? We have to finish it. We're

stuck here.' Marandëi glanced over at the door. 'How long till those beasts break through?' She looked at the älf. 'And where are your weapons, my warrior?'

He racked his brains. *She's got to risk it.* 'What kind of spells can you cast that won't make the tower react?'

Marandëi hurried to the door, clambering nimbly over the piled-up obstacles, and looked into the stairwell. Because of the sloping floor it was difficult to get a true picture. 'I'll try to frighten them first,' she said. 'Let their hearts be filled with fear.' She pointed to the heap of furniture. 'Pray that the tower doesn't punish me for it and do your best with that battering ram. I'll cover your back for as long as possible.' She left the room.

Right, then! Sisaroth was at a loss for what else to try, so he seized two large gold jugs, lugged them to the far corner of the room, then turned and ran with them in his arms, flinging his weight against the outer wall. He repeated this again and again until he realised he was having no effect whatsoever. *I've got to think of something!*

The tower went on humming and shaking. It was drawing in as many beast attackers to fill its belly as it could.

But it was this magic shuddering that eventually brought the first signs of success. Cracks appeared in the floor.

The tower is so eager to get rid of us that it is bringing itself down. 'Marandëi! It's starting!' he yelled through the doorway. 'Get ready! Mind falling beams and . . .'

The cracks got bigger and bigger and bricks started to crumble away. Stones that had been dovetail-joined began to pull apart. The building was clearly breaking in two.

The upper part, where Sisaroth was, began collapsing in on itself. As the walls shifted, a cloud of dust hurtled at Sisaroth, making it difficult to breathe. Over the rumbles of the crumbling building, he could hear the shrill cries of terrified beasts.

The roof gave way and beams and huge stones thundered down.

I've got to get out of this alive! So near to freedom and yet so far! Sisaroth could avoid the falling masonry as long as he could see it coming, but the clouds of dust soon made this well-nigh impossible.

A lump of stone hit him on the shoulder and forced him to his knees. Another struck him on the back and felled him completely.

The attic room separated from the bottom half of the tower, crashing down into the encompassing moat. The älf fell with the rubble, landing in a whirl of bubbles in the foaming waters with no protection from the crashing beams and falling debris.

Sisaroth struggled to the surface and grabbed the side of the basin. He looked around wildly just in time to dodge an axe-blow.

'Missed, dammit!' cursed a tough-looking gnome in rusty chainmail as he lifted his weapon for a second attempt at Sisaroth's neck. 'I'll get you this time, my little Black-Eyes! Where do you keep your treasure? Huh?'

Sisaroth slid back down under the water and launched himself upwards when his feet touched bottom. He shot up as swift as an arrow in flight, landing next to the knee-high gnome. He punched him on the jaw then seized the axe. 'I haven't escaped the clutches of the tower just to be killed by you, you misbegotten freak!' He hefted the axe straight through the pitiful creature's neck.

'Marandëi!' *Where has she gone?* Sisaroth wiped the water off his face, tossed back his dripping dark locks and took in the devastation.

All around was nothing but ruins. The tower as it fell had destroyed most of the stone colonnade and the edges of the artificial lake. Even great boulders from the cave wall itself had become dislodged by the tremendous impact.

He could see crushed limbs sticking out from amongst the rubble. Dying beasts' cries of agony filled the air. There was no immediate sign any of the aggressors had survived.

First the tower enticed them, pulled them in; then it swallowed them up and crushed them to death. 'Marandëi!' he shouted, pulling a sword out from under a horizontal beam. 'Marandëi, can you hear me? Where are you?'

Two small gnomes appeared, scavenging among the wreckage.

Sisaroth took careful aim and hurled his axe at one of them. *Disgusting little rats!*

The blade hit its target and the gnome collapsed screeching.

The companion dived for cover, launching a torrent of gnome curses. Sisaroth recognised the golden necklet in its hand as Marandëi's. The two gnomes had been ripping valuables from crushed bodies.

Is she lying there dead or injured? Picking up a discarded morning-star, Sisaroth headed in his direction. He chucked the multi-headed flail at the scarpering gnome.

The metal globes flew through the air.

The chain wrapped itself around the gnome's neck as a lethal throttling collar. Two of the heavy iron balls slammed into the ugly face, smashing nose and temple, while the third ball shattered the back of the creature's head. The impetus of the spiked metal missile threw the gnome off its feet, and it gasped its last in the mud.

Something in a muddled heap of broken beams from the tower caught Sisaroth's eye: it was a tattered piece of Marandëi's robe. *Please be alive!*

Despite his own painful injuries, he set to work hauling heavy stones and timber aside until there was room to retrieve the unconscious älf-woman.

He was relieved she did not seem to have any broken bones. He carried her out of the debris to the edge of the water.

Just cuts and grazes, I think. She's been lucky. He collected a little water in his hands and knelt down, sprinkling some drops on her face to bring her round.

Marandëi opened her eyes, completely bewildered at her surroundings. 'So . . . I'm no longer in the tower?' she stammered through dust-caked lips. She sat up slowly, gingerly touching her head, and turned to take in the scene. 'We've . . . done it!' She gave a cry of delight, embracing Sisaroth gratefully. 'But for you, I'd have been a prisoner forever.'

'True,' he said, grinning. 'But if I'm honest, it wouldn't have happened without you. The escape needed both of us.' He helped her to her feet and she brushed the dirt from her dress. 'Look, I've saved something else, too.' He pointed to the glittering necklace in the grimy hand of the gnome who had stolen it from her.

'That was good of you.' Marandëi checked herself for injuries. 'I've been extremely lucky. I think the gods of infamy must have been watching over us.'

'I shall be sure to ask them as soon as I get a chance.'

He went over to the dead gnome and extricated the golden chain for her.

'You're going to *ask* them? What do you mean?'

'I am a priest for them.' Sisaroth could see she wasn't taking him seriously. 'I admit that I was still very much at the start of my training when I was sent into exile, but I can do a proper ritual.'

Marandëi was impressed. 'Not bad. I hope you'll let me come along to see you do one. A close friend was training to be a priest but he nearly killed himself doing his first incantation. The gods of infamy are terribly choosy about who serves them.'

Sisaroth wondered whether he had said too much, but blundered on. 'The gods have high standards.' He left it at that and turned away to survey the immediate environment to change the subject. 'What shall we do now? Where shall we go?'

Marandëi fastened the chain round her neck. 'By the way, I intend to keep my promise to you,' she said soberly.

'Your promise? Oh, I remember!' He had indeed nearly forgotten the oath she had sworn. 'You don't have to do that. You can go wherever you please. I'll be off to try and find my brother and sister. You are released from any obligation towards me. I'm sure you have plans of your own.' It was hard for him to show this generosity to another, but he felt it was right. *I hope I don't live to regret this.* 'What would be the point of exchanging physical captivity for an oath that enslaves you?'

But she was resolute. 'I gave you my word. I think the gods of infamy sent you to me to demonstrate that their power extends to the dark realm of Phondrasôn and that they care for those who do not give up. This means that I shall serve you for five divisions of unendingness.'

'Your decision.' He was pleased, though he would not admit it. *Generosity is its own reward, it seems.* He had not yet seen any example of her cîanai magic abilities. *But there'll be plenty of opportunities. I'm sure Phondrasôn holds monsters enough for her to destroy.*

Marandëi pointed to the cave entrance. 'We should go that way. As long as the cave walls haven't moved much I should know my way out. Let's go to my palace. We'll be safe there.'

'Just to make sure we understand each other here: I don't want to dwell there, even if it's a perfectly lovely palace.'

'I know. Don't worry. We won't stay long.' She brushed down her tattered dress. 'I've had to wear this same threadbare garment for ages and however fond I used to be of it, I would like to see the end of it now. I really need to pack a bag of clothes.' She spied something in the rubble. 'Ah! My trusty staff!' Marandëi bent down and pulled the tall metal-trimmed stick out from under a pile of stones. She was delighted to find that it was all in one piece. She strode off. 'Come with me.'

Sisaroth followed her. As they walked, he helped himself to a selection of weaponry dropped by the óarcos, choosing a small shield, a better sword than the one he had been using, and three daggers which he stuck in his belt. *If I have to, I can defend myself.* 'Who built your palace for you?'

'Nobody. I just took it. The owner did not know how to appreciate it.' Marandëi stepped lightly over the ruins, using her staff to help her along. 'He hadn't realised the foundations were in a magic source. Quite handy for me as a cîanai.'

'Why did you leave it? How did you end up in the tower?'

'I was bored. I was exploring and I came across the cave; that was all it took.' She looked back over her shoulder and spat.

'And you've no idea how long you were there?'

'No. I can only guess.' Marandëi sighed.

While they were marching through the desolate scene, Sisaroth wondered about the original reason for her banishment.

He was there despite being innocent, he had told her. He had not been able to read her expression and he did not know whether she believed him. She evaded giving explicit details about her own history. 'By the way, you don't have to be afraid of repercussions when we get to Dsôn Sòmran. It was only Dsôn Faïmon you were expelled from, after all.'

He and Marandëi were entering the tunnel behind the cave and found walls and floor decorated with the älfar runes that had led Sisaroth to the tower initially. Now the symbols looked lifeless and charred, fractured and harmless.

Marandëi kicked the remains of the runes to one side. 'The spell will have been broken when the tower collapsed. No älf will ever again be tricked like we were.' She struck the floor with her staff and the inlaid pattern in the wood glowed softly. This gave them enough light to see by. 'Let's get out of here.'

Sisaroth and she walked side by side and he held his sword and shield at the ready. *It's so quiet. All the monsters must have died in the hail of stones.*

They walked along in silence, exercising every precaution.

'You still owe me an answer,' Sisaroth reminded her.

'I wasn't exiled,' she countered, sticking her chin out. 'I . . . ran away.'

What threat can have been terrifying enough to force her to seek refuge here? 'I suppose you came here because you had committed murder and needed to get away from the victim's family?' he suggested.

Marandëi banged the ground with her stick. It could have meant Yes. Or it could have meant No. 'I was trying to escape from my own guildsmen,' she confessed. 'I knew the scholars were after me. I could never have found anywhere in Dsôn Faïmon to hide. And they would not have accepted banishment as a suitable judicial sentence for me.'

This piqued Sisaroth's curiosity. 'Had you stolen from one of the other cîanai? Did you take a magic artefact?' His eyes were fixed on her staff. *Perhaps that's what she stole?* 'Or did you plagiarise a colleague's spell?'

She shook her head. 'I killed my own master. Quite deliberately.' She bit down on her lower lip, causing a bead of blood to form. 'Because I wanted to prove to him that I was better than he was.'

Chapter VIII

Night-dark is the oak – lit by the moon –
  leafless now, its branches dead,
    the strangest fruit are the crown on its head.
      The smell of decay brings carrion crows and swarms of
flies.
    A hungry fox waits under the moon,
      slavering for its prize.
The tree-fruit sways in the wind,
    the tree-fruit rots in the air,
      the tree-fruit is spurned
        by wanderers
          anxious to hurry by.
And the wind plays with the dead man,
    making him dance on his rope.
      Insects roam the rotting flesh, drinking their fill.
        The fox leaps up
          and bites off a chunk of soft thigh,
            devouring it in the shade of the oak.
The tree-fruit sways in the wind,
    the tree-fruit rots in the air,
      the tree-fruit is spurned

by wanderers
anxious to hurry by.
Hanged without cause
by those who relish cruelty
and who rejoiced about their deed.
But now plague runs wild,
brought unwittingly into their ranks
by their victim.
This gave Death twofold cause for merriment.

'Strange Fruit' from the epic poem *Young Gods*
composed by Carmondai, master of word and image

Phondrasôn, some time after the 5427th division of unendingness.

Firûsha's terror grew as more of the berry-like cocoons burst open, releasing their insects. The buzzing sound got louder and louder until it sounded like a rushing mountain torrent. Clouds of the flies swarmed around them.

We'll never get through. 'Come on, you're too slow. Let me out!' she shouted, rattling the bars of her cage. 'If you let me out at least I can run away from them.'

He did not answer; instead he concentrated on hauling the heavy sled. He was putting on a good turn of speed, all things considered. But things weren't going fast enough for Firûsha.

The hatched insects spread their wings and sailed through the cave, swirling dangerously close to the two älfar.

It would only take them five or six little skips to catch up with us.

'Crotàgon, you must let me out!' she pleaded, desperate now. 'Please! Just leave all the supplies. It's life or death.'

The broad-shouldered älf halted, but it wasn't because he was doing as she asked. It was because their way was blocked. A landslide had rendered the cave exit impassable.

'We can't go that way,' he said – and at long last he opened the cage door. 'We'll go to the right here. I think there's a second way out.'

'You *think*?' She clambered out of her prison. 'I don't see that we have time to look for it.'

'Do you have a better idea? I warned you that it's dangerous out here away from my home. Don't you dare complain.' He ran, Firûsha following at his heels.

Despite his armour Crotàgon moved swiftly; she struggled to keep up with him.

They headed in a straight line through extremely dense under-growth, but at least there weren't any insects here. An unpleasant smell of lilies overrode everything else, and clouds of yellow pollen were released when they brushed against branches, making it difficult for them to breathe.

Crotàgon cut a swathe through the thick foliage, chopping at the heavy branches and twigs that were getting stuck in Firûsha's hair and the billowing skirts of her dress.

Have they reached us yet? When she looked back over her shoulder she caught sight of a huge swarm of the insects hovering under the roof. Long black lines of the creatures jutted out like fingers from the main swarm; the lines reached almost to the cave floor. One of these exploratory strings was pointing directly at the two älfar and was horribly close.

I don't want to bleed to death! 'Crotàgon, hurry!' Firûsha yelled, wanting to push him bodily onwards. 'They're getting closer!'

'I can't go any faster,' he replied. 'The undergrowth is too thick. It's slowing me down.'

Firûsha was about to frame a retort when she managed to tread on his heel by mistake. Crotàgon stumbled but kept his balance, while she toppled over and fell.

The insects' wild buzzing hummed in her ear.

You shan't get me! Firûsha struggled to her feet but nearly immediately tripped over a root. Her foot was stuck fast. *No! Not now!*

Suddenly a barbarian came leaping out of the undergrowth and thrust himself into the insects' path with outstretched arms. He wore nothing but a loin cloth.

The flies crashed into him – and within the space of four heartbeats they turned into dried-up husks that rustled as they slid to the ground. Their legs, chitin plating and wings fell off. Whatever touched the barbarian's skin seemed to lose its life-strength immediately on contact; everything shrivelled and died.

Firûsha freed her trapped foot, got slowly to her feet and without taking her eyes off the spectacle, started backing away. *How does he do that?*

The barbarian was tall and strong and his upper body was covered in tattoos that seemed to come alive as his muscles rippled. The flies were aware that destruction was near at hand and they surged away from him. The dark swarm retreated.

The barbarian laughed and turned to face the älf-woman.

By all the unholy ones! She staggered back; the stranger had the head of an ancient old man, his furrowed face radiating cruelty. His brows, drawn together in a grimace, gave him a mad grin. Remains of the insects fell from his open, toothless mouth. The beast seemed to have been put together randomly. The head and the body didn't fit, age-wise.

'Run!' Crotàgon urged, tugging at her sleeve.

She did not question his order. The barbarian had saved her from the insects, but she was not safe yet. 'Who is that?' she panted, not daring to look round. She could not risk tripping again.

'It's an ukormorier. I'll explain later if we get out of here in one piece.' Crotàgon changed direction, following a well-trodden path.

Judging from the sounds, the barbarian was following them.

Firûsha could make out further figures to the right and to the left; they were emerging through the bushes, flanking the fleeing pair. All the shrubs, the scarce grass and the flowers shrivelled and rotted immediately on contact with the ukormoriers, creating a brown swathe through the cave's luxuriant vegetation.

I don't want to know what happens if they touch me. Firûsha tried to pick up her speed; their pursuers were catching up. Crotàgon pulled her away from the cave wall. *What's he doing? 'Where are we going?'*

The path gave on to a clearing about ten paces wide. Crotàgon stopped in the middle. 'Stay behind me,' Crotàgon whispered, holding fast to the spear with the long, wide blade.

Firûsha realised he was about to challenge the barbarian to combat. 'Give me a weapon,' she said quietly.

He stared at her intently and passed over a dagger that felt to her as heavy as a sword. This was not a weapon she felt at home with. 'If you are in a fight, aim for the breastbone. The heart lies directly beneath it.' Crotàgon turned his attention to the nearest foe and swore.

Can it get any worse? Firûsha looked past him.

Eight ukormoriers reared up in front of them out of the thicket of dead wood; all of them were naked and sported tattoos; their heads were those of very old men. They had no need for weapons of any kind. It was clear that the slightest contact would spell an enemy's death.

She was shocked by their appearance. *Is it the tattoos that make them look so frightening?* Firûsha glanced quickly at Crotàgon's spear and then down at the dagger in her own hand. She did not want them close enough to use it. *What happens if we actually hit one of them? Will our weapons rust and crumble away?* She grimaced. *What appalling-looking creatures! What is the best way to fight them?* She bent down to pick up some large stones.

The ukormoriers stood in a line, biding their time, looking at the älfar with derision.

'What have we ever done to them?' Firûsha whispered to Crotàgon.

'I have no idea. You've seen what they are capable of. I'm not going to try to take any of them on,' he answered, his voice brittle with tension. 'But they're not going to let me off lightly.' He twirled the spear in his hands and watched his opponents closely.

'Maybe they want to negotiate?'

'No, they don't,' came a reply out of nowhere. The language was a barbarian dialect that slaves in Dsôn used.

Firûsha looked round but could not see anyone. Crotàgon seemed equally at a loss. The body of one of the ukormoriers began to shimmer and change shape: they were now facing a squat creature with six arms. The skin was pale yellow and the eyes a striking green. 'They're waiting for my order to attack.' The mouth had no lips and hardly moved. It was as if the words were issuing directly from his throat. 'I am Hopiash, overlord of this part of Qchior.'

I suppose he means what we call Phondrasôn. Firûsha swallowed hard, but her mouth was dry with fear.

'We would like to thank you for saving us from the wyde-flies,' Crotàgon began, his manner courteous but not effusive. 'We have no quarrel with you. Let us pass.'

Hopiash crossed three pairs of arms. It was clearly the gesture of a ruler not acceding to the wishes of a subject. 'We may have no quarrel with each other but I have been waiting for you for a very long time. You hid in that stone house of yours. It was fate that our paths have crossed at last.' He pointed at Firûsha. 'And I can see you have brought me something interesting.' The sound of his voice was grating and when he smiled he showed a row of sharp-pointed teeth. He tossed his head to fling back his long greasy mane.

'What do you want?' Firûsha saw Crotàgon change the grip on his spear almost imperceptibly, readying himself to throw the weapon.

'I want the two of you.' Hopiash leaned forward. 'I need you! You're what's missing from my collection. The others will be so envious.'

'The *others*?' Firûsha breathed, horrified, making Hopiash laugh. 'There are *more* like you?'

'Oh yes. We karderiers are a close-knit little family,' Hopiash replied, transforming himself into a beautiful älf-woman. 'We do like your kind. Very rewarding.'

Crotàgon was astonished by what he saw. 'That's Tûrshai's form.'

'Of course, she mentioned that she knew you.' Hopiash placed his hands on his hips. 'I'm afraid that was quite some time ago. We weren't able to preserve her. Something went wrong with the embalming process.' As he said this, he frowned at one of his tattooed colleagues. 'I may have misjudged Tossàlor on that score; I have a shrewd suspicion that one of this lot brushed against her corpse.' He smiled. 'But now, here are the two of you.'

Tossàlor? First he uses his own kind for his sculptures and then he lowers himself to carry out embalming for this monster? Firûsha was growing more and more opposed to the idea of locating Tossàlor and taking him along.

'What exactly do you mean by *rewarding*?' She saw Crotàgon's shoulder muscles tense up.

Firûsha knew what he was doing. *He's trying to divert attention with all these questions from the attack he's about to make.*

Hopiash transformed himself back into one of the ukormorier. 'I extract the latent magic in a creature and I preserve it for my own use. It enables me to change shape whenever I choose,' he explained. 'Magicians and witches are not bad but the best source of magic is in creatures that have it inherent in them since birth. Like the älfar race. I don't come across them often enough and when I do they always fight like stink.' He laughed. 'My ukormorier warriors will change your mind about defending yourselves. If there is the slightest contact you start to fall apart. Not immediately; maybe not even tomorrow or the next day. You people are immortal so it takes a little longer for you to decay completely. And it's an extremely painful process. But it happens.' He grinned.

Firûsha shivered. *And* we're *known as the cruel race! The whole of Tark Draan should have a look at what's happening in Phon-drasôn. They'd be forced to recognise what true cruelty is.*

'Best find yourself a different source. We've got to get on our way. But I'm happy to send you a little of my own magic.' And Crotàgon launched his weapon.

The spear struck Hopiash full in the chest, the wide tip splitting the ribcage as easily as a spade going into soft earth. A dull thud was heard as the shapeshifter was thrown on his back by the impact, his body returning to his original, squat, yellow form. Blood shot out of his open mouth, gushing round the long teeth, running down his face and forming a pool on the ground.

The ukormoriers were not dismayed by their leader's demise. They promptly rushed forward, charging at the two älfar.

'Watch yourself,' said Crotàgon, drawing his broadsword from its scabbard. 'I've got to concentrate now. May the forces of infamy be with you, little älf-girl. If you run I won't take it amiss. I've no idea how this is going to go. You have to save yourself.' He ran to meet the foe.

Firûsha weighed the heavy dagger in her hand. *But I'm a singer,* she thought in panic. She suppressed her fear as much as she could. *My combat skills are so much weaker than Tirîgon's.* In the whole of her life she had only fought three mock duels, all against her brothers, of course. And she had lost each time. Her only hope was that Crotàgon would somehow manage to defeat all of the ukormoriers by himself.

The älf slit the bellies of three of them with a scythe-like sweep of his blade. The sword dripped with white blood but started to decompose immediately. Reddish-brown rust spread upwards to the grip.

When Crotàgon raised his arm the sword crumbled in his hand. The blade was corroded through and splintered to pieces when he swung it at another.

Ukormoriers destroy everything they come into contact with, whether it is dead or alive! Firûsha's heart beat wildly when she noticed two of the ukormoriers stepping round the muscular älf and heading for her. On their hideous old men's faces stood pure lust to kill. Their toothless mouths were open in a soundless battle cry.

'Get back! I'll kill you!' She hurled stones at them, temporarily felling the first one with a double hit to the forehead. Bright blood flowed into his eyes from the cuts on his wrinkled brow. The second attacker leaped at her.

Firûsha dodged and swung her knife. The sharp tip buried itself in the hairy belly of her assailant. He groaned but lunged at her once more.

'Don't touch me!' She kicked him back with a cry of desperation. The sole of her shoe heated up and started to disintegrate, with the rest of the leather following suit. She was forced to go barefoot.

The ukormorier pulled the dagger out of his flesh. A thick gout of white blood sprayed towards Firûsha. She jumped back, holding her eyes and mouth tightly shut. The sound of his falling body told her she had eliminated one enemy.

But am I infected now? Am I starting to disintegrate? She opened her eyes to see where her other attacker was. The knife in her hand crumbled, from the metal blade to the material used to cover its hilt. *I've no more stones left and now the dagger is useless!*

Crotàgon stood facing own two assailants, desperate for a solution to the problem of defeating them without making any kind of contact. Firûsha's first attacker was rising. *I am a singer,* she thought. *I ought to be able to use the talents I was born with.* She opened her mouth and sang the first song that came into her head. The notes were clear and pure as they formed in her throat and the cavern's walls magnified the sounds, making the tune swell and reverberate in the empty space. *I want to make you stop to listen to my song.*

But the ukormorier was completely unaffected.

Before she could move safely out of reach, he grabbed her arm. He pulled her towards him, yanking her long black hair with his other hand to get her to the ground.

She was aware of a burning sensation all over her body. *It has touched me! I shall dissolve away to pieces!*

Knowing herself to be a lost cause, she battered at him, screaming, until she broke his hold. Lines of fury burst across her face in an angry web. 'You are stealing my immortal life. I shall kill you for that!'

She stabbed the ukormorier in the eyes with two fingers, kicked him in the groin and knocked him to the ground. He was on his knees, gasping for air; she belted him on the ears with both fists and kneed him in the face.

He fell over backwards and tried to crawl away.

I won't let him escape! Firûsha jumped on him, put her sweet, white, soft hands around his throat and throttled him. 'You have taken my immortality!'

The ukormorier was beyond defending himself now but flailed at her weakly; when she released her hold, his death-rattle heralded his passing. She had suffocated him.

'Your death bears the name of Firûsha,' she spat, as she rose to her feet.

Over to one side Crotàgon was still trying his best to dodge his opponents' touch. Firûsha thought it was like a child's game of *It*.

I have actually won a fight now. Two! Tirîgon would have been amazed. She ran over to Hopiash's corpse and pulled out the spear. 'Wait, let me help you!' She nearly laughed at the comic situation. Here she was, a weak älf-girl, racing to the aid of a warrior built like a wardrobe.

'Stay where you are!' Crotàgon called out. 'They must not touch you!'

'Too late. It's already happened. I've nothing to lose.' Firûsha rubbed her arm. It felt numb. A tuft of hair fell out when she touched her head. 'Look out, beasts! Here comes your death. It bears the name . . .'

But her strength failed her. She fell senseless to the ground, her eyes rolling up into her head.

Ishím Voróo (Outer Lands), Dsôn Sòmran, Dsôn, in the northern foothills of the Grey Mountains, 5427th division of unendingness (6241st solar cycle), spring.

Aïsolon was sitting on a wooden chest in the attic room. All around him were smoking blackened beams and his nostrils were filled with the smell of a recently extinguished fire. And of freshly spilt blood. Ranôria's perfume could only faintly be detected, but he recognised it as being one he had once given her.

He stared at the dead body lying under the roof window. The eyes were still open, reflecting the grey sky. The fog masked the brilliance of the distant stars the dead woman would never see again.

The still-smouldering timbers crackled and a charred lump of wood clattered to the floor joists.

The sound died away. As Ranôria's soul had done.

Aïsolon wanted to leap to his feet and shout and scream and weep; a second later fury shook his body and he was consumed with the desire to plunge his sword into the unknown perpetrator, to split him limb from limb and fling the remains from the highest point of Dsôn's ramparts. At his third breath, he found he had no energy at all and he sank down next to her body, wanted to do nothing more than lie with her in his grief. His emotions were as violent as any thunderstorm.

Rain falling through the open skylight had cleansed Ranôria's countenance, removing the traces of blood on her skin. But the marks and wounds her body had received left no doubt that there had been a struggle; her killer had stalked her and deliberately taken her life.

It was clear how she had tried to escape.

The guards had found the shattered body of two älfar in the ruined transport lift that had crashed to the bottom of the quarry. The bodies belonged to the lift operative and a passenger. The injuries had not all come from the fall. They had been murdered with the same blade that killed Ranôria.

A witness had turned up, stating he had glimpsed four älfar inside the car he had tried to board.

She leaped free of the lift before it fell. She must have jumped down onto this roof and the murderer must have followed her. Aïsolon took Ranôria's cold hand in his own. 'I swear I shall find whoever did this. They will die at my hands. And my investigations into the deaths of Sémaina and her family will be re-opened. I will have justice for you.'

Aïsolon guessed what had happened. Ranôria must have made certain people in Dsôn nervous with her enquiries. They would have paid an assassin to silence Ranôria before she could uncover the truth. There was no other interpretation for the death of his beloved former companion.

If only I had believed her. She would still be alive. He reproached himself with her fate.

If it had not been for the rain putting out the fire the murderer had deliberately started, there would have been three unidentifiable blackened corpses and a mystery concerning a celebrated singer. Whoever was behind this killing will have had a store of rumours ready to explain away Ranôria's disappearance. There would be witnesses bribed to say they saw her throwing herself in despair from the ramparts, or fleeing for Tark Draan. The homeowner and his daughter would be lives claimed by a tragic house fire.

Clasping her icy fingers, Aïsolon covered his eyes, trying to stop the tears flowing down his face.

He was determined not to collapse into helpless mourning. It was vital that he begin the search; he would pit all his strength and fury against the perpetrators and those who had commissioned this cowardly murder.

However strong his resolve, his emotions were stronger still. He simply could not get up and leave her. The most powerful figure in the whole of Dsôn, the city governor, wept for the mother of his children. The hardest thing to bear was the innocent son who had followed his siblings into banishment of his own accord. *I have lost everything.* He sobbed. He found it hard to look at Ranôria through his guilt and grief. *Samusin, where is your sense of justice?*

A woman called his name quietly. He heard the rustle of dress fabric on the stairs.

Hands placed on his shoulders and the warmth of her body against his back as he sat calmed and comforted him. It was Cèlantra, his current partner. She had been looking for him.

'Look at her injuries,' he said, his voice hoarse.

'Yes,' she said, with great sympathy. 'It must have been terrible. She was made to suffer so much before she was killed.' Cèlantra did not try to evade the shocking truth of the situation.

The young, brown-haired woman was from the upper echelons of älfar society and lived on the eighth ring with her family. She specialised in magic healing. Cèlantra had an eye for assessing wounds. Aïsolon had chosen her as his companion because of her sharp intellect. He could only assume she had been attracted to him on the grounds of his heroic past deeds.

'Can you imagine what it will mean for the city when word gets round?'

Cèlantra hesitated. 'There could be different reactions. Some will be upset about the breakdown of community ties, some will accuse everyone who envied Ranôria, and a few will say her death was due to her disputing the story about her children,' she said, appraising the situation soberly. 'Not more than a handful will believe it was a random attack, a robbery. Perhaps even I'll be suspected of involvement. They might say I was jealous.'

Aïsolon nodded. 'I have to find the murderer and deliver him to justice. Can you make a plaster cast of her wounds for me?'

'If the blade went deep enough to damage a bone, it should work.' Cèlantra pulled Aïsolon's head gently back against her belly, swollen with the child she was bearing. 'Do you think the attacker still has the knife on him?'

'Älfar do not kill each other without very good reason. Not here in Dsôn Sòmran. Everyone knows we depend on our sense of community for our survival. Envy or malice aren't sufficient motives for murder,' he said. 'I've come to the conclusion that someone has hired a hit man, perhaps one of the assassins that Virssagòn trained. If there's one living here in the city I'll bring him in and interrogate him. If you could get me that cast from the weapon?'

'Of course, my dear. And have Gàlaidon carry out the enquiries about hired killers. He is a good deputy governor. He's clever. If there are assassins living here in Dsôn, he'll find them.' Cèlantra bent her head to kiss his hair. 'She was beautiful. Beautiful to look at and wonderful to listen to. A great loss,' she whispered. 'Nothing can justify such a deed. You must find the murderer.'

'I have already sworn to do so. I have made my vow to her.' Aïsolon loved the woman at his side but he was very aware of his deep feelings for Ranôria. *Yes, truly a great loss. My heart is like a heavy millstone in my breast. Every heartbeat hurts.*

He gently placed Ranôria's hand back down on the floor and Cèlantra wiped away his tears. He said, 'I expect she went to see Wènelon first of all. And after that she will have gone to see the story-teller. She was checking out the witnesses closest to where she lived. She will have been on her way to see Nomirôs, when ...' He broke off. 'It's so absurd, the idea that the perpetrator could cause the lift-car to crash and that we'd somehow not notice. That we'd not work out what had happened.' *To show such a callous attitude to one's own kind.*

'If I can be of any help with the investigation ... ?'

'Please check the body for any clues. Any traces he could have left on or near her. And be discreet. Take care that word doesn't get out. We don't want to alert the killers to our suspicions. Who knows how they might react if they think we're onto them?' *I can't have Cëlantra placing herself in danger for my sake, too.* Aïsolon stood up. 'I'll get the body brought to your institute.' He looked deep into her light green eyes. 'Remember, nobody else gets to hear what you discover. Your report comes to me alone.'

'Of course,' she agreed.

'I'll have one of my best warriors detailed to protect you and our child at all times.' With a tender kiss on her mouth, Aïsolon embraced her. The two of them went downstairs to leave the house.

At the bottom of the steps Aïsolon gave his instructions to the älfar who served him; taking two guards with him, he headed towards the nearest lift platform.

It will soon be getting light. That is, if it gets light at all with this heavy fog. It's been a hard winter. He paced through the streets with his escort.

He was afraid there would be more deaths if he did not solve the murder quickly enough and uncover the plot behind it.

Of course, they'll be watching me. Aïsolon could not understand what was happening in the city he was holding, waiting for the long-awaited call from the Inextinguishables for the älfar people to join them in Tark Draan. He was a governor, nothing more. And he bore this simple title although his function was in reality closer to that of a ruler. *Why is all this happening now?*

There had never been more than a handful of killings in the years since the founding of this interim Dsôn state on the slopes of the volcanic basin in the Grey Mountains. Any previous murder would have been an act of passion or the work of a mentally disturbed älf. And when the offenders confessed, as they always had, they were exiled to Phondrasôn. When their sentence was over they could return, but the majority never made it back. This made him even more worried about the fate of his triplets.

I ought to have given ear to their versions of the incident. But the evidence had been so clear, so cut and dried.

They took the lift cabin down to the fourth ring.

His soldiers did not talk, and, as ordered, kept watch assiduously, making sure no one came too close to Dsôn's governor. It was doubly important considering the recent events that would soon be the talk of the town.

I hope I can find the killer in the next few moments of unendingness and break this plot – this vicious conspiracy – wide open. His emotions were in turmoil and he could not dispel the image of Ranôria lying there with those horrifying injuries. Cèlantra had managed to calm him, but only temporarily. Now his fury was reignited. The tugging on the skin told him the threatening black anger lines were spreading across his face.

They alighted at the fourth ring and made their way to Wènelon's house, where one of the guards hammered on the door.

When the door opened slightly and a sleepy face appeared in the slender gap, Dsôn's governor delivered a hefty kick to the wood, flinging the surprised älf into the corridor.

You are going to tell me the truth! Aïsolon bent down, grabbed Wènelon by the collar of his mantle and hauled him to his feet, slamming him against the wall. 'I have just come from Ranôria,' he said darkly.

'Have you gone completely mad? My nose! You've broken my nose!' Wènelon protested, whimpering with pain.

'She was lying dead in an attic, with multiple stab wounds to her body. And I know,' he said, banging Wènelon's head hard against the wall again, 'I know she'd been to see you to ask about the night Firûsha and Sisaroth apparently committed that murder. It was on your say-so, and the evidence your friends gave, that I banished my own children to Phondrasôn.' He punched Wènelon in the face. 'You swore to me they were guilty! And I'm here now to put the question again: exactly what happened that night in Tênnegor's house?'

'Maybe Ranôria was attacked by a robber?' Wènelon sought to distract Aïsolon.

'NO!' Aïsolon shouted into his face. The anger lines chased across his visage like black lightning. The tightening of his facial muscles spurred him on. 'Don't you dare lie to me or I'll drag you straight to the top of the wall and hang you up by your own guts!'

'But Governor, I...' Wènelon's eyes were darting wildly hither and thither. 'I can't do it!'

'Oh, but I can!' Aïsolon drew his dagger and pressed it against Wènelon's stomach. 'No one will ever learn what happened to you,' he growled, his voice full of hate and rage. 'You will simply never be seen or heard from again. Now start talking, or ...' Aïsolon pressed the knife-point harder, piercing the skin.

Wènelon cried out in anguish. 'Acòrhia! It was Acòrhia! She made us!'

The story-teller! Aïsolon had to fight to control his temper and stop himself from plunging the knife deep into Wènelon's gut. 'You're all together in this plot, aren't you? You and the other six?'

The älf nodded. 'Please don't kill me!'

I want all of them – the whole damn pack of liars. Aïsolon withdrew the blade, stepped back and motioned one of the guards to approach. 'Go and tell Gàlaidon he is to collect all the witnesses to the crime my children were punished for. He should do this discreetly and have them taken to the citadel. No one else should notice what is happening.' The soldier saluted and ran out. 'Right, then, back to you, Wènelon. You are now going to tell me why you all conspired to destroy my children's reputations and to ruin their lives. What was the reason?'

Chapter IX

The three are as one.
  Whisper soft
  the tale of death;
  here it comes, unlooked for
  and easy as breath.
The three are as one.
  Night shapes, dark thoughts
  cannot be subdued.
  Beguiling siblings striking fair
  kill their victims in the open
  or stifle them unseen.
Three are one.
  Three are everything.
  Three not to be parted,
  three not to be mistaken,
  three everywhere, eternal.
  Sisaroth, Tirígon, Firúsha.

'First Song of Praise' from the epic poem *Young Gods*
composed by Carmondai, master of word and image

Phondrasôn, some time after the 5427th division of unendingness.

Murdered her own master? Sisaroth thought he must have misheard.

But when Marandëi fell silent following her confession, seemingly wishing she had left the fateful words unsaid, he was forced to assume that she had indeed spoken the truth.

They walked wordlessly on through the labyrinths of Phondrasôn, at crossroads speaking briefly about which tunnel they should take.

For some time now they had been in a section with coloured sandstone walls. There was a smell of damp. Tiny plants in crevices shrank away and cringed when any light touched them.

Right you are. Get back in the niches and leave us in peace. In the dim light from the inlays in Marandëi's staff Sisaroth could make out various tracks in the sand. Some he thought were made by óarcos, but others had clawed feet that were four times as big. He wondered how beasts of those dimensions could ever get through these constricted shafts.

He decided against calling out for his brother and sister because of these tracks. He would need better armour and weapons if he were to face new assailants. *And I need to fortify myself with food and sleep.* 'Are we nearly there yet?' he asked Marandëi quietly.

'We'll need to set camp twice more at the rate we're going,' she said, shining the staff-light around her. 'I'm starting to recognise this place. It's a lobby cave that leads to the palace. This is where they had tents to entertain visitors.'

'Why not put visitors up in the palace itself?'

'They didn't want any foreigners in the palace overnight, according to what I've read.' The cîanai put her staff down and turned to look at him. 'It does make sense. We're in Phondrasôn, Sisaroth. Never forget that, however nice the creatures you meet may seem to be.'

'Maybe I should apply that advice to yourself?' he joked.

'When I have finished my term serving you, you should indeed do so. Until then you have optimum protection: my oath of loyalty.' Marandëi seemed deadly serious. 'We must go that way,' she said, pointing, and took the lead, confident of her whereabouts.

Sisaroth still did not know what to make of her. *I shall take her advice to heart. It's a good thing she is pledged to serve me for the next five divisions.* 'Can you tell me a bit more about your master?'

'Do you really want me to?' She did not seem keen. She walked on.

'You don't have to. You are in my service but you are not my slave. I'm just curious, that's all.' He could see she was unwilling so he tried a different tack. 'I've got a better idea. Fill me in about what happened when I arrived. I'd come across a groundling and we were both engulfed in some sort of energy field.' He described how the surrounding air had fizzed and sparked and how his own anger lines had burst out in spite of himself, and how he had been unable to move while the energy surge had tortured him.

Marandëi came to an abrupt halt, turned round and held the light so that she could see him better. Sisaroth felt as if a medical healer looking for signs of disease was examining him.

'It's one of the most dangerous of the Phondrasôn phenomena,' she said slowly. She put out a hand to run her fingers over his face. 'Tell me, does it hurt when I do this?'

'No.' Sisaroth's suspicions increased. 'What would that mean?'

'That you had been altered in some way by the magic. The strangest things can happen. There's all this latent energy on the loose and sometimes it just picks a place and settles there – like in the tower walls, for example. Other times it sweeps through the passages tearing at everything in its path.' He was surprised to see she was examining the walls of the tunnel in the light from her staff.

'What are you looking for?'

'Seeing as you emerged unscathed yourself, I want to check out your immediate aura to see if there has been any change,' she explained. 'I'm not inspecting the rock walls. It's your shadow I'm observing. I want to see how it behaves.'

She is a strange one and no mistake. Sisaroth laughed. 'What's wrong with my shadow?'

Marandëi lowered her staff with a tight-lipped expression. 'We'll find out when we get to the palace. It's too dark here.' She resumed walking. 'I was told I couldn't win.'

'You were conversing with my shadow?'

'No. My master,' she replied matter of factly. 'I learnt a lot from him and I knew I was more powerful than he was. He realised it, too, and did his best to humiliate me at every turn in front of the others. He was afraid of losing his reputation.'

'I thought things were more progressive in Dsôn Faïmon,' Sisaroth said. He wished he could forget what the groundling had told him about the destruction of Tark Draan's älfar empire and the death of the Inextinguishables. *Nonsense, of course. He invented the story to confuse me.* Sisaroth tried to discard the notion.

Marandëi made a sound somewhere between laughter and sobbing. 'I keep forgetting that our city is long gone.' She led the way down a long corridor with a vaulted roof. Faint paintings were visible on the stonework. 'Life without the radial arms, without the Black Heart, without the Bone Tower...' She shook her head, the blonde curls bouncing. 'It's inconceivable. But I fear it is true what you say.'

'I wish I could see where our parents grew up. They miss their homeland so much.' Sisaroth thought back to things his father had said about the sheer beauty of the old Dsôn. He was not paying attention to the pictures on the ceiling as they walked. They were clearly of älfar origin. As was the roof construction itself. Time had robbed the colours of their vibrancy and damp had added to their deterioration.

'Well, I used to live in Wèlèron, the radial arm where the magic arts were taught. Most of those in our institute were scholars rather than practising magicians. They researched the magic powers inherent in every älf. They were working on how those powers could be perfected: throwing greater shadows, creating more intense fear in others, things like that. Very few could do anything more than basic magic,' she told him.

'But you were different.'

'Yes. I think there were only three of us who were authentic cîanai and cîanoi. Three out of a thousand. They kept quiet about us in Dsôn Faïmon so the populace wouldn't be worried. You know that magicians are ... were ... always thought to be something extremely rare and peculiar.' Marandëi sighed. 'I admit I was proud of my gifts. There was nothing I did not think I could do. And the head cîanoi was furious when most of what I attempted worked the first time. He was envious. He made me an object of scorn and ridicule.' Her voice faded. It seemed to be difficult for her to talk about what she had been through, or what she had done. 'The rivalry between us turned into a proper feud. I was arrogant enough to provoke my master to such an extent that he swore I would never beat him, no matter what I did. He said whatever magic spell I employed on him he could fend off and return against me threefold.'

'And then?'

'He insisted on a contest – a duel. In front of all the other scholars. He wanted a big audience to witness his victory over me. It happened just as I knew it would. My friends encouraged me and he rose to the challenge.' Marandëi's speech grew hesitant. 'His key spell was to conjure up a black fog so heavy with fear that no living creature, whether barbarian, bird or älf, could survive for long under its oppressive weight.'

Sisaroth was all ears. Marandëi was a relic of the old days. There were no cîanai at all in the new Dsôn. *She is talking about a way of life that has totally disappeared now.*

'He called up the black fog and was preparing to hurl it in my direction,' she went on, speaking so quietly that he could hardly hear her voice. 'I had to defend myself. I caught the cloud in mid-flight and made it grow bigger and stronger, adding more and more magic to it. You can guess the effect.'

Did she kill all of them? The spectators as well? Sisaroth was stunned. *And she looks so ordinary. So unassuming. Harmless.*

'It was completely out of hand, the whole contest. By the time it was over, I was nearly broken from exhaustion. And my master was dead. Twenty-eight of the spectators were killed. It was a terrible blow to the entire guild.' Marandëi's shoulders shook. 'It was awful, just appalling. I never meant for it to happen! My master pushed me to the limit! It was his fault,' she insisted. 'Afterward, I was in despair and terrified my former friends would turn on me, so I ran away and came here to Phondrasôn.' Marandëi drove the end of the staff into the sandy ground and twisted it around.

'You should be forgiven,' Sisaroth said soothingly. 'It was an accident.' *I'll take her back to Dsôn. We could really use someone like her. One of the legendary cîanai would do wonders to lift the spirits of our dejected race.*

They left the corridor with its painted ceiling and found themselves at the edge of a cool cavern where vegetation was rampant. There was an overwhelming scent of lilies that made it difficult to breathe. A pale gold light shimmered out of the mist high above them.

Sisaroth was perturbed to hear nearby fighting. 'Is this where you intended for us to come?' he asked.

'We must have taken a wrong turn.' Marandëi frowned as she contemplated the trampled path in front of them. 'Let's turn around before we get involved in a battle.'

Suddenly they heard the sound of a woman singing – a clear and beautiful voice.

Is it possible? Sisaroth would have recognised those dulcet tones amongst thousands of singers. *Firúsha!* He raced along the path.

Ishím Voróo (Outer Lands), Dsôn Sòmran, Dsôn, in the northern foothills of the Grey Mountains, 5427th division of unendingness (6241st solar cycle), spring.

Aïsolon was in his office in the citadel. 'You are not being reasonable.'

Acòrhia hung slumped in a chair opposite him. One of the guards held her shoulder, preventing her from sliding to the mosaic-inlaid floor.

She attempted a grin but her face was too swollen and covered in bruises and cuts. Her thin clothing was stained red from broken blood blisters. It was still the simple housecoat she had been arrested in. 'Your actions will get you sent to Phondrasôn yourself,' she babbled and spat a piece of broken tooth that landed on his desk. 'You are not an Inextinguishable ruler – only the governor here. You are not above the law.'

'Nobody knows you and your fellow conspirators are here. The walls of the cells are solid and my guards will hold their peace. They know what you did and they are happy to keep silent. They will smile to themselves when they drag you to the top of the wall and throw you over.' Aïsolon picked up the bit of tooth and studied it. 'This fragment of tooth will be the only bit of you remaining in Dsôn. The beasts will fight each other for your cadaver, Story-Weaver.' He put the ivory shard down. *I'll have it set in a ring. As a souvenir.* 'But if you confess, I'll arrange a trial. It's up to you ...'

'I don't know what you are talking about.' She looked to one side in feigned boredom.

Aïsolon motioned to the guard to let go of her.

Acòrhia crashed to the floor, hitting her head on the stone tiles. She groaned and tried to get up. Her red hair hung unkempt over the sorry remains of her face. 'Does that mean I'm free to go?'

'Yes, but you'll be taken back to your cell first, where they will cut you and burn your flesh and let the rats gnaw at you. Your orifices will be filled with boiling water, then I'll have you locked in a cage of wild jerm cats,' he answered harshly. 'Afterwards, whatever's left of you will be free to return home. A home that will be demolished and chucked over the ramparts.' He waved his arm in dismissal. 'That is so you know where you belong. I'm sure you will enjoy your freedom on the other side of the protective walls.'

Acòrhia struggled back into her seat, visibly shocked.

'Bring Wènelon in here,' he ordered.

The door opened. Aïsolon's deputy, Gàlaidon, came into the governor's office with the conspirator, as yet unharmed. He was placed next to Acòrhia and forced to look at what they had done to her.

Wènelon, dressed in tunic and mantle, paled visibly. 'What do you want from me, Governor?' he whispered, shocked to behold the story-teller's state. She was staring at him intently, as if trying to hypnotise him.

'As you can see, we have been talking. I confronted Acòrhia with a few truths. As you can see, the truth is often painful. We're about to discuss the events of the night of the murder in Tênnegor's house.' Aïsolon pointed to the broken tooth. 'I wonder if I'll have to use the same methods for you when we have our little conversation?' he said, his voice deceptively friendly and low.

Wènelon pulled back in his seat but Gàlaidon shoved him forwards again. 'I have ...' He glanced at the story-teller, drew a deep breath and gathered his courage. 'We have told you every-thing, Governor. What you are doing is not right. I insist ...' Wènelon stopped, seeing Aïsolon's stormy visage.

'You insist? You INSIST?' he shouted, slamming his fists down on the table. 'I'm the one doing the insisting here,

Wènelon. I'm going to insist that you be my guest. I want you to consider a particular plant.' He indicated his deputy. 'A speciality of Gàlaidon's. It's a quick-growing blood-shadow grass with sharp blades the size of your little finger. From sun-up to sundown they will grow nearly a hand's span and can penetrate wood. Do you think your skin could withstand that force? We can find out. I'll have you tied down on a bed of shadow grass and we can watch it grow right through you.'

'Because the growth is gradual,' added Gàlaidon, 'you should be conscious for most of it. You must let us know how it feels when the buds open inside you. I tried it once with a rat, and then with an óarco. Both of them lasted eleven moments of unendingness before they died. Their bodies looked just like a piece of my lawn by the time they died.'

Wènelon looked over at the tale-weaver, who was uttering imprecations. 'I . . . I . . .' he stammered, tearing his eyes away from her fixed stare. 'I must insist on your protection, Governor. For myself and for my family.'

'Shut your cowardly mouth!' shouted Acòrhia. Gàlaidon punched her in the face, sending her back to the floor again. Her lips were badly split but she struggled up onto her knees. 'Don't you say a word. No one can protect you, no one! Not even him!'

I knew he would break under pressure. Aïsolon smiled in triumph. 'I guarantee nothing will happen to you.'

'You can't promise that,' the story-teller objected. 'The assassin is in Dsôn and he already has his instructions . . .'

What is she afraid of? 'Then call him off,' Aïsolon snarled at her. 'I swear you won't leave this place alive if you don't.'

Now it was Acòrhia's turn to laugh, but it was a laugh of quiet despair. 'As if that were in *my* power.'

'Of course she can do it,' a frantic Wènelon interrupted. 'She's lying. She talked to him at the payment handover. I saw her. I didn't see his face, but she must know who he is.'

'At the payment handover?' Aïsolon and Gàlaidon exchanged glances. 'So you were paid to give false witness against my children?' He quickly wrote an order for the other five witnesses to be brought up and sent a guard out with the note. 'How much did you get?'

'One day you won't wake up because he will have killed you,' whispered Acòrhia, spitting out blood and phlegm. 'You idiot! You weakling! You deserve death. I hope he spares me.'

And now the bricks are starting to fall out of their wall of silence. Aïsolon was relieved. He was starting to get information that would bring him closer to the ring leader. *She'll be the only one to hold out, I reckon.* The door opened quietly and the other five witnesses were ushered in without Acòrhia or Wènelon noticing. *Excellent.* 'So, Wènelon, tell us exactly what happened.'

'We arrived at Sémaina's and the evening began pleasantly enough. Then Sisaroth turned up and insulted our hostess. She laughed at first and took it as a joke . . .'

Aïsolon raised his hand. 'It's the truth I want. Not the version you trumped up between yourselves.'

'But that is what happened,' Wènelon insisted. 'They wrangled. It was harmless, really. Sisaroth was chucked out and his shirt got torn. And he dropped a talisman his sister had once given him. That was used in evidence against them both because you as their father would recognise the objects.'

Malicious pack of scoundrels. Cleverly done. He picked up the fragment of tooth again. 'Go on. Go on!' He was on tenterhooks. It was important, all of this, but he wanted to get to the heart of the matter, and find out who was behind it. *Who could have plotted this so thoroughly?*

'Everything had settled down but then a masked figure jumped down into the room. He must have been waiting in the shadows all that time. He stabbed Sémaina several times. It all happened so quickly. We were taken by surprise . . . and we had all been drinking. He threw a bag over to Acòrhia – tionium coins, as it turned out. Then he ran out of the room to kill the rest of the family.' He pointed to the story-teller. 'She told us we would all get fifty coins if we stuck to her version of events.'

'It was the coins and lifelong silence *or* death. That was what I said,' Acòrhia corrected him. 'You made your choice. Not just for you but for the others involved. We all had to keep quiet or we would all be killed.' She spat out a ball of bloody saliva.

Aïsolon watched the horrified faces of the other five captives and knew Wènelon and Acòrhia had been telling the truth. *The others will want to pretend they had no choice in the matter.* 'The assassin gave you the money,' he said to Acòrhia. 'You already had the story prepared. You must have met with him beforehand. Were you in on the arrangement?'

'He was in disguise,' stammered Acòrhia. The blows to the face she had received prevented her from speaking clearly. 'So I can't describe him. He didn't tell me his name. And he spoke in a whisper so I wouldn't be able to recognise his voice.' She leaned against the chair.

Aïsolon believed her now. Her eyes had lost the fire of resistance. She had given up on hearing Wènelon's confession. 'And then?'

'He told me he had measures in hand in case my version of events was doubted.'

Aïsolon felt a stab to the heart. 'What were those measures?'

'He said there was a trained killer in Dsôn who would do his bidding.'

A cold shiver went down his spine. *So it's not over yet.* 'And who is the hit man? Did he give any clue?'

She shrugged her shoulders. 'He didn't say. What kind of a plot would that have been if he told me the details?'

'And Sémaina's murder? Did he indicate there was a conspiracy aimed at my children?'

'Only that the murder was to take place and that there was a greater cause behind it. "The killing will provoke great things," he said. He sounded odd. Confused.'

'Yet you still took him up on it and did what he demanded?'

Acòrhia stared at Aïsolon in amazement. 'Of course. He was offering me money or death. What should I have done? Come knocking at your door claiming a masked älf had threatened me? I know exactly what you would have done: you would have laughed me to scorn and told me I was starting to believe my own tall tales.'

'Hardly, in those circumstances.' *What is the way forward here? How do I discover the killer and find out who is really the mastermind of the whole conspiracy?* Aïsolon quickly planned a strategy. The First Sytràp would start a search for Virssagòn's trainees. Those that remained would be thoroughly interrogated. This should lead him to the killer, and the instigators would soon follow.

In the meantime I will keep an ear to the ground for rumours regarding any enemies Sémaina and her family may have had. I can't afford to discount other possibilities: potential feuds between other influential families in Dsôn. Aïsolon did not need to carry out investigations to tell him that Sisaroth had not been one of the dead woman's greatest admirers. Certainly not after her malicious slandering of his mother. Every Dsôn citizen knew about this and it could easily be used to divert attention from the truth. *But what was the truth?* He raised his head and confronted the seven false witnesses. *I fell for it and I brought nothing but suffering to my own family and to my former partner.* 'I take note of Wènelon's confession and assume that he is telling the truth.'

They all, with the exception of the story-weaver, nodded. She stared down at the bloodstains on her clothes and the dark drops forming on the floor in front of her.

'But the false evidence you gave and the items you planted at the scene of the crime caused the unjustified banishment of my children Sisaroth and Firûsha to Phondrasôn. You are responsible for this.' Aïsolon saw flashes of indignation cross several faces but none of them dared contradict or beg for mercy. 'And because you also closed your eyes to the matter of a murder, your silence allowed other killings to take place, therefore doubling the guilt you bear. Do I hear any suggestions for restitution?'

Acòrhia gave a weak attempt at laughter. 'Tell us what you have come up with,' she said slowly and indistinctly. 'And then tell us how you are going to present this to the rest of the city. It will attract a certain amount of attention if seven celebrities suddenly disappear, notably following these other deaths.'

She is cunning. 'I have come up with a scheme that gives you the opportunity to remain part of society's elite with your reputations intact,' he announced generously. 'I shall give you a potion to drink that will do away with you within a division of unendingness.'

The accused groaned and whispered amongst themselves. One of them rushed forward in indignation but Gàlaidon stopped him by slamming a fist into his belly so that he doubled up, gasping.

'But ... Governor!' stuttered Wènelon. 'I thought ...'

'Wait. I'm not done,' said Aïsolon, fetching seven glass leather-encased phials out of his desk drawer. He held one carefully between his thumb and forefinger. 'This contains a remedy which will slow down the decay to your vital organs. But it will not overturn the process. The only full and effective antidote is in my possession and I shall take it with me to the top of the defence wall to wait for you.'

Wènelon looked round at his friends and then back at the governor. 'I don't understand. Are we supposed to have a race up the mountainside to see who gets there first?'

'Think about it,' Acòrhia grunted. 'He wants to send us to Phondrasôn to fetch his children home.'

Yes, she is shrewd. She will be the one that succeeds. Aïsolon raised his arm in acknowledgement. 'She is correct. One of you will be granted life in return for bringing back my children. If you manage to do that, the antidote will be yours and there will be no further word spoken about your misdeeds. You will be free. You will remain one of Dsôn's respected elite and part of the entourage that proceeds to Tark Draan to greet the Inextinguishables. So do your best.'

Their horror at the prospect stood engraved on their features for all to see.

'Phondrasôn and a lethal medicine in our bloodstream,' said Wènelon in chilly tones. 'What could be worse?'

'It should stop any monsters from wanting to eat you. They'll pick up the smell of the poison in your veins,' replied Aïsolon with a malicious grin. The guards and Gàlaidon laughed. The governor pointed at the door. 'There you have my decision. You will be sent over the wall tonight. You will be given equipment and,' he said, tapping the phials, 'your important medication. Take a thimbleful as soon as your skin starts to crawl and itch. Don't delay or it will shrivel and fall off and your flesh will decay. The gods of infamy may . . .'

'And my family?' objected Wènelon. 'What do I tell them about being sent to Phondrasôn?'

'Nothing at all.' Aïsolon leaned back in his chair and put his feet on the desk. 'Before you leave, you will each write a message stating that the governor has asked you to help him formulate a plan for the future of Dsôn Sòmran. You are on a secret mission to find out how to reach the Inextinguishables. It will take as long as it needs to. You will also write additional missives that we will send in the future: *I'm fine. We are making progress. I'm looking forward to seeing you all again soon. There will be a new start for Dsôn.* Believe me, the city will be at your feet in gratitude.' His voice became sharp with sarcasm. 'Now get out, you despicable cowards. Bring back my children. Or die in Phondrasôn.'

The guards shoved the condemned group out the door. The phials were collected. Acòrhia dragged herself to the entrance, too weak to walk.

Aïsolon was alone with his first deputy, and despite the pain at his loss and his fury at the conspirators, he felt a certain satisfaction at what he had achieved. He could not think of anything more he could do for his children.

He had thought carefully whether to broadcast the truth

about Sémaina's death and drum up a volunteer troop to go in search of his children. *But there aren't enough of us. We need every single able-bodied älf for Dsôn's defence.* He was also reluctant to make the seven witnesses' immediate families suffer. *Not to mention the killer would strike again and cause more distress still.* 'If I could go to Phondrasôn myself to bring them back, I would,' he muttered.

Gàlaidon jammed the thumb of his right hand into his leather belt. 'I understand how you feel. But I think the seven have good motivation for their task.'

'They are no warriors.'

'They haven't even been sent over the wall yet, and already you are doubting your decision?' The blond älf gave him a questioning look. 'It was a good idea and it's the best you could do in the circumstances. We need all our guards and warriors here on the defences. We can't spare a single one.'

'I know,' said Aïsolon. *Was my decision really right?*

'Do you want me to go along with them?' Gàlaidon offered. 'I can see you don't really trust them.'

'Send you to Phondrasôn?' he took his booted feet off the desk and sat up in his chair. 'That would be just as much of a waste as sending my children was,' he muttered. 'You are needed here. It's me that should go.'

'But that's impossible. You are much more important than I am.' Gàlaidon completed Aïsolon's thoughts. 'I am honoured that you think highly of me, but the älfar need their heroes – the ones that founded the city for them and protected them after the destruction of their original homeland. You make the people feel safe. I am nothing but your assistant and I respect you just as they do. Without you, Dsôn Sòmran would be in peril.' Gàlaidon came around the desk and clapped his superior on the shoulder. 'Acòrhia has left you her souvenir piece of tooth, I see.'

'What would she do with it? She can't plant it back in.'

'No, but it would make a nice piece of jewellery set into a ring.'

Aïsolon was sunk in thought. 'Have you heard anything at all that would give us a hint about Sémaina's killing? Heard any rumours? Any long-standing feud with other powerful members of our community?'

'No. Sémaina was a fool, but generally well liked – apart from by Sisaroth, of course. What was the phrase Acòrhia said the ringleader used? *The killing will provoke great things.* Gàlaidon looked lost for an answer. 'At first I thought it implied a rebellion, but that – excuse the thought – would have meant doing away with you. Why kill some overestimated singer and her family? What was the point? I don't have any idea what kind of greatness is supposed to arise in Dsôn as a result of this.'

He's doing his best to calm me down. Aïsolon laughed out loud. 'That's true. We'll just have to find the killer.' There was something that he wanted to ask Gàlaidon about, but for the life of him, he couldn't remember what it was.

'One? I thought there were two?'

'No, I don't think so. Whoever it was that paid Acòrhia was leading her down the garden path, trying to confuse her on purpose. Sémaina's murderer is the same as Ranôria's, and he also killed the two älfar in the attic and the ones in the lift cabin.' *Eight murders. It doesn't bear thinking about.*

'You're still convinced it's a trained assassin?' The First Sytràp rubbed his lower lip. 'If that's the case, it'll be hard to find him.

And we'll have to be careful not to alert him that we're on his trail. Who knows what he'd get up to if he suspected?'

He is one of my best guards. So cautious and wise. 'That's why I gave you the task, Gàlaidon. I can always rely on you. You have excellent instincts.' Aïsolon smiled at Gàlaidon in encouragement.

'My instincts tell me I'll be spending a lot of time in dusty archives, looking at the old registers of citizens.' Gàlaidon sighed and smiled. 'I'll let you know the instant I find anything unusual.'

'Good. Cèlantra will approach the task of finding our hit man from the other direction. From the scientific perspective.'

'Oh?' Gàlaidon raised his eyebrows.

'I asked her to examine Ranôria's body and the other corpses for clues. There might be indications of the weapon used left on the bones.'

Gàlaidon nodded, impressed. 'We're sure to find our killer with that.' He patted Aïsolon on the shoulders one more time. 'You see? That's exactly why we need you here in Dsôn. Your mind takes us along paths no one else would think of.' He passed the governor's chair. 'I'll get to work. Have you got any documents here that might help?'

'No, only my notes about the seven false witnesses.' *Watch out, assassin. You will soon feel my blade.* Aïsolon suddenly remembered what he had wanted to ask as he bundled up his notes to hand to his deputy. 'Tell me, how long have you had that ring? It's very unusual. A present from a grateful mistress?'

'Oh, did you notice it? I'd call it more of a parting gift.'

'A broken heart leaves you a nice keepsake?' Aïsolon was about to turn around when he heard Gàlaidon draw his dagger.

The blade touched his throat. 'Gàlaidon, is this some kind of a joke?'

'No. Virssagòn gave me the ring; I wear it on special occasions,' said the älf at his back in icy tones. 'You should know I was his best pupil.'

Chapter X

People doubted
   that älfar ruled
in empires in Tark Draan.
Suns went up and suns went down
and never a word from the Inextinguishables.
Hope dwindled.
Proud civic spirit faltered;
   a grievous rift appeared.
The binding rings were broken
and citizens of every band
thought only of themselves;
even the border guards on the wall
began to think like this.
When need was at its greatest
   all was turmoil in Dsôn Sòmran.
   Who might bring order?
   Who might close the gap
   that opened in their midst?

Excerpt from the epic poem *Young Gods*
composed by Carmondai, master of word and image

Phondrasôn, some time after the 5427ᵗʰ division of unendingness.

In the firelight Tirîgon lay stroking the älf-woman's magnificent back. The fish she had caught had been tossed aside. They had more urgent business than eating.

Touching her naked skin sent shivers down his spine and there was a burning fire in the centre of his being. Black butterflies danced inside him; his head was as light as a feather. He was in such high spirits that for once he spared not a single thought for his missing siblings.

The female älf turned to face him, her hair brilliant with silver dust. Her chestnut-brown eyes gazed into his and they were without guile. 'Let us return, Tirîgon,' she said, laying a hand on his chest. 'Let us go back to Dsôn together to enjoy life.'

He kissed her forearm. 'We shall.' *Everyone will envy me when I bring her home!*

She relished the tenderness of his caress. She combed back her long black hair with her hand. 'I have been missing people's company, conversation and sense of community,' she said sadly. 'You remind me of what I've been deprived of all this time. The way you are and how you make love to me.' She gave him a long warm kiss on the lips. 'I never want to give you up, Tirîgon,' she whispered devotedly. 'I want to belong to you alone.'

'I feel the same,' he murmured hoarsely. *And I don't even know her name.* He was full of admiration for her naked body in all its perfection. Her mysterious effect on him had not diminished. *I would do anything for her.*

Noting his expression, she smiled and covered herself with

the wet fabric of her dress. 'In that case, let us head for the surface and travel with all speed to Dsôn Sòmran.'

Before answering, he remembered Firûsha and Sisaroth. He was ashamed to admit he had forgotten his mission in the heat of love. Love could make you blind, indeed. *A dangerous emotion. I must try to keep a clear head.*

A warning voice inside him counselled extreme caution: perhaps he was being manipulated by this älf-woman. Maybe she had anticipated this strong response in him. There might be a secret agenda she was pursuing; perhaps getting his support to lift her imposed sentence. He knew nothing about her for certain and there was no way of verifying what she had told him.

She had risen to her feet and was brushing down her dress. 'Why do you look so worried all of a sudden? I hope I haven't displeased you in some way?' She fastened the last of the buttons and tightened the lacing around her waist. 'What's troubling you?'

'Your name.'

'You don't know what it is.'

'Exactly.'

She laughed and held out her hand. 'Stand up and kiss me and I'll tell you my name.'

'Simple as that?'

'Simple as that.'

Tirîgon took hold of her hand and jumped to his feet; he kissed her wildly, revelling in the softness of her warm mouth. His hands drifted to her hips.

She drew back. 'Slow down! That's more kisses than I have names, Tirîgon.' Slipping out of his embrace, she went over to the cave exit and picked up the fish. 'Let's eat first, my young warrior.'

He grinned. 'Fine with me. Something seems to have made me extremely hungry.' He dressed quickly, clamped his armour under his arm and followed her. 'So was my kiss so bad that it did not earn your name?'

She turned to face him but kept walking. 'Esmonäe. That's what they call me.'

The warning voice stoked his suspicions. 'Is that the truth?' he said, forcing a light-hearted tone.

'Are you really called Tirîgon?' she countered, not seeming flustered by his question.

'I am truly Tirîgon, as sure as I am a warrior,' he assured her.

'I do not doubt either assertion.' She stopped, placed her arm round his shoulder and kissed him passionately, then laughed and ran off. 'Last one has to gut the fish!' she called out.

That's not going to be me. He ran after her, following the torch glare.

He was astonished at himself. He had allied with other females in his past – some fairly seriously, others casually – but he had *never* felt the way he had in Esmonäe's arms. He only had to catch sight of her, and even Phondrasôn became bearable. *She has bewitched my soul.* He was sure of it.

By the time he arrived at the fire, Esmonäe had already slit open the fish and gutted it. She was threading it onto a spike to grill it and laying the special yellow stones on the embers to make the fire burn higher. 'Oh, there you are. I knew you would take ages so I went ahead and got started. I'm famished.' She winked at him. 'You'll do it next time. Whatever we catch.'

'Right you are. As long as it's not an óarco.' Tirîgon sat opposite her, after putting his armour down in the sand for her to lean against. 'I hope we find my siblings soon.'

'If we have Tossàlor to help us and the map you told me about, we're sure to.' Esmonäe browned the fish on both sides. 'I've been thinking: even if you don't like him, I expect he knows these tunnels better than anyone. He can tell us how to read the map and suggest places to start looking for your brother and sister. As long ...' She cut her words short and cleared her throat. 'As long, I mean, as long as they are still alive.'

Tirîgon's concern for them and his guilt about the fact he was sitting by a warm fire while his siblings might be in acute danger made him uncomfortable. 'I know they're not dead,' he said, staring into the flames. 'I would have felt it in my bones. Until I know where they are and whether they are safe, there is no way I can go back to Dsôn. How could I face our parents?'

Esmonäe nodded. 'Of course, Tirîgon. I never doubted that. But I have spent untold divisions of unendingness here in this maze of caves and I know how dangerous it is. You're a warrior and can defend yourself. But what about your siblings?'

'They are still alive,' he insisted. The smell of the roasting fish and the prospect of the meal no longer appealed to him. *Firûsha is bright enough. She'll know what to do. And Sisaroth can fight.* But he was frightened for their safety.

The two of them fell silent as they watched their dinner cooking.

'Have you thought about how long you would give yourself to search for them?' she asked gently.

'What do you mean?'

'I really want to go back home, Tirîgon. With you,' she said quietly, taking a deep breath. 'Don't get me wrong: I shall be at your side. But I cannot stay here for all eternity, amongst beasts and shadows and the rest of the horrors Phondrasôn may use against us. This is a mere fight for daily survival; it is not a life. There's a limit to what I can cope with.' Esmonäe was on the verge of tears and stopped turning the stick she was using as a spit for their meal.

She is demanding you abandon your siblings for her sake. That is too much to ask, murmured his inner voice of doubt. *You have only slept together once. It's not as if she were your official partner. How can she ask it of you?*

Tirîgon's face closed up. 'Careful. You're letting the fish burn.'

Esmonäe lifted the spit and examined the fish's scorch marks. 'It's done.' She cut herself off a portion and placed it on a stone to cool, then handed the spit to Tirîgon. 'Please don't hate me for what I've said,' she said, her voice fearful.

Hate her? 'No, Esmonäe!' He looked shocked at the thought. 'No. I understand why you said it.' He picked bits of fish off the bones and put them in his mouth. It tasted of nothing at all. 'I promise we shan't look for them forever,' he heard himself say.

When Esmonäe smiled at him, it made his heart leap for joy. The warning voice was stilled and then smothered.

Tirîgon and Esmonäe picked their way through the corridors, tunnels and caves.

She led them to one of the places Tossàlor sometimes stayed. She explained to Tirîgon on the way that Tossàlor kept several homes; he got different inspiration from each location.

While they walked they made plans for their future together back in Dsôn. It seemed as though the two of them shared similar dreams, Tirîgon was delighted to learn. When they rested they always slept close in each other's arms.

At long last they came to a cave that opened over a hilly landscape with a jagged roof vaulting high above.

'Here we are.' Esmonäe clapped her hands. 'Let's have a bit of appreciation for getting us here safely.'

Tirîgon kissed her. 'I'll appreciate you whenever you want.'

Glowing stalactites produced the effect of petrified lightning. There were cracks in the walls and huge holes a dragon could have got through.

Pale green conifers grew in the dim glow of the calcium formations, with orange grass in the forest clearings. Deer-like creatures grazed and birds flew in the treetops. Simple shacks were visible, with smoke coming from the chimneys; farms had been cultivated and there were wheat fields and vineyards. Several miles away, at the other end of the valley, there was a tall fortified building hewn into the rock. It had a large orange banner adorned with an indecipherable symbol flying from the top.

It all looks peaceful enough, Tirîgon was surprised to discover. *No monsters and no barbarians attacking us. It looks as if it were possible to lead a normal life here.* He turned to Esmonäe. 'Is this the Island of the Blessed Ones?'

She laughed. 'No. It is the Cave of the Warfaring Ones.' She indicated the fortress. 'The inhabitants are from a barbarian tribe originally and they keep a monster in there. They let it free as soon as they feel they are threatened by danger. It is huge and it can fly, but it always returns to its eyrie when things calm down again. It seems quite happy there.'

'And they let Tossàlor stay here?'

'More than that: they *like* having him. It means we'll be safe from the monster, too. The creature recognises älfar and has been trained not to attack us. Well, that's what Tossàlor told me anyway.' Esmonäe looked around. 'If I remember correctly, that's his house down there on the right. Look, between those tall trees.'

Tirîgon could see the large hut on stilts and the bones piled up outside according to size. *Probably remnants from his works of art.* The white roof reflected the light and made the home visible from afar.

They hurried down the winding path past the vineyards where bright red grapes hung full and luscious on the vines. Tirîgon resisted the urge to pick some. He didn't know whether they were safe to eat. 'Is there anything else I need to know about Tossàlor?'

'You sound a bit scared,' Esmonäe joked. 'Don't worry, he's not going to launch himself at you with his de-boning scalpel.'

He bit his tongue and did not ask why Tossàlor was no threat to Esmonäe. *Perhaps because he has a shred of decency while he's stranded here in Phondrasôn and wants to respect his own kind?* 'I'm not scared. I'm looking for some reason he might agree to help us. Some kind of enticement, I suppose.'

'I know you'll come up with something. You are clever.' Esmonäe led the way through the wood to where the black house stood on its sturdy wooden supports.

Closer up, the house appeared to be a place most rational creatures would avoid like the plague. The roof tiles were actually thin slices of bone, protected from the weather with varnish. The gutters and downpipes were hollowed bones, and the fixtures were fashioned from jawbones.

Like in some savage nursery tale. Wherever Tirîgon looked he could see that Tossàlor had decorated his home with the mortal remains of others: paintings on stretched skins, little sculptures and carvings on the roof. *You could not buy it with money.*

As they walked round the house they passed a heap of discarded, broken bones that must be the artist's rubbish tip.

They climbed the bone steps up to the veranda. Esmonäe knocked at the door, which was made from black wood and decorated with white ornaments. 'Tossàlor, it's me – Esmonäe.'

Tirîgon made a mental note to ask Esmonäe about her relationship with him. 'Let me go first,' he said, moving in front of her.

After a series of clicks the door opened.

An älf appeared wearing a purple robe with vertical stripes on the sleeves. His hands and forearms were dripping with blood and his face and clothes were also spattered. His hair was covered with an embroidered black hood, but one pale green curl had escaped. The artist clearly liked to dye his hair. The dark eyes inspected Esmonäe first.

'What a pleasure to see you,' he said with a smile. Then he turned to Tirîgon and the smile vanished. 'What do you want?'

'Greetings.' He felt like an animal being assessed for slaughter. 'Esmonäe was good enough to bring me to you.'

Tossàlor grinned. 'How kind. She would not have had much use for you in the long run, and I am running out of material.' The artist looked at Esmonäe. 'It's unusual to have my subjects come knocking at the door in their eagerness. He obviously appreciates the importance of art.'

Tirîgon stepped smartly backwards and placed his hand on the hilt of his sword. 'That is *not* why I am here.'

Esmonäe laughed. 'No, Tossàlor, he's not a gift. This is Tirîgon and he belongs to me. He is looking for the way out of Phondrasôn; he has not been exiled here.'

'Because he is innocent, I'm sure.' Tossàlor smirked, his face relaxing. 'How original. That's a very good reason for wanting to go home. Good luck.' He started to close the door.

Tirîgon placed his foot in the doorway. 'I've got a map but there's a vital bit missing, I'm afraid,' he said, fishing out the elven chart. 'If you could tell me how to get out of here, I'll give you anything you want as soon as we are back in Dsôn. My family is powerful.'

'Anything I want?' Tossàlor scrutinised him carefully. 'Nice. I'll have your fourth rib on the right, a thighbone, your right hand and your eyelids. That should do it. I'll be quite gentle. Do we have a deal?' He grinned demonically.

He's serious! Tirîgon swallowed hard. 'I'm afraid not.' He did not know how to respond.

'Is the price too high? Well, what would you give me of your own free will?' Tossàlor laughed. 'Or in your last will. Oh, that's funny. I must remember that one.'

Tirîgon took a deep breath and glanced at Esmonäe, who shrugged her shoulders. 'I've got money ...'

'What would I do with money?' the artist snarled. 'I want something unique so I can make a work of art out of it. *Then* I'll show you the way out of here.'

'The beast,' said Tirîgon promptly, before he had time to think. But he saw a gleam of interest in Tossàlor's eyes and proceeded. 'The beast that protects the valley. Would that be unique enough?'

The artist älf pursed his lips and considered the offer, nodding his head slowly. 'But they can't suspect me. You have to get into the fortress, kill it and take the cadaver to the cave of Frempâion. Esmonäe can show you where that is. But take your time and do it properly, I don't want a bloody mess to work with. Then tell me when it's done.' Tossàlor looked pointedly at Tirîgon's boot. 'And now, if you'd let me close my door?'

'Could you give us something to drink? We've come a long way and could do with refreshment,' Esmonäe said quickly. 'Then we'll be underway, High Master.'

'If you want.' He moved aside. 'This way.'

Is this a good idea? Tirîgon crossed the threshold gingerly. *But when will I ever get another chance to see his works?* Curiosity won out over caution. 'Keep your eyes open,' he mouthed to Esmonäe. 'I don't trust him.'

'I'm glad you trust me,' she whispered, stroking the back of his neck. 'Don't worry. I'll look after you, darling.'

He did not have time to resent that she was making fun of him again. The sights that greeted him made all thought impossible.

The first room was clad in grey bone panelling. Chandeliers fashioned from skeletons hung from the ceiling. Holes had been drilled through the limbs to allow the candlelight to shine out. The effect was remarkable. *I could learn so much from him.*

They walked through the room and crossed two more similarly decorated.

When Tirîgon inspected the translucent slices of bones, Tossàlor came up close behind him and placed a hand on his shoulder. 'I see you are a connoisseur, young friend.'

'And he's quite good at carving,' Esmonäe chipped in from the background.

'Nothing special. It's just a hobby. I like to do it when I've finished sentry duty on the wall,' he stammered. The artist's thin and bloody fingers were hurting him. *I've got to change the subject. I don't want to talk about myself.* 'Are the bones painted? It doesn't look as if they are.'

'Well spotted, young älf.' Tossàlor seemed to be considering a course of action. Then he took Tirîgon by the sleeve and led his visitor off. 'Come and see my studio. I can show you how I work.'

He was amazed when they reached his workshop. Cupboards were labelled with the type of bone stored in each. A cabinet held paints and tools. On the floor there was a wide trail of blood leading to a trapdoor. The artist must have disposed of a cadaver shortly before his visitors had turned up.

Against the far wall there were four small cells containing apathetic-looking elves. They had lost the will to live, it seemed. One of them had violet-coloured hair and another's was tinted a shocking yellow. Apart from the scars on their forearms, they did not look maltreated or even under-nourished. *He looks after them properly.* Tirîgon turned to face the artist and looked at the strand of green hair.

'You're trying to puzzle it all out, aren't you?' Tossàlor was enjoying this.

'I assume you keep them here as a resource. And you've clearly been experimenting with dyes. You've tried them out on your own hair, too. Do you create them with blood platelets?'

'Certain races here in Phondrasôn have bones with a distinctive coloration due to their nutrition. It can vary based on the algae, plants, moss or insects they eat. I've been collecting these ingredients and grinding them to a powder that I then put in their food,' he explained proudly, pointing over to the elves in the cages. 'These contain my next works of art! Elf bones infused with different colours! I'm so excited!' Tossàlor pushed his green curls back under the rim of his hood. 'That was my first attempt. I was a little too impatient.' He looked at his visitors, expecting admiration.

He is completely mad. Tirîgon was well aware the artist would employ exactly the same practices on an älf, given half a chance. *It would be best if I killed him before he tries to work on either of us.*

'Extraordinary,' Esmonäe praised the artist's endeavours and applauded. 'You know, you could make a fortune back in Dsôn with these ideas.'

'I shall indeed.' Tossàlor grinned. 'But not yet. I've got more testing to do first. Who knows how long our young älf here will take getting me my beast? And I'm still trying to perfect a formula for the soft bones.' Before Tirîgon could stop her, Esmonäe went on to ask what he meant.

Tossàlor went over to a store cupboard and took out a ribcage; the bones had lost their original white colour and had taken on a milky tinge. Tirîgon was astonished to see how the ribs could be twisted like the pliable young branches of a tree. 'I use vinegar,' Tossàlor said, 'and two or three other additives to remove most of the calcium. Then I can make any shape I want. Afterwards I apply a coat or two of clear varnish to hold the shape.' Tossàlor handed the bones to Esmonäe for her to examine. She tested the substance with her fingers.

'You are indeed a master of your craft,' she said, admiringly.

And you are totally out of your mind, thought Tirîgon, catching Tossàlor's assessing glance. *What a nuisance that we actually need him.*

Tossàlor clapped Tirîgon on the back. 'Right, that's enough. Get yourself off now and come back when you've got my new toy.'

Tirîgon would be relieved to get out of Tossàlor's place in one piece. 'I'll start straight away.'

'I'll help him,' Esmonäe added. 'We'll be back before you know it.'

'Sure.' Tossàlor did not sound convinced. 'You can both find your own way out. I've got to check the colour of the yellow-head's bones.' He took out a long, thin knife with a flat blade. 'I may have to adapt the composition of the powder I've been adding to his food.'

Tirîgon realised what the scars on the elves' forearms were from. *He cuts through their flesh to look at the bones.*

The two of them left the artist's house and headed back through the wood to where the vineyards started.

'Ye gods of infamy!' Tirîgon exclaimed. 'How insane is he?'

'He's an artist. Some people say art is just a different form of insanity,' Esmonäe answered.

'That would mean that nearly all älfar are mad,' he conjectured. *And it's not like that.* 'In my opinion, Tossàlor is as crazy as it gets.' Despite his interest in the topic, Tirîgon left the subject of art and started to work on his campaign. 'We'll climb that slope at the entrance and take a good look round,' he said to Esmonäe. 'Have you ever been inside the fortress?'

'No, there's never been any reason to. And I don't want to get too close to a monster like that one.' She laughed. 'I'll have to now, thanks to your suggestion. It was very brave of you, of course . . .'

'I'm not going to let some beast hold me up.'

'I meant it was brave of you to trust what he said,' Esmonäe amended. 'Tossàlor might be tricking us.'

She's saying just what I fear myself. 'If he tries that, he will die.' Back in Dsôn, Tirîgon would have demanded some kind of surety from a new ally. A pawn. *They do things differently here.*

'Our advantage is knowing the beast is trained to not attack älfar,' he said as they made their way along the winding path up the incline. He looked over to the fortress. 'So it will be . . .'

She halted suddenly and grabbed him by the arm. 'Look!'

Tirîgon had been concentrating on the distance and had not seen the large ship she was pointing to. The vessel was floating over the top of Tossàlor's bone-clad wooden house.

Figures were ascending the ropes and ladders and a cage was being pulled up on deck. A captive in bright purple clothes was protesting loudly before the cage disappeared through a trapdoor into the belly of the ship.

What's happening? Tirîgon could see that the runes on the mast and on the vessel's stern started to glow when the last of the crew had swarmed back over the railings. *They have taken Tossàlor prisoner!*

The ship gained height, swung round and headed for one of the clefts in the rock wall. 'Elves!' cried Esmonäe in horror. 'He always thought he would be safe among the barbarians because of their beast. But they found him at last! And we have only escaped by the skin of our teeth!'

Smoke rose from the artist's house; soon orange flames leaped from the rooftop.

There goes our only real chance to learn how to navigate Phondrasôn. Disappointed and unsure what to do next, Tirîgon watched the ship pass close overhead. All his hopes of finding his siblings quickly were now dashed.

I cannot let this happen.

The elves did not seem to have noticed their presence. Or perhaps the two älfar were not thought worthy of attention. The air vessel inclined slightly to one side and then undertook a course correction and came nearer. Three ropes were still hanging down and as the ship moved, they swung to and fro in the direction of the slope where Tirîgon and Esmonäe were watching.

It's now or never! He gave Esmonäe a quick kiss. 'Follow me!' he said and ran to the edge of the ridge they were standing on.

With a mighty leap he launched himself into the air and stretched his arms out towards one of the dangling ropes. The abyss yawned far below him.

The heartbeats in which he hung in the air seemed endless.

The dangling rope swung closer with a jolt of the ship.

Tirîgon's fingers grabbed it and he reinforced his hold by making a loop for his foot. *Wherever you are going with our guide, you've got me on board now and I'm not letting you have him.* If Tirîgon succeeded, Tossàlor would be indebted to him – much more so than if he brought him the carcass of some weird beast.

He turned to Esmonäe – but he could not see her anywhere. Neither on the ridge nor below on the plain.

Phondrasôn, some time after the 5427th division of unendingness.

Acòrhia came to her senses because of the intensity of the awful smell. She opened her eyes.

Her cage lay in a puddle of excrement that must have issued from a monster of the most terrible kind; the little lantern she had been allowed to take with her shone on half-digested food items, bones, and rags of familiar clothing.

Isn't that Nomirôs' robe? Acòrhia released the bolt on her cage door and clambered out, lugging the rucksack packed with her meagre supplies. She waded through the mire. *How did he get here before me? And how did he manage to get eaten so quickly?*

She jogged over to the shelter of a rock and took a look around from its relative safety.

The little light she had was enough to show her the extent of the cave. She was at a crossing of five ways. A hole two paces up explained how her cage had arrived. The ground was sandy and drenched with urine and faeces. She gagged at the stink and nearly vomited.

Only now did the story-teller notice the second cage – the one that Nomirôs had arrived in, she realised. *Yes, and there is his food-pack. The beast must have turned its snout up at that.*

She ventured cautiously out of the shelter and held her lamp and a dagger aloft as she ran over to the abandoned cage through the disgusting puddle.

She rifled through the large sack until she found the small phial with the remedy. There was a chinking sound. *It's broken! Curses!* The disappointment made her check on the where-abouts of her own flask of medicine. *Where can it be?* Before she was heaved over the wall in that cage she had hung the phial round her neck. She felt her throat.

The leather necklet was missing.

No! No! I need it! Acòrhia patted her clothing, checking the folds in her robe and the pockets of her undergarments, desperate to find the vital elixir. *Did it . . . ?* She looked at the puddle of excrement. *Surely it can't have fallen in there?*

There was nothing for it. It was a matter of life and death.

Groaning and gagging, she made herself sift through the muck with her bare hands. She almost passed out, the smell was so bad. Her eyes were streaming and she heaved again and again, adding the contents of her stomach to the mire. She examined every tiny object she came across.

It was all to no avail. Soon she was seated by the edge of the pool, filthy from head to foot, with nothing to show for her trouble.

It means I'll be dead soon and what's more, I'll stink worse than any decaying óarco carcass.

She got up and trotted back to the rock where she had put her things. *More than anything, I want a bath in clean water.* She presumed the beast that had eaten Nomirôs tasted the poison and spat most of him out again. *The monster will probably not touch me, the way I must smell.*

She took the bag of provisions and slung it over her shoulder before marching off with her lamp aloft. *Which way shall I go? The toxin will kill me soon. Even if I were to find the triplets, my fate is sealed.* She might as well sit down and wait for death.

She dragged herself along the tunnel, following the sound of running water. Perhaps she could at least get something to drink and have the opportunity to clean herself up a bit.

In the lantern's flickering light, she saw an alcove with a fountain spurting brownish water that ran down the reddish rock to sink into a small basin full of pebbles on the ground.

Acòrhia tossed her rucksack from her back, sniffed at the water and decided that it did not smell too bad, despite the unwholesome colour. *And what if it isn't safe? I'm going to die, anyway, and it has to be better than what I'm currently covered in.*

She washed her arms then splashed her face and tasted the water carefully. It was slightly salty and had a grass-like essence, but it was better than nothing.

She pulled off her stinking clothes and washed properly from top to bottom; she then scrubbed her dress to get the excrement out. Leaving the garment in the water to rinse, she wrapped herself in the mantle that had been stowed in her rucksack. She settled on a rock to wait, warming herself as much as she could by the lantern.

She heard a loud oath and then a splash.

That was Phodrôis' voice, I'm sure. Acòrhia drew her dagger, but concealed it under the folds of her mantle. *To be on the safe side.* 'It's me,' she called. 'Follow my voice and you'll find me. There's water here to drink.'

The light of a second lantern approached and she found herself facing the älf with the dyed purple hair.

Unlike herself, he had only got shit on his shoes and the hem of his black robe. His white shirt and his mantle had stayed clean. 'That is so disgusting,' he said. He put his rucksack down and went over to the water source to wash his things. The story-teller watched him. His physique showed that he was not used to exercise or hard work. He was one of the audio-art specialists of the city; he liked to use special metallic paints for his pictures. When the paint was dry it would emit different tones when hit softly with a beater. Themes, colours and sounds acted in harmony to produce a comprehensive artwork. However celebrated he was, though, his reputation had not saved him from banishment.

'Good to see you, too,' Acòrhia said sarcastically, nodding in his direction. 'Did you meet Nomirôs?'

'No. Why do you ask?'

'He was in that cave. Parts of him were floating in that ghastly puddle you've just splashed through. He was half-eaten and then sicked up.'

'No! O ye gods of infamy! Dead?' Phodrôis sat down opposite her and had the air of an älf ten divisions of unendingness older than he was in reality. 'So soon? Phondrasôn doesn't give one much time to get used to things.' He looked at her. 'I am glad to see you, you know. Not being alone is good. Your cage ended up in the mess, then?'

'Difficult to avoid on landing, I'm afraid,' she said. 'Do I still smell awful?' She already had a plot hatching in her head; it was instinct from her former life.

Phodrôis motioned a yes. 'On the bright side, we shan't be attending any formal functions for a while, so it doesn't matter. Bit annoying, though.' As he surveyed the surroundings his expression was one of disbelief and despair. 'Passages, caves and then tunnels. And more passages. How are we going to find the governor's three children, I wonder? We've got about as much chance as if we'd chucked a gold coin down off the wall with our eyes shut and expected it to turn up again all by itself.'

Acòrhia held her mantle tightly closed, but stole her hand out to run it through her red hair. 'I've got no answer for you. All the gods of infamy, Samusin and Inàste will have to be on our side or we don't have a hope of fulfilling our task.'

Phodrôis thought hard. 'We've lost Nomirôs. That leaves six of us. Perhaps the others won't be far off. We stand a better chance of survival if we can find them and stay together.'

Oh yes, that's exactly what I want. 'I can't wait to see Wènelon again,' she said sarcastically. Now she had rested a little she was aware of the pain in her face from the ill-treatment she had received during the interrogation.

'It was hardly his fault. Anyone would have given in under

pressure. Apart from you, of course.' He gave her a friendly look. 'Under the circumstances, I think the punishment the governor handed down was reasonable.'

'What are you talking about?' Acòrhia was furious. 'Aïsolon was acting outside the law – breaking all the rules of governance!'

'We broke the law ourselves by taking bribes,' Phodrôis reminded her. It was as if he was relieved to have received punishment. 'We hid and lied about a murder. No one in Dsôn will be on our side.'

'If we had not done what the masked älf demanded, we would all have been killed. Like Sémaina. Like the älfar in that attic. Like the ones on the platform.'

The story-teller despised the älf for his cowardice. 'Without Wènelon and his botched confession, we could still be sitting in Dsôn at our ease, counting out the tionium coins we earned.'

Phodrôis' mouth narrowed. 'It wasn't supposed to be like this,' he said, speaking quietly and placing his hands on his thighs. 'I for one want to do everything possible to get back home.'

'Me too.' She smiled. *And how!* 'It will work out.'

'Yes, it will,' he said, not suspecting anything. 'I hope our disappearance is causing Aïsolon a whole load of trouble right now.' He paused for a moment and then shook his head. 'No, perhaps not. It would not help our cause any. Perhaps it's for the best that we simply find the triplets and get back home without anyone knowing the true reason for our absence.'

'Exactly.' Acòrhia pointed to her robe that was lying in the water. 'Would you be good enough to fetch my dress and wring it out for me? I don't want to expose myself unnecessarily.'

Phodrôis laughed. 'I could always wait out there in the

tunnel.' He got up and went over to the fountain to lift the dress out of the water. He leaned forward and twisted the roll of fabric in his hands, then slapped it against the rock a few times to expel the moisture. 'I'm pleased to tell you it doesn't smell too bad now, though there's still a definite aura about it. They should use the beast's urine as a weapon of war.'

'I'm sorry you've had to dirty your fingers for my sake.' While he was still preoccupied, she moved behind him and stabbed him between his neck and collarbone. Blood sprayed out of the gaping wound and when he tried to defend himself, she kneed him in the face, leaving him to sink unconscious to the ground. His life's blood mingled with the water in the fountain basin and almost disappeared on the red stones.

'Your death bears the name Acòrhia,' she panted. 'By dying you safeguard my own survival.'

She searched his body and found his leather-covered phial with the restorative. *All praise to the gods of infamy!* she rejoiced, holding it tight in her fist. This would preserve her from the effects of the poison for the present.

Without a second's regret she dragged the dead älf to the edge of the cave and ripped off his outer garment; she scrubbed out the fresh bloodstains and put it on. It did not smell of piss like her own soaking wet dress. The hem was sullied but she cut that off with her dagger.

Then she transferred her own food supplies into his rucksack and shouldered it, grabbing his dagger as well. Equipped with double provisions, two lamps and the remedy, she set off – but almost immediately stumbled over a small object.

She saw it was another of the little bottles, caught on her boot by its leather strap.

But that's mine! It must have been in her rucksack after all and fell out when she transferred her stuff. She picked it up and hung it around her neck. *The gods have granted me a double dose. They obviously set more store by me than by him.*

'Acòrhia!' It was Wènelon's friendly voice greeting her. 'I was beginning to think I was on my own here!' As he approached he exclaimed in horror, having seen the body in the light of his lantern. 'Is that . . . Phodrôis?'

'Yes.' The story-teller had not turned round yet and she placed her hand on the handle of the dagger. She bent over and groaned as if racked with pain. 'We were just resting and some óarcos attacked us. They killed him and wounded me.' She stretched out an arm as if wanting help, drawing her weapon cautiously. *The infamous ones really do love me. They're sending me a third phial.* 'Can you give me a hand? I don't think I can walk otherwise.'

'Of course! Let me have a look at your wound.' He dropped his rucksack. 'I'm so sorry. I really did not want to betray us all. But I couldn't help it. I'm not as strong as you are.' Wènelon set his lantern on the ground.

It was this sound that alerted Acòrhia. *Why is he putting the lamp down over there when he says he's going to come and look at the wound in my leg?*

She threw herself to one side.

His sword whizzed over her head, slicing off two long strands of red curls before clanging against the rock wall, splintering the stone. Wènelon kicked at her but she had her dagger ready.

The blade passed through the sole of his boot, went right through the foot and came out the other side covered in blood.

She let go of the handle. 'You were trying to kill me!' she fumed. *But it was my idea to kill all of you.*

Wènelon hopped backwards in agony. He could not put his foot down with the knife still in it. 'You were about to do the same to me! Admit it,' he hissed. He tripped over his own rucksack and fell.

The story-teller pulled out the second knife and set after him. 'And I'm not finished yet!' She kicked pebbles into his face, slid her rucksack off her shoulders and hurled it at him.

He rolled to one side, waved his sword about and managed to make Acòrhia keep her distance. 'Wait! Wait! We really should not be trying to kill each other,' he groaned. 'Let's stick together and get rid of the others. If we do that we'll have plenty of the antidote; that'll give us enough time to find Aïsolon's brood and get them home again.'

'What a good idea, Wènelon.' Acòrhia was four paces away. *He's tougher than I thought he would be. Because his own life is at stake.* 'That means we each get three phials. I'm afraid one of them got broken.'

'Right you are,' he replied and took a quick look at his injured foot, moaning with pain. The knife was still sticking out of it. 'Do we have a pact?'

'You won't be able to walk,' she commented, putting her dagger away. 'And you certainly won't be able to fight. Don't you think that using the remedy on yourself would be a terrible waste?'

Wènelon glared at her. 'I'll soon recover from this.' He put out his hand and lifted his leg so that he could pull the blade out of his foot.

'I don't think so. I just used that knife to cut the dirty hem off my clothes. It was covered in waste,' she told him callously. 'The wound will become infected and you'll die unless you cut your foot off.' Acòrhia gave him a cruel smile. 'I shan't have to do anything except sit and wait.'

Wènelon froze. 'I see. Well, you're not having that pleasure.' He reached under his robe, extracted the fragile container and hurled it against the rock wall. Acòrhia made a flying leap into the air to intercept it. She landed hard on the stones and her ribs cracked under her, but in her upheld hand was the little bottle, its precious contents unscathed.

Holding her ribs gingerly, Acòrhia got to her feet, carefully stowed the valuable flask and picked up her rucksack. She extinguished the lantern Wènelon had brought and hung it from her belt. Working in silence, she sorted through his provisions and took everything she could use.

Wènelon protested loudly but could not prevent what she was doing. No point in trying to attack her – she was quicker on her feet and more agile than he was.

That should be enough. She heaved the overfull rucksack onto her back; it was a weighty burden but would see her setting off on her Phondrasôn adventure extremely well equipped.

'You're really going to leave me here?' Wènelon whimpered. 'After you've taken all my food?'

'I shall leave you your pathetic little life, you traitor. Enjoy the rest of your time and don't forget about your infection,' shot Acòrhia cruelly as she strode off. 'I'll let you keep the knife as a souvenir.'

She stepped out into the corridor and gave no further thought to her one-time co-conspirator. It was vital she find the triplets.

And not just to guarantee her own safe return to Phondrasôn.

Chapter XI

I shall always love you,

I shall always love you,
the älf-woman swears.
I shall never deceive you, my beloved,
but I beg you:
Always tell me the truth.
I shall, replied her lover.
Because she was precious to him
and because he wanted to keep his promise,
he told her
he no longer loved her.
Then he stabbed her.

'Insights' from the epic poem *Young Gods*
composed by Carmondai, master of word and image

Phondrasôn, some time after the 5427th division of unendingness.

Sisaroth sprinted up the thicket path in the dark, sword and shield to hand, until he reached a clearing.

He saw his sister lying motionless, eyes closed, at the edge of the open area.

'Firûsha!' He squatted over her and shook her by the shoulder but there was no reaction. The skin was warm to the touch and he could feel a pulse at her neck. *She is alive! Praise be to the infamous ones!*

He stood up to ascertain what the giant älf and two barbarians were doing. The savages had revolting, grimacing old heads on their young bodies. *What sort of creatures can they be?*

Marandëi reached him, holding her staff in the air. 'You have found your siblings?' she asked.

'This is Firûsha, but I don't know the other älf.' He was amazed at the älf's height and broad-shouldered stature. *I wonder if he was born like that or if it's what Phondrasôn has done to him?* He could not think of another instance in which one of his race achieved such physical proportions. The spear that his sister was still holding, which she must have pulled out of the nearby corpse, looked as if it belonged to the tall älf. *He ought to be able to down his foes with his bare fists, the way he is built.*

The two barbarians had noticed Sisaroth and Marandëi approaching and could not make up their minds whom to deal with first; one turned on the two of them and the other went for the giant.

'Watch out!' warned the älf. 'Make sure they don't get close. These ukormoriers are lethal. They destroy everything with their mere touch.' He dodged his opponent's attack.

Ah! So that's the answer! Sisaroth saw the enemy running up, toothless mouth agape. He was uncertain about using his sword. 'Does that hold for metal as well?'

'Everything means everything,' came the sarcastic comment. *What's the point of having a magic cîanai in my service if not for moments like these?* Sisaroth glanced over at Marandëi. 'I wonder if you could spare the time to get rid of these guys for me?'

'Does that include your titan over there?' She did not move a muscle.

'No, of course not. I mean, for now.' He decided in favour of the huge älf, though her question had been justified. In Phondrasôn the only älfar you were likely to come across would have been vicious outcasts expelled from decent society. *We haven't met any älfar who just lost their way in the maze on a legitimate adventure. Only the hardiest criminals can survive here.*

Marandëi lifted her staff and pointed its silver tip at the barbarians. She recited a few syllables.

The dull buzzing sound reminded Sisaroth of what had happened in the tower; a black ray the diameter of a finger shot across at the attacker with a hiss.

As soon as the dark energy struck the creature's breast, the blackness spread, eating into the skin and burning its way through flesh and bone, so that the blood turned to steam and the internal organs shrivelled and fried. The ugly barbarian was transformed into a pile of ash within seconds.

'That was impressive,' Sisaroth said in admiration.

'I can do better than that. Watch.' Marandëi lowered her staff and put her hand in the air, with the palm directed towards the second barbarian.

This time a bright white ray of light shot out from the gemstone on one of her rings. She wore the ring with the jewel turned inward; Sisaroth understood why now. The light enveloped the human. The cîanai transformed him into a single flame that then consumed itself within the blink of an eye. Neither ash nor bones remained.

Sisaroth congratulated himself on his choice of companion. *I wonder what else I can do here in Phondrasôn with her at my side?* He gestured to the perplexed älf, who was staring at the vacant spots where the barbarians had been. 'Come over here!' Then he knelt at his sister's side. 'Wake up!' he urged, stroking her face.

'She's been in contact with one of the ukormoriers,' the älf explained, leaning to collect his broad-bladed spear, which was big enough to use as a shovel.

But Sisaroth prevented him from doing so by placing his hand firmly on its shaft. 'Tell me your name.'

'Crotàgon.'

'You'll get your weapon back as soon as I know what happened here and when my sister can tell me how she is.' He glanced at Marandëi and received the silent indication that he should be wary of this stranger. She was bound to be able to hold him back with her magic powers. He knew that he stood absolutely no chance against this älf on his own. *He could pick me up with one hand and throw me through the air.* 'What happens if one of the monsters touches you?'

Crotàgon made an apologetic face. 'You decay. Everything decays. Metal. Plants. Everything except for stones.'

Sisaroth's heart was gripped with fear for his sister and his mouth went dry. *I can't have found her only to lose her immediately, forced to watch her die!* Crotàgon passed him a flask of water, and he dampened Firûsha's face gently.

Her eyelids flickered, but that was all.

'This is a new phenomenon for me,' said Marandëi. 'But I do know this creature over here: a karderier. They hunt anything magic.'

'He was their leader,' said Crotàgon. 'He called himself

Hopiash and made no secret of the fact he wanted our innate magic powers.'

Sisaroth noticed that whole clumps of hair were falling away from Firûsha's scalp. *Is that one of the first signs of decay?* He ran his hands gently over her and found that her skin and bones still seemed to be intact. *Oh ye gods of infamy, what can I do? What do you expect of me?* 'Marandëi, have you any ideas?'

'Not off the top of my head,' she said, 'but back in my palace I have a number of books I brought with me when I fled from Dsôn. I might be able to find some remedy. It must be some kind of magic process, so there should be something we can do if I find the right spell.'

'How long would it take us to get there?'

She looked unsure of herself. 'Trying to work out any timings in Phondrasôn is an illusion. I thought we would have got to my palace a long time ago. But as you see we have ended up in this cave instead.' She looked questioningly at Crotàgon. 'Do you know your way about this area?'

The älf nodded. 'I know of a palace. Maybe it was yours. But I haven't been there for some time.'

'You're sure to have been there more recently than myself.'

'It's decided, then: Crotàgon shall guide us.' Sisaroth got to his feet and lifted his sister onto his shoulder.

'Best let me,' offered the giant älf. 'I'm stronger than you.' Sisaroth agreed and Crotàgon took the älf-girl in his arms.

Their little group made their way along the well-trodden path, with Sisaroth in front and Marandëi bringing up the rear. Sisaroth carried the giant's spear.

As they walked, Crotàgon filled them in on how he had found Firûsha in her cage and took her to his house. They also learned the reason for his banishment: he had been accused of inciting a rebellion against the Inextinguishables.

'Firûsha persuaded me to return to my own people,' he told them, finishing his tale. He wasn't even out of breath, in spite of the extra weight he was carrying. 'I have done my sentence and I want to go back to Dsôn.'

Sisaroth, listening attentively, thought it was amusing that his sister had won them an ally with the magic of her singing. *I got a cîanai companion and Firûsha got a warrior who must be twice as good as any in Dsôn. If we get home safely, this outing might have been well worth the trouble. I ought to be grateful to the enemies that got us exiled.* His high spirits soon departed, however, when he remembered his sister's parlous state of health and the fact that he had no idea where his brother was.

'Firûsha and I agreed to take a friend of mine with us,' Crotàgon continued. 'I don't want to abandon him here.'

'Is he a warrior, too?' Sisaroth asked, taking the path the broad-shouldered älf indicated.

'He's an artist. He is wonderful at carving bone and he will be a great asset back in Dsôn. He knows his way around these mazes better than anyone else here, and he will know a route back to the surface.'

Marandëi laughed incredulously. 'Sure he will. And that's why he's still down here in Phondrasôn. Too fat to crawl through a tunnel?'

Crotàgon grinned. 'He's an artist, like I said. His mind works a little ... differently.'

The group left the round tunnels and came to a rectangular corridor where walls and ceiling were decorated with marble tiles. The three of them stepped over fallen marble chunks, which must have come from a more recent excavation.

'This is starting to look familiar,' Marandëi muttered, looking around. The runes on her staff were starting to glow more strongly, shedding light on the scene. She went ahead a few paces, leaving the others behind.

Perfect! This is getting better all the time. The warrior claims to be bringing us a map on two legs. But Sisaroth wasn't entirely convinced, having noticed a slight hesitation in Crotàgon's voice when he spoke about this unknown friend. 'What name does he go by, your friend?'

'Is that important?'

'If he was banished to Phondrasôn, yes, I'm afraid it will be important.'

'Tossàlor.'

Tossàlor! Of course Sisaroth knew the sculptor's story. Aïsolon had talked about it. 'Did you tell my sister who it was you wanted to take home with you? Did she realise what sort of crimes he committed? He never repented at all, I understand.'

'Yes. And I know you are the children of the Governor of Dsôn,' said Crotàgon, looking at him intently. 'If Tossàlor can get us out of this labyrinth and I can bring you back to your father, he'll be sure to agree to a pardon.' He placed a hand on Firûsha's back. 'You're not stupid, Sisaroth. Marandëi may be a cîanai, but she can't be at your side at all times for protection. Am I supposed to be intimidated by you, the little warrior cadet?' His voice took on a sharp edge. 'This is what I propose: we collect Tossàlor, find your Tirîgon and head back to Dsôn. Your father lets him stay. Leave it to me to make sure there'll be no more älfar sacrificed for his art works.' The powerful muscles on his chest and upper arms rippled as he transferred the weight of Firûsha to his other shoulder, his hand on the nape of her neck in a gesture that was at once tender and threatening. 'I can assume you are in agreement?'

'Over here!' called Marandëi, pointing to an opening. 'I know where I am now.' She waved her arms in delight. 'Come on! My palace is round the next bend. This new tunnel has saved us an awful lot of walking.'

'So? What do you think?' asked Crotàgon, slowing to a stop. 'I wouldn't take too long to decide: the sooner we are in the palace, the sooner we can get help for your sister. I saw the ukormoriers turn a dagger to dust and a sword to a rusty splinter of metal. Imagine what that can do to . . .'

'I agree, I agree,' Sisaroth acceded with frustration, consumed with impotent anger. The other älf had him pinned! Without him, he would struggle to get his sister to the palace in time, and there would be no Tossàlor and no way home. He was sure the mad artist would refuse to show them the way without Crotàgon. *It's sheer coercion!* 'I shall ask my father to do as you suggest.' He strode off.

Crotàgon did not move a muscle. 'Asking won't be enough.'

'I shall see to it,' he shouted angrily. 'I swear by Firûsha's life.' *And I vow that you will receive a special reception when we get back to Dsôn.*

'That's all I needed to hear.' Crotàgon walked on without further ado, overtaking Sisaroth and catching up with Marandëi.

They stopped in front of a closed gate of rusty metal which showed signs of having been hammered with a battering ram, mallets and other tools.

The dents and scrapings in the decorations and ornamental symbols were not new. It appeared that nobody had bothered with it in recent times; the besieging force had left broken handles and useless bits of equipment scattered around.

This is getting us nowhere. Sisaroth's bad temper did not improve. 'Marandëi, I thought you told us this was the answer?'

The cîanai said nothing, but she lifted her staff in the air. With the silver tip she traced the symbols and the reliefs on the gate, muttering incantations under her breath. When the point of the staff reached the eye of a carved beast, it pushed through.

The door suddenly glowed and gave a crash, dust rising off in a cloud and flakes of green patina peeling off to shower the four älfar standing below. The doors creaked noisily open.

A corridor appeared with a glass bridge at the end, spanning a sea of liquid glass that seemed to have the properties of ordinary water.

A wave of searing heat swept towards them, making Sisaroth break out in a sweat. 'And this is where you lived?'

'Nothing wrong with warmth when you're getting on a bit, my boy,' replied Marandëi with a happy sigh. 'I do believe we are in luck.'

They went through the gates.

Ahead of them was a lake containing a mountainous isle, washed by the waves of glass. As the molten glass cooled on the shoreline, bizarre shapes were formed, reminding the älfar of frozen waterfalls in winter. On the headland they saw a small palace. Sisaroth noticed two bridges that connected with the island.

'So this is your home,' commented Crotàgon. 'No, I've never been in here before. Will that bridge take my weight, do you think?'

'It will bear your weight because I shall instruct it to do so. Otherwise it would collapse under you and send you into the molten waves. Nothing can survive down there.' Marandëi wore a seraphic smile. 'I rather thought my security measures would function.' She turned round and motioned for the gate to slam shut behind them.

'Not entirely.' Sisaroth caught sight of a ship sailing in the sky above, heading slowly down towards the palace. Magic symbols glowed on the mast and sails and presumably were responsible for the craft's ability to fly. *Is there no end to the wonders of Phondrasôn?* 'Are those people yours?' he asked.

The cîanai wheeled round, furious. 'Certainly not! Who dares . . .'

'Elves,' Crotàgon said. 'They've hoisted their banner over your palace.'

So the elves have invaded. Sisaroth looked first at the giant älf and then at Marandëi. *Oh well. Perhaps it's all for the best. Samusin has brought us our deadliest enemies so we may defeat them and destroy them with zeal.* 'They stand between me and saving my sister. I need those books that are in your library,' he said firmly.

'Then we all know what we have to do.' Crotàgon laid the unconscious Firûsha gently down on the ground, cushioning her softly with her own mantle. He twirled his spear, tapped it once against his armour to give a metallic clang and aimed the point at the palace. 'Tell your bridge thing I'm about to cross, cîanai.'

Marandëi touched the first of the planks with the silver staff tip and lightning flashed the length of the causeway. 'We can cross.'

'Then let's chuck those elves out of your palace.' *And let us save my beloved sister.* Sisaroth ran ahead with Crotàgon at his side; Marandëi followed closely and kept up a continuous recitation of spells.

It took some time to cover the four hundred paces between the two shores.

Hot waves crashed, hissing against the support posts, and glowing spray spurted occasionally onto the bridge, making them dodge.

By now the elves' ship was hovering low with its bow over the roof of the palace. A trapdoor opened and a cage was let down. They saw a captive sitting inside.

'I can hardly believe my own eyes, but I'd recognise that figure anywhere. Tossàlor!' Crotàgon cried out in surprise. 'They've taken him, even though he was safe in the Valley of the Beast!'

It gets better and better. This'll save us some time. Sisaroth did not bother to ask what the Valley of the Beast meant. He was clear on one thing: this palace now housed two items he desperately needed and he was not going to leave them to the elves.

The tension became almost unbearable when he realised the significance of the coming confrontation: *My first ever clash with my sworn enemies!*

And he did not have either his father or an army of veterans to support him in the endeavour. His fighting force comprised one giant älf, one female sorceress, and himself, a young priest. And they were about to meet a ship full of elves in full combat.

Phondrasôn, some time after the 5427th division of unendingness.

'Look up! I'm up here!'

Tirîgon raised his head and saw Esmonäe hanging from a rope; her feet were just over his head. 'How did you do that?'

'You always underestimate me, don't you?' The älf-girl laughed and grabbed a second rope that swung past them; she transferred to it and slid down a little to be on the same level as him. They sailed through the air at a dizzying height.

Isn't she amazing? When their ropes came together, Tirîgon put an arm round her and they kissed.

The elf ship was heading out of the cave through the narrow fissure at the end. The two älfar found the wind pulling at their clothing and their hair.

Tirîgon had no option but to trust the rope he was hanging onto. *If the elves decide to haul us up we've got a problem.* 'We'd best stay down here and wait and see what happens,' he told her, shouting over the gusts of wind. 'If the wind gets any stronger we're going to find it difficult to climb up.'

'I can see it might be tough for you,' challenged Esmonäe with a teasing flutter of her eyelashes. 'But I am going to suggest we get higher up. Just in case we need to get on board quickly.'

If you say so. He nodded despite his better judgment and they worked their way up until they were about ten paces below the keel. They each knotted a loop in their ropes to give them a foothold. 'When is the best time to attack?'

'When they're busy. When they attempt their next landing, I'd say.' Esmonäe looked over at the cliff face that was coming closer.

They flew through the tight opening. The vessel had to correct its course several times to avoid the huge stalactites and outcrops of rock on both sides. When the ship manoeuvred, runes on the planks shone out brightly. The passage proved increasingly dangerous for the two stowaways, who were swung violently to and fro on their ropes.

'What do you think they will do with Tossàlor?' Esmonäe wanted to know.

'They could easily have killed him if they'd wanted to, so I'm assuming they want to keep him alive. They must want to torture him and draw out his death.' Tirîgon supposed they were heading for a place where more elves lived. 'I expect they're taking him to one of their floating islands.' He told her briefly about his previous encounter with the obboona.

'You ought to be a story-teller. You've had so many adventures and yet you've only been here in Phondrasôn for such a short time.' Esmonäe gave him another kiss. 'We'll beat them, just you wait. I've got a few tricks up my sleeve.' She winked at him and then turned her head in the direction of travel. A rosy glow fell on her beguiling face and her hair swirled about her head.

I believe you there. He looked to the front, aware of the wave of heat that was rolling their way.

The ship entered a cave at considerable altitude. Below them lay a lake of molten glass, an island situated in the middle of the lethal waves. Four slender bridges led off from the island in different directions and connected with corridors capped by great gates.

The island itself was overgrown and desolate; the outlines of an abandoned garden were just visible still. There was a palace built on the highest point of the headland. It was not an elf construction but there was a banner hoisted with elven writing on it. It was not the usual sort of edifice that elves went for. It was all straight lines and corners rather than adorned with the decorative, playful elements they typically liked. The mottos chiselled into the stone over the entrance were in the älfar language, but they were still too far away to be deciphered.

'What do you think that says?' he asked, pointing.

'*Not for eternity but for a very long time*,' Esmonäe answered.

Wow, she's got good eyesight. He could only just make out the shapes of the letters. Tirîgon had a closer look at their surroundings. The bridges were damaged, badly so. *Those gates don't look as though they've been opened very often. They're all rusted up. Nobody's looking after the entrances at all.* This meant the only approach for the elves and anyone else must be via that fissure they had come through, about three hundred paces away from the island. You could only do it with a flying ship. 'They've taken over the palace. It's a perfect stronghold for them.'

'And what about that älfar motto?' Esmonäe was voicing his own thoughts.

'Perhaps it used to belong to some älf. They must have killed him when they conquered the place.' *If I were to stay in Phondrasôn I'd want a castle like that one, to be safe.*

The ship lost height and steered straight for the turrets.

'What shall we do? They'll see us if we hang about here like glorified wind chimes.' Tirîgon could not think of what to do. Enveloping themselves in shadow was unlikely to help much because black shapes on the ropes would be just as noticeable.

Esmonäe took charge. 'Climb down to the end of the rope.' She undid the loop and slid down her own. 'We'll jump down as soon as we're over the island.'

He slid down, and the warmth from the molten glass hit him. The waves seemed to behave exactly like normal sea water, rolling in towards the coast and up the beach. *The rocks must be the same temperature, otherwise the glass would cool and harden.*

The next thing he would encounter were the trees, with their blackish green leaves. The tree tops were less than ten paces below his feet. *Still too high.*

'Do you remember what you said back there in the other cave?' Esmonäe called to him.

'What do you mean?'

'You said *Follow me.*' The girl let go of the rope and dropped. *She is . . .* Tirîgon followed suit and fell. *This is utter madness.* He landed in a soft tarpaulin of leaves. Spreading his arms he tried to grab at branches to break his fall, but they broke under his weight, whipping against his face and body.

Tirîgon crashed onto a thick branch and held on for dear life. *Done it!* His back hurt, his arms were shaking and his heart was beating fit to burst.

He clambered down cautiously and with great difficulty, finally jumping to the ground to find Esmonäe waiting with a smile on her inviting lips.

'Well, look at you! The young warrior as a climbing bear, old before its time. Were you picking fruit on the way down? What kept you?' She greeted him with a kiss. 'There, that was your first reward. You shall have the second one when we've killed all the elves and saved Tossàlor. I promise you won't regret it.' She sped off.

'How do you know which way to go?' he asked, following her.

'We've been floating over the island. Didn't you work it out? We had plenty of time up there.' She disappeared between tall fern leaves which hid her from view. 'Stay close or you'll get lost.'

Tirîgon followed, sword in hand, watchful now in case the elves had posted sentries. His right leg sent stabs of pain all the way up his spine if he put too much weight on that foot. *And she's absolutely fine, as if she'd just jumped off a little wall.*

They kept close as they ran up the hill, grinning at each other.

It's fun going into battle with her at my side. Her confidence was infectious. It did not matter which of them was in charge. He was keen to see the tricks she claimed to have up her sleeve.

Esmonäe gave him a sign to stop; she ducked down and crawled through the undergrowth up to the edge of the wood.

Tirîgon followed her, doubled over. Through the foliage he caught sight of the ship hovering above the palace. The trapdoor in the bow of the ship opened up and Tossàlor was let down in the cage. They could not see exactly where it landed. *There don't seem to be any elves on watch. They must feel so secure up here. All the better for us.* He swapped glances with Esmonäe. 'Do you have a plan?'

'A very simple one. We go in and do away with every elf we come across.'

Her brown eyes shone with the prospect of killing. 'There is one thing I want to ask for.'

'What's that?' *Anything, anything at all.*

'If we catch an elf that's really, really old, please don't kill him. Leave him for me.'

Tirîgon thought the request odd but he was happy to agree. 'Sure. Let's get going.'

Esmonäe smothered him with excited kisses before she wrapped herself in darkness and made for the building.

Tirîgon had not seen any weapons in her hands. He followed, admiring the intense degree of blackness she had conjured up to conceal herself. *It's as if she carried a piece of the night and has dressed herself in it.* His companion seemed to have many secrets.

They hurried along the overgrown path and ducked behind a pillar to watch the entrance.

'The gate is open,' Esmonäe whispered and she slipped through before he could restrain her.

A stifled shout of surprise came from within, followed by a dull thud as a body hit the ground.

'Esmonäe!' Tirîgon ran through the entrance, his sword ready. He saw the älf-girl kneeling over the bodies of five slaughtered elves. 'By all that's infamous! How ... ?'

'Don't overdo the admiration thing. Those ones were already dead,' she said, nodding to four of them as she took her hand away from a dead elf's mouth and removed his sword. 'He came down the stairway and found the bodies at the same time I did. I had to kill him or he would have raised the alarm.'

Elves never killed each other as far as he knew so there must be someone else in the palace beside themselves. 'Perhaps some of Tossàlor's friends are trying to free him?' That would complicate matters. *It would be much better if he were obliged to us for freeing him. We need his help.*

He could see from her expression that she was thinking along the same lines. 'We'll have to be quicker than the others. I don't want them doing me out of my share of elves!' Esmonäe bounded up the steps.

Or let's find the others and kill them, too. Tirîgon picked up a shield from one of the slain elves and hurried after her.

They soon came across other corpses.

The elves had been dealt hefty blows with some type of blade, leaving broad cuts that couldn't come from a sword or an axe. Other injuries had been made with conventional weaponry. Footprints in the dust led further into the palace and through two long hallways.

It occurred to Tirîgon that the attackers must have known

exactly where to go. It did not look as if wild hand-to-hand combat had ranged randomly through the rooms. *Perhaps the original owner of the palace has come back to get his revenge?*

He and Esmonäe came up to a high set of double doors behind which the sound of fighting could be heard. 'Let's wait till they've finished fighting and then we'll get whoever the winners are,' was his suggestion.

Esmonäe shook her head. 'Those elves will kill Tossàlor first. We must step in.' She lowered her head, eager to attack. 'And they've deprived me of two of the old ones I wanted to kill myself. They'll pay for that!' She pushed open the doors and was about to rush in, weapon raised.

I've got to show her I'm a decent warrior, too. 'Stop!' Tirîgon pushed past her. 'You've made me follow you all the way here. Now it's my turn to lead!' He was never going to admit to her how fast his heart was racing.

Esmonäe smiled in response.

Tirîgon slipped through.

A tumultuous fight was taking place in the hall. Three älfar were facing down a whole host of elves. Tossàlor's cage stood in the middle of the room.

A huge, heavily armoured älf was dealing out blows and jabbing with his spear. He had cut off the limbs of several opponents and was shattering helmets and breaking shields to bring death to as many as he could reach. An older älf-woman stood at his side sending out lightning bolts from the staff she held. Whoever she hit disintegrated in a puff of smoke and dust.

But the third figure, driving his sword through an elf's neck and laughing triumphantly, he recognised immediately.

'Sisaroth, it's you!' he cried in delight. *Everything's going to be all right! We'll win!* 'I'm with you, brother! Hold on!'

'Tirîgon!' panted his brother. 'Tirîgon! How wonderful to see you!'

The last row of elf warriors turned their fury on Tirîgon.

He mowed down three or four before finding himself wedged between a corridor and a wall made of shields. He was immobilised; there was no room to manoeuvre his sword arm.

A spiked spear tip jabbed at him and nearly grazed his chest.

'Cursed pack of light worshippers!' Tirîgon pushed against the shields wildly hoping to get through them, but had no success.

Another spear came hissing out of nowhere and would have slit open his belly if his armour had not protected him.

I can't let myself get trapped. I'm not going down like this! With a shout he transferred his entire weight backwards, pushing with both feet on the shields opposite and forcing the elf behind him to retreat. Then he dropped down and swept about him with his sword, hitting at the unprotected legs of those who had surrounded him. The blade severed muscles and sinews.

The wounded fell on top of him and together they shielded him from the spear throws from the rest of the elves.

He slipped through the mass of injured elves as a snake would slither. He switched to his dagger to stab the bodies closest to him. Blood flowed all around. *You shall die!*

Tirîgon jumped to his feet, hammering the grip of his knife against the nearest elf's nose-guard to blind him and then jabbing the dagger tip through the elf's throat. 'I'll show you how an älf fights, no matter how he is outnumbered!'

From the corner of his eye he saw a thin-bladed axe thrust

coming. There was no way to fend it off with his knife and no time to dodge out of its path. *No!*

Before the axe-blade could strike home, the handle was seized by a mighty hand. The huge älf reared up in front of him.

'You need to watch out for yourself better,' he grunted, stabbing with his spear. The elf's head was struck from his shoulders.

'That would be my advice to you, too,' said Esmonäe, fighting next to Tirîgon now. She drew her long-bladed dagger out of the back of an enemy's neck and watched him collapse at her feet, his cudgel tumbling harmlessly to the floor instead of stamping a hole in Tirîgon's head, as intended. 'We've still got a lot to do when the fighting's over, you know.' She nimbly avoided the corner of a shield and dealt with its owner.

How lucky I am. Tirîgon wiped the elf blood from his eyes. There were no enemies left near him now. The final struggles were taking place in the middle of the room around the cage that held Tossàlor. *I have killed masses of elves but I've only survived thanks to that huge älf and Esmonäe helping me.* He was embarrassed at this, and his excitement at having killed his foes disappeared. *I wasn't taking sufficient care.* He watched how Sisaroth wielded his sword. *I'm either not careful enough or I'm a rotten soldier. Everyone here seems better than I am. Even the bloody elves.*

Suddenly the fighting stopped. Tirîgon had not seen exactly what had happened.

There were heaps of corpses piled on the floor. Groans betrayed the wounded, whom Esmonäe cheerfully finished off, slaughtering them like animals.

Sisaroth rushed over and embraced his brother. 'Tirîgon! So

brave! My brave brother! We were in the same battle without knowing it and together we've won!'

He clapped Tirîgon on the shoulder. 'It is so good to be with you,' Tirîgon replied, no less moved than Sisaroth. His sibling had emerged pretty much unscathed, with only superficial injuries.

I've found him! We're together again! 'Who are your friends?'

'Crotàgon and Marandëi. I'll fill you in on the whole story later. But let's get our sister first.'

'Firûsha? She's here?' Tirîgon was not ashamed of the tears that welled up. *The three of us together again!*

'We've got her with us, but . . . . she's in a bad way.' Sisaroth shot his companions a fierce glance. 'Get Tossàlor out of that contraption and see to the ship.' Then he ran off. 'Come with me. We will collect our sister.'

He's the one in charge. As usual. Nothing's changed. Tirîgon addressed Tossàlor: 'Didn't I say we'd be meeting again soon?'

He and Esmonäe hurried off with Sisaroth and as they moved, he briefly introduced them. Apart from that they did not talk; they needed their breath and their concentration for running.

The battle and the journey beforehand had demanded a lot of him. Tirîgon's arms were weary and the cuts he had received were smarting badly and needed attention. However, the thought of holding his beloved sister in his arms made him forget his discomfort.

They hurried across the bridge that was still intact. Firûsha lay on the mantle where she had been left: her breast rose and fell regularly.

There she is! Tirîgon sank to his knees at her side and threw his arms around her. *It's as if she were asleep.* He let tears of joy run down his face, unashamed, but he was extremely concerned at her state. 'Tell me what happened.'

Sisaroth gave a swift summary of what he had learned. 'Marandëi will find a remedy to stop this terrible decay. That's why we came here, to her old palace.' He motioned to his brother to get up. 'We need to get her inside, now.'

'Of course! We must get her to safety. I'll take her head and you take her feet. That'll be the best way to carry her.' He placed his arms gently under her shoulders. Together the brothers carried her across the transparent boards over the raging molten sea.

They saw the elf ship attempting to move away but a glistening bolt of lightning shot up from the palace roof and lodged in the stern of the vessel, cutting it in half.

The shimmering runes in the ships side ceased to glow; the craft plunged to the waves and erupted into flames before sinking to the bottom.

'What was that?' cried Tirîgon. *I've never seen anything like it!*

'That is Marandëi's work,' Sisaroth commented, unfazed. 'She is a cîanai.'

Esmonäe kissed Tirîgon on the cheek. 'You see? I told you we'd kill them all,' she said enthusiastically as she rushed off. 'We'll meet in the hall.' She ran along the walkway. 'I've got to see if there are any elves worthy of my sword still alive.'

Tirîgon was speechless. His mind could not keep pace with events. He may have been utterly exhausted by the fighting and the confusion, but his heart was brimming over with joy at having located his siblings. *It's all coming together! It's more than I ever dared hope for! Which gods should I send my prayers of thanks to? I'll make proper sacrifice to them if my sister is restored to health. If they don't save her life, I shall forswear the lot of them.*

'It seems,' Sisaroth remarked, 'that each of us has found a treasure here in Phondrasôn: two warriors and a cîanai. They brought us together and gave us Tossàlor. With his help we will get back to Dsôn.' He gave his sister a tender glance. 'And then we shall bring death to the slanderers who sent us here.'

Tirîgon was silent. His train of thought differed from his brother's. He was thinking about the opportunities that Phondrasôn had to offer.

With this unique group of gifted people, we could build an empire that is impossible to destroy. He was lost in this dream of grandeur. *We would be the unquestioned rulers. No one would tell us what to do.* He, too, stared at his sleeping sister. *And back in Dsôn, what could we ever achieve?*

Phondrasôn, some time after the 5427th division of unendingness.

'Let's stay here. Not forever, you understand, but until we've found a safe way out.' Firûsha looked at the expectant faces. *I want them to stop talking. They're going on and on. I can feel the anger rising.*

She passed a hand over the headscarf she wore to hide where her hair had fallen out. Marandëi had found a spell that saved her life. Only time would tell whether the improvement was permanent or whether the ukormoriers' poisonous touch would win out. She had lost her hair; Firûsha prayed to the gods of infamy that this was the whole extent of the damage incurred.

The seven älfar were in the palace library drinking a

restorative herbal tea that Marandëi had made to help their wounds heal quickly. The cosy book archive was a comfortable room with thick ornamental carpets on the floor and decorative carved wood panelling. The shelves could have done with a few more books, it was true. Perhaps the elves had thrown out some of the works, or the previous owner had had little time for reading.

Before meeting like this, there had been a great deal of tidying up to do. It took a long time to get all the elf cadavers piled up on the jetty exactly as Tossàlor wanted. He was going to take the best of the bones. He did not have the necessary preserving chemicals here in the palace to keep entire skeletons, so after he collected the pieces he wanted, he'd throw the rest into the boiling glass sea. He had already embarked on retrieving the best material. Firûsha was curious to see what he would make out of it.

But before they let him get down to work, the triplets insisted on discussing a plan of action.

They were all washed and changed, after selecting appropriate dress from the old wardrobes. The fabric smelled musty. But they preferred to wear the old robes of the first owner of the palace than to wear anything belonging to elves. There would be time enough to make clothes of their own that were more to their liking and embroidered with älfar motifs.

Firûsha looked at Tirîgon, who smiled at her gratefully. Her suggestion that they stay in the palace for the time being had placed her on his side. *My view is the most sensible, after all.*

Sisaroth did not hide his displeasure. 'Why?' He indicated the map that Tirîgon had brought with him. 'We have many good, possible ways to escape from our prison.'

'But there's no tried and trusted passage up to the surface. No guarantee of success. I don't want to do endless forced marches or face hordes of monsters we can't defeat or wind up at a dead end. We have wonderful headquarters right here. Let's stay and take our time with our plans. We can explore Phondrasôn and find out its mysteries. And anyway, there's a bit of the map that's missing,' his brother objected. 'Tossàlor said that he knows tunnels that might lead to the surface but that he can't be sure.'

'I'm afraid that's the truth.' The bone-carver crossed his arms stubbornly. 'I'd really like to get away from here, believe me, but I've absolutely no wish to be devoured by monsters when we're only halfway home – and I'm sure any tunnel going to the surface would be full of them.'

'We'll never have a total guarantee of safety,' Sisaroth snorted. 'Look around you. We've got excellent warriors and a cîanai. Our fine little army ought to be able to make it!'

'But it's a large army we need,' Tirîgon said crossly. 'Hundreds of warriors afraid of nothing, who can take our enemies apart as easily as Tossàlor does his cadavers.'

'Are you looking to start your own Dsôn here? A third Dsôn?' Sisaroth pointed at the ceiling, meaning the surface. 'Have you forgotten why we landed in this maze of terrors and dangers in the first place? Our parents are waiting for us up there and our revenge awaits us; we have to retaliate against those who accused us. You were the one that followed us of your own free will to help bring us home. What ties you to this place all of a sudden?'

'Nothing. But I am against risking our lives unnecessarily after we've been through so much to survive so far.' Tirîgon hurled the words back at his brother.

Crotàgon, Tossàlor, Esmonäe and Marandëi kept out of it.

Firûsha understood them only too well. *They don't want to join the argument and are waiting to see how it ends.*

They had already voiced their opinions: Marandëi followed Sisaroth's line, as she was in his service. Crotàgon and Esmonäe wanted to go back with Tossàlor, but they wanted the same certitude that Tirîgon was demanding.

I can't watch this happening. They'll end up in a feud! That would be the worst possible outcome Firûsha could imagine. She got to her feet. 'My dear brothers, let me suggest a compromise,' she said, her voice quiet and calm. 'We come to an agreement right now about the length of time we remain here in the palace, regardless of what we discover before that point – but if we find a safe passage exists, we travel back to Dsôn immediately.'

Sisaroth nodded in agreement though he seemed not totally sure. 'I concur, as long as the departure point is not too far in the future.'

'But also not too soon,' countered Tirîgon aggressively.

They are like shadow-wolves fighting for supremacy in their territory. 'This is getting us nowhere. If we are not capable of reaching an agreement, we shall have to leave it up to the gods of infamy.' Firûsha spoke hastily to prevent the next confrontation. She asked Tossàlor to select an elf bone from his collection. She did not meet his eyes because she found his cold stare unpleasant. He always gave the impression he was assessing her for her usefulness as material. 'Not too small a bone.'

He rustled about in his shoulder bag and brought out a long thigh bone that had been thoroughly cleaned. It shone white in the light. 'This one is good.' He laid it on the table.

'Now Crotàgon, strike it with the flat side of your spear,' directed Firûsha.

Tossàlor objected to destroying the beautiful bone but he was overriden.

'Shouldn't have given you such a good one,' he grumbled. 'May this dead elf serve our unity of purpose.'

'Thank you. Off you go, Crotàgon. The number of splinters from his blow will indicate the number of tenth-divisions of unendingness that we remain here.' Firûsha regarded her brothers in turn. 'Do you two accept these terms and agree to abide by them?'

'I don't know if this is a good –' Tirîgon began, but Esmonäe placed her hand on his thigh. He said nothing more.

Marandëi saw what happened and her eyebrows shot up. It did not escape Firûsha's notice that Esmonäe gave the cîanai a challenging look. *What does that mean?* She groaned inside. *Not another quarrel in the group?*

'I call on Inàste, Samusin and the gods of infamy! We ask you, gods young and old, to send us a sign, a decision.' Crotàgon struck the bone.

The table shuddered with the force of the impact and the bone shattered into dozens of pieces. Tirîgon and Sisaroth counted them assiduously. Seventy-seven. Neither of them was pleased.

They'll be coming up with objections, trying to outdo each other. They'll find excuses for not keeping to the agreement. I've got to make peace here. We need to stay strong, all of us. 'We hereby swear a solemn oath,' Firûsha spoke in ceremonious tones. 'Let us swear that none of us shall harm another of the group for as long as we remain here in Phondrasôn.'

'What's the point of that?' Esmonäe had been taken by surprise, but she immediately realised her objection made her look suspicious so she tried to make light of things. 'I mean, of course we'll all support each other, won't we?'

It was evident from the sour expression on Tossàlor's face that he had planned to acquire some of their bones. Apparently elves were not enough to satisfy his artistic cravings.

What a splendid, united community we are, Firûsha thought in quiet despair. *Does every single one of us have a different agenda to pursue?* The sense of community that had upheld society in Dsôn did not exist in Phondrasôn.

Crotàgon supported Firûsha's motion. 'It seems like a sensible oath to swear. It might give us more protection than we may at present think we need.'

'As if some oath could give protection against a traitor's blade,' scoffed Tirîgon under his breath as he turned away to study the books on the shelves.

Marandëi struck the ground with the end of her staff. 'I know a way to give the oath more power. A little ceremony: each of us selects one of the splinters. A small one.' Her peaceful voice carried through the room.

The assembled company did as she had suggested. Some were obviously just going through the motions. Esmonäe's scornful expression made it clear she thought this a childish trick of some kind.

'Now hold them up and let them touch.' They did this and the cîanai intoned a magic spell.

Suddenly a blackness enveloped the united bone fragments and each splinter took on a dark hue, crackling and fizzing, as if roasting in some invisible fire.

'They're ... heating up,' said Tossàlor in surprise. 'And they've gone dark as the night.'

'There is a death curse on them,' Marandëi explained with a sly smile. She breathed a sigh of relief. 'Whosoever discards his fragment or harms another of us will be overtaken by it.' She was the first to take her own splinter out of the circle; she stowed it in her pocket. 'If I were you, I'd make sure you look after them extremely carefully.'

Esmonäe stared at her incredulously. 'Are you mad? You told us it would be a ritual, not some lethal spell, you crazy witch! Remove the curse at once!'

'It can't be done, impetuous älf-girl,' the cîanai retorted. 'I would only be able to break the spell when at least one life has been lost to it.' She tilted her head to one side. 'Why are you so upset? Have I foiled some secret plan of yours?'

Esmonäe was furious, but said nothing. Tossàlor dropped his gaze and put his sliver away.

'Why did you not warn us first?' Sisaroth was exasperated. 'You're supposed to be in my service ...'

'You would have refused,' Firûsha broke in, taking the sorceress' side. *The curse was not what I had in mind, but at least it should prevent us trying to kill each other.*

'But what if I lose mine or someone steals it?' Esmonäe was not giving up. 'I'm not dying because of some stupid accident.'

'Then mind you look after it.' Crotàgon nodded at Marandëi. 'I would never have agreed to the curse being imposed on the oath, but I'm starting to think it's no bad thing. It makes us safe. All of us.'

Firûsha felt slightly guilty. It was she who had suggested they all take the oath and Marandëi had shamelessly exploited the idea. *Why is she looking at Esmonäe like that? Is she afraid of her?* She decided to speak to the cîanai alone after the meeting.

'We can't change it now. Let's get to work.' Sisaroth stood up. 'Friend Tossàlor, let us inspect the places you thought might lead up to the surface. We'll take paper, pen and ink to fill in the missing parts of the elves' map.' The artist nodded and got to his feet. The two of them left the library together.

The company drifted apart. Tirîgon went with Esmonäe. Marandëi had removed a book from the shelf and went to a seat by the window to read.

Now we are united. But there can be no joy in this. Firûsha looked out of the window at the sea of molten glass and the jetty with its rows of elf corpses.

On seeing the dead bodies she was reminded of her own fight against the ukormoriers. She would never have survived without Sisaroth, Crotàgon, and Marandëi's intervention.

I have criminally neglected my weapons training. Fate had decreed they were going to be spending nearly eight divisions of unendingness in Phondrasôn and there was certainly going to be fighting involved.

We need every arm that can hold a sword. Tossàlor could not be relied on. He was only concerned with his art and was probably looking forward to the first älf dying so he could use their bones.

Firûsha knew that she had the build for a warrior and that she was nimble enough. *I must work at it.*

When the giant älf stood up to go, Firûsha called to him. 'Crotàgon?'

'What is it?'

'I have not told my brothers how you treated me when I

arrived in Phondrasôn. I think you owe me for this.' She looked at him determinedly. 'Teach me to fight properly and I'll sing you all the songs you want. I want to outdo my brothers in swordsmanship.'

'Why is that?' Crotàgon was intrigued.

'Because I might have to keep them from hurting each other. Sisaroth is impetuous and Tirîgon is stubborn and although they love each other, there was a lot of brawling back home in Dsôn. I can only stop them from fighting if I can take their weapons. I need to be able to beat them both.' Firûsha saw Marandëi smirking into her book. *She doesn't think I can do it.*

Crotàgon nodded with a smile that spoke volumes.

SECOND BOOK

The Tested Ones

Time went by
    and the siblings pursued their aims.
The centre of all their endeavours was the island in the sea of
molten glass.
    Inaccessible for any enemy and completely impregnable,
    unless the enemy could fly.
Sisaroth, Tossàlor and Marandëi tirelessly explored
    the caves and tunnels of the underground region
    and discovered the secrets of the deadly labyrinth step by step,
    constantly expanding their field of enquiry.
Tirîgon followed his brother with Esmonäe for company.
    They searched for any älfar who might have been banished
here, or lost.
    All should be won for their cause: community was
everything.
    Each of them was under a deadly curse,
    welding them together with an oath.
Firûsha was schooled in combat
    and trained her voice in the concerts
    she gave for Crotàgon and the others on the island.
    Her voice held them together

and furthered unity and harmony in the minds of the
älfar.
  Her singing was like a drug for their immortal souls.
  They could never have enough . . .
As exploration continued
  their älfar numbers grew.
Buildings were constructed on the island to house the
newcomers.
  An immense stronghold grew up round the palace,
  and the fragile walkways were replaced with solid bridges.
  The scattering of warriors became a fearsome army
  and the original refuge became the centre of an empire.
Beasts and monsters hid away
  on hearing the älfar bugles.
  Óarcos paid tribute,
  warlords bowed their heads to the Triplet Siblings,
  and whole caverns surrendered to their rule.
But one thing plagued them still:
  no exploration brought them to a path
  that led back home.
The success of these Young Gods
  caused envy and malice
  in Phondrasôn's other rulers
  who had held sway and had felt safe.

        'The Beginnings' from the epic poem *Young Gods*
        composed by Carmondai, master of word and image

Chapter I

Name me a weapon
more lethal
than the sharpest of blades.
You choose duplicity?
You are nearly right.
The sharpest weapon
you can use
is reason.
Blessed is he
who knows how to use it,
for many people
confuse duplicity
with reason.

'Aphorisms' from the epic poem *Young Gods*
composed by Carmondai, master of word and image

Phondrasôn.

Sisaroth stood lost in thought in the library of the palace that
had once belonged to Marandëi. The cîanai had relinquished

the palace to the siblings, wanting the young rulers to have a suitable home. The floor-length robe Sisaroth wore was equally appropriate to his station in life: a high collar and black embroidery stitched so densely over the entire garment that its original light grey was hardly visible.

Sisaroth studied the map he was building. It extended over the surface of an entire library wall. Records of other explorations were to be seen on the ceiling, the floor and the other walls.

There was still no end in sight. He would need a separate map room soon.

Phondrasôn must have been created by more than one god. Sisaroth clasped his hands behind his back. *Endless paths and mazes, but no road seems to lead back to Dsôn! How ever did we reach this place in our cages?*

He was convinced that the tunnels changed from time to time: they would disappear or change direction, taking a sudden upward or downhill turn. Magic must be responsible for these phenomena. Enchantments were making fun of their endeavours by transforming the environment at random.

Tirîgon laughed at him for thinking like this and demonstrated that it was not the case by placing markings on the walls. Sisaroth would object that those very symbols had also been altered by the magic powers to complete the deception, but Tirîgon would have none of it.

When he surveyed their empire, however, Sisaroth had to admit that Tirîgon had done well as a conqueror. *I have become an excellent warrior but he is a better strategist.*

The map showed their ever-increasing territory. The caves under the triplets' direct control were designated in blue, the areas that paid them tribute were in yellow and the regions governed by their own deputies were green.

Red lines denoted the caves that constituted danger for the älfar, be it due to a monster that was difficult to defeat, a strong population, or an environmental hazard.

Notes pinned to the map bore letter and number combinations summing up the properties of individual areas. The code keys were held in books on the library shelves.

Sisaroth had marked the position of certain grottoes yet to be thoroughly explored. He and Tossàlor were often attacked and forced to withdraw before they could complete their investigation. Some areas were too large and too inaccessible even to be mapped provisionally. When they went on their exploratory excursions, they took lengths of cord and chalk to mark the walls so they could find their way back.

There is so much still to do. He looked out of the window. He often doubted that the seventy-seven tenth-divisions would ever prove sufficient for the task. He was hoping against hope for a lucky discovery. *I should consult the gods of infamy.*

The kind of ritual used for speaking to the old gods who had lived before Samusin and Inàste was dangerous in the extreme. Dangerous for himself and for any other älfar who attended. His own training as a priest had barely begun back in Dsôn when they were banished. He was in no way confident with the gestures and phrasings.

But I think I should try. First, however, he wanted to expand the exploration with Tossàlor and the other scouts. *Let's hope he's not deep in his next creative phase, or I'll have to wait till he's finished.*

The artist was making the most of the expeditions by collecting as many different bones as possible. His studio and store-rooms in the palace were piled high with the raw materials for his works of art. He could fashion practically anything out of bone – from huge chandeliers to delicate hair ornaments to a mosaic composed of the finest fragments. He would stay in his studio for moments of unendingness at a time, then he would emerge and show off his new creation. Sisaroth had a few of his works himself. But there was still an uneasiness if he looked too deep into the sculptor's eyes. Tossàlor radiated an uncanny aura.

A detachment of forty warriors left via the north gate to march out along the broad causeway with orders from Tirîgon to deal with the state of affairs in the Efrigûr province. Tribute had not been paid and the soldiers would be investigating the cause: it could be local unrest or possible invasion by a foreign power.

My brother really enjoys his role as commander in chief. Originally he only wanted to build up an army to get us back safely to Dsôn, but his field of influence has expanded beyond that. Sisaroth had warned Tirîgon not to deploy his forces too widely; he didn't want to lose any of their number. But the gods of infamy seemed to be on the side of the älfar military units. Phondrasôn was simply not prepared for a disciplined army and their losses were always low. *He knows what he is doing and his tactics are paying off.*

What made Sisaroth uneasy was Tirîgon's unquestioning acceptance of any älf that turned up. Occasionally whole bands of exiles would congregate by the gates, hoping to be allowed in. And regardless of their previous history – whether guilty of the most gruesome crimes or suffering from extreme mental derangement – Tirîgon didn't care.

He is too dependent on the magic oath of allegiance. Sisaroth took down a volume containing details of their recent conquests. *Be that as it may – I have my own tasks to carry out.* He opened the book to the sketch maps of the seventh cavern. That was the one causing him headaches.

It was a wonder the cave had not collapsed. Hole after hole had appeared in the walls. The cylindrical shape of the tunnels made him believe they had originally been formed by underground rivers. *If that water flowed down from the surface, then one of the tunnels must surely lead to the outside.* He had already explored four of the possibilities with Tossàlor and now he was researching a fifth.

There was a knock at the door.

A palace guard entered the room and bowed, wearing elegantly decorated armour made of an alloy of iron and tionium to protect the älf from swords and missiles. 'Excuse me, Sisaroth, but a messenger has arrived.' He spoke from under a simple helmet.

'Bring him in.'

'He's not one of ours.'

Sisaroth looked up from the papers he was studying and pointed to the maps on the wall. 'Which cavern or cave is he from?' He wanted to know roughly what to expect before welcoming barbarians, óarcos, or worse.

'He did not say.'

A newcomer? Sisaroth turned to the guard in surprise. 'What race?'

'A groundling, I'd say. I've never actually seen one, but judging from the stature and the apparel, he corresponds to the usual descriptions,' the soldier answered, a little unsure of himself. 'For the most part, that is.'

'Is he armed?'

'Yes. He's got . . . it's kind of a sword. Blackest black. Looks like pure tionium to me. That's odd, I thought. But then, in Phondrasôn there's a lot of oddness around.'

'And why are you bringing him to me? Aren't the orders to keep all the lower creatures and unidentified beings out at the second wall?'

'Yes, but I'm not sure that he *is* a lower being,' the guard confessed. 'If he's important, I did not want to incur your displeasure or risk possible war with another cavern, so I thought it best to let you decide. I've left him in the care of four warriors.'

Sisaroth became curious. 'What made you hesitate?'

'He says he's an envoy from the prince of Phondrasôn,' the guard said reluctantly. 'He doesn't look very intimidated by us.'

So he's not frightened about the possibility of death or imprisonment? 'Well, well! So now the groundlings are claiming our caverns, are they? Perhaps because they fancy the tunnels?' Sisaroth snapped the book shut so sharply that the draught made his hair rise up round his face. 'Bring him in.'

The guard bowed and shouted out an order.

The double doors swung open to admit four armoured soldiers escorting a one-eyed groundling in silver chainmail reinforced with tionium plates. He carried his black and silver helmet under his right arm while the stumpy fingers of his strong left hand gripped the hilt of the weapon that hung from his belt. He had constructed a specialised scabbard that would not catch on the jagged end of the sword.

Sisaroth was familiar both with the weapon and the furrowed features of the face before him. His brown beard was still kept short. *The groundling who tried to kill me!* He instinctively placed his right hand on his dagger.

The remaining right eye of the messenger flashed and the facial expression was one of astonishment. The groundling slowed. He, too, was remembering. He approached Sisaroth and addressed him in a melodious bass voice. 'I bring you greetings from my master. If I am not mistaken, we have met before?' He seemed to be racking his brain. 'How long ago would that be?'

'Yes, we met in combat. For mortals it would have been a very long time ago. For immortals, of course, it was but yesterday.' Sisaroth was cautious and gave his soldiers a sign to train their spears on the groundling. Silently, his warriors moved their weapons round to point at the newcomer. 'So you have found a prince to serve?'

'And you have made yourself prince to get others to serve you. How nice.' He was unperturbed by the fact that four weapons were trained on him. 'In fact, it was my prince that found me. I am obliged to serve him. I can think of many other things I would rather do than be subject to a gålran zhadar. But one does not always have a choice in these matters. My name, in another place and in another time, was Tungdil Goldhand.'

'I am Sisaroth, as I am sure you are aware.' The little fellow was impudent as hell and stubborn as they come, but Sisaroth was rather taken with him. *I wonder what a gålran zhadar is.* He indicated the sword-like weapon. 'So, you are still using it?'

'Bloodthirster has served me extremely well. The blade can sever any and everything it strikes. It's the sort of thing you need if you are abroad in Phondrasôn.' The groundling gave a smile and rubbed a hand over his trim brown beard with its silver strands. 'Right, let's get down to business. I have a message to deliver. You and your black-eyes have founded an empire without asking my master's permission. So . . .' He came to an abrupt stop, annoyed that Sisaroth had burst out laughing. 'I shouldn't do that, if I were you.'

'What? Laugh at you?' *The odd fellow is funnier than I thought.* He wished his brother and sister could see this. He pushed the book to one side and wiped tears of laughter from his cheeks. He plunged his hands in his pockets and leaned forward. 'I shall laugh just as long and as hard as I choose to. Tungdil. That was the name, wasn't it?' He straightened up, grinning. *Too funny, really, too funny.*

'You're making a big mistake, Black-Eyes. I've seen mightier folk than you die laughing. My prince is a master of turning hilarity into fatality.' Tungdil stayed calm and passed his hand over his silver eye-patch, which was fashioned with a black inlay design studded with small diamonds and held in place by a black leather band.

The pattern reminded Sisaroth of something he had seen in one of Marandëi's books. *Is there some magic happening here?* 'Say I were to believe you about there being a prince. What does he want?'

'He wants you to present yourself to discuss what happens next.' Tungdil leaned slightly forward, mirroring the movements Sisaroth was making. 'Perhaps your empire will be allowed to continue. But if you fail to come and meet with him, you will all die quicker than a herd of unicorns in Phondrasôn.' Now it was his turn to laugh, and his laughter was dark and full of threat. Sisaroth's face had lost any trace of amusement. 'You see, it's starting already: you are losing your sense of humour. I'm not surprised, given the circumstances.'

Sisaroth pointed to the enormous map. 'Can you see, with your one eye, the extent of our power? In the whole of that territory, I have never come across any creature calling itself a gålran zhadar.'

'I can see, with my one eye, where you and your lot have never been, and that's far more significant,' replied Tungdil with a grin. 'You have not travelled anywhere near my master, yet he still knows everything that you are up to.' He slowly extended his arm towards the charts on the wall. 'There are maps I've seen that are ten times as big as this one.' He sustained his grin. 'By the way, you *and* your deputies are expected.'

'When?'

'At once. I'll take you.'

No manners at all. No respect! This was all too much for Sisaroth. 'Tell me why I shouldn't have you killed here on the spot.'

'Because if you were to lay hands on me, there would be nothing left of your palace, your fortress or the entire cavern,' he countered. 'The gålran zhadar would interpret my death as refusal on your part to enter into negotiations and that in turn would lead to his refusal to allow your continued presence in his empire.' Tungdil stamped his foot for emphasis. 'You don't seem to understand: you are *guests* here. You are not rulers.'

The impertinent grin that had initially amused Sisaroth now invoked his fury. *I'll carve that insolent expression off your face with a knife and Tossàlor can stick it on his gallery wall.*

He did not know whether or not to believe what he had heard. It seemed strange that the name gålran zhadar had never cropped up in any of the conquered territories, and that none of the governors of their barbarian provinces had ever mentioned it. Surely the groundling must be lying.

Or have we been told nothing about this powerful prince because our subjects are hoping he will suddenly appear? He devoutly wished he had Tirîgon and Firûsha with him to help him decide. 'I must consult the others.'

'Right you are.' The groundling crossed his arms across his chest, making the silver-plated chainmail jingle. 'I'll wait.'

'It will take some time.'

'It had better not.' Tungdil grinned.

'No,' Sisaroth said after a short pause. 'I need proof that this prince really exists. I can't lead my siblings into the unknown just because some groundling turns up out of the blue and says he does. What evidence can you offer me?'

Tungdil sighed. 'I'm used to that; there've been quite a few sceptics. And I do take your point. So my prince and master gave me a present to convince you and your siblings with.' He slowly reached into his belt and pulled out an ornamental brooch in white gold, with a black onyx at its centre. 'This is for you. You shall have your proof if you press the stone.' He tossed it over.

I'm not touching it. Sisaroth stepped back and the jewelled piece fell to the floor with a clink. He did not trust the gift.

Nothing happened.

Tirîgon entered the room in the black armour of a conquering general. He was accompanied by Esmonäe. They were laughing and joking together in the way of young lovers.

Sisaroth stared at the älf-woman who he was starting to find more and more attractive.

Esmonäe liked to dress in a way that flattered her figure and drew attention to her obvious charms. Today she was wearing a tight-fitting dark red robe with slits in the fabric at strategic places. Her modesty was not in question; her pure white skin was on display.

She would look good next to me. Sisaroth cast the thought aside. She belonged to his brother. *It would only cause discord. Firûsha has her work cut out keeping the peace between the two of us as it is.*

Tirîgon noticed the guards and the groundling. 'Oh! A captive? Or do we have a visitor, brother?'

'Or perhaps it's just half of a normal visitor?' Esmonäe said scornfully. 'Oh no, I see: it's a groundling, not an underling.'

Tungdil's smile was vicious. 'When do an älf's eye-sockets go black?' he jeered. 'When you tear his eyes out!' He threw back his head and bellowed with laughter. 'See, I am witty, too.'

Tirîgon glanced at Sisaroth. 'Is he your new court jester? If so, he needs to work on his repertoire.' Esmonäe saw the brooch and bent down to pick it up.

'Don't touch it!' Sisaroth quickly told them why the groundling had come. 'The brooch is supposed to be evidence that what he says is the truth. He claims that if we press the stone in the middle we'll be given proof that his master exists.'

Tirîgon was clearly not enthusiastic about the sudden appearance of this messenger and he was not keen on the message, either. He considered himself the overlord of Phondrasôn. 'Gâlran zhadar? That name doesn't mean anything to me,' he sneered. 'And if he were really a prince, he'd have an army with him to impress us. He'd hardly send along a groundling, even an insolent one in a suit of fancy armour. Would we send a gnome to represent us at important talks?' As he spoke, Esmonäe had her arm around his shoulders and stroked the back of his neck.

My brother will definitely not be agreeing to a meeting with the gâlran zhadar, then. Sisaroth nodded. *And nor will I.* Even if Firûsha decided differently she was now outvoted.

'To help you understand: here is our answer.' He stamped on the brooch and ground it with his foot.

There followed a huge explosion outside the fortress.

Sisaroth whirled round in shock. The northern gate had been blown off its hinges and blasted to smithereens, with the iron shrapnel raining down on the stunned guards as they lay sprawled on the ground, thrown off their feet by the strength of the detonation. Some of the soldiers had been hurled into the lethal molten glass of the sea while others were horribly mutilated and died on the bridge. A cloud of dust rose in the air.

This was not, however, the end of the destruction; a large block of stone from above the entrance slipped and crashed down through the wooden bridge, making a seven-pace-wide gap. The northern causeway was now totally impassable.

'It appears not to matter whether you press the gemstone with your finger or foot,' Tungdil remarked. 'I ought to have mentioned that I happened to drop the second brooch by your gate there. Now, let's imagine the second brooch had been in the fortress. Or here in the palace. In this room. An army is not always necessary when you have other means at your disposal. Magic, for example. Shall we say this was a preview?' He rubbed his chin and looked thoughtful. 'I know I'm a bit slow on the uptake, like all groundlings. So take me through this again: is your answer a Yes or a No?'

'I'll give you my answer!' raged Sisaroth, his hand on the hilt of his dagger.

But Tirîgon restrained his brother with a nimble movement. 'We have been given an impression of your master's power and we appreciate that it would be sensible not to resist.' His words were calm and controlled. 'My siblings and I will be accompanying you.'

Tungdil stuck his square hands in his belt. 'Don't worry. I know a short cut.' He nodded to them and marched out. 'I'll wait down in the yard.'

Tirîgon whispered to Sisaroth, 'Go and get Firûsha.'

'You want to drag her into danger?' A thought occurred to him. He gestured to Esmonäe. 'Why not say she is Firûsha? Then we can leave our sister here to look after things. We don't know how long we'll be away.' *Did I suggest that so that Esmonäe would be near me?*

'No. Firusha's voice will have more persuasive power with this prince than any amount of tionium we could offer him. She could win him round with her singing.' He clapped his brother on the shoulder. 'I tell you, we'll emerge triumphant. And there won't be any fighting involved.' He stood tall and ostentatiously embraced Esmonäe.

Sisaroth watched, almost able to feel the älf-woman's lips on his own. He was unable to suppress the emotions of jealousy and greed he was going through. *How I long to be in his place!*

Esmonäe observed Sisaroth closely all the time she was being kissed by his brother. He could read a definite invitation in her chestnut-coloured eyes.

His heart skipped several beats and his whole body flushed. He had to avert his gaze to prevent her noting his desire.

Phondrasôn.

Firûsha had completed her combat practice session with Crotàgon and was doing a strip-wash in her own quarters. *He is making me work harder each time.*

Her arms ached from the constant thrusts and parrying

strokes and she had hurt her ankle in a misjudged leap, but she was not going to complain. She was getting stronger by the day.

Most of the old bruises from her opponent's blunted sword were fading but today new ones would appear. The only part of her anatomy he was careful to spare was her face.

She studied her naked reflection in the polished silver mirror and could not help noticing the changes her body had undergone since starting weapons training with her outsized mentor-älf. The physique was still decidedly feminine but her muscles were more pronounced, longer and leaner.

I'll soon be as good at fencing as I am at singing. She was not going to risk challenging her brothers yet. But Tirîgon had suggested she could fight with one of the best of the palace guards.

And we'd use unguarded rapiers, to make it more fun. Firûsha smiled to herself and applied a perfumed herbal lotion to her skin before dressing in a flowing bright blue robe. She held her black hair out of her eyes with an ivory and silver circlet studded with diamonds. It was one that Tossàlor had made for her.

Refreshed, fragrant and ravenous, she made her way downstairs to the kitchen.

Here in Phondrasôn they had none of the slaves that would have served them back in Dsôn Sòmran. Tirîgon had insisted on this, to avoid introducing any unnecessary vulnerability to their community. There was already enough tension in a society composed of criminals, exiles and älfar who had simply got lost in this underworld. They all fixed their own meals, but Firûsha didn't object. She enjoyed preparing food for herself and her two brothers. *I'll never be as good a cook as Marandëi, of course.*

The dimensions of Marandëi's palace were generous, but sometimes she thought it could have been bigger. She got the impression that the thickness of the outer walls must have been miscalculated, taking up too much of the interior space.

One evening as they sat together by candlelight the cîanai had told them about the original inhabitants of the castle. She described them as creatures of glass who had emerged in some mysterious way from the broiling sea. Roaming fields of magic were probably responsible for this transformation.

Who knows what they intended when they planned these huge walls. Now we'll never know. She went into the vaulted kitchen area. *What shall I have today?*

She placed two logs and a bucket of coal in the stove and lifted the trapdoor to the cellar, climbing down the ladder to gather the ingredients for a stew. Food kept well in the subterranean space because – somehow, in spite of the molten glass sea – it always remained cool.

Barrels, crates and open store boxes crammed the floor space. The whole room smelt of earth, roots and smoked meats.

I'm going to cook something really filling and hearty today. She picked up a small basket and made her selection.

Only herself, her brothers and their four colleagues were permitted to use the kitchen facilities. They acquired their provisions from various other caves in Phondrasôn, where everything was available: meat, cereals, spices. It was really easier to get what you wanted here than it had been in Dsôn.

They never suffered from food shortages, though some of the fare took a little getting used to. The fruits and vegetables grown under the mysterious cavern light effect and watered by underground rivers tasted different to those exposed to rain and sunlight.

With her basket full, Firûsha made her way back up.

Next the wine. The bottles and barrels were in a room adjacent to the kitchen. Leaving her basket behind, she went through and checked along the shelves. *I want a bottle of the red from Himayn . . . Let's see where Sisaroth has hidden it.*

All of a sudden she heard a clatter of cutlery from the kitchen. She peered back through the doorway and saw Marandëi standing at the stove shaking the contents of a round-bottomed glass flask. Sisaroth had asked the cîanai to create a concoction to promote wound-healing, and he wanted it as soon as possible.

Marandëi was currently experimenting with a bubbling, thick, golden brew giving off green vapour. This she collected and condensed in a second vessel. Every so often she checked the sand level in the timer on top of the woven box she had brought into the kitchen with her.

She's going to stink out my whole kitchen. Why can't she do that in her laboratory?

'Oh! I wasn't expecting to find you here,' Esmonäe said as she strode in, wearing an impossibly tight dress. 'I was looking for Firûsha.'

'She's not here but she should be back soon. She's making her supper.' Marandëi indicated the basket of provisions.

Firûsha kept silent to watch the two of them. Esmonäe's sudden appearance seemed to be awkward for the cîanai, who had the look of a hunted animal. *Why would she be scared of anyone? She has her own magical powers as well as the oath's death threat to protect her.*

'Fine! I hope she's making enough for us.' Esmonäe had a knife in her hand and was playing with it. 'And how are you doing?' she asked sweetly. 'Have you got over your time imprisoned in the tower?'

'Of course. Forgive me, but I really need to concentrate on this experiment.'

'What are you making?'

'A remedy to help injuries heal faster. Our army numbers are low enough as it is. We can't afford to lose people. I'm doing what small part I can.'

'Is this Sisaroth's idea?'

The cîanai nodded.

'Do you do everything he asks you to?' Esmonäe tossed the knife into the air and caught it neatly, swirling it about like a trained swordswoman.

Not even my brothers could do that kind of trick! This is starting to get interesting. Firûsha made sure she did not betray her presence.

'What is it you're really asking, Esmonäe? Are you trying to find out whether I am his partner?' Marandëi sounded amused. 'I doubt he would go for someone my age.'

'Have you lived through very many divisions of unendingness?' Esmonäe had come quite close and was examining the droplets condensing in the glass vessel. 'I'm bad at working out people's ages.'

'A few.' The cîanai was trying and failing to keep distance between the two of them.

'You don't remember? Or you don't want to say?'

Marandëi tapped the collecting vessel, pleased with her results. 'I don't see why I should tell anyone my age. Now, if you will be good enough to excuse me . . .'

'You know – that cursed oath you got us to swear – it really took me by surprise,' Esmonäe interrupted.

'I could see that it did. All the more reason for me to think it was the right thing to do.' Marandëi put the large round-bottomed flask down and disconnected the second vessel. She had collected only half a thimbleful of liquid but she was satisfied. 'Given how different we all are, I think our little community's definitely benefited from the extra safeguard.'

Esmonäe perched on a corner of the table, with her dagger in one hand, tip downwards. 'I would have been ready to swear,' she said quietly, 'that you knew exactly what I was *really* convicted of in Dsôn Faïmon. That would explain why you created the death penalty like that. But perhaps it was all just a coincidence.'

What is she getting at? Tirîgon had told Firûsha that circumstances had forced his companion to kill an armed älf, and that the weapon had disappeared by the time the watch had arrived. This had made her guilty of murder in the eyes of the court. *So was she lying to him, I wonder? Or has he been covering for her?* Firûsha was eager to see how things developed.

Marandëi closed the flask carefully. 'The thing is, you know – every single one of us here: whether a criminal, in despair, or simply a failure in life – we all have our little secrets. If you sit in the middle of the rumours, you get the whole picture.'

'You forgot to mention the young älfar who come to Phondrasôn to prove themselves as warriors.'

'I include them with those in despair.' Marandëi was still taking care to stay as far away from Esmonäe as possible.

'I suppose you heard rumours about me?'

'One of the criminals whose wound I was dressing told me he knew you and that he wouldn't need to worry about being safe as long as you were nearby. In spite of your fourteen älfar murders, he said.'

Esmonäe gave a sly smile. 'Aha, so the old witch has her ear to the ground.'

'Knowledge helps keep one alive. The ones who aren't prepared tend to be the first to die.' Marandëi took her staff in her left hand. 'I make a point of being prepared.'

'I suppose he told you who it was I killed?'

She nodded. 'You killed venerated members of society, he said – a real loss for Dsôn Faïmon. But he had no idea why you picked on the old ones. He also said you were mad. Opinions differed about why you lost your mind.' While she held her staff low, her thumb and forefinger touched two runes. 'Tell me why you hunted the oldest ones.'

That's news indeed! Firûsha assumed the cîanai was holding herself in readiness to cast a spell. Whether in self-defence or to force Esmonäe to speak the truth was not clear.

Esmonäe watched Marandëi carefully and laid her knife down on the table, relaxing visibly. 'You have to understand: I'm an artist, same as Tossàlor. I think the death of any immortal creature is something uniquely wonderful. Way more satisfying than the death of a normal being. The older the älf that I kill, the more I get out of it. It was always my secret wish to slit the throat of one of the Inextinguishables!' Madness shone in her eyes. 'Children and young people are quite safe.'

Firûsha, in the pantry, clapped a hand to her mouth. *She is demented. As crazy as Tossàlor! I must warn Tirîgon about her!*

'To what creative use do you put such a death?'

'The death of an elderly älf inspires my art.' Esmonäe was going through the items in Firûsha's supper basket. She selected a piece of fruit, rubbed the skin clean and sniffed at it. 'My paintings and drawings hung on every free bit of wall in my house in Dsôn.' She raised the forefinger of her right hand and pointed at her eye. 'That's what I capture: the expression at the point of death. When the soul departs. When the living creature becomes nothing but a husk. I'm not interested in the bones like Tossàlor is. My art is more abstract.' Esmonäe stretched out a hand, almost tenderly, towards Marandëi's features. 'What I do, witch, is to capture the vanishing of immortality. If you could only experience that feeling! An old soul is radiant in death! It warms the whole environment! I find it intoxicating – even more so than vintage wine or love-making or the glorious bloodshed of battle. Nothing can touch it.'

Her pupils glittered more and more as she went on, so obsessed was she.

'And I think,' she whispered to Marandëi, who was staring at her in horror, 'you are quite old enough to serve, witch. I would enjoy killing you. I *shall* enjoy it.' Esmonäe put the fruit back down. 'You put a curse on me and so I put this vow on you: I shall be your death. Your soul passing will provide the best high I can imagine. It will inspire the most beautiful painting.' She leaned forward gently.

Marandëi could not move a muscle and had to accept the light kiss on her cheek with closed eyes.

'What do you think of that?'

Staring out agog through the gap in the door, Firûsha saw the cîanai's hand shaking as if she were forcibly restraining herself from using the staff. *How can I tell Tirîgon?*

'I think the soldier was right. He told me you were driven mad by being forced to watch your long-term partner die,' Marandëi said. 'Your mind was damaged irrevocably by that.'

'Nonsense,' retorted Esmonäe. 'No, I wasn't driven mad.

I . . . It was an accident. He fell on his own sword and I held him in my arms while he died. I watched as his soul departed . . . through his eyes . . . and entered endingness,' she sobbed, collapsing onto a nearby stool. 'I am not mad, I am an artist,' she murmured. 'An artist. An artist.'

Marandëi had managed to turn things around. 'Do you think Tirîgon will still want you when he hears you have been so deceitful?'

'You won't tell him!' Esmonäe hissed back.

'Or have you already mentally discarded him and now you want Sisaroth? I've seen you looking at him. And at the palace guards. You flirt with all the platoon sytràps, with every älf who glances your way. What is your plan? I don't believe your heart is altered so quickly. I think you're following a definite strategy. You are trying to drive a wedge between the brothers by making them jealous. And while they're at each other's throats because of you, you'll step in and seize power. Is that it? And the army would be on your side because you've been fluttering your eyelashes at all the commanders. But that's unthinkable, really, isn't it?'

Esmonäe struggled to regain composure. She slid off her stool and stood over the cîanai menacingly. 'It's best you keep your mouth shut, witch. Keep quiet about my past and keep quiet about what you've seen.'

Marandëi leaned on the staff. 'I could. But what's in it for me? The old lag who told me your story will be demanding payment, too.' She smiled. 'Don't try to find out who it was, either. I know him. That's enough.'

Firûsha admired the way the cîanai now seemed to have all the strings in her hand. *Maybe she is the more dangerous of the two after all.*

Esmonäe had run out of steam. Instead of offering Marandëi some kind of a deal in exchange for her silence, she whirled round and stormed out of the kitchen back up the stairs.

It's disturbing, what's happening all around us. Firûsha shivered. There was a cold draught in the drinks pantry where she was hiding, but she did not dare come out yet. It was vital Marandëi did not realise she had been eavesdropping.

The cîanai exhaled loudly and slumped down. 'That wasn't easy,' she muttered to herself. She put the experiment equipment and the time-glass back in her wicker basket. Time was very much up. 'Oh, that took too long. He's going to be angry.'

Looking frightened, Marandëi picked up the basket and hurried upstairs.

Angry? Why would he be angry? Firûsha crept out of the tiny pantry. She could not imagine that Sisaroth had been so demanding about timing. Surely a sand-grain here or there would make no difference to him? *Could she have meant someone else?*

Her curiosity piqued, she scooted after Marandëi, who was slow on the stairs, hampered by her heavy basket. Firûsha stayed back, out of sight.

Marandëi disappeared into the laboratory next to the library.

That's a shame. I can't go in there without a good reason. And I really wanted to know who . . .

The door swung open again and the cîanai emerged.

Great! I still get to follow her.

Firûsha learned much about the palace's secrets as she and Marandëi scurried through its corridors and rooms. She was amazed to see the cîanai go through hidden doorways whose existence she had kept from the älfar triplets. Activated by pressing a certain carving, pulling at a certain stone, the doors opened up into new corridors that wove their way through the building.

That is why the rooms seemed too small. There's another palace inside the palace. Firûsha kept close to Marandëi and used her powers of shadow-making to conceal herself.

The hidden passages were extremely narrow and there were steep stairways to negotiate, leading to tiny rooms the cîanai had adapted for her own use. It had been such a generous gift to Firûsha and her brothers, ostensibly, when she gave them this palace. But these false walls also provided her with the perfect listening posts.

That's why she said we could have it. Firûsha was furious. *She just wanted to be able to spy on us.* She had counted on having Marandëi as a reliable ally because of the oath of service she had given to Sisaroth. *She is nothing but a rat in the castle walls.*

The excursion continued. Firûsha's dress was too flimsy by far for such an adventure. The delicate fabric kept catching on sharp bits of stone.

Ahead, the cîanai suddenly vanished through an opening in the floor. Firûsha could see the glow of candlelight and hear a sing-song recitation and a lot of clattering.

What's she up to?

Firûsha waited a little while and then crawled close to the aperture, bending her head to see what was happening. Marandëi was kneeling before an altar and on the altar was an ancient, weathered skull.

The skull was not the right size for an älf. It must have belonged to a smaller race. And it had probably been very ugly when it was alive. The bones seemed deformed, with an elongated head shape and a forehead as flat as if it had been slammed into a plank. It was adorned with carvings, painted symbols and ornaments.

The sounds the cîanai was making seemed to follow a tonal pattern rather than belong to any particular language. She was making obeisance to the skull. Suddenly she stopped intoning and savagely bit open the veins at her wrists, letting the blood drip onto the skull itself.

The blood was mysteriously absorbed by the skull; not a drop remained on the surface.

Firûsha thought it wise to withdraw at this stage. *I must tell my brothers! We must find out what Marandëi is up to.*

But no matter which passages she went along, which steps she went up or down, no matter how she concentrated and used her senses, she could not find the way out.

It appeared that all the secret openings had simply ceased to exist.

Chapter II

As long as you think
    you are the spider in the middle –
make sure you know
    how your web is secured.
And remember:
    if you sit in the middle,
    everyone is watching you.
If you ask me,
    I'd tell you to choose
    not to be the spider,
    but the bird
    that will eat it.

'Aphorisms' from the epic poem *Young Gods*
composed by Carmondai, master of word and image

Phondrasôn.

Where can she have gone? She's not in her room and there's no one in the kitchen. Tirîgon ran through the courtyard where the groundling stood waiting impatiently. 'We'll be with you really soon,' he muttered to the dwarf as he hurried past. 'My sister seems to have got lost in her own palace.'

'Oy! Black-Eyes!' Tungdil uttered a piercing whistle that brought the älf to a halt. 'This is taking far too long. Do you think I don't notice when I'm being strung along? Either we all four leave now to my master or I'll go back and tell him you tried to trick me.'

The pint-sized bastard! I'd like to . . . Tirîgon swung round with a false smile planted across his features. 'I'm not stringing you along.'

'That's what you get for hiding in shadows and creeping about like cats in the dark,' Tungdil mocked. 'You can't even find your own sister.' His one-eyed gaze assessed Tirîgon's armour. 'Your breastplate's not bad but it's old and you haven't looked after it. I can see three weak points where I'd be able to slide Blood-thirster straight through your skinny body.'

'Nice of you to warn me. I'll have a word with our smith.' Tirîgon saw Sisaroth and Esmonäe coming out of the main entrance. Both were in light armour and had weapons at their belts. He thought this odd. *Surely they won't be trying to pretend . . .*

'Found her!' Sisaroth called, his hand on Esmonäe's shoulder. 'Firûsha was just gathering things together. We looked every-where except the cellar.'

'Imagine that,' she carried on. 'I never even heard you both calling.'

Are they really going through with this charade? Tirîgon drew his brows together in a frown. This play-acting was dangerous. What would happen if the groundling worked out what they had done? Or his master, the prince? He needed to speak to the two of them.

'Great. So we can get going. Does this mean provisions are sorted?' Tungdil asked.

'Yes. Our escort is waiting down at the fortress. They'll have everything we've packed – ' Tirîgon attempted to downplay his displeasure.

'No, you're not having any escort. Just you three and me. That's all,' the groundling interrupted him. 'You need to bring enough food for the four of us. If I get hungry on the march you'll find me really nasty company. You've been warned.' He turned round and stomped off.

Esmonäe caught up with the groundling and started chatting, apologising for her flippant underling remark earlier. The two brothers followed behind.

'Have you lost your reason? Have the gods deserted you?' Tirîgon hissed. 'How can you pass her off as our sister? We needed Firûsha's captivating voice.' He indicated Esmonäe. 'She's not going to be any good!'

'Hey, she's your partner. Don't insult her. She's extremely attractive and that'll help,' Sisaroth protested. 'Anyway, you ought to be grateful to me for bringing her along. She'll stop you feeling lonely.'

'Of course she's pretty. But I have no idea what a gâlran zhadar is. How do we know whether or not he'll find her attractive? What if he likes them fat and ugly?' Tirîgon was finding it hard to keep his voice down. *What were they thinking?* 'But singing appeals to every race. Firûsha can even make an óarco's heart melt.'

'Yes, yes, I get it. But the mine maggot was champing at the bit. I didn't want him leaving without us,' Sisaroth snapped. 'We searched the entire palace and couldn't find her. I had to do something.' Sisaroth avoided meeting Tirîgon's eyes. 'Marandëi will tell Firûsha what's happened.'

Tirîgon doubted that this deception would prove useful; it would not help their case to start off negotiations with a failed con-trick. 'I hope it works, for *all* our sakes,' he emphasised, showing Sisaroth he would accept no responsibility if things went wrong.

'You should have taught Esmonäe how to sing instead of diving under the sheets all the time.' His brother tried to lighten the atmosphere, but it sounded more like bitterness and envy.

I get it. You are hurt because she's mine, not yours. 'I can't help it if the älf-woman you freed is so much older than mine,' Tirîgon retorted. 'And we usually don't bother going under the sheets when we make love.'

Sisaroth did not deign to reply.

They went through the west gate of the fortress, collected their provisions and set off, rucksacks on their backs. No horses. No escort. The groundling took the lead. He put on a surprising turn of speed, given how short his legs were.

The quartet took the bridge over the glass sea and passed through the mighty iron portal which opened for Tungdil as easily as it had done for Marandëi. They entered Phondrasôn's warren of tunnels.

Each of them carried a petroleum lamp with the wick shielded so as not to attract beasts. With their excellent eyesight, älfar and dwarf coped well in the half-light.

They initially walked in silence. The groundling showed no interest in conversation. Tirîgon was lost in thought, pondering what he gleaned about the gâlran zhadar race in the few moments he had with Marandëi's books; occasionally he stopped to check their progress on the folding chart acquired by the elves.

Esmonäe had a permanent grin on her face; she was enjoying her actressing role. Sisaroth, unobserved, left marks on the walls.

Tirîgon quietly motioned the other two to his side. 'Do you know anything about this mountain maggot's master?' The groundling glanced over his shoulder but did not bother to find out what they were up to. *He doesn't seem to care about much.*

'Nothing at all.' Sisaroth was surprised by the question. 'If we'd heard of him before, we'd have gone and sought him out.'

Esmonäe shook her head.

'I don't mean that. I mean his race.' Tirîgon could tell neither of them had done any preparation – *no surprise there* – whereas he had consulted the archives, albeit fleetingly. 'One of Marandëi's folios said something about them being easily confused with groundlings. But they're not related at all. They are comfortable with magic and very good with weapons.' He kept his voice low so Tungdil would not overhear. *I expect the sound of his chainmail clinking is louder than my words.* 'It said there used to be just a handful of them in Ishím Voróo.'

'And they steal stuff.' The groundling turned to go down a vertical shaft. The steps jutting out unsupported from the wall did not inspire confidence. Tungdil had to jump the gaps between them. 'I heard you. Ask me anything you like. He is my master. That doesn't mean he's my friend.'

The älfar followed him into the unknown depths of the rock-chimney. The air that streamed up was warm and there was a distinct odour of hot metal ore and molten rock.

Tirîgon checked the chart. *This shaft isn't marked. But I'm pretty sure I've been here before. There should be a wall through here. Maybe Sisaroth was right about things changing.* He put the alteration down to the magic power fields or some trick of the gâlran zhadar's, and resolved to revisit the matter later.

'Watch out,' the groundling called up in warning. 'Miss your step and you're lost. You'd die of thirst before you ever hit the bottom.'

Tirîgon took a look down into the abyss. 'I thought it was all solid rock here.'

'You've got me to look after you. I'm a dwarf. The rocks obey me,' was Tungdil's answer, given in all seriousness.

'What name does your master go by?' Sisaroth took him up on the suggestion that they could ask questions.

'Different ones all the time. That's why I just call him Master. Simpler. The heralds he negotiates with use all manner of names. He seems to have got around in his time.'

'Does he have weaknesses?' While he climbed down, Tirîgon maintained contact with the rough stones of the wall.

'No. Neither in combat nor in magic skills. His sore point is when his things get pinched. He's quite funny about that. Ironic really, seeing as he's constantly helping himself to other people's property.' Tungdil spoke each word with utter contempt.

Can we get the mine maggot on our side against the gâlran zhadar, I wonder? 'Why do you serve him?'

'Because I have to. Same as you will,' Tungdil snapped. 'You'll see what I mean soon enough. There's no alternative. Sinthoras and Caphalor found out to their cost. Do you know of them?'

'Of course,' laughed Esmonäe. 'Did they fight the zhadar?'

Tirîgon vaguely recalled his father once telling him about the exploits of these two commanders. Long before the Tark Draan campaign the famous nostàroi had attacked the fortress of a gâlran zhadar. *Surely it can't be the same one, living down here in Phondrasôn?* 'They killed him, didn't they?'

The groundling nodded. 'Exactly. At least, that's what they thought. He let them escape because he wanted to see where they would take their plunder. By the time he had realised what a danger the demon represented for the whole of Ishím Voróo, it was too late. So he got permission from the Inextinguishables to go to Phondrasôn. That's the story as I know it.'

'Danger?' Sisaroth's insatiable curiosity was wide awake. 'Do you mean the demon who was our ally for a time? And the zhadar knew about the threat?'

'I think our groundling is telling us nice little stories to make himself feel important,' Esmonäe said.

It is the same zhadar his father's companions fought! Tirîgon needed to know more.

'I can only tell you what I heard. I wasn't actually there.' Tungdil had come across a corridor leading off from one of the wide steps. He motioned the others to go past him into it. He leaned back into the vertical shaft to let out a piercing shriek.

There was an answering roar from down below. Golden light started to glow lower down the shaft and grew brighter as it neared.

'We have to get out of here. I've alerted the Grey Amdiu.'

'What's that?' Tirîgon asked.

'A worm-lizard. They come in different colours and sizes. The grey one likes fighting. He hates high notes. I've made sure he'll come and see who's annoying him. He's too fat to fit in this corridor but he's got a very long reach with his tongue.' The groundling jostled past them. 'Get moving, Black-Eyes! We're running for our lives.'

'What did you do that for?' Esmonäe started running with the others.

'To make sure we don't have anyone following us,' was the good-humoured response. 'You lot can creep and you can hide, but you won't escape an amdiu's exquisite sense of smell. Should one of you have instructed the fortress to send an escort, your soldiers are done for.'

He knows his way blindfolded in these mazes and he has the ability to manipulate the rock walls. We need this guy on our side. Tirîgon was losing confidence in his own map. What he wanted was an opportunity to put the groundling in his debt. *Something to make him grateful. Like saving his life.*

They climbed up a copper ladder that led to a vaulted hall.

Without a moment's hesitation, Tungdil took the left-hand door and started singing so loudly that the älfar's ears hurt.

'Can't you stop that?' Esmonäe asked.

'Because you don't care for it?' The groundling gave a belly laugh. 'It was a song a good friend of mine liked to sing. He was called Bavragor, the singing drinker. He only had one eye, just like me.'

'And are you . . . ?' Sisaroth ventured to ask.

'A drinker? Used to be. Phondrasôn could have driven me back to it, but I've been steadfast. Never touch a drop. Important to keep a clear head down here. Danger everywhere, you know.' Tungdil fell silent and his furrowed face was dark.

'I assume the friend is dead?' Tirîgon wanted to keep the conversation going while trying to locate their surroundings on the map. *I've got an inkling I know where we are. But how did we get here? All the paths I know about would have taken much longer.*

'Yes. He died when I made the Fireblade that we used to destroy the mist demon. That was in . . . It doesn't matter.' The groundling looked at Sisaroth over his shoulder. 'Did you tell the others the Inextinguishables are dead and that I made my own weapon out of your Super Black-Eyes' sword?' He tapped the hilt and gave an evil grin.

Tirîgon and Esmonäe laughed and after a short pause, Sisaroth joined in.

'Ah, I see. You don't believe me,' the dwarf said.

He's funnier than I thought he would be. 'How did you come to be roaming round Phondrasôn, then?' Tirîgon wiped the tears of laughter away. 'Do the groundlings send their banished criminals here, too?'

'A mischance. After we had vanquished the Inextinguishables' – Esmonäe burst into gales of laughter again but Tungdil continued unperturbed – 'we had to leave Girdlegard to put a stop to a catastrophe threatening from the Black Abyss. We fought a battle against countless beasts who came storming out, and we beat them back. But a protective shield was set up to cover the entrance. I could not get out in time.' He touched the wall with his strong hand. 'So I'm here, cut off from all my friends. But it won't be forever.'

I've never heard of this Black Abyss; it can't be in Ishím Voróo. Not unless it's a very long way away from Dsôn. But it's another way out of Phondrasôn, if this story is true. Ye gods, how big is this netherworld we're stuck in? In his mind Tirîgon saw the Phondrasôn chart expanding to cover not only the walls and ceiling of the library but the entire palace. 'When was it you met my brother?'

'Ages ago.' He gave a quick résumé and Sisaroth nodded

agreement. 'After that I wandered round and got ambushed by a load of orcs. I would have died if my master hadn't saved my life. I was badly injured by their crossbow bolts.' He brought his tale to a conclusion.

'You serve him because he saved your life.' Esmonäe took some food out of her bag and ate a few mouthfuls.

'And also because he can tell me how to get back to my friends.' Tungdil took a side turn and led them to a cave with an artificial fountain. 'We'll stop here for a rest. You can drink the water and monsters don't come in here. We'll leave one of us on watch.' He took up a position at the right-hand wall where there were small niches to sleep in. There was a fireplace equipped with cooking pots and pans. 'I put down a barrel of black beer if one of you fancies a good hangover?' He grinned and settled himself into the embrasure, without bothering to take off his chainmail or his boots. 'I'm going to have a nap. Make a fire and cook yourself something. Use the red coals. They make the best flames.'

He closed his eyes and folded his hands across his belly, keeping Bloodthirster within easy reach. 'If one of the monsters should come in, though it's very unlikely, will one of you please press that stone over there with the green markings.'

He was soon snoring away.

We don't seem to have any choice but to wait till he wakes up. Tirîgon exchanged looks with Sisaroth and Esmonäe. 'Right. I'll get a fire going.' He went over to the hearth, swept out the ashes and piled the kindling up before lighting it with the wick from his lamp. 'What shall we make?' Then he caught sight of their reflection in the mirror of his lantern.

Sisaroth's hand was on Esmonäe's hip. She smiled at him in

a certain way before turning aside and moving over to where Tirîgon was working. He knew that smile well. It was suggestive.

He pretended not to have seen the exchange but he suddenly knew why his brother had insisted Esmonäe accompany them. *It was nothing to do with having to hurry because of the groundling's impatience.* Tirîgon was not prepared to simply overlook the matter. *I'm going to tell him to keep his hands off her as soon as she's asleep.*

Esmonäe was crouching at his side putting coals on the burning twigs. 'Well done. We can start making the meal now.' The firelight emphasised her enticing looks and the shimmering hair.

Tirîgon bent over and kissed her soft mouth, placing his hand on her thigh and stroking her. 'It was hard having to wait until the groundling went to sleep,' he whispered. 'I hate not being able to touch you whenever I want.'

Esmonäe ran her fingers over his cheek, pulled his face towards her and pressed her lips to his own. 'Let's get over to one of the bunks,' she murmured seductively.

'But what about supper? And Sisaroth?' he objected weakly. The thin curtains would not provide much privacy and any moaning would immediately be heard.

'So what? Your brother can do the cooking. We'll be needing sustenance.' She undid her belt and got to her feet, laying armour and padded tunic aside. 'I want you, now!' She washed her face and hands at the fountain, slipped into one of the bunks and gestured to him.

Tirîgon, after a slight hesitation, followed suit.

Any resistance and inhibition melted away in her arms.

Phondrasôn.

Firûsha drummed her fists against the wall as hard as she could. 'Can anyone hear me? Help! I can't get out!'

At first she had hoped she might be able to loosen some of the stones but she soon had to give up that idea. Kicking had no effect, nor did hurling herself against the wall. She had searched in vain for a hammer or some other kind of tool.

Being stuck was not the worst thing; she was hopelessly lost. The palace was twice as big on the inside as in the normal accommodation.

I can't die here like a rat in a trap! Firûsha cursed and went distractedly back along the slender corridors, sometimes turning sideways to squeeze through. Anyone built more solidly than she was would get jammed.

She was so desperate to get out now that she considered the prospect of finding Marandëi to let her out. Anything, as long as it meant escaping from this prison. She'd be able to come up with some excuse for her presence here. *But I shan't forget what I saw. That altar with the peculiar skull. And those strange incantations . . .*

Suddenly she came up against an unlatched metal grille. She almost fell through it into a chamber.

A diffused light came from overhead. It did not look as if Marandëi had been here recently. Dust lay thick on all surfaces. Firûsha saw a desk with a tilted top; sketches and formulae were pinned to the walls.

What have we got here? She studied the drawings: there were exact representations of the depth of the palace foundations, room dimensions, lists of materials, pillar cross-sections, designs for metal supports, rows of engineering calculations, buttress diagrams, copies of ancient runes . . .

Firûsha came across the plans for a tower.

She couldn't believe what she held in her hands. *By all the gods of infamy. Marandëi erected that prison tower she and Sisaroth were trapped in! No one else built it!* She folded the blueprint and stowed it under the pitiful shreds of her filthy dress. *Something malicious is afoot. She's playing with us, this is a game to her. My brothers will . . .*

'Firûsha!' came a soft friendly voice. 'Where are you?'

She pressed her face against the wall. 'Tirîgon! Here I am! Here!' she shouted, hitting the stones as loud as she could.

'Go along to your right,' she heard the voice say. 'I'll guide you to where the walls aren't as thick.'

'Okay! Please keep talking!' She was so relieved. Now everything would be all right. She ran along, following her brother's instructions – and the floor opened up beneath her feet.

Twisting in her fall, she narrowly missed the long upright floor spikes as she landed. They bore the skeletons of less fortunate intruders.

She rolled to one side, panting hard. She had ended up in a room with no other exit than the shaft she had fallen down. *Another of Marandëi's secret traps for unwanted visitors.*

Firûsha collected some sharp bones to help her climb. She made use of the cracks in the rock and worked her way back up, jamming bones into any gaps that were too small to get a finger hold. The fragile bones protested but held her slight weight.

I'm not due for endingness yet! Bathed in sweat, she crawled back into the design room.

'Firûsha? Are you still there?'

'Yes,' she groaned. She realised now that the voice did not

belong to either of her brothers. *Is it the walls themselves that are speaking? Trying to entice me along to the next death-trap?* Marandëi was a cîanai; she might have put a spell on the walls of the palace. *The first assault failed. What will the next one be?* 'Which way do you want me to go?'

'Follow my signals, sister.' A soft knocking sounded from the other side of the wall.

'I will.' This time Firûsha was more wary. Feeling her way cautiously, she managed to avoid two further traps: poisoned spikes shot up from the ground and blades darted from the wall. The knocking led her from one trap to the next. *You won't get rid of me so easily.*

She heard a loud impact. Dust came raining down on her from the roof. 'You wretched little rat,' the voice raged. 'Why don't you die like all the rest?'

'Because I know you are trying to kill me. I knew you weren't trying to help. Who are you?'

'I am the master of this palace,' the voice said winningly. 'I'm sorry I was so unwelcoming. I thought you were a monster. Nobody has come to visit me for such a long time – apart from Marandëi, of course. She's a good friend. Let us be friends, too, Firûsha. We should get to know each other, face to face. I love the way you sing. When you practise, the sound travels through the stones. Come to me and we'll talk.'

A spirit? A shiver went down her spine. She was not taken in by the change in approach and wanted to find out more about her foe. *I'll pretend to trust him.* 'Where shall I find you?'

'Follow the sounds. Nothing will harm you.'

Firûsha heard a bell. She intended to look carefully at every stone she passed.

She soon started to recognise her surroundings and ended up in front of the trapdoor that led to the opening above the cellar room with the small altar. That was where the sound of the bell was coming from. She could see candlelight.

So it is Marandëi after all, doing her best to make a fool out of me. She went carefully down the steps. 'Where are you?'

'Over here.'

She looked round but could not see anyone in the flickering candlelight. 'Come out of the shadows,' she demanded, thinking the cîanai had concealed herself in a blanket of darkness.

'You are standing right in front of me.'

Firûsha turned to the altar. *The skull?* 'Is it you I'm hearing or am I going mad?' she mouthed.

'No. What you are thinking is correct.' The eye sockets of the decorated skull were black and empty. 'I am the lord of the palace and of the molten glass sea that surrounds the island.'

She knelt down by the altar, fascinated by the skull's appearance. She had no explanation for the misshapen dimensions and she had never seen a forehead as flat as this. *A birth defect?*

'Not at all. My parents went to some trouble to make my skull this shape,' it retorted. 'You can touch me if you like.'

Firûsha did not have the slightest intention of laying a finger on that head. Not until she knew what was happening here in these secret passageways. There was powerful magic streaming out from the artefact; it was making her face tingle. *Whatever it is is pretty potent. I must keep my wits about me.* She examined the carvings, which had without doubt been executed by an älfar craftsman.

Decorating an object to such a high degree of perfection must have taken a considerable time; even at this distance she could see some of the fine detail: pearls were embedded, silver beads, gold leaf. The precious materials were polished to a high sheen. The yellowish tinge and general state of the old skull itself only served to emphasise the splendour of the ornamentation.

What cult does Marandëi follow? 'Tell me what you are,' said Firûsha hoarsely.

'I am everything and anything you desire,' the skull replied in velvet tones. 'I am your fate, and your fortune.' The dark sockets grew larger until they swallowed up Firûsha's entire field of vision. 'I am here to fulfil all your dreams, my child.'

Her temples throbbed and ached, her eyes smarted and her mouth went dry. She blinked and when she looked up she saw the smiling face and dear features of her own mother. There was Ranôria in her favourite black dress with the white embroidery.

'But how . . . ?' Firûsha scanned the room. But it was no longer the cellar room. She was standing in Dsôn Sòmran in her own chamber, looking out past Ranôria and down to the town itself. 'What happened?' There was a spring fragrance of blossoms in the air and the gentle sound of music from outside.

'You just had a bad dream, my darling girl,' her mother reassured her. 'You had a fever and we have been so worried about you.' Ranôria turned to the door and called for Sisaroth and Tirîgon to come. 'Your sister is awake!'

Her brothers hurried into the chamber, one of them in armour, the other in the robes of a priest. They embraced her warmly and she was overcome with joy, sobbing and pulling her family tight to her. 'It was only a bad dream? I'm awake now?'

'Yes, indeed.' Ranôria took half a step backwards and clasped her hands, so that the bone jewelled rings clinked. 'My child, I can't tell you how delighted I am. Let us sing together. The competition is nearly upon us and I want to establish you as my successor. Your voice is my legacy to you.'

'Sing for us, sister,' Tirîgon encouraged her.

'Oh yes, that would be splendid,' Sisaroth urged, clapping his hands. 'Show us what Mother has been teaching you.'

Firûsha felt completely at home. The sounds and smells of her hometown, the sight of her family, that dress, it was all so familiar . . . *How marvellous! I am awake now!* She smiled at her brothers and sang a ballad about homecoming, the joyous celebrations that followed the return.

Hardly had the last note faded when Tirîgon asked for an encore.

Firûsha was flattered and fulfilled his wish; Sisaroth asked for more and she consented graciously. Finally her mother requested a whole song cycle.

One melody gave way to the next. Firûsha did not notice how much time was passing.

All that mattered were the syllables she was forming, the lyrics of the songs, the dynamics and the melodies, the glowing faces of her appreciative audience. She sang and sang and sang until she was near exhaustion.

'I must have a rest,' she finally croaked. 'Can I have a herb tea sweetened with honey for my throat?'

'No, you can't,' roared Tirîgon, grabbing her arm and holding it in a pincer grip. 'Don't stop singing.'

'But I can't,' she protested, crying out when Sisaroth pulled at her other arm.

'Sing!' her second brother insisted menacingly. His fingers hurt like ice cutting through the flesh.

'Mother, help me!' she implored in terror. 'Tell them to leave me alone!'

Ranôria slapped her across the face and her head jerked back; the diadem slipped from her black hair and fell to the floor.

'You ungrateful piece of nothingness,' snarled her mother, grasping her hair and yanking whole tufts out of her scalp. 'Do what we tell you to do!' With her right hand she clasped Firûsha by the chin and forced her to look out of the window. 'Can't you see what is happening? And it's all because you are refusing to sing.'

Firûsha opened her eyes wide: a monster the size of a house, a cross between a human and an óarco, was stamping its way through the city and punching holes in the rooftops, plucking out the residents to hurl them into the depths of the funnel-shaped valley where an abyss had opened up. The beast's victims hurtled screaming to their deaths.

'Only your voice can halt its progress,' Tirîgon whispered in her right ear.

'Only your voice,' muttered Sisaroth on the left.

'Now raise that voice of yours,' their mother said, her smile as lifeless as that of a painted doll, her face motionless as a mask.

Ranôria's black chignon came loose and her hair with the eleven fair streaks fell loose on her shoulders. Her scalp rotted away from her brow to the back of her head, her hair dropping to the floor in clumps. Her ears turned into shrunken beans and fell off. The skin came away from the skull, which shone damp and bloody and before clearing to a white gleam.

Tossàlor stood behind her mother and laughed as he carved designs into her head as Ranôria went on calling for her to sing, sing, sing . . .

Sisaroth and Tirîgon and the dying hordes from Dsôn joined in the shrill plea, torturing Firûsha's soul even more than the sight of her poor, tormented mother.

I have to do it! The young älf-woman opened her mouth to sing. But the sound that she uttered made all the glass in the room shatter.

Tossàlor drew back in horror and drove a needle into Ranôria's brain. She shrieked with pain.

By the gods of infamy! Firûsha attempted to shout her mother's name but could only make the ugliest of sounds.

'What are you doing?' Tirîgon kicked her in the stomach, making her retch.

'Are you trying to kill her?' Sisaroth kicked her, too, striking his sister on the chest.

Ranôria's arms shot up and her hands grabbed Firûsha's face, squashing it with all her might. 'Are you trying to kill me?' she snarled reproachfully. 'Are you trying to kill us all? Dsôn will collapse! The whole city! All because of you!'

This is lunacy! Firûsha threw herself this way and that but could not escape the älfar grip on her arms. 'You are not my family!' She stared at the needle sticking out of her mother's skull. *Tossàlor has never been in Dsôn. I am here, in the cellar, by the altar. I am not at home. Focus, focus.*

Firûsha shut her eyes, pumped her lungs full of air and gave the loudest scream she was capable of. No tune, no words. Just pure, ear-splitting noise.

When her eyes snapped open she recognised the painted and engraved skull in front of her. She was in the small room, kneeling at the altar, her whole body shaking violently. The spell was broken.

But for how long? Before the magic being could address her again, Firûsha seized a candlestick and slammed it into the flesh-less ancient head.

The fragile bone shattered into many fragments. The lower jaw broke in two and yellow teeth rolled out and onto the floor.

'What do you say now?' Firûsha groaned as she went on smashing at the skull until there was nothing left of the eye sockets but a handful of splinters, 'Have I shut you up? Have I made your evil illusions vanish?'

She got to her feet and swayed as she climbed the steps.

The lord of the palace and the glass sea was gone. If it were up to Firûsha, Marandëi would soon be following him.

Chapter III

Arithmetic
can be a demanding branch of knowledge.
One and one
makes two
But one and one
are not one,
they become one.
So it is
that two and one
can only make one.

'Aphorisms' from the epic poem *Young Gods*
composed by Carmondai, master of word and image

Phondrasôn.

Tirîgon woke, sensing Esmonäe was not at his side. He missed
the warmth of her body. *Where has she gone?* He could see the
firelight glow even through his closed eyelids and could hear
stifled laughter. The mood out there seemed to be excellent.

Something told him not to show he was awake. He cracked
an eye open.

The curtain across the sleeping niche had not been fully closed and he could see Esmonäe sitting with Sisaroth by the fire. She was feeding him pieces of bread dunked in sauce. She wiped his lips and sucked her thumb. Sisaroth had his arm round her and the message in his eyes was urgent and clear.

Tirîgon's suspicions were substantiated. He felt rage against his brother. *Who does he think he is?*

It was the norm among his own people that sexual relationships never lasted long. The creator goddess Inàste gave them the gift of immortality; nobody would wish to spend eternity with the same person. However, the moral code dictated that partners stayed true to each other until the end of the relationship was officially agreed upon and declared in front of witnesses. The partner being left should be the first to know.

Tirîgon was not aware of having released Esmonäe from their understanding, and she had never mentioned the possibility of leaving. That meant the partnership was still valid. So what she and his brother were up to was . . .

Well, what is she actually doing? They're good friends, aren't they? Why shouldn't they share a laugh? They're not doing anything wrong.

His reasonable side said he was kidding himself and his emotions demanded that his companion explain her actions.

Tirîgon turned over in bed so as not to be tempted to watch the pair. *Esmonäe isn't doing anything forbidden or morally reprehensible. If anyone's guilty then it's Sisaroth. He knows she and I are an item and yet he's not holding back.*

Tirîgon forced himself to take deep breaths. Tactical thought must take precedence over clamouring emotions and growing indignation. He did not want a confrontation with his brother.

Not during their mission. He was unable to prevent his hand from forming a furious fist. *Self-control. That's what is needed here. Always gets you what you want.*

'Aha, the lovey-dovey black-eyes are having breakfast!' chortled the groundling. There was a metallic clanging sound. Everything about Tungdil was noisy. Even his boots squeaked.

'Hold your tongue!' Esmonäe hissed. 'We were cooking together.'

'Indeed you were. Sibling-love is quite usual among black-eyes, I understand. It didn't do the Inextinguishables much good in the end. Think on that.' Tungdil came and shook Tirîgon by the shoulder. 'Up you get. We need to move on. My master will be waiting.'

Tirîgon feigned waking; he stretched his limbs and then swung his legs over the edge of the bunk.

Sisaroth and Esmonäe were now sitting a good arm's length apart with no hint of the previous intimacy. *I can't see any trace of guilty demeanour.* He jumped to the floor. 'What a night. Don't usually sleep so soundly. Have you two been up long?'

'No,' Sisaroth replied cheerfully.

'But plenty long enough to get breakfast on.' Tungdil went over to the fire and took a look in the pot. 'And long enough to eat it, I see.' He picked up a bowl, spooned himself a hefty portion from the pot and broke off a piece of bread to go with it.

Tirîgon's common sense told him to pretend he saw nothing going on between his brother and his companion. He came over to where they sat. Esmonäe handed him a bowl with a warm smile. A loving smile. *You see? It's all fine.* 'You sound as if there's a big hurry, groundling. Is there a set time we have to be there by?' he asked.

'We shouldn't take too long about it, that's all. Else the palace and the sea will disappear.' Tungdil dipped the bread in the sauce and ate quickly; some of the juices trickled down into his beard. 'It's a security arrangement my master came up with. If anything happens to me on the journey, then you and your headquarters also have an accident. Give a little, take a little.'

Esmonäe frowned. 'What if it isn't our fault? What if you just tripped and fell?'

The groundling grinned, wiping the crumbs from his mouth. 'As I said, if I have an accident, the palace and the sea will go. Look after me well!' He washed his face at the fountain and adjusted his eye patch before stomping off down the passageway.

The trio grabbed their things and followed him.

Tirîgon kept close to Esmonäe, letting Sisaroth go a few paces ahead. Whenever his brother and the groundling went round a corner, Tirîgon kissed her. She always responded passionately. If the group leader had not yelled at them to catch up they would have stayed behind and made love in an alcove somewhere. For him it was heaven to be touching her and inhaling her scent.

She knows I am looking for reassurance, the suspicious, calculating part of his mind insisted, starting to suppress the maddening intoxicating emotions he felt towards the älf-woman. *I must be watchful.*

'You are mine,' he said, kissing her on the forehead, and stroking her shimmering hair.

'Yes, I am,' she answered breathlessly, pressing her body against his.

'Hurry up, the two of you. There's no point trying to find where we are on your precious map. Let's get on,' Tungdil bellowed. His heavy footsteps echoed in the corridor. 'We'll be there soon, anyway.'

Tirîgon grinned. 'Did you hear that?'

'Just as well that's what he thinks we're doing.' She set off, pulling him after her, only letting go of his hand when they reached the corner. Tirîgon was the last of the little band to leave the passage and enter the cave. He put his head back to look up; there was a high wall directly in front of him. He reckoned the height up to the battlements must be about a hundred paces. You could see nothing at all of what was on the far side.

'It goes all the way round,' Tungdil explained. 'It's the outer wall and it's twenty paces thick. But wider still in the foundations, of course.' He indicated the gate over to the right. 'That way. We're nearly there.'

There was only a small space, about an arm's length, between the massive fortification and the cave wall. Tirîgon thought it would be easy to climb. *Like going up a chimney.* He made a mental note of this: a useful strategic advantage should they ever choose to wage a campaign against the gâlran zhadar in the future. *You wouldn't even need ladders or siege engines to get over that.*

'I can see what you're thinking!' laughed Tungdil. He slapped the stones with his broad palm. A thin black surface layer rubbed off. 'Can you see where it's been burned?' What the älfar had thought was black paint was in fact soot. 'If any monsters get the notion to climb the wall, they're met with a burning mixture of pitch, sulphur and petroleum.'

I should have guessed. It couldn't have been that easy. Tirîgon and Sisaroth looked at each other and nodded. 'I can't make out any guards up on the walkway. How do you know if there's anybody down here in this ravine of yours?'

'Magic. Simple. My master has thought of everything, don't worry your little heads.' Tungdil halted in front of the small gate and pressed one of the runes, murmuring a phrase.

The symbol glowed and the heavy door swung open to reveal a dimly lit corridor with a bright light at the far end.

'Onwards and upwards. You'll be meeting my master any time now.' Tungdil waved them on past him, and pulled the gate closed behind them. 'It'll open easily. The wall knows we're allowed through.'

That's like what Marandëi did with the causeways over the glass sea. Tirîgon was aware of the slight tingling that usually meant magic. He guessed it would be a lethal spell that would activate if intruders appeared.

Tirîgon counted thirty paces before they emerged into the open.

What they beheld was more magnificent than any building any of them had ever seen in Dsôn.

The cave itself must be a good ten miles high, he reckoned. And twice that distance in length. A gigantic edifice reared up in the middle of the cavern. It was almost impossible to take in at first glance.

Four square towers a mile high supported a huge construction on the same rectangular principle. On top of each supporting tower was a taller version, twice as high. Above that again a new, larger tower, and a fourth surmounting that one. The lowest of the towers was also the narrowest, bearing twelve times its own weight.

These four edifices were connected by a series of rope bridges which gave the place the appearance of a giant cobweb from this distance.

If the bridges give, each of the towers can be defended as an independent unit, thought Tirîgon. *Very hard to attack.*

Because each of the three upper storeys was wider than the one immediately below it, the castle's defenders could repel a besieging army by raining a veritable hail of missiles down on them.

The clear geometric lines of the design had no superfluous embellishment whatsoever. The walls were stark, grey and forbidding. The massive dimensions would make even trolls and ogres feel small.

If there were a weak point, it would be the relatively slight foundation sections.

It's a miracle it can take the weight. What material did they use to build it, I wonder? The individual towers would have a very high centre of gravity. If a tower could be induced to sway even a little bit, it would eventually collapse.

The cave's light all came from the lower tower windows. The surrounding land was composed of fields and lush meadows; the artificial sunlight even allowed a small forest to flourish.

Esmonäe, Tirîgon and Sisaroth were speechless with wonder but Tungdil did not pause. He was already halfway along the road. 'Come on, hurry up,' he urged them. 'Your nice little palace will be going up in smoke if we don't get a move on.'

'But... this... it's incredible! Impossible, surely!' Sisaroth was impressed. 'Do you see how far up it goes? And those walls must be tremendously thick, or they'd give way.' Tirîgon saw him stretch out to take Esmonäe's hand, but he thought better of it and pretended he was brushing dirt off his tunic instead.

Esmonäe stumbled, her eyes fixed on the top of the towers. 'Who will have helped him build these towers? Where does he keep his slaves?'

Tirîgon stepped to her side and observed the cultivated fields. *Advanced agriculture. They won't be lacking good food.* 'The slaves will be in one of the towers.'

'My master prefers not to have many creatures near him. He is very retiring and he keeps to his quarters at the top.' Tungdil called, pointing to the towers and slowing down to allow them to catch up. 'He resides in the one at the back. If you like, I'll show you how the towers differ from each other. Just in case you decide to attack the castle one fine day,' he said scornfully. 'The other three are subdivided. That one on the right houses an óarco who's a whole lot cleverer than any black-eyes. In this one here there's a being too weird to be given a name and in the tower on the left there's a long'un. You'd probably call him a barbarian.'

Esmonäe paused to take a draught from her flask. 'Why do they live here? Are they allies of his?'

The groundling chuckled. 'No. The Master doesn't have allies. He has slaves to serve him or creatures that earn their daily bread. The three I mentioned are all mercenaries and the armies they lead are accommodated in the towers. There's a specially trained and specially equipped regiment assigned to each of the caverns. The Master has a fleet, too. He conquered whole marine empires. The ships were taken apart and stored in the towers.'

They were only a few miles off now and the towers were looking more impressive than ever.

And there I was, making my little plans to invade and vanquish. Tirîgon could not imagine how one would begin to defeat this place. *Without using magic, that is. That and the support of the gods of infamy.*

The gålran zhadar's towers would spew out thousands and

thousands of warriors. *They will have their own stables, their own forges and workshops to make siege equipment.*

Tirîgon's troops – infantry and cavalry – numbered four hundred in total. Until Tungdil had turned up, Tirîgon had thought Marandëi would be their secret weapon.

We are a ridiculous little band compared to what they have here in these towers. He was furious to have to discard his dream of a Phondrasôn ruled by himself and his siblings.

'Down in the basements, in the foundations, is where the slaves for menial tasks are kept. Then in the next block above that, we have the basic soldier ranks and associated workshops and stables. The third block unit is for the elite troops. The masters reside in the top units. They like to have plenty of space.'

Sisaroth glanced at his brother. 'I told you right at the start we should get out of Phondrasôn.' He pointed to the colossal buildings, where great flocks of birds were wheeling. Mist from the meadows swirled round the foot of the towers so the tops seemed to float in the air. 'Our warriors are nothing in comparison. We aren't building an empire.'

Are you trying to show me up in front of Esmonäe? 'You're right. Tell me again how many exits you've found that lead to Dsôn?' he snapped, as they slipped into the cool fog. 'Which of us would you say has had more success so far?'

Sisaroth opened his mouth to reply but thought better of it.

He couldn't think of an answer that would make him look good. Under cover of the rising mist he reached for Esmonäe's hand and pressed it.

After a short march Tungdil led them inside one of the towers. They stepped into a lift operated by a slave; it pulled them up through the edifice.

Ropes rolled up over pulleys. Tirîgon was impressed. The mechanism recalled the cabin gondolas in use in Dsôn.

They alighted and had to go the rest of the way on foot. The steps were broad, but there was no handrail or wall to hold onto. The stairs led over the top of the lift shaft. If you slipped you would fall all the way to the bottom.

At the end of the stairs there was a lobby enclosed by gates the width of a barbarian. Tungdil touched runes once more to gain access.

Tirîgon's mood was growing darker and darker. At the outset he had believed they had a chance at victory against the gâlran zhadar, but all optimism was now in dust and ashes.

The groundling brought them to a room on the outer wall of the fourth block. 'Wait here. I'll come back with my master.' Tungdil left the room via a different door.

Tirîgon's despondency did not last. He looked through the rounded window, examining every aspect of what he saw in search of vulnerabilities. *Tungdil could be an ally; a useful idiot who could turn traitor and open the towers for us. We'd need more älfar. We must get our army numbers up to a thousand at least. Then we might succeed.*

He could feel his brother's eyes on him. Sisaroth was shaking his head. *He knows me too well.* Tirîgon decided to save his snide remark for later because Tungdil was coming back in. With company.

The gâlran zhadar stood next to the groundling. His squat body was strongly muscled and his forearms were thick from heavy work. He wore an extravagantly ornate breastplate of dark red metal with brilliant white palandium inlay over a padded black tunic to protect him from cold and from blows.

'My guests.' He greeted them in a sinister-sounding voice as deep as any troll's. His short black hair shone as if dressed with wax. Hair from his sideburns was long enough to reach his chest. His face had more wrinkles and furrows than Tungdil's – even the silver headband did not distract attention from that. He looked at them genially. 'Let's get our business over with quickly. My dinner is waiting, and I'm sure you'll be wanting to get back home.' He gestured to the empty armchairs and took a seat at the head of the table. He had a leather folder in his left hand and extracted a document from it. Tungdil remained at the window.

I wonder how I'm supposed to address him? We forgot to ask. Tirîgon noticed the scent the gâlran zhadar was wearing. It reminded him of home, of his father and the incense they used to burn to the gods of infamy and to Inàste.

Esmonäe spoke first. She tested the gâlran zhadar with a delightful smile. 'Do forgive us for not being appropriately dressed for our audience. Your messenger brought us through the filthiest tunnels he could find.'

'That was what he was supposed to do,' the gâlran zhadar replied, his manicured hands placed flat on the table top. They could have belonged to a scholar or a scribe, rather than to someone who could strangle an ogre with his bare hands. He waited until they were all seated and surveyed the group. 'There they are, our triplets. They're not quite as similar as I had expected.'

I knew he'd be difficult to fool. Why did I agree? Tirîgon stayed calm. *Perhaps it's not too late to explain.* He thought it would be better not to appear confrontational right from the start. 'Do you know . . .'

But Sisaroth was nodding. 'Yes, my brother and I are

practically identical but with Firûsha, the gods must have thought it better just to make her beautiful.'

Esmonäe's smile became more charming than ever.

Tirîgon clamped his jaws shut. Now the lie was out there and could not be traversed. 'What have you heard, then, sir, about us three, the älfar triplets?'

The gâlran zhadar sat upright in his chair, his piercing gaze fixed on Tirîgon. 'That you have made yourselves a little kingdom on an island and that älfar from all over Phondrasôn are flocking to you. I was surprised how quickly you managed to conquer the various caves and hold them.' He inclined his head in acknowledgement of this achievement, the diamonds on his silver circlet flashing cold fire. 'And I will point out that the preferred form of address is *Master*.'

Sisaroth stressed that the empire-building had been his brother's work. 'I draw up the maps.'

'Excellent. And Firûsha, of course, sings to keep the troops happy?' The gâlran zhadar opened the leather folder and took out several sheets of paper. 'I have detailed things you may need,' he said, passing the pages to Tirîgon. 'I'll see that you get them.'

Astonished, Tirîgon skimmed the lists of provisions, pack animals and mounts, weapons, items of equipment. 'But why? We've already got most of this.'

'Oh, come on!' A look full of pity. 'Your tribute vassals won't have delivered their best quality, now will they? You won't know the difference, of course, so they can diddle you. I can supply the finest range of hard-wearing armour and the sharpest sword blades. Your small army will be unbeatable. And it is also *my* army. You will be under my command.' He jerked his thumb towards Tungdil. 'He's my top blacksmith. No one can work with metals like he can. He is at your disposal if you wish. I can cope without him for a bit.'

Tirîgon felt he was taking part in alliance talks between equals – except for that reference to the fact they would be under his command. *Play along with it for now. Perhaps he'll reveal his true intentions.* 'Fine by us.'

'You are too gracious, Master,' Esmonäe said swiftly.

'Never. Ask Tungdil.' The gâlran zhadar laughed coldly. 'If I were gracious, I'd let the three of you carry on what you're doing. But you omitted to come and pay your respects and present your claim to the caves.' He extracted further pages. 'Here I have drawn up a list of the conquests you have made that have not been sanctioned by myself.' He glanced over his shoulder. 'Tell them what the penalty for transgression is, Tungdil.'

'Extermination, Master,' the groundling announced in bored tones.

'Or you buy your way out.' The gâlran zhadar clapped his hands once. 'You have seen that your deeds have placed you in a serious position. You have been in my realm for a considerable time; the fees, together with their compound interest, amount to more than you will be able to pay.' He inserted a sly pause. 'Well, with coin or treasure, at any rate. But you can settle your debt in the form of service.'

The älfar exchanged looks. Sisaroth was poleaxed by the turn negotiations had taken. Esmonäe looked confused.

Now we're getting to it. 'I can't imagine there's anything you need doing that you can't do yourself,' Tirîgon eventually responded. 'We saw the power that was unleashed when the magic brooch exploded.'

The gâlran zhadar tapped a forefinger on the table

thoughtfully. 'I won't deny that there is much I am capable of. But sometimes one can benefit from the skills of others. For example, a smith like Tungdil, who forges exceptionally good weapons. Or the fighting prowess of an älf like yourself, when sending an army would arouse suspicion. Oh yes, and there's always the artistry your race excels at: your gift of song. Nobody can sing like the älfar.' He smiled. 'I think you get my meaning.'

'Not quite.' Sisaroth leaned forward. 'Do you want us to kill someone?'

'You creep in the shadows, you bring darkness, and you instil fear in others. You can slip past guards unnoticed, kill silently, and leave no traces; no one will see you unless you wish to be seen,' he went on. 'If you carry out the tasks I give the three of you, without complaint, you may keep your nice little älfar realm. You will only have to pay for the supplies I provide.'

Tirîgon felt a surge of anger that he knew was unwise. Nobody had ever spoken to him in this manner before. He was being demoted to the status of a vassal! All the battles he had fought, all the enemies he had killed, all the victories he had won were as naught to this gålran zhadar. A hot tugging sensation on the skin indicated the lines of fury were spreading across his face.

'Before any of you says something you may have cause to regret,' the gålran zhadar said charmingly, 'take your time. Chew over your words. Swallow them rather than spitting them out.'

'The thing is . . .' Sisaroth started.

'The thing is that you are *not* in one of your Dsôns. You are in *my* domain! Your so-called Inextinguishables brought disaster to their own empire and half of Ishím Voróo with their insatiable greed. *That* is why I will never allow an älf to rule Phondrasôn. Understand?' His genial mask had fallen away to an expression of distaste. 'You are arrogant like the rest of your race. You are power-hungry. Look how far it has got you!'

'But surely it is that same lust for power that made you ruler of this underworld,' contradicted Esmonäe. 'Why are you any whit better than us?'

The gålran zhadar sprang to his feet and slammed his hands down on the table. The circlet on his forehead flashed and lightning bolts shot out of his fingertips, snaked across the table and struck the girl.

Esmonäe cried out and lifted her arms to defend herself. She seemed not to have suffered.

'I can easily expel magic with many times that force; nothing but ashes would remain,' he growled. 'I will not tolerate resistance that has neither thought nor content. I am the ruler here and you are the subjects. My leigemen. Dependent on my good will. Dependent on the grace of your master,' the gålran zhadar bellowed. 'If you serve me loyally and well, I will show you how to get out of the labyrinth. But you have to work for it.' He sat down and waited.

Tirîgon put his arm round his companion and looked to see if she was harmed.

'I'm all right,' she breathed, trying to look normal. Her chestnut brown eyes were full of shock.

Sisaroth cleared his throat. 'Excuse me . . . you actually know the way out?'

'Yes.'

'But you are still here?'

'Because this is where I wish to be. I have everything I need. You and your siblings have not yet learned of Phondrasôn's advantages. If you carry out all the assignments I set, I'll take you back to Dsôn Sòmran. Or to Tark Draan. Whichever you prefer.'

'Would we each be able to choose our own destination?' Sisaroth was enthusiastic at the prospect.

'Of course.'

Tirîgon looked at his brother. 'What do you mean?'

'I just wanted to know. Hypothetical question.' Sisaroth wouldn't make eye contact.

'Each of you can choose a place outside Phondrasôn and you can take as many companions with you as you like.' The gâlran zhadar placed his hand on his chest where his heart would be as a symbol of the oath he was swearing.

'Accepted, then,' said Sisaroth.

Esmonäe nodded. 'It's a deal.'

Tirîgon felt the two of them had rushed into an agreement and was about to protest.

'It's not a business deal. It's a bonus I will grant you when you have done what I demand and served me for the duration I see fit.' He leaped to his feet. 'I'm off to have my meal while you start on the first task. Tungdil will show you where you can sleep and he'll explain what needs to be done. We'll meet again on your return. You are all to address me as Master when you speak to me; I'll pardon you for getting it wrong today.' The gâlran zhadar hastened out of the room, ignoring Tirîgon's call.

'So the black-eyes are to learn how to serve.' Tungdil came over, smiling. 'How does it feel when you have to swallow your pride? Have you choked?'

'I'd ask you the same question,' Tirîgon threw back at him.

'It was easy,' he answered, lowering his voice, 'because I made a vow that I'd kill him at the very first opportunity. Try it. It's a lovely thought.'

He's not acting. That urge to kill is real enough. Now Tirîgon was absolutely convinced Tungdil could be won over as an ally. *I shall kill the gâlran zhadar. And I'll take over his empire. That will be my bonus.*

Phondrasôn.

Firûsha had taken the tall candlestand out of the chamber with her and dragged its heavy base along the floor as she struggled, famished and exhausted, through the corridors. She was not even aware of the metal scraping noisily on the tiles. She stumbled along in a daze. She had hardly any voice left from shouting for help. *No one's ever going to find me. That skull put a curse on me before I smashed it to pieces.*

From time to time she allowed herself a short rest, and once she stopped to drink water she found running down a wall. She did not care where it came from. It tasted of decomposing grass and slate but it slaked her thirst.

She did not know exactly when Marandëi's infuriated and despairing scream had rung out, but it must have been when she discovered the shattered artefact she worshipped.

It does not matter. At least she can't do us any more damage with the skull. Firûsha pounded the wall. The candlestand broke in two. *She can't harm my brothers, that is. It looks as if I shall be the new palace ghost.*

'Is someone there?' It was an älfar voice coming from the far side of the wall.

'Yes,' she croaked. She swallowed to moisten her throat and repeated the word louder this time. 'Who's there?'

'It's Tossàlor. And who is that behind the wall?'

'Firûsha! Firûsha! Break it down, do you hear?' She leaned against the stonework and wept with relief. Her tears coursed down the wall in dark lines. 'Hurry! I've got to get out of here. Please help me! Can you find my brothers . . . ?'

'They're not here. Wait. I'll get Crotàgon. He'll be strong enough,' he said.

She waited in the silence.

Found! At last! Firûsha sank down to the floor and fell into a half-sleep. The broken candlestand rolled on the ground.

She did not wake up until a hole was hammered through the wall. Two strong arms reached through, picked her up and pulled her out of her prison. She was carried to a couch where she looked around in dazed bewilderment.

She seemed to be in Tossàlor's studio, a place strictly off limits to visitors. *Well, at least I'm getting to see his workshop.*

Tossàlor in a purple robe, and Crotàgon in a black tunic, stood side by side with worried expressions on their faces. Her fencing master passed her a goblet of water and then brought her a platter with bread, cheese, fruit and some cooked meat spread with a savoury paste.

Thank the gods of infamy! I'll eat it all. Every last morsel! Firûsha drank her fill and started shovelling food in as fast as she could. She could not tell them what had happened until her hunger was satisfied.

Neither Tossàlor nor Crotàgon tried to make her talk. They waited patiently. Crotàgon put a blanket round her shoulders. It was obvious that she had suffered.

The room they were in had open shelves for storing the bones the artist had been collecting on his expeditions with Sisaroth.

These were carefully graded and grouped according to size, shape and hue. There was a cupboard with a label stating it contained teeth; another held samples of hair.

Firûsha recalled hearing that Tossàlor never painted or dyed the bones he used; he had discovered other races here in Phondrasôn whose skeletons were different colours due to the type of food they ate. Sisaroth had permitted him to use the dungeon cells in the palace to keep captives he fed specially prepared diets: algae, plants or insect chitin was ground to powder and mixed with their food. When Tossàlor judged the bones had attained the desired shade, he killed the prisoner and extracted their skeleton. For art, of course.

Firûsha was no longer bolting her meal, but chewing slowly. She scrutinised the meat with its paste layer. *I wonder if this will make my bones change colour?*

Tossàlor's true speciality, though, was carving. Occasionally he would show Tirîgon how he went about his craft: cutting the finest of details without damaging the integrity of the bone. Various tools were hanging on the walls, but she could only hazard guesses as to what their particular uses might be.

'You were half-starved,' said Tossàlor, stroking her matted, filthy hair. He went over to the gaping hole in the studio wall and poked his head through. 'I'd really like to hear how you got in there,' he said, returning to her side. 'That corridor doesn't look as if it just happened by chance. It's been specially constructed, surely?' His eyes narrowed. 'I know you don't like me because of what I did that made them banish me to Phondrasôn. Were you in there spying on me, maybe? To make sure I'm not up to my old habits?'

'What?' Firûsha washed the final mouthful of food down

with a swig of water. She had definitely been eating far too fast. Her stomach was protesting, but she felt the energy flooding back into her. At last she could collect her thoughts. 'I . . . got in there by mistake, pure chance. When the palace was built, they constructed a second one within the first. But there's no way out once you're in.' She was reluctant to let on about the altar room until she had spoken to her brothers. *These two don't have to know the whole story.* 'Thank you. If you had not heard me, I would have starved. It was driving me mad to be able to smell the food cooking in the kitchen.' She gave them both a grateful smile.

The thought occurred to her that the decorations on the skull might possibly have been Tossàlor's handiwork. *He's certainly capable of exquisite ornamentation like that.* She stopped feeling quite so grateful. *Did he and Marandëi have some kind of a pact? Or maybe he carried out her commission without knowing what it would be used for?*

Crotàgon brushed the cobwebs and dust off his robe. 'You need to get cleaned up. I'll take a look at this second world behind the wall.'

'No, don't do that. You'd never get through the passages. In places it's really narrow. Your shoulders are too broad.' Firûsha had a mental picture of the muscular älf getting wedged in or falling prey to one of the many traps she had avoided. 'I need to tell my brothers. Where are they?'

'A messenger turned up and they went off with him.' Tossàlor sat down in a wobbly armchair and Crotàgon leaned against a table that bore a row of skulls with the tops drilled off. They would be used as wind chimes; Firûsha was familiar with the kind of souvenirs soldiers liked. Thin sheets of painted bones and pieces of silver were fastened together with plaited hair.

'What messenger was that?' Her eyes darted from one to the other. Crotàgon told her what had occurred while she had been the unwilling prisoner of the palace's walls. 'So someone is claiming the right to rule Phondrasôn?'

'The bit we are in, at least. Let's hope your brothers are level-headed enough not to declare war against the gålran zhadar. We'd never win.' Tossàlor picked up a small bone and fiddled with it nervously. 'Marandëi has some old writings about the gålran zhadars that I've read. Nasty pieces of work, the lot of them.'

'The explosion that blew the gates off their hinges will mean some difficult repair work.' Crotàgon looked out of the window. 'Parts of the bridge have been damaged and we'll have to post extra troops at the entrance until the gate's been replaced ...' He broke off and stood up slowly, his brown eyes filled with horror and disbelief. He was staring out of the window. 'I don't believe it! The sea has solidified!'

Tossàlor turned his head.

Can it be true? Firûsha got up from the couch to look.

The raging waves of liquid glass they were used to seemed to have turned to ice. Under the bridges, the surface was flat and the red glow had faded.

All the heat is draining out of it. 'Another gålran zhadar trick?' Firûsha saw one of the palace guards running to the castle, probably to find them and report the phenomenon. On the battlements, soldiers stood around in groups, staring incredulously.

'Perhaps the underground fire that kept the glass molten has been extinguished,' suggested Tossàlor. 'Curses! If I'd known that was going to happen I'd have made sure I had a good store of glass bones. They're popular with everyone. It's not only our people that collect them.' He gestured to the strange seascape. 'I can't make anything now with that the way it is.'

'I'm much more concerned about our security. Enemies can reach the island from anywhere now, without having to use the bridges. The stupidest of monsters might take it into their heads to try their luck.' Crotàgon was already considering the strategic implications. 'If the surface of the glass cools down to the point where it's safe to walk on, we'll have lost our decisive defence factor.'

'But we still have the fortress.' Firûsha looked at her mentor. *Perhaps it was nothing but a passing whim of Nature.*

'The fortress can withstand a preliminary attack. But remember what kind of monsters abound here.' Crotàgon folded his arms and turned to her. 'What shall we do, Firûsha?'

A shiver went down her spine when she realised that with her brothers both absent, she would be expected to take command. She had made good progress with her military training but she had no idea how to organise the island's defences. *I have no choice. Where are my brothers when they're so badly needed?* She seemed fated to have to cope on her own.

'An attack by a horde of monsters would be just the trick! I want a lot of long thighbones for my next project. I'm almost out.' Tossàlor went to check one of the shelves. He was in his creative mode again and blind to wider issues.

I'm pretty sure I can do it. I'll take responsibility. 'We should start by closing all the gates and trebling the guard on the northern side,' she said after a moment's consideration. She noticed Crotàgon's expression of approval. 'That should do for the present.'

'Good call. I agree.' Crotàgon nodded. 'I'll get the command passed round. Oh, and don't worry about singing for your training today, Firûsha. I'll let you off this once . . .'

The workshop door crashed open.

Marandëi crossed the threshold with her staff in her right hand. On her left palm she held out fragments that she hurled at Firûsha's feet. 'It was you. I know it was!' she shrieked. Her grey dress was streaked with dirt from the secret passageways. 'You stole him!' Her pale eyes filled with tears as she stared at Firûsha with contempt and hatred. 'If we weren't all bound by the oath, I swear by the infamous gods and by Samusin that I would kill you for this!'

'Nobody is killing anybody round here!' Crotàgon thrust himself in front of Firûsha to protect her. As he did so, fragments of bone crunched under his right foot. 'Explain yourself! What do you mean by this unacceptable conduct?'

Marandëi had spotted the hole in the wall. 'So that's how you escaped!' She pointed the silver tip of her staff at Firûsha. 'You have absolutely no idea the consequences of what you have done. The sea will harden and all the heat will be lost. The palace will be destroyed. The entire cavern will cease to exist!' She wagged her forefinger accusingly at the girl. 'It can only be rectified by your sacrifice!' The cîanai turned and stumbled out of the room, distraught.

Crotàgon could hardly believe it. 'Marandëi *knew* about the other corridors?'

'Yes,' she muttered, cowed. *What can I tell them?* She was reluctant to give more specific information.

But her trainer insisted. 'She was storing something that you found and have now destroyed?'

Tossàlor bent down to examine the splintered fragments,

turning them in his hand, examining the patterns and shapes that were still visible. He picked out a couple of pearls from the handful of fine debris. 'I've only ever heard tell of this in tales!' He was enthusiastic. 'Was the skull a strange shape? Quite long? And flat at the front?'

'Yes. And yes,' she conceded. *He knows about it!*

Excited and yet horrified at the same time, Tossàlor groaned. 'Oh ye gods of infamy! It *was* long and flat. But now . . .' He dropped the fragments he was holding. 'It's lost forever.'

'So what was it?' Crotàgon asked impatiently. 'How could some old bones manage to control the glass sea?'

Firûsha was afraid of what Tossàlor was going to say. But she told herself that she was free of guilt. *It was destroy or be destroyed. Or be driven crazy, like Marandëi.*

The artist's tone was heavy with significance as he dropped to his knees and brushed all the pieces into his hand. 'That,' he said, 'used to be the skull of a god. One of the gods of infamy.'

Chapter IV

A fire
  I can extinguish
A heart
  I can stop
But a feeling
  can unsettle me
Who has the greater power here?

'Aphorisms' from the epic poem *Young Gods*
composed by Carmondai, master of word and image

Phondrasôn.

Tirîgon woke with a start, for the same reason as before:
Esmonäe was not there. *Again.*

He sat up and looked around the room the groundling had
assigned them. The Zhadar, as they called him, rather than using
the hateful title of Master – was permitting them to refresh
themselves before embarking on the first of the duties they were
to carry out. The way Tungdil had explained it, it was going to
be relatively easy. Too easy, perhaps. Suspiciously easy.

But that was not what was worrying Tirîgon.

Where has she gone? At the back of his mind the answer was clear, but he did not want to jump to conclusions. There was more than one reason why she might have left the room. *Perhaps she's exploring the fortress?*

In spite of his determination not to act hastily, his jealous heart forced him out of the comfortable bed. Sensibility lost to emotion yet again.

Throwing on a robe, he left the room to look for her.

There was no guard on duty. The Zhadar had put no restrictions on their free movement within the fortress, making clear that he had other means to guarantee security and that he was not afraid of these älfar visitors.

Tirîgon stole along the corridor, past windows that showed how high above ground level they were; he could see slaves working the brightly lit fields, irrigating the crops, tending the fruit trees, or driving a herd of cattle across the meadows to the shade of a small wood.

Even if he did not want to find out that his fears might be true, he found himself standing in front of the accommodation that Sisaroth had been given.

He hesitated, and then placed his hand on the latch, his muscles tensing.

If I open the door and find her with him, my life will never be the same again. And the change won't be for the better. I would have nothing but contempt for them both. I'd have to leave the palace, or send them away, and our new empire would fall apart. He stared at his hand. *What's more important?*

He slowly drew his hand away. He did not enter to have his suspicions confirmed.

Mentally he went one step further still: he would ignore any hint of an illicit affair unless they made it obvious. Esmonäe had not officially thrown away their relationship and he would not give her up. His desire for her was too strong for that.

That will be best. The alternative means wrecking my dream. He turned on his heel, went back to his room and tried to sleep. It did not work. He stayed awake and troubled until Tungdil knocked.

'Half the sand has gone through the time-glass. Get up, Black-Eyes! The others are up already.'

Tirîgon leaped out of bed, put on his armour and left the room. Theoretically that information was evidence she had spent the night with his brother. *Or maybe it wasn't. I didn't actually see them in bed together. She could have slept elsewhere.*

Esmonäe and Sisaroth were at the door, armed and ready to go.

'My brother the Sleepyhead,' Sisaroth joked. 'Firûsha and I have been discussing how best to carry out the Zhadar's mission.'

'Welcome to his army of unwilling servants,' the groundling said bitterly. 'But it should be worth your while because I'm making you the most perfect weapons and armour you can imagine. The dwarves have always been the very best smiths, and I am the best of them all.' He stomped off and the trio followed him to the lift.

'Did you make your own armour?' Tirîgon enquired, exchanging a loving smile with Esmonäe; he pretended not to have noticed that she had left his bed.

'Of course. And I'm currently working on my most advanced project. The Master has shown me some magic formulae for strengthening the armour. You can do it during the forging process. I'm still perfecting the technique, but I've had quite a bit of success so far.' He stepped into the cabin, waited for the others to get in and then sent the lift downwards. 'He thinks he's the only one to get the benefit of my skill, but I'm not having that. He should come up with his own ideas and sweat at the anvil like I do. He's not short of free time.'

Tirîgon was astonished at how the groundling spoke so openly of his dislike. 'Aren't you worried he'll kill you if he finds out how you feel about him?'

'No. He needs me. Like he needs you. We are better at certain tasks than he is.' They had reached the bottom level now. They stepped out of the lift to head across the rough ground to the other gate.

From time to time Tirîgon turned round. Not to watch Esmonäe and Sisaroth but to look at the towers from the new perspective. The groundling was not the only one to have rebellious thoughts. *But it must wait. It would have to be carefully planned.*

They went through the defence ramparts and Tungdil led them to a broad tunnel on the other side. 'Keep straight. You know what you have to do.' He turned to go.

Sisaroth caught him by the arm. 'Not so fast. How are we going to get back in?'

'We'll see you coming.' Tungdil's one eye glared at the hand on his sleeve. 'Touch me again, Black-Eyes, and Bloodthirster will split your arm from the shoulder down to the little finger. We may all be obliged to serve the same master, but that doesn't make us friends. I hate your race for what you have done to us in the past and I don't trust you.' Then he left.

Well, he made his point. Stubborn. But straightforward.

Tirîgon looked at his brother. 'Tell me the plan the two of you came up with while I was asleep.'

'The Zhadar is testing us with the task he's given.' Sisaroth seemed to want to change the subject. 'We don't really need a plan as such.'

'We get to the area, sneak through their defences and steal the barbarian leader's chain,' Esmonäe said. 'All we have to do is bring it back and we've shown the Zhadar that we're reliable.'

Tirîgon forced a smile. *You weren't discussing anything at all. You were all over each other.* 'And that's why you got up so early? I thought you were sorting out all the details.' It was meant as a joke but it fell rather flat. Now that Tungdil had gone, he could not help himself. He went up to his companion and embraced her, kissing her tenderly on the mouth. 'I missed you when I woke this morning,' he said, twisting a shining strand of her hair around his finger.

'I hadn't been gone long,' she replied, pressing her body against his. 'We should get going. The sooner we complete the task, the better the Zhadar will like it.' She ran off.

Tirîgon deliberately avoided looking at his brother, so that Sisaroth would not catch the jealousy in his gaze. He did not want proof that they were going behind his back, that she was lying to him. 'She doesn't take the mission seriously.'

'Nor do I, really. It's not much of a challenge, is it? The barbarians won't be expecting us.' Sisaroth moved off. 'It'll be a walkover.'

'Do we know anything about this chain we're supposed to steal?' Tirîgon was looking for snags. 'Tungdil said nothing.'

'It's just some chain or other,' Esmonäe called back blithely.

'Probably some frippery dedicated to the gods. Or perhaps it's a gift. Stop worrying.' She ran her hands over her breastplate. 'Do you think the Zhadar will let me keep this if I ask nicely?'

Sisaroth laughed and moved to catch up with her, touching her elbow as if by accident.

Tirîgon had a different view of the Zhadar's intentions. *There'll be a reason behind this thievery. The chain won't just be a piece of jewellery.* The self-appointed overlord of all Phondrasôn was cruel and kept an army that could sweep away all resistance and force others to do his bidding. *If he really wants that chain, he has a wealth of resources to get it. He could even send the barbarians one of his exploding brooches. But no, he's sending three älfar he doesn't know. There's something fishy here.* Tirîgon determined to stay vigilant. 'In my opinion, we do need a plan. Let's see what it looks like when we arrive.'

It was a long march; they slid down inclines and crossed fields and forests before climbing a stairway of a thousand steps. At the top was a broad corridor with a sharp right-hand bend an arrow's flight ahead.

Before they got to the corner they heard voices: men talking quietly to each other.

'Guards,' mouthed Esmonäe.

Sisaroth crept forward to spy round the corner, then waved the others up. 'It's very odd,' he whispered.

Tossàlor would love it. Tirîgon saw five barbarians standing in front of a primitive grating. They were armed to the teeth. The only vulnerable point would be their heads. They had circular hauberks over the shoulder, neck and lower face, but from the eyes up they were unprotected.

But the men seemed to have scalped themselves! The skull

was bare bone from the top of the ears. Somehow they had removed the skin and prevented it from growing back.

Perhaps they used some kind of alchemical tincture. Tirîgon noted metal inlay, painted sections, and symbols carved into the skull bone, presumably indicating the wearer's status. *We're used to tattoos but this is new to me. Must be a special Phondrasôn thing.*

'It's a good thing Tossàlor didn't come, too. He'd walk straight up and invite them all back to his to find how they've done it.' Sisaroth checked them out again. 'Armour is simple enough. Bronze, I think. Soft metal. Should be like butter to cut through.' He looked at the other two. 'Who wants to go first?'

Esmonäe put herself forward. 'Let me show you what I'm capable of!' Drawing both of her daggers from the scabbards on her back, she ran forward, enveloped in a cloak of älfar darkness.

The barbarians were leaning on their spears, chatting away, obviously not expecting trouble.

One of them was telling a story of some kind, gesticulating wildly. Esmonäe confronted him, slipping out of the shadows she wore as if emerging from black water that pearled off her, reluctant to let go. Plunging one blade horizontally into his neck and the tip of the second dagger through his companion's ear, Esmonäe released her hold on the knife hilts and snatched the soldiers' own daggers out of the sheaths they wore.

She smiled and stepped forward to deal with the remaining three barbarians. She cut the eyes of one, rammed a dagger into another's open mouth, and kicked the third so hard that she sent him flying into the wall. Whipping around, she killed the barbarian she had blinded by pushing the sharp blade through a gap in his armour.

She picked up a spear and flung it at the last survivor.

The weapon crashed through the hauberk and left him dead.

Unbelievable. It had all happened so quickly; Sisaroth doubted he could compete with her speed. Not even Tirîgon could have outperformed her. Not one of the guards had been able to utter a shout of warning. The only noise had been the sound of the armour on stone as they fell. The brothers hurried over.

Esmonäe withdrew her own daggers and wiped the blood off on her victims' clothing. As she did so, she checked the corpses for valuable items. 'Satisfied?' She gave a happy smile, her eyes gleaming with excitement at the success of her deadly mission. Her soul thirsted for further bloody deeds.

'Very,' replied Sisaroth, giving her a kiss on the top of her head. 'You make an excellent *sister* for us.' They both laughed.

It should have been me giving her the praise. And the kiss. 'Well done,' Tirîgon muttered. He stared straight ahead through the railings. There was another stretch of corridor behind it that led into a brightly lit cave.

He opened the gate and stole up to the entrance.

After all the time he had now spent down here, he thought he had seen everything Phondrasôn had to offer in the way of caves, caverns, hollows, tunnels, shafts, corridors and holes.

But what he saw now was completely new.

An uneven floor of basalt tiles dipped away at his feet. The spaces between the mosaic-like stones were as fine as horsehair. A trodden path indicated the way the barbarians were wont to take.

Animal carcasses and barbarian corpses lay scattered everywhere. At the lowest point of the cave, in the centre, there was a pile of decomposing remains emitting a foul stench.

On the opposite side of the mass grave, a good half-mile from the entrance, winding paths climbed the steep incline and led to a village with houses built of stone. *So the only protection they had for their settlement was that fencing?* Tirîgon was astonished. Perhaps the heaps of dead bodies were intended to deter invaders.

'Well, what have we got here?' Sisaroth came up to him. 'More cadavers to de-bone. Tossàlor would have been a kid in a candy store.' Esmonäe joined them and stared at the pile of corpses and then up at the steep path. 'Can't see any other guards. They'll never notice who's come visiting. Shall we do them all in? They're not old, but killing is still fun.' *What difference does the age make?* Tirîgon quashed the thought. 'No, it's not what we were sent to do.' He restrained her with a hand on her hip.

'But if we kill them, we don't have to worry about them coming after us on our quest,' Sisaroth butted in. 'I think it's a good idea.'

'And *I* say we do what we were told to: we get the leader's chain and we go back. If the Zhadar wanted a village to be slaughtered, he could have sent his army.' Tirîgon thought the area was strange. 'So no more mass killings. And if one of you tries, I shall stop you. We don't need to be concerned about them pursuing us if we do this right.'

Esmonäe turned away from him and held out a pig's bladder. 'I found this on one of the barbarians. In a bag on the belt.'

'I don't want to imagine what they do with that.' Sisaroth took it and tossed it aside. 'Probably keep something revolting in it to eat. Don't you think?'

Tirîgon caught the item in mid-air and examined it. It stank of alcohol and resin and there was a layer of fine powder on it to prevent it sticking to itself. A thin wooden pipe allowed the bladder to be filled. *With water? With air? What was the purpose of it?*

Esmonäe had already set off across the hollow wrapped in a shadow; she wouldn't be seen by anyone in the settlement watching the plain or the hill paths.

Tirîgon did not like her aggressive approach. *I'm sure she's determined to go against the Zhadar's explicit instructions.* 'We've got to stop her committing indiscriminate wholesale slaughter,' he warned Sisaroth.

His brother nodded in agreement. 'Let's hurry before she gets to the village and starts a massacre.' Like Esmonäe had done, he wreathed himself in a robe of shadow. As he stepped forward, the strap accidentally came loose from his belt and his sword touched the ground.

A loud hissing sound issued from between the basalt stones.

'Did you hear that?' Sisaroth looked enquiringly at Tirîgon.

'Is it gas of some kind?' He crouched down and sniffed carefully. 'There's no perceptible odour.' One of the characteristics of his race was the ability to leave no footprints. They could even run through the snow without leaving a mark, unless they dropped something – like this sword, for example – or carried a heavy load that increased their natural weight. Perhaps some mechanism under the stones had been activated.

Tirîgon pressed his hand against the black stone and a constant hiss ensued. It did not cease until he removed the pressure. It made him feel giddy. *So it is a gas.*

'I see,' Sisaroth said. 'As soon as you walk on the stones, the vapour is activated.'

'I would think it's more likely to be a natural phenomenon.' Tirîgon stood up and took lungfuls of fresh air. In his left hand he still held the pig bladder. *They must fill them with air and use them to breathe when they have to cross the plain. Otherwise they would die. Like those animals back there, and any enemies that arrive unaware of the danger.* Esmonäe would be fine, as long as she did not drop anything. 'That will be why the Zhadar sent us. We can get over to the settlement safely.'

'But why wouldn't his army be able to do the same as the barbarians and use the pig bladders? I think his mission has another purpose.' Sisaroth secured his weapons belt anew and set off.

'Didn't he say he didn't want to be noticed? If he sent an army, that would not work.' Tirîgon pocketed the pig bladder and ran after his brother.

'Dead bodies always attract attention,' was the reply.

They reached the steep paths without hearing any more gas escape.

Esmonäe was already making her way swiftly up the incline. However much they tried, they could not catch up with her. They had to call out softly to her and when she finally stopped to wait, they saw the blood lust in her. The brothers explained briefly about the toxic gas before they entered the village together.

The streets seemed deserted. Tirîgon assumed everyone was at home asleep. *Good. They won't provide Esmonäe with temptation.*

Under the cover of their shade, the älfar swept past the few barbarians who were up and about. They considered the men and women ugly, with their crude features. Esmonäe struggled to control her desire to kill. It would be so easy to take these humans by surprise.

They moved into the centre of the village without making a

sound. A large, decorative building covered with symbols was presumably where the chieftain lived.

Let's find out if this is the leader's house, and get what we've come for. Tirîgon was afraid there might be further surprises ahead. He led them cautiously through an open window to find four children asleep. They could hear men and women moving about in the next-door chamber.

'Where will the chain be? What did the groundling say?' Sisaroth whispered to the others.

Don't! Tirîgon grabbed Esmonäe sharply by the arm. He had noticed her sidling up to the bed where the barbarian brood were sleeping. 'No killing!' he hissed. 'We leave no dead bodies unless we're forced to defend ourselves.' He gestured to the ceiling. 'Upstairs. Where the guilds meet.'

They crept out, climbed the stairs and searched through the upper chambers.

It was Esmonäe who found it. 'The Zhadar can't have been serious, surely?' She was amazed and stepped aside for the brothers to take a look.

In a room furnished with a long table and many chairs, a long chain hung from the ceiling beams, its links as thick as a finger, entirely made of the purest gold. A sword was suspended from the end of the chain, its pommel welded to the final link.

The brothers exchanged glances, aware that it would take all three of them to carry the heavy prize.

And this would increase their weight. The basalt stones would register their presence and release the poison gas, threatening their lives.

'The Zhadar is a . . .' Sisaroth clenched his fists. 'He can kill us with that!'

It's more than a test of courage or strength. He wants to see if we are clever enough to get round this trap. Tirîgon checked the stairs: it did not sound as if the barbarians were intending to leave the downstairs room.

A scroll on the long table bore over thirty signatures and several wax seals. *Is it a proclamation? A treaty of some kind? What is being decided?*

He skimmed through the text and found a reference to Black-Eyes.

Does this mean us? I'd better take a closer look. He pushed the roll inside his breastplate to peruse later.

'Well?' Esmonäe urged.

'He doesn't want to kill us,' said Tirîgon. 'He wants to see if are bright enough to master the challenge he's set us.'

'Of course we are.' Esmonäe jumped up onto the table and released the chain from the hook in the beam overhead. 'But I want my fun with the barbarians!'

The sword plunged down, its tip burying itself in the wood by her feet. The chain crashed noisily onto the table.

Esmonäe giggled with delighted anticipation. She had been hoping it would make a lot of noise.

Voices were raised in the room below and footsteps sounded on the stair.

Tirîgon sent his companion a furious look; now the älfar would *have* to fight.

Phondrasôn.

Firûsha, Crotàgon and Tossàlor sat opposite Marandëi at the table in the simple dining room. They had chosen the meeting place deliberately. From her long wanderings inside the second palace, Firûsha was relatively confident that there was no entrance to it from this room, and thus no easy escape route for Marandëi. Although she couldn't be sure

'What's this game you've been playing with us?' Firûsha touched the pile of fragments on the table, the remains of the skull alleged to have belonged to one of the gods of infamy. *An artefact of immeasurable power and worth but destroyed by a strike with a candlestick.*

Firûsha had wanted to await her brothers' return for this meeting but the recent startling turn of events made immediate clarification essential. She was glad they were all covered, under pain of death, by their mutual oath of non-aggression. This was their best hope of protection against the cîanai.

Crotàgon and Tossàlor were to back her up and show Marandëi that she was on her own.

'You have not understood anything!' Marandëi murmured, staring at the splinters of bone.

'Did you build the tower in order to capture älfar?' Firûsha asked her. 'Why did you keep the skull concealed behind the palace walls?' She swept the pieces of bone, the pearls, the gold leaf and the silver beads to the floor with an angry gesture; they collected in a strange pattern on the tiles. 'Start talking!'

Marandëi flinched and raised her head. Her white eyes pierced Firûsha with disdain and a deadly chill. 'You have destroyed the skull of Shëidogîs, the greatest of the gods of infamy. It protected the palace; it was the heart that beat behind the walls, our shield against all danger. I found it and cared for it. I worshipped it and made sacrifices.'

'Älfar lives,' Firûsha spat. 'Caught by your tower.' *It really was her, all along.*

Marandëi ignored the accusation. 'The palace was already here when I came. I overcame the previous residents and their subjects with my magic and they served me and built the tower. Then I gave them to the glass sea and Shëidogîs.' She surveyed the remaining pieces of the skull. 'But I made a mistake in my calculations and walled myself up in my own prison. I owe your brother too much, Firûsha, to want to put him in danger.'

She heard the subtle distinction. *It's only Sisaroth she'll make the exception for.*

'Why didn't you tell us about the skull?' Tossàlor wanted to know. 'We worship the same gods.'

'Shëidogîs said he didn't want me to tell you. He said the time was not ripe.'

Crotàgon snorted. 'I never believed in the gods of infamy. I valued the power of the Inextinguishables more highly, even if I didn't approve of everything they did. But I consider it extremely unlikely that the gods of infamy would have an actual bodily form whose remains can be crushed so easily.' He pointed at the fragments. 'What makes you so sure it was him? Couldn't it have been a demon that was influencing you?'

Her contempt turned to high indignation. 'Never! Shëidogîs was one of the infamous gods.'

'Then how did he come to be in Phondrasôn? And who placed his head behind those walls?' Tossàlor chimed in. He seemed to be enjoying the intellectual sparring; it was obvious he did not believe the cîanai, either.

Marandëi was angry. 'You doubt too much. If the skull were still intact I could prove it all.' She glanced at Firûsha. 'Without his influence on the sea, the lava underneath and the invisible magic fields that rule the caves, we shall have to give up the palace. Shëidogîs was keeping all those forces in check.'

'It won't be up to you to make that decision,' Firûsha objected.

'The bolts on the gates won't close now. They have lost their magic. A child could push the gates open,' Marandëi snapped. 'You destroyed more than an artefact and the soul of a god of infamy. You have brought about the end of the älfar empire in Phondrasôn. Your brothers will never forgive you. I shall make sure of that.'

She can't. 'This skull, or demon, or whatever it was, tried to drive me mad!' Firûsha protested, defending her actions.

'Nonsense. It wanted to drive you out so that you would not stumble into things that were not good for you. It was trying to protect you. But you were too small-minded. You have ruined everything. All my efforts and all my hopes. I wanted to tell Sisaroth everything on his return and to complete his training as priest for the gods of infamy. Now that will never be possible. Thanks to you and your cowardice, you stupid little älf-girl.'

Firûsha noted that Marandëi was trying to take the heat off her own part in the disaster. She had not broached the subject of why the tower had been built. *What shall I do with her? How do I restrain a cîanai against her will? Will the oath of obedience she swore to Sisaroth be sufficient?* 'You are absolutely right. Let's leave it to my brothers to decide what we should do next. Until they come back, I'd like to ask you to remain in this room.'

Marandëi looked at her with indifference. 'I will do that. Until I decide otherwise, that is. But I shan't be disappearing. I am in Sisaroth's service and only he can release me. I don't have to accept any orders from you.' She glanced at Crotàgon and Tossàlor. 'None of us do. Bear that in mind.'

I knew she would cause trouble. Firûsha was at a loss over what to do. She could not have the cîanai roaming freely through the secret places of the building spying on them all.

'That may be so. But I'm not having you telling me what to do, either.' Crotàgon stood, drew back his fist and punched Marandëi on the temple so that she fell unconscious to the ground, landing in the pile of skull remnants. 'I suggest we keep her quiet with a potion,' he said, circling the table and dragging the cîanai upright to throw her over his shoulder. 'It's for our own safety. Who knows what spell she'd use on us if the fancy took her?'

'Have you got a potion in mind?' Firûsha was grateful to her mentor for taking the initiative in this way.

'I don't. But she will have.' He grinned. 'There was something she was working on, meant to put you into a healing coma and spare you pain if you were injured. It'll be just what we need to send her into dreamland.' Crotàgon strode to the door. 'Let's hope your brothers get back soon. She only made a small sample.' He carried her off.

Tossàlor bent down to collect the pieces of bone, placing them on a cloth he pulled out of his pocket.

'What are you planning to do with that?'

'Stick it all back together,' was his laconic reply.

Firûsha was not ready to confront those empty eye sockets again. 'No.'

Tossàlor continued regardless. 'I want to find out how much of what she was saying is actually true.' He felt around on the floor with his fingers to see if any tiny pieces had escaped. He did the same with the table top. 'There were symbols on the artefact. I want to recreate them and try and decode their meaning.'

'I did not see you as a research scholar,' she said.

'I'm a sculptor, a bone-smith, and an älf who specialises in art of all kinds. What good would I be if I did not study the ancient runes and scripts of our people?' He smiled and picked a tiny fragment out of a crack in the table. 'I'll try to put it back together. Then we'll see where we are. Marandëi might have been telling the truth. It could turn out to be Shëidogîs' skull.'

'Where does that get us? If I have really shattered the soul of one of the gods of infamy?' Firûsha stared at the pieces and heard the sound they made as they were moved. *I really don't want him to do this.* She was frightened the reconstructed being would exact its revenge.

'It's not the mystical significance I'm interested in, but the symbols on the bone,' Tossàlor said. 'I'm sure your brothers will be keen to see what I can come up with.' He raised his arm in a wave. 'Excuse me. Someone's waiting for his head to be restored. Don't worry, all it will be is an empty skull with some pretty drawings on it.' He left the room.

Firûsha tried to assess the situation. *Should we leave the palace?* She tried not to feel guilty. *If Marandëi had told us about Shëidogîs, none of this would have happened. She's still not revealing the entire truth. Sisaroth can make her tell the truth. We can't.*

Getting up, she ran her fingers through her hair and plaited it. She gazed out of the window at the guards and the supervising engineer attempting to repair the damaged causeway. They had already fastened extra supports in the newly hardened surface of the sea.

The lengths they're going to. In the end it made no difference whether there was a bridge or not: enemies could reach the island by marching over the sea itself. They could attack from any side they chose.

Firûsha was downcast and dreadfully homesick. *I want to be back in Dsôn. I miss my mother. I do hope she is well.*

Chapter V

If you ask
    the purpose of our immortal existence
    you will hear many answers.
Some say it's to let us extend our power,
    some feel the gift is to let our knowledge grow,
    some, to let us reach perfection in our skills,
    some, that it will allow us to attain the love we crave.
Why should I seek power, knowledge, skills and love,
    without ever having lived?

'Aphorisms' from the epic poem *Young Gods*
composed by Carmondai, master of word and image

Phondrasôn.

Tirîgon vaulted over the banisters to land on the shoulders of an astonished barbarian, whom he forced to the ground with a thump while simultaneously slicing a second adversary ear to ear with a horizontal sword swipe. Then he thrust his blade through the spine of the man at his feet.

'Come on!' he called up to the others. 'The coast is clear! Only the children left. Let's get out of here!'

They did not come, so he ran up a few steps to see what was happening. Perhaps the trophy was too heavy for just the two of them.

He peered over the top stair and saw Esmonäe and Sisaroth locked in a passionate embrace.

No! How could they? With great difficulty he suppressed a shout of outrage, but the tightening skin told him the anger lines were on his face. The proof of their faithlessness was before his eyes.

The certainty he hadn't wanted shook him to the core. His mind was paralysed and there was a gaping hole in the centre of his being where his stomach seemed to have fallen away like the sudden collapse of a volcano.

They are mad! They'll ruin everything! Tirîgon could not think clearly. He took two steps back and stumbled, slowly returning to the ground floor.

Sisaroth and Esmonäe did not know he had observed them. They ran down the stairs carrying the chain and the sword that was attached to it. It was strange to hear the unusual sound of älfar feet making the floorboards creak. The chain was heavy. They had to stop and adjust their hold several times.

His muddle-headedness disappeared and his strategic thinking came to the fore, pushing away the shock he had received. *We shall have to make rest stops on the way if we are to take this weight back with us.*

He did not want to contemplate the difficulties they would encounter crossing the plain. They only had one of the pig bladders between the three of them.

Tirîgon opened the door and peered out. The open square in front of the house was empty.

'Out with you,' he whispered, going ahead, wrapped in dark shadow and pressing himself close to the wall. Every time a board creaked behind him he broke into a sweat, and the clink of the chain being moved was horribly loud to his ears. He feared the whole village would be down on their necks in an instant.

They made their way painfully slowly through the settlement. The two brothers took the full weight of the chain when Esmonäe could not carry it any longer.

'I still think we should kill them all,' she said quietly. 'We are taking too long about this. But if we kill them all first, we'll be safe.'

Esmonäe is complaining because she did not get her way about killing the barbarians. The brothers said nothing and put their burden down for a brief respite.

After another twenty paces they would reach the steep path that led down to the plain.

'I hate the Zhadar,' said Sisaroth, his hands massaging his lower back.

'Talk to the groundling if that's the way you feel,' called Esmonäe. 'You could start a rebellion. It would be a good idea.'

'Not at the moment.' Tirîgon gave a signal for them to lift the chain once more. 'Onwards. We'll let it slide down the slope under its own weight. They won't hear it back at the settlement and it'll allow us to save our strength for the plain. We'll certainly need every bit of our energy for the crossing.'

The two brothers dragged the chain. When they reached the last house in the village, a door flew open.

Five armoured barbarians stepped out, spears in hand, presumably on their way to the gate to relieve the watch.

This is the worst possible moment for them to be diligent and punctual about guard duty. Tirîgon glanced at Esmonäe, who crouched down and pulled out her daggers to go on the attack. *Not yet! Wait till we can be sure there are only these five to contend with ...*

Esmonäe's black shadow cloud leaped between the men and her knife blades found their targets as swift as lightning, so that the barbarians sank to the ground as one, with not a sound from their fleshy lips.

She turned round with a triumphant grin – and was struck in the side with a sword. Pieces of armour flew off and her blood came pouring out. She stumbled and fell.

'No!' cried Sisaroth, dropping the chain. He drew his sword and ran towards her.

Tirîgon observed his brother's reaction. It would be more proper for him to fly to her aid. *But she betrayed you and deceived you*, his inner voice whispered. *It didn't get her very far, did it? This is the penalty for not being faithful.*

A six-armed being stepped out of the house, his stature squat like that of the Zhadar. He wore substantial metal armour over his pale yellow skin and his piercing green eyes were focused on Sisaroth and Esmonäe.

'I don't believe it,' the creature yelped delightedly, pointing its bloodied blade at the injured girl-älf. 'We're in this forsaken hole looking for numbers to make up an army to strike your colony, and here are the leaders, right in front of me. Right here! What do you want?' The lipless mouth hardly moved while he spoke. 'Have you come to surrender?'

A karderier! Tirîgon knew what the creature was. Firûsha had told them she met one in her battle with Crotàgon. Tossàlor's name for them was rîconiers; he occasionally did business with them and knew their natures were far from noble. *This creature wants to destroy us to obtain our innate magic gifts.*

'You're never going to find out,' taunted Sisaroth, as he flourished his sword at the karderier, only to be repelled by a wall of whirling steel blades.

Tirîgon hesitated a moment before joining his brother in the fray. He completely ignored Esmonäe's moans as she lay bleeding at their feet.

'Another one! Excellent!' The karderier bellowed loud enough to rouse the entire village. 'You will leave me a decent portion of your magic. It shall be a foretaste of what we will have when we take over your empire!'

The two young älfar fought in circles around the tenacious veteran fighter until he was exhausted and struggling to breathe. Saliva dripped from his sharp incisors.

He squirmed out of reach, dropped one of his daggers and caught Sisaroth by the wrist. 'How does that feel!'

Sisaroth screamed with pain and lines of fury sped across his countenance. His eyes turned black with anger.

'Let him go!' Tirîgon hacked through the karderier's arm and stabbed him in the armpit through a gap in the wall of blades. When he withdrew his sword, pale yellow life-juice sprayed out of the wound like putrid milk.

The karderier collapsed, his eyelids closing, and to be safe, Tirîgon cut his head from his trunk.

Shouts rang out. The settlement had heard the sounds of the skirmish.

'Get going!' Tirîgon said to his brother, who was rubbing a

painful wrist where the enemy hand had inflicted damage. 'The chain!' *Esmonäe will have to look after herself.*

But Sisaroth stopped to help her to her feet, one arm round her in support. He appealed to his brother for assistance, 'She can hardly walk.'

'But she's going to have to. You and I will have to carry the chain.' Tirîgon attempted to lift it by himself but could not manage more than a couple of steps with the load.

'Leave the chain here. Let's get Esmonäe to safety first.' Esmonäe placed a grateful hand on his chest.

Everything changes. Now it's him that has to wait and help her out – until she decides to drop him and go for someone else. 'They know what we came for. Do you think they'll leave it lying about, ready for us next time we come?' Tirîgon dragged the chain and the sword along to the slope and let it slide over the drop. *She deceived me. Now it's his turn.*

'Don't you care about Esmonäe?' Sisaroth was shocked by his attitude.

'What's she to you?' barked Tirîgon. 'You've been sleeping with her, so it's up to you to save her. I prefer to put my trust in the Zhadar.' He leaped down the incline.

He slipped and slid his way down to the bottom, inflated the pig bladder and stuck the wooden pipe between his teeth. *If Sisaroth is clever he'll get himself one of these from a dead barbarian's belt.*

Tugging the sword and chain behind him, he stepped onto the basalt stones, which immediately sank under the weight of the golden trophy. Silent puffs of odourless lethal gas were emitted from the ground.

Tirîgon felt it move past his face. He remembered only to

breathe air from the bladder as he began the strenuous crossing. He was soon drenched with sweat.

He had to make sure the air supply would last. When he got halfway over he realised he would not have enough and quickly altered his plan. *I've got to leave the chain here, sprint to the other side and refill the bladder before coming back.*

This is what he did.

When he returned to the sword and the chain there was still nothing to be seen of Sisaroth or Esmonäe. He was all by himself in the middle of the low-lying plain.

The gas turned to a layer of fog that enveloped the village. The fog smelled of bad eggs and made his eyes sting and water. Without the air in the pig bladder, he would surely have been dead by now.

Sisaroth and Esmonäe will be in combat. So she's getting her own way after all. If she can even stand. He dragged the chain to the edge of the plain where the barrier was, and sank down, his legs folding under him. He took a draught from his flask to moisten his dry throat.

The stench of sulphur was intolerable, even here above the mist. A breeze was carrying the lethal cloud of gas over to the houses.

Well, well. Tirîgon's laughter was hollow. *If we'd only known, we could have saved ourselves a great deal of trouble. And I need never have learned the truth about my partner.*

It would have been simple: all they would have had to do was to roll heavy boulders across the basalt to release the gas, thus ensuring the barbarians all died in their sleep. Eventually the air would have cleared again and they could have walked right in.

He heard the sound of his brother's voice calling for help. It came from the gas cloud in the middle of the basalt stretch.

They'll make it. Tirîgon was not sure whether this made him glad or not. He was still smarting from their treachery and he never wanted to see Esmonäe again. He put most of the blame on her. *Sisaroth is the victim, just like I was.* But he was still furious with his brother. He forced himself to shout, 'I'm over here! This way. This is the way out.'

He could hear swords clashing and the dark, death cry of a barbarian.

'Tirîgon, where are you?'

He took another mouthful of water. 'Over here! You've nearly done it!' He tapped the chain with his sword as a signal. 'Follow the sound.'

There came the noise of renewed fighting from within the mist. Another barbarian hit the ground, with the sound of a death-rattle.

'We'll die if you don't come and help us!' Sisaroth coughed. 'Please! Brother!'

Tirîgon recalled the oath they had made. They had vowed to return to Dsôn together. How could he ever face Firûsha or his mother or his father if he left Sisaroth to die in a field of poison gas?

I curse the day I met Esmonäe. Tirîgon stood up, filled the pig bladder and tied the end of his rope to the gold chain, keeping the knot in his hand so that he could let himself down gently. Rope and chalk: part of the basic equipment for every journey in Phondrasôn.

Tirîgon was soon swallowed up in the yellow fog and could hear a body being dragged along in the vicinity.

Then his brother's back became visible. Sisaroth was swaying; the bladder hanging from his mouth was almost empty. He was pulling Esmonäe's body by the arm with one hand, while his other hand held a bloody sword.

How long had the älf-girl been breathing in the lethal gas?

She can't have survived! Tirîgon touched Sisaroth gently on the shoulder and pressed the rope into his hand. He threw Esmonäe over his shoulder, carrying her because he feared his brother would otherwise refuse to follow him.

Together they made their way up the slope to safety.

Sisaroth hurled the bladder away and drew deep racking breaths. He lay on the ground and struggled in vain to speak.

Tirîgon placed Esmonäe on the ground. Her eyes were wide open but her gaze was empty. He put his fingers on her neck, trying to locate a pulse. 'She is dead,' he confirmed. He felt a certain satisfaction but, confusingly, also a rush of pain. *Now both of us have lost her.*

'She is dead . . .' Sisaroth groaned through his tears, 'because . . . because you wouldn't help us!'

'She is dead because she was unfaithful. I did everything for her sake,' he replied. 'I would have given my life for her back there in the settlement if I could have been sure of her love.' His steel-blue eyes fixed on Sisaroth. *It's clear as crystal. I was a fool, blinded by love. And so were you.* 'She was deceiving both of us. The only person she ever loved was herself, brother.'

His grief still overpowered him, eradicating any smugness he might have felt. Tirîgon could not hold back his sobs as he knelt at her side. He kissed her brow and smoothed her eyes shut with tender fingers. *Why did we have to come to this wretched place? Why did you cause me this pain? I am losing you for a second time.*

He made a solemn vow to bring death to the Zhadar, no matter what he might promise them, or what treasure and favours he might bestow. He would kill the Zhadar and all those who followed him. Had it not been for this hopeless mission, Esmonäe would still be alive. And Tirîgon would never have had to know that she was being unfaithful to him.

Phondrasôn.

'Aha, so you're back! You were quick.' The gâlran zhadar and Tungdil entered the room where they had their original audience. He examined the golden sword and the chain it was attached to; they had thrown it down on the table, ruining the surface of the wood. 'I'm a bit disappointed. I thought it would be more impressive. The Wolrak humans worship it but as far as I can see, it's just a gold chain with a sword on it.' He turned to the groundling. 'Melt it down and make something decorative out of it if you like.'

'You are too kind, Master,' Tungdil answered with no trace of gratitude in his voice.

'What?' Sisaroth pulled himself up to his full height. 'You mean to say we risked our lives ...'

'I know,' the Zhadar interrupted, grinning broadly. He stroked his black side whiskers. 'It was a test to see if you were worthy of being my allies. You've shown you know how to handle yourselves. I never thought you'd both come back.' He indicated the gold. 'It wasn't the gold I was interested in. It was your ingenuity. I don't need any more riches. You lost the girl, then?' The brothers nodded. 'What a shame. Tell me what happened.'

The Zhadar took his seat and Tirîgon made his report, having to bite his tongue so as not to show how bitter he felt about the whole incident. *The sooner you die, the better.*

He could feel Tungdil's gaze on him. The groundling knew exactly what was going through his mind. His grief over the loss of Esmonäe – despite what she had put him through with her game-playing – caused strong waves of emotion to wash over him, making it difficult to exercise self-control. He had to clench his jaw tightly.

'Excellent, excellent. So that village will have ceased to exist.' The Zhadar got to his feet and walked to the door. 'The sulphur gas will have finished them off; anybody still alive won't last long. Phondrasôn is too cruel to allow that. If I were you, I'd watch out for the karderiers. They don't just need magic energy for their shape-shifting tricks; it's essential for their very survival. They are extremely keen on forming an alliance against you. Don't underestimate them.' He left the room.

Tungdil looked at the silent brothers. 'You see how deep his emotions go. He must have a stone instead of a heart. But you will understand that I shan't be wasting sympathy on you. Älfar and dwarves have never got on.' He indicated they should follow him. 'I've had a preliminary shipment of armour and weapons put together for you. It should be sufficient to improve your army's capability.'

'What about cavalry animals?' Tirîgon enquired.

'You mean night-mares, I assume?' Tungdil grinned broadly. 'Bad luck. Not even my master keeps those. We once had a few but they're long gone and we never managed to tame them anyway.' He walked them to the lift and they travelled down to the plain where the groundling's forge was located.

'The Master has a gift for you . . . well, there were actually three, but you'll only be needing the two, I suppose.'

'We'll take all three,' Sisaroth said quickly. 'Including our sister's.'

'I thought she died in the basalt gas?' Tungdil gave Tirîgon a shrewd look, narrowing his one eye. 'Which one of you is speaking the truth, I wonder?' After a second of study, he gave a belly laugh, having seen through their subterfuge. 'That's a good start! You've resorted to deception the very first time you met my master. We can see the death of your fake sister pains you, but it's nice to know your real sister is still alive.'

'If we'd had her with us, we wouldn't have been in this awkward situation in the first place.' Tirîgon was thinking of Firûsha's incredible gift of song. *She would have wound the Zhadar round her little finger and melted that heart of stone. He'd have accepted us as his allies rather than treating us like lowly slaves.*

They reached Tungdil's warm workshop, where they found three forges burning brightly, each at a different heat. The air was oppressive and smelt of smouldering coals. The visitors' mouths filled with a metallic taste; hammers clanged repeatedly on the anvils. Sparks flew and there was constant noise: warnings shouted, instructions barked. Steam hissed in clouds when the hot metal was plunged into the water tubs to cool.

The groundling explained that his workforce of apprentices and journeymen was toiling away at the capacious cauldron to extract iron and other metals from the basic ore, mixing them with other substances to form alloys.

'That's the way I like it. If you add a smidgeon of magic to the mix, the result is quite extraordinary. You have an amazing advantage when you're locked in a fight for survival.'

What a ghastly place. Tirîgon was repelled by the filth everywhere. The crude barbarians working here were covered from head to foot in soot and sweat. Their skin showed multiple superficial burns and none of them could stand properly erect. Their bodies were ugly enough to begin with and were definitely not improved by this unpleasant labour.

He was familiar with smithies in Dsôn, but there was absolutely no comparison. The älfar used the same equipment as the groundlings, but it was never this dirty because the work processes were organised differently. This forge just further emphasised the differences in their races.

Tungdil led the brothers over to a quieter corner, where smaller tools were used: special mallets, small chisels and tongs for fine detail. Pieces of steel and tionium were spread out ready on a long table. Together these components would represent a complete set of body armour and arm and leg protection.

'I've left space for älfar runes to be engraved,' he explained, taking each piece in calloused hands that looked too crude to have executed such exquisite craftsmanship. 'I can write your language but I thought you'd want to choose your own motto and engrave it yourselves. That way the armour becomes truly yours and is bound to you.' He picked up the pieces of armour from the third set and placed them in a small metal chest. 'The first is for Sisaroth. The second is Tirîgon's and the third one is for your sister. It was built to fit the other älf-girl, so I hope they're similar in size.'

The brothers scrutinised the workmanship.

Tirîgon held up the arm greaves and tried them on. 'A perfect fit!' he said, astonished. 'When did you take the measurements?' *This squat fellow is good.*

The groundling touched his right eye. 'I see you and I know how älfar are built. I've killed plenty of them, after all. Put the two together. Though I expect there'll be a few adjustments still to make.'

Tirîgon had not intended to accept the Zhadar's gift, but the quality of the product changed his mind. 'Are there secret weaknesses built in?' he asked.

'Stupid question. If I had done, I'd hardly admit it, would I? And you'd never know until you were locked in combat. But I am prepared to swear by our gods – both yours and mine – that I have worked with the same care I would have employed if the armour had been intended to protect one of my own.' He disappeared through a side door and returned with three basic sword forms. 'I've only done the first pass; I wanted to ask you how you'd like me to finish them off.'

'Long. As long as I am tall. Well balanced, naturally. Sharper than your own Bloodthirster, and as light as a one-hander,' was Sisaroth's request.

'I'd like a double dagger with parallel cutting edges,' Tirîgon chipped in.

The groundling nodded and pulled over a piece of paper and started sketching with a piece of charcoal. Each brother added further specifications for his own weapon, and they suggested Tungdil include throwing discs for Firûsha.

Tungdil studied his final drawings, considering the project. 'Would you like for the parrying guards to be extra-long, too? They could be used to provide added power to a violent thrust.' The älfar agreed to his suggestion. 'Right. I'll get to work. By the time the master gives you your first real mission, I'll have everything ready for you.' He bowed. 'I wish you luck with your endeavours,' he said quietly. 'You are capable of victory. But keep your emotions under control.'

He's known all along what our plans are. 'That sounds as if you are going to be leaving soon?' Tirîgon was alarmed. *We could have used his help.* 'Will he be sending you to one of the other caves?'

Sisaroth weighed the breastplate in his hands and tapped the metal sharply so that it gave a clang. 'Or will you be marching with his army, perhaps?'

Tungdil gave a sly grin. 'No, it won't be that. Let's just say I might have found an escape route and may want to absent myself from his service. Can you imagine his face when I'm gone?' He laughed. 'It would probably look much like your own. Now, let's get the fit checked on this armour.'

However hard the brothers pressed him for more details as they tweaked the armour, Tungdil refused to divulge any more information. But they did extract a promise that he would not disappear until the weapons were finished. He handed them a drawn map showing how to get home from the Zhadar's stronghold. 'Not all the tunnels in Phondrasôn are subject to change,' he explained.

Equipped with their new armour, Sisaroth and Tirîgon began their return trip to the palace. The chainmail wore like a second skin, giving them unhampered freedom of movement. They were also equipped with a wealth of knowledge they would have preferred to have done without.

'I owe you an apology,' Sisaroth said on the way home. 'I knew that Esmonäe and you . . . But I did not turn down her advances. It was wrong of me. She was so hard to resist. I've been thinking about what you said back there and you were right: she would have thrown me over for her next victim if it had served her purposes. I know that she went about flattering and flirting with many of the älfar, getting their hopes up.' He sighed. 'But it still makes me sad. More than sad. My heart mourns for her, even if my head tells me I'm well rid of her influence.'

Tirîgon was relieved to hear it. 'Thank you. Let's leave it at that, brother. I don't want to waste another word on Esmonäe and her machinations. It's still too raw and . . .' *And I don't know how honest your remorse is. Time will tell.*

'. . . painful.' Sisaroth filled in the missing word. 'How I wish I had never taken her along with us. It had seemed such a good idea at the time. I . . . really wanted her near.' He wiped away a tear.

'Enough.' To distract himself and his brother, Tirîgon took out the scroll taken from the council chamber in Wolrak; he started deciphering the script as they walked. 'Look what I found in the village.'

An untutored hand had scratched a treaty in barbarian writing. Forty settlements including Wolrak had undertaken to support the karderiers' cause in the planned assault on the älfar palace in the cave of liquid glass. In return, they were to be granted the caverns of the Okmains and the caves of the Smahu, currently under älfar control.

'I'm afraid it doesn't say how many other alliances the six-armed creature had already entered into,' he said. 'We can only hope the delegates from the other settlements were there to sign the treaty when the vapours wiped out the entire village. We've got the right number of signatures here.'

'But the karderier might have been the last one to sign. We could be faced with thirty-nine settlements ready to fight us,'

Sisaroth pointed out. 'Not to mention however many other karderiers.' Both of them found this distraction a welcome relief from their thoughts about Esmonäe. 'We were lucky you found that treaty.'

'So there was one good thing that emerged from the Zhadar's ridiculous test, even if he knew nothing about it.' *Though it's been dearly bought.* Tirîgon tried to calculate how strong a force they might expect from an alliance of barbarian settlements. *I wonder if the other villages are about the same size as Wolrak?* Perhaps one third of their inhabitants might be capable of bearing arms.

'We must try to find out who has already joined an alliance against us. And what exactly they are planning to do, and when.' Sisaroth shouldered his pack.

He's looking older and more tired. Esmonäe's loss has left its mark. On me, too, I'm sure. 'Perhaps the others will have something to suggest.' Tirîgon pulled himself together. *Concentrate on the task at hand, saving the empire. Not on the pain in your heart.* He was consoled by the fact that the planned attack on their palace could not yet have taken place. *We're safe as long as the karderiers are still trying to assemble their army.*

'So do you think we'll see the groundling again? What do you reckon? Will we get our weapons or will he run before he delivers?' Sisaroth seemed to be considering the consequences of a possible flight. 'I wonder what he'll do? And how is it he suddenly knows the way out? Do you think he'll confront the Zhadar before he goes?'

He wants to get away, that's clear. Tirîgon shrugged his shoulders. 'I don't know. The armour is really good. It would be a pity not to get the swords to go with it, but he won't change his plans for our sakes.' They could always betray the groundling to his master, but Tirîgon was not going to entertain that idea. On the contrary, he wished him well. *Without Tungdil, the Zhadar will be weaker. It'll be harder for us to capture the fortresses without his aid, but I'll think of something.*

But Tirîgon had something more urgent to contend with before he could entertain a plan for storming the Zhadar's defences and occupying the four towers: the imminent assault on the älfar palace.

'If we can find out where the karderiers intend to assemble their troops and their idiotic allies, we could send Marandëi out to deal with them,' Sisaroth said, thinking out loud. 'It would be a real blow to their morale.'

Nobody would ever join the karderiers after that. And we could take over their territory. Tirîgon thought his brother was right. 'We will muster our troops and send them out to reconnoitre all the caves.' He recalled that one of the provinces had defaulted on its tribute obligations. 'Do you think it might be worth investigating Efrigûr?'

'Are you suggesting they haven't paid up because they're already aligned with the karderiers?' Sisaroth smiled. 'Good point. I'll go there myself.' He placed a hand on his brother's shoulder.

We seem to be back to normal. We trust each other again. Tirîgon was moved by the gesture. He turned his attention to the runes under the list of signatories. 'I may be mistaken, but I'm seeing a similarity with our own script.' He held the treaty out to his brother.

Sisaroth studied the curvilinear symbols. 'I'm not sure ... is it possible you might be imagining it?'

'Perhaps. Tossàlor will know.' Tirîgon raised his arms and was gratified to note that the armour did not creak or restrict his movements in any way. *The little guy has done sterling work in his forge.* 'Tell me, are you as pleased with the fit of your armour as I am with mine?'

'Indeed. That groundling knows his stuff, doesn't he? I wouldn't say it to his face, of course, but he's as good as anyone we have at our disposal.' He thought far more highly of Tungdil's skill than his words suggested, though his admiration was evident in the tone of his voice. 'I can't wait to see what he makes of the swords.' He was overcome with breathlessness all of a sudden and succumbed to a fit of coughing, spitting out a red-tinged clot of mucus. 'The after-effects of the poison gas,' he commented.

'Are you all right?'

'I hope so. One lung feels shrunken to the size of a newborn baby's. When I breathe I can hear it rattling away. And walking takes it out of me.' He coughed again. 'I'll be fine once I'm back in the fresh air of our own palace, I'm sure.' He laughed. 'Once I hear Firûsha singing, all my symptoms will disappear.'

'I hope so, for all our sakes. I need you, you know.' Tirîgon meant what he said. 'Our opinions may sometimes differ on the subject of Phondrasôn and our immediate future plans, but in the long run, we both want the same thing our sister does: to get back home. To Dsôn. To our parents. And to bring the evildoers to justice that accused you so falsely.'

'Exactly. And I'd like to congratulate you for your initial wise decisions concerning our palace and the creation of our empire.' Sisaroth had the map in his hand and was leading them through the passages. 'If we didn't have our safe refuge established before we attempted the journey to the surface, the karderiers would be able to harass us all over Phondrasôn – and eventually perhaps even corner and defeat us. Your actions have kept us safe.'

Tirîgon was touched; he saw in his brother's clear blue gaze that the sentiment had been sincere. 'And I shall change my attitude, I promise. I'll put more effort into finding how we can get back up and go home. I'm considering using some of our serfs as scouting parties. That is, as soon as we have dealt with the karderiers.'

Sisaroth said nothing.

What's the matter now? 'I thought you'd be pleased?'

'It's just that I remembered Firûsha telling us the karderiers can change their shapes.' He grimaced and stifled a cough. 'What if they are already amongst us back at the palace? Maybe as guards, or soldiers on the defences?'

'By all the gods of infamy!' This possibility had not occurred to Tirîgon and he could have kicked himself for having overlooked it. *It would be so easy for them. We have taken on a number of new älfar recruits recently.* 'You're right! They could have infiltrated our army already.' They had assembled a force of about eight hundred älfar. *How are we going to find out if all of them are truly of our race?* 'We'll ask Marandëi what she thinks. Perhaps she'll know of some spell she can use to reveal any spies.'

'It might be enough if we gather the troops and pretend we have the ability to expose the fake älfar. We might catch someone reacting shiftily,' Sisaroth suggested. 'That's what we should do first, as soon as we get back to the palace.' He increased his pace, although this meant he suffered a renewed bout of coughing.

Tirîgon hurried along, stowing away the treaty the karderier and the barbarians had signed. Without comment, he took his brother's rucksack and added the load to his own. He was also carrying Firûsha's set of armour. His reward was a brotherly smile of gratitude. A sincere and heartfelt one.

Did it have to happen like this? Did Samusin impose this trial on us to make us stronger? Tirîgon found his thoughts returning to Esmonäe; he could think of her now without succumbing to grief or hatred. At long last he began to see a purpose in what they had gone through. *Her death was a sacrifice.* She had been sacrificed for the good of him and his brother. A sacrifice to rekindle their brotherly affection and harmony.

Their sibling bond would be stronger in the future than it had ever been back in Dsôn.

Chapter VI

Anyone with the choice of two things,
if others expect him to make that choice,
should leave
without choosing.
This is the greatest freedom.

'Aphorisms' from the epic poem *Young Gods*
composed by Carmondai, master of word and image

Phondrasôn.

Firûsha was overjoyed to hear from the sentries that her two brothers had returned. As if she had sensed their approach, she had that morning chosen her most beautiful robe, a fine black and green lawn worked with silver thread and embroidered in white silk.

She hurried to meet them, welcoming them out on the causeway with warm embraces and walking back with them through the fortress gates and courtyards to the palace itself. As they walked she told them in full detail everything that had happened since their departure. She was so excited and relieved to see them that she didn't even notice Esmonäe wasn't there.

They related the events on their journey to meet the Zhadar and told her how the älf-girl had died.

Neither looked particularly upset at the loss, which surprised Firûsha. There seemed to be a new understanding between the brothers; the bond was stronger, more harmonious. *Their experience has brought them closer and healed the rifts.*

She was also aware that this first impression might not be complete. She knew that Tirîgon suppressed personal problems to let external goals take precedence. Firûsha had spent many nights in Dsôn singing softly at his bedside when the pain in his soul had not allowed him to sleep. But anyone coming across him in daylight hours would never have seen his distress, so great was his self-control. She thought it better not to enquire further at the present. *I shall be able to soothe him if he asks for my help.*

On their arrival in the palace, they entered Marandëi's chamber, where the cîanai lay sleeping, watched by two guards.

Tirîgon sent the soldiers out and they woke Marandëi with a few drops of cold water on her face when she did not respond to a gentle shake of the shoulder.

The cîanai opened her eyes and looked around the room in confusion. She did not smile until she saw Sisaroth standing beside the bed. 'So considerate to put me in a healing coma after that awful blow,' she said sarcastically. 'It's nice not to wake up with a painful jaw.'

'My sister has told us what happened,' Sisaroth said, not wanting to deal harshly with her. 'Now I should like to hear your version of events. I insist that you only speak the full truth.'

What will we hear? Firûsha was eager to learn whether the cîanai had previously been lying when questioned. She was relieved to hear the same version this time, although she noticed there was still a glaring omission. She prompted her brother to ask Marandëi about the tower's original purpose.

'I built it,' she admitted reluctantly, 'with the aim of capturing älfar. I was under orders from the gods of infamy.'

The siblings exchanged glances.

She's been lying through her teeth this whole time! 'So you wanted to make us think we were safe and then you were going to kill us as soon as this Shëidogîs asked you to!' Firûsha cried. 'The more älfar we assembled in the fortress, the happier you were. We were being kept to sacrifice to your god. Is that not the case?'

Tirîgon raised his hand. 'One moment, dear sister. We need to hear why one of the gods of infamy would demand sacrifices from a race that reveres and worships them.'

'It is the first I have ever heard of any Shëidogîs cult,' said Sisaroth. 'Neither Father or Mother ever mentioned älfar souls being demanded by the gods of infamy.'

Firûsha did not like the expression on Sisaroth's face. Back in Dsôn he had started training to be a priest for the gods of infamy. His devotion to the gods had remained key in his character despite his prowess as a warrior. *I hope he is not intending to follow the cîanai's way of thinking?*

'The Inextinguishables suppressed this particular form of worship,' Marandëi explained. 'This is why the gods of infamy are failing to support us as they have always done in the past. They are not getting anything valuable in exchange.'

Tirîgon, resplendent like his brother in his new set of armour, crossed his arms defiantly. 'So the gods of infamy are becoming fussy? Not satisfied with all the prayers and incense now?'

Marandëi cast a condescending glance at him. 'Would you be satisfied with just prayers and incense if you were hungry?'

'I suppose not,' he answered with a grin.

'Well, why should a god?' She asked for something to drink and was handed a cup of water. 'I studied the old writings and read how the gods had originally been appeased. Ninety älfar a year: thirty young men, thirty women and thirty newborn babies.'

'By all the . . .' Firûsha was horrified. *I refuse to believe that.*

'The Inextinguishables outlawed the practice, claiming it endangered the survival of their race. It was merely an excuse. The truth was they envied the gods the miracles they could perform and the popularity they enjoyed. It was considered a high honour to die for them. Once we stopped sacrificing, the gods stopped bestowing their favours. They were no longer worshipped with the previous intensity and the Inextinguishables found their own esteem increasing.'

Firûsha thought about the terrible end that Dsôn Faïmon had suffered. She could not help wondering how much better the empire might have fared with the gods of infamy fully behind them. *But it is still out of the question to sacrifice our own kind!*

'The end of the university you told me about: it was not an accident, was it? It was deliberate.' Sisaroth confronted Marandëi with the unpleasant truth.

'Yes. I dressed it up as a tragic accident, but I was making a sacrifice to the gods,' she confessed. 'I found the holy skull of Shëidogîs concealed in the crypt that housed historical relics. They had attempted to wipe out any memory of the old religion and I took it upon myself to put the blasphemers to death. Shëidogîs awarded me special powers for the occasion.' Marandëi took another mouthful of water. 'The Inextinguishables quickly worked out what had happened and they sent the other cîanai to hunt me down. In my view, it seemed Phondrasôn would be the safest option. For me and for Shëidogîs. Until the headstrong young älf-girl shattered the skull with a candlestick.' She fixed Firûsha with an icy stare. 'All that effort. For nothing.'

'Have I got this right? You wanted to entice Phondrasôn's älfar into your tower in order to sacrifice them to your skull?' Tirîgon wanted to confirm.

Marandëi did not answer.

'Answer him,' Sisaroth commanded. 'And speak the truth to him just as you would have to me.'

'Yes,' she snapped back. 'That was it. My own stupidity thwarted my plan.'

She is insane. Completely mad! She would have killed us all for the sake of this . . . demon . . . this Shëidogîs . . . if her own creation had not imprisoned her and held her fast. Firûsha looked at Tirîgon to see his reaction to the revelation.

There was a knock at the door.

Tossàlor entered the room in a deep purple robe, with a fully armed Crotàgon at his side.

'I understand our leaders are all assembled.' The artist had a cushion on his right hand, bearing an object with unmistakeable outlines covered by a velvet cloth. 'Let me present my newest creation in this auspicious gathering.' He nodded; Crotàgon removed the cloth with a grand gesture.

The skull had been skilfully rebuilt and glued together. While the cracks were visible, it was clear that every fragment had been recovered. There were no gaps. All the gold leaf, all the pearls and all the silver adornments were back in their rightful places.

Marandëi beamed. Firûsha froze.

'In truth, my masterwork. When it comes to restoring works of art this is undoubtedly my supreme achievement. I constructed a series of vices and grips that allowed me to put the fragments and splinters together. When I was sure the glue would hold, I put the inlays back and buffed out any rough edges. Thanks to the inscriptions, and with Marandëi's archive for reference, I've been able to rebuild . . .' Firûsha stopped listening. The cîanai had already told them everything they needed to know about Shëidogîs. She avoided looking directly at the skull, terrified of its empty eye sockets and dreading having to hear the sound of the infamous one or the evil spirit that inhabited the skull.

'I recognise the symbols,' said Tirîgon in surprise. 'There, on the side. And on the top. The soldiers in the barbarian village had the same signs on their skinned scalps. If the settlements are in thrall to the gods of infamy, this could be good news for us. We could turn the tables and get the barbarians to take arms against the karderiers with the help of this relic. I'm sure Shëidogîs will appreciate being adored by more than just Marandëi. We could offer a few barbarian souls . . .'

Firûsha realised Sisaroth was deep in thought. *Surely he won't . . .* She leaned towards him. 'Brother, think, please. The only reason you are still alive is because the cîanai made a mistake with her calculations when she built the tower,' she whispered urgently in his ear. She shuddered. 'She would have tossed you to that thing for her own advantage if she wasn't trapped in there herself. She cares nothing for our community here. For her we are merely souls to sacrifice to her god.' But Firûsha was aware her words were not getting through to him. *I can see it in his eyes. He has made his decision.*

Sisaroth took the skull gently, turned it around and handed it to Tirîgon. 'My thanks, Tossàlor. Marandëi, can you tell if the spirit of the infamous one has returned to the skull?'

'We won't know that until a sacrifice has been made,' she said, not without ambiguity. 'We can try to entice the spirit back into its former home . . .'

'With what aim?' Firûsha interrupted her. 'Merely for us to resume sacrificing to it? The miracles a god of infamy can perform won't be worth waiting for, surely? There's an attack imminent. Armies are gathering, intent on stealing our magic. We need every hand that can hold a sword. And you're contemplating sacrificing some of our own soldiers?'

'To start with, it ought to be enough to sacrifice just one life,' the cîanai said gently. 'That won't be too much to ask if we then are granted a miracle?'

'Most of them are criminals anyway. It's not so awful if we kill one of them.' Sisaroth obviously shared her point of view. 'In fact, it would be quite justified.' He stretched out his hand for Tirîgon to pass the skull back to him.

But his brother was firm. 'It's not just us bound by the oath of loyalty. All the älfar in the palace have sworn the same pledge; we have vowed to protect one another,' Tirîgon reminded his brother. 'If one is killed, his death would be avenged. And remember, Marandëi said even she can't lift the curse.' He smiled at her smugly. 'You seem to have a few problems controlling your own creations. The tower first, then the oath.'

'I still think it's worth a try,' said Tossàlor.

'You're just drooling at the mouth waiting for the victim's bones,' Firûsha snapped at him.

The artist burst out laughing. 'Well said, young älf-woman. You may have hit on a grain of truth there. But I've got an idea how we can get round the curse.' He looked at Crotàgon. 'Correct me if I'm wrong, but while our good Marandëi was getting her beauty sleep, three new älfar recruits have turned up. They haven't taken the vow yet, so they are free. For whatever purpose . . .' He gave Sisaroth a sly sideways glance. 'It's up to you . . .'

'Up to all of us, you mean.' Again, Firûsha interrupted. *I'm not letting you get away with that, Tossàlor.* 'We make all our decisions as a group.' *I can only hope Tirîgon takes my side.*

Tirîgon tossed the skull into the air and caught it, ignoring Marandëi's horrified intake of breath. 'I don't think we should start reducing our own forces for the sake of some ritual. We've got no guarantee Shëidogîs will return.' He repeated his juggling trick. 'But we shouldn't forget that our best defence, the molten glass sea, has gone hard and that means enemies have free access to the island. The fortress walls will withstand an assault, but if we consider the number of barbarians that may be on the march . . .' He tossed the empty skull to Marandëi, who caught it with a stifled moan of terror lest she drop it. She began to kiss and caress it. 'In the circumstances I'm for giving it a go. The loss of one soldier won't damage our chances.'

'But we must keep this to ourselves. There'll be trouble among the troops if the truth gets out,' Tossàlor objected. 'We can say the älf has had an accident out on manoeuvres. While he was scouting out one of the caves, for example.'

They all agree and they have no idea what the implications are.

'You didn't see what that thing is capable of!' Firûsha had lost but she was not going to give up. 'There'll be no miracles! There'll be nothing but disaster!'

'There'll be disaster if we do nothing, sister dear!' Tirîgon came over and put his arm round her shoulders. 'I know how you feel. I can understand your view entirely. But in our situation…'

I cannot let this happen. We can't shed älfar blood. Firûsha leaped forward and grabbed at the skull.

Marandëi must have been expecting this move and she yanked the precious object out of harm's way. Sisaroth grasped his sister's arm and pulled her back.

The warrior training she had undergone with Crotàgon served her well now. She twisted out of his grasp with a nimble movement and drew her sword out of its sheath, striking at the skull…

… but the thrust was parried by Tirîgon's armoured forearm and her blade shattered.

Her jaw dropped as she stared at the useless hilt and guard. She dropped the ruined weapon at her brothers' feet. 'You are making a terrible mistake.' She turned and ran out of the room. *Am I the only one thinking clearly here?*

An idea occurred to her.

Firûsha ran through the palace as quickly as she could until she reached the courtyard nearest the troops' quarters. She knew where the three newcomers would be.

If I can get them away, there'll be no sacrifice. Firûsha wanted to make use of the head start she had. She could use the extra time to talk to her brothers and make them realise how wrong their decision was. She had to make them see sense.

Phondrasôn.

I have come so far. Acòrhia held the little flask up to the light to look at the contents. *I shall manage the rest as well.*

'What's that you've got there?' Bephaigòn came up to her wearing wide black trousers. His feet and torso were naked; drops of water that had escaped the towel ran down his skin.

'It's a souvenir of Dsôn,' she replied, putting the phial back into its protective leather cover. She was kneeling by her rucksack, which she had been looking through again. However carefully she searched, this was the only bottle remaining. The others lay discarded and empty in some corridor or in a far part of the labyrinth. In her quest to find the triplets, she had used up nearly all her supply of the precious remedy, even counting those of the fellow conspirators she had killed. *The dose we were allowed would not have kept a single one of us alive to the end of our mission. Aïsolon was sending us all to our deaths.*

Bephaigòn scraped his wet hair away from his face. 'What's it got inside?'

'My mother's tears,' the story-teller invented. She did not like this brown-haired älf. He was constantly eyeing her. It was obvious he had not enjoyed an intimate touch for a very long time. Acòrhia did not find him attractive and he was not going to get anywhere with her. She sent him packing. 'Get back to your own bed.' She stood up and adjusted the clothing and armour she had been given to replace her own ruined robe.

Bephaigòn withdrew to the lower bunk. Iòsunta was sitting upright on the top bunk thumbing through a book with a tattered cover: another souvenir of home. 'There's no need to be nasty. He was only showing an interest,' said the blonde älf-girl, turning slowly to face Acòrhia. 'This is such a godforsaken place. Is it wrong to seek comfort and affection?'

Acòrhia made a dismissive gesture. 'I'll be the one to choose whose affection I want. I'm not as desperate as you seem to be.' She placed a hand on her belt where her new sword and her old dagger hung.

Iòsunta closed the book and gave her a challenging stare before lying down and turning on her side to sleep. 'I shall get to see the triplets before you do.'

'Is that what you think?' Acòrhia leaned against the bunk beds. *I am sure only one of us will meet them.*

Iòsunta was one of the group who had borne false witness against Sisaroth and Firûsha. Back home in Dsôn she had earned her living as a caterer. She could conjure up a dish that was a delight for both palate and eye from the simplest of ingredients. The most powerful citizens would engage her to cook for them. She had arrived at the palace just after the story-teller and had likewise been told she must wait to see the leaders of the älfar colony. It was said that the two brothers were on a mission and Firûsha was too busy to speak to new arrivals. However much they insisted that their affair was of vital import, their pleas fell on deaf ears. Bephaigòn had been brought in first thing in the morning. Three new recruits for the small army.

'Of course.' Iòsunta sat back up and put the book aside. 'How many did you kill to get their phials?'

The redhead smiled. 'All the ones that escaped from your clutches.' She looked at Bephaigòn, steadily snoring on his bunk. *He's making a show of being asleep.* 'We've come far. The gods of infamy have been with us all the way.'

'They will have to decide which of us they favour,' said Iòsunta, indicating Acòrhia's rucksack. 'I don't have any more reserves than you do. That means that we either die together, or . . .' She pulled her legs up under her.

Is she preparing to launch an attack? 'Oh, that's where you are wrong. It's only you that will die.'

'Because you are going to kill me?' Iòsunta spoke calmly, playing with the hem of her underskirt.

'No. Because I know a way home.' This was a lie but the other girl did not know it. 'I don't care if you get to Sisaroth, Tirîgon and Firûsha before me. You'll never see Dsôn again. I shall take the triplets back to the light of the sun and you will be rotting here in Phondrasôn.'

Iòsunta frowned. 'What's to stop me coming with you?'

Acòrhia gave a sly grin. 'I've had a look at your phial. You have less in your bottle than I do. Do you suppose I shall select a route that permits you to make it all the way? I will return home triumphant with the triplets and Aïsolon will heap praises on me. He will give me the proper antidote and any reward I care to name. Or the triplets themselves will pay me for my efforts and the time I have spent here in their cause.' *Particularly Tirîgon. He will be especially pleased to see me.*

Iòsunta slipped nimbly down from her mattress. 'That means I shall only survive if you do not leave this room.' She drew both sword and dagger from their sheaths hanging off the end of the bed. 'I must kill you for your flask and my reward. I also know the way back up to the light.'

The älf in the lower bunk muttered, apparently in a deep sleep, and turned over to face the wall. The sound of his snoring increased in volume.

Acòrhia laughed. 'You're nothing but a cook. You won't be any good with a blade.'

'You're mistaken. I can butcher you like a trussed boar and cut out the best bits to throw to the beasts. Why should I be afraid of someone who can only make up stories?' She took a step backward and raised her weapons. 'We have established that the gods of infamy have so far supported us both equally. Shall we see which one of us they favour now?' Iòsunta attacked.

Acòrhia ducked, allowing the sword to pass over her head and strike the bedpost, where it jammed in the wood. Iòsunta thrust her dagger and kicked upwards.

The story-teller avoided the knife-tip but the kick hit home, hurling her backwards onto one of the other beds. She did a backwards roll and landed on her feet on the far side, while Iòsunta took a flying leap over the bed, aiming both feet at Acòrhia's face.

It was a surprise twist too far for the story-teller: the heels crashed into her face, felling her. A hundred stars exploded inside her head, tears coursed down her cheeks and she could taste blood.

Where did she learn to fight like that? Only half-conscious, she dodged a plunging shadow. The knife clanged to the floor, but Acòrhia had received a cut to her upper arm, initially deflected by her armour. She stifled a cry and slid under the nearest bed for shelter.

Iòsunta shoved the bed to one side and stamped on her. 'I will have your phial!'

Acòrhia wrenched her opponent's foot and twisted it until it snapped. 'That should put an end to your attack.'

The other fighter staggered back, howling; she wrenched her sword out of the wooden post.

Acòrhia used the bedframe to lever herself up and she was able at last to bring her own weapons into play. Iòsunta was handicapped by the broken ankle, but Acòrhia could only see out of one eye and her head was bursting. She began to suffer double vision. The two circled each other, neither daring to make the next move.

Bephaigòn had placed a pillow over his ears so as not to hear the sounds of their struggle. He was an outlaw and knew when to keep his counsel. It was wise to avoid getting involved.

Acòrhia passed her injured left arm over her face and groaned with pain. The side of her head was badly swollen and her nose felt broken. She started to feel unsteady and nauseous. *If I wait too long, I shan't be able to defend myself at all.* She spat and launched herself on her opponent. *Gods of infamy, stand by me!* she implored, with a silent promise to make a sacrifice to them if they helped her win.

Iòsunta tried to avoid the onslaught but was badly compromised by her ankle. She managed a side-step shuffle but tripped when her sound foot caught on the leg of a chair.

I've got you! Acòrhia followed through, smashing first her opponent's defensively raised dagger and then her sword aside. Iòsunta was struck as she fell. She lay convulsing on the floor, where blood from her head wound collected in a pool.

'I told you you'd never reach Dsôn alive.' Acòrhia revelled in the other's distress. She sauntered over to the rucksack by the bed. 'You won't mind if I help myself to the remedy? To the victor the spoils, and all that?'

Iòsunta's heels continued to drum on the wooden floor. The

death agony was a long process; the body shook with tremors, the eyes wide open.

Don't look at me to put you out of your misery. Acòrhia located the precious phial and placed it inside her armour.

She caught sight of Bephaigòn sitting bolt upright in bed, his face on a level with her own. He stared at her expectantly.

Just as I thought. He was only pretending to be asleep. As swift as lightning she saw that if she were not compliant he would blackmail her. She was disgusted at the prospect of having to buy his silence in his embrace.

Her decision took no time. She stabbed without warning.

But Bephaigòn avoided the blow and landed a murderous uppercut that threw her off her feet to land against the wooden frame of a neighbouring bed. 'You are a murderer,' he said bluntly. 'But I don't understand why.' Through a red film she could see him approaching. 'Tell me why you did it. And what's in it for me if I . . .'

At that very moment the door opened.

A young dark-haired female älf in a green and black embroidered dress stepped into the room, to pull up short in horror as she took in the scene.

'He's trying to kill both of us,' Acòrhia moaned. It was only then that she realised that it was Aïsolon's daughter. 'Firûsha! I . . .'

Bephaigòn catapulted himself up, grabbed a spear from the wall and stormed at the defenceless Firûsha, who just managed to dodge the attack. 'That was easier than I thought it would be,' the älf chortled. 'Hold still. It will soon be over! And then I will be beautiful, too!'

Acòrhia pushed herself up. *What is happening?* Holding her

sword as firmly as she could, she began a steady advance on Bephaigòn, distracting him from his attack on Firûsha.

Bephaigòn was good with the spear. He used the blunt end to strike Acòrhia in the solar plexus, driving the air sharply out of her lungs in spite of her armour's protection, then twirled it and felled Firûsha with a blow to the head using the sharp end.

Acòrhia lay gasping. *Why didn't he kill her? He could have split her skull in two.*

Bephaigòn then did something she could not understand. He put his fingers onto the young älf-woman's face. She screamed as black lines of fury shot across her visage and her eyes turned black.

Acòrhia was exhausted and weakened by her injuries but she attempted a renewed assault on Bephaigòn.

The älf had seen her coming. He jabbed at her, catching her with the blade-end, which pierced leather and shoulder and kept her at a distance, like a speared fish.

I'm not going to let you jeopardise my return to Dsôn! Moaning, Acòrhia hacked at the spear shaft with her sword, falling forward. Blinded by blood and pain, she stabbed in the vague direction she thought the älf would be standing.

A vicious blow struck her on the temple, and Firûsha screamed anew . . .

'. . . she comes round, I'll explain,' she heard an älfar voice.

Acòrhia opened her eyes and saw Tirîgon in armour, seated at her side. She was in a different chamber now and a number of älfar were standing staring down at her. Their eyes were full of admiration. *I am still alive! And I have found him.* 'What . . . what happened?' she stuttered. The blow to her temple had made the whole side of her face swell up, making her speech slur like a drunkard's.

'Get out, the lot of you,' said Tirîgon with an imperious wave of his hand. As the door closed, he turned towards her. 'Well, this is a surprise. I would never have thought to find *you* here in Phondrasôn.'

'I did not expect to be here, either,' she responded. *My thanks, o gods of infamy!* 'And where am I, exactly? And what did that älf do to your sister?' Acòrhia struggled up and then sank back into the cushions with a groan. 'His name is Bephaigòn and he ...'

'My sister sends her greetings and her apologies. She needed to get her injuries attended to. She will come by later.' Tirîgon placed his hands in his lap. 'She did not recognise you; she thought you were some banished criminal from Dsôn.'

'Well, that's what I am.' Acòrhia made an effort to get her eyes to focus. *I have barely escaped endingness.* 'But I'd like to know what Bephaigòn had in mind with your sister. He was acting oddly.'

'Because he wasn't an älf at all; it was a shape-shifting karderier. He had taken on the form of an älf he had killed elsewhere in Phondrasôn. The karderiers are after us for our magic. They're assembling an army. I assume he was sent here as a spy. Or as an assassin.'

'Or to be a doppelgänger.' Acòrhia recalled what the shapeshifter had done and said. *That was it! He had wanted to take on Firûsha's external form!* 'Just think what harm he might have caused.'

'That's why we are so grateful to you.' Tirîgon smiled. 'Now. About you. What was the reason for your exile? What can a story-teller have done to make my father banish her?'

'Your father and your mother . . . they uncovered some of the truth concerning Sémaina's death. Aïsolon sent everyone who had given false witness – all seven of us – to Phondrasôn, to bring the three of you home.'

Tirîgon's eyes were narrow slits. 'What do you mean, they *uncovered* the truth?'

'They know it wasn't Sisaroth and Firûsha who killed Sémaina and her family. It was some other älf they are now trying to track down. Your mother was very . . . persistent.'

He went pale. 'Persistent?'

They haven't heard the news. 'She was making her own enquiries. She came to see me. She interrogated a couple of the witnesses, and . . . then she was dead.'

'Dead? How? An accident?'

Acòrhia shook her head. 'A paid killer, they think. He must have stalked her halfway across the city to an attic where he stabbed her to death. He did not manage to obliterate his tracks. Aïsolon took over the investigation she had begun. Wènelon caved under questioning. He told them about an unknown figure who had given us money and threatened us.'

Tirîgon's face was frozen. 'Dead,' he repeated to himself.

Acòrhia regretted having to break this news to him. *I wish I could have told you something nicer.* 'Your father made us all take a slow-acting poison and gave us each a small amount of a remedy to keep the effects at bay for a short time, to encourage us to find you quickly and bring you home,' she continued. 'I'm the only one to have made it. Iòsunta was killed by that karderier.' She stroked his face. 'I'm sorry about your mother.'

Tirîgon got unsteadily to his feet, like someone many times

his age. 'Did they find the murderer?' His question was spoken so softly that she had difficulty making out the words.

'No, they didn't. That is to say, they hadn't by the time they banished us.'

'How long ago was that?'

'Time is different here in Phondrasôn.'

'I said how long, Acòrhia?' he barked at her, grasping her by the shoulders and shaking her violently. 'Two divisions? Four? Or...'

Waves of pain swept through her and she felt her head was on the verge of exploding. 'Very soon after you three left. I warned your parents not to do anything.'

'By all the gods of infamy!' Tirîgon released his hold and sank down on the chair. 'What have I done?' He stared right through her. 'My plan...'

'It was a good plan. Many welcomed Sémaina's death.' Acòrhia attempted to rally his spirits. 'Nobody could have guessed your mother would get involved. There was no reason for her to doubt the evidence.'

His eyes raced here and there. 'All I wanted was to make a little more of myself. With my siblings at my side. We could have been undisputed rulers here in Phondrasôn. It was all going so well, too,' he said tonelessly. 'We had a palace. We had an army. Successful conquests. But now there's the Zhadar. And the shapeshifters bringing war ... and – ' he said, turning to face Acòrhia, ' – you bring me this horrendous news about our mother.'

'I can't help that.' She gave him a sympathetic look.

'I was so foolhardy!' he exclaimed in sheer despair. 'What right did I have to inveigle my siblings into this Phondrasôn adventure, with the murder claim and the false evidence against them? I should have gone on my own, without telling anyone.' Black tears slipped down his cheeks. 'My guilt would have been nothing in comparison.'

'It is not your fault that your mother ...'

'Yes, it is. It is my fault. I should have known how she would react. I knew how tenacious she was. All the precautions I left in place closed as traps around the ones I love.' He wiped away the dark tears. 'I must get back there immediately.'

'That would suit me. The medical remedy I have is running out. And Phondrasôn is a dreadful place. Why did you want to found an empire down here in these awful caves?'

'What could I ever achieve in Dsôn? In a realm that does nothing but wait and wait for something to turn up? I wanted to have the chance to rule, share power with my siblings.' Tirîgon stood up. 'It was a mistake. The whole plan was a terrible mistake. I have to try to put things right.' He turned to go.

'Do you think your father will still be alive?' Acòrhia could not stop herself.

Tirîgon halted. 'Why shouldn't he be?'

'Do you remember the instructions you left? If Aïsolon has not stopped his investigations, he will suffer the same fate as your mother.' Acòrhia watched him turn round and come back to where she was. *That expression on his face! It's terrifying!* She started to quake with fear. 'You can't hold me responsible!'

'You could have stopped him.'

'How? You never told me his name.'

'That's because I didn't know it. And I never knew what he looked like, either. But I gave you a description of the ring he wears and told you how to find him.' Tirîgon stared down at her.

'I must get back home. I have to save my father's life.' He wrenched the cushion from under her head. 'I will make sure they all hear about your heroic deeds here in Phondrasôn and how you saved my sister. Other story-tellers will relate your achievements and turn you into a true legend.'

'What...?' Acòrhia tried to struggle to one side to escape the cushion he was bringing down over her face. 'No! No! I did everything you ever asked me to.'

'I know, my dear. And I enjoyed my time with you, but I cannot risk a word of this coming out. You have succumbed to your injuries. These things happen. The gods of infamy are not always merciful.' He pressed the thick fabric onto her mouth and nose. 'Believe me. I know that only too well.'

No! No! With all her remaining strength, Acòrhia tried to push his hands away.

Chapter VII

Consider the fact that we need light
to protect ourselves from the darkness.
But what about those
who are born blind
and are thus
not afraid of the dark?
I can only say:
these are the most dangerous ones.

'Aphorisms' from the epic poem *Young Gods*
composed by Carmondai, master of word and image

Phondrasôn.

I wonder how effective our efforts will be with the reconstituted skull?
Sisaroth watched Tirîgon return from the patient's sickbed. 'I was
just coming to find you. We need to get Acòrhia into the palace so
we can use her as a sacrifice.' He was tingling with anticipation.
His long-held vocation as a priest for the gods of infamy was now
reawakening. He felt tremendous. 'We'll have to come up with a
story to account for how she died. Some injuries turn out to be
more serious than they may appear on first sight.'

'You are absolutely right there, brother.'

'You mean . . . ?' His exuberant hopes took a nose-dive into disappointment.

'Yes. She died of her wounds before my very eyes. It happened so quickly. No one could have prevented it.' Tirîgon looked truly distressed, unusually for him. 'And I am starting to agree with you. We should abandon any plans for Phondrasôn. With her final breath, Acòrhia told me your sentence of exile has been repealed. In Dsôn there's a big hunt on for the real killer of Sémaina.'

Repealed? He was exonerated? Sisaroth's spirits soared again as he took in the import of his brother's news. 'Can it be true?'

'I gather so. She told me messengers had been sent out to find us, but she fell into the sleep of endingness before she could explain.' Tirîgon wiped the tears from his eyes. 'We need to get ourselves organised to eradicate these karderiers so they can't attack us on our return journey. As soon as we have dealt with them, let's be on our way. I want to see Father again.'

'And Mother, too, of course.' Sisaroth could not work out why his brother, normally such a tactician, should suddenly have become sentimental. *The news from Dsôn seems to have affected him deeply.* 'Don't tell me Acòrhia put a spell on you?'

'Forgive me if I give way to my emotions for once.' Tirîgon gulped down a sob and struggled to contain his feelings. 'She opened my eyes to what is truly important. But I don't think the good news she brought you will make up for the loss of a sacrifice for Shëidogîs.'

They walked up to the palace side by side.

The next älf who turns up won't be covered by the death curse. 'Was she able to give you any clues about the route to take up to the surface?' Sisaroth asked. 'I know we want to go back, but without knowing the way . . .'

'The Zhadar knows the way.'

'Well, he says he does.'

'We'll ask him. Or we'll force him to tell us. Let Marandëi show what she's capable of.'

Sisaroth was more and more confused by the change in his brother's attitude. He seemed to be contemplating an immediate attack, eschewing a strategic plan, on an enemy power that vastly outnumbered them. *What has brought about this change of heart, I wonder? This is the first time he has shown himself desperate to go home. He always wanted to create an invincible empire here in Phondrasôn.* 'What's the matter? What did Acòrhia say to you?'

Tirîgon's pace slowed.

'Excuse me,' came a call from behind them. 'I have a message for you.'

Sisaroth saw a soldier hurrying towards them with a leather roll in one hand. 'Who is it from?'

The älf handed him the roll. 'The same groundling that came to see you before. He said to tell you these are his master's instructions. And he said to give you his own final greetings. He would not be coming back.'

Tirîgon asked urgently, 'Has he been gone long? Did he deliver any swords for us?'

'No, no swords. I came as quickly as I could from the gate.'

So the little mountain maggot is carrying out his plan. Sisaroth could guess what his brother was thinking. 'Forget it. The groundling would never have taken us with him. He hated his master but he'd have led us to our doom rather than take us to

Dsôn or Tark Draan. He told us clearly that he considered all älfar his enemies.'

Tirîgon uttered a curse. 'It would have been too good to be true,' he muttered. He looked about to set off. 'Perhaps I can catch up with him.'

'Wait.' Sisaroth opened the leather folder. Out tumbled another example of the fateful jewelled breastpin and a parchment whose contents he quickly skimmed. The document was written in perfect älfar and headed *My trust in you.* The piece of jewellery was presumably intended as a reminder and a warning.

Our first real mission. This is not coming at a good time. 'Brother, come. We've got something more important to sort out. More important than Tungdil. Let's speak to Firûsha.' He rolled the parchment up and entered the palace.

The guard saluted and returned to his post.

Tirîgon accompanied him in obvious ill-humour. 'I suggest we take Marandëi along. Whatever the Zhadar wants us to do she should be able to deal with easily. The sooner we're done with that the sooner we can come back, take on the karderiers and set off for home.'

'So you've no idea what he's asking us to do?'

'It won't be anything the cîanai can't pull off. Apart from maybe working out the design specifications for building a special tower ...'

'... that I'll then have to liberate her from.' Sisaroth could not help laughing.

They called Firûsha, Crotàgon, Marandëi and Tossàlor to meet in the library.

There was dismay about Acòrhia, with the cîanai in particular devastated by the news of her death. But when Tirîgon explained that they did not intend to place the next arrival under oath, with the explicit intention of making him or her a sacrifice, she began to smile. She had placed the skull in a padded casket and carried it about with her everywhere she went. This and the staff she used gave her the look of an eternal wanderer.

Firûsha made no comment, not even when she heard that their sentence of exile had been repealed.

She is still terrified of the potential power of the skull. Sisaroth put his arm round her shoulders. 'You'll learn to see Shëidogîs as a friend we can confide in. We shall need his protection if we are to survive.'

His sister indicated the box. 'Will you be taking it with you to Dsôn?'

'Of course,' he replied. 'The gods of infamy belong to our race.'

'But didn't the Inextinguishables themselves ban this form of worship?'

'Didn't you say the Inextinguishables are in Tark Draan now?' Marandëi interjected, one hand on the casket. 'And that they have been there for a very, very long time? Perhaps they will welcome what Shëidogîs can do for them. Or the Dsôn Sòmran älfar may take to him if the Infamous One performs some miracle to improve their situation.'

An impatient Tirîgon broke into the discussion. 'Can we not postpone this decision? I want to know what that bastard, the Zhadar, wants us to do.' He took the leather document roll from his brother and extracted the instructions. 'We only have to obey him one last time.' He read out the Zhadar's demand.

My trust in you

I am sending you to the Cjash region in the triple caves of Whifis. In the middle cave there lives a creature I once showed a favour to. It has not repaid the debt.

It calls itself the veyn. Do not be taken in by the way it speaks. It is neither male nor female; it likes to speak the truth and will attempt to read your minds. As you know, in many a head, it is better if the truth stays hidden.

The veyn wears a silver bangle and a circlet of tionium connected to a palladium chain from which it derives strength, power and authority.

You will act as my strong arm to collect my outstanding debts. Bring me the creature's malicious tongue and the bangle and circlet. Act with all speed. Do not delay, and above all, avoid entering into bargains with the inhabitants of Whifis.

I am only concerned with getting the bracelet and the circlet. Tungdil will show you the way. Make haste. The quicker you are, the sooner your return to Dsôn or other place of your choosing.

Tirîgon cursed. 'The groundling was to have taken us? Why didn't I run after him? I wish I had.' He tossed the paper down onto the table.

'We'll have to go and find the Zhadar first to let him know the dwarf has deserted,' Crotàgon proposed.

Sisaroth noticed the corner of a second piece of paper jutting out from the leather case. It was a note with a sketch map and a written description. *That's not the Zhadar's handwriting.* 'Tungdil read the instructions and has given us a route plan,' he said with relief.

'Right.' Tirîgon was already on his feet. 'Let's get started.

Sisaroth, Marandëi and myself. That should be enough. The rest of you stay here to hold the palace and the fortress.' He went to the door. 'I'll get provisions made up. When we're back we'll discuss how to locate where the karderiers are assembling so we can find them and destroy them before they get a chance to attack us.' He left the room.

Initially all was silent in the library.

Finally Crotàgon cleared his throat and spoke. 'It's remarkable how he always seems to be the one to make decisions.'

'I would have said exactly the same,' said Sisaroth in defence of his brother. Firûsha indicated her agreement. 'You must excuse his uncouth manners. He is upset about the news from Dsôn.'

'One would have thought he'd be pleased about what he heard.' Tossàlor played with a piece of bone, examining it under the light. He removed a thin slice with his pocket knife. It was impossible for him ever to leave his art at the door. 'After the incident over there in the barracks he's a changed älf. Where is that calm sense of reason?'

How would I know? Sisaroth had no explanation for the change in his brother's attitude.

'I think it's because he volunteered to join us in our Phondrasôn banishment and now the longed-for return is within our grasp,' Firûsha proposed. 'He misses our parents and friends just as we do.' She looked at the others, a happy smile on her face. 'Isn't it amazing to know we can all go back soon?' But she could not help sending a sickened glance at the casket.

'It certainly is,' Tossàlor agreed. 'I'm eager to know what kind of a reception they'll give *me* in Dsôn.'

'I get what you're hinting at.' Sisaroth smiled. 'The three of us will make sure our father issues a pardon. We'll tell him how

much you have helped us. He'll have no choice but to be
gracious.'

He would never admit that he had any doubts in that respect.
The artist was guilty of such perfidy and atrocities against his own
people in the name of art that his deeds eclipsed any straightforward murder. *My father will have great difficulty in dealing generously
with the case. It might be better for Tossàlor to stay here in Phondrasôn.
He's just waiting for the next set of curse-free bones so he can get his new
project started without having to fear the consequences.*

At the same time he was well aware that Crotàgon would insist
that Tossàlor accompany them. The warrior was fond of him, even
if the affection did not seem to be mutual. Crotàgon was very popular among the troops and was regarded as the army's unofficial
commander. They could not afford to slight the statuesque älf.

'That goes for every älf who has shown us loyalty during our
time in Phondrasôn,' Firûsha added.

The others nodded and clapped.

'Do you think you three can carry out the Zhadar's mission
by yourselves, or would it be a good idea if I came along, too?'
Crotàgon asked, flexing his muscles.

'It'd be better if you stayed with Firûsha and the army, just in
case the karderiers try anything while we're gone,' Sisaroth said
after a short pause for thought. 'Tirîgon is right to suggest we
take Marandëi with us. We should have no need to fear any
opponent if we have her magic skills.' He got to his feet. 'Till we
meet again.' He embraced his sister. 'Be good, and if you can't be
good, be careful,' he joked.

'She'll be fine,' Tossàlor remarked. 'If anyone attacks she'll
hew their skull into tiny pieces and sing a song of victory when
she's finished.'

All the älfar joined in the general laughter. Sisaroth left the library in Marandëi's company, so that they could prepare for the journey.

'I shall be taking the skull with me,' she told him.

'Don't you trust Firûsha?'

'She destroyed it before and I'm sure she'd do it again, given half a chance.' She carried the casket by its handle. 'It'd be better to take Shëidogîs with us. After all, we might come across a superfluous älf on our travels.' A smile of anticipation played about her lips. 'I know the Infamous One will return to us. I can feel it in my bones. We must ensure Tossàlor is given due recognition for his masterly reconstruction.'

Sisaroth recalled the frightened expression on his sister's face. 'Firûsha certainly does not share your enthusiasm. What exactly did the skull do to her?'

'Nothing. Obviously, nothing. Otherwise she'd be dead, wouldn't she?' replied the cîanai. 'Shëidogîs wanted to drive her away. He was frightened for his own existence.' She stopped and looked him in the eye. 'Believe me, Sisaroth: Shëidogîs is perfectly capable of driving anyone mad. That would have been your sister's fate if he had decided to try.' Marandëi walked on, striking the ground with the silver-tipped staff as she did so. 'Is it your wish to become a priest?'

'Yes,' he replied quickly. 'I have studied all the rites.'

She smiled. 'You mean the rituals the Inextinguishables allowed before they lost faith with the gods of infamy and condemned all forms of their worship?' She moved the casket. 'You have absolutely no idea what powers Shëidogîs has. The miracle of the glass sea is just one of the wonders to come. Imagine the force of a god of infamy riding on an untameable night-mare! A magnificent specimen brim-full of fury and able to carry its rider through any battle, trampling the enemy under its hooves!' Her features darkened. 'What the Inextinguishables did by outlawing the religious practices was to shackle this stupendous animal, to curb the mouth with its formidable incisors, to hobble the lightning-hooves, leaving nothing but the extraordinary coat.' She tapped the casket lid with the end of her staff. 'Dsôn Sòmran won't know what's hit it. The power of Shëidogîs will astound them all. They'll love it, I promise you.'

Sisaroth could hardly wait to try out the sacrifice to invoke the spirit of the god and entice it back into the skull. He had paid attention to his sister when she had tried to warn him that the spirit might not be that of one of their own gods, but he had dismissed her objections. He was convinced by what Marandëi was telling him. *I shall sacrifice all the älfar that bore false witness against us. All of them!* 'Can you teach me more about the old forms of worship? We'll have plenty of time before we reach the triple cave. You could teach me on the march.'

'My word! You remind me of myself when I was younger, Sisaroth. All that passion.' Marandëi nodded to him. 'Of course I will. You should learn how to pray properly to the gods of infamy and understand how to free them from their chains. The two of us will be instrumental in returning our race to the old ways.' She turned to enter her own chamber. 'I won't be long packing the things I need. I'll see you at the gate.'

Sisaroth walked on to reach his own quarters.

What will the Inextinguishables say when we bring the gods of infamy back with us, I wonder? Are we heading for a conflict here? Could it be that we will cause a schism amongst our people?

He stepped into the first of his suite of rooms, removed his armour and undergarments and got dressed for the journey.

He was still considering the ramifications. He wanted to find out the extent of Shëidogîs' power before making his final decision. *Shëidogîs must convince me himself.*

Phondrasôn.

Firûsha was in the guardroom at the fortress. She was wearing the armour that the groundling had made for her. The metal plates fitted round her body perfectly, never making a sound when she moved; the black metal suit, partly decorated, was not heavy at all.

She was going through the effects that had belonged to Iòsunta and Acòrhia. Her motivation was mostly curiosity, but she was also hopeful she might come across something with good news from home. *A note, perhaps, or a letter, or maybe even a map indicating the route they had taken from Dsôn!*

But apart from two small phials in leather protective cases there was nothing out of the ordinary. Any knowledge about the route home would have died with the two älfar women.

I wonder what's inside these? Both of the little bottles had been with Acòrhia's things. One of them had been inside the armour she had been wearing and the other one was in her rucksack.

Firûsha undid the stopper and sniffed. *Cloudy yellow oil. It's gone a bit rancid.* She did not understand what its significance could be.

What caught her attention were the splashes of a similar liquid staining Iòsunta's rucksack and also her collar. They were the same colour and consistency as the contents of the phials, but there was no corresponding bottle to be found in Iòsunta's things.

She started to suspect that Acòrhia might have purloined Iòsunta's phial. *Did that happen before the fight with the karderier? And what for? Why would the little vessel have been important?* These thoughts made the heroic älf-woman appear in a different light. And Firûsha was increasingly sure that she had seen the dead woman once before, back in Dsôn. *Wasn't she some kind of celebrity? And when would I have seen her?*

The door behind her opened quietly.

'Forgive me for interrupting you,' said Crotàgon. 'But we have a new arrival.' He looked concerned.

A new arrival, who will soon be sacrificed to the skull . . . Firûsha could see from his expression that the älf shared her misgivings on that score. 'Do you think we should turn him away?' It might seem cruel to refuse entry to one of her own kind, but it would be saving his life. *At least for the immediate future.*

'You should speak with him first. He . . . comes from Dsôn, but he hasn't been banished,' Crotàgon replied.

'You're absolutely sure he isn't a shapeshifter?'

'He has wounds he would never have inflicted on himself purely to trick us.'

'Then our father must have sent an extra volunteer to find us.' She stood up and went with Crotàgon, who avoided giving a direct answer. 'No?' she insisted.

'No. But you should hear for yourself. I've called Tossàlor over as well. I hope you don't mind. I know that he . . .' Crotàgon looked for the right words. 'None of you can see any use in him because he refuses to take up arms. But he is intelligent. Sharper than any knife.'

Firûsha placed a hand on his broad back. 'I'll be happy to listen to his views.' *As long as he doesn't have any immediate plans for my skeleton.*

She stepped into the sickbay to find a blood-smeared älf lying on a red-stained sheet. A pool of blood was collecting on the floor. It was obvious that the ghastly mutilations he had received would transport him into endingness. His bandages were soaked through and the blood was still flowing.

The two healers Draïlor and Horogòn were comparing notes at his bedside, their aprons stiff with blood from the injured new arrival.

'Thank goodness you have come. I don't think he'll be conscious for much longer,' Horogòn said quietly. 'These wounds have been made with a poisoned weapon. Even putting a compression bandage on is having no effect on the haemorrhage. We have given him a pain-relieving potion. If you want to ask him anything, you'd better hurry.'

Firûsha stepped close, passing through the puddle of blood so her boots left red footprints on the stone tiles. *This was never a karderier spy.*

The stranger had lost both arms; one had been cut off below the elbow, while the other stump stopped below the shoulder joint. The wound in his left thigh had gone through to the bone and his clothing and skin had been burned off on the right side of his body. His face was swollen and disfigured and great handfuls of his grey hair had been ripped out of his scalp.

It's a miracle he's still breathing. 'Brave warrior,' she said in respectful greeting. 'I bid you welcome. What shall I call you? I am Firûsha and I command this small älfar empire together with my two brothers. Whoever has done this to you . . .'

'Firûsha?' He stared at her in amazement. 'Oh, if only Aïsolon could know that I have found his daughter. I am Naïgonor. I was one of the wall defenders, and I knew your father before...' He coughed and looked at them imploringly. 'You must save the others!' he gasped. The dose of pain-relief the healers had given him was starting to fail.

'The others?' *Does he mean further envoys?*

'The people of Dsôn Sòmran,' he breathed. 'We were...' He was overcome with emotion and despair reduced him to a storm of passionate tears.

Battling her instincts to grab him and shake the truth out, Firûsha gently sat down on the blood-soaked sheets and stroked his matted hair. *There's a remedy that is stronger.* She raised her sweet voice and sang him a tune she had learned at her mother's knee.

The melody seemed to calm Naïgonor. His breathing became less laboured and the fear of death disappeared from his gaze. Clarity of thought had returned.

Firûsha sang two more verses to ensure lasting peace of mind for him. *I hope that is enough.* 'Now tell me what you know,' she begged.

'It was ... some time ago. Quite a while after you three had gone. Much of the city was lost in a landslide, the likes of which we had never known. Over a third of the buildings were dragged into the valley, burying the inhabitants and any out on the streets in that quarter. Then an earth-fall broke a huge gap in our northern defence. The rubble that plunged down onto the city caused even more damage. It was dreadful!'

Mother! Father! Firûsha was thunderstruck. The hand on the soldier's head froze in mid-stroke.

'We were still searching the ruins for survivors when a horde of óarcos and trolls overran the city. They had heard or seen the ramparts were down.' Naïgonor was in great distress. 'There was no way we could hold the breach against the sheer mass of the beasts' onslaught. We tried to put up barricades in the streets. No one knew what had happened to Aïsolon. We needed him to organise our resistance; there was total chaos and we were scattered around the city. We decided we should all flee to Phondrasôn and assemble here rather than be slaughtered in the valley.'

Firûsha began to tremble. *This is not the news I wished to hear! I'm sure my father is still alive. He . . .* 'Did the trolls do this to you?'

'No. We gathered about a thousand älfar and swept through the tunnels of Phondrasôn. Where we met opposition, we were able to defeat our attackers. But then some other creatures joined the fray. A mere touch produced fatal wounds. When their victims died, they assumed their bodily shapes.'

Karderiers. O ye gods of infamy, how could you allow this to happen? Firûsha held back her own tears. Her insides were cold as marble and her fingers had lost their sense of touch. *Is there no hope for my race? Where can I go back to with my brothers now? All is lost!*

'They took over our leader and led us into a trap.' Naïgonor's eyes implored Firûsha for help. 'Our people are imprisoned like cattle.'

A slight hope was rekindled in her heart. 'Is my father amongst them?' Firûsha knew what had happened to the survivors from her city. *The karderiers ambushed them.*

'No. I never saw him after the landslide.'

That need not mean he is dead. She did not permit herself to explore this possibility, for the sake of her own sanity. 'How many of us are still alive?'

'When I escaped, there must have been roughly six hundred.' Naïgonor closed his eyes, exhausted now. The pulse at his throat was slowing. 'You have to save them or these terrible beings will kill them all.'

'And my mother?' Firûsha saw that he was past being able to respond. 'Naïgonor! Tell me! What about my mother?'

But the älf did not open his eyes. His heart had stopped forever.

It is up to me to liberate the captive älfar. Firûsha got slowly to her feet with the warrior's blood sticking to her armour. She had been tasked with an enormous responsibility. She looked at Crotàgon. 'Was Naïgonor able to explain where our people are to be found?'

The broad-shouldered warrior nodded. He was obviously dismayed at what he had heard. 'He gave me a rough idea of where they are imprisoned. I'll consult Sisaroth's map.' He did not look pleased at the prospect of carrying out what she was planning. 'I know what you have in mind, but there are not enough of us, Firûsha. If the karderiers' army were to attack . . .'

'. . . we definitely need the assistance of those six hundred souls who are currently held captive,' she broke in. Her mind was made up. *Every second's hesitation may mean further loss of precious life.* 'Give me fifty of the best soldiers. You stay here and hold the fort.'

She might have been expecting her mentor to object, but he

stroked her face tenderly, staring intently into her eyes. 'Your brothers will kill me if anything happens to you. So it's quite selfish of me to ask you to come back in one piece.' His gaze was that of a teacher assessing an esteemed pupil who was leaving as a journeyman on a quest to become a master. 'I'll draw you up a chart of the route to take.'

Firûsha stood looking at the dead älf and heard the sound of the last of his blood dripping from the soaked sheets to the floor. 'You did not go into endingness in vain. Your message has reached us and we shall avenge you.'

She left the sickbed and attempted to control her stormy emotions. Her priority was to release the imprisoned warriors. One of them was sure to have some knowledge of her parents' fates.

I may already be an orphan. I may have no home to return to. She was still trembling all over and she went weak at the knees. The significance of what she had learned hit her with the force of a landslide. She sank to the ground, sobbing. *What shall I do? What shall we do?*

Firûsha stared into an abyss. Ever since her banishment she had kept alive the hope of eventually being reunited with her parents in Dsôn Sòmran. She had lived and breathed the longing for the embraces she would be greeted with on her return. *Now I have nothing. The gods have forsaken me. I have nothing except for my brothers.*

She felt her stomach turn and she vomited several times.

Firûsha was in a bad state, shaking from head to toe. She took some time before she felt able to get up from where she had cowered. She walked as if in a trance on her way from the guard-room back to the palace.

Terrified to think about what the future might have in store, she discarded any plan other than the immediate one of procuring the liberation of the captives. And she would need to confer with Sisaroth and Tirîgon. *They'll be as shocked as I am.*

To her surprise she found she was expected.

In the palace hall ten guards stood encircling two filth-encrusted, starving new arrivals, holding them at bay with their spears.

Firûsha halted. 'What is this? Why haven't they . . .' Then she recognised one of them. *Can that be Father's deputy?* She approached. 'Gàlaidon? Is it you?'

Her emotions were in turmoil. This was her father's First Sytràp; he had been the one to arrest her in the middle of the night and have her thrown from the walls, showing no mercy. *It was unjust. Everything that went wrong started when he turned up.*

Yet she also felt a certain relief at seeing him: he was a familiar face and a close friend of her father's. Perhaps his sudden appearance on the scene was a good omen. *Was he sent to find us? Has Father got to the bottom of the conspiracy?*

'It is me, indeed, my little songbird,' the blond älf said. His perilous state of health was obvious despite his joyful reaction at seeing her. His right hand was bandaged but the linen was soaked with pus. 'Praise be to Inàste that I have found you.' He tried to step towards her but the ring of spears remained rigidly fixed.

'Watch out, Firûsha!' one of the guards warned. 'Remember that the karderiers are shapeshifters. We only brought them here because he swore he'd be able to prove he's really Gàlaidon if we let him speak to one of the triplets. He said he would know many things to which an imposter would not be privy. You and your brothers know him better than anyone else. You should be able to judge.'

We'll soon see about that. Firûsha looked at Gàlaidon. 'My Father's Golden Time of Immortality, where was that held?'

He answered with a grin. 'In a cage. In the citadel.'

'Tell me why that was.'

'Because he wanted to test it for strength.'

'And what was the purpose of the cage?'

'It had to hold an óarco. We wanted to try our new steel arrowheads and see how deep they could penetrate óarco flesh.'

Firûsha was nearly convinced. 'And what did he call me?'

'Apart from *Daughter* and *Songbird*?'

'There was a special name.'

Gàlaidon's smile widened. 'My blue-eyed star of the night.'

It is him! To hear those missed terms of endearment eradicated all her resentment against Gàlaidon. She was reliving happier times in her homeland. She signalled to the guards to let him go and she moved forward to embrace him. 'It is good to see you. You are forgiven for what you did. There was a plot against us and we were condemned in error. You had no choice but to follow Father's orders and send us into exile.' Her words were delivered firmly to dispel the last of the shadows. 'I have heard such awful tidings about Dsôn.' She gave a summary of what she had heard from Naïgonor. Gàlaidon confirmed the truth of it. She was reluctant to pose the next question. 'And my father?'

'I haven't seen him since Dsôn. Back in the guardroom. Then the landslide happened. Most of the citadel was destroyed. But I feel that he will have survived. We must not assume his passing.

I shan't believe he is dead until I see his corpse.' He stroked her dark hair consolingly.

'And my mother?'

'I don't know.' Gàlaidon pointed to the unknown companion who was still held back by the sharp spear blades. His armour was similar to the First Sytràp's own, and he carried a large rucksack. His long brown hair was dirty and unkempt. 'This is an älf I met on my journey. He saved me from some fierce barbarians as big and broad as trees. They wore animal skins and used scythes as their weapons.'

Firûsha looked closely at the other arrival. He was finding it hard to stay upright, he was so weak. *Is that ink on his left hand?* 'He doesn't really look like a better warrior than you.' She pulled Gàlaidon's head down so she could whisper in his ear. 'You know what the karderiers are capable of? They can take on the shape of those they have murdered.'

'Yes, your guards gave me that impression.'

'How can we find out whether or not he is one of their spies? We've had a recent problem with that.' Firûsha could not think how to test the stranger to establish his identity beyond doubt. 'He is to be kept prisoner until my brothers and I return.' She cast her eye on Gàlaidon's injured arm. 'Is the wound infected?'

'It's starting to heal, I think. But it's very painful. And bad news for an älf like me, who is right-handed in combat.'

'Our healers here are good. They will look after you.' Firûsha turned to her soldiers. 'Take the älf to . . .'

'My name is Carmondai,' the other new arrival interrupted her. 'Perhaps you have heard of me?'

'You?' Firûsha could not believe her ears. *How ever did he get here?* Every älf alive knew the name of the celebrated master of word and image who had accompanied Sinthoras and Caphalor on their famous first campaign in Tark Draan. She had always loved his tales of bravery and battle. *Now I figure in just such a saga myself.* 'I can hardly believe it.'

He rolled his eyes. 'Which of my poems would you like me to recite? What do I need to tell you about my long wanderings through the cursed and magic-infused land of demons in order to be spared getting dumped in some cold, dank cell?'

Firûsha looked down, shame-faced. 'You are claiming to be the master of word and image? The founder and designer of Dsôn Balsur? The älf who went on the first campaign and preserved its history for posterity?' She understood the significance of his being there. *There is a way through to Tark Draan. We could all get to where the Inextinguishables are if what he says is true!*

'No, I'm not *claiming* to be him. I *am* him,' Carmondai retorted. 'And I want a bath.'

Firûsha did not have time to waste. *Lives are at stake.* She pursed her lips. 'I'm sorry but you will have to wait. I have to go and save my people.' She issued instructions to put Carmondai in a cell and to take Gàlaidon to the guest rooms. 'We will speak later,' she said as she took her leave.

'Where are your brothers?' Gàlaidon called after her. Carmondai was complaining loudly about his treatment. The ten spears remained trained on him.

'They'll be back soon.' Firûsha hurried off. Crotàgon had prepared her well for the battle to come. *It is time to drive my sword into the flesh of my enemies!*

Firûsha took the map her mentor handed her and set off with fifty of the best male and female warriors the fortress had to offer to liberate her people.

She would eliminate any karderier or opponent who stood in her way. She would take no prisoners.

Chapter VIII

Paint your blade black
  so it won't flash in the light.
Paint your face black
  to hide its radiance.
Turn your soul black
  and the darkness will belong to you alone.

'Aphorisms' from the epic poem *Young Gods*
composed by Carmondai, master of word and image

Phondrasôn.

'Whifis really is a cave within a cave.' Tirîgon looked at the
cocoon-shaped stone formation that hung from the roof. He
could feel the air vibrating and his skin tingled. *We are enveloped
in magic.* 'How wide do you reckon this cavern is?'

'I'd say it was at least a mile in diameter.' Sisaroth peeked over
the rock they were hiding behind.

'It reminds me of a nest.' Marandëi put down her skull casket and scrutinised their target, which was now less than one
hundred paces distant.

'That thing probably contains a second cocoon containing this veyn we're supposed the steal the items from.' Tirîgon looked at the free-standing helical staircase which wound its way upwards like a rearing snake about to strike; it had neither central post nor handrail. On each of the stone steps stood an armoured guard holding a shield and a spear.

Tirîgon found his mind wandering back to Esmonäe in spite of himself. He missed her and his feelings for her were still strong. It occurred to him that she, as an accomplished assassin, would have been an immense help in the present circumstances. However hard he might try to fill in the gap her absence left, the wounds kept reopening. And bleeding.

The only thing he could do by way of diversion was to concentrate on the task at hand. *Open combat is useless here. It would take us a long time to fight our way up and the alarm would be sounded immediately. The gods only know how many troops they have in reserve.* He cast a sideways glance at the cîanai. *I'm glad I insisted she come with us.* 'Can you get rid of the guards with a spell?'

Sisaroth spoke up. 'Brother, I've no idea what Acòrhia did to you but you seem to want everything to happen yesterday. You're rushing at this like the north wind in Dsôn. What happened to your cool temperament?' He nodded at the floating interlocking caves. 'What if they are all full of waiting troops?'

'Do you suppose that thought hadn't occurred to me?' Tirîgon looked amused. 'Then our nice little skull will have a chance to show it really *is* the remains of an infamous god.' *And I'm not convinced that's what it is.* During the course of the journey his brother and Marandëi had been chattering away together, practising gestures and sing-song prayers. He had had enough.

The skeleton head had no effect on him, as far as he was aware. It did not seem to be imbued with magic or power; it did not make him quake with fear. *What happened to the skull when it was shattered will have destroyed any force it once had. What a fate – to be unmanned by a candlestick.*

'No need to mock,' Marandëi said.

'I'm not. I'm waiting for some sign to show me the light,' he answered.

'You will have your sign when I have made Shëidogîs his first living sacrifice. I'm afraid Acòrhia was gone too quickly for us to use her.' She kept up the friendly tone of voice. 'I have been able to generate enough magic power to use for my spells. There must be a force field hereabouts.'

'Then get to work.' Tirîgon drew his sword. 'We may have the gift of eternal life but time is passing fast.'

'Don't tell me you're basing your strategy on Marandëi killing all the guards, and us storming up the staircase?' Sisaroth was not happy with the plan. 'This has not been thought through. It's not worthy of a brother of mine.'

Tirîgon turned his head to his sibling. It felt as if he were looking at his own reflection in a mirror. 'I should prefer it if we had a layout of the interior of the double cave, but I'm afraid we don't.' *Who does he think he is?* 'So unless you have a better plan, we'll get inside and see what's there. Then we look for this veyn. You can draw a map as we go, Sisaroth. It'll be just as much help as the ones you've got plastered over the walls of our library in the palace. They've got us nearer getting home, haven't they?' He had spoken more loudly than he intended to, and an echo went round the cave. The pain of his loss had shortened his temper; he had allowed himself to get irritated. *That was the wrong time to let off steam.*

His brother studied his face. 'I hardly know you, you've changed so. It's as if your form had been taken over by a karder-ier.' He drew his own sword. 'Right. Let's go for it. I don't have a better idea. But I had hoped you would approach this more calmly. You are always so level-headed.' He nodded to Marandëi. 'You've heard what we want you to do.'

The cîanai got to her feet, rotated her staff and intoned some cryptic syllables.

Three fine cracks appeared in the stone at her feet to extend and race across the intervening ground towards the staircase.

The guards noticed what was happening; one by one they turned to where she stood. Behind their visors their faces glowed green. Each in turn banged once on his shield with his mailed fist so that a continuous metallic clanging tone resounded, drowning out Marandëi's voice.

Tirîgon wondered what her spell was designed to do, if the ground was the only thing touched by it. *Furrows – is that it?*

The cracks had reached the first step, ebbed away in the speed of their progress, then spewed out a crackling whirlwind of sparks to attack the guards. As soon as one of the armoured sol-diers was hit by one of the glowing, dancing sparks he turned into a ball of fire.

That's quite impressive! Tirîgon watched in awe.

Exploding clouds of ash sent limbs, armour-plating, and hel-mets into the air. Figures plunged down off the steps to whirl around like nothing more than rag dolls, with arms and legs forced into unnatural angles.

And there was something else he noticed.

'Time to attack!' Sisaroth jumped up and was about to rush off but Tirîgon grabbed him by his armour and pulled him back down. 'What's the idea? Just now things couldn't go fast enough for you and now you're holding me back?'

'Tell Marandëi to destroy the whole staircase.'

'I don't understand.' Sisaroth was crouching down behind a boulder. 'Tirîgon, how are we going to get up there to explore and find the veyn if we do that?'

'Trust me. Trust my tactical abilities. You wanted me to employ them, didn't you?' What he had in mind was a radical, but simple solution. *If I am right, this staircase bears the entire double world and it is supported on a force field of magic.* 'We don't have to climb up there to get to it. We will bring it down to us.'

'Make up your minds!' Marandëi was keeping her gaze fixed on the double cave. 'And do it fast!'

Sisaroth exhaled and indicated to the cîanai that she should demolish the whole flight of stairs.

He will see what I'm trying to do. Tirîgon rose and took a look over the rock that protected them. His brother stood at his side.

Marandëi went into action once more. She executed sweeping gestures with her arms and used her staff like a cudgel. There was a dull thud. A pressure wave shot out from the end of the staff and sent stones hurtling through the air.

The invisible wall swept towards the stairway. At the same time new soldiers were storming down to replace those lost in the first attack.

Marandëi's spell collided with the steps – and resolved itself into an opalescent bolt of lightning that dazzled and blinded the älfar.

Is it done? When Tirîgon's sight returned he could see the lower portion of the stairs had gone. There were huge gaps all the way up. It would be impossible to climb up or down. The enemy warriors stayed where they were and took counsel with each other.

Sisaroth turned to Tirîgon. 'What did you hope to get from that?'

'Look over there,' he countered. 'And take your hat off to me. Me and my bright ideas.'

The floating double cave was starting to lower with audible creaks and rumbles, as if it were being crushed under the weight of its own stones. Then it tipped to one side and flipped over, its entrance swallowing up the waiting troops.

The floating steps, drenched with blood, now burst apart under the pressure from above. Corpses and rubble rained down.

Neither Sisaroth nor Tirîgon could tear their eyes away. Marandëi was also staring in amazement at the effect of her spell. 'How did you know that would happen?'

I hoped it would. Just as Tirîgon was opening his mouth to reply, a double sphere collapsed to the ground as if the cords suspending it had suddenly snapped. It buried the remains of the stairs.

The cocoon-like case crashed down, making the entire cavern rock and quake. It split open like a pottery vase dropped onto a stone floor. Black and red clouds of dust swirled up on all sides.

Shrapnel from the explosion shot through the surrounding space. Sisaroth and Tirîgon both felt impacts on their helmets as they ducked.

Why is she still standing up like that? Tirîgon pulled Marandëi down under cover and they threw themselves to the ground.

The ground shook under their feet and the rumbling noise did not stop.

When the cloud of dust reached the älfar's shelter they were swamped in it. A storm-like wind howled past their ears.

This is more violent than I had imagined. Tirîgon kept his eyes tightly shut and wrapped his arms around his knees so he wouldn't be blown away. He had no idea where his brother and Marandëi were.

Thunder claps sounded.

It seemed as if the whole of Phondrasôn was in turmoil, shaking itself in fury. Boulders fell from the rock ceiling, crashing to the floor and sending up sharp splinters.

When the noise gradually abated, Tirîgon opened his eyes and looked around. *Now to look for the veyn. It will be out there somewhere. Somewhere under all that rubble.* 'I told you the being would come to us and we wouldn't have to go up and get it.'

Then he saw Sisaroth. He was bending over Marandëi, who was lying full length by the rock wall with her torso crushed under a rock that had fallen from the cave roof. Her staff lay in several pieces at her side. It seemed that only the casket with the skull had remained intact.

That should never have happened! Tirîgon stood up and raced over to help his brother try to lift the huge stone. Blood was trickling out from under it, making a line through the ubiquitous dust.

Her white eyes were wide open but they saw nothing at all. She turned her head from side to side.

'Mistress!' Sisaroth cried to her in despair. 'Save yourself! Try a spell! You must have one!'

Tirîgon gave up trying to move the boulder. *It is far too heavy.* He picked up part of the staff and attempted to use it as a lever, but it did not work. *No! We can't afford to lose her! We'll need her spells and magic for our journey home to Dsôn.* 'Marandëi, you must do something to save yourself! We can't help you,' he urged. 'Do you hear? Use a spell. Your people need you!'

'And who but you will bring Shëidogîs the fame he deserves?' added Sisaroth, kneeling at her side. He held her head as she tossed it constantly from one side to the other. 'Marandëi! Marandëi! You must . . .'

She focused on him. 'Take the Infamous One back,' she breathed. Blood came out of her mouth and she choked on it and coughed. Red droplets spattered his face. 'You must promise me that you will be his priest.'

Sisaroth shook his head. 'No. I cannot do that. My training . . . you have to . . .'

'Back in the palace locate the secret door behind the library. In the second chamber you will find my writings,' she explained. 'Study my instructions, give Shëidogîs his blood sacrifice and he will protect you and lead you.' She coughed up more blood and it ran down the side of her face.

Noises became audible through the clouds of dirt that were starting to retreat. Some figures stumbled coughing and swaying out of the fog of dust. There was the clattering of armour and weapons to show that some soldiers had survived the collapse of the double cave.

They won't put up much of a fight. Tirîgon had his sword in his hand. With his foot he slid the casket over to Sisaroth. His level-headed temperament led him to his next inspiration. 'You could use her for your sacrifice, couldn't you? She'll die anyway. And if she self-sacrifices, it won't trigger the death curse. I'll make sure you have the time you both need.'

Tirîgon took several steps forward, and came round the side of the rock. He struck off the head of the first figure to come near. He pierced the next through the stomach and cut off a third warrior's raised sword arm. He sent the badly injured barbarian to the ground with a kick and stamped on his neck. *Just what I needed! Your death bears the name of Tirîgon!*

The älf made steady progress.

The sandy fog that gritted between his teeth started to dispel.

Tirîgon could only see about thirty opponents struggling through the clouds of dust, and all of them were injured in some way. *You belong to me.* He could see scratched and broken limbs sticking out from the remains of the broken hollow spheres. The scene reminded him of a sea of stone with drowning mariners wading through petrified waves.

He had no mercy for them. *I shall tell Tossàlor where the cave is. He'll be pleased to get all this new material.*

As soon as any soldier came too close, Tirîgon struck him swiftly down with a precise blow. None of the enemy could match him for skill. 'I want the veyn,' he called out. 'The gâlran zhadar, lord of Phondrasôn and sovereign ruler of these caves, has sent us. I challenge the veyn to surrender to us and then your survivors will remain survivors.' He stabbed an injured warrior to death as he lay on the ground. 'If he does not surrender, my name shall be the death of many, many more of you.'

A barbarian in dusty, battered armour came up and fell to his knees. 'Mercy, Shadow Lord. The one you seek is dead.'

'How do you know?'

'I saw the corpse.' The barbarian pointed towards the place. 'I can show you.' He stumbled off across the rubble.

Tirîgon followed him. This time he did not pause to stab any wounded warriors he came across. *I can do that on the way back.*

He found himself confronting a humanoid creature whose skull consisted of a single lump of an indefinable mass. Severe injuries to the ruined body made it impossible to see the original form. Two arms, two legs, a wiry trunk with bloodied rags that must once have been clothing. At once he recognised the items the Zhadar had described. Relief flooded through him. *Are the pieces of jewellery intact?* He told the barbarian he was to go and bent over the cadaver.

Tirîgon prodded around with his sword tip in the remains of the creature's head until he found the tongue. With deep distaste he took hold of the dripping flesh and cut it out, placing it in a bag he found amongst the stones. He tossed the bangle and circlet into the same bag and went back to his brother. He spared the wounded. Not because he was benevolent but because he was in a hurry.

Sisaroth was still seated by the body of Marandëi, whose throat had been opened up. It looked as if the reconstituted skull had bathed in her blood and the decorative grooves in its surface were bright red.

Tirîgon knew what had happened – or rather, hadn't – when he caught sight of the disappointment on his brother's face. *Shëidogîs has not returned to the artefact despite the brilliant sacrifice that has been made.* He raised the bag. 'I have what we came for. Let's get going. There's a lot to do.'

Sisaroth looked up with an expression of sheer grievance before getting to his feet, packing the skull away in its casket and striding out of the cave.

He can't hold me responsible for her death? Tirîgon guessed there would be more to contend with than a silent accusation.

With this second loss, the brothers' hard-won unity was already in jeopardy.

Phondrasôn.

Firûsha and her fifty soldiers soon found the entrance to the cave where the älfar from Dsôn Sòmran were awaiting death. The charts and Crotàgon's descriptions had been meticulously exact.

We need a miracle now. The gods have tested me for long enough. Firûsha sent out four scouts to appraise the situation. They created passwords they were to use on their return to certify that their forms had not been usurped by shapeshifters. She and the remaining troops would conceal themselves and wait.

One of the spies returned quickly and stated his keyword. 'I've found the groundling. The Zhadar's envoy. He's in a terrible state. Looks like he's been in combat with a formidable enemy.'

This was news she had not expected. She frowned. *So he did not get far when he made his escape.* 'Where is he?'

'I found him floating in a shallow pool by a waterfall. Over there. I pulled him out, thinking he might be useful. His heart is still beating.'

Alive! Wasn't it said that he knew the way out? 'Bring me to him.' She told her unit to follow her and they moved slowly into the main cave.

The squat figure of the groundling lay almost naked at the side of the pond. His body showed such serious injuries that they could have been inflicted by any barbarian or even an óarco.

Firûsha bent over him. *These mountain maggots are tremendously tough. It must come from the rock they live in; it must get into their blood.*

The eye patch for the left eye was missing. There was only an empty socket of pink flesh where the old wound had been. The process must have been overseen by a competent healer.

He needs another specialist now if he's ever going to recover from this. Tungdil had taken a violent blow to his forehead. The bone of the skull was visible beneath a vicious cut on his brow. It was difficult to assess through all the dirt and clotted blood but Firûsha thought she could see a fracture. The wound reached up from the right eye through his brown hair to the top of his head.

The groundling gods must be with him to let him survive thus far. Firûsha gave instructions to carry the half-dead Tungdil back to the fortress, where he should be carefully tended to and watched. *If his mind has been affected he will be of no use to us. If that's the case, Tossàlor can have him.*

The other scouts came back and made their reports, sketching out a map to show exactly where the cages of the captives were located.

The reports sounded encouraging. There were not more than five hundred barbarians, though ten of those were of colossal size and wearing wild animal skins over their armour. There were also three karderiers in their natural six-armed formats.

It's do-able. 'I want ten of our archers to deal with the big ones and the karderiers when I give the signal. The rest of us will approach quietly in a circle formation. As soon as the first arrows have flown, we attack the guards.' Firûsha gave her orders and divided her force into groups. Each group was to target a different cage. 'Make sure our archers know that the karderiers must be their priority. If they change shape and hide amongst the älfar, we'll never know friend from foe.'

'Excuse me,' said one of the sytràps. 'If I were a karderier, I'd already be one of the älfar and in that cage with them, listening to the plans they hatch.'

Firûsha blinked. 'That . . . is a good point.' *Curses! What are we going to do? How can we test them before we take them back to the fortress?*

She knew the karderiers might well be using that very strategy. They only saw three, but there could be others hiding in the midst of the captives. Naïgonor's escape was sure to have been noticed, and the shapeshifters would likely be expecting an attack.

But I cannot abandon our rescue attempt. She stared at the chart in her hands. *Now, how could I . . .*

She had an idea. It would help even though it was not entirely satisfactory. 'We'll bring all the älfar back with us and place them in the ditch between the first and second ramparts. They'll be safe there until we have time to sort out how to tell the real ones from the false. I'm sure Marandëi will have some magic spell to help with that.' Her troops nodded eagerly. 'To your posts.'

The älfar spread out.

The archers took up their positions, while the other warriors encircled the cages.

Firûsha drew her sword and crept forward with her own unit. They had been allotted the largest of the four cages to liberate.

There was a terrible smell of urine and faeces. The starving älfar behind the iron bars had not been treated with respect.

The odour of rotting flesh was overpowering. Dead bodies piled up next to a hut were decomposing in the warm, damp air of the cave. The corpses were blackened and bloated. The karderiers did not grant burial to the bodies of those whose magic they stole, and they did not bother to burn the corpses.

Vermin crawled among the bodies; rats and dog-like animals

were gnawing at the carrion flesh or fighting with each other over torn-off limbs.

You six-armed monsters! Firûsha could not help the lines of fury taking over her countenance. She almost wished her archers would miss their targets so that she could be the one to kill the karderiers with her own hands.

One of the karderiers looked over at the cave entrance and barked an order. A giant barbarian in a fur-covered armoured coat with a horned helmet on his head stomped over to the cage.

Perhaps they need a new victim. Firûsha glanced at her warriors. Each bore the black lines of anger on his face. 'Bring them their death,' she mouthed. 'Let them suffer as they die.' She took a deep breath and started to sing. This was the signal. It gave hope to some and meant death to others.

Long black arrows sped through the air, piercing the chests of the imposing fighters and felling them, apart from the one who had already entered the cage. He was hit but the wounds appeared to be superficial. Arrows ricocheted off the bars.

Two of the karderiers died under the feathered onslaught, but the third took cover behind a heap of bodies.

Good. I'll take that one. But let's deal with the barbarian giant first. Firûsha raced ahead of her unit to storm the warrior, who had grabbed an älf-woman by the scruff of the neck and was holding her as a shield in front of himself.

All of the captives were shackled; none could move to protect the unfortunate victim.

'Let her go!' Firûsha approached slowly, her sword held out in front. 'Or you will meet the same fate as . . .'

The barbarian tightened his hold fatally, snapping his hostage's neck. He laughed and tossed the body at Firûsha.

Firûsha dodged and leaped up onto her opponent's shoulders and from there diagonally up to the bars of the cage compound. She catapulted herself above the foe to land on his back, where she stabbed him with her sword.

He roared and whirled to spin her off, his scythe-like weapon just missing her legs.

The barbarian was not able to halt his momentum and he spun towards the crowd of tethered älfar with a hideous grin on his face.

His curved blade beheaded several älfar and sliced off limbs. There was a terrible shrieking and fountains of blood spurted up. Firûsha sprang through this chaotic scene; at least seven or eight älfar had been killed.

The monster! When the barbarian twisted round, her own flight ended close to him. Hardly had her feet touched the ground than she delivered swift blows to his middle, all of which he was able to fend off. He was extremely tall but not corpulent.

With great agility Firûsha executed a somersault between his legs, coming up on one knee to give him a mighty swipe across the back of his thighs.

Leather and chainmail offered little protection; her blade sliced through muscles and tendons.

With a loud scream of pain he keeled over, lashing out backwards with his sword.

Firûsha leaped to her feet, fending off the scything blow using both hands and jerking her own sword sharply upwards. The surprise impact gave her the momentum to do a back flip over the pile of wounded älfar. She sprang up to stand by the fallen man's head and rammed the blade down through his helmet.

The giant gave a cry, slumped and lay still.

'Your death bears the name of Firûsha.' She stood up and looked over at the surviving älfar, who were aghast and obviously terrified. 'Stay calm,' she told them. 'We shall come back and free you. But first we have to kill the last karderier and the enemy force.' Panting, she ran out of the cage and threw herself into combat with the other guards. Barbarian reinforcements had arrived.

Their superiority of numbers did not worry her. One trained warrior älf could take on and defeat ten barbarians at a time. She hurried over to where the karderier had hidden behind the tower of rotting älfar bodies.

With her sword gripped in both hands, she tiptoed over to the grisly, stinking pile.

The shapeshifter had gone.

Exactly what I was afraid of. She heard a whimpering from the pile of corpses.

A child's hand pushed its way out, the fingers covered with corpse secretions and crusted blood. 'Help me, please,' the little voice cried. 'Before the monster comes back.'

Can I trust it? Or is this a trick? Firûsha hesitated then grasped the small hand and pulled.

A young boy tumbled out of the gruesome heap. He was covered in scraps of decomposing flesh and the smell that he gave off was appalling. It was hard to imagine what he was wearing in the way of clothing. 'Thank you,' he gasped, sobbing with relief. 'I . . .' He stared at her in horror when she put her sword to his throat. 'Why are you doing that?'

Is this the shapeshifter? Is he taking me for a fool? Firûsha's heart was pounding and she could not think straight. The smell of decay and the sight of her mistreated kinsfolk made her keener than ever to locate and kill the karderier to punish him for these misdeeds. But she could not be sure that the young boy was, in fact, the quarry she sought. 'How did you get out of the cage?' she asked him.

'Through the bars. They're quite wide.' He pointed to one of the other compounds. 'They told me to steal the warder's keys. I was waiting in the dead bodies until I had a chance.'

'Sintholor! My child!' an älf-woman's voice called out from far behind Firûsha. 'The gods of infamy are on our side. They have saved us!'

He did not dare raise his hands to wave at the approaching älf. His eyes were glued to the sword. 'I am not the bad one! The karderier crawled into a pipe.'

Firûsha saw the hole in the rock, wide enough to admit the six-armed creature. *He might be telling the truth. Or it might be a lie.* The child's bright blue eyes were clear and he did not seem afraid. In fact, he showed no emotion at all. She was reluctant to trust him. *Is he in shock? Or is he waiting for me to turn away so he can attack?* 'Where in Dsôn did you live?'

Sintholor stared in surprise and said nothing.

Firûsha increased the pressure and cut into the boy's neck. 'I'm going to count to three and if you don't tell me exactly which ring of Dsôn your house was in, I'll cut your head off. One . . .'

'Sintholor!' A thin blonde älf-woman wearing rags that had once been a dark green dress rushed up, disregarding the sword and sinking to her knees to embrace the boy.

'Two . . .' Firûsha's heart rate increased.

'I'm too confused,' he stammered.

'What do you want from him?' the mother demanded.

'She wants to know where we live, Mother. If I don't tell her, she's going to kill me. She thinks I am the karderier,' he said, starting to cry.

His mother opened her mouth.

'No. Don't help him,' Firûsha snapped. 'It's your son's answer I need. That is, if that's who he really is.' *Of course, she might be one of them, too. How did she get out of the cage?* She swallowed. 'And the last number is . . .'

The boy gave his mother a shove, making her stumble against the sword, resulting in a deep gash across her face. Sintholor vaulted past Firûsha with a yell.

I was right! 'You won't escape your punishment!' She had been watching him closely and anticipated his move. She whirled and kicked him in the side, then struck him on the back with her weapon.

The sword blade sliced deep into the spine. Sintholor collapsed without a further sound. The distraught mother shrieked and threw herself over him to shield him from any further attack.

'Get away from him! Don't you see? It's a karderier. Not your son at all.' Firûsha waited to see if the creature would change shape on death.

It did not happen.

Firûsha felt sick. *Ye gods!* She stared at the dead child and the mother cowering over the body, drenching his face with her tears and blood. *So why did he . . . ?*

A warning shout made her whirl round.

An älf came crawling out of the tube and ran off down the slope towards the pool where they had found Tungdil.

So that's where he is. 'No!' Firûsha shouted to the archers, who had seen what was happening and had drawn their bows to fire at the fleeing figure. 'He's mine!'

She raced after the figure who had caused the young boy's death. She was convinced that the karderier had deliberately waited to see what she was going to do. *He turned me into a murderer. He let me kill an innocent child!*

The false älf had reached the top of the hill and disappeared down the other side.

Firûsha stormed after him and saw him spring into the pond the groundling had been found in. *Is he trying to escape me through the water?*

She hastened to the side and struck out with her sword which cut through the waters with a great splash. 'And now? Are you going to turn yourself into a fish?' she shouted, plunging into the pond after him. At least the immersion would remove the blood of the injured and the ghastly smell of decomposed älf bodies clinging to her.

Firûsha waded further in, discovering that the ground fell away sharply under her feet. There would be a basin hollowed out where the waterfall cascaded in. *He'll be hiding down there, where it's deep!*

She dived, still wearing her armour; the weight pulled her to the bottom.

The pond was clear and only bubbles obscured her vision. The water cooled her hot-headedness but not her hatred of the karderier.

She spotted an opening behind the waterfall.

A second cave! She felt her way up along the pond wall and surfaced cautiously.

A six-armed silhouette leaped out, smashing down at her head with a raised cudgel.

Too slow! She dodged the crushing blow and plunged her sword into the karderier's belly; pushing off from the edge, she leaped out of the pond and pushed her adversary backwards. He stared in horror at her sword and his own gaping wound.

'Did you think I was going to let you go?' Firûsha bawled, wrenching the blade out of his flesh to slice sideways, cutting off the first of his arms. 'No, I'm going to make sure you suffer before I let you die! I'll trim you to size!'

With sharp blows she removed the other five upper limbs as if they had been branches of a tree. The karderier stumbled backwards screaming. He fell with the loss of his sixth arm and spat blood and saliva at Firûsha. He rolled about, uttering incomprehensible sounds.

'Are you begging me to put you out of your misery?' Firûsha laughed at him. 'I pray Samusin will keep you alive so that I can enjoy your pain. It is revenge for what you have done to my people and to me.' *I'm a murderess. Now my banishment is justified.*

The dying shapeshifter's movements slowed. He lay still, fighting for breath, his ugly head thrown back. The lips drew back in a grimace, revealing his sharp teeth. 'Never reach,' he muttered. 'So easy ... so easy ... the dwarf ...' He died.

She contemplated the hideous body and the odious face with its cold, dead eyes; she raised her sword high over its head and slammed the sword down with a yell of fury.

The blade pierced the karderier's skull and met the ground underneath, causing the tip to snap off, but the violent blow split the upper body. The sword remained firmly lodged upright.

A shame. I should have enjoyed torturing him some more. She let go of the hilt and jumped back into the pond to cross the waterfall and return to her people. She had to take them to the safety of the fortress.

The sword stayed where it was. Firûsha never wanted to see it again. It was contaminated with innocent älfar blood.

Chapter IX

The loss of the Young Gods
seemed irredeemable.
Esmonäe – dead.
Marandëi – gone.
These would not be the last friends
to be lost.
But fate
had compensation in store
for the Young Gods.
The price they paid for it was incalculable.

Excerpt from the epic poem *Young Gods*
composed by Carmondai, master of word and image

Phondrasôn.

Tirîgon played nervously with the quill in his hands. The page in front of him was empty. *It should be covered in notes and ideas by now.*

He hoped the meeting with his siblings, Tossàlor, Crotàgon, Horogòn the Healer, and Gàlaidon (who they had appointed

Sytràp of the guards) would produce something useful. They needed to come to a decision and take courage, although it was difficult to stay positive.

They were all sitting around the library with doleful faces, each pursuing his or her own train of thought.

Everything's gone wrong. This is not what was supposed to happen. Not here in Phondrasôn or back there in Dsôn Sòmran. Esmonäe's image flashed into his mind. He saw her sparkling hair and her reproachful expression. *It should never have ended like that.* He was torn apart by conflicting thoughts of her, alternating feelings of longing and hate. In order not to detest his own brother to the same extent, he tried hard to condemn her utterly. But it didn't always work.

'How is the patient's state of health?' Sisaroth asked the healer, to get the conversation going again.

'We have managed to keep the groundling alive, but that's about it,' Horogòn replied. His white garb had a red design of stylised splashes of blood: the badge of his guild. 'The superficial wounds are healing well and we have given him strengthening tonics. But the blow he received to the head has severely affected his mind, I fear. He lies in bed, his one eye open and staring at the ceiling.' Horogòn drank from the water-filled goblet in front of him. 'I don't see that he will ever be able to tell us how to get out of Phondrasôn.' Horogòn addressed Tossàlor. 'As far as I'm concerned, you might as well take him now. I can't see the maggot being any use to us at all in this state.'

The sculptor grinned in anticipation.

Just what he was waiting for, Tirîgon thought. There was little point in recording what was being said. It was too depressing. *Another hope bites the dust.*

'Let's wait and see. As long as he doesn't require too much looking after, let's not turn him into a work of art yet,' Sisaroth protested. 'What about the Dsôn survivors?'

Horogòn accepted the reprimand and bowed in apology. 'We are doing everything possible to aid their recovery. Some of them are extremely weak and on the point of entering ending-ness. The karderiers had removed much of their magic. My staff and I have been trying to understand what happens to the älfar bodily processes when our inherent magic is lost.' He shrugged. 'I regret it is taking so long, but we have never come across any-thing like this before.'

'How many are affected?'

'At the present time thirty-two, but it may turn out to be less. Five of them have died already, despite our efforts. I think the others will recover eventually.'

'Our problem is provisions,' Gàlaidon commented. 'I've cal-culated how long our supplies will last with so many mouths to feed, and it's vital we start cutting back. Tirîgon sent units to squeeze more tribute from the vassal caves, but until that food arrives, rationing is essential.' Aïsolon's one-time second in com-mand had found his feet quickly, becoming an invaluable support to the triplet rulers. He took his office very seriously and had evaluated the current practices in place in the running of the fortress. He might have been with them for whole div-isions of unendingness, he was so well informed.

'How are the interrogations going?' Sisaroth asked.

Tirîgon made an effort and started to take some notes. *It all seems like such a waste of time. Nothing is going to prevent the coming conflict. The last surviving älfar from Dsôn will end their days in misery in Phondrasôn.*

Gàlaidon reported back: 'So far we've been able to firmly eliminate three hundred and eighty from our enquiries. There are fifty-one
where we are in some doubt and eight positives – definite karderiers
in disguise.' He looked grim. 'If the Siblings will permit the use of
force, I can get the truth out of the prisoners much quicker.'

Firûsha refused immediately before her brothers could
respond. 'I want you to continue questioning them, but you are to
use the power of words, not violence. We cannot risk harming or
even mutilating innocent parties purely because they have kept
silent. They could still be in shock. They have been through a terrible ordeal and will need time to get over what they have seen.'

She's saying that because she feels so guilty about that young boy.
Tirîgon had tried, as had Sisaroth and Crotàgon, to talk her out
of this self-castigation, but she remained immovable. Nobody
had reproached her, not even the child's mother. They all knew
it had been unintentional, a chain of unfortunate circumstances.
Quite different from Esmonäe.

Gàlaidon continued, 'We can add a good two hundred of the
survivors and cleared älfar to our army, but given how low we
are on equipment, I felt it would be wiser to keep them here in
the fortress or use them as scouts rather than a fighting force.'

A fighting force that can't fight. Tirîgon started doodling in
the margins. At first he drew abstract shapes, but then he realised he was sketching things that had belonged to his mother.
He gave a heavy sigh, scribbled through his drawings and laid
his quill aside. *I sent death to her. If Sisaroth kills an innocent älf,
too, like my sister has done, then we'll all be guilty of murder and
will deserve to spend our lives in exile.*

'What about this Carmondai character?' Crotàgon wanted
to know if his identity had been verified.

'We'll be talking to him after this meeting,' Sisaroth announced, sending his brother a questioning look. He seemed well aware that Tirîgon was not taking any active part in the discussion. 'As soon as the troops get back here with the food we need we will seal the entrances. We'll treble the number of sentries on duty at the gates and I want high alert status for the defenders along the first rampart.'

Gàlaidon was surprised. 'Are you expecting the karderiers to strike back? So soon?'

Tirîgon raised his head. 'He's expecting the Zhadar to turn up as soon as he finds out how we got the veyn's tongue and valuables. He might not like the fact that we've destroyed the triple caves of Whifis.' He kept the rest of his thoughts to himself. *There's nothing we can do to defend ourselves against his magic. Without Marandëi we've no chance.*

Sisaroth reached for his goblet and saw it was empty. 'We've got nothing to fear. He didn't expressly tell us not to damage the area. He told us to get the circlet, the bangle and the tongue, and we did as he asked. He seemed pleased enough and he said we could go.'

'If he is a threat, then we need good weapons and we need them now,' said Gàlaidon. 'According to what I've heard, the Zhadar is not known for his generosity.'

'What we need is the way out of here,' Crotàgon corrected him. 'That's our only hope. We stand very little chance against him in direct conflict.' Firûsha agreed.

They're talking as if it was that simple. Tirîgon slammed his fist down on the table. 'The way out? The way out to where, exactly? Where are we going to go?'

The others looked dismayed but said nothing.

'There you have it, you see. There's your answer,' he said glumly, pointing to the expanse of the Phondrasôn map that covered the walls, the floor and the ceiling of the library. 'We've explored and explored but we're going round in circles. Or we come across a new tunnel, a new cave, a new region that has to be conquered. But has anyone ever found an exit? The älfar who used to come down here in the past for a challenge – to prove themselves worthy as warriors – how did they get back to Dsôn?'

'Well, for a start it would have been Dsôn Faïmon they went back to in those days,' said Gàlaidon. 'I expect Phondrasôn would have been quite different from that area. And where the groundling came through, as well. In the Black Abyss.' He looked over at Sisaroth. 'That's what he called it, didn't he?' The young älf nodded. 'We have no choice but . . .'

'But *what*?' objected Tirîgon's defiantly. *He's only just arrived and he's already muscling in on decision-making.* 'Listen. We are never, ever, going to see the moon and the stars again. Get used to it.'

'Tirîgon! Don't give up!' implored his sister. 'Our beleaguered people need to trust in our leadership.'

'We are three young älfar. Any of the survivors from Dsôn would be able to carry out our tasks.' He leaped to his feet. 'Why don't we ask Crotàgon to decide? Or Tossàlor? He could slaughter his way through the lot of us and produce some nice little carvings before the Zhadar turns up and hacks him to pieces.' His voice cracked and his fists were tightly clenched with desperation. 'Can't you see? It doesn't matter what we decide. It makes no difference at all. It's all over. We are lost down here. It is utterly ridiculous for immortals to be discussing a future that is not going to happen. For the älfar in Tark Draan perhaps, but not for us.'

'There are no älfar left in Tark Draan,' a sonorous voice announced from the library door. Everyone turned and saw Carmondai on the threshold escorted by two guards. 'You are the last of our kind.'

Sisaroth gave a derisive snort. 'Come off it! Tungdil tried to sell me that one, too. He also said the Inextinguishables were no more.' Gàlaidon and Crotàgon both laughed and Tossàlor joined in. 'The groundling even carries a weapon he claims to have made out of our ruler's sword. He calls it Bloodthirster.' He motioned the guards to let the celebrated älfar poet step nearer. 'But please, enlighten us. Or entertain us, rather. My brother Tirîgon could do with cheering up.'

A murmur went around the table.

Tirîgon studied the famous älf's features. All of them were aware of Carmondai's reputation as the famous master of word and image, whose tales from the first Tark Draan campaign were so well known in Dsôn Sòmran.

He had been one of those who had never returned, remaining on the far side of the Stone Gate to found a new älfar state. Before contact with the other side broke down when the groundlings re-conquered the gateway, it was even rumoured that Carmondai had provided the initial concept for the new Dsôn, or at least had been a major contributor in the design process.

More bad news. Tirîgon wanted to leave them to it. Wanted to get away from the all-pervasive misery and guilt. He slumped back down in his seat. *There is no god for the älfar. Tion has abandoned us. Inàste has forsaken her people and the gods of infamy have turned away their faces. Are the älfar truly doomed to disappear without trace?*

Carmondai remained standing at the head of the table and let

his gaze take in the assembled leaders. In fresh but simple clothing and with his long brown hair loose on his shoulders, he had
a distinguished and authoritative air. He addressed them with
dignity. 'I could not wait to be summoned any longer and asked
the guards to bring me here.' He bowed to them. 'I speak the
truth. The groundling speaks the truth. Much has occurred in
Tark Draan in recent divisions of unendingness. Hear what
I shall relate and you will understand your own vital role.'

More dead älfar. More despair. Tirîgon at first refused to listen. But the poet's compelling narration conjured up such a
vivid picture of the tragic events that he was forced to pay attention. He could not escape the power of the words.

Carmondai told them of the immense successes the Inextinguishables had achieved; he told of the progress made into the
Dead Lands; of the fall of the elf-kingdoms; of the beauty of
the älfar state in Dsôn Balsur; of the desperate struggles against
the combined armies of Tark Draan; of the collapse of the whole
älfar empire; of the devastation caused by the Testing Star when
it struck, wiping out the majority of all óarcos, trolls and beasts,
as well as the älfar; he spoke of the Inextinguishables' attempt to
seize power. And he spoke of their end.

'The dwarf in your sickbay is Tark Draan's greatest hero.
Humans and elves alike owe their deliverance to him. It was he
and his companions who killed the Inextinguishables. The
weapon he bears did indeed belong to our ruler.' Carmondai
concluded his narrative. Gàlaidon passed him a cup of water.
'You and the few remaining survivors in the fortress are the last
älfar in the whole of Ishím Voróo *and* in Tark Draan. You have
a duty to safeguard the continued survival of your whole race.'

Tirîgon blinked a few times to moisten his eyes. *I must have almost held my breath to hang on his words.* He had no idea how long Carmondai had been speaking, but he realised he was hungry.

Sisaroth was visibly shaken. 'How is it that you survived the Star?'

Firûsha had tears glistening on her cheeks. 'How did you get here? Can you lead us out of this place?'

Such, then, is the fate of Tark Draan, the land free of monsters. Tirîgon's mind was fizzing. Carmondai's report had renewed his hope and he was coming up with a plan as bold as it was reckless. A project ideally suited to the new circumstances.

He exchanged glances with Crotàgon. The one-time rebel was of a similar opinion. *No one in Tark Draan will be expecting us to come back. Following the strike of the Testing Star and the loss of the Inextinguishables, they think they are safe. We could take them completely by surprise. And we have their greatest hero in our own ranks.*

In his mind's eye Tirîgon saw a new älfar empire emerging, its dark splendour and fearful reputation surpassing that of any previous Dsôn.

He had no need of the gods that had deserted them. Gods who had failed to protect his mother and who had allowed his father to die crushed under rubble. Gods who abandoned their people to the clutches of the karderiers. *We will be our own gods!*

'At the moment the Testing Star flashed out and sent its rays of destruction throughout the lands, burning all the älfar to ash, I was below the surface, spying in the groundling tunnels. That is what saved my life. I learned what had happened and decided to leave Girdlegard – Tark Draan – when the Inextinguishables ceased to be. I went to Ishím Voróo to see who had survived. On my journey I fell through a cleft in the rocks and found myself in Phondrasôn.' He pointed at Gàlaidon. 'The two of us met and we ended up here. I'm afraid there's no chance I could ever find my way back to the gap I came through.'

Gàlaidon, whose right hand was still bandaged, offered Carmondai his seat. 'That was very moving, poet-master. I'll carry on from where you left off, though I shan't be able to compete with the way you told your story.'

Not more horror. I can't bear it. Tirîgon clenched his fists. His guilt at the death of his mother was eating him up from inside.

The longer Gàlaidon spoke about Dsôn Sòmran, the more Tirîgon felt the urge to stab his father's friend through the heart to stop him – to wipe out the terrible truth that he alone knew. Firûsha sobbing at his side made his pain all the greater. *It is my doing that my siblings were sent to Phondrasôn and it is my fault our mother met her death. How could I ever wash my soul clean of this guilt?*

'Aïsolon and I were in the guardroom. He had arranged to have all the conspirators sent secretly to Phondrasôn to look for you. Shortly thereafter, the mountain took issue with us and threw all the buildings off its back. The landslide buried us. When the dust settled, the beasts stormed in. I fought them off and came here with the others in search of a safe haven. That's why I can't tell you whether or not your father is alive.' It was difficult for Gàlaidon to speak of these terrible events. He cast his eyes down to the bandage on his arm. 'I can only second what Carmondai told you: we are under an obligation to survive.'

'We must do more than survive,' Crotàgon spoke up passionately. 'Let us go to Tark Draan. They think they have nothing to fear from us. It will be so easy to attack them. We will avenge the

Inextinguishables.' He looked at the others to assess their opinions. 'What do you say?'

No one answered.

I will have to back him up. Tirîgon stood up. 'Are we going to spend the remainder of unendingness skirmishing with the Zhadar over turf and having to submit till he grows tired of us and slaughters us? Let us show Tark Draan that all attempts to vanquish our älfar spirit have failed. And let us exterminate the elf-brood once and for all!'

'I would not attempt the break-out if we are not sure of a safe passage.' Horogòn was not convinced. 'Too many of our people are still in a vulnerable state. And we would have to leave behind all those whose identity remains in doubt – the ones who might be karderiers.'

'Or we could process them, of course,' Tossàlor suggested. 'Don't get me wrong, I'm all for you healers doing what you can, but if there are any wounded that need putting out of their misery, let me know. I'd be happy to help.'

Tirîgon did not like the mood round the table. *They will need time to digest Carmondai's words.* 'I suggest we postpone our decision. Carmondai, you are no longer a prisoner, but a guest. No need to return to your cell.'

Firûsha got to her feet. 'I'll come to the dispensary with you, Horogòn. Songs from the homeland will raise their spirits.'

'A noble offer. It will indeed improve morale amongst the sick.'

The company broke up, with the brothers being the last to go.

Sisaroth went over to look at the map. 'All that work creating this,' he murmured. 'The time Tossàlor and I invested in exploring every inch of Phondrasôn we could reach. All wasted.'

'As were my attempts to conquer as much territory as I could lay my hands on. An equal waste of effort. All we have to show for it is some paltry barbarian tribute and the wrath of a local lord.' *And we have lost Esmonäe. The only winner in all this is the wretched Zhadar.* Tirîgon joined Sisaroth by the map. 'What are you thinking?'

His brother smiled. 'It seems to me there are two missing keys to open the prison called Phondrasôn. One of them is very much alive right here.' He drew a throwing knife from his belt and stabbed at the chart. 'The Zhadar. It would be hopeless to think that he might open the locks for us, even though he has promised. I don't trust him an inch.'

So Sisaroth is going to support me and Crotàgon, after all! Tirîgon was relieved. 'And the second key?'

'Is in our fortress and is in dire need of repair. Whatever it costs.' He tapped his brother on the chest. 'And I think the time has come.' Sisaroth went over to the bookshelves and took out two volumes. Then he stepped through the secret door.

'Time for what?' Tirîgon was at a loss to understand. *What's with the riddles, Sisaroth?*

'May I have a word?' Gàlaidon's voice came out of nowhere. 'I need to speak to you without the others.'

He whirled round and saw the sytràp coming from behind a set of bookshelves. *Didn't I just see him leave the room?* 'Of course.' With increasing astonishment, Tirîgon watched Gàlaidon remove the bandage from his right hand. 'I'm not much of a healer, if that's what you're after.'

'No,' Gàlaidon replied coldly as he unravelled the remains of the long strip of material.

The fingers that emerged were strangely unaffected in any

way. There was no visible bruising, cut or scar. A spectacular ring made of silver and tionium sparkled on his forefinger; there was an inlay of ivory and a deep purple stone.

Immediately Tirîgon knew who it was facing him now. The ring had been the sole means of identification connecting perpetrator and contractor of the murders.

Gàlaidon placed his hand on the grip of his dagger. 'That's not what I've come for.'

Phondrasôn.

Sisaroth entered the chamber where he had installed the skull of the Infamous One. He lit the candles and then laid his armour aside and put on an embroidered dark brown vestment.

He had placed the artefact here for safekeeping, not trusting Firûsha. As long as he was not being followed, the skull was safe from discovery.

Climbing up a set of steps, he reached into a false wall, pulled the casket towards him and jumped back down with it.

How are you faring, Shëidogîs? He opened the lid and took the skull reverently in his hands.

Sisaroth saw it as Marandëi's legacy. The cîanai had deepened the apprentice-priest's rudimentary knowledge and since her demise he had been religiously studying the tracts in her archive. She had collected information about the cult of the gods of infamy and he was learning the necessary symbols and rituals.

But all my book-study is no good if the god's soul cannot be enticed back into the relic. Sisaroth examined the decorated surface of the ancient skull, noting where Marandëi's dried blood still adhered. Whereas his sister had been terrified of its empty eye sockets, he experienced only fascination. *Why did the sacrifice not work?*

Tossàlor's proposal had given him an idea and he wanted to attempt a new invocation, using as offerings those älfar who were beyond the healers' powers. He reasoned that sheer volume of sacrificial blood was probably the key. The god desired more lifeblood and more energy before deigning to reappear. This, at least, was what Sisaroth hoped.

He had read in Marandëi's notes that the Infamous One could work miracles. *And it would be a true miracle if the groundling's mind were restored and he were able to lead us out to Tark Draan.* A certain amount of persuasion would also be necessary. Dwarves were known, as a race, to be extremely stubborn.

He sat down at the desk and started searching through the notes.

He was intending to win friendship by magic means. The cîanai had made a collection of recipes for potions suitable for winning over hearts and minds.

In combination with the correct runes inscribed on the groundling's skin, the effect would be permanent. The dwarf, on awakening, would consider himself a lost brother to the Triplet Siblings. Until the end of his days.

But for this I shall need Shëidogîs to grant me the power that Marandëi had. He skimmed through the handwritten pages, comparing paragraphs, trying hard to decipher illegible sections that might well be the ones holding the secret.

A sudden draught made the candles flicker.

This was, in itself, nothing strange in the draughty chambers concealed behind the palace.

But the young älf felt he was being watched . . .

Am I imagining it? Sisaroth stopped what he was doing and turned round slowly.

He found Tossàlor in his purple robe immediately behind him, a cool smile playing on his lips. He was looking not at Sisaroth, but at the lovingly restored skull. His eyes shone with eager delight.

None of the älfar of the inner circle were forbidden from moving freely within the concealed rooms and corridors, but Sisaroth was indignant at this interruption. 'Did you want me for something?'

Tossàlor shook his head.

'Were you looking for my brother or my sister?'

This question was also met with silence and a shake of the head. Tossàlor's pupils were dilated as he stared fixedly at the relic.

This was too much for Sisaroth. 'Then I must ask you to return to your studio and get on with your carving – '

'Since being allowed to touch the skull and work on its restoration, I have become totally fascinated. The artefact is uniquely beautiful. Sensational. It should not be confined to a secret room where only you can view it, Sisaroth.'

His tone of voice was a warning; Sisaroth realised that the bone-carver was in a state of trance and unable to formulate clear thoughts. *Is it Shëidogîs? Has the god affected Tossàlor's mind?* 'I needed to conceal it from my sister. She might attempt to destroy it again.'

'I would have ripped out her heart. No one must harm the skull.' Only now did Tossàlor focus on Sisaroth. 'It was a good hiding place. I had been trying hard to find it.'

Sisaroth was starting to fear that the artist's brain was being manipulated in the same way Firûsha's had been, but to the opposite extreme. *The relic has dragged him here.*

'I felt such longing.' Tossàlor shyly stretched out an arm to brush the skull with his fingertips. He touched the gold leaf and the pearls reverently, a satisfied smile on his face. He kept his hand on the artefact. 'Marandëi would never let me borrow it, no matter how I begged.'

'I shan't let you have it, either. It might get damaged.' The other's attitude and conduct made Sisaroth more wary than ever. *Marandëi never breathed a word to me.* Maybe she had not taken his effusive enthusiasm seriously.

'But why would I want to damage it?' asked Tossàlor, suddenly outraged. 'I would put it on a shelf where it could watch me working. It would be my inspiration. I would work with the best bones available and create a shrine dedicated to the god. Shëidogîs would love it.' He stroked the top of the skull and then enclosed the item in his long fingers.

'I told you: it's to remain here!' Sisaroth grabbed his wrist.

'Without me, it would still be smashed to smithereens. I have a right to it.' The sculptor stared angrily down at Sisaroth. 'Permit me to take it. Please.'

'No.'

'You have to! I made it what it is. It calls me!'

Sisaroth stood up without releasing his hold on Tossàlor's hand. 'Your behaviour is unacceptable. You are aware that my word is law.'

'Yes, but I'm an outlaw,' Tossàlor responded, his piercing eyes fixed imploringly on Sisaroth. 'Give me the skull. I'll ask you again one more time . . .' He bit his lip.

'Or what? Was that a threat?' Sisaroth increased the pressure on Tossàlor's wrist. 'Let go at once or I'll break it myself and you'll never be able to mend it. Is that what you want?'

'I'd get Crotàgon to kill you, if you did,' Tossàlor hissed.

'And the death vow curse would kill him.'

'He would still do it for my sake. There could be an accident. The curse would not be invoked if you fell into a trap.'

Vicious, raving maniac! 'You take advantage of him all the time. Do you think he doesn't realise? Do you think he enjoys it?'

Tossàlor laughed in his face. 'Do you think I care about him? He's useful. That's all.' He looked past Sisaroth and grinned. 'Oh, there you are! Kill him for me,' he commanded into thin air.

Curses! Sisaroth whirled round, dagger drawn.

No Crotàgon to be seen.

A hefty blow to the back and a burning hot pain. His legs threatened to fold under him and he felt warmth streaming over hip and thigh. He slumped down, gasping for breath, to see Tossàlor beside himself with merriment.

'He really believed it!' In his hand he held a slim carving tool he had pulled from inside his robe. 'Fine warrior you turned out to be. Not wearing your armour? It would have saved you having your back split open.' He cradled the skull in his other hand. 'You should have let me have it straight away. Saved yourself a great deal of trouble. I regret the fact of your death, which carries my name, of course, but there was no other way.' He turned to leave.

'Wait!' groaned Sisaroth. *It cannot end like this.* 'My death should not be in vain. I will sacrifice my life to Shëidogîs. That will bring his power back. You must swear to become his priest from this day forth.'

Tossàlor considered the prospect.

'Make haste,' said Sisaroth, sinking back under the waves of pain from his back. The blood loss was weakening him. 'My life force is ebbing away. Don't make a second-rate offering to the god.' He shut his eyes. 'My dying is my final service to him as his high priest.'

'That shall be so. Shëidogîs will be gratified at the extent of your offering.' There was a rustling of material as Tossàlor knelt by his side. 'Tell me what to do.'

Without opening his eyes Sisaroth stabbed upwards, his aim guided by the sound of the artist's voice.

The blade pushed through against little resistance. Sisaroth opened his eyelids. His knife had struck through the breastbone and entered the solar plexus. 'You die for the god,' he mouthed, tasting blood on his own lips.

Wrenching out the blade, he took the skull from Tossàlor's grasp and drenched it in blood. He was beyond caring that his actions would bring down the cîanai's curse. He was dying anyway.

'The god of infamy accepts your generous sacrifice, Tossàlor.' Sisaroth recited the formal words Marandëi had taught him. He was trying not to faint but knew he was powerless to survive his injuries.

It was essential that he place the relic on his own breast, but its weight felt like that of a thousand óarcos perched on his body.

I hope Tirîgon finds me before Firûsha does. He will know how to handle the skull. His greatest fear was that his sister would find him and destroy the artefact after the infamous soul had returned to it. *They will need his power to conquer Tark Draan.*

Sisaroth's vision was failing and darkness closed in on him.

Tossàlor collapsed in a heap on top of him, muttering something incomprehensible, and causing sudden gouts of blood to gush over the skull. Its black eye sockets were turned towards Sisaroth. Then the skull of the Infamous One tumbled to the ground.

Sisaroth lost consciousness.

Phondrasôn.

Tirîgon stared at the sparkling ring on Gàlaidon's hand. *The assassin! Can it be that he has come all this way to Phondrasôn to follow me?*

Back in Dsôn he had always dealt with a masked individual who would identify himself as Virssagòn's student by presenting this ring for inspection. He had long been investigating how best to engage a paid killer without being observed doing so. It was better for both sides, the masked figure had maintained, if he stayed anonymous and did not display his features. Dsôn was a small city and they might meet again. *I would never have believed it was him!*

'I completed my mission and accomplished the task you gave me,' intoned the älf smoothly. 'I prevented the truth coming to light. It was not revealed who was behind Sémaina's murder; all the witnesses are dead. As are those who proved too inquisitive.' He threatened Tirîgon with his dagger. 'I have come for my payment.'

'What?' Tirîgon felt as if he were trapped under a huge boulder. The room started to spin and he had to sit down. 'You . . . killed my mother . . . and you are demanding . . .'

The blond-haired älf raised his eyebrows, his green eyes cold. 'I kept to my side of the bargain. My orders were to silence everyone in Dsôn who could reveal the truth. Not just the original witnesses, but also anyone who was set on investigating the incident. Don't blame me for taking you at your word. Believe me, Tirîgon, I really did not want to kill Ranôria. And it was a pity about your father and Cèlantra. Though, if truth be told, I'm sure the two of them would have died in the landslide anyway. Better to be safe than sorry.'

Dead? Murdered, too? And all because of how I worded my instructions? Earliest memories flashed into his mind: images of his mother and of Aïsolon. A childhood of warmth and safety, love and adventure. Tirîgon stared at the hired assassin. *This is merely a bad dream. I am imagining this!*

'Your silence speaks volumes,' said Gàlaidon. 'If you are considering asking me to carry out subsequent contracts I must insist on payment of the outstanding amount, Tirîgon.'

'Subsequent . . . ?' he croaked incredulously.

'In case anyone else starts to get suspicious. But disguising a death and disposing of a body is simpler here in Phondrasôn – in fact, you could do the deed yourself if you prefer. Name your victim and I'll create a backstory. Perhaps before Aïsolon died, he had accused your target of Sémaina's murder; I could implicate them in hatching the plot against Sisaroth and Firûsha. It would all be over and done with.'

Tirîgon was unable to think clearly. He was overcome with encompassing feelings of guilt, as his mind flooded with sacred memories of his childhood and dread intimations of the future. *I had Mother and Father put to death!* He could hardly breathe, so sharp was the pain in his breast.

'Did you have anything else in mind?' Gàlaidon was growing impatient. His grip on the knife hilt tightened and the metal grated audibly against his ring. 'If you want me to do away with your siblings, just let me know. You can't kill them yourself. Family blood doesn't wash off.' He held out his free hand. 'But my payment first,' he insisted.

'You get nothing,' Tirîgon whispered.

'What did you say?'

'I'm not paying you for turning us into orphans.'

The killer laughed contemptuously. 'Are you trying to rid yourself of guilt? I told you beforehand you ought to think about the consequences.'

'But not the death of my parents!' he yelled, leaping to his feet.

'You never specifically excluded that.' Gàlaidon took a couple of steps back. 'My fee. Now. Or I'll kill *you* for free.'

I'll have to do it. I owe it to them. Tirîgon swallowed and drew his sword. 'I carry your fee on my person, assassin.'

Gàlaidon stood tall and drew a second dagger from the sheath on his leg. 'You have no moral strength or honour, my young älf. Otherwise you would pay me what you owe before attacking me.' With these words he kicked a chair on his right, propelling it towards Tirîgon, who fended it off with his plated forearm. Before he could recover his balance, he was struck on his side and thrown. He heard a metallic clang and a clinking echo when a broken blade fell to the floor. The assassin's blade had been foiled by the armour. His life had been preserved by the groundling's superb forging skills.

Without knowing exactly where Gàlaidon was standing, Tirîgon did a circular sweep with his sword to gain time. He took his own dagger in his other hand.

The assassin leaped back and jumped at a bookcase, which tipped forward under his weight so that books cascaded onto Tirîgon. He vaulted to one side to avoid being hit by the heavy shelves that crashed down behind him. Out of the corner of his eye he could see his adversary on his left. He ducked back out of the way.

A jabbing blade narrowly missed his throat and then he was kicked in the mid-section, sending him flying across the room to land on the conference table.

'You stand no chance against me.' The assassin leaned over him, gripping his arm to immobilise the dagger, and head-butting him.

Stunned, Tirîgon shook his head to clear his vision; his eyes were watering and he was seeing stars. But he was not going to give in. A sudden instinct urged him to move his head to the side.

The plunging dagger lodged in the wooden table surface. Gàlaidon uttered a curse. 'You make it harder for me than your father did.'

Tirîgon was able to bring one knee up under his opponent's torso to push him off, but the trained assassin forced the leg aside and launched himself onto Tirîgon – and straight onto the tip of Tirîgon's drawn sword. Given his own momentum, Gàlaidon effectively impaled himself.

'Your death,' the younger älf intoned grimly, 'bears the name Tirîgon!' He delivered a kick to force Gàlaidon backwards, pulling the blade out before thrusting again, using his sword as a lance. Half the length of the blade sank through his body.

Bounding up from the table, Tirîgon placed one hand at the

nape of Gàlaidon's neck and his other on the sword. 'Here, take your fee!' He shoved the weapon brutally through the assassin's torso and hurled him to the ground.

He had no inclination to watch him die or listen to his dying words. He could not face hearing further implications of his own guilt.

Sure that life had left Gàlaidon, he dragged the corpse to the fireplace and left it to the work of the flames to burn off any identifying features. After that he alerted the guards and said he had found and killed another karderier.

Tirîgon did not enjoy the praise he was heaped with.

Phondrasôn.

'Wake up, Sisaroth!'

At the sound of the friendly voice he opened his eyes. He was lying in the chamber with Tossàlor's dead body on top of him; he shoved it off and sat up with some difficulty.

The first thing he noticed was that there was no trace of any pain or discomfort.

What can have happened? He felt the place where his back had been sliced open and noted warm blood sticking to his fingers – but there was no incision. He explored with his fingers, but no injury was found. *Was that him?* He focused on the skull, which was sending off a soft red glow.

'I accepted your offering,' said the voice. 'I was impressed at your willingness to sacrifice your own life in addition. Marandëi chose well in selecting her successor.'

I hardly dare believe it. Sisaroth lifted the relic carefully. 'Shëidogîs?'

'That is my name. I have returned to support you and to lead the älfar to Tark Draan. They will worship the gods of infamy, they will pray to me and they will make you the most powerful of their number in the älfar realm that is to come. You and your siblings will become gods.' The voice insinuated itself into Tirîgon's head; the skull's eye sockets glowed red and the inset pearls and rubies shone with an inner fire.

'You have healed my wounds!' he exclaimed.

'To indicate my favour. It was a beginning, merely a beginning,' the Infamous One replied. 'We shall have to work quickly if we are to get you up to Marandëi's standard. You have many enemies in Phondrasôn. Your race is in need of a cîanoi like yourself or it will not survive. But you are young and bright and quick on the uptake. It will not be hard for you to follow what I tell you. Marandëi was sometimes slow to understand.'

'How . . .'

'Pay attention to my voice,' he heard in his thoughts.

Sisaroth listened, waited, listened, waited. 'I can't hear anything yet.'

It started with a repeated whisper increasing in volume until it became a roar that was hard to tolerate. *That is far too much . . . too loud!* He was moved to release his hold on the skull and press his hands up against his ears – to no avail.

The books in the chamber all sprang open and the pages flapped and fluttered, causing a mighty draught that quelled the candles. Whole sentences, words, syllables and letters floated out shimmering, forcing themselves through his eyes and into his mind.

All the concentrated knowledge that was being infused into

his brain threatened to rob him of his sanity. The pressure in his head intensified. There was no room for all the texts and the sentences jostling urgently for admittance.

The stress he was under released itself in a wild cry.

Then it was done.

Sisaroth was crouched down with his head in his hands to stop it bursting open. He sat up gingerly, noting how his head was buzzing and his fingers were twitching. He felt hot. Incredibly hot.

But I feel . . . splendid! He stood up with his bloodied mantle about him.

'I have given you all the researched wisdom that Marandëi recorded. All her knowledge and skills are now yours. You must work to increase your own store of knowledge, but first you will need to process this new information,' the skull told him. 'Hold me in your hands and you will be capable of any magic.'

Sisaroth was overwhelmed and desperately keen to experiment. *All that effort was worth it! I can . . .* He thought of the älf-woman who had taught him, he thought of his siblings and of the future that would compensate in untold measure for all the ordeals and privations Phondrasôn had imposed. He lifted the relic reverently. 'I thank you, Shëidogîs,' he said.

'I accept your thanks. Now hurry and put your preparations in place. Gather all the things your people are going to need before they leave these depths and return to the surface to make a new and glorious beginning.'

'This I shall do!' With the precious skull in his right hand he left the chamber to find his siblings and report to them about this astonishing turn of events.

After that he would hasten to the groundling.

I shall make of him an ally such as the world has never seen. Tark Draan will not stop him or us.

He thought it best not to let on that the death curse no longer existed.

THIRD BOOK

The Conquerors

And so it was that the Young Gods
   were given support in many forms.
Shëidogîs, the Infamous One,
   instructed Sisaroth
   in the magic arts.
   Random älfar encountered in the caves
   were offered in all secrecy in sacrifice.
   Sisaroth's power thrived.
And with this power
   he made a friend of the groundling
   whose race are deadly enemies to the älfar.
   He scored älfar runes in his skin as he slept,
   laid spells upon him and gave him potions
   that effected transformation.
On rising from his sickbed he saw the Triplets as friends
   and did not doubt the story that they told him.
   They named him Balodil
   and from then on he was on the älfar side.
Balodil was untiring at his forge,
   making weapons and armours of the best.
   Thus equipped, the Siblings feared no enemy.

He was tutored in the älfar tongue
and shown the cîanoi magic
with which to reinforce his metals.
With his blacksmith skills and magic art
he produced the strongest plates and mail.
Nothing approached the standard of the armour
he had fashioned for another.
Designed for the Zhadar, and thought of as his own.
The Young Gods worked tirelessly at their task
— to lead the älfar to Tark Draan.
They sent out scouts
and abandoned their conquests;
ignored commands from the Zhadar.
All efforts were expended on the Quest:
The Flight from Phondrasôn.
But despite themselves
they proved an inspiration
to the plotters and insurgents –
those the Zhadar kept oppressed.
Murmurs of protest soon became a steady roar.
A front was formed in Phondrasôn
and Balodil nurtured their rebellion.
He befriended the älfar,
forging alliances like steel.
He furnished the foes of the Zhadar
with the tools of insurrection
and in secret watched the progress of their battles
as he had so often done before.
A storm broke in the land,
and the Zhadar's mighty towers were attacked.

Firûsha, Sisaroth and Tirigon held sway
    but did not use nor want their power,
    choosing to ignore the war
    and chaos at their feet.
Until the time arrived
    when all was set to change.

Excerpt from the epic poem *Young Gods*
composed by Carmondai, master of word and image

Chapter I

*Only the veritably dead
know what it is to die.*

'Aphorisms' from the epic poem *Young Gods*
composed by Carmondai, master of word and image

Phondrasôn.

Firûsha stood at the window and looked out on the waves of liquid glass. *How glorious! How unique!*

The waters played around the mighty pillars of the bridge, forming a transparent crust like ice or sugar-coating on the stone. Sisaroth was responsible for the miracle of recalling the god of infamy and restoring the previous conditions in the cave. As cîanoi to Shëidogîs, he was servant and master alike to an ancient godhead now manifested in the gruesome artefact.

I would not hesitate for an instant to destroy the relic once again. Firûsha kept her thoughts, however, to herself; it was essential her brothers did not know her attitude. She simply did not believe that they were being aided by a god. *It is a demon, a terrible spirit.* She feared Shëidogîs (or whichever spirit dwelt within the skull) would destroy them all, turning against them at some vital point in battle.

Firûsha suspected Sisaroth was offering sacrifices to the skull and was firmly opposed to it. Tirîgon, on the other hand, accepted the practice, seeing the benefits. Thinking strategically, he preferred to ignore any possible disadvantages.

Her only ally in the palace was Crotàgon. The death of the object of his secret passion, Tossàlor, had led him to utterly reject the gods of infamy.

Crotàgon had heard Sisaroth tell how he and the artist had struggled over possession of the skull. Stony-faced, he talked about the change he had noticed in Tossàlor's behaviour following the intense period of reconstructive work that the artist had done on the relic. The word obsessive was used.

Crotàgon demanded the artefact be destroyed, but the brothers refused: one of them for purely personal reasons and the other from tactical considerations.

Firûsha found the sight of the ochre-coloured waves fascinating. She raised her voice in song, creating the lyrics spontaneously: an ode to the Sea of Glass, where beauty merged with danger. The slightest contact with the waves would suffice to lose a finger, a limb, a life. The heat of the molten glass would ensure nothing would remain. Yet Firûsha was thrilled by the thought of immersion in this lethal material.

Her song ended but her train of thought continued.

How would it feel to be swallowed up by liquid glass? What kind of favoured creature might survive? She leaned against the window frame, enjoying the warmth reflected upwards by the sea.

There was a knock at the door.

'Come in.'

Crotàgon entered, dressed in light attire. He bowed and approached. 'It is time.' He had brought wooden swords with him in a long sack.

Firûsha stared in surprise. 'Already?'

'The watch have been given their duties, the scouts are still out, and the gates are invulnerable, thanks to Sisaroth's magic security measures. What could go wrong?' He had arrived earlier than arranged. He laid the sack on the table, removed the cord and shook the practice weapons out. He threw two of them over to Firûsha, and took one for himself. 'I know you don't need any more instruction. You are at least as good as I am, and you are certainly much more agile. The training practice is for my benefit now.' He tensed his muscles. 'I enjoy a challenge.'

Firûsha laughed. 'Flatterer!'

'Not at all. You beat Tirîgon recently. And I'm sure you could beat Sisaroth, too, especially now that he spends all his time with that wretched skull and neglects his swordsmanship.' He took up a stance in the centre of the room. 'Firûsha, show me what you are made of!'

She was wearing only a flimsy robe so a strike would be painful. She might suffer a broken limb. *Here's to the challenge.* She grinned. 'Let's see how many hits I can score, my dear Crotàgon.' They were about to proceed when they were interrupted.

From the doorway came the sound of someone clearing his throat. It was Balodil.

'Training?' The groundling was carrying a wooden crate and was followed by a female älf guard bearing an extra-length sword. 'I seem to have arrived at the right moment,' he joked.

Balodil appeared to have come directly from his workshop.

His boots and breeches had scorch marks and his torso was bare under a battered leather apron. The empty eye socket was hidden under a decorated golden patch fixed directly into his skin with thin wire, obviating the need for leather fastenings.

'You are always welcome, Balodil,' said Firûsha, but her words were not sincere. She glanced at Crotàgon, who looked annoyed. They both shared the same concern that the groundling might someday regain his full senses and overcome the combined effects of the potions, tattooed runes and incantations that bought his loyalty. They always went through the motions of welcoming him as a friend but neither of them trusted the relationship.

They watched him carefully any time he was near. If his old identity, answering to the name of Tungdil, were to re-emerge and become aware of what Sisaroth had been doing to him, there would be hell to pay. *And he is enormously strong.*

Balodil came over and put the crate down on the floor. 'I've given it all a thorough overhaul,' he announced proudly. The long scar on his face and forehead had healed but would never go away, Horogòn the Healer had said.

'Is it my body armour?' At this Firûsha was excited. 'That's wonderful! And you had so much other work to get through in the forge.'

'A labour of love while I'm waiting for my next commission from whatever tribe or race calls on me for help. They're all coming together in the name of the Young Gods, though of course in secret. We don't want to risk alerting the Zhadar at this stage.' He smiled and bowed his head. 'It is an honour for me to serve the three of you and to call you my friends.' The groundling opened the crate.

The Young Gods. Firûsha looked at the symbols tattooed on Balodil's skin. The pictures seemed to come alive with the play of his muscles. Sisaroth and Tirîgon had created excellent work. The runes and symbols incised on his skin would stay with him until the end of his days. 'Is the sword for me as well?' she asked.

'It is,' he replied, taking out the pieces of armour, which had been carefully wrapped in fabric to protect them. 'I've followed the original design but it's better balanced now. The tip has been tempered several times over. You won't find it breaking or bending or ever getting blunt.' He stood up and motioned the female soldier over. 'Because the cross-guard is so long, you can use the sword to help you vault. I know the älfar don't just hack away with their swords like a barbarian might. You like to show your expertise in combat.' He tapped the steel. 'This should guarantee your skills can be fully deployed. Take care with the tips of the cross-guard. They are sharp.'

Firûsha took the weapon the soldier handed her and practised a few sweeps. *It is perfect!* 'You are a Master of Steel, Balodil! It feels like an extension of my own arm.' She passed it to Crotàgon and he nodded approvingly. 'Excellent handiwork!'

'I'm delighted you are pleased with it.' He undid the cloths to reveal the armour.

'Do people really call us the Young Gods?' she asked, inspecting the items. *How swiftly we have risen! The Zhadar will not like it. He will hate the idea that we might be more powerful than he is.*

Balodil nodded and polished a few places on the metal before gesturing to his companion to come over and help attach Firûsha's armour. At first glance it looked as if it had been fabricated from burnished black leather. 'Some use that name. Since you have rebelled and have been supplying the insurgents with arms, sometimes I go along when there's a fight, to see if I can win over a few of the Zhadar's men to your cause.'

'Your hatred of the Zhadar should not lead you to actions that would make him take up arms against us. Provoking him would be unwise,' Crotàgon advised. 'We have Tirîgon's army, it is true, but . . .'

'I would never do anything to endanger my friends,' said Balodil sharply.

Spiky black lines shot out from under the eye patch and covered the weathered face, similar to an älf's anger lines. *That must be the effect of the potions and the rituals my brothers have been subjecting him to.*

The groundling gasped, pressing a clenched fist against the eye patch until the lines faded.

He's been turned halfway into an älf! Firûsha picked up the sword again.

'The Zhadar has no proof of my involvement,' he said, in a quieter voice, lowering his hand. 'The weapons could have been supplied from anywhere.'

'But they've got älfar runes?' Crotàgon was not convinced.

'We can say they're from some fallen älfar city,' said Balodil. 'There have been plenty of those recently, after all.'

We have so many deaths to mourn. Mother and Father are foremost in our minds. Firûsha, stepping into her armour, was hurt by the groundling's thoughtless remark.

Balodil assisted where necessary and observed carefully to see if adjustments would be necessary.

'It fits tightly,' Firûsha said. 'Very tightly.' The armour let her breathe freely and did not restrict her movements but it crushed her breasts like a laced bodice.

'I wanted to make it as slim-fitting as possible with no jutting shoulder plating so it can't catch on anything,' he explained. 'In battle your opponents will see you not as an attractive female älf but as a female warrior. But they will hold their breath in admiration when they catch sight of you.' Balodil noticed there was a long mirror in the corner of the room. 'Have a look and see if I'm not right.'

She had to agree with him. The armour emphasised her slim figure without letting it become a diversion. The älfar engravings and inlaid metal patterns led the eyes upwards to her face. The dark combination of tionium and steel brought out the brilliant blue of her eyes and clear features, framed by her long black hair.

Crotàgon made appreciative noises. 'Any male keen on women will be distracted by the sight of you.'

Firûsha picked up her sword and checked her reflection. '. . . and will receive his death from me,' she added grimly. The armour suited her and it was lighter than she had expected. She noted the iron comb arrangement along the backbone for extra protection.

Balodil took out two double-bladed daggers and affixed them to unobtrusive fitments on the thigh-guard plates. 'These should complete the picture.'

There was further weaponry in the form of palm-sized discs, which clicked easily into place on the metal upper arm coverings.

'Your brothers recommended I make these throwing discs for you. Practice is essential but you will find them easier to handle than knives. They fly well and the weight makes for a strong impact.' The groundling stood back to admire his handiwork.

'Yes,' he judged. 'That is exactly how a Young Goddess would look.'

'Armed with a lethal sword and a magnificent singing voice,' added Crotàgon. 'You are beautiful enough to be knelt to.'

Firûsha was pleased. *I can think of worse titles than that of Young Goddess.*

The girl-soldier said, 'The Zhadar will be afraid of you. Phondrasôn's people would still flock to your banner, though death were a certain outcome.'

Balodil gave a quiet laugh. 'She's right. And my ex-master was always afraid of the Triplet Siblings.'

Firûsha sheathed the long sword in its fastenings behind her back. 'Why? He treated my brothers like useless servants, come begging at his door.'

Balodil was surprised. 'I thought we had discussed that?' He touched the scar on his brow. 'Or did I imagine it?'

Crotàgon and Firûsha exchanged looks. They sent the female soldier out of the room. 'No, my dear Balodil. We have not talked about it. Your mind is still affected by the Zhadar's attempt on your life.' She drew on her deceptively fragile-looking decorative metal gauntlets.

The armoured gloves slipped like a second skin lovingly around her hands and wrists. There were raised surfaces over the knuckles and these proved at second glance to be equipped with tiny blades, so that a punch would split open an unprotected face. *Fantastic!*

The groundling muttered, 'The bastard! Curse him! I'll take my armour and I'll kill him! I've got plenty of reasons. Then the four of us will be rulers here.' His right eye was focused on the surface of the lake.

Firûsha watched the eye change. The brown disappeared, supplanted by bright green rings and yellow spots for a while. *The inner transformation will continue to progress as long as he takes his medicine – the potion Sisaroth gives him.* 'Balodil,' she asked gently. 'Why does the Zhadar fear us?'

He was still deep in thought. 'Some melody, if you would?' he murmured. His right arm underwent a sudden tremor. 'The pain is excruciating but your voice always helps. Your singing calms my troubled spirit.'

Firûsha had to suppress the pity she felt. They had, after all, saved his life. *He should be glad he is still breathing.* She granted his request and intoned her ode to the glass sea.

When the last note died away Balodil shook himself out of his daze. 'Sometimes,' he said quietly, 'I feel quite strange. It is as if there are two of me. One sees you as my enemy and wants to leave and the other . . . the other one is stronger. I know you are my friends. My family. My allies in any battle.' He looked at Firûsha. 'When you sing the discord in my soul is settled and I know I am in the right hands.' He smiled a little. 'I thank you, Firûsha.'

In order not to have to answer and perhaps be caught in a lie, she merely nodded.

Balodil got on the window seat to look out, fascinated by the sight of the molten glass. 'The Zhadar knows of a prophecy about the three of you,' he told her. 'That's why he enticed you with promises to show you the way home after you complete your service to him. He wants to keep you here and make you dependent on him.'

Firûsha's eyes grew wide. 'This prophecy . . . What does it say?' she urged.

The groundling rubbed his scar. 'I can't remember all the details. There used to be an oracle in Phondrasôn and all his predictions came true. Mostly they were riddles that had to be deciphered. The saying went that the Three would come, young in age-cycles, and accompanied by loyal allies. *The Three* would accomplish great things beyond the capacity of others. Beyond the powers of the Zhadar himself.'

That could mean anything. Firûsha was disappointed, having hoped for something more specific. 'I see,' she said, downcast. 'So that is all?'

'All?' Balodil laughed. 'The Zhadar is the mightiest figure in the whole of Phondrasôn. He can be stopped by no one. No one can defeat him.' His expression became enthusiastic. 'Don't you understand? The prophecy could mean that you three may vanquish him!'

A wave of heat swept through her.

'Is that why they call them *the Young Gods*?' Crotàgon was getting equally excited.

'Of course. It was all kept secret for ages. But every time there was a battle I would help to spread the rumour,' Balodil admitted slyly.

'Wouldn't the Zhadar be better served if he had us killed?' Firûsha poured drinks from the carafe on the table. 'We must have represented a threat from the day we arrived.'

The groundling shook his head. 'You are a useful and effective tool. The prophecy can be interpreted as meaning that with your help he can achieve any goal he had previously found impossible.'

'I thought you said he was all-powerful?' Crotàgon took the cup Firûsha offered him.

'He holds supreme power in Phondrasôn and he likes to claim it all belongs to him.' The groundling waved a hand over the territory shown on the maps that covered walls, floor and ceiling.

'Tirîgon and Sisaroth have surveyed much of the cave system, but it . . .' He looked round and placed a hand on the table top. 'You have explored these areas but the rest is still unknown. Not even the Zhadar has travelled through it all. Nowhere near all of it.' He rubbed the scar. 'Did I tell you about the trade he runs?'

The älfar shook their heads.

'He is keen to avoid peace in Phondrasôn at all costs. Until he is the overall ruler, that is. He supplies the arms and the troops to both sides in any conflict. For some reason he took a liking to me. He taught me new techniques and showed me how to forge with charmed runes even though I don't have a cîanoi's magic skills,' he went on, staring out at the molten sea. 'I watched him bargain with beasts from territory on the far side, places your brothers never got close to mapping. The Zhadar trades with them, providing them with armour and weapons. Sometimes the wares are of good quality and sometimes poor. That way no one side ever gets to win. But he never wanted to take on leadership of their armies. After a while he started to trust me and he'd send me out to negotiate for him. That's why I came to you, if you recall.' He looked at Firûsha.

'Praise be that you did,' she said, and this time her warmth was not all pretence. *And I shall praise the day we get rid of you again.*

'I can't imagine anything better. I'm afraid I've lost my memory of our many adventures with each other, but your brothers have told me about them.' Balodil's regret was obvious. 'I secretly went behind the Zhadar's back. He did not want to command the armies so sometimes I would take that office. As I do for you. He was unaware that I was creating my own realm with the covert aim, given the right opportunity, of absconding. I know many of his secrets.' He frowned. 'Was that really what I wanted to do? Or maybe . . .' He looked pensive. 'Forgive me. I am occasionally confused and names of fellow-groundlings swim into my mind, but I can't place them.'

Firûsha smiled encouragingly. *The spirit of the old Tungdil is still floating around in his head.* 'Do go on.'

'I had thousands at my command, but at the same time I was undermining the Zhadar's trade arrangements. I had forged my final armour masterpiece and I decided to take off. To escape to . . .' He halted, as if he did not know what to say next.

I think I know what happened. 'But he caught you, seized the armour, and left you for dead,' Firûsha supplied. She made a mental note to tell Sisaroth to increase the dosage. If the old Tungdil broke out, the groundling would be worse than useless. She touched the armour. *It would be a shame. His skills are irreplaceable.* 'The Zhadar is an arms dealer and a behind-the-scenes fixer serving his own ends in pursuit of total power in Phondrasôn,' she said in summary.

'Yes, and he needs you to achieve those ends.' Balodil looked over at the fortress. 'A visitor, I see! A barbarian messenger. It'll be for me. Someone wants a general for their army.' He clapped his stumpy-fingered hands together. 'No more boredom for me!'

'Not so fast!' Firûsha decided to receive the new arrival dressed in her impressive new suit of armour. *I'd like to gauge the effect.* 'I'll come with you. I want to hear what he has to say.'

Together they left the room.

Phondrasôn.

Tirîgon sat opposite Carmondai, drinking an infusion of the bittersweet oltrû herb and reading through the historian's notes. It was the summary of the report he had given them, but expressed in such a richly decorated way that it was moving and tragic to read.

This was how my race was lost for the second, even the third time. No älfar realm has ever survived for long. This knowledge etched its way into his consciousness where it melded with his terrible recriminations concerning the deaths of his parents.

The guilt he bore for their loss would never fade. He had already avenged their deaths by killing their murderer. The truth about those crucial, incriminating events in Dsôn had died with the assassin. Nobody in the fortress doubted that Gàlaidon had been a cleverly disguised karderier. Tirîgon knew himself to be safe from discovery.

That knowledge did not mean he was happy. Esmonäe's infidelity and her subsequent death only added to the heavy burden he would bear until the end of days.

While Carmondai kept busy filling page after page with his impressions of life in the Phondrasôn älfar realm, Tirîgon was lost in contemplation of the concept of atonement.

He could not be forgiven by those whose lives had been lost and he could never admit to his siblings what he had done: the intrigues that meant a normal life would never be possible. It was immaterial that he had saved their lives. *I ought to have asked them whether they would follow me to Phondrasôn instead of subjecting them to the pain they went through.*

Tirîgon looked up.

Inside him a second, mollifying voice sang out. His guilt, it told him, was not so severe, after all. *What would have happened to my people if we had not been here to offer them an älfar realm to join? What would have become of them without the refuge and protection we have been able to offer? They would have become victims of the karderiers and the other beasts, they would have been sucked into Marandëi's magic tower, or pulled firmly under the Zhadar's yoke. My dubious actions still produced a beneficial result.*

Tirîgon was happy to go along with this interpretation. He liked the idea that he had saved the inhabitants of Dsôn and thus preserved his own race.

He shared the generally held view that they should get out of Phondrasôn as quickly as possible. There were better opportunities awaiting them than a potential empire in the depths of this netherworld, surrounded by scum. *Tark Draan must be recaptured and must be punished for the deaths of the Inextinguishables. We shall rule over the humans with a rod of iron and we will make certain the elves get what they deserve.*

Tirîgon was eager to ride into battle with drawn sword, storming through barbarian ranks in a magic cloud of destruction.

Carmondai gave them various maps of Tark Draan for their campaign. The historian-poet was a vital component in their planning, as he was able to tell them about the geography of the area and where there might be weak spots in the defences.

The siblings had worked through different scenarios. They had discussed ways of using their troops, which strategic targets should be attacked in which order, which leaders to take out of action. The threads were spun and woven in the skilled hands of the Young Gods.

There was one imponderable: everything depended on where exactly in Tark Draan they would surface. This was the deciding factor.

Tirígon picked up the papers again and skimmed them for the hundredth time. This time something new occurred to him.

Yes, that is a weakness there! I think I've found something. He looked over to Carmondai. 'Do you mind if I disturb you?'

'You already have. Is it important?'

'You tell me. The groundling tribes are united, aren't they? Apart from the Thirdlings?'

'Yes.'

'Nothing's changed there? Even though Tungdil Goldhand was a Thirdling and he's the greatest hero in Tark Draan?'

'Why don't you ask him yourself?'

Tirígon shook his head. 'No. The potions and the spells have made him think his name is Balodil. I don't want to risk reminding him of his previous existence.'

Carmondai laid down his compressed-charcoal writing tool. 'What are you getting at?'

Tirígon lifted up the page that dealt with the notes on the tribes. 'If I've got this right, the groundlings stick together to defend Tark Draan in spite of any internal differences they may have. The Testing Star eliminated most of the monsters and the Inextinguishables have ceased to exist, so the passes will all have fallen quiet.'

'I suppose that's so.' Carmondai was listening attentively.

'The groundlings have been able to expand their trade.' Tirígon traced the four regions with his forefinger. 'We must have been mad not to make use of that fact. The Thirdlings are the best warrior tribe of all five. And they can't stand the other four.'

'That's true. But not the other inhabitants of the Girdlegard. Their god Vraccas insisted they protect all the humans, magicians, elves and good creatures,' Carmondai objected.

'Well, I think we can use the Thirdling forces to our own advantage,' he said, completely convinced. 'For them the conquest of the four tribes would be the biggest coup imaginable. They'd surely pay any price for that.'

Carmondai laughed. 'You don't know the groundlings very well. They'd never . . .'

'And you, if I may point out,' Tirîgon said with some arrogance, 'do not know me and my siblings very well, either. We have the Infamous One on our side and my brother is a cîanoi. We can offer the Thirdlings so much power and riches that they won't be able to refuse.'

'But that's not the way their minds work.'

He may be good at writing stories, and apparently he's not bad at town-planning, but his intellectual capacity falls short of greatness. Tirîgon gave a sly smile. 'We won't give them any choice in the matter. Did you think that Tungdil joined us as a soul mate of his own volition?'

'I know you put him under a spell.'

'With the power of the Infamous One. Sisaroth can do the same with the leader of the Thirdling tribe. If we have them onside, all the clans will follow because they are bound by their oaths of allegiance.' Tirîgon leaned his elbows on the table by the map. 'You'll see, Carmondai. We know how to make use of the groundlings. We'll be able to found the next älfar empire with their assistance.' He gave a quiet laugh. 'I shall enjoy that.

Have you seen the magnificent sets of armour Balodil made for us? And his own he fashioned from a tionium alloy that is engraved with älfar runes. He almost thinks he's one of us. I'm confident my brother can bring off the same miracle with the Thirdlings.' His visage showed him certain of his own invincible powers. 'We are the temptation none can resist.'

The door was thrust unceremoniously open.

One of the guards stumbled across the threshold, slipped and fell to his knees. 'I— we couldn't— ' he gasped, fighting for breath and holding his side.

Carmondai and Tirîgon sprang to their feet. In the doorway lay three palace guards, dead or unconscious.

In strode the gâlran zhadar over their bodies. He wore costly black tionium armour and bore in his hands two short-handled war hammers whose heads shone silver and gold and were set with radiating diamonds and other gems. They emitted a crackling sound as if superheated.

This must be the armour Tungdil was describing. He says it belongs to him. Tirîgon hoped the groundling was not going to suddenly turn up. The armour showed imperfections in the inlay and runes, but those parts of the inscriptions which had been completed gave off a threatening glow. The blast of air that accompanied the Zhadar tasted of hot metal and charred meat.

What can he want? 'Welcome,' said Tirîgon, bowing his head in greeting. *Good acting skills called for here.* He did not believe the Zhadar wanted him dead. *If that were the case I would already have been killed.* And he was keen to find out how the Zhadar had got into the palace without the alarm being sounded.

The soldier at their feet tried to stand up but collapsed again, clutching his side.

'Welcome? Hardly,' came the deep voice. The Zhadar's long black side-whiskers dangled and quivered. 'I am rarely welcome. Not even to those who should be serving me.' The tone of voice grew ever more unpleasant. He took up a stance in the centre of the room, looking first at Tirîgon, then perusing Carmondai from head to foot. 'Where are your brother and sister?'

'They are busy.' Tirîgon moved in front of the table to hide the pages of Tark Draan sketch maps from view. 'You'll have to make do with me.'

Carmondai sat down as though to get back to his drawings. As he did so, he shuffled the maps and invasion diagrams out of sight.

The Zhadar tossed one of the hammers into the air, spinning it and catching it again as if it were made from the lightest of woods. 'As you see, I had no difficulty entering your fortress and coming straight in here,' he said in a bored voice. 'It would be equally easy for me to kill you and your scribe there. Like bothersome insects.' He weighed the weapon in his hand, stepped forward and struck a mighty blow.

It landed on the älf at Tirîgon's feet.

The gemstones flashed and there was a detonation and a wave of heat when the flat side of the hammerhead hit the soldier's helmet. Metal and skull were fused. The guard was smashed to the floor and did not move again. Blood from the älf's shattered face trickled across the mosaic floor.

'I am well aware of that, and I am glad you are not doing it.' Tirîgon would have loved to fling himself upon the creature but knew he stood no chance. *I must remain calm if I want to survive to defeat him on another occasion.* 'So what have we done to provoke your anger?'

'Do I look angry?'

'I don't know of anyone who kills guards from sheer *joie de vivre*. I presume it was intended as a warning.'

'You are correct, *Young God*.' The Zhadar was ridiculing him. 'I am the only one in the whole of Phondrasôn to be known as a god. Neither you nor your siblings have any right to the term. Continue using it and I'll put your divinity to the test. And I showed divine restraint and mercy in letting you get away with the silly trick you played with the female you pretended was Firûsha.'

'That is generous. But let's get back to our supposed elevation to godheads. I don't know what you are talking about.' Tirîgon made every effort to control his temper. 'We are living here in peace and caring for the survivors of our race. We take no notice of what happens in the surrounding caves.'

The Zhadar's eyes narrowed. 'I see. You take no notice. And you take no notice, I learn, of my instructions. You have been ignoring the missions I have tasked you with.' He slammed the bloody hammer into the table top. 'The deal we have is that you carry out the tasks I set.'

'Pardon us. We were occupied in looking after our own folk. A terrible misfortune struck the älfar who lived outside Phondrasôn, in Ishím Voróo in the Grey Mountains. We had to free them from the clutches of the karderiers. It was your advice, I recall, to make war on the six-armed monsters. We are in the middle of planning our strategy.' Tirîgon bowed and feigned extreme humility, though this drove him to the limits of what his pride would allow. 'Hundreds of lives depend on us. We are the last of our kind.'

'Did you think that would make me more kindly disposed? I have eliminated so many peace-loving peoples and gentle species that I have lost count. And you thought you'd touch my heart with your story of the sad fate of the cruel shadow-creepers? Don't make me laugh!'

Tirîgon was aware their visitor had come with the sole intention of intimidating them. *He does need us. He needs us because of the prophecy.* 'I ask your pardon for . . .'

The Zhadar punched him hard on the chin.

It felt to Tirîgon as if an iron bar had struck him. The impact sent him sailing through the air to collide three paces back into a set of shelves.

Stunned, he still managed to land on his feet and to jump aside as the piece of furniture crashed to the ground. The room was spinning.

He never saw the next blow coming.

His adversary's knuckles slammed into his belly and left him gasping and retching. Two further blows to his knees felled him. The Zhadar had shouldered one of his hammers and was showing him an open hand.

'You do see, don't you, my Young God, how quickly one can lose one's splendid status when one meets an Old God?' the Zhadar thundered. 'I don't even need to use my weapons to destroy you and your siblings.'

'You . . . took me by surprise,' Tirîgon gasped, struggling to breathe. There was an excruciating pain in his abdomen. It felt as if a vital organ had burst.

'I shall *always* take you by surprise. Even when I've announced

I'm going to attack, you'll never be able to stop me. You älfar are good, agile and swift. But *I* command *you*.' He brought his hammer down slowly, close to Tirîgon.

The heat the hammer radiated struck his face and he could see the detail of the engraving on the flat surface. *You shall not brand me like one of your slaves!* Beside himself with fury, he moved to fend off the iron brand.

The Zhadar only laughed. He removed the hammer. 'Disobey me one more time, Tirîgon, and I shall cover your älfar flesh with my decorations, believe me. No salve or potion will undo the marks.' He went over to the table and pulled his second weapon out of the ruined wood.

Tirîgon resisted the urge to vomit and his stomach burned like fire. His throat was full of blood. Those bare-fisted blows had been worse than any cudgel. *He is ten times stronger than Crotàgon.* His pride forced him to his feet but it took him some time to stand firm. He felt humiliated by having to haul himself up on the furniture.

The Zhadar had been observing his movements without compassion. 'You will tell your brother and sister that I expect the following: you will go to my troops. They are stationed in Sojól. You know where that lies. The commander, Korhnoj, is expecting you. He will give you your instructions when you arrive. The main task is to take the fortress, remove the ringleader and ensure the region is calm.' He stroked his whiskers smugly. 'I thought it would be a good idea to have the Young Gods that they all so admire put down their rebellion. It will make it clear to the insurgents exactly who is in charge here.'

The Zhadar turned and left.

Carmondai drew a deep breath. 'I thought I'd seen everything,' he commented. 'That speed, the magic aura . . . it's nearly like the Inextinguishables!'

It's absolutely nothing like the Inextinguishables. That's where you're wrong. Tirîgon opened his mouth to protest and vomited a gush of blood.

Chapter II

Where there is no necessity
nothing is proved
by the killing of another being
other than it is possible.
How much easier
will that killing be
when necessity dictates it.
Hesitation
brings nothing
but hastens one's own death.

'Aphorisms' from the epic poem *Young Gods*
composed by Carmondai, master of word and image

Phondrasôn.

Firûsha crossed the courtyard behind the first defence wall in the company of Balodil and Crotàgon. This was the place where the guards had stopped the barbarian and taken him to an interview room outside the complex. Nobody got any further than this point and any messenger or visiting envoy had to wait until one of the Triplets found time to speak to them.

Crotàgon stayed behind with the watch and the groundling entered the chamber with Firûsha. She saw an armoured barbarian whose face was unfamiliar. She glanced at Balodil. *I wonder if these two know each other?*

Balodil greeted the man and introduced him as Shucto. 'We've come across each other a few times and we've fought in the odd skirmish together. He's one of the Shuctanides, a race that's aiming to rise up against the Zhadar. He, his father and his three sisters reign over five of the caves.' Balodil sat down opposite the man and then pushed his chair back a little so as not to be on the same level as the älf ruler. He knew his place; Firûsha was thus not put in the uncomfortable position of having to assert herself. She met the barbarian's gaze and assessed his body language. She could see that he admired her appearance and was surprised and fascinated in equal measure. *He is staring at me as if I had stepped down from the stars.* 'What do you seek here?'

Shucto watched her in silence, his jaw slightly agape. It did not make him look any more intelligent.

'What do you seek?' she repeated, her hands on her hips. There was a metallic scraping sound when her gauntlets touched her armour.

The barbarian could only stare. His lips moved and some mumbled syllables emerged.

Balodil kicked the man's chair. 'Hey! Wake up, you!'

Shucto jerked upright and leaped to his feet, tugging off his fur cap, stared at Firûsha again and then went down on one knee. Then both knees. Then he lowered his gaze to her feet. 'I offer you my most humble of humble greetings,' he stammered. 'My thanks for granting this audience to an unworthy subject; you are most gracious. How was I to know that Firûsha herself, one of the favoured Siblings, one of the Young Gods, would address me in person?' His emotions were getting the better of him.

Balodil smirked, but said nothing.

The four guards in the corners of the room started to smile.

Firûsha had noticed how respectfully they treated her, as well. *I obviously impress them, too, not just this barbarian fellow.* She approached him. 'You may look up at me. Now tell me why you have come.'

Shucto gulped, twisting his cap in embarrassment. 'I wanted to ask Balodil to put in a good word for me so that I might speak to the Young Gods,' he stammered. 'I have a request.'

'We are not the right ones to grant requests. It's the Zhadar you must address on that score.'

'No, Young Goddess! You . . . your brothers. You are indeed the ones who can come to our aid,' he said fervently, spreading out his arms in entreaty. 'We are suffering under the Zhadar and his forces. The mercenaries will arrive soon. I know they are encamped in Sojól, and from there – '

'That's nothing to do with me,' Firûsha cut in. She turned to go.

'But the Young Gods showed us that it is possible to defy him. You are our role models in this. We worship you. We pray to you at night!'

'We never asked you to,' she said firmly but not unkindly. 'You chose this situation for yourselves.' She motioned to Balodil to accompany her out of the room. 'There is nothing we can do.'

'I implore you!'

Firûsha did not answer. *They are the best possible distraction to divert attention from our plans. Let them rub up against the Zhadar. That'll keep him occupied.*

'Please let me finish. Please hear me out. We are offering a special incentive, seeing as you . . .'

'Did you say *incentive*? You're offering an incentive to a god?' Firûsha laughed. 'That's absurd!'

'We had heard the Young Gods were looking for a way to get back to the surface,' said Shucto shyly.

Yet another one who thinks he knows a secret way out. 'Isn't everyone in Phondrasôn looking for the same thing?' Firûsha halted in her tracks but did not turn round.

'We aren't. My family and I . . . would be happy here, if it weren't for the Zhadar.' Shucto's voice bore a trace of hope. 'We have always lived in these caves. My forefathers, our earliest ancestors, the Oldest Ones, were the first to settle here. But your race, Young Goddess, does not belong in this place. It is not your world.'

'Are you telling me you really know a way out of here?' Firûsha had lost count of the number of times she'd been told a similar story. She had even heard it from her brothers, of course. She turned.

'Yes,' Shucto answered promptly. 'But it won't stay open for much longer. You'll have to act quickly.'

'And where does the exit lead to?'

'It comes out in a body of water the elves call *Suamotil.* It means something like *Pond of the Moon.*'

Firûsha felt the hairs on the back of her neck stand up. 'What did you say? Why do you understand elvish?'

'My family once saved the life of an elf who had got lost in Phondrasôn. He wasn't one of the ones that travel with the flying ships. He didn't want anything to do with them. He taught us some basic things in his language. That's why I'm able to read some elvish writing, Young Goddess,' Shucto explained. 'I know they are your mortal enemies and that you want to exterminate them just as passionately as they want to wipe you out.'

'The elf you are talking about – is he dead?'

'Oh yes, he died fighting with us in an óarco attack, Goddess.'

That's a shame. I would have liked to interrogate him. Firûsha fixed her blue gaze on the barbarian. 'The passageway emerges into a pond?' He nodded. 'Why did you say it would soon be closing up?'

'It only came about through magic. You know about the magic power surges that plague us. One of them affected the course of a river,' he told her, nervously wringing his cap between his hands. 'It was completely reversed. Instead of drawing water out of the pond it pumped water in. The cycle reverses at intervals, but the sequence has started to slow down. I think that means the magic is losing power.'

Firûsha walked back to where the barbarian was standing and looked down at him. 'Go on.'

'I was on a boat when the river changed direction. I swear by the perfection of your countenance, Young Goddess, that I was veritably sucked up the length of a waterfall. There were crabs and fish swirling round my ears and I was in the middle of the rushing water. I emerged in the Moon Pond and swam to the bank. There was an elf settlement nearby.'

'So how did you get back here, if the river had reversed its course?' Firûsha asked sharply.

'And how did you manage to breathe underwater?' Balodil wanted to know. 'Why didn't you drown?'

'I waited. I just waited until the direction of the river's flow switched again. And I can breathe because of this . . .' Shucto swept his hair back and showed them the gills at the side of his neck. 'The magic affected us as well. We can exist on land or in water. That is, in water for a considerable time.'

'Really?' grunted Balodil. 'I don't like that idea. I know if I fall in a river I'll drown, just like any sensible creature that wasn't created for life in the water. There's a terrifying goddess of the waves called Elria.'

Firûsha was disappointed. 'We are not like the Shuctanides,' she said. 'We are not half-fish. I wonder if there's a solution?'

Shucto had to admit he knew of none.

'How long were you under water before surfacing?'

'I'd say about seven hundred heartbeats.'

I'd never be able to hold my breath for that length of time. Four hundred I could manage, but not seven.

She suddenly recalled something her brother had told her.

Tirîgon had explained the trick with the pig bladders. She reckoned the air in an inflated bladder would be sufficient to get them through to the Moon Pond. Provided, of course, that the whole thing wasn't a trap, something cooked up to get rid of the Triplets and the rest of the älfar.

She briefly considered the possibility but decided it was an unlikely scenario. Shucto had admitted he and his family had had dealings with elves. If the whole thing were a plot he would never have mentioned elves at all. *And if he were out to trick us he'd hardly have started negotiations by asking for a reward. Could he be a karderier, though?* She motioned to him to stand up. 'Did

I understand you correctly before? You were proposing some kind of a deal? A trade of sorts?'

Shucto stepped back. 'My family decided to suggest it. We are desperate. We thought we'd ask you for help.'

'You thought you would force us to do what you want, you mean.'

He bowed his head humbly. He did not seem to be enjoying his role as negotiator in chief. 'We are . . .'

'. . . desperate. Yes, I know.' Firûsha decided to listen to the request. 'Go on.'

'It's . . . the Zhadar is going to launch an offensive against the rebels. His forces have them pinned down on the Sojól heights and the fortress is under siege. Korhnoj is the name of the Zhadar's commander there and we think he's about to storm the stronghold.'

'And?'

'You . . . could prevent it happening. You could do something. Kill their officers?'

Firûsha looked at Balodil, who was considering the options. 'What do you think?' she asked.

'Not a bad idea,' he said. 'I know this Korhnoj. He's cunning. His unit is efficient and reliable. If the officers are put out of action the soldiers will be clueless.' But his eyes told Firûsha that he was not speaking his mind. He did not want to talk openly with the man in the room.

'That's exactly what we're hoping,' said Shucto urgently. 'As soon as we get your signal that the officers have been eliminated, the rebels can pounce on the army. Then we'll march on the Zhadar himself and force him to surrender.' Balodil burst out laughing, which disconcerted the barbarian. 'We will. We'll force him to give up,' he insisted.

'What makes you so sure?' Firûsha asked. 'I know the Zhadar. I know his four towers. I know his defence wall and the sort of magic he's capable of. An attack by a force such as yours is not even going to spoil his breakfast.'

'We . . . we will succeed,' Shucto repeated. It seemed that he was not being completely truthful. Being so close to the august älfar personage was disturbing for him. He was unsure of himself and overwhelmed in her presence. 'Really. We will.'

Balodil's eyes narrowed. 'What are you not telling us?'

'Nothing! Nothing at all!'

'Oh, yes, there's definitely something. I know a lie when I hear one,' Balodil growled.

'There is one thing . . .' Shucto implored them to trust him. 'Please don't ask me to say it . . . We just need the leaders defeated, then we can finish the rest. We don't want you to take this war on yourselves. You need to take your people out to Girdlegard. Whether we win or lose against the Zhadar in the long run must not concern you.'

Even if he's keeping something back, there's something to be said for this. It won't be difficult to take out a few barbarians. Even if they are in an army camp. Don't I command the shadows, after all? 'All right,' said Firûsha, 'it's agreed. But first I need to see that the access passage via the Moon Pond actually exists.' She stood in front of Shucto, who was quaking in his shoes. 'Take me there. Prove you are not lying. If what you claim is true, then I promise my brothers and I shall fulfil your request.'

Shucto looked nervously between Firûsha and Balodil, weighing up his chances. He agreed. 'I'll take you to the river. Straight away if you like.'

'A good idea,' said the groundling.

'Yes.' *Is it?* She told one of the guards to bring her a leather drinking pouch that she could use as an air supply. *It's probably not going to work, but it's best to find out. I have to know.* 'I will go with Shucto on my own. If it is a trap and I don't come back,' she told Balodil, 'you must inform my brothers. And then,' she said, looking directly at the barbarian, 'they will ride to the five caves of the Shuctanides and will destroy every living creature they come across. If I die my death will bring down havoc and thousandfold devastation. Be sure of that.'

He stammered in protest.

This was not the sole reason Firûsha had for travelling alone. She knew Tirîgon and Sisaroth would simply forbid her to try out the underwater passage through a raging torrent. It was a dangerous undertaking. Extremely dangerous.

If it were up to my brothers they'd send one of the soldiers through first. But this would not satisfy her. He might come back without finding the exit. Or he may not return at all. She wanted to go to Tark Draan herself. *They'll believe me if I can get back in one piece. And if I don't make it, they'll avenge my death.*

There was a commotion outside.

One of the guards opened the door and looked out. 'It's the Zhadar,' he announced. 'He's heading up to the palace with our warriors escorting him.'

Shucto went pale. 'He knows what we're doing,' he whimpered. 'Oh, I knew this would happen! He knows what we've been plotting!'

Firûsha looked at him and smiled. The barbarian was comforted by this and fell silent. 'Don't worry. If the Zhadar knew you were here he'd be in this room and you'd be dead. You'll be all right here.'

She was, however, afraid that the Zhadar had yet another task for herself and her brothers to carry out. She would not be able to refuse. The fact that he had appeared in person, she thought, showed he was losing patience.

She was not concerned for the sake of her brothers, but she was worried it would scupper her planned expedition to Tark Draan. As soon as the Zhadar left, Tirîgon and Sisaroth would send for her. *I must set off before that happens.* 'Shucto, show me the way. Now.'

They left the room together, but she paused to talk to Balodil. 'I'll wait here till my master goes,' he said, taking a drink of water to which he had added a few drops of liquid from a phial at his belt. This was the medication Sisaroth had prescribed. The drops were to treat the headaches he was suffering from, he understood. 'He would be angry if he found me here with you. He would be so angry he would forget himself and kill you in spite of the prophecy. It's better all round if he goes on believing I'm dead.'

Firûsha thought he was right. 'You know what is to be done if I don't return.'

'My dear friend, I do indeed,' he replied. 'Look after yourself. And bring me back something nice.' He grinned. 'I wouldn't mind a barrel of black beer.'

'I'll check out the elves' food stores.' She raised her hand in farewell and pulled the door closed behind her and Shucto. She was in a state of high excitement as she accompanied the barbarian across the bridge. *Tark Draan.*

The land she had heard so much about in stories. The land they would conquer.

The land which held the secret hopes of her people.

Her expectations were high. She would not be satisfied with anything less than total success. *There has to be a Moon Pond. There just has to.* Her blue gaze was fixed on the nape of Shucto's neck as she followed him, planning how she would take the bones out of his body while he was still alive if she found he had betrayed her.

Firûsha listened to the voice of her heart; apart from the exhilaration and the anticipation there was a new feeling: fear.

Phondrasôn.

Sisaroth held his scythe-like knife in his right hand and heated the blade on the furnace fire until it glowed red and the inlays shone green.

He was concentrating on the phrasing. The ritual was all-important and the smallest detail had to be observed minutely: the rhythm of the words had to be exactly as Marandëi had coached him in their short partnership.

He was now unaware of anything but the immediate task in hand. He was not alone in the room but had the impression that the whole world revolved around him. Even if an unthinkable catastrophe broke loose he would not interrupt the incantation. *I am offering him another sacrifice. It shall not be the last.*

The knowledge about the ancient älfar language and the prayers to the gods of infamy which Shëidogîs had breathed into his mind came from the old books, but he was able to apply them as if he had been performing these rites for decades. Once he held the skull in his hands everything just flowed.

He pulled the blade out of the glowing coals and held it over the naked torso of the älf lying on the stone table before him.

Sisaroth plunged the knife in and the red-hot blade slipped through the skin up to the hilt. *Perfect.*

With one powerful movement the priest opened the flesh from the navel to the chin. The älf's animal scream ended in a gurgling sound. Blood surged out along the length of the wound into a chiselled gully on the stone to collect in a wide and ornately decorated bowl.

In the base of the bowl sat the skull of Shëidogîs.

The blood ran, like thickened juice, splashing onto the centre of the relic, filling the carved engravings and following the convoluted patterns traced into the bone to cover the gold leaf, the pearls and the tiny spheres of silver.

But the mutilated älf still breathed.

'Accept all the strength his immortal life has stored. Take it!' Sisaroth replaced his blade on the forge and plunged both hands into the gaping cut. He rooted through a jumble of sliced intestines and vital organs until his hands located the heart in the chest cavity.

He wrenched it out and tossed it onto the coals.

On its bed of stone the body contorted and foamed at the mouth but the light in the eyes was not breaking.

The offering bowl continued to fill, with the blood reaching the eye sockets.

Sisaroth picked up the scythe-knife and sliced deliberately round the crown of the victim's head. He took a silver axe from his belt and struck the head forcefully.

The top of the älf's head fell off, releasing brain liquid which ran down to collect in the same channel as the blood.

There must be no mistakes made. Sisaroth's red fingers retrieved the brain mass and placed it next to the burning heart.

'Accept his mind. Take the mind that kept him alive so long. Accept it!' he called out, raising his blood-covered arms. 'Shëidogîs, reveal yourself in the blood of this älf! Reveal yourself to protect us all, to lead us all.'

The relic was now submerged under the congealing fluids, which bubbled and hissed, sending up a whitish steam.

A fountain of blood shot up out of the vessel. It squirted like a geyser and formed the silhouette of a bloodied älf with his dark mouth agape.

Yes! Yes! My reward! The murky cloud of breath drifted across the victim's body and infiltrated itself into Sisaroth through his nose and mouth, causing fury lines to erupt on his face and his eyes to become shadowy holes. His body cramped and his back spasmed as he gasped and choked, needing to steady himself by grasping the table edge. *The effect is even stronger than before . . .* He stretched out an arm for support.

And Tirîgon was by his side, holding him fast.

The blood silhouette crackled, ignited and turned to ash and smoke; the relic skull lay pristine in its dish, as if nothing had touched it.

'Thank you,' groaned Sisaroth. Absorbing the residual force was always a thorny problem. A cîanoi could be in shock for some time while the energy was redistributed. Sisaroth's vision began to clear and he took in his surroundings again.

Balodil and Tirîgon were with him in the largest of Marandëi's secret chambers, standing by a chimney vent that prevented suffocation during these smoke-filled rituals. The stench of burning organs from the charred brains and heart of the victim was sucked up the ventilation shaft.

The groundling had wanted to be present during the

ceremony. This was now the fourth time. The tattoos on his skin made him sensitive to the spirit force. He had become a fervent worshipper.

No mention of Vraccas or the Tark Draan divinities. Sisaroth was still gasping for breath as he nodded to Balodil. *Tirîgon and I did a good job with his conversion.* The potion he had created had overcome any mental resistance without the groundling noticing what was happening to him. The effect had been instantaneous and was, if anything, intensifying.

'Are you feeling better?' Tirîgon gradually removed his supporting hands.

'Yes.' Sisaroth wiggled his fingers, which were sticky with the victim's clotted blood. 'I'll be fine soon.' He leaned on the sacrificial table. 'Shëidogîs has been generous this time.'

He watched as his brother carried the corpse with Balodil's help over to the forge. The groundling activated the bellows. The heat increased to facilitate the cremation process.

This had been the seventeenth sacrifice in total that had been offered to the unholy skull.

They no longer searched the tunnels and caves for lost älfar; they took the ones who had arrived from Dsôn when it was not immediately clear whether or not they might be fakes.

When these älfar did not return after their interrogation, their disappearance was read as a confession of guilt; the presence of a karderier. No questions were ever asked because the word of the Triplet Siblings was never doubted.

Balodil enjoyed watching the flames do their work. The corpse shrank in the heat. 'We still haven't slit open a real karderier,' he noted with a sinister laugh.

'All the better,' said Sisaroth. His veins were pulsing

alternately hot and cold. Rubbing his arms free of the clotted blood he decided he needed a bath. 'The Infamous One wants älfar. Only älfar.'

Tirîgon lifted the dish with the relic and handed it to Sisaroth. 'Do you think you are prepared for the task the Zhadar wants us to perform?'

'Yes,' he replied. 'I feel strong enough for that.' *Marandëi would have been proud of me.*

'Excellent.' Tirîgon waved away the cloud of stinking air that the vent was slow to remove. 'But I do think we should wait until Firûsha gets back. I want to know what she thought she was doing, going off on her own with that Shucto.'

'Nothing wrong with that, surely?' Balodil spoke up. 'The Songbird's sword skills are better than your own,' he teased. 'She's just the one to explore our way out to Tark Draan.'

Sisaroth smiled. *The little mountain maggot thinks he's one of us. Perhaps we overdid the dose?*

'Shucto is a barbarian. They can't be trusted,' Tirîgon complained.

'Shucto is an exception. I've known him a long time. He would never dare set a trap for us. He knows exactly what will happen if Firûsha doesn't come back. His family, his whole race will be wiped out.' Balodil worked the bellows steadily, the muscles on his torso and arms swelling up like mountain ridges. 'And there's a service he wants from the Young Gods.' He winked at them with his good right eye. 'I'm looking forward to seeing home once more. To go back there with you. Who's going to stop us?'

Sisaroth noted Tirîgon's broad smile. *That's true enough.* 'Absolutely,' he said. 'Who's going to stop us, Balodil?'

Tark Draan.

Wearing full armour underwater, Firûsha stalked along the bottom of the pond through the murky black before kicking towards the lighter grey shimmer that must signify its surface. The moon, suspended high overhead, was an elliptical disc shining through the water.

The leather pouch had proved a success and had survived the rough journey. She had enough extra air to travel underwater. *Without it, though, I would have drowned.* She calculated the submersion totalled eight hundred heartbeats.

It had been a long time since she had last seen the moon and its glow lifted her soul. The world on this side was a thing of mystery: there were water lilies growing on the mirror-like surface above her head.

The pond floor rose sharply near the bank and it was spongy in feel. She was an arm-length's away from breaking through.

Is it Tark Draan or is it another cave and I've been tricked? She took the leather air pouch out of her mouth and drew her dagger. She lifted her head slowly out of the water.

She could hear the sounds of frogs and crickets. A soft breeze from the west brought the fragrance of warm grass, blossoms and ripe cherries. Someone was playing the lute and singing.

O ye gods of infamy! Firûsha was overcome.

Looking up into the night sky to see the moon and the stars in all their glory, she was overwhelmed by their sparkling beauty. She saw a shooting star ride through the sky with a fiery tail, while the cool waters of the pond lapped around her.

She had been under such stress that the joy released a flood of tears. Shucto had told the truth.

I am in Tark Draan. This is not just yet another cavern full of madness and idiosyncrasies and monsters. She made her way slowly forward, creating as little disturbance as possible. She glided up the bank, heading for the nearby wood in search of cover from enquiring eyes.

It was vital that her arrival were not discovered. But in her elation she wanted to sing at the top of her voice, whirl and dance. She had been doubly fortunate in her escape: she had found the way out of Phondrasôn *and* out of Ishím Voróo.

I wonder who our musician is on this balmy night? Firûsha followed the tones of the instrument, creeping round through the undergrowth until she reached a clearing.

There she saw a pair of elf lovers. He was playing and the female raised her voice softly in song. Their garments were delicate and translucent and the two were lost in contemplation of each other.

Firûsha stared at them. *My mortal enemies. Within my grasp. They are unarmed and not encumbered with bags or equipment. That means their village cannot be far off.*

She didn't intend to stay. Shucto had warned her about the stream reversal. The current would change direction soon. She was aware of the water lilies drifting towards the centre of the pond. As yet it was only a tiny movement, the leaves' movement barely perceptible.

Our attack on Tark Draan is imminent. Firûsha permitted the lovers to enjoy each other's company a while longer. *I shall soon be back.* She studied the faces of her victims carefully and withdrew in silence.

On her way back to the Moon Pond she relished the evening's pleasures: the fragrances, the starlight.

Taking a deep breath of the fresh air, she collected grass stems and flowers as evidence to show her brothers. There must be no doubt in anyone's mind that she had truly set foot in Tark Draan and been in an elven grove. She even took down a rune-etched lantern to convince them of her story.

Sitting on the bank, she stared down into the pond. *This would be a good place to found our new Dsôn. We would be the Dsôn Aklán: the gods of Dsôn.*

She gave a nostalgic smile. There was much to be accomplished. A new beginning with neither father nor mother at her side. Her parents had waited for such a long time for the Inextinguishables to return. *We will look after your legacy.*

There was a sound on her left.

She drew her long sword and gathered the darkness around her, crouching in wait.

A magnificent white horse stepped out of the wood and approached the pool five paces from where she hid. It lowered its head to the water to drink. Firûsha suddenly realised what the animal was.

She had thought at first that it was a trick of the reflection on the ripples. There was a twisted horn as long as an arm jutting out from the creature's forehead, with lines resembling the blood channels on a sword.

A unicorn! Firûsha gulped. *It is sure to attack me.*

Her next thought was daring in the extreme. The magical stallion was her opportunity to create her own night-mare.

But this was not something that could be done in Tark Draan on elf territory. It had to be in the dark lands of Phondrasôn with her brothers' help and the powers of the god of infamy. *If I bring back a unicorn, they'll all have to believe me.*

She had to work out how to get the animal to accompany her through the underwater passages. She could intimidate the creature and frighten it into the pond, but would the undertow be sufficiently powerful to drag the animal down? Could it possibly survive the long moments with no air to breathe? Or would it suffocate on the way?

Who cares if it does drown? That would merely be one less unicorn to bother about. Firûsha circled the beast and approached it from behind.

The magical creature had quenched its thirst unaware of the danger. It raised its broad head and uttered a loud whinny.

Its call was answered from the outlying forest. *There are more of them.*

The water lilies! They are drifting faster to the middle. Firûsha dropped the dark shadow and used her inborn gifts to weave a net of fear which she threw over the unicorn's head.

The animal bucked and reared and stumbled into the cold, dark waters.

'Off with you!' Firûsha whirled her sword above her head to intensify the terror the creature felt. She employed all her strength to drive the unicorn before her. Had she used the same amount of energy against a troll or a barbarian horde, her enemies would have collapsed with their hearts burst open. The stallion tolerated a far greater degree of evil.

The unicorn galloped away into the depths of the pond, finally leaping and swimming when it could no longer feel the ground under its hooves.

'That's a nasty surprise, isn't it, meeting an älf-woman?' Firûsha set off after the unicorn, sheathing her sword and swiftly inflating the leather pouch. *Well, you can be forgiven for being surprised. You will soon serve us. You will be ours.* She quickly sank to the bottom from the weight of her armour and the surface closed over her dark head.

In front of her she could see the pale body of the unicorn and the hooves kicking out wildly as it trod water dangerously close to her head. The undertow began to pull at her legs. The stream was changing direction.

You shall accompany me or die with me! Firûsha put the mouthpiece to her lips and grabbed hold of the animal's plunging back legs with both hands.

The stallion increased its attempts to resist the pull of the current but the added weight and the increased drag gave it no hope of escape.

Together, the älf-girl and unicorn rushed into the depths.

Chapter III

DARK PATHS

Moon Pond, Moon Pond!
Flat as a mirror,
dark as the night.
We slip out unseen
and emerge into the light
Moon Pond, Moon Pond!
May your secret lead us
to the enemy's elven heart.
Let our fight be unceasing
and let fame be our part.

Excerpt from the epic poem *Young Gods*
composed by Carmondai, master of word and image

Phondrasôn.

'She is back!' His brother's voice rang through into the laboratory Sisaroth had installed in what had been Tossàlor's studio. Tirîgon put his head round the door. 'Firûsha's come back. And you'll never guess what she's brought us from Tark Draan!'

Praise be to the gods of infamy! Wait, Tark Draan? Sisaroth put the distilling experiment to one side. He had been making a concoction for Balodil out of the concentrated essence of älfar resulting from the sacrificial offerings; the aim was to produce a substance that would stabilise the groundling's mental capacities. 'She got to Tark Draan? Up there?' But Tirîgon had disappeared. 'Tirîgon, come back! Tell me what . . .' With a mild curse Sisaroth wiped his hands clean and rushed into the corridor.

He raced along the passageways behind his brother, up and down staircases and through the halls, with an excited Carmondai and Crotàgon joining them on the way. Crotàgon hardly deigned to greet him, even fleetingly. The two of them had had their differences since the death of Tossàlor.

He'd love to know where I keep Shëidogis' skull so he could destroy it. Sisaroth nodded to him.

Even following the extinction of Marandëi's death curse, everyone kept the peace. In fact, all the exiles and refugees were collaborating well. There had been no killings or feuds. Being surrounded by Phondrasôn's dangers seemed to consolidate the little community.

They reached the courtyard together and heard furious neighing from afar.

Are my senses deceiving me? Or is it the vapours from the new potion affecting my brain?

Sisaroth saw a tethered and blinkered unicorn fighting against its chains. The hooves struck the cobbles repeatedly but the creature could not get free. Straps from the leather bridle and halter were held fast by eight älfar. *What a magnificent play of muscles!*

The horn, long enough to skewer two älfar at a time, whistled through the air like a sword every time the creature tossed its head.

'Unbelievable! No question! It must have come from Tark Draan!' Carmondai was opening his sketch book to record the wild movements and to write a few notes.

Firûsha stood next to the groundling and one of the barbarians. She looked exhausted but triumphant. 'Proof enough?' she asked, reaching into a bag and taking out wet flowers, grass and twigs, tossing them merrily into the air. 'My brothers! I have been to Tark Draan! I have seen the stars and stood in the moonlight and I found some elves just waiting for us to come and kill them.' She threw herself into her brothers' arms in turn. 'We are going to leave Phondrasôn and we're going to fulfil the destiny of our race . . .'

'. . . and reign in Tark Draan!' Tirîgon completed her sentence joyously. 'You have brought us a unicorn!'

Firûsha laughed. 'I thought that would convince any älf still suspicious of my claim. The flowers and leaves I possibly could have obtained from another part of Phondrasôn, but there are no unicorns down here.' She indicated the barbarian. 'Shucto of the Shuctanide tribe in the Sojól cave showed me the way.'

She told them quickly what had happened. She did not attempt to gloss over the fact that the journey had been fraught with danger. Travelling the river was not easy and she had nearly lost the magic stallion on the way. She did not forget to mention the agreement reached with the barbarian.

Sisaroth and Tirîgon looked at one another. *That directly clashes with the task the Zhadar's given us.* Sisaroth motioned Firûsha and Tirîgon to his side. 'What's to stop us going back to the waterfall without Shucto? We can swim through to the Moon Pond without his help, surely?'

'He blindfolded me! I might be able to try to reconstruct the journey by the sounds I heard, but only Shucto understands the timing sequence by which the current goes into reverse. We can't afford to trick him. Or at least, not yet, certainly,' she stressed. 'Why don't we just do what he's asking us to? We're leaving anyway, so it doesn't matter what happens after we kill the Zhadar's officers.'

'We can't, because the Zhadar has told us to do the exact opposite,' replied Tirîgon tersely. 'We can't risk it. You should have seen what he is capable of. Balodil warned us not to provoke his former master in any way unless we can kill him at the same time.'

'Then we need a plan that will guarantee Shucto helps us *and* keep the Zhadar at bay long enough for us to get to Tark Draan through the Moon Pond,' Sisaroth murmured. He could not take his eyes off the unicorn. *I can turn it into a night-mare.*

He knew there was a ceremony that would transform this basically good-natured creature into a wild flesh-eating beast as swift as the wind. He did not know exactly what had to be done but he remembered his father Aïsolon saying Caphalor had created his stallion Sardaî from a unicorn.

Shëidogîs will help me, I'm sure. In his mind's eye he could already see the horrified expressions on the faces of the elves he would confront, riding his magnificent and malevolent nightmare. *I will make Shëidogîs a sacrifice of the elves' eternal life.*

'That's exactly what we need,' agreed Firûsha. 'We have to make sure that the Zhadar doesn't get wind of our intentions. I don't like the notion of relying on the vagaries of a capricious waterfall to protect us from his wrath.'

'I can't see a quirky cascade stopping him.' Tirîgon looked at Sisaroth. 'Any ideas?'

'Not yet. I'll consult the Infamous One and offer . . .'

'Are you not keeping count?' His brother put a restraining hand on his shoulder. 'We don't have any more älfar to sacrifice. We've run out of possible karderier suspects.'

All of them? 'But surely there are enough criminals?' Sisaroth was not going to accept his brother's objection. *I must ask Shëidogîs what he thinks.*

'They used to be criminals, perhaps. Now they are the last few survivors of our race.' Tirîgon was firm. 'I can't allow you to jeopardise our chances by reducing the numbers in our ranks. And it would ruin the soldiers' morale. We'll need every sword at our disposal once we're in Tark Draan. The initial advantage of surprise won't last long. The Infamous One gets no new älfar sacrifice right now. Tell him he'll have to make do with the elf blood we'll give him. He can swim in that to his heart's content.'

Sisaroth did not bother to contradict him. He knew his brother was right.

'Why can't we do both tasks?' Firûsha was rubbing her temples. 'We can help Shucto first, then get him to lead our people to the waterfall while two of us stay behind in Sojól and carry out the Zhadar's mission.' She smiled. 'If we're going to be pedantic – as I understand it, he gave the task to you both. I was off with the barbarian at the time, wasn't I?'

Tirîgon grinned in response. 'Good point. But that won't convince the Zhadar not to make a fuss when his officers are wiped out. Shucto said the rebels were planning to storm the four fortress towers and they had a surprise for the Zhadar, but how are our allied forces going to cope if they've no officers?'

Sisaroth was annoyed. 'We need more time.'

The siblings were silent, thinking hard.

The unicorn calmed, snorted a little and uttered an enquiring whinny, desperate to return to the herd.

Balodil was waiting a little apart and studying the stallion; from time to time he grinned over at the triplets. Tirîgon watched him. 'Firûsha, didn't you say the groundling refused the river trip?'

'Yes. He was adamant. He's not going into water for anyone. He doesn't trust the water goddess, Elria, he said.' She waved at Balodil and he raised his hand in greeting.

'And he hates the Zhadar, doesn't he? The Zhadar nearly finished him off.' Tirîgon tapped himself on the chin. 'Why not leave him here and get him to attack his old master's officers?'

'No,' Sisaroth said. 'Are you forgetting he is the greatest hero Tark Draan has ever seen?'

'I know. But do we *need* him?'

'Yes. You've got your plan to use the Thirdlings.' Sisaroth looked over at the groundling. *It's really only going to work if we have him with us.*

Carmondai was still rooted to the spot, sketching away obsessively. The siblings would get no sense out of him.

'As it may be. But I am absolutely convinced we have to leave him behind.' Tirîgon addressed his brother and sister. 'Listen. We kill the commanding officers on *both* sides and put Balodil in charge of two leaderless armies. He might be able to defeat the Zhadar while we're making our escape. If he fails, the Zhadar will put all the blame on him. If he wins, he can take over Phondrasôn and impose the worship of the infamous gods everywhere. What do you say?' He noticed a shadow fall across them. 'Crotàgon. How long have you been standing there?'

Crotàgon had come up to them unobserved. 'Sounds like a plan to me.'

Sisaroth felt uneasy when the tall warrior was near him. Crotàgon was too big to be able to get into the secret passages behind the main palace. He tried to keep as close as possible to the Sibling Rulers. *I think he's spying on me. He wants to get at the skull. I know he does.*

Firûsha was in favour of Tirîgon's proposal. 'One of you go and explain the plan to Balodil. You get on with him better than I do.'

'Are you implying we've got a little too close to our half-älf, half-dwarf creation?' Sisaroth gave an apologetic smile. 'I trust my potions and elixirs. They have made our groundling a reliable servant. And he doesn't suspect a thing.'

'Will their effect be sustained if we leave him here on his own?' Crotàgon had doubts.

'I'll leave him a store of medicine to take. Parts of his brain have undergone permanent changes. We've been inculcating him with the arts of the infamous and he's combined that with his knowledge of the Zhadar and his existing skills at the forge.' Sisaroth indicated the dwarf's squat form. 'What you see there is no true groundling any more but a crossbreed permeated with our älfar influence.' *All my own work.*

'Right. That's decided, then.' Tirîgon got ready to move off. 'I'll talk it through with him while Firûsha and Shucto finalise the details of their campaign. Don't tell Shucto what our mission for the Zhadar is.'

'That way everyone's deceived to a similar degree. Excellent!' laughed Firûsha. 'I'm so looking forward to getting back to Moon Pond, I can hardly wait. I already have two elves on my hit list: the lute-player and his little friend.' She pointed at Crotàgon and then at Sisaroth. 'They're mine, remember!'

'But if we don't know what they look like ... ?' the statuesque warrior objected.

'I'll draw you a picture. Don't you dare touch them.' Firûsha went over to the barbarian and led him down to the gate. She was going to take him to her rooms to discuss tactics.

Tirîgon and Balodil went off into the palace. The groundling's furrowed features glowed with grim eagerness.

'And us two?' Crotàgon asked.

'We get on with our own affairs,' Sisaroth answered. 'In my case it's the elixirs I'm working on. I need to get some supplies ready for Balodil. You assemble the troops and tell them that in our name, the Young Gods are preparing a return to the surface and they will overrun and conquer the elf realms.' He turned to go. *I want to get away from him before ...*

'Are we leaving the skull with Balodil?' the warrior asked.

... before he asks me questions I don't want to answer. 'Why would we do that? We'll be needing the god's power once we get to Tark Draan.'

'Wouldn't it be better left in Phondrasôn?'

'Shëidogîs wants elf-blood. Unfortunately there aren't any elves left in Phondrasôn. I rather think we killed the last ones when we took over the palace.' Sisaroth strode off and left the warrior standing there. *I'm not having you making decisions about what I should or should not do.* 'The skull definitely comes with us!' he called back over his shoulder.

He found himself thinking Crotàgon would look good on the sacrificial stone table. He was fed up with being followed around all the time. *He's stalking me and he's not going to stop till he's found and destroyed the skull. He and Firûsha are as bad as each other.*

Sisaroth went back to his laboratory and completed the distillation of the boiled älfar essence, but he did not give the process his full attention.

The idea of having the majestically built warrior follow in the path of Tossàlor, his secret love, was too tempting. On the other hand it would be very difficult to come up with a cover story for his disappearance; Crotàgon was incredibly popular with the troops. *And Firûsha would know straight away.*

He tried to suppress the thought by concentrating on how to turn the unicorn into a night-mare.

Shëidogîs must help me. I'll win him round with the prospect of what our future holds in store. Sisaroth hurried through the gap in the wall and into the narrow passageways. He listened carefully before daring to take the artefact out of safe-keeping.

Placing the relic on a cushion on the small altar in front of him, he related the recent events, speaking intimately as if to a close friend.

He described the forthcoming attack on Tark Draan in glowing terms and spoke of the veritable mountains of slaughtered elves he intended to offer up in honour of the god of infamy. 'I need your help. Firûsha has brought us a unicorn and I want to turn it into a night-mare. I'll give it to my sister as a reward for her courage. How do I go about it?'

Shëidogîs gave Sisaroth all the necessary details.

Phondrasôn.

Tirîgon poured Balodil some wine and drank a toast to him. *He has a good head for wine. I'd have thought beer would be more to his liking.* 'So you agree?'

The groundling took the goblet, turning the stem in his calloused fingers and staring into the drink.

'I'm more or less sure,' he said slowly. The alcohol had affected his speech and his mind. He took a deep breath, his chest expanding. 'There is a desire in me to go back with you to Tark Draan but I could never go through the water as you are planning to do.' He looked miserable. 'I got to Phondrasôn through the Black Abyss and it seems I'll have to return the way I came sometime in the future. Impossible to determine in advance.' Balodil placed the rim of the cup to his lips and drank. 'Is it very bad of me to be unhappy about it?' He turned his brown eye on Tirîgon and smiled. The lines on his face seemed deeper. 'When you go I shall lose my main support, my friend. You saved my life, all of you, and I have fought many a battle for you.' He was lost in thought as he drained the cup. 'Now you are leaving me.'

'Don't forget what you stand to gain. The death of the Zhadar. Your special set of armour – the one he stole off you. You will command territory and caves. And you can encourage the worship of the god of infamy, who will support and stand by you. And when the time is right, you can rejoin us through the Black Abyss.' Tirîgon refilled the groundling's cup. 'Make absolutely sure you keep taking the elixirs Sisaroth is brewing for you. The effect of his remedies will restore your mind and help you recover from that blow to the head.'

Balodil answered with a vague mumble, then raised the cup and studied his own reflection in the polished metal. He traced the scar on his forehead. 'It's true,' he said. 'I can't leave here until I've exacted justice from the Zhadar. I can't let anyone get away with trying to kill me.' He turned his head from side to side to examine the line of the injury and the swollen scar.

'That's the way I see it, too,' said Tirîgon, sipping his own drink. *I've set you on the right track. Get going, you stubborn dwarf.* 'You are assured of the grace of the ungodly. You have always worshipped faithfully and have assisted the cîanoi in the religious rites. The god will remember your loyalty. You will see: your successes will outdo those of the Zhadar a hundredfold.'

'If this is what I must do to get back through the Black Abyss, then I shall do it,' Balodil mumbled, replacing the cup on the table. He placed one hand on his breast. 'I can feel it inside me, Tirîgon.'

'The burning desire for revenge?'

'The god.'

He's talking rubbish. Tirîgon nodded. 'Of course. He is in us all.'

'No, I don't mean that. I mean I can actually feel him in me. He speaks to me. It's like there's a part of him sitting inside me.' The groundling groaned and held his hand tight against the eye patch. 'That is his gift to me, my friend. There can't be better protection than that.'

'I shouldn't contradict you but there's a possibility that what you are feeling is the effects of the drink.'

'That's what I thought at first. But something occurred to me. It happened at the ceremony before last. You weren't there, so I had more duties than usual. We were sacrificing an älfar child whose parents had gone missing. When the Infamous One was about to show himself, the dish his skull was in started to wobble. Sisaroth was in a trance – I could see his black eyes and the black lines on his face. So it was down to me to do something.' Absently, he stroked the hand with the golden mark.

Tirîgon was listening intently. *What has the mountain maggot been up to?*

'Some of the älf-child's blood spilled onto my hand as I steadied the bowl and it seeped in through the pores of my skin. It was as if my skin were made of paper. Before I could wipe it off, it had entered my body.' Balodil showed him his hand. 'You can't see anything, I know. But since that day a part of the Infamous One has been in me. He is in my blood.'

'And my brother did not notice?' *It's probably his imagination.*

'No. Everything proceeded normally. Shëidogîs appeared in his blood silhouette form and blew the black breath of power over Sisaroth. But ever since, my work in the forge has been of a much higher quality and the special älfar runes are so much easier to apply. I have been creating armour with built-in magic spells, I think.' He sighed. 'I never dared tell Sisaroth. I wonder if I should?'

'I don't think so.' Tirîgon was wondering about the occasional convulsions the groundling had been experiencing. He had recognised a greater preponderance of älfar nature in Balodil recently. He did not want Sisaroth's attention drawn to this as he feared his brother would insist Balodil accompany them to Tark Draan because of the infamous presence inside him.

He took another drink of wine. *It's nonsense, of course. Shëidogîs would never choose to enter a dwarf, rather than myself or my brother.* Tirîgon put the whole thing down to Balodil's imagination.

'Right. Let's keep that between the two of us.' Balodil seemed relieved to have got the confession off his chest. 'When do we start moving? The sooner I lead the army against the Zhadar's towers, the sooner I can smash his face in. I want to kick him to death like a dog. I want his armour. I made it for myself.'

'Did he not commission it in the first place?'

'I created it for myself and after he saw how it good it was, he insisted he ordered it.' The skin surrounding the eye patch turned dark and sent fury lines across the groundling's face. 'I saw the Zhadar when he came to speak to you. I was by the guardhouse.' His hand gripped the goblet so hard that the metal started to bend as his knuckles whitened. 'He took over my masterpiece and made adaptations. He even carved his own runes into the metal. I'm not letting him ruin my work!'

From outside came a shout, and the sound of the unicorn's protests.

'That was Sisaroth! It's coming from the hall!' Tirîgon leaped up and ran out. The groundling's faltering drunken steps followed at a considerable distance.

Tirîgon heard the clatter of hooves, loud shouts and the animal bellowing and kicking against the palace walls. Crockery and other items crashed to the ground and wood was shattered.

Is it inside the palace? Reaching the gallery, Tirîgon looked two storeys down.

The unicorn was wildly thrashing out, its tail raised up as it cantered through the hall, slamming the hooves of its hind legs repeatedly against the doors, but not succeeding in breaking them down. It evaded all Sisaroth's attempts to drive it into a corner with the tionium and silver axe he used for his sacrificial rites. In his left hand he held the Infamous One's skull.

Sisaroth barely dodged a full frontal attack by the creature as it tried to drive its horn through his body.

'Are you out of your mind? It will skewer you through!' Tirîgon yelled before rushing down the staircase. *He's not even got his armour on!*

'Just let it try! That's what I've been waiting for,' Sisaroth wheezed, gasping with the exertion. He had a cut on his arm and there was blood soaking his priestly robes from another injury on his flank.

Tirîgon was downstairs by now at his brother's side. 'What are you trying to do?'

'I'm going to turn it into a night-mare,' he panted. 'The god has explained how.'

'Did he say you had to get yourself impaled on its horn first?' Tirîgon was impressed by the powerful elegance of the magnificent creature's movements. Its large eyes were fixed on both älfar, and it stood ready to lunge.

It was not put out by the sudden appearance of a second adversary. It neighed aggressively and gave a loud threatening snort, tossing its white mane. Its bright tail whisked from side to side.

It turned and faced the brothers and lowered its head in preparation for a new attack with its horn.

Tirîgon noted that all the doors were heavily barred. Only a battering ram would enable anyone to come in. The hall had been transformed into an arena for a final confrontation between unicorn and älf.

Holding the animal continually in his sights, Sisaroth said, 'I must cut off the horn and introduce my own blood onto the stump. Our own magic will drive out all the good in the creature.'

'Oh, is that all? Didn't Father say Caphalor . . .'

Sisaroth raised the decorated skull. 'Shëidogîs will tell me the right spell to recite. Go back upstairs. You can't help me. Go and stand on the stairs, at least, so that it can't . . . Watch out! Here it comes!'

Tirîgon had not dared move his eyes away from the unicorn and could see it bearing down on the pair of them.

Its hooves beat on the mosaic flooring and crushed the little stones. Furiously it charged, aiming the tip of its horn first at him and then at his brother. It seemed to be revelling in the älf-baiting exercise.

Tirîgon was so mesmerised by the creature's beauty that he failed to spring completely clear.

He avoided being struck by the horn but the creature's body collided with him and sent him flying through the air.

That was close! Too close! Tirîgon used the momentum to make a backward roll and regained his balance before the next onslaught from the plunging horn.

Curses! It's so quick! The tip of the horn grazed his armour, gouging a deep channel in its metal surface. He was forced backwards again, struggling for breath. Any other set of armour would have failed.

He landed up against a door, spluttering; turning to the right he avoided the unicorn's charge, which left its horn lodged in the wooden planks of the door.

Tirîgon could see the look in the reddened eye of the unicorn: hatred and iron will and the determination to kill his tormentors. *You beast! We'll tame you yet!*

The thick muscles in the creature's neck swelled. Instead of pulling its horn free, it whipped its head in a horizontal movement, slicing the heavy door through until it met the masonry frame. When the unicorn raised its head, stones and a cloud of dust came out of the wall.

What strength it has! It's inexhaustible! Tirîgon stepped behind a pillar, his vision hampered by the dust.

'Move!' his brother shouted beside him.

Tirîgon ducked, attentive to the warning. Above his head a unicorn hoof crashed into the marble of the column he had been sheltering behind. It had the force of a catapult hurling a boulder. The animal followed through to ram him.

Tirîgon had to execute a second roll to escape and could feel the draught as the kicking hind hooves narrowly missed his head. He took cover behind a different pillar. *Why does it hate me so?* He made an effort to control his breathing so as not to betray his location. *I wonder if the armour has something to do with it?*

The hooves clattered past.

He got up and saw the unicorn's tail and hind quarters go by, while Sisaroth jumped around on the steps trying to provoke the animal. *How does he hope to calm it? Surely if Sisaroth cuts off the horn, the beast will be maddened with pain and its strength will increase tenfold?* He looked around at the devastation wreaked on the hall. *Not even solid stone and heavy wood were able to withstand its attacks.*

The unicorn focused on Sisaroth now, snorting wildly through its nostrils.

It's looking for a way to escape. Tirîgon crept closer, but kept a respectable distance away from the powerful hind legs. 'Watch out! It will knock you down. It wants to get up to the next floor!'

The unicorn charged, its head lowered slightly.

'Let's be having you!' mocked Sisaroth, offering his broad

chest as a target. 'Kill me if you can!' He danced to the side but slipped in a puddle of his own blood. The cîanoi did not lose his footing completely but the ensuing loss of concentration threatened catastrophe.

No! You shall not rob me of my own brother! Not when we're on the point of leaving for Tark Draan! Triumph is so near! Tirîgon slipped off his weapons belt with its heavy sword and hurled it overarm with all his strength between the animal's feet. The unicorn shrieked with fury, intent on killing its foe.

The belt caught in the unicorn's hooves and the long sword impeded its progress.

The stallion crashed down and slid towards Sisaroth; älf and unicorn ended up in a confused heap.

'Sisaroth!' Tirîgon ran over to where his brother lay, drawing his double daggers from their harness as he ran. *I will stab it while it's down. I don't care that it means we don't get our nightmare. My brother's life is a thousand times more important.*

The horn had penetrated Sisaroth's belly and emerged out the back. Blood poured down the grooves and collected on the floor. Sisaroth was struggling for breath. The unicorn was struggling to get to its feet.

No. Tirîgon lifted his daggers, aiming at the creature's white-maned neck. 'You accursed . . .'

'The axe,' croaked Sisaroth. His grasp loosened and the silver weapon clattered to the floor. 'Hack off the horn with the axe. Then put your own blood on the stump and listen for the words Shëidogîs will give you.'

Tirîgon's eyes welled up with tears. 'If you think either Firû-sha or I would ride a night-mare that ended our brother's life, forget it!' He replaced one knife in the sheath anchored on his thigh armour and picked up the axe. With a nimble foot sweep, he prevented the unicorn getting to its feet. 'It shall follow you to endingness.'

Tirîgon took careful aim and struck out – but at that moment and in spite of the terrible horn piercing his body, his brother forced himself to his feet. The movement resulted in Tirîgon's weapon striking through the horn rather than the vertebrae.

Freed from the ballast of the älf's body, the stallion's head reared up, smashing into Tirîgon's chest.

The älf's dagger was forced into his own neck and he felt the blood pour out: the wound was a deep one.

This is going to end badly. Staggering, Tirîgon dropped his weapon, grabbed hold of the bannister to steady himself and tried in vain to stem the bleeding. *I need a healer. And fast . . .*

The unicorn, teetering, had managed to get upright but was screeching with pain. The horn stump gushed blood and the white muzzle and blaze now streamed red.

'It shall not defeat us.' Sisaroth was still on his feet and stretching out an arm to his brother. Tirîgon assumed it was for support but realised Sisaroth was extracting a throwing disc from his armour. He drew it through blood from both siblings. 'We shall create it together.' Then he tossed the disc onto the unicorn's stump.

Älfar blood combined with the beast's own. There was a hissing and a bubbling as black foam formed on the open surface.

The stallion went wild, bucking and prancing through the great hall, shattering anything its hooves came into contact with.

How could such a wound be overcome? Only the power of the infamous god can have kept life burning. Tirîgon could hear

Sisaroth muttering certain words. His brother's body remained skewered on the unicorn's severed horn.

At that moment the main door burst open.

In strode Balodil with his weapon Bloodthirster in both hands. The groundling must have left via an external staircase. His one eye scanned the scene. He saw the state the brothers were in. 'By the god of Infamy! Tirîgon! Sisaroth!' He stepped back to avoid the shrieking unicorn. 'We've got to get out of here! Get out of the palace!' he yelled, running up to the two älfar. 'Now!'

Sisaroth sank to his knees, continuing the incantation that would complete the unicorn's transformation. His eyes were fixed on the stallion; it was as if a strong bond existed between the two of them.

'What's happening?' asked Tirîgon, his voice slurring. *I think the bleeding's letting up.* The pains in jaw and neck remained hellish.

'How can he be alive?' Balodil tried to help Sisaroth to his feet but the älf pushed him off.

'It is the power of the Infamous One,' Tirîgon replied, coughing blood. He was confused and did not know what he was supposed to be doing. 'What do you want?'

The groundling pointed at the open door with his sword. 'A magic force field! It's heading for the fortress. There've been two detonations. The bridges . . .'

As he spoke a whizzing sound was heard over their heads accompanied by the crack of an invisible whip.

The whole roof lifted off in an incredible explosion that stopped Tirîgon's ears. The shockwave threw him against the steps.

We are done for. His senses were affected. Falling masonry, Balodil shouting, the unicorn's screams, collapsing columns and plunging balustrades all produced but a shrill whistle in his head. The ground under his feet was shaking but he heard no rumbling sound. Merely a high piping. Nothing more.

Tirîgon's skin tingled as if ants were crawling over him, biting at him. *We are completely cloaked in magic power!*

There were further flashes in the hall; now the roof had gone it was an open yard, with clouds of dust from the damage rising to the sky, chased away by a hot, scented wind. Even great lumps of marble were whisked away by the violent currents of magic air. Rubble was swept upwards as if it were dry leaves.

Above him was the cave roof, where sparkling spheres danced and dazzling stars shot past, streaming bright tails behind them, raining down on what remained of the palace.

His face was burning hot. *My dream is lost. We were nearly home. My triumphant return! All the bad had been turning good! So nearly there!*

Balodil stood over him and was obviously shouting something. He could smell the wine-laden breath on his face but all he could hear was the whistling sound in his ears. Looking past the groundling he could see the unicorn lying on the ground, its coat turning dark and then black. *There's one thing we managed to do right. So we'll be dying with a night-mare at our side.*

Two stars collided, causing an explosion loud enough for even Tirîgon to hear. A red magic curtain was formed, reaching right down to where they were. A new bolt of lightning danced and flashed over the mosaic flooring, bringing fresh destruction and leaving a scorched black line until the bolt of fire got near Balodil.

Tirîgon saw how the zigzag of light struck the groundling's armour and made all the inlaid work glow. His golden eye patch shone out, illuminated from within, as if the sun were hidden behind the covering. Balodil's face was a network of black lines.

Then something happened that made Tirîgon doubt his own mind. The single figure of the groundling was suddenly two!

The lightning strike had brought a second Balodil to life, an imitation created from the original in a shower of sparks. Posture, body shape, hair, weapons, every tiny detail was identical.

Tirîgon's jaw dropped as he stared at the doppelgänger. Then the red curtain reached them and its enormous force dazzled and blinded him completely.

Everything was excruciatingly painful.

Tirîgon cried out and uttered curse after curse until the torture suddenly ended. After a few heartbeats he started to regain his sight and then his hearing.

What . . . what has the magic done to me? His wound had stopped hurting. Feeling for the injury with his fingers he found the skin smooth and whole. *It's gone! Healed over!* He looked around.

He saw Sisaroth standing next to him holding the unicorn horn in his hand. He was touching his belly carefully. 'I . . .' Then his gaze fell on the magic skull at his feet, totally unscathed.

'Was that the magic?' Tirîgon got to his feet and looked at Balodil. He saw only one Balodil. *I must have imagined it.* A trick of the light – a reflection, perhaps, caused by the detonations. 'Balodil?' He rubbed his temples to deal with the dull ache collecting there. He could still see little stars in front of his eyes.

The groundling shook himself as a dog might do emerging from water. 'Did that have to happen right now?' he grumbled. 'We were in the middle of our preparations for our ventures.'

Balodil rubbed the back of his neck. 'It feels like a band of óarcos have been thrashing me with a cudgel.' He scrutinised the brothers. 'Your wounds!'

'The Infamous One sent a miracle,' Sisaroth decided, not wanting to concede that magic could have had anything to do with his recovery. 'The god transformed the force into a healing spell.'

They heard a dark, low neighing.

They turned their heads.

A night-mare came trotting out of a far corner. It had glowing red eyes and a coat as black as coals. When the stallion gave a snort its vicious incisors showed. The beast appeared weary but in good condition.

What a magnificent creature. And from now on it belongs to us. Tirîgon was speechless with emotion.

'Didn't I tell you we would do it?' Sisaroth whispered in awe. 'It is wonderful. Firûsha will be thrilled . . .'

Balodil turned his head. 'Not only Firûsha,' was his comment. He drew slowly back. 'I just hope we have enough meat for them.'

What's he talking about? Tirîgon rubbed his eyes to make the light flashes go away. He thought it must be his hearing coming back that made the beast's snorting louder and louder. Then he saw what the groundling meant.

They came out of the dark ruins, heading for the brothers as if suddenly released from the enveloping shadows: night-mares! The magic force had duplicated their first specimen, many times over.

Sisaroth stroked the skull of the infamous god. 'Aren't they incredible?'

'I shan't trust the beasts till they've been fed. And I don't want to be their fodder.'

More and more of them, identical in every single respect. Tirîgon stopped counting once he reached forty. 'It looks like we'll be riding to Tark Draan.' He approached the herd cautiously. 'Come on, Sisaroth, we need to get Firûsha and find out what else those explosions have destroyed.' *We can only hope for the best.*

He chose to ignore the possibility that his seeing a double groundling might not have been a fleeting illusion. Locating his sister had priority.

And thus he chose to go nowhere near the question of whether the Balodil in front of him was the original, or the copy.

Chapter IV

Do you think
  Death has a smell?
  A form?
  A weapon to take a life?
Death has none of these.
Death is everywhere,
  and inhabits all things:
  from a knife slicing open your gullet
  to the smallest of breadcrumbs
  in the very same throat
  choking you to death.

'Aphorisms' from the epic poem *Young Gods*
composed by Carmondai, master of word and image

Phondrasôn.

Firûsha struggled out from under the rubble of the guardhouse. *Was that the Zhadar? Was it intended as a warning? Or was it the long-feared magic storm?* She slipped and slithered her way, snake-like, to freedom.

Her armour had been largely responsible for her survival; she suffered no serious injury. But she wasn't completely unscathed by her immersion in the torrent of falling debris: the beams, roof tiles, and blocks of stone left painful grazes on her arms and legs. The all-pervasive smell of fresh blood told her that other älfar had not been so fortunate.

I would never have thought those massive walls would succumb to magic. I am lucky to be alive.

She made her way forward towards a bright gap in the rubble and pushed her arms through to get a hold.

'Firûsha!' Crotàgon appeared and helped her out of the constricted aperture. Like her, he was covered in dust and dirt. 'Are you all right?'

She nodded. 'Where are my brothers?' Firûsha stood upright and stared round at the devastation that was all that remained of the palace and the fortress. *That was never the work of the Zhadar.*

Apart from the destruction, there were odd occurrences resulting from the uncontrolled magic strike: some parts of the fortress had duplicated themselves and were placed randomly all over the island, together with their teams of älfar.

Now there were seven new main entrance gates: some even in the middle of the forest. One was spotted poking up through the surface of the molten lake and there was another on top of the palace ruins.

The defence ramparts were projecting vertically out of the ground but starting to crumble under their own weight.

This is ghastly! Firûsha surveyed the scene. *Our own residence has suffered the same magical onslaught as the fortress.*

The magic had provided four copies of the main and side wings of the building. They were interconnected in the most illogical manner and were causing untold further damage to the structure as they balanced on top of each other.

The attack had caused the molten sea to burst its banks, flooding a third of the island with lethal liquid glass that was starting to harden. Anything touched by it would have been charred into nothingness or trapped in a transparent coffin for all eternity.

Nothing is as it should be. Firûsha gave silent thanks to the goddess Inàste that she and her brothers had already made their plans to leave Phondrasôn. *Neither the Zhadar nor the karderiers are the main danger here. It's the place itself we have to fear most.*

They were lucky that the molten sea had not completely swamped their island. There was one bridge leading out of the cave that was still intact, but it was coated in a strange fluid that was slowly solidifying.

The weight of the extra glass will test its stability to the limit . . . Firûsha caught sight of the älf struggling up from the ground behind Crotàgon with a strangled cry. The whole of his right side was missing. So was part of his head. Like those of the randomly duplicated main gates, all the edges were clean cut and the inner organs and the brain were visible.

She suddenly realised that it was not only the inanimate masonry sections that had multiplied.

Crotàgon turned and stepped away from the gruesome magic-generated being. 'By all the gods!' he breathed in horror.

The body confines of the weird figure gave way with a disgusting squelching sound and the vital organs slid to the ground. The mutilated älf fell down and remained motionless.

This is worse than any night terror Phondrasôn has inflicted on me.

More misshapen älfar duplicates were sliding, limbless, over the rocks, crawling through the ruins, groaning or screaming or shouting for help.

Limbs were also present in ridiculous extra configurations; there were even älfar with two heads shrieking in a unison of agony and despair.

The horrors did not end there. Some of the victims were missing their skin, or had an extra layer covering the entire face like a gruesome flesh mask. Intestines burst forth and dragged along the ground.

Crotàgon had drawn his sword. It was all far too creepy for him. 'What has happened here?' he murmured.

Everywhere she looked, Firûsha saw extra copies of members of her own race. Twins, triplets, full-grown quadruplets or even quintuplets stood around in dazed confusion. Those who had recovered from their astonishment were starting to quarrel as to who was the original and who was the imitation. Scuffles and armed combat broke out in a hopeless attempt to establish unique and true identity.

'I don't know,' she answered hesitantly. Her stomach churned. Not because of what she saw here but because of a thought that shook her very being. *Am I really Firûsha? Or am I a copy?* She looked over at her mentor. *How will I know whether he is the real Crotàgon and not a magic imitation?*

She heard a familiar voice.

My brother. Firûsha turned her head. 'Sisaroth?' She clambered over the ruins as quickly as she could, following the direction the sound was coming from.

She found him half-buried under a collapsed wall, calling out in pain. She could not understand what he was trying to say.

Nearby another Sisaroth was missing both arms. And there was a lower torso, by itself. Undoubtedly also belonging to her brother...

All fakes! Firûsha looked at the one stuck under the wall. *A copy, too?* She whispered his name and supported his head gently. *How will I ever know which to trust?* 'Look me in the eyes, brother. Is it really you?'

Sisaroth was still for a moment, staring at her, with the light of recognition in his eyes. He opened his mouth and showed an incomplete row of teeth. And no tongue.

No. That's not you. It can't be. Firûsha took her hands away and picked up her knife to ram it through the heart of the false brother. The figure died with a horrified hiss. 'We have to find my brothers,' she told Crotàgon, as she put her hand in the blood of the corpse she had stabbed. With her forefinger she painted a rune first on Crotàgon's forehead and then on her own. 'Kill any Firûsha you come across that doesn't have this mark. And I'll do the same with any multiple Crotàgons I meet.'

'Good idea.' He looked her carefully up and down, then looked at the slaughtered Sisaroth-copy. 'How will I know your brothers? Which ones are real?'

That's the question that's bothering me. She took a deep breath. 'We'll have to get them all in the same place and figure out how to determine which is the original.' She wanted to go back in and start searching immediately but then she saw a black cloud billowing out of the devastated palace. There was the thunder of hooves and the sound of neighing.

She could not believe her eyes. *Night-mares?*

A whole herd of the black-coated magical equines streamed

out of the building with Sisaroth and Tirîgon in their midst, followed by Balodil.

But are these the genuine versions? Firûsha hurried off to meet them, lifting a long spear high in case she should need to defend herself against any overly insistent night-mares. The animals would never normally attack an älf, recognising a certain affinity, but clearly these multitudes had come about by magic. *And they'll be hungry, at that.*

Her brothers approached.

The bloodstains and torn holes in Sisaroth's tunic were evidence of severe injury but he was walking without any apparent discomfort. She assumed he had been able to use his spells to heal his wounds. The brothers looked utterly astounded at the devastation outside the palace but it was obvious they were relieved at the sight of their sister.

'May Samusin, god of the wind and of justice, be praised that you have survived, my brothers!' She quickly reported on events and told them what she had observed.

Following her example, the brothers and the groundling made marks on their brows to ensure there was no confusion with their imitations.

They held a short discussion and decided to destroy any copies of themselves they came across, but to spare any newly created älfar as long as they were physically complete. Their army was in sore need of reinforcements and these double, treble and fourfold copies would help with making up the numbers. The arrival of the night-mares meant they would now have a cavalry unit. It only remained for the älfar to get used to riding the new steeds.

All the surviving älfar gradually assembled where the siblings were, but out of respect remained at a distance. They had recognised their leaders and looked to them for advice and instructions as to what they should do. The company talked quietly together, wondering what the future held.

'Those that are crippled but still alive, leave to me. And any imitation of ourselves,' Sisaroth told them. It was a command rather than a request. 'I shall sacrifice them to Shëidogîs and increase the god's divine power. We need every miracle he can give us.' He looked around. 'How fortunate that he was able to turn this catastrophe round in our favour.' Sisaroth laughed quietly. 'It will be strange to sacrifice a copy of one of you. Or of myself.'

Tirîgon and Firûsha exchanged glances and Balodil laughed in disbelief.

'You're saying we're supposed to be grateful to Shëidogîs for the destruction of our home here?' It was Firûsha who spoke first, unable to credit what she was hearing from her brother. *He's ascribing everything to the demon. He's completely taken in and obsessed by this being.* 'Listen. If he's so powerful, why didn't he prevent all this?'

Crotàgon pushed his way to the front of the crowd to join the siblings and heard Firûsha's protest. He did not say anything but his face was dark. It was clear what his opinion was.

Sisaroth was unconcerned. Holding the skull relic in one hand he said, 'Of course we must thank him! We would have been done for without his intervention. He transformed the effects of the magic storm and donated a whole herd of night-mares and new troops to our cause, so we can march off against Tark Draan and the elves . . .'

'Utter nonsense!' Crotàgon shouted. 'That skull has abso-lutely nothing to do with what happened here. And whatever is in there, it's certainly not the soul of one of the gods of infamy.'

Silence fell. The älfar gathered around them were eager to hear what the response would be.

'How dare you . . . ?' Sisaroth began.

'I'm ready to dare anything. That thing,' Crotàgon said, pointing at the skull, 'stole what was dearest to me. There is a demon, an evil spirit, in there. It's taken you prisoner just like it captivated and enslaved Marandëi. It doesn't care who gets sacrificed to it – the souls of älfar, elves, groundlings or barbarians – to that demon they're all the same. It only cares it gets living energy.'

Crotàgon's words could have come from Firûsha's heart. *But it's unwise to be saying this now.*

'Silence!' Sisaroth took a step forward and was about to strike Crotàgon.

Crotàgon raised his spear and held the tip aimed at Sisaroth. 'Keep your distance, cîanoi. I've been silent for long enough and I've let you carry out those sacrificial rituals. You've killed our own people . . .'

'Crotàgon, what are you talking about?' Tirîgon interrupted him roughly, using all the acting talent at his disposal. 'You must be confused.' The spectators muttered to each other in alarm.

'I reckon this is not the genuine version of Crotàgon,' Sisaroth growled. 'It's a fake. We should get rid of it.'

You wouldn't! 'No! He is the real one!' Firûsha went to stand at the warrior's side.

'I am the real Crotàgon,' he declared, not lowering his weapon. 'I owe nothing to any of you. On the contrary. I have saved Firûsha's life, served the Triplet Siblings and commanded the troops in the fortress for them. But enough is enough. I can't stand idly by while this skull is worshipped and deified. It has brought nothing but death and destruction and it must be destroyed.'

Sisaroth lifted the relic high above his head so that all might see. The gold shone out brilliantly and the pearls gave off a bright sheen. 'This is an artefact that contains the soul of Shëidogîs, one of the gods of infamy, the divinities worshipped by our ancestors,' he announced. 'Marandëi instructed me in the ancient rites and I have studied the old language. The meaning of the runes inscribed is clear: they stand for us, the älfar. Only for us. It is utterly impossible that a spirit of another kind might inhabit this skull. Crotàgon, can you tell me what kind of a demon you think it might contain?'

Surprisingly, Crotàgon retained his composure. Firûsha had been dreading he would charge at Sisaroth with the spear and kill her brother. 'I'm under no obligation to tell you anything at all,' he replied. 'It is how it is: we are serving an idol here instead of worshipping the Inextinguishables or venerating the values our race holds dear.'

'I have brought new life to the old traditions!' Sisaroth insisted.

'Even if what you say is correct and the runes are an old älfar inscription and you can read the old writing, who can guarantee that what our forefathers used to do wasn't wrong in the first place? There will have been a good reason for outlawing blood sacrifices to the gods of infamy. We should leave things as they were. No more sacrifices to the skull demon.' Crotàgon looked round at his audience and lowered the spear. 'Not a single älfar life more to be lost. If Sisaroth is so keen on feeding the skull, let him sacrifice himself. Or one of his siblings. If that god of his had wanted to protect us our island would not be in this terrible state. A true god would have prevented the disaster. Our gods are named Inàste and Samusin. They are our älfar divinities.'

He's doing what he's best at. Inciting rebellion. That's what got him sent to Phondrasôn in the first place. Firûsha looked round. The other älfar were silent but their expressions showed that they agreed with the demagogue's speech. It was a terrible shock to hear that their own kind had been secretly killed as blood-offerings. Sisaroth had not denied anything. *We are fortunate that no violence has broken out yet.*

Tirîgon laid a hand on Crotàgon's broad shoulder. 'Enough. We have all got the message. Let's direct our efforts to looking after the survivors and gathering our strength before starting out for Tark Draan as we have planned,' he said, speaking reasonably. He addressed the other älfar: 'I give you all my word that there will be no more sacrifices made. Unless it's by a volunteer.'

That's a clever move. Firûsha gave thanks for Tirîgon's more sensible nature. *That should calm everyone's fears.*

Nobody spoke.

Crotàgon nodded agreement. 'I accept that and will hold you personally accountable, Tirîgon. If one of us dies to feed this demon without having announced loud and clear that it's of his own free will, it'll be your life as well that's at stake.' He planted his spear in the earth. 'Let's get this place sorted out. We must round up those night-mares. We haven't got long to learn how to ride them.'

The älfar dispersed and started removing the rubble.

There's no disputing it. The troops love and respect him. Firûsha watched the ease with which the tall warrior organised the älfar into work details. Carmondai had found a seat on a block of masonry and was writing in his journal. He represented the group memory.

'They listen to him and obey,' said Tirîgon thoughtfully. 'He as good as belongs to the Young Gods, doesn't he?'

'There are only the three Young Gods,' Sisaroth growled, holding the intricately decorated skull lovingly in the crook of his arm.

I know what you're going to do. 'My brother,' said Firûsha, stepping in quickly because she guessed what was being planned. 'Please don't be hasty. We need Crotàgon. The island has to be restored to some sort of order. He has already taken that in hand. And if we get to Tark Draan we'll certainly need him when we ride against the elves. His military skill and his reputation with the soldiers will be decisive in battle. We cannot think of going ahead without him.'

Sisaroth gave her a scornful look. 'If I didn't know better I'd think you were his mistress.'

'Don't be childish,' she snapped.

'It's not being childish at all. I know what I know,' he replied. 'I know you are as keen as he is to have the skull put out of action permanently. You are allies. And you've been trying to argue Tirîgon and me out of getting rid of a real threat to our power.' Sisaroth got to his feet and leaned towards her threateningly. 'Be careful when you take sides, sister.' He turned on his heel and headed back to the ruins of the palace.

He had hurt Firûsha. She was upset. 'Tirîgon, was he really threatening me?' *Is my own brother wanting to get rid of me?*

'It certainly sounded that way. Forget it, though. You know what he's like. He feels as though he's been humiliated in front of everyone. He'll settle down. He knows we all have to stay calm and reasonable. That magic storm has caused a massive disruption to our plans. We haven't got much time left if we're to make it through the passage to the Moon Pond.' Tirîgon bent and gave her a gentle kiss on the forehead. 'Forgive him his outburst. He is under a lot of stress. I'll talk him round when he's ready, you'll see.' He placed an arm comfortingly round her shoulders and hugged her. 'Come on, let's find Crotàgon. We need to show ourselves to the troops and make it clear that we are the masters, the Young Gods, and that Crotàgon is in our service.'

Firûsha made herself nod in acquiescence, but she did not take her eyes off Sisaroth's retreating figure. *Crotàgon was speaking the truth. That skull has got to go. It's up to me to make sure the bad spirit does not come to Tark Draan with us.* 'Yes, it must be done,' she said ambiguously, and went with her brother to start tidying up the island.

Phondrasôn.

The three siblings trotted through the caves of Phondrasôn: their first outing on night-mares. As the hooves struck the ground, flashes and sparks hissed out from under the animals' fetlocks.

For once I am travelling as befits my station in life. Tirîgon was enjoying the new sensation; he was pleased with his stallion. As an interim measure they got their saddles and tack from Shucto's tribe of barbarians, adapted for their own use.

He was learning fast. Tirîgon responded easily to the movements of his black steed, revelling in the creature's stamina and strength. The night-mares gave their riders confidence. *I can hardly wait till we get out onto open country for a proper gallop.*

Their route took them to the location of the Zhadar's army encampment, where the rebels had dug themselves in.

Shucto and Balodil were riding with them, but on clumsy, crude animals that were closer to a cross between a giant frog and a horse than anything else. The Shuctanides used these mounts to speed up their own journeys but they were quite unable to keep pace with the night-mares. This was another reason the älfar were not letting their mounts canter.

Tirîgon wondered what else was happening while they were underway. The four hundred head of älfar troops commanded by Carmondai and Crotàgon had already set off for the cascade through which they all hoped to make it through to the Moon Pond and the rest of Tark Draan.

The underwater bit should work. They would be using inflated pigs' bladders and soft leather flasks to help them with the breathing. Special breathing equipment had been devised for the night-mares. *We have completed our preparations.*

Shucto would only tell them about the vital final few miles to the waterfall when he had received assurances that the Zhadar's commanders had been eliminated. Such was the agreement they had reached between them. *And why not? But he'll have quite a surprise coming to him after that.*

They had discussed with Balodil at length the detail of what was going to happen after the commanders' heads were handed over to the barbarians. Shucto had been kept in the dark about this aspect of the arrangements.

He'd hardly be likely to guide us to the waterfall if he knew what was in store. Tirîgon suppressed a grin.

Shucto rode into a low-roofed tunnel. Night-mares and älfar alike had to duck their heads. As the ceiling got increasingly low the riders had to dismount and walk beside their animals.

'We've got to get up that rock chimney,' their guide explained, taking the lead and lighting a small lantern. 'We'll have a good view from there.'

Balodil looked enquiringly at Tirîgon. 'Why don't you just go straight in? The Zhadar gave you the commission and he'll be expecting you, won't he?'

'All in good time.' He gave the groundling a smile. 'It's not always the best tactic to do the obvious thing, precisely because it's expected.'

'And anyway Shucto wanted to watch from up here, to see what we do,' Firûsha added.

'I can't wait,' said the barbarian, climbing up the tapered shaft. In spite of his armour he was agile and made swift progress.

After a strenuous ascent they crawled out onto a rock spur and wriggled into place at the edge.

The cave they were in was a mile or so in height and illuminated by the light of numerous campfires. In addition there were lights attached to huge hot air balloons tethered at the end of long ropes. Mirrors directed the beams of light down onto the camp and on the beleaguered fortress.

It's as light as a sunny day in Dsôn. No shadows anywhere, though. Tirîgon noticed that the balloons were moving slightly in the steady draught. If they had not been tied down the breeze would have driven the floating lights to their observation post. He scrutinised the slopes and found traces of the burned-out remains of others than hadn't been secured. *Distinctive and original Phondrasôn flotsam and jetsam.*

The rebel camp had erected star-shaped fortifications. No lights were showing down there, as if the encampment were stubbornly opposing the overwhelming dominance of overhead lighting. Occasionally an armoured solider or two could be seen crossing the yard. There were a few catapults at the ready, loaded and aimed. But so far there was no indication of imminent troop movements or any sign they were expecting trouble.

These floating lamps are a clever idea. No one will be able to get out of the fortress unobserved. Tirîgon guessed the balloons had been made from animal skins or intestines. He tried to assess troop numbers by counting the tents.

'My one-time master seems mightily angry about the rebellion! He has sent the entire squad from the Draiben Tower,' Balodil announced to the siblings. 'I can see their banner down there. If that's the case, we'd be looking at about eighty thousand, including their entourage.' He whistled through his teeth. 'Few enemies could amass that amount of hatred against themselves.'

'And he still won't force his way in. He's going to need us,' Sisaroth said. He did not have the skull of Shëidogîs with him and had not told anyone where it was concealed. He had hidden it in the consignment of luggage heading for the waterfall. He could not trust Crotàgon or his own sister. 'Those star-shaped fortification walls make it possible to hit an attacking force from two sides.'

'What cowards,' Balodil muttered, spitting disgustedly down at the Zhadar's army. 'I know how to break down ramparts. If I had a few dwarves I could have had those walls tumbling, no problem.'

I expect the Zhadar is of exactly the same opinion. 'Of course they aren't cowards. These are intelligent and experienced commanders,' Tirîgon countered, pointing to a badly burned part of the stronghold. 'It looks like they've had a go over there.' On more careful scrutiny they could see that the tiny black dots in front of the walls were dead bodies. 'How many, do you think?'

'I'd say roughly two thousand,' Balodil answered flatly. 'That would be the first wave, sent to test the defences. They wouldn't

be trained troops, just the normal poor swine – prisoners guilty
of some minor misdemeanour.' His laugh sounded malicious.
'Fine kind of pardon, if you ask me, freeing them to use as bait.'

The siblings agreed.

'My own father and the most important of the rebel leaders
are in the fort. They had gathered there for a secret meeting.
Someone must have betrayed them for this army to show up.'
Shucto's words cut through the jollity. 'The Zhadar will use every
method at his disposal to capture them all. The fact he's marched
up with eighty thousand warriors speaks volumes on that score.'

'I'm surprised he hasn't come along in person with a bit of
magic to toss those walls aside. Something doesn't add up.'
Tirîgon could not understand why the Zhadar was relying on
his troops and risking so many lives. *It must be something to do
with the way that fort has been constructed. What could be making
the Zhadar hold back?* He would have loved to be able to send
out a scout. Esmonäe suddenly imposed herself on his thoughts.
May Tion take her! Am I never going to be free of her?

'Perhaps he just wasn't in the mood,' Sisaroth suggested. 'You
never know where you are with him.'

Tirîgon turned his head and looked sharply at Shucto. 'Can
you give us any clue?'

'It makes no difference,' the barbarian said, avoiding a direct
answer.

'But maybe it does,' Firûsha chipped in.

'No. You don't have to get into the fort at all. You just have to
eliminate the army commanders.' Shucto snorted. 'When are
you setting off?'

He's keeping something back. Secrets. Tirîgon could sense the
barbarian was determined not to enter into a debate on this.

Before the älf was able to feed fear into Shucto's mind, Balodil seized the barbarian by the nape of the neck and shook him violently. 'Tell us what it is. Or the Young Gods'll find their own way to the waterfall and I'll teach you how to fly!'

'It's nothing! Nothing important at all,' Shucto insisted, dangling in the groundling's grasp like a rabbit in a trap. 'I'll tell you. I'll tell you!' Balodil released him. 'There's a magic field inside the fort. It won't go away . . . we think it's jealous. If anything magic approaches it erupts and goes wild.'

'So if the Zhadar were to use a magic spell against the fort . . .' Sisaroth began.

'. . . it would come back at him threefold.' Shucto indicated the army. 'That's why he's using numbers rather than sorcery.'

And that's why he's sent us here to intervene. He wants our help to obviate the need for a long siege. Tirîgon pushed a strand of black hair out of his eyes. 'Makes sense. Good thing we don't have to break into the fort.'

Balodil smacked Shucto on the back of the head. 'You know what, my friend? You and I are in for a whole load of fun together. Just make sure, from now on, you tell me everything you know. I really don't like surprises. Nor do the Young Gods.'

Shucto stammered out an apology, although his attitude showed he thought he had been within his rights.

Firûsha was examining the huge cave from their vantage point. 'There's no shadow anywhere,' she commented. 'Every tiny section of the place is fully lit.' Her steely blue gaze was focused on the balloons. 'Those aerial lamps are a clever idea.'

Things in the camp started to move.

Fanfares were the signal for soldiers to emerge from their

quarters armoured up. Several units started preparations, with hand carts being trundled out. There was no sign of battering rams or catapults.

Tirîgon counted at least a hundred and ten of the wagons with ladders. *They might be able to get up onto the walls with those.*

Shucto was tense. 'The Zhadar has got fed up with waiting! You've got to hurry!' he urged, and would have stormed to his feet had Balodil not restrained him and forced him back down on the rock. 'Get down there and kill their officers! Go now or all is lost!' He unwound a sash from his hips; it was a banner. 'Look. These are my family colours. When you kill their commanding officers, put this banner by the bodies to show the rebels are more powerful than the Zhadar.'

'I know where you'll find their leaders.' The groundling nodded to the siblings.

Let's get started. Tirîgon was excited and apprehensive. The slightest miscalculation would spell disaster, with repercussions for the survival of the whole älfar race.

Shucto waited behind on the spur of rock while the siblings and Balodil went down to retrieve their night-mares. They hid the groundling in a large sack together with the barbarian's banner and stowed it on Firûsha's mount behind her saddle. A small hole enabled him to see out.

This was a concealment Tirîgon had insisted on. There was no need for any of the Triplets to hide from the Zhadar's troops. They were expected. But because it was not clear whether word of Balodil's disappearance would have reached the army, it seemed sensible to hide their companion. *In the beginning.*

They rode up to the sentries, who stood back to admit them.

The night-mares' blood-red eyes and lethal incisors made the soldiers quake with fear.

'Welcome,' one of the soldiers said in greeting, keeping a healthy distance. 'We had thought you would arrive before this. We've been expecting you.'

'We couldn't come sooner,' Sisaroth said arrogantly. 'Your commanders? Where will we find them? The Zhadar told us to ask for Korhnoj.'

'The instructions have changed,' came the response. 'You're to go straight through the camp to the first tent. The Zhadar's envoy is waiting to speak to you. It'll be him rather than Korhnoj, as I understand it, giving you your specific orders. Our captain is busy at the moment giving a briefing.'

Tirîgon cursed inwardly. *The plan was definitely that we get straight to the commanding officers.*

The siblings' gazes met as they hastened past the sentries.

'We need to get to Korhnoj, whatever we've just been told,' Tirîgon said. *We can always say the guards at the gate gave us the wrong information.* 'Balodil, you'll have to tell us which way to go.'

Following Balodil's instructions they made a sharp turn and eventually reached a large tent with dark yellow hangings. It was modest in its markings and the älfar would never have suspected that this was where they would find the officers.

Here, too, the guards backed away from their night-mares, holding up their shields in fear.

'Greetings,' said Tirîgon, swinging down from the saddle. He was well aware of the impression he made in his fine armour. 'We have been sent by the Zhadar.' Going over to Firûsha's mount he took down the sack with the groundling inside and heaved it up onto his shoulder. *They won't be able to refuse us entry.* 'We've his gift to deliver and then we'll be off to deal with the rebel fortress.'

The soldiers were unsure what to do. 'Masters, Mistress. The commanders are discussing the attack, so you ought . . .'

'. . . so we ought to go straight in and raise their spirits for their imminent victory.' Sisaroth strode forward followed by his brother. Firûsha brought up the rear.

One sentry felt it his duty to protest. He had his orders, after all. He laid a hand on Firûsha's arm. 'Stop! You are not to . . .'

Firûsha half-turned, lifted her arm and smashed her elbow into the barbarian's face, shattering his nose and cheekbone. His face was streaming blood and he fell to the floor.

'Don't any of the rest of you try anything,' she warned the other guards. 'Or I'll make use of my sword. The Zhadar has sent us and only he is authorised to hold us back. We are here on his mission. You are nothing,' she said, raising her voice. 'You should be grateful he did not task us with decapitating the lot of you.'

Tirîgon nodded to his sister. *Sometimes I forget our little song-bird has grown up.*

They strode into the roomy tent unannounced. The place smelled of straw, sweat and cheap candlewax. It seemed the commanders placed little importance on cleanliness.

Upwards of forty heads turned in unison towards them; mostly men, perhaps ten women in total. And none of them were pretty.

Crude-featured, the men had wild beards and unkempt hair; their appearance presented an insult to älfar sensibilities. *Reason enough for doing away with them.*

The officers were gathered round a table-mounted model

of the fort. Some were drinking wine, others were partaking of fruit or other food that was piled on large dishes next to the model.

To Tirîgon the meeting had more the air of a social occasion or nostalgic celebration of past glories rather than a military briefing.

A bald-headed barbarian in heavy armour was holding a pointer and appeared to be going through tactics with the other men. It was he who first spoke, having challenged the visitors with his eyes. 'Who have we got here? Would these be the Master's shadow watchdogs, I wonder?'

'And who have *we* got here? A tent full of fools, I think,' Sisaroth retorted scornfully. A rising mutter of protest went through the gathering. 'That's the only interpretation I can put on the fact you have failed to greet us appropriately.'

'I have taught better folk than you how to behave,' Firûsha said, indicating they should kneel. Fresh bloodstains were obvious on her armour. 'Down! In the name of the Zhadar!'

One of the women spat directly at Tirîgon's boots. 'The Zhadar may pay for our obedience but we don't have to take that kind of talk from his henchmen.'

Tirîgon saw that bits of food were stuck to her leather armour. 'Wipe yourself off or I'll grant you a cleaner, quicker death,' he said, putting the sack down that contained the groundling.

'Nobody's killing anyone in my tent,' said the barbarian in shining armour. 'I am Korhnoj. I am the leader here. And as far as I know, you three are supposed to be with Ehiow, not here. Go and tell him I'm calling off the attack. Tell him our threefold salvation has finally arrived.' Korhnoj's tone was sarcastic. 'You'll find his tent . . .'

There was a loud metallic clang.

Korhnoj stopped speaking and looked down, staring at the throwing disc that had cut through his breastplate. 'What...?' He staggered and fell back onto the table, crushing the model of the fort.

Firûsha lowered her arm, but it was still pointing in his direction. She had hit her target. 'If you want the pack to obey take out the one with the loudest voice,' she said sweetly, but with an undertone of steel. She pulled the next disc out of its fixture and hurled it at the woman who had spoken out of turn and spat at her brother's boots.

The sharp edge of the disc sliced through the woman's unprotected throat; the vocal cords were severed, so that no protest sounded.

I wouldn't have wanted to wait here any longer. The smell is intolerable. Tirîgon and Sisaroth had already drawn their superlength swords and were advancing on the officers.

No hesitating. No holding back. Tirîgon selected his victims from those on his right. It was vital not a single one escaped alive. If the alarm were sounded the whole enterprise would founder; they had to be quick and they had to be thorough.

He decapitated two barbarians before they had even had a chance to put down their wine goblets. The drink ran out of their sliced open gullets instead of down into their stomachs.

Tirîgon took a run and jumped over his victims and grabbed hold of a tent pole with his left hand. The momentum let him swing round with his sword arm outstretched. A single blade thus felled a good dozen of the barbarians.

Four others launched themselves at him but his weapon brought death to all four; the blade of his sword cut through chainmail, knives and armour like a knife through warm butter. *All praise to our groundling for his work at the anvil.* On his third revolution of the tent pole Tirîgon landed in a crouch in front of one of the women trying to get out of the tent. Hacking at her ankles to bring her down, he cut off her head before she could scream.

Balodil had freed himself from the confines of the sack and was thrashing around with his sword Bloodthirster in his hands. It was a bravura performance. The men were taken by surprise; they had only been concentrating on fending off the triplet siblings. Even the guards on watch at the door, storming in to see what was happening, had been swiftly dealt with.

So far no alarm had been sounded. The men were being killed at lightning speed and without a sound, apart from the dull thuds when bodies, limbs or heads fell to the floor. The odd chair got broken, but not a single voice had been raised.

Tirîgon saw that his siblings were having the same success as he was. *Oh, but there's another one over there.*

A woman who had been playing dead was crawling round behind Firûsha and making her way to the wall of the tent. She had a deep wound in her chest and was therefore unable to cry out.

Isn't that the bitch with the loud mouth? Tirîgon rushed over.

He saw he had been wrong. They really all looked the same to him. 'Do just wait a second,' he said. 'I want to give you something to take with you.'

She rolled over and tried to injure him with her short-handled axe.

Let's see what happens. Tirîgon put his trust in the armour Balodil had made.

The impact was painful but not dangerous. The sharp edge bounced off the leg protector, leaving only a small dent.

'Do you get it now? You mocked and disrespected us.' He raised his sword, ready to strike, all the while fixing his gaze on her terror-filled eyes. *I don't want to miss seeing how her eyes change as she dies.* 'It's just as my brother said: nothing but a tentful of complete fools.'

The weapon cut through the rusty chainmail, splitting some of the metal rings, and then it sank into the barbarian's belly. She died instantly and her head slumped to one side.

That was too quick. 'Shame. I didn't see her soul depart!' Tirîgon was cross with himself. He looked round. 'Are there any left for me?'

Balodil was standing over the unconscious figure of one of the guards. 'Forget it, friend. This is the only one whose heart is still beating. We have to keep it that way. He didn't see me killing anyone so he's my expert witness for the role I'll be playing when you've all gone.'

'Are you sure they'll believe you?' Tirîgon asked. He looked at his brother and sister in their regal black armour towering over their victims like death-bringing deities. *What a picture this would make. Where's Carmondai when you need him?*

'I took lessons from the best actor of his time. His name is...was...was it Rodario?' Balodil was having trouble remembering. 'It doesn't matter. I'll have no difficulty convincing the army. As we heard: they're being paid for what they're doing.' He cut the leader's head off his shoulders. 'Right. Get moving. You've got to take off all the heads and deliver them to Shucto. He'll be waiting for his proof. Then it's off to the waterfall and away you go back up to the surface.'

'Forty heads.' Firûsha was thinking. 'That's an awful lot. Any idea how we're going to get them all past the guards?'

Tirîgon noticed the sack in which they had concealed the groundling.

'I think I know,' he said cheerfully.

Chapter V

Name three things
that can trounce death.
Art
Song
and Fame
but forget about Love.
Relish it.
Enjoy it.
But be sure of this much:
it will pass and must die
like an opening flower captured in ice.

from the epic poem *Young Gods*
composed by Carmondai, master of word and image

Phondrasôn.

'Nearly done.' Firûsha was spying through the gap she had cut in the canvas tent wall and she was following the flight of the last packet as it swept upwards.

She admired her brother's ingenuity. Tirîgon had simply marched out of the marquee and used Korhnoj's name to commandeer a number of the floating airborne lamps and a supply of the thin skins to use in an experiment. He told the quartermaster the idea was to use them to set fire to the fort if necessary.

The items he ordered were brought promptly and were quickly dispatched again in secret: each thin leather skin wrapped around the severed head of an officer and carried off by balloons.

Firûsha had watched them climb on the breeze and head towards the spit of rock where Shucto was waiting. Tirîgon had worked out in advance that this was where the prevailing air current would drive them. As they caught on the sharp stones of the cliff, the balloons shredded and burned up, dropping their grisly cargo of trophies.

All Shucto has to do is pick them up. The last of the bags reached its destination. 'You can set off now,' Firûsha told them. 'Lead our people to Tark Draan.' She embraced her brothers. 'And don't you dare take the lives of my lute-player and his little turtledove. They are mine.'

Tirîgon laughed. 'We won't. We promise.'

'We'll mark the path you have to take to reach the waterfall, but don't forget to clean up after you. We don't want anyone following you,' said Sisaroth, trying to conceal the anxiety he felt. 'You really want to do this on your own?'

Firûsha nodded. *I have to prove to myself that there's more to me than just a singing voice.* She looked down at Balodil. 'The two of us are going to re-write the history of Phondrasôn.'

He grinned up at her. 'I am ready.' He bade the brothers farewell with a firm handshake. 'We shall meet again. In Tark Draan. Woe betide you if you are not in charge of the whole region by then, my conquering heroes! I'll bring my own army to test you out.'

The two älfar laughed, pretending their friendship was genuine. Firûsha was quite taken with their performance. *I would never be able to hide my feelings of distaste as convincingly as Sisaroth and Tirîgon are doing.*

'What are you going to do before joining us?' Sisaroth wanted to know.

'Are you quite sure you won't come with us now?' Tirîgon made a token attempt to change the groundling's mind.

'No. Nothing can make me go through some stupid waterfall and a wretched pond. I'll make good use of my time here; there's a fair bit of tidying up to do down in these caves and tunnels,' Balodil replied with a knowing smile. 'And somebody down here is wearing a suit of armour that isn't his.'

'That's one way of looking at it. I doubt the Zhadar sees it like that.'

The groundling bared his teeth and touched the scar on his head. He ran his fingers over the eye patch. 'Exactly. It would be boring if he agreed with me.' He turned serious. 'I want to thank you for everything you have done for me. I owe you my life, my memories; I can't repay you.'

The two brothers looked at him with satisfaction.

Firûsha knew what they were thinking. *Didn't we do well?* They were patting themselves on the back. He was their own creation, through and through.

'Don't forget to keep taking the medicine,' Sisaroth reminded him. 'I've left you a good supply and the recipe is in the little box next to the ingredients if you need to make more up. There should be plenty for the next few divisions of unendingness.'

'I won't need it as long as that. I'll find a way out, you'll see,' Balodil countered. 'You can brew me up a fresh supply when I see you next. Perhaps I shan't be needing it by then. Once I've killed the Zhadar,' he vowed soberly, 'I'll make a complete recovery. I'll be healed from all the effects of the wrong he has done me.'

They shook hands once more and the älfar brothers cantered away from the tent on their night-mares.

Now it's up to me. Firûsha fought down the fluttery sensation in her stomach. It was one thing to prevail in combat against a horde of enemies, but the challenge facing her now was of a completely different kind.

Balodil was surveying the headless barbarian corpses strewn round the tent, their blood soaking into the ground. 'No one will notice the guard has gone missing but the stains will seep up into the canvas,' Balodil said, wiping Bloodthirster clean on a dead man's cloak. 'When they see that they'll know something's up.'

Yes. We've got to act before we lose our advantage, our head start. 'That's when you'll have to give your performance.' She tossed the sack over to him. 'You should get back inside if it's going to be believable.' Firûsha cleaned the broad blade of her sword, admiring yet again how light the weapon was in her hand. The extended cross-guards had been a great advantage in combat, especially at close range. At one point, she had thrust the sharp end right through an enemy breastplate. She held it up. 'This weapon, Balodil. Perfect work.'

He grinned at her. 'I've done a lot of perfect work in my time. Your armour, your swords, the weapons for all your troops . . . and that won't be the end of it. I love forging metal. The things

I produce are of higher quality than ever, now that I can incorporate my knowledge of magic and älfar runes.' Balodil ran his fingers carefully along the blade of his eccentric-looking sword. 'If I had only known that älfar and dwarves could be good friends, I would never have attacked your leader long ago. I'm missing Sisaroth and Tirîgon already. I shall miss their conversation.'

My brothers can be proud of their achievement. Firûsha nodded. 'I'm sure they'll make friends with the Thirdlings in Tark Draan,' she said. 'Don't worry. Your folk and my own race will be allies.'

Balodil looked at her. He seemed concerned about something. 'Before we part, Firûsha, tell me. Have I done anything to offend you?'

'What do you mean?'

'You have always kept your distance, whereas I feel very close to your brothers. We have hardly talked and I've always had the feeling you don't like me. So I've been wondering what the reason is.'

Firûsha gave a faint smile. 'You are imagining things, Balodil. I have always valued your friendship, just as the others do. I'm just less demonstrative than they are,' she lied, forcing herself to pat him on the shoulder. She was not about to confess that she did not trust him and that she had been expecting the true Tungdil to emerge any second and try to kill her. If she been honest she would have told him she was delighted he would be staying behind in Phondrasôn. *As soon as I leave, you can do whatever you want.*

'Thank you for that,' the groundling said, greatly relieved at her response. 'I didn't want ...'

The sound of loud footsteps intervened.

'By all the demons of Zrôl ! What's happening? Why have the älfar ridden off?' Before Balodil could wriggle into the sack, the tent flap was flung open and a broad-shouldered warrior stormed in, only to stop in his tracks, finding his way barred by a heap of dead bodies. His boot splashed into a puddle of blood.

He was probably more than two and a half paces tall and was wearing a grey animal skin over his armour. On his head was an impressive horned helmet.

Gripping the hilt of his long scythe-like weapon, he stared into the gloom, catching sight of Balodil. His eyes widened in astonishment. *'You?'*

Firûsha listened carefully but could not hear anyone else approaching the tent. *He was on his own. Excellent.*

'What an unpleasant surprise. This is Ehiow, who has been secure in the knowledge that I was dead. He has been really glad about that.' Balodil laughed as he made the introduction. 'He is another one of the Zhadar's trusted men, but he's never been as high up the pecking order as me. I mean, back when the Zhadar still had need of me. Ehiow was always jealous of my status and tried many times to get rid of me.' The groundling lifted Blood-thirster and pointed it at the intruder. 'Was it *you* the Triplets were supposed to report to? Was it *you* the Master sent?' He gave a spiteful laugh. 'That was thoughtful of him. Now I can kill my rival before moving on to deal with the Zhadar himself!'

Ehiow surveyed the scene of slaughter. 'Was this a rebellion against the Master?' He drew his weapon out of its sheath. There was a damp sheen to the blade. 'He will reward me for stamping it out at the source.'

Firûsha was astonished at the barbarian's brazen courage. *He must know what he's letting himself in for.* She was relieved that he was not alerting the camp. No alarm was being sounded. *He is one of those who overestimate their own capabilities.*

'Ehiow uses poison,' Balodil warned her. 'And he's full of tricks and deception. Don't trust your eyes.' He raised Bloodthirster and attacked the Zhadar's envoy.

The barbarian uttered a curt laugh – and vanished!

'What the . . . ?' Firûsha held her sword horizontally in front of herself as a protective barrier. She caught sight of a flicker from the corner of her eye to the right. *That's him!* She ducked.

She felt the air whip past her and there was a snapping sound as one of the supporting tent poles was sliced through by an unseen hand. The tent was still erect.

Firûsha executed a wide sweep, taking full advantage of her sword's unusual length. The blade met no resistance. *Where has he gone?*

Balodil seemed able, even with his single eye, to see more than she could. It looked as if he were attacking thin air but she heard the crash of Bloodthirster meeting metal. 'To me!' he yelled over to her.

Firûsha hastened over to the groundling's side. He had been thrown backwards by a powerful blow. She felt ungainly as she fumbled with her sword like a novice. 'Coward! Show yourself!' The unseen opponent laughed, provoking her further.

She hit out to the right, but the enemy struck her on the other side, glancing off her armour with a harsh abrasion, sending up a shower of sparks.

She whirled round in a reflex action and crouched down, catching sight of the corner of a bloodied leg guard.

Ah! I see! Where the blood's splashed up his leg! She wasted no time. She jabbed the spiked end of her sword's cross-guard through the metal leg protector. The enemy's leg and her weapon were now fused.

Grabbing her sword with both hands she forced it to one side and heard the barbarian crash to the ground. As she had hoped, Ehiow had tripped over the pile of fresh corpses, and now he was marked with their blood.

Now I can see what I'm aiming at! She swung her sword with both hands up over her head and hurtled it down with all her strength.

The blade struck him in the chest and Ehiow reappeared in view. The blow had knocked a horn off his helmet. But he had a small silver pipe between his teeth . . .

No! Firûsha tried to exert more pressure, to dispatch her opponent before he could give the alarm signal.

But with his last breath he gave a shrill whistle that seared through the canvas and penetrated the far corners of the camp.

When the sound had died away voices were heard on the other side of the tent walls. Some soldiers had already approached at the sound of fighting, even before the alarm was given.

'No time left.' Firûsha picked up Shucto's banner and helped the groundling into the sack he had travelled in before. She fastened it with a knot so there would be no dispute when Balodil claimed to have been taken prisoner. She was relieved to have seen the last of her unwelcome ally. She had even considered killing him – secretly, without telling her brothers, of course. *But I need him alive now as a diversion, so I can get away.*

'Yell as loud as you can!' she urged, before racing out. The men had taken up their positions outside the tent, but she was so quick that they were taken completely by surprise. She wounded and killed several of them with her circling blade, slicing through armour and opening up barbarian flesh.

She heard Balodil shouting from inside the tent at her back. 'The shadow warriors of the Zhadar! They've killed our leaders! Stop them! Stop them! They've cut down Korhnoj and all the commanders! The Zhadar's special warriors have done it!'

Not bad at all! He knows his stuff. Firûsha jumped onto her night-mare and raced through the advancing throng of soldiers, knocking them to the ground. She used her sword mercilessly, to incite as much hatred towards the Zhadar as possible. 'Die! In the name of the Master! Die!' As she yelled she laughed scornfully at the dead and dying at her night-mare's feet.

She murdered her way through the enemy ranks, through the camp and out, leaping over the ditch and the palisades, and off into open country.

She headed for the stronghold where the rebels were holding out, the hooves of her snorting mount throwing up clods of earth from the floor of the vast cave.

'Shucto has sent me!' she called, looking up at the imposing walls of the structure. 'Let me in! I need shelter! I have killed Korhnoj and his commanders for you! They're dead!' She waved the banner that she was supposed to have left behind in the tent near the slaughtered officers. *Inàste! Make sure they recognise it!* 'See! I bear your colours!'

She was being hotly pursued by four dozen furious soldiers on horseback and arrows were whizzing past her ears, but the Zhadar's archers were not up to the challenge of hitting a speeding rider on a night-mare. Not so far.

The night-mare raced on, bearing her towards the large entrance gate.

But it refused to open for her.

Phondrasôn.

Sisaroth, Tirîgon and Shucto rode to the meeting point previously agreed with Crotàgon and Carmondai.

'At last! My father will now be able to free himself and the other rebels. Thank you!' The barbarian was overjoyed at the apparent success of their venture.

He had the severed heads in their leather sacks like trophies, dangling from the saddle of his mount.

Without Shucto noticing, the älfar had left signs all the way along their journey, so that their sister would see the markings on the cave walls and be able to follow them to the waterfall.

'Of course. Shëidogîs was on our side.' Sisaroth had to restrain himself from trying to goad the barbarian's horse into speeding up. The ride was taking far too long because the ugly beast was burdened with the extra forty heads. Sometimes the bags would get twisted up between the horse's legs. 'Do you think we could go a bit faster now?'

Shucto did not seem to mind the brothers' attempts to hurry him along. He had what he had asked for. 'Doing my best,' he said.

The trio eventually made it to the cavern where the other älfar had encamped.

'There's suddenly an awful lot of us Siblings,' Tirîgon remarked, seeing the faces turned towards him. 'I shall have to get used to the Triplets not being anything special.'

'We are still special. Our parents took great pains to create the miracle we represent.' Sisaroth surveyed the surviving älfar. 'It's only magic that's produced all these.' He still thought it likely the imitations would suddenly cease to exist. *That would be disastrous in the middle of a battle.* He watched Crotàgon give the signal to begin departure. *He wasn't even interested in hearing how it all went.* 'It seems our deputy is in a hurry.'

'So am I.' Tirîgon told Shucto to take the lead for the rest of the journey to the cascade. He pointed to Carmondai, who was sitting at one side, closing his notebook, ready to go with them. 'He's still writing his notes and making his sketches, I see.'

'The records he has made will bring us great fame,' Sisaroth said firmly. 'Fame for ourselves and fame for our infamous god.' *Shëidogîs deserves it.*

'So where have you got him hidden to keep him away from Crotàgon and Firûsha?'

'Somewhere safe.'

His brother grinned. 'You're so suspicious that you're not even going to tell me? Remember, I was the one who assisted with your rituals and helped you find your sacrificial victims. And with keeping everything secret.'

'Until you told me I had to stop doing it,' Sisaroth flung back at him. *I shan't be forgetting that.*

'I see. You're angry at me for that.'

Exactly. 'No,' he lied. 'I could see where you were coming from. But it has not been easy for me to keep to what you said.' Sisaroth watched Crotàgon organising the column of riders.

The warriors, the women and the children took up their pre-arranged positions. Carmondai walked round, helping where necessary and sometimes stopping to make further notes.

Sisaroth had plans for their writer. *He will be the one to spread our message. He is so good with words; he'll have them converging on us in swarms to sign up for the new religion. The älfar and Tark Draan are ripe for a new creed.*

'So tell me where the skull is.' Tirîgon was not letting go. He teased his brother, aware of how Sisaroth was torn between revealing it and keeping it secret. The two of them rode past the column and the baggage wagons to get to the front where Shucto was.

I'm . . . I'm not going to tell him. Sisaroth could hear the warning voice of the god inside his own head. *Keep it secret. There is no Tossàlor to restore the skull if it gets damaged this time.* He instinctively looked at the supply wagon and regretted it immediately.

But he had been observed.

'You hid it in there? In a barrel full of blood, I expect?' Tirîgon laughed.

'Stop looking at the wagon!' Sisaroth hissed angrily. *He's winding me up.*

'It's quite a high load on there. I expect the skull will be right in the middle,' teased his brother.

'Will you hold your treacherous tongue?' snapped Sisaroth at a greater volume than he would have liked. He looked to see whether Crotàgon could have overheard. He was nowhere to be seen.

'So I'm right?' Tirîgon patted him on the back consolingly.

But Sisaroth brushed him off angrily. 'Go and do something useful. Ride with Shucto. And don't forget to leave the marks for Firûsha.' He turned and pretended he was heading over to the group of riders to check if things were in order. In reality he was trying to work out where the tall warrior was. *I can't relax until I've located him.*

He found him at the far, rear end of the column. He was assisting one of the älfar, a pregnant female. She was having trouble packing her bag.

Good. He was quite a long way away from where we were talking. Shëidogîs is safe. Sisaroth was relieved. He turned his night-mare's head and rode over to them. 'Everything all right?'

'It will be,' Crotàgon answered coldly. 'If you and your brother are back now, does that mean your part of the venture has worked?'

'Yes. Firûsha has taken over.' *Do you think I can't see what you're doing, pretending to be so helpful?* Sisaroth dismounted and offered the woman his assistance, which she gratefully accepted. *I can win hearts and minds, too, by being nice.*

The woman spoke the words 'Young God' as she thanked him. Crotàgon reacted with a snort of suppressed laughter. The woman mounted her night-mare and rode to catch up with the others.

'Well done,' he said to Crotàgon, turning back to his dark stallion. *I'm not spending longer than absolutely necessary at your side, Crotàgon.*

'What do you mean?'

'Well done for minding the camp while we were away. No one's missing and we can set off for Tark Draan with our full complement. I hope we don't have any losses on the way through the cataract.' Sisaroth placed his foot in the stirrup.

'I hope the losses we have are the right ones,' the warrior said to Sisaroth's back. 'Perhaps I should help them along a bit.'

So the friendly mask is being tossed aside. Sisaroth took his foot out of the stirrup and turned round. He was expecting an assault. 'And just what, in your estimation, would constitute *right losses?*'

'Anything dead? Anything possessed?' He held his arms away from his sides. 'They call you all the Young Gods. If you're wise, you'll make proper use of the way they respect and worship you, instead of palming them off with some trumped-up demon that'll only weaken our people.'

'I assume you had a good look for the skull while we were away.'

Crotàgon nodded. 'I did. Without success, unfortunately, or else I'd have got rid of it.' Crotàgon walked past, barging into Sisaroth as if by accident and knocking him slightly off balance to stumble against his night-mare. 'I shall be biding my time, cîanoi. I'll be watching you. I'm sure you'll want to grab hold of the artefact before you go through the waterfall. Then we shall see what we shall see. Not all demons are happy in the water.' He swung himself up into his saddle and rode off.

So he's not going to do me that favour. Sisaroth mounted his own steed and followed, furious. *I should love to kill him.* He was itching to use the sword stowed on his back. Trying to maintain as cool a head as his brother usually did, Sisaroth placated himself by imagining exactly how the giant warrior would meet his end.

No. I shan't kill you now. I think you'll make a good sacrificial victim for Shëidogîs. You could be the first one we offer to the god when we get to Tark Draan.

Phondrasôn.

'Can't you see I'm waving your colours!' The gate stayed firmly shut even though Firûsha was less than forty paces away from it. She would be crashing straight into the iron-reinforced wood at her night-mare's stupendous speed if the rebels did not react. *What are they waiting for?*

Arrows rained down around her; her pursuers' aim was improving.

At long last a small opening appeared in the gate.

A semi-circular shield formation stepped out of the fort, spears poking out of the gaps.

They don't want to let me in! They want to stop me out here! Firûsha guessed the obstacle they presented was five paces long and two in height. Behind it was the opening she needed.

'Out of the way!' she shouted, holding the banner up to flutter in the breeze. 'I've been sent by Shucto. I've got an important message from him!'

The shield unit did not budge. They were preparing to spike her.

She had very little time left.

Up! She pressed hard against her night-mare's flanks and hoped against hope she would survive the leap. If she flew out of the saddle now she would be skewered.

Snorting loudly, the stallion rose through the air over the wall of shields, its hooves clanging against the men's helmets. It landed safely behind their line.

She was nearly hurled out of her seat with the impact of the landing, but she was holding so tightly to the black mane that she stayed upright in the saddle. *Once we're in Tark Draan I'm going to have to take some riding lessons.*

They shot through the open gate and galloped through a troop of warriors on their way out to swell the defenders' numbers.

The night-mare snapped viciously at the nearest soldiers, tearing hunks of flesh from the unprotected shoulders and necks of three men, who fell shrieking to the ground. It all happened too quickly for her to prevent.

That's going to make it difficult to persuade them I'm here in peace. She reined the animal in when they arrived at one of the larger buildings. Holding the banner aloft, Firûsha felt a tingling permeate her body. She was in a state of high excitement.

'I am a messenger! I have something to report! Something wonderful has happened. Take me to your leaders!' She sprang out of the saddle and went up to the door.

The soldiers she had ridden down caught up with her and barred her way with their drawn weapons. 'Who are you?' the tallest of them asked furiously. He was covered in red splashes. He must have been standing next to one of the victims of the night-mare's feeding frenzy. 'What kind of a demon horse is that?'

'That was a mistake. The creature is terribly hungry.' Firûsha folded the banner over her arm like a towel. 'Why didn't you open the gate and let me in? You could see my flag with the Shucto family colours. I'm here at his bidding and speak for all the rebel peoples.' She glared at him. 'My name is Firûsha and I am one of the Young Gods. Had you been told nothing about the treaty we signed?' *This is the tone to take with these barbarians. They are confused.*

Their captain was unsure what to do. His men surrounded Firûsha; behind them came the screams of pain from the soldiers lying wounded by her night-mare. Healers were hurrying over to the injured. 'Yes . . . Yes, they told us . . . but we thought . . . Forgive . . . We were to be your escort and protect you from your pursuers.'

Firûsha laughed. 'Well, that went well, didn't it? If my night-mare had not been clever enough to jump over your men's heads I would have been stuck through like a wild boar caught by hunters.'

'Let her pass!' It was a woman's voice from overhead. 'We want to know what has been happening and whether she has been successful.'

Looking up, all Firûsha could see was an armoured arm pulling the window shut.

The captain issued his orders and the forest of spears disappeared, leaving a path for Firûsha. 'But you need to offer compensation for what your demon horse has done,' he told Firûsha as she drew near.

'I see that differently. Your men provided only inferior quality fodder. It is you who owe me.' *Barbarian scum.* She left him and his unit open-mouthed with indignation.

She was expected. A page greeted her with a bow and led her through several passageways and up some stairs to an opulently decorated hall.

Around thirty men and women, mostly in armour, were talking at a long table. There seemed to be differences of opinion. It was clear the rebels were composed of several factions and that they did not all agree on strategy.

Well, well. The brave ringleaders of the revolution. Firûsha recognised the symbols some of them wore on their tunics. Two different caves were represented that had previously paid dues to the Young Gods. The rebellion was not only directed against the Zhadar. *The spark of revolt. Once it has been lit, it will ignite everything around it. The fire will only be quenched with blood-letting.*

'. . . have to be sure we don't get something worse in his place,' one of them was warning the company. It was a corpulent barbarian woman in a dark purple dress overlaid by black armour. She wore silver bracers to protect her forearms and her long grey hair was held in a circlet of steel round her brow. Ugly but impressive, Firûsha had to admit. 'We may think the Zhadar rules the underworld but this realm is so extensive that we can never know what may be lying in wait. There might be some as yet unknown beast waiting for the Zhadar to fall before it makes its move on us.'

'That's a risk I'm willing to take!' shouted one of the others. He was wearing a cloak far too large for him. When he bent forward to speak, he looked thin enough to break in two. 'The main thing is to put an end to the Zhadar's incredible cruelties. What do we need to fear, once we've got rid of him?'

'We must consolidate and establish a joint empire,' said the woman who had called out of the window earlier. Firûsha recognised her voice and her arm protectors. She was dressed from head to foot in metal armour; two axes and two daggers hung from the weapons belt at her hips. 'And a combined army. Only if we are united do we stand a chance. The caves that refused to join the insurgency will be brought in but they will be made to pay.' Her blue-green eyes focused on the älf-woman. 'You are the Young Goddess we sent Shucto to appeal to.'

All heads in the hall turned towards Firûsha.

She threw the folded banner onto the table so that it covered their goblets and jugs. The tingling she had experienced on entering the fortress had intensified. 'My name is Firûsha. My brothers and I have complied with the Shucto tribe's request. Shucto is at this very moment underway with the severed heads of the commanders of the besieging army. He will be showing them first to your allies outside Sojól. Korhnoj is dead, and we beheaded forty of the Zhadar's main commanders. The army at your gates has no leadership. A good opportunity to attack them.'

The armoured barbarian grinned. She said, 'If we had an army here in the fortress that is just what we would do. But with only two hundred warriors, our bodyguards' – she indicated the assembled men and women – 'we might just as well fall on our own swords. But Shucto will turn up with some troops. Our pleas have been heard.'

'How soon will he come?' Firûsha's heart was beating faster now. *Shucto didn't mention troops.*

'As soon as he's escorted your people to the waterfall. It's all planned. We had established a hidden army before we were caught in Sojól.' She pointed at an empty chair. 'Take a seat and tell us exactly what happened. We want to relish the victory in every detail.'

The company murmured assent. The banner was shifted and goblets and cups were recharged.

I ought to be quick. 'I've got a better idea.' Firûsha climbed onto the chair, with one foot on the table; then she raised her voice in song. Her improvised ballad told of all the events of the battle in the marquee. As she sang, the prickling on her skin became almost painful.

Even though Firûsha found it distasteful in the extreme to have to sing in the barbarians' crude language, the effect of her song was mesmerising. Her audience was entranced.

Her voice took her listeners directly into the heat of battle; she summoned up the atmosphere and the action, firing their imaginations.

I have them all in the palm of my hand. Just as I planned. She stepped onto the table without interrupting her song. She drew her sword as she sang and acted out the strokes she had made in the tent, underlining the action in her ballad, all the time moving her booted feet carefully amongst the crockery.

Firûsha danced her dangerous dance, captivating the minds of the audience – until the second when she brought the sword blade down and decapitated two of the men. Fountains of blood shot up and splashed down on their companions. The severed heads bumped along the floor and the headless bodies jerked and collapsed.

Nobody moved!

The audience were securely rooted in the ballad's magic and they confused what was happening here with the events of the narration. They were not surprised to hear the sound of the sword or to see and smell blood and feel it splash upon them.

Yes, hear my song! Hear my song and die! Firûsha sang herself into a trance. Her long sword swished through the air, cutting life-thread after life-thread. Piercing chests and hearts and severing heads in rhythm with her song, she reduced by two the number of her listeners with every alternate line of melody.

She sat herself down on the table in front of the final survivor, the armoured barbarian woman who was hanging on to every word from the singer's lips in fascination. Firûsha let the sword rest on the woman's right shoulder before sounding the final note of her song and falling silent. *What do you say now?*

The woman blinked. Focusing more and more intently on the älfar singer, she at last registered the sight of the blood running down her armour. She woke from her daze in horror and took in the scene of slaughter. She became aware of the sword at her throat. 'What have you . . . ?'

Firûsha placed a finger on her lips. The exaltation she felt even suppressed the tingling. *Doesn't she look horrified?* 'Shh, shh, quiet now. What is your name?'

'Kiumê.'

'You were asking what I've done? I'll tell you. You won't scream. You'll listen, Kiumê,' she whispered. 'My brothers and I have worked out that there is a certain logical justice to be had by killing the commanders on both sides. The Zhadar's officers and the rebel leaders alike. We älfar worship Samusin, the god of justice and fairness. The mercenaries outside are running around like headless chickens. Your army will be turning up here soon and will have no one to give them their orders. Rebels without a leader.' *I am really enjoying seeing how distressed she is.* Firûsha furrowed her brow in feigned sympathy. 'Oh, you poor things! What will happen to your little revolution? Do you think the Zhadar will take as long as you will to replace his officers? Or won't he just send more of his forces out to crush you? He has four towers, after all.' Firûsha smiled. 'Yes, me too. I think the Zhadar will be quicker than you to recover from this blow. Your houses will all burn. Your families, too.'

'But you encouraged us . . .' stammered Kiumê. 'You said . . .'

Firûsha kicked the woman on the breastplate, shoving her against the chair back. 'Did I tell you to speak?' she hissed. 'We do whatever we want to do. We trick, we deceive, we make you believe whatever we want you to believe. Anything to achieve our goal. That's what we've done with the Zhadar and that's what we've done with you.' She inched the blade nearer the woman's jugular. 'But we would not be the Young Gods if we didn't leave a gift for you. As a token of our fairness. A gift that brings freedom. The perfect weapon against the Zhadar.'

'What do you mean?'

'The gift is called Balodil. His true name is Tungdil, the greatest hero ever to emerge in Tark Draan. He hates the Zhadar and he will be taking command of the combined armies. He will perform the miracle of uniting the mercenaries besieging you here with your approaching forces when they arrive. We have thought everything through. The armies will both obey him and join to march on the Zhadar's own stronghold.'

Kiumê's eyes jerked away from Firûsha and surveyed the slaughter.

'I know what you're thinking. You are wondering why they had to die? The answer is: to increase the hatred you all feel against the Zhadar, so no one will hesitate to join the new commander, although he can offer nothing but promises.'

'We can't hate the Zhadar more than we do already,' Kiumê protested.

'Oh yes, you can. And yes, you will. I shall be strolling out of this hall to make a speech announcing that the Zhadar will not rest until the last child has been dragged from its rebellious mother's breast. The guards will hear my words and they will not be able to forget. And that is exactly what will happen.' She smiled. 'We have been very thorough.' *It will happen just as we have planned.* The unpleasant tingling set in again; it was giving her a strange headache.

'And what is *your* reward?' Kiumê was trying to understand.

'We are modest in our demands. While the Zhadar is occupied, we shall vanish and be off to conquer Tark Draan.' Firûsha leaned forward. 'Between ourselves, I don't think the groundling will manage to overthrow his one-time master. But his attempts to do so will serve us well. The Zhadar will be kept busy and his hatred will be directed at Balodil rather than ourselves. That's enough.' She jerked her thumb to indicate the scene behind her. 'So, do you think this bloodbath will be sufficient to anger your people enough?' she asked, pressing her sword into

Kiumê's neck. 'Or should we crown events with a display of your own cold corpse?'

'Please, I . . .' Kiumê desperately tried to find a reason for Firûsha to spare her. 'I can help with your plan. I'll join Balodil and win our people over to him. Things will be easier for him if he has my support. Then we can storm the oppressor's towers together. Please, I swear.'

'You want to stay alive, don't you?' Firûsha jumped up onto the table and pointed to the door. *Let's see what a barbarian is capable of.* 'Let's make a wager. If you reach the entrance before I do and can touch the wood first, I'll let you live. If I win, you die.' She kicked one of the corpses and it fell off its chair. 'This one wasn't given that chance. Make use of the opportunity.'

'I accept. Let me drink to my victory.' Kiumê took her cup and put it to her lips, then chucked the contents at the älf-warrior woman before sprinting off.

Firûsha wiped the wine from her eyes. *Good try, barbarian.* Taking one of her throwing discs she fired it at Kiumê.

The weapon hissed through the air and caught the woman behind the right knee where there was a slim gap in the armour.

Kiumê screamed and hobbled along, hampered by the injury and the weight of her armour. She picked up a fallen shield and held it behind her as protection should Firûsha throw more discs.

Aha, she knows how to help herself. Firûsha picked up a jug of oil from the table and threw it. It broke open on the floor very close to the barbarian's feet. The oily contents quickly spread on the tiles, making them slippery.

Kiumê's feet started to slide and she struggled to keep her balance. She fell with a crash and dragged herself along on the floor. Her right arm was broken.

But the door was almost within reach.

She is strong-willed even though she must know she doesn't stand a chance. We should learn from this for our battles against the peoples of Tark Draan. Firûsha ran along the table, jumping off to land in front of Kiumê. *I wonder how long she can hold out?* 'I admire your courage, but I'm sure you can remember the wording of our agreement. You have to touch the wood before I do.'

'I know,' Kiumê replied, clenching her jaw. She stretched out her left arm, but Firûsha's sword slammed down and severed her hand. Blood spurted out of the stump. She screamed and stared at her mutilated arm.

'You have to touch the door with your hands. Go on. Try,' Firûsha taunted her. She crouched down next to the barbarian. *My brothers must take care not to underestimate these barbarians. They can be as stubborn as the groundlings, it seems.* 'Oh, what a shame. One arm is broken and the other hand is lying on the floor somewhere. Your death bears the name of Firûsha, in that case.' She smiled and raised her right arm to touch the door with her fingertips.

Chapter VI

If I have one
I'll want two
If I possess two
I'll want three
And if I own three,
I'll want four.
Where will it end?
Be content
with one
If you lose it
take another
It matters not
from whence.

'Aphorisms' from the epic poem *Young Gods*
composed by Carmondai, master of word and image

Phondrasôn.

Sisaroth stood looking at the cataract of water that surged
upwards from below, contradicting every known law of nature.
Incredible.

The wide stream of water roared and splashed wildly, sending clouds of spray into the air before the top of the waterfall disappeared through a hole high above their heads. The hole led to the passage that ended in the Moon Pond.

But what is normal anyway, down here in Phondrasôn? Sisaroth was at the head of the column together with Tirîgon. It would have attracted too much attention if he had checked out the provisions wagon to keep an eye on the box that held the skull. Now his brother knew about the hiding-place, he was afraid to betray himself further by looking directly at its location. *Crotàgon has always got his eyes on me.*

Shucto reined in his horse on the bank of the lake. 'We're here. This is the place. If you go into the water and let yourselves be drawn up in the cascade you will end up on the surface. The cycle is nearly through. Then the current will change direction and the waterfall will come down rather than going up. It will be another two thousand heartbeats until the next change after that. Make your preparations.' He pulled his ugly mount away from the water and was about to ride off, his grisly sacks dangling from his saddlebow. The trophy heads thudded together as he swung round.

'One moment.' Sisaroth noticed some large cracks in the roof of the cave. Rocks and large stones occasionally fell from where the waterfall surged in. He grabbed the barbarian's reins. 'What's the significance of that?'

Shucto seemed to be in a terrible hurry to get away. He scowled. 'I don't know.'

'Looks to me as if the roof might cave in,' Tirîgon said. He had noticed the cracks, too. 'The constant changes, and perhaps the magic, are damaging the rock formation here.'

'Balodil could lecture us on that,' laughed Sisaroth. 'We could do with him for once, but where is he when you need him?' *In the best place he could possibly be.*

A large lump of rock broke away from the roof and crashed into the water, causing a wave to surge out and cover the nightmares' hooves.

'It's not going to hold for long,' Tirîgon guessed. 'Look! It's already changing direction!'

In the blink of an eye the waterfall had altered its current and was behaving as one would expect a waterfall to do. The thundering at the base made it impossible for the column of refugees to hear themselves if they did not shout. Water vapour and spray soaked their clothing and settled on their weapons and baggage.

'We ought to get through on the next cycle,' Tirîgon shouted, not taking his eyes off the damaged roof. 'I think we're in trouble otherwise. The cascade isn't operating properly. I don't think we can rely on having more than one attempt at crossing through. Unless you can do something with one of your spells, cîanoi, to repair the roof?'

Sisaroth had already been considering his options. 'Too dangerous. The water itself seems to be imbued with magic and it's impossible to predict the effect of a clash.'

Shucto tugged at the reins. 'Good luck. May the gods be at your side. I must leave.'

'Why are you in such a hurry?' Sisaroth kept hold of the reins. *You knew perfectly well the cave was unstable.* 'Why not stay and keep us company? We would appreciate it. The Zhadar commanders are gone. Your people are safe now.' *But that's immaterial, isn't it?*

'I've got to get back. We're expecting an army to arrive to march on the mercenaries. And I want to take these trophies home to show everyone.' Shucto looked round. 'Where's Firûsha? I'd like to say goodbye and wish her well.'

'She is making sure our night-mare tracks are removed,' Tirîgon replied. 'The iron shoes leave burn marks on the rock. She'll be setting fire to the tunnel to eradicate our tracks.'

Shucto's eyes grew large. 'But how am I supposed to get back, then?'

'Not at all, really. You've served your purpose now.' Sisaroth let go of the bridle. Tirîgon drew his sword out of its fastenings and stabbed Shucto through the chest. The blade made a half-turn. 'Your death bears the name of Tirîgon,' he intoned, looking the dying man straight in the eyes. 'And I shall be the last thing you ever see.'

Shucto slid from the saddle with a groan. The movement pulled the sword free of his body. He landed on the ground with a thud.

'Follow your master, hideous fish-horse.' Tirîgon severed the creature's neck and it collapsed, burying the barbarian under its mass.

Come on, Sister-heart. Where are you? Sisaroth looked back at the entrance to the cave. 'It's time Firûsha caught up. I have the feeling our Shucto took us the long way round. I expect he was hoping the roof would fall in with us under it.'

'Firûsha will be all right. She had an excellent fighting tutor, even if you can't stand him.' Tirîgon studied the copper-coloured blood on his sword. 'Look how shiny it is! That must have happened when the life-juices of the two species mixed together. I'll take a sample with me. I can use it on my carvings.'

'Good idea. I'll tell the others to get ready.' *Two thousand heartbeats will soon pass.* Sisaroth was pleased his brother would be temporarily occupied by his aesthetic pursuit; this way Sisaroth could do all the organising and check on the skull's box away from prying eyes.

Sisaroth rode along the column, issuing instructions.

Leather bags and pig bladders were inflated and provisions securely stowed in such a way that they would float to the surface when the current pulled them through to the Moon Pond. Nothing was left to chance.

He approached Crotàgon towards the end of the column. He was too close to the provisions wagon holding the skull for Sisaroth's taste. *Does he know? Did he hear Tirîgon and me talking about it? His ears can't be that good.*

Carmondai was perched on top of the box, an open notebook in his hands. 'What a moving sight,' he called down from his vantage point. 'This is such a significant moment in our race's history. As good as exterminated, we were, but now we shall rise again out of our place of banishment, to regain power. An actual re-birth.'

'With the help of the Infamous One, we shall succeed,' Sisaroth replied. He could have bitten his tongue. *Why did I say that?* The last thing he wanted was to provoke Crotàgon now. He vowed silently to him: *Once we are in Tark Draan, it will be over. You will be the sacrifice I offer to Shëidogîs and he will bathe in your blood and your life force.*

'Indeed. And we shall be accompanied by the Young Gods,' Carmondai added happily. 'It's a title that I've established will go down in history.'

Sisaroth raised a hand to acknowledge his words and then

turned to Crotàgon. *I have to get him to move away. Otherwise I can't take the relic out.* 'Please ride to the front and check on our progress. As soon as the cascade switches direction, the first ones need to go straight in, even if I'm not there. Your presence will calm them if they're feeling nervous about the venture.'

'Shouldn't you and your brother go in first?' he protested. 'The honour of leading the entry to Tark Draan must be yours!' Crotàgon placed his broad hands on one of the heavy boxes of food. 'I'm needed back here. We have to accelerate the unloading. Muscle power will help.'

He knows what I have in mind. 'You have your orders,' Sisaroth said coldly, keen as a sharpened blade.

'I don't take orders from you,' the warrior replied calmly. 'I joined you of my own free will. The others may look on you as a Young God, but in my eyes you are nothing but a cowardly murderer, hiding behind lies and deception.' Crotàgon's true emotions were hidden. He exercised strong self-control. 'I am going to work on the unloading and if you try to stop me because of something concealed in one of the boxes, you will have to kill me first to get at it. Do you dare to do that, Sisaroth?' Crotàgon drew himself up to his full height. 'It might be problematic to kill one of your own kind with everyone watching; it's quite different to driving a red-hot knife into the body of a chained victim in a darkened chamber where no one else can see.'

Sisaroth looked up towards Carmondai, who was busy scribbling his notes. 'For pity's sake, don't write this down!' he shouted.

'I, on the contrary, would request that you record everything, the whole truth,' Crotàgon interjected. 'Our descendants should learn what the cîanoi and his private demon have based their power on: the sacrifice of his own people's lives.' He turned back to the work he was doing and unloaded the first of the many boxes.

'Mind you don't go too far!' Sisaroth urged his night-mare forward, to push against the warrior, but then thought better of it. *It would be stupid to make the scribe suspicious. When Crotàgon dies I've got to show as much surprise as everyone else. And I shall be seen to be mourning him.*

'You have already gone too far,' was Crotàgon's response.

There was a cracking noise as two boulders came loose from the roof to crash into the lake, sending up fountains of spray and surging waves.

'The waterfall!' the call went from mouth to mouth. 'It's changing direction! Everyone into the water now! At once! Forget about the luggage. Leave everything behind!'

That was not a full two thousand heartbeats. Sisaroth cursed out loud and glared at the heavily overloaded wagon. *The relic is right at the bottom.*

'So what do you do now, cîanoi?' Crotàgon grinned knowingly.

Phondrasôn.

Let the final stage follow, completing my mission. Firûsha took a deep breath and opened the door. *Inàste, be at my side!*

She left the hall laughing out loud; this drew the attention of the two guards.

One she stabbed, the other she kicked, throwing him against the wall so that he let go of his halberd; he flourished his second weapon, a short sword.

Ramming her blade through his right shoulder, she pinned him to the wall. With her extra-long sword, the man was unable to reach her with his own weapon. 'You barbarians are such simple creatures,' she mocked. 'Do you think the Zhadar doesn't know what you are up to? I'm to present my master's compliments. Before the army takes over your ridiculous fortress I killed all your commanders. I shall let you live so that you can report it all. Take this as a warning!'

The soldier groaned and battered away at the long sword with his puny blade to demonstrate that he was not giving up. 'We shan't surrender to anyone! You traitor! What you have done will only make our hatred grow stronger!'

Excellent. I shall make my message clearer still. Firûsha made use of the powers she was born with, and produced fear to envelop her victim. 'I shall report to the Zhadar and then go to your own home cave to kill all the children. I won't stop until I have speared every newborn baby on my sword!'

The first black waves of fear rushed out of her eyes towards the man – but then a flash of intense light pierced her head, causing unthinkable pain. She screamed. It was as if she had been struck by lightning.

What was that? She drew back, yanking her sword out of her enemy. She took shelter in the darkest corner.

She had forgotten the peculiarities of the fortress. *It will react to any enchantment that is deployed. That funny feeling I had, the tingling, it wasn't just excitement. It was magic!*

Her heart was beating fit to burst and she could hardly breathe. Firûsha was trembling like the foliage of an aspen tree and she felt sick. Had she not been wearing gauntlets her sword would surely have slipped from her grasp, her hands were sweating so. *I have been given a taste of my own medicine. This terror is three times the strength of what I expelled.*

The injured sentry swapped hands on his sword and retreated, calling for reinforcements. 'To me! Murder! Murder! The messenger is a traitor!'

She heard boots approaching and armour clanging.

His reaction was exactly what she had wanted but she was in no fit state to take on a large number of opponents.

Every rustle, every movement she heard terrified her. She cowered in the corner where she thought she might be safe. *Where are you, my brothers? I need you!*

Soon she was surrounded by armoured barbarians in tunics of various colours. A sea of spear points swirled around her.

The injured guard told the others the threats she had made and how she had betrayed them. Some of the soldiers hurried into the hall and returned horror-struck and quivering with anger. There was a lot of shouting; curses flew through the air in condemnation of the Zhadar; there was a heated discussion about what the fate of the captured traitor should be.

I have to eradicate this fright or I'll never be able to defend myself in combat. I'll be easier to kill than a wounded gnome. Firûsha calmed herself and attempted to shrug off the paralysis that had taken over her body. She was lucky the soldiers were so conflicted about what should be done; their arguing had won her some time.

She counted twenty-two barbarians, male and female, surrounding her, and thirteen weapons. *I ought to be able to cope.* She breathed in and out a few times. *I can cope!*

'. . . take her to Sojól Keerin. She can stand trial and give evidence that she was sent by the Zhadar,' said a sensible-looking barbarian.

'Rubbish! She's already confessed,' shouted the injured sentry. 'My word will be sufficient. I say let's kill her now, before she . . .'

Firûsha could see in people's eyes that the decision had been made. *Against me. A wise decision, but it comes too late. I am stronger now.*

One of them lunged forward to jab the sharp tip of a halberd through her throat, but she leaped up and pushed herself away from the wall, executing a forward roll in mid-air over the heads of her captors.

Below her came the sound of metal crashing as their weapons collided, leaving her untouched.

As she flipped through the air she struck out with her sword, slicing three guards on the backs of their necks, where they wore no armour. She landed in a crouch and attacked the knees of five more with a hefty swipe.

You ought to have killed me immediately. She whirled round, rising to her full height as she did so, taking her sword in both hands and cutting into the approaching soldiers.

Her blade laid low several more and then got stuck in the armour of one of the dying.

Firûsha remained collected, although two solidly built enemies were swiftly bounding towards her. Keeping one hand on the hilt of her sword, she retrieved a throwing disc from its fastenings with the other and tossed it at her foe.

The circular blade sliced into the leg of one, halting his progress.

She pushed her foot against the dead man and pulled her sword out of his body.

His comrade in arms reached the älf-woman and belaboured her with blows that she warded off, ducking down under the broad blade of her sword and using it to protect herself – until she saw the chance to thrust the sharpened end of the cross-guard into her adversary's hip.

The barbarian gasped audibly.

The two of you are too slow for me. Or maybe it's that I'm too fast for you. With her free hand Firûsha drew her double-edged dagger and stabbed it home through the gap between helmet and body armour. The enemy fell with a gurgle.

She whirled around to hack at the last opponent, striking through his armour into the collar bone. *Not too deep. I don't want him to die. I must not kill all of them or there'll be no one to carry the tale. No one to spur the barbarians on against their overlord.*

She pulled her blade out of his neck and ran up the steps. *I'll be able to see from up there how to get back to where my night-mare is.*

Running up the spiral staircase, she found herself on a narrow walkway where she had a good view over the star-shaped fortress and the besieging army.

The Zhadar's troops had got into formation. There was a small figure in the middle of the army. It could be the groundling, she thought. *It looks like he is holding his pre-written speech.* She grinned. *The little mountain maggot will be winning over hearts and minds by talking to their money-belts.*

Ten warriors came storming across the courtyard and disappeared into the building. She was spotted by one of the opposite watchtowers and a warning went up.

'Long live the Zhadar!' Firûsha vaulted over the stone surround with a laugh and landed several paces below on a sloping roof. She surfed across the shingles to the edge, where she took her sword to the tiles and hacked herself a hole to slip through.

She vanished through the newly created opening to find herself in an attic room, with a trapdoor to the building below.

Not a lot of ways to escape. Pulling up the hatch, she met a soldier coming up the wooden ladder and kicked him in the teeth, sending him flying. *It's a good job these humans are so slow.*

She clambered down. She did not know where she was, but she broke the nearest window and jumped out.

Firûsha landed on the stable roof and ran along until she reached the edge. From here she could see her night-mare, fighting the barbarians wildly as they did their best to kill it. A large wound gaped open on its flank and there was a stream of blood coming from its neck.

You will pay for that with your lives. She leaped off the roof without making a sound. She killed three of the warriors before they even knew she was there, and the night-mare's kick took care of the fourth.

Firûsha tossed one of the bodies over her shoulder and climbed up into the saddle, storming for the gate which was now closed and barred. 'Open up!' she yelled. 'Open up or I'll kill him!' She held her sword at the neck of her pretend hostage. She knew how to manipulate humans. Their weak points were obvious. *Soft-hearted and simple-minded. Inàste, make it so this time, too!*

And it happened as she had hoped. The gate was opened for her and she galloped out.

'Long live the Zhadar!' Firûsha threw down the corpse and directed her night-mare towards the cave entrance. *I need to get back to my brothers.*

A shudder went down her spine when she thought of the terror-wave that had struck her back in the fortress. If the barbarians had made use of their opportunity and attacked her when she was in that state, there'd be no more talk of triplets, only twins. *The creating spirit was protecting me.*

She had carried out her task. The rest was up to Balodil.

It looked as if his speech had gone down a storm. Soldiers were cheering and enthusiastic shouts accompanied her ride. *Lead them against your ex-master, and die in battle, Balodil! That way you'll be no more bother to us.*

It was easy to find her way following the markers that her brothers had left.

But it was a long ride. The night-mare had been badly injured and was losing pace. Finally, it gave a neigh of defeat and collapsed.

Firûsha rolled nimbly off. The creature had lost too much blood and the exertion had finished it off. 'Curses!'

Firûsha was in a extensive passage and had no idea how long it would take her to get to the waterfall. She did not think she had ever been in these sections of the caves before. *Did Shucto show them a different route from the one he took me? Then again, I was blindfolded.*

There was nothing for it but to set off on foot. She started to run, watching out for her brothers' signs.

She saw her way by the glowing mosses, which gave off a dull brown or greenish light. Humans would have been forced to light themselves torches in such darkness but she had enough night vision.

As she kept up a steady jog she breathed evenly.

What worried her was the fact that although she had shaken off the last effects of the terror, she was still experiencing that same tingling. She wiggled her fingers to dispel the sensation, but it would not go away. *Am I suffused in a mysterious charge of some kind, or is this some damage I sustained from that last magical event?*

She ran and ran and ran without feeling she was making any progress. She would have been three times as quick if she still had her night-mare.

She imagined her brothers emerging from the surface of the Moon Pond in Tark Draan and invading the elf settlement.

She frowned crossly. *They'd better not have touched my lute-player.*

She heard a dull roar followed by the sound of rushing water.

The floor, the walls and the entire passageway rocked and heaved, requiring her to deploy all her agility and skill to keep her balance.

It's the whole cavern! It's collapsing! Firûsha waited for the space of two heartbeats until the quaking had subsided, then she took off at a sprint.

Fear had returned with a vengeance, but this time it had a totally different cause.

Phondrasôn.

Sisaroth watched as the älfar under his command hurriedly inflated their leather breathing bags and rushed into the churning waters to reach the bottom of the cascade whose mighty force was sucking up everything in the vicinity and conveying it through the aperture at the top. Anyone colliding with the edge might be hurled against the rocks and badly injured, but there was no alternative.

'Well, cîanoi?' Sisaroth heard Crotàgon's harsh tones. 'What are you waiting for? Are you going to get the skull out? Or are you contemplating going to Tark Draan without it?'

A further lump of stone crashed down from the cave roof to fall on a group of älfar who were swimming towards the cataract. Their heads looked like corks bobbing on the waves.

The cavern is collapsing. Sisaroth turned to the warrior.

Carmondai sprang down from the wagon and picked up a small box in which he carefully placed his manuscript. He lit a bar of wax and sealed the edges with flying fingers to make it watertight. 'May Samusin be with us,' he said. 'May we all reach Tark Draan safely.' He stepped into the turbulent waters. 'Quickly, Sisaroth. Your people will be needing their Young Gods when they come up on the other side.' He plunged in.

Tirîgon rode up looking worried. 'Brother, come on!'

'I'll catch you up,' he called. 'Someone has to watch out for the stragglers. You go ahead. You're the better strategist. People will be needing your direction on the other side.'

'And I'll be needing a strong hand and a sharp sword.' Tirîgon turned his red-eyed night-mare's head to face Crotàgon and tried to propel him towards the waters. 'Crotàgon, come and help me protect our people.'

The grey-bearded warrior looked at him. 'I shall. But don't be angry with me for this.' He grabbed Tirîgon and threw him into the middle of the lake where the current took hold of him. Tirîgon barely had time to inflate his pig bladder before being forced upwards in the torrent.

Let's fight it out. Sisaroth drew his sword. 'I was planning to use you as a sacrifice when we reached Tark Draan, but you are making me dedicate your life to Shëidogîs right here in Phondrasôn.'

'We shall see about that. I wonder what your demon will say?' Taking hold of the side of the wagon, Crotàgon tipped it over.

A veritable flood of boxes, crates and bags tumbled onto Sisaroth. He rolled aside to avoid being buried.

One of the sacks burst open. The flour it contained spread like a white fog and made Sisaroth cough. *I can't see him!*

When his vision cleared he saw Crotàgon wildly smashing any container he came across using planks of wood.

Where is the little box? Sisaroth looked for it frantically but could not find it. He confronted the warrior, the greatest threat to the relic. 'You shall follow your sweetheart!' *And I won't let you take me by surprise ever again.*

'Tossàlor didn't deserve to die like that!' Crotàgon said accusingly, chucking the planks of wood at his head before grabbing his sword. Balodil had manufactured a cross between a cudgel and a spear for the heavily built warrior. It was almost two paces in length and bore a long thin blade above a metal sphere the size of an älfar head. 'If it weren't for your accursed demon, he'd still be alive.'

'No, he wouldn't. The Infamous One gave me the power to protect the gates and transform the solid lake back to its original molten state. Without the god, we would have been overrun and he would've died in conflict.' He circled the warrior, who mirrored his movements, all the time searching in the widely strewn luggage. *I have to distract him somehow.* 'Do you know how much pleasure I got from killing your dearest Tossàlor?'

Crotàgon's face turned black with a network of frenzied anger lines. He lashed out, uttering an unintelligible shout.

Sisaroth did not make the mistake of attempting to parry the blow from the deadly weapon. The force of it would have driven his own sword from his hand. Instead he ducked out of the way, only just avoiding the follow-up with the blunt end of the spear. *Oh, yes, I shall continue to torture your soul.* 'He was lying in front of me, whimpering, pleading to be spared.' Sisaroth backed slowly away, trying to entice his adversary away from the upturned wagon. 'But I slit him open and let Shëidogîs bathe in his blood.' He laughed, pulling his head in to avoid a blow.

'You shall forfeit your life, cîanoi. I swear it.' Crotàgon made a series of quick thrusts, not pausing for breath. In his powerful hands the weapon seemed weightless.

Sisaroth held his sword in both hands to deflect the attacking blows. He did not risk a step to the side, not wanting to leave any gap in his defences. The hefty opponent was unexpectedly agile.

But he was keen to inflict further damage on Crotàgon's soul and drive him to utter despair. *I shall keep needling him until he is overcome with emotion. Only then will he weaken.* 'Do you know Tossàlor kept a secret from you? He never wanted you,' he panted with exertion. 'He *despised* you.'

'No!' shouted Crotàgon.

'He valued your protection; he enjoyed having you serve him. That's what he told me. He said you were a useful fool, blinded by love so that you could not see how he was exploiting you.' Sisaroth had enticed the warrior a good ten paces from the wagon. *Wonderful! He is so easy to lead if I call his love into question.* He risked a quick look at what was happening around them.

Night-mares and älfar were swimming determinedly; a number of bold ones were on the bank throwing provisions, weapons and other equipment into the water. The cave roof was showing several dangerous cracks, and parts of the rock ceiling were sagging ominously. The cave was nearing its end.

And that will mean the end of the waterfall! Sisaroth became impatient. *Enough playing around. I've got to get out of here.*

Crotàgon had noticed. 'Fine by me. Let's die together if we have to. But that skull won't make it through.' He grinned. 'Did you think I wouldn't see how you're trying to get me away from the wagon? Wrong! It's me that's moving you away from the cascade.' The next arrow-swift thrust came too fast.

The spear blade struck Sisaroth in the stomach, but slid with a metallic clang to rest in his groin. The iron-ringed leather absorbed most of the impact but the tip caused intense pain.

Before Crotàgon could twist the blade or push it further in, Sisaroth jumped backwards, gritting his teeth against the pain.

'Well, cîanoi? Why don't you use your powers to blow me to smithereens?' The warrior looked at the blood on the tip of his spear. 'Oh, have I exposed your secret? You need the skull before you can do anything special. The old witch was better than you. If you don't have your demon and its skull to hand you are nothing but empty words. What a shame that it seems to be buried under all that lot.' He twirled the spear over his head and aimed at Sisaroth's middle with the heavy end.

I underestimated him! Sisaroth limped to one side but could not escape the blow.

The spherical weight hit him on the right side and sent him flying two paces off, further still from the chests and crates that lay fallen in a jumble.

He landed in soft sand and somersaulted. The wound in his groin seemed to tear and get bigger and he felt warm blood running down his leg under the armour. *I took on too much. It was arrogant. I mustn't hesitate again . . .*

He got to his feet – and was greeted by a fist to his lower

jaw that had him sagging. His knees hit the sand and a black veil in front of his eyes told him he was about to lose consciousness.

Crotàgon stayed back, his cudgel aimed at Sisaroth. 'It would be so easy to kill you. There's no one here to stop me. Our people are on their way to Tark Draan. Without you and without me. That makes for a good new beginning, I would say. Let them worship your brother as the Young God. I don't care. But there's one thing I am going to make sure of.' Another punch knocked Sisaroth sideways. 'Wait here. I'm going to bring you your precious skull. In tiny little pieces. And when you're putting them back together you can think about Tossàlor.' Crotàgon raced over the sand to the wagon.

Shëidogîs! No, he mustn't . . . Sisaroth dragged himself along on the soft ground, getting grains of sand between his teeth and on his armour where the blood had stuck to it.

His progress was slow but determined as he made his way back to the spilled crates. Crotàgon was moving between them, breaking open boxes with his spear and rummaging through the contents.

I am a servant of the Infamous God. I shall give my life to save him. Älfar will come to Phondrasôn in the future and they will find him and honour him. Sisaroth loosened a throwing disc from its fastening, sat up and hurled it with all his strength. 'You shan't touch him!'

Crotàgon shot upright, raising his spear, and used the guard to fend off the missile. The blade edge stuck in the wooden shaft. 'Almost,' he said with a grin, holding out his other hand. 'Go on,' he taunted. 'Throw something else. I'll catch it with this.'

I have failed. Sisaroth gave a cry of frustration. Crotàgon's large hand held the relic. 'Put the god down! This is blasphemy!'

'What I see here is a demon you have fallen prey to.' Crotàgon inclined his head slightly. 'How sure are you that this is Shëidogîs?'

'Absolutely positive.'

'So you would die for it?'

'Without question!' Sisaroth crawled forwards and was just three paces away.

'Then I suggest you kill yourself,' snarled Crotàgon. 'I swear by Samusin that I shall not destroy the skull after you reach end-ingness. It will be your life in exchange for Tossàlor's. If you do not agree, I will destroy it now.'

Sisaroth clamped a hand over the wound in his groin. He looked up at the cataract, where more and more of the roof was caving in. 'I do not believe you.'

'I swear by Samusin, the god of justice and of the winds.' Crotàgon slowly closed his hand and there was an audible crunch, but the glue held and the skull was still intact. The first of the beads came loose and a silver ball fell onto the sand.

The dark red glow in the eye sockets was pleading and demanding at one and the same time. The soul of the infamous god, enticed at great cost to re-enter the artefact, was in peril once more. This time it would be final.

I cannot allow the god to be destroyed. 'Wait!' cried Sisaroth, drawing his double dagger. *I have to do this. Shëidogîs is worth more than my life.* His emotions were running riot. So near their goal, and forced to do away with himself to save the Infamous One, the god to whom he had planned to sacrifice Crotàgon. In Tark Draan. 'Here! Do you see?'

'I know that dagger well. It would be good if you sank it into your flesh.' Crotàgon increased the pressure on the skull in his hands. A crack started to open up where the skull had been mended.

'No! Stop!' Tears of anger and self-pity obscured his vision. *I shall never see Firûsha or Tirîgon again. I hope they will think of me and put up a statue to my memory.* 'Look! I will slit my own throat!' Sisaroth placed the double blade against his throat and chin. *God of infamy, protect my soul. Let there be some miracle . . .* He observed the tense expression on Crotàgon's face.

The crunching sound grew louder and another pearl rolled out of its mounting.

He will break his word! He hates Shëidogîs!

A thunderclap sounded and the roof fell in. The falling boulders crashed into the lake causing a tidal wave that swamped the two älfar.

Chapter VII

Co-operation
  is important
Even more so
  is the strength of each individual
Make sure you are not a bundle of flimsy twigs
  but a bundle of mighty trunks!

'Aphorisms' from the epic poem *Young Gods*
composed by Carmondai, master of word and image

Phondrasôn.

I can't get left behind! I would be the only female älf in Phondrasôn, and surrounded by enemies. Firûsha hurried through the tunnel. After what she had done in the Sojól cave there would be no warm reception for her anywhere. *I could not even apply to re-enter the Zhadar's service.*

A riderless night-mare came snorting up to her. The stallion already had the breathing equipment with the leather bag fastened to its bridle but the älfar rider seemed to have gone astray before affixing the animal's mouthpiece properly.

A gift from the gods! She took hold of the reins and mounted, turning the animal back in the direction it had come. She once more followed the signs her brothers had left for her.

The thundering quake did not recur, but now there was water rushing down the tunnel, steaming and hissing when the lightning flashes from the creature's hooves met the wet element.

What has happened? Firûsha was afraid the cave must have partially collapsed.

The night-mare carried her onward. The stream at its feet swelled until the water reached the creature's knees.

But suddenly the current seemed to alter. The water was sucked back, the level getting lower and lower.

What is happening? Did Shucto trick us? At last she reached the entrance to the cave and rode through.

What Firûsha saw made her distraught.

The small aperture in the ceiling had opened up to a large hole and the water was being sucked out of a lake that was practically empty. The shimmering column of water was now no more than a hundred paces wide. The last of the chests and boxes dragged upwards by the current were heading out through the opening on an uncertain journey.

Firûsha saw shattered wooden crates, sacks that had burst open and any number of twisted älfar corpses drifting on the water. *They must have been thrown violently against the stone rim by the force of the surge, only to fall.* Her eyes searched the cave ceiling, where cracks and fissures were testimony to its imminent total collapse. *I have to get away from here!*

Firûsha turned her mount's head towards the base of the upturned waterfall.

There was little water left. Only a small amount remained in the middle of the basin. Even the mud was being sucked up through the aperture.

'Sister!' She heard a familiar voice shout through the noise of the cascade.

'Sisaroth?' Firûsha stopped and sat up tall in the saddle, craning her neck to see. 'Where are you?'

'Under the overturned cart,' came the answer, the voice low and pain-filled.

Locating the semi-destroyed vehicle high on the bank, she cried, 'Wait! I'm coming!' *Fate delayed me. What luck!* She raced up the incline, passing discarded items and debris, and jumped out of the saddle to look for her brother. *There he is!*

He was lying under the axle covered in mud. He looked more like a monster than an älf. Blood trickled from his mouth and the right side of his face was badly swollen as if he had been struck.

'Let us thank the gods for sending me to save you,' she said cheerily, touching his hand before attempting to lift the heavy axle. 'How did this happen?'

'Huge blocks of stone fell, sending a massive flood wave that swept everything away,' he explained. It was obvious he was in pain. 'Can you see Crotàgon anywhere?'

'Is he still here?' Firûsha applied all her strength to the axle. *The wagon is heavy.* 'I could use his help for this.'

'Not me. He tried to kill me.'

'What?'

'About the skull. I hid the relic before he could smash it.' He placed his hand protectively round a mud-splashed object which she had thought was a stone.

My good Crotàgon. Determined to the last. He was right. The skull should not survive. Firûsha stopped for a second while she tried to think but then she noted the cascade stream was growing weaker. She redoubled her efforts. *The pull of the current is decreasing. Soon there'll be no water left at all.* 'Come on!'

Sisaroth dragged himself out from under the vehicle. 'Thank you. Thank you, my sister! And thanks be to Shëidogîs!' He gave the muddy artefact a kiss and then wiped it to free the eye sockets of the slime and filth from the flood. The inlays glowed faintly in return. 'The god has closed the wound I suffered to my groin. I was stabbed – '

'Tell me later. We have to get away now or it will be too late.' She helped her brother onto the night-mare and urged the stallion into the water.

Firûsha was dismayed at the thought of leaving her mentor behind. She thought it more than probable that he had tried to kill her brother. And while she condemned him for it, she could understand his motives: he had been robbed of the one he loved and he was convinced the skull had played a decisive part in his loss. *Who knows what Sisaroth might have said to him.* 'Did you challenge him to a fight?'

'What?' he shouted against the roar of the cascade.

'Crotàgon. Did you challenge him? You said he tried to kill you?'

Her brother said nothing and gestured to imply that he could not hear what she was saying.

I bet you provoked him. Firûsha's mouth narrowed to a bitter line. She had long forgiven Crotàgon for his initial coercion when they first met. After all, he had taught her all she knew of swordsmanship. It wasn't her brothers that had made sure she could handle herself in combat. *Such a shame. A terrible shame. I have lost my friend. And all on account of the evil demon skull.*

She considered continuing the mission that Crotàgon had pursued.

But it mustn't look deliberate or my two brothers will hate me and we will sacrifice our unity. They were invulnerable if they stayed united. They could only provide the älfar folk with a new home, a new realm, by working together. *Let Samusin decide whether the skull should travel to Tark Draan or not. If I see an opportunity I shall take it.*

The mud at their feet started to spurt up and a broadly built creature emerged to fling itself on them.

Firûsha and Sisaroth were dragged from the night-mare's back. The animal neighed and snorted and moved aside.

'I promised you the demon would remain here in Phon-drasôn,' said the mud-encrusted figure, grabbing Sisaroth, punching him twice and flinging him three paces away. Sisaroth landed in shallow water and choked and spluttered in the mire. He was too dazed to get to his feet but he pressed the relic tight against his chest.

He's sure to use a magic spell! That would truly bring the cave down! 'Crotàgon!' Firûsha was on her feet, sword drawn. She took up a stance in front of her brother to protect him, and she pointed the blade towards her one-time fencing master. It occurred to her in that instant she did not know which of the two älfar she was trying to protect. 'Don't touch him! Don't either of you do anything!'

'I won't hurt him. I shan't hurt your brother unless he insists on dying for the sake of the skull,' replied the warrior, brandishing his spear-cudgel. 'The same goes for you, Firûsha!'

Is this our chance to get rid of the skull? Firûsha glanced over at the waterfall and back again. 'We don't have time for this. If we don't leave now, we're exiled forever.'

'Then get out of my way!'

Firûsha saw how steadfast and full of integrity Crotàgon was. *I will have to choose.* 'You will have to kill me too if you want to kill my brother.' *I only hope he can understand what I'm trying to tell him. Or Sisaroth and I will both die.*

'Your decision, Young Goddess.' Crotàgon made a startling attack with the heavy cudgel.

Two things came together now and chance had no part in it. Firûsha parried the blow more slowly than she could have and her mentor put less force behind the blow than he could have.

She was struck lightly on the helmet and dropped to the ground, giving Crotàgon an imploring look, warning him to remember his vow. *Don't kill him!*

He gave her an almost imperceptible nod and rushed past.

She turned over to see what would happen. Her sword was ready to throw if she needed to intervene for Sisaroth's sake.

Crotàgon had reached her brother. Sisaroth had rolled himself into a ball, with the skull pressed to his middle. He felt for his knife.

The warrior pulled him up by the nape of the neck and shook him violently. 'Give me the demon and you can become a god in your own right in Tark Draan!' Crotàgon dropped his spear and tried to grab the skull.

Sisaroth kicked out, striking Crotàgon on the chest and in the groin, but the warrior hardly seemed to notice. 'Die like your lover died!' Sisaroth yelled, wielding his dagger blindly. The double blade sliced the warrior's upper arm but his grip remained strong. 'Except I'll let you die in your armour!' Sisaroth closed his eyes.

'So you will accept death for your demon!'

No, he won't. Firûsha leaped up, preparing to throw her sword, when Sisaroth muttered a spell.

The relic's eye sockets glowed red and a deep blue flash settled round Crotàgon, who sank to the ground with a moan, releasing his hold on Sisaroth.

There was a hiss and the smell of burning flesh. Every piece of armour the warrior bore turned red-hot and scorched away the skin underneath, fusing metal with flesh, causing intense agony.

Sisaroth staggered to his feet. 'There you have it. You have seen what the god of infamy will do for his servant,' he said triumphantly. 'You shall roast in your metal armour as long as I please.'

Firûsha suppressed an oath. She was dismayed for Crotàgon. *He deserved a different end.*

Unexpectedly and with a tremendous effort, the burning warrior reached into the mud and grasped hold of his own discarded weapon.

Only the armour he wore prevented Sisaroth from being slit open by the spear-blade, but the hefty cudgel homed in on the skull Sisaroth was clutching under his arm.

The relic flew through the air and landed in the mud at Crotàgon's feet.

Yes! Do it! Firûsha ran toward them, but did not know what she intended to do. *Please, for the sake of Tossàlor. Don't leave it up to me.*

'No! You won't harm Shëidogîs!' Sisaroth hurled his dagger, striking the warrior full in the face.

Crotàgon fell forward, burying the skull under his broad torso and the glowing armour. There was a sharp noise and a dull hissing sound as the muddy puddle below him boiled and turned to steam. The fiery heat was abruptly halted and the armour restored to its normal metallic hue.

The skull has been destroyed! Firûsha was enormously relieved and felt such gratitude towards her one-time tutor. Crotàgon had gone to his Tossàlor in the endingness, having avenged his loved one's death. *That will be the end of the demon.*

She could not allow herself to brook a second's further delay.

Firûsha hurried to her brother and dragged him along after her. 'Come on! We must get to the cascade before it fails entirely. Let's hope it still has the power to send us up to Tark Draan.'

Sisaroth offered little resistance. He stared at the bone fragments round Crotàgon's body in dismay as they were gradually sucked into the watercourse. He knew perfectly well there was no chance of repeating the masterly work Tossàlor had produced. 'Shëidogîs,' he murmured, distraught. 'Shëidogîs! Don't abandon me! Pardon me. Forgive me for not preventing...'

'You are not alone, brother. You have me and you have Tirîgon,' Firûsha told him as she manhandled him onto the night-mare. She inflated two pig bladders and gave one to her brother, then she fixed the apparatus round the horse's muzzle. *Samusin, my thanks! You have allowed three gods to be born rather than letting their unity be destroyed by hatred.*

Firûsha rode the stallion into the dwindling flow just as the cave roof collapsed. She heard a deafening crunch and crash as it fell and the passageway through to the Moon Pond disappeared forever.

The siblings were drawn up into the wild, mud-filled torrent.

We are a good eighty paces above the ground! If we fall from this height, we're done! Firûsha clutched her night-mare's mane as the animal struggled in the flood of murky water and debris. She held tight to her brother and concentrated on not losing the breathing mouthpiece. *If I can't breathe I'll arrive in Tark Draan as a dead body.*

It turned dark around her.

She was travelling deep inside the stone chimney, hoping desperately the journey would end well.

Tark Draan.

'Where are they?' muttered Tirîgon impatiently, his bent spear held at the ready. He had been using it as a type of boathook. He was worried about Sisaroth and Crotàgon. *And how is Firûsha ever going to find her way to us?*

He blocked his growing despair and went back to watching the troubled surface of the muddied water.

It was dark brown in colour and there were broken crates and the remains of supply containers and weapons chests floating everywhere. Drowned älfar and night-mare cadavers bobbed, face-down in the water, limbs at unnatural angles.

He thought once he recognised his Esmonäe's features on a dead body but it had been his imagination. It served to show him that the älf-woman still had a hold on him.

Fifty bodies and thirty lost night-mares. There was a small cave in the sandstone cliff behind him. The walls and ceiling were running with moisture which splashed down on the sheltering älfar. This was where the remains of their force had gathered to wait.

According to his calculations, they were in an intermediate cave under the actual Moon Pond. Scouts he had sent out came back with reports about a further opening in a second basin they would all have to dive through to get to Tark Draan and their foes, the elves.

I feel for Balodil, being terrified of water. He's got a point. Tirîgon watched the rescue squad, who had previously been occupied with dragging survivors to the safety of the bank.

But recently there had been no more survivors arriving.

He saw cracks in the ground where fine sand was drizzling away and vanishing. 'We won't be able to wait much longer,' he told the others. He felt deeply troubled. He did not know how he could rescue his sister. If necessary, he would have to go back to Phondrasôn on his own to fetch her. *It's my fault she went to Phondrasôn in the first place. I have to make sure I can get her out again. And if . . .*

He noticed a strong disturbance in the water.

'Over there!' he called. 'I think . . .'

The first thing they saw were two red glowing dots and then a night-mare's head broke the surface. Snorting wildly, the stallion charged up the steep bank, pulling two älfar behind him: Firûsha was hanging down sideways, her fingers caught tight in the mane. Sisaroth was attached to one of the stirrups. His sister still had her breathing equipment but Sisaroth's had gone missing.

The rescuers hurried up from all sides to give aid, calming the night-mare and pulling off its breathing mask, freeing Sisaroth's foot from the stirrup and wrapping the disorientated young älf-woman in blankets.

Tirîgon would not have been able to describe his relief when he saw his siblings. Laughing, he embraced his sister and then quickly moved to where his brother lay.

He waited in vain for a sign of life. No choking or coughing.

'He's not breathing!' he shouted in horror, turning his brother onto his side to let the water run out. 'Quick! I need two of you over here!'

With combined force they unstrapped his armour and pressed on his abdomen and chest until the cîanoi vomited a gush of brownish fluid and gasped for air.

I have not lost him! Tirîgon patted his brother's cheek. 'Can you hear me? You'll soon be in Tark Draan. Together with me and our sister.'

Sisaroth tried to sit up, grabbing his brother by the shoulders. His grasp was so desperate that it was painful. 'Did you collect the skull fragments?' he mumbled before being sick again.

Tirîgon knew what he must mean and looked over at the slurried mixture of brackish water, corpses and debris. *We won't find anything in that mess.*

'It has been annihilated,' said Firûsha, her lips quivering.

Sisaroth looked straight ahead emptily, his face falling in like that of a corpse. 'It is my fault,' he whispered. 'I ... my knife ... he fell on top of the Infamous One. I have lost all my powers! My magic arts, gone!' He shut his eyes and sobbed like a young child. 'I have extinguished Shëidogîs. The other gods of infamy will surely punish me ...'

Firûsha knelt at his side, stroking his black hair and humming softly.

Tirîgon weighed up the situation objectively. *Should I be pleased?* Crotàgon could have become difficult, stirring up trouble, and Shëidogîs, and the attendant blood sacrifices, would certainly have been a problem. *On the whole, yes, I think*

'Follow us!' Firûsha drew her sword and stretched it to the roof. Sisaroth copied them. 'Follow us!'

The cave filled with the rumble of numerous weapons being unsheathed.

I shall rule! Tirîgon was overcome with emotion: his flesh had goose-pimples and his eyes filled with tears. A sense of his own supremacy flooded his being.

Tark Draan.

Firûsha found the swim pleasant this time; she had had sufficient practice underwater. Here there was no relentless pull of current causing the mass of air bubbles that had masked their vision in the other body of water, and she was in control of her trajectory. *I can see where I am.*

As on her previous visit, she found large-leaved water-lilies bobbing on the Moon Pond. The setting sun sent blood-red beams down through the surface to the army that was marching underwater toward the elves. The night-mares' saddlebags were filled with stones to stop the animals shooting straight up to the top, thus alerting their foe.

Unseen, unnoticed, they slipped straight into the heart of enemy territory.

Firûsha had taken command at the head of the column because she knew the lie of the land. The air in her breathing equipment would last for eight hundred heartbeats. She took her time and enjoyed each step of the way. *We are returning to Tark Draan and we shall be avenging the Inextinguishables.*

Two figures were moving about in the water above their heads. It seemed they were teasing each other.

An elf and his girl at play. Is that my lute-player?

The male elf dived down and headed in their direction without noticing the älfar and then he swam around under the lilies to hide from his girlfriend, who was climbing out of the water.

The sun now dipped below the horizon, giving way to star shine. Silver light penetrated the water and welcomed the approaching älfar force.

The elf swam underwater over to the bank and left the Moon Pond.

A night-time arrival. Firûsha gave the signal to move forward. Her army was only minutes behind her. *It could not be better.*

She saw the elf-girl splashing into the water as if she had been pushed. She concealed herself under the leaves. Perhaps this time it was she who wanted to frighten her lover.

I can help her there. Firûsha had a wicked idea. *We are masters of fear.* She slid from the saddle, and taking a final deep draught of air from the air bag, put her knife in to deflate it. She drew her sword and strode up towards the bank.

Firûsha saw the elf waiting expectantly. *My lute-player!* She cut her way through the lily stems. *You belong to me!*

The elf came nearer to the edge and stared into the dark waters, looking for his mistress.

You will be getting a surprise. Firûsha shot up out of the Moon Pond to face him. *Beautiful and deadly!*

Firûsha was obscured by a high splash of water when she surfaced and the elf didn't immediately realise she wasn't his girl. He smiled at her happily and placed his hands on her shoulders. But when he felt her armour and the water fell away, he looked at her in horror, realising that this was not who he had thought he would be embracing.

Firûsha thrust the broad blade of her sword into his abdomen up to the hilt. *This is what I shall do with all the elves I find.* Pushing him backwards, she wrenched her weapon out of his guts, widening the cut. A rush of blood and liquid from the intestines shot out of his belly.

The musician collapsed and sank into the shallows.

His sweetheart will soon come looking for him. Firûsha climbed out of the Moon Pond, and raising her left hand to sweep the long black hair out of her eyes, she took in her surroundings. *No one to be seen. Excellent. I'll lie in wait here. If the girl doesn't turn up of her own accord, my brothers will drive her towards me when they arrive.* Silently, she slipped into the wood.

At that very moment the elf-girl leaped out of the pond.

The noises she made were intended to sound like the cries of a monster, but she burst out laughing. 'I can't do it,' she spluttered in a dialect Firûsha roughly understood. The young elf stopped to rub the water out of her eyes. 'Did I scare you to death, my darling?' she giggled, catching sight of the body at the edge of the pond.

She bent over him, still laughing, and turned him onto his back. When she saw the wound, guts spilling from his body, she dropped to her knees with a cry. 'Sitalia, save him!' she cried, distraught. 'Fanaríl, open your eyes! Wake up! You've got to wake up!'

Firûsha was about to step out of her hiding place when she saw her two brothers emerging silently out of the deep. *I'll wait. If she runs away I'll go after her.*

The elf-girl was alerted by the sound of dripping water and looked back over her shoulder to find Tirîgon's night-mare standing over her, snorting.

What will you do now? Firûsha waited. *Go on! Run away and show us where the village is. That will save us the trouble of looking for it. Then I will enjoy your death.* The elf was drawing her dagger with quivering fingers.

Night-mare after night-mare rode out of the pond, hooves flashing, lighting up the water; älfar forces surrounded the elf-girl, who had frozen, staring at the brothers, unable to take her eyes off their dark armour and the night-mares' red glare. Firûsha was sure the elf-girl knew who it was that had come to kill her.

Tirîgon drew his long sword and placed its tip against the centre of her back. Drops of water ran down the blade and onto her skin. She began to tremble.

'Tell us who you are, elf-woman,' he commanded.

'Alysante,' she breathed. She was unable to get over the paralysis that had struck her. Seeing her people's deadliest enemies appear out of the depths of the Moon Pond like avenging demons was too much of a shock.

'Is your settlement far from here?'

Alysante did not reply – and Tirîgon applied pressure with his sword, so that the tip pierced the gossamer-thin clothing and her skin, driving a little way into her flesh.

From where she was hiding, Firûsha watched the dress staining red. *Don't go too far! Her life belongs to me!*

'Answer me!' he snapped, urging his night-mare forwards.

The elf-girl came to her senses and realised this was not some bad dream. She turned away, jumped up and ran past Firûsha into the heart of the wood.

At last. Firûsha took up the silent pursuit.

She could hear Alysante sobbing and the rustling of twigs

and branches as she ran through the trees. Sometimes she paused to wipe her bloodied hands on her shift, or to stare at the blood that had come from her lover's body.

Firûsha watched carefully. *Oh, I can imagine what you are feeling. You are trying to understand how we got round the groundlings' defences.*

She remembered the prophecy Balodil had mentioned as the reason the Zhadar had insisted on pressing the Siblings into his service. *The Three will achieve what no one else can. Not even the Zhadar.* Firûsha was ecstatic. *The oracle spoke true!*

Alysante was beginning to struggle for breath and her pace slowed. She stopped and climbed a tree, continuing her journey at tree-top height, flitting from branch to branch.

She's trying to avoid leaving any prints. Firûsha followed her up. *As if that would prevent me tracking her!*

The chase was on.

Firûsha spotted light shimmering through the upper branches. *That's it! You have led me well, little lute-player's mistress.*

Alysante climbed down and headed for the edge of the village. There was the illusion of safety and a warm glow from lanterns on the carved façades between the ancient trees.

So, here we are. This will be the site of our first victory. Firûsha swung down from the branches, landed on soft earth and charged at the elf-girl, seizing her and hurling her to the ground. *In the dirt where you belong! You and the entire brood!*

Before Alysante could recover, Firûsha put her boot on her arch-enemy's neck and mercilessly pressed her face into the forest floor, then knelt down next to her. 'Tirîgon asked you whether the village was far from the pond,' she whispered in her ear. 'I shall be bringing him your answer, elf-woman.' She took her double dagger slowly out of its sheath, enjoying the threatening metallic noise, creating as much fear as possible. 'Now I am going to send you to your sweetheart. Rest assured that all your relatives will follow you this very night.' She used her special powers to put terror into the elf's soul.

Alysante attempted to cry out to alert the settlement.

I am enjoying seeing you flounder. Firûsha stabbed the girl in the back, all the way through to the racing heart, sending her to endingness. *It begins. Now to retrieve my brothers; the blood harvest draws near.*

She got to her feet and ran straight back to the Moon Pond.

By the time she reached the bank, the älf-warriors were in formation on the grass; the young and the weak who would not be taking part in the fighting were to remain in the shelter of the trees and follow later.

'Do we have everyone?' Firûsha asked, out of breath, as she wiped the sweat from her brow.

'Yes. All of us got through safely to Tark Draan.' Tirîgon took a deep breath and addressed his soldiers. 'Taste that air! So pure! And look at the stars! Drink your fill of these sensations and rejoice that you will never have to lose them again,' he encouraged. 'Did your little elf mistress lead you to her home?'

'She did, indeed. And she has received her reward.' Firûsha mounted her night-mare. Sisaroth seemed frustrated. He still hadn't come to terms with the loss of his special priestly status and the destruction of the unholy artefact. *That is all right by me. He deserves to suffer after what he did to Crotàgon.*

Carmondai was sitting on a log writing and sketching like one possessed. He looked up in delight. 'What joy to be able to see the stars once more! If I remember aright we must be in the elflands of Lesinteïl. It's just as I thought: the elves would not have found shelter anywhere else.'

Firûsha gave a wicked smile. 'Samusin knew it was time for the two races to meet in conflict. Why else would he have allowed us to find this passage out of Phondrasôn?' *And Inàste held her hand over me. More than once.*

Sisaroth opened his mouth and was about to object, but then he thought better of it, his sister noted with some satisfaction. It would be unwise to speak the name of the gods of infamy and bring up unfortunate memories. They had achieved the most perilous part of their escape without the slightest intervention from Shëidogîs.

'I say again: we do not need a god.' Tirîgon raised his sword so that all might see, then used it to point the way over to the wood. This was the signal to move off. 'Let us prove this to ourselves. And to our enemies – the elves.'

'We shall prove it to the whole of Tark Draan.' Firûsha took the lead and led her small army towards the elf settlement.

Epilogue

The light
    that shines on your path
    may betray you to your foes.
Use it wisely!
    If your foes can see you,
    use the light
    to set fire to them.

'Aphorisms' from the epic poem *Young Gods*
composed by Carmondai, master of word and image

Tark Draan.

'Left! To your left! There is another one . . .' Tirîgon uttered a curse and flung the throwing disc with all his might.

The missile spun through the night and cut into the elf's side as he fled. Blood spurted out, staining the large green leaves; the elf disappeared into the murk.

'Firûsha, give the last instructions. I don't want to lose this one.' He ran off in the direction his victim had taken. *My sword needs to drink elf-blood this night! I swore this to my parents.*

'Will do, brother!' she called back. She gave the command to set fire to the houses.

Tirîgon's ambition was aflame. He had not yet killed a single elf during the battle. The village their army had forged its way into had been so small. Once the command was given, there were soon seventy elf corpses, from the youngest to the oldest, slaughtered in their beds or killed in combat. Sisaroth had enjoyed cornering a large male elf and slitting him up the middle. His death brought him some respite from his dark mood.

Now it's my turn. Tirîgon saw the elf's shimmering hair. *There you are!* The dim starlight was enough for him to get his bearings. He was helped further when he spied dark drops on the ground and foliage.

The blond-haired elf did not seem to be hampered by the wound he had received. He hastened through the undergrowth along a rarely used path, fastening his leather armour as he went.

He knows he's being pursued and that he's going to have to turn and fight. Tirîgon was considering throwing a second disc when the elf suddenly turned and leaped at least two paces. *I wonder why?* Tirîgon copied his victim's movements.

He did not land exactly in his quarry's footsteps – there was a loud click under the soles of his feet.

Before he could leap ahead, the ground opened up.

An enormous trap! The pit split open, revealing blades shining below. Tirîgon balanced on the last support just as it started to fold under him.

This could mean the end of me! Jumping up, he tried to reach the edge of the hole. He failed.

Positioning his sword horizontally under his feet, Tirîgon landed on the broad edge as if he were on a wooden spar.

The knives set into the pit floor were bent flat by his blade and weight and none of them penetrated his boots.

That was a close thing. Tirîgon hurried over the floor of the pit back to the edge, crunching over small skeletons of rodents or game animals. He sheathed his sword and climbed back up using his daggers and ran along the path, being more cautious than before.

He could no longer see the elf he was chasing, but the spots of blood made it clear which way to go.

He assumed the path was planned for emergencies, and designed to trap any attacker who took it. *That was probably not the last snare.* He needed to moderate his pace; the hunt had become more of a challenge.

Just as he was thinking this, he felt something like a spider's web brush across his face. The ensuing faint click alerted him to the direction the danger would come from.

He executed a sideways roll and almost escaped the crossbow bolts that shot out of the darkness. Balodil's perfect armour absorbed two hits but a third bolt got past the neck shield and scored the skin on the back of his neck.

It could be poisoned. How will I know? Tirîgon swore – and when he stood up he trod on a further trigger.

Toothed metal jaws came snapping down out of the trees. Only his efficient forearm protectors saved him from serious injury. Dirt and moss came raining down on top of his helmet.

Tirîgon took a deep breath and looked at his arm. If it hadn't been for Balodil's skill, he would have been killed or at least badly mutilated.

He used his sword to lever the trap open and release his arm and then he climbed the nearest tree, moving, as Firûsha had done, from branch to branch. It seemed safer than taking the path below him. He could now see exactly what that path threatened: further surprises and ambush devices easily triggered by an incautious pursuer. He could see that the ropes and chains strung across the path would strike an älf at hip height or below. He came to the conclusion that the mechanisms were not designed for defence against his own race.

Perhaps it's to keep out the groundlings? If so, Tirîgon was surprised. He knew the elves could not stand the mountain maggots, but he was stupefied to think they were afraid of an attack by the short-legged brigades here in their own territory.

What has happened in Tark Draan? Carmondai's knowledge could not have been completely up to date.

Tirîgon decided to find a barbarian to interrogate on the subject. But first he had unfinished business to take care of.

Beneath him he spied his chosen quarry.

The blond-haired elf was covering his wound with leaves and using his belt to secure them. Then he replaced his armoured jacket and pulled the buckles tight.

Then he did something that intrigued Tirîgon.

The elf upturned the pommel of his sword and shook out a map from a hidden compartment. He unfurled it and raised his head to refer to the stars.

Tirîgon enveloped himself in darkness so that he would not be spotted.

A messenger, I suppose. He's probably making for other settlements to warn them of danger. He was surprised that the elf was consulting a map. *They can't visit each other very often. Or he's a young one and hasn't travelled widely before.*

The elf rolled the parchment up and stored it back in the hilt of his sword.

Tirîgon was most keen to get hold of the chart. *It will save us a lot of work and give us the advantage of surprise.* He hurried through the trees, following the elf as before. He noticed something glittering in the starlight and heard the sound of rushing water.

Spying through the foliage of the branches below him, he saw a swift-running river, the black wavelets crowned with silver.

The elf stepped into a hollow tree and vanished.

Curses! Tirîgon jumped down and cautiously approached the tree trunk. As he did so, he noticed a movement on the water.

It was the elf, standing upright on a boat, pushing it away from the bank and manoeuvring it out into the current. When he looked back to the river's edge he saw Tirîgon. He pulled the punting pole inside the boat and picked up his bow and arrow and started shooting.

Tirîgon took cover – but the metal tip caught him on the breast. It broke open on his armour as if made of glass and the fine splinters pricked his face, stinging badly. It was painful, but could be tolerated. *Now I wish we hadn't left Balodil back in Phondrasôn. His work is irreplaceable.*

He slid over to the tree trunk, slipped inside and, after feeling around, found a hidden opening. A ladder led down to a concealed boathouse where ten more boats were rocking on the water.

He shan't escape me that easily. Even though Tirîgon had absolutely no idea how to steer a boat, he threw off the tether on one of them and pushed the craft through the reeds and hanging plants covering the entrance.

He leapt nimbly on board, pushing off with the long pole and taking the boat into the middle of the river. The current caught him and carried him off.

Doesn't seem to be particularly difficult, after all. He spied his target up ahead, standing at the back of his craft, using the pole to speed his progress.

The pursuit continued. Neither was at any advantage, it seemed. The current treated both boats equally. The elf's efforts with the pole were not making any difference.

Dense woodland skimmed past on either bank and here and there shelters and small houses could be seen. They were overtaken by an enormous collection of tree trunks bound together as a raft, floating downstream with no passengers. It bobbed harmlessly behind Tirîgon's vessel.

We can't go on like this forever. Tirîgon was getting impatient. It was important for him to get back to his siblings quickly. He would have to work against the current on his return journey or go back on foot. *What can I do to catch up with the elf?*

The elf fired a volley of arrows in quick succession, but he was not aiming at Tirîgon's boat. Instead, he was firing at the ropes connecting the tree trunks!

Released, they came rolling through the water, going much faster than their boats.

He knew I couldn't steer. Tirîgon found himself surrounded dangerously by these enormous logs, some of which crashed into his boat. Thus far no damage had been caused, but he could hear the noise of rapids about half an arrow-flight away. The unruly tree trunks would present a lethal threat in those whirling waters.

I shan't survive this! Tirîgon racked his brains. *What can I do?*

He jumped overboard and landed on one of the rolling logs.

Balancing carefully, he jumped from log to precarious log as they thundered downriver. He was losing so much time.

The bank is too far away! He catapulted himself up into the air just short of the rapids, grabbing hold of a thin willow branch. The tree protested but the branch held his weight.

His muscles were screaming at having to pull his armoured weight up, but he was immensely relieved to be away from the water. Seconds later, his boat smashed to pieces in the rapids, crushed by the floundering logs.

That would have happened to me. Tirîgon was exhausted but he did not give up. *I must get that map!* He climbed out onto the bank to search for the elf's tracks. At last he came across tiny spots of blood. Filled with renewed confidence, he resumed his pursuit.

By the time dawn announced the return of the sun, he had caught up with his enemy. Tirîgon found him asleep at the edge of a clearing, huddled under a blanket of leaves.

He thought he had escaped. He approached cautiously, sword in hand. He placed the tip at the elf's throat. 'Wake for the last time,' he whispered, sending a cloud of fear towards his victim.

The metal against his skin and the panic startled the elf awake. Any further movement on his part was prevented by the pressure of the blade on his unprotected throat. He stared at the älf with eyes full of hatred and enmity.

'I can see you are wanting to ask certain questions,' said Tirîgon, drawing his double dagger. 'So let me answer them for you: we came through the Moon Pond from the depths of Phondrasôn in order to avenge the deaths of the Inextinguishables and to exterminate your race.'

'You have done that,' spat the elf. 'That village – they were the very last of my people. The dwarves had already wiped out the rest of us.'

Tirîgon raised his eyebrows. So he had been correct in his assumption. 'I am sorry to hear it.' He grinned. 'Not out of sympathy, but because I had expected to enjoy killing more of you.'

The sun rose over the horizon and sent its beams shining through the tops of the trees. Tirîgon felt the pull around the iris of his eyes that denoted the change in light. The white of the eyes was replaced with black. *How I have missed this sensation!*

The elf uttered a loud curse, his face contorted with loathing. 'Sitalia will destroy you! Girdlegard will rise up and attack you and send you back into the dark waters you came crawling out of!'

'We have thrown off all the old gods,' he replied. 'Away with Samusin and the gods of infamy and Tion. We are our own gods. Let others worship us. If you want to let higher beings decide your fate you'll be waiting a long time. I learned that much in exile.' Tirîgon let his eyes rest on the sword hanging from the elf's weapons belt. 'Tell me about the map.'

For the space of one heartbeat the elf's eyes widened in surprise. 'What do you mean?'

'The rolled parchment concealed in the handle. If you unscrew the pommel you can shake it out. I watched you studying it.' He observed the expression on the other's face closely, to assess how close he was getting to the truth. *Will he be provoked?* 'You were working out the quickest way to one of the other settlements, weren't you?'

It was obvious how horrified the elf was. 'No. No. I was going to an ally of ours, a prince . . .'

'You are a miserable liar. Are there more elves elsewhere?'

'No. I told you, the dwarves...'

'You are trying to deceive me just like you tricked the ground-lings,' barked Tirîgon. *This elf is easier to read than a child's story-book.* He gave a quiet laugh. 'Oh, so that was your strategy. You made Tark Draan believe your race had been wiped out. You wanted to gather secretly and hatch new plans. You are a messenger, setting out to warn the others. I expect we killed your regular messenger when we attacked the village, so they sent you instead,' he said, noting from the reaction that his hypothesis was correct. 'That's why you were unsure of the way. If I hadn't seen you look at the map, I'd never have known about the other elves, would I? You can rest easy – the groundlings shall never learn your secret from me. The älfar always carry through their plans. What we begin, we see through to the end.'

The elf thrust Tirîgon's sword aside with his bare hand, ignoring the resulting cut. He pushed himself backwards into a roll, drawing his own weapon ready to fly at Tirîgon.

Tirîgon dodged the lightning rapier thrusts and kicked the elf's side where he had been wounded. 'I wanted to draw your attention to the steel greeting I gave you not so long ago.' The injured elf groaned and doubled up, failing to follow through with his next attack.

Pinioning the elf's sword arm, Tirîgon kneed him repeatedly in the same place until he saw blood flowing from under the armour. 'I see the wound remembers me.' He avoided a head butt and slammed the hilt of his dagger against the elf's nose. 'Here! Take that! Another souvenir!' He let go of his adversary and, putting his dagger away, stepped back far enough to be able to use his long sword.

The elf wiped the blood from his nose. 'Sitalia stands by me!' he cried, charging wildly.

The combination of stabs and sword strikes he employed caused Tirîgon great difficulty. *No one in Phondrasôn fought like that.*

An unexpected kick on his right knee swept the legs from under him and he could only deflect the oncoming blade with his forearm protector. The elf's sword plunged into the leaf mould of the forest floor uncomfortably close to Tirîgon's head.

Tirîgon thrust a metal-plated gauntlet under the elf's armour and tore at the open wound.

The elf rolled to one side, screaming with pain and dropping his weapon.

There's the end to it! crowed Tirîgon. He raised his own sword in both hands and slammed it down with all his force, so that it cut through the elf's leather breastplate, straight into the torso. At the level of the solar plexus the cut ran parallel to the belt, slicing through heart, lungs and, finally, spine. The elf lay at Tirîgon's feet in two halves. The light in the eyes fluttered and broke.

'Your death,' he panted, 'bears the name of Tirîgon. You shall not be the last of the elves my people will kill. And remember, it was you,' he said, staring into the elf's blind pupils, 'who gave us all the help we needed.' He drew himself to his full height and shouted his triumph to the day star.

His initial elation was followed by disappointment at having no more elves to slaughter. He consoled himself with having won the map that would lead his siblings and him to the secret elf refuges.

Tirîgon took the elf's sword and head as his trophies.

He did not know what he would do with the head, but Tossàlor had taught him well. *A decorated elf skull on the roof of my house, perhaps. I like that idea.*

Time was short but he stopped to cut the largest bones out of the corpse, wrapping them in the elf's tunic to carry. *Let the scavengers and crows deal with the rest.*

Tirîgon started his return journey in a state of euphoria.

The smoke caused by the burning settlement guided Tirîgon on the last stage of his journey.

When he reached the ruined village towards sunset, he was met with an eager reception by a concerned Firûsha. Sisaroth also hastened over to greet him, relieved that he had returned safely.

The älfar had set up camp and elf corpses were being prepared, with individual body parts set aside for future use. This was a procedure many of them had never seen carried out; they needed detailed instruction.

'I've come back but not empty-handed.' Tirîgon placed his trophies aside and showed his siblings the chart he had stolen, on which seven further settlements were marked. *I wonder what they'll say?* He took an apple and bit into it with gusto. *What a wonderful taste! No fancy banquet food can come close!*

Before he was given a chance to tell them what he had experienced, his brother and sister grabbed him by the arms and escorted him into the wood in the direction of the Moon Pond. They were being very mysterious.

'We've sent scouts to spy out the land,' said Sisaroth, who was much more cheerful today. 'They're disguised as elves and will bring back news from the barbarians.'

'There were three elves that escaped, but we'll soon have them rounded up. I've dispatched small units to go after them,' Firûsha chipped in.

'And what if they reach the other settlements?' Tirîgon asked. The idea did not appeal to his tactical mind. *We'll lose the advantage of surprise.*

'It doesn't matter if the villages are warned about us. It won't make any difference. They'll still be wiped out.' Firûsha was too excited to wait any longer. 'Brother, something wonderful has happened!'

'Over there. Be careful. Don't get too close. There might be a further landslip,' Sisaroth warned him as he pushed the undergrowth to one side to allow a good view.

Tirîgon turned, expecting to see the dark waters of the Moon Pond – but it had vanished!

Where the pond had once been there was now an enormous cavity a good mile in depth and width. Tumbled bushes and rubble cloaked the slopes of the new crater, and just a few remaining trickles of water were gradually seeping away into the subsoil. Piles of water lilies lay jumbled at the bottom, catching the evening light.

Could this be the crater for our new Dsôn? Tirîgon gave a joyous laugh. 'It's a sign!' he exclaimed, embracing his brother and sister and kissing them on the forehead. The cavern below the Moon Pond must have collapsed and the water had drained away through the cracks. 'This will be our new home. A new Black Heart, beating strongly for all to hear. Every creature in

Tark Draan will quake before us!' He studied the excavation. 'It won't be big enough for what I have in mind. We are the Gods of Dsôn, after all! We'll increase its size until it is the most impressive crater ever!'

'And we have Carmondai to do the town-planning for us,' Firûsha continued eagerly. 'We'll be continuing in the traditions of our forefathers and of the Inextinguishables.' Her darkened eyes shone with excitement. 'Mother and Father would be proud of us.'

'Yes, they would.' Sisaroth was less enthusiastic than his sister. 'We are their legacy. They waited so long for the chance to go to Tark Draan. If they had been able to come with us, Father would be the new ruler.'

'And he would have been an excellent ruler indeed.' Firûsha took a deep breath.

Sisaroth sighed. 'No. He already *was* an excellent ruler,' he amended, choking with emotion.

Their words dealt a red-hot needle stab to Tirîgon's heart. He tried to think of a suitable rejoinder but guilt rendered him incapable of speech.

They stood around in silence, contemplating the huge natural basin, while the sun sank further and the älfar's elongated shadows reached the centre of what was to be their new empire. The siblings each followed their own trains of thought and memories. The wind rose and played with their long dark hair.

Tirîgon could see the new city in his mind's eye. Proud and mighty, sombre and magnificent, full of art and beauty. *Towers, houses, bridges, decorative runes, sculptures and statues!* There was so much he wanted to plan with his brother and sister. The most important item right now though was the coming negotiations with the Thirdlings. Talks would have to be held in secret. It would be an alliance such as Tark Draan had never known.

'I wonder,' said Sisaroth quietly, 'what our Balodil is up to at the moment? Do you think he has defeated the Zhadar yet?'

'I hope he doesn't ever get back through the Black Abyss,' said Firûsha. 'We don't need someone trying to steal our thunder in Tark Draan.'

Tirîgon could not help thinking of Esmonäe and how they had talked together of the future. *We had such dreams. Now she is a spirit, roaming Phondrasôn forever.* 'Forget about the groundling.' Tirîgon placed his arms round his siblings' shoulders.

In close embrace and in silence they stood at the edge of the crater, thinking of the future.

The day star disappeared and the älfars' eyes turned white. White with steely blue.

We have so many plans. For Father and Mother. Tirîgon cleared his throat. 'No matter when it may be,' he said, 'let us make certain that by the time Balodil returns, nothing in Tark Draan will be the same as when he left it.'

. . . you think they achieved their goals?
    You think they exterminated the elves?
    You think they subjugated Tark Draan
    in an alliance with the Thirdlings?
The Young Gods dispensed with their old title
    and became known as the Dsôn Aklán,
    the gods of Dsôn.
And out of the small hole
    that the Moon Pond left when it emptied
    they created Dsôn Bhará,
    the true Dsôn.
And even if they were now Aklán,
    the genuine gods were above them,
    however strongly the Siblings denied this.
    Samusin, the god of justice and the winds,
    laughed with joy as he put them in their place.
And so there appeared on the scene, mightier still than the Dsôn
        Aklán,
    Aiphaton, child of the Inextinguishables,
    and from the south he led a second älfar people,
    born of elves and älfar who had left Tark Draan

many divisions of unendingness in the past.

These enemies had become one folk,
wild, stormy, filled with inner discord, hating themselves and
others.

And so the Aklán had to accept him as their overlord,
their emperor, although they considered themselves the sole
rightful rulers
of the älfar people.

The wild älfar attacked Âlandur and the one-time Dsôn
Balsur.

The Aklán remained in Dsôn Bhará and feigned subservience.
Samusin took pleasure in punishing the Aklán
for their arrogance.

Together the älfar ruled the east
but the north belonged to a beast by the name of Kordrion,
the south to a malcontent sorcerer who went by the name of
Lot-Ionan,
and the west to a dragon called Lohasbrand.

The Aklán did not cease in their endeavours to gain total
power.

Together with their cousins they wiped out the last of the elves
and waged war,
making an alliance with the Thirdlings.
Sisaroth used his knowledge about potions
to win over a special unit from the ranks of the Thirdlings.
They were the backbone of the insurgency.

The preparations advanced,
the intrigues became more complex,
and when Firúsha, Tirîgon and Sisaroth
forged ahead with their plans against all-comers,

their forgotten one-time ally arrived from the Dark Paths:
Tungdil Goldhand.
This changed everything.

End of the epic poem *Young Gods*
composed by Carmondai, master of word and image

Afterword

This was the third instalment ...

After dealing with the prelude to the first attack on Girdle-gard in the first two parts of the *Legends of the Älfar,* now I had to enter the netherworld.

Phondrasôn.

This was the place of banishment and the site of signifi-cant events touching the whole of the älfar race, and also Firûsha, Tirîgon and Sisaroth in particular, as well as Tungdil Goldhand.

If you have read the Dwarves cycle of novels, you will now understand why Tungdil, on his return, knew the Triplet Sib-lings and why their reunion was, relatively speaking, friendly.

The present novel explains the marvel of the älfar's return and how they arrived through the Moon Pond.

I took enormous pleasure in connecting up the threads of the two novel cycles.

I concerned myself primarily with the back-story of the Tri-plets, who will go on to be the greatest adversaries. I wanted to show what had happened to them before they rose to become rulers of the älfar and were designated the Dsôn Aklán. More of their adventures and what happened to them you will find next in the fourth Dwarves novel: *The Fate of the Dwarves*.

The fourth instalment will follow.

The last of the individual Legend novels (without excluding the possibility of publishing anthologies penned by Carmondai) will deal with Aìphaton and will pick up the story from the end of the fourth Dwarves novel. There is much excitement to be had about events in Girdlegard!

... if you are wondering what happened to Tungdil Goldhand during the attack on the Zhadar castle, and about the truth concerning a possible doppelgänger for the dwarf, you must be patient.

I know there are many eager Tungdil fans out there, but I must ask you not to pester me with questions.

At this point I should like to refer you to the project led by the group BLIND GUARDIAN.

The musicians asked me for a story to go with a particular orchestral album; there is obviously a dwarf in the story. Further details will be made available later on the website www.mahet.de

My special thanks as always to my much-appreciated test-readers: Yvonne Schöneck, Tanja Karmann and Sonja Rüther.

I don't want to forget our top fantasy master and editor at PIPER, Carsten Polzin, whose comments helped the älfar wander through the pages of the novel with typically evil style and grace.

Many, many thanks also to Anke Koopmann from the guterpunkt agency for her wonderful cover again.

And last but not least, my thanks to my many loyal readers,

without whom I would not be able to devote myself to my calling to the same extent.

Without you, the protagonists are mere actors in an empty theatre.

Thank you for reading!

Markus Heitz
Summer 2012